Victoria Routledge worked in publishing for three years before her first novel, FRIENDS LIKE THESE, was published. She was born in the Lake District and now lives in London, and writes full time as a novelist and a journalist. She is the author of FRIENDS LIKE THESE and KISS HIM GOODBYE.

. . . *And For Starters*

Victoria Routledge

POCKET
BOOKS

LONDON · SYDNEY · NEW YORK · TOKYO · SINGAPORE · TORONTO

First published in Great Britain by Pocket Books, 2001
An imprint of Simon & Schuster UK Ltd
A Viacom Company

Copyright © Victoria Routledge, 2001

This book is copyright under the Berne Convention
No reproduction without permission
® and © 1997 Simon & Schuster Inc. All rights reserved
Pocket Books & Design is a registered trademark of
Simon & Schuster Inc

The right of Victoria Routledge to be identified as author of this
work has been asserted in accordance with sections 77 and 78 of
the Copyright, Designs and Patents Act 1988

1 3 5 7 9 10 8 6 4 2

Simon & Schuster UK Ltd
Africa House
64–78 Kingsway
London WC2B 6AH

Simon & Schuster Australia
Sydney

A CIP catalogue record for this book is available from the
British Library

ISBN 0 743 41518 3

This book is a work of fiction. Names, characters, places
and incidents are either products of the author's imagination
or are used fictitiously. Any resemblance to actual people, living or
dead, events or locales, is entirely coincidental.

Typeset in Sabon by
Palimpsest Book Production Limited, Polmont, Stirlingshire
Printed and bound in Great Britain by
Omnia Books Limited, Glasgow

Acknowledgements

Thank you to Dan and Fiona Evans, who run the fantastic Anglesea Arms in Wingate Road, W6, for letting me research behind the bar, to the bar staff who didn't brain me when I accidentally rang £14,000 through the till, and also to the very patient customers who explained how to make the drinks they wanted, checked their change, and smiled kindly when I served them chilled Guinness rather than the real stuff, because it was easier to pour. The Bunch of Grapes isn't based on the Anglesea: the Anglesea has much better food, much funnier barmen and no weirdo regulars.

Also in the name of fearless research, I am forever indebted to Helen Stockman of BSM, for getting me through my driving test without the use of hypnotherapy, sedatives, bribery or threats. Not that they'd done any good before.

Usual grateful thanks to James Hale, for comforting half-time pep talks and inspirational liquid lunches, to Suzanne Baboneau for brilliant and thoughtful editing, to my sister Alex Cooper for the technical educational details, to the whole team at Simon & Schuster for encouragement and enthusiasm, and to the irregular Tuesday night Clapham pub quiz team for the crates of Becks. Especially to whoever is still 'looking after' them.

Thanks, Dillon, for everything else.

For Shona Sutherland, and Jimmy Page.

Driving down to Rosedale
Got my rider by my side
She bakes my bread so soft and sweet
Sure keeps me satisfied
She's my hot stove lady
She's my jelly roll bride

Oh, honey, won't you come into my kitchen?

Red Hot Blues, Blind Willy Kipling

Chapter One

The red Lancia Integrale screeched to a halt at the traffic lights and stopped three precise centimetres behind the cyclist waiting at the line. According to Angus, that was the beauty of rally cars – stopping distances only slightly longer than the car itself.

Iona averted her eyes from the traffic warden staring nervously from the pavement and wondered whether she should just cut her losses and get out. Walk away. While she could still walk. After all, she had only been living with Angus for five years. Five years was a long time to cheat death like this. It might suit Angus to expire at high speed in the car of his dreams, but airbag earrings had never been her thing.

The cyclist, who must also have felt as though Death was filing his nails at his shoulder, turned round and saw Angus's scarlet face glaring over the steering-wheel. He wobbled violently on his pedals. Then, despite the fact that the lights were now red *and* amber, the cyclist dismounted and began wheeling his bike round to the driver's side of the car.

Iona drew in an involuntary breath and gripped her seat. Please no. Not again. All right, so she couldn't drive herself, but she was London's leading expert on passive road rage.

'Oh, my *God*,' said Angus in a voice heavy with disbelief. 'What *is* his problem?'

'Angus, please,' Iona began desperately. 'Don't shout at him. He nearly came off round that corner. And you . . .'

Angus swivelled his head round to her. Iona blinked at the

sudden piercing eagle-eye Action Man glare. 'For Christ's sake, don't *you* start!' His eyes narrowed.

How can he go from looking so handsome to so mean so quickly, wondered Iona, and then hated herself for thinking it. He's had a long day at work. He's tired. He doesn't really want to have supper at Jim's. He doesn't want to make chitchat with Tamara about ascendants and clunk-click-clash astro-compatibility charts. If it wasn't for the promise of Ned cooking, we'd probably still be at home with a curry, watching *The Italian Job* on video for the millionth time, instead of sitting here simmering.

The cyclist leaned into the car and pulled the earpieces of his Walkman out one at a time in a menacing fashion, glaring at Angus all the while. Angus glared back.

Iona looked at the traffic lights, which seemed to have been on red and amber for an eternity. What if the cyclist were an off-duty policeman? Or an off-duty martial arts instructor? He looked pretty scary. Apart from the Michael Jackson face mask.

There was a brief moment of silence and then a torrent of abuse from both sides, which streamed into one violent jam of obscenities. Iona shut her eyes. The cars behind starting hooting, bleeping out the normal words, so all she could hear was a *Jerry-Springer*-in-reverse babble of fuck, shit, bastard and, for some reason, near-side mirror.

It was twenty past six.

Jim stretched out his legs beneath the kitchen table and tried to get them on to the chair opposite his own. They didn't quite reach. Instead he twisted his chair round and hoisted his feet on to the metal dustbin, then found he couldn't reach his beer on the table.

He flailed an arm helplessly at the bottle.

'Ne-ee-ee-ee-d,' he began, and then remembered that he didn't share a flat with Ned any more. So no help there. With a sigh he put the cookery book on the table, grabbed the beer and swivelled his long legs round to rest on the stainless-steel vegetable rack. Which made a good footstool, since it was always empty.

Jim didn't mind admitting that he hadn't quite got the run of the new kitchen yet. For a start, there was a massive gas cooker hob flame-thrower thing down one side of the room that looked as though it had been installed by either Gordon Ramsay or Conan the Barbarian's head chef. His absent godmother, whose flat it technically was, had also invested in a waste-disposal unit that had so far only vomited old coffee grounds up at him. Not even his own coffee grounds either, since he hadn't got round to making coffee yet – there was a perfectly good Portuguese café next door and the espresso machine was a foreign country to him without Ned to explain it.

He gave the cooker another suspicious look over the sticky pages of a *Lads' Cookbook* Iona had given him the previous Christmas, to try to encourage a little more participation in the kitchen, aside from opening the wine. Living with Ned had had its definite advantages. First of all, the visual effect of standing next to stringy 'Just Say No, Kids' Ned was as good as a makeover, and secondly, Ned was a sous chef in the West End. Chicks beat a path to their door. Admittedly, since he had moved in here on his own, in a last-ditch attempt to create a swinging bachelor pad, and Ned had gone up to Archway with some other chefs, to pursue his studies in magic mushrooms, both the chicks and the nutrition had slid a bit, but things were going to change.

Jim had been saying this loudly for ages and had even written it in his diary. However, after a little over a fortnight in the flat he still hadn't broken his three-year sex drought, or got round to turning any of the flame-throwers on.

And that was a sign of encroaching age, he thought, trying miserably to find turkey in the index. Two years ago Angus and Chris would have been straight round with a crate of beer and the four of them would have spent a whole evening playing Top Gun with the cooker. He peeled 'Beef and Dumplings in Beer' apart from 'Roast Beef and All the Guff', sheering off a whole-page illustration of mashed potatoes as he did so. Mind, Top Gun could still be an option. Iona and Marie, Chris's wife, permitting. He cheered up considerably.

'Tam!' he yelled towards the bathroom. 'Tam, there's nothing here I can cook!'

'Isn't Ned coming over?' Tamara's voice was indistinct beneath the sound of running water. 'You told me Ned was coming over!'

'Are you having a shower in there?' asked Jim hopefully. He put the book down. Tamara having a shower had been number one in Jim and Chris's list of Millennium Fantasies; number seven for Angus, who was after all effectively married to Iona, Tamara's best friend, and therefore stood a better chance than the rest of them of actually seeing it in real life. Ned's number one had been, inscrutably, Julie Christie.

Yet here she was, in his flat, showering – and there was no one here to witness it! 'Tamara's having a shower? In this house? In my house? Oh, my God . . .' he added in an amazed whisper to the fridge. Inevitably, panic overcame the initial excitement and he started biting his nails urgently.

'No,' Tamara shouted back. 'Don't get excited, I'm just washing my . . .'

At this critical moment, the pile of Sainsbury's bags which Jim had piled optimistically on top of one another in his haste to get the beer in the fridge slid down the side of the work surface, scattering bird's-eye chillies all over the tiled floor, and it was left to his imagination to supply whatever it was that Tamara was washing as he grovelled around trying to pick them up and listen at the same time. Then the front doorbell rang and he smacked his head on the kitchen table trying to work out which door the sound was coming from.

'Tamara, can you get the . . . No, I suppose you can't, really, if you're in . . .' A lascivious thought passed down the one-track urban highway of Jim's mind and, finding its route clear, picked up speed. 'Oh, Tamara, there's someone at the door, and I really can't leave the, um . . .'

He looked at the flame-throwing hob. What would you call it? Baby griller? Torture device?

'. . . I can't leave the stove, so could you get it?'

The doorbell rang again more urgently and Jim hovered by the open door, looking down the long hall. The bathroom was on the left and any minute now . . . He held his breath. Any uncovered portion of Tamara was worth feeling like a fifth-form stalker for.

'Jim, I can't really . . .' Water dripped on the tiles inside the bathroom.

'Please?'

'Oh, for God's sake! Where are your towels?' The water was switched off and the lock rattled as she tried to get out.

Jim bit his lip in anticipation, and then squealed in agony as a pair of hands settled on his shoulders and his front teeth nearly went through his lip. He twisted round as far as the hands would let him and got a noseful of unwashed male and fresh basil. Which contrasted painfully with the fragrant gust of expensive shampoo from the bathroom as Tamara stormed out and down the hall.

'There's no one *at* the door, Jim!' she shouted from the front door. 'Do you mind if I carry on washing my hair now?'

'Ned,' muttered Jim under his breath. 'You bastard.'

'What?' Ned loosened his bear hug on Jim's shoulders and dumped the bunch of basil on to the kitchen table. 'Thought you might like this to put in the supper.'

'You need to put herbs in Pot Noodles?' Jim picked it up suspiciously. 'There's a perfectly good door in the front incidentally. Just because that window's open it's not an invitation for freelance burglars.'

'It's nearest the street, isn't it? Man, why do you always buy corn on the cob? You never cook it and it always ends up rotting the rest of your veggies. Just because it's reduced . . .' Ned was sifting through the split bags of shopping with despair written all over his face. 'Anyway, wasn't sure if it was your door once I'd rang the bell. Too posh for me round here, like.'

Jim ignored this. It was a bit posh for him too. Bit posh for everyone, with the possible exception of Angus. 'Where've you been anyway? I thought you were doing a shift at the Uxbridge.'

'I was, like,' said Ned, chewing a basil leaf. 'But things were slow, so they put me on to doing puddings for supper. Did a fridge full of crème brûlées and left.'

'Then?'

'Then I had a walk down to the common to see if there were any new mushrooms, OK? What is this, *Twenty Questions*?' Mushrooms were Ned's obsession. For cooking and other medical uses.

'No, it's *Ready Steady Cook*.' Jim emptied the bags on to the table.

'Oh, God, Jim. Not turkey pieces again.'

'They were going cheap.'

'Ho ho.'

Jim looked confused. 'Was that a joke?'

'No more than usual. Never mind.' Ned sifted through the ingredients. 'Jim lad, do you ever go to Sainsbury's with a list? Do you still not have any idea about what goes with what? I mean, tell me, what *do* you imagine goes with ginger in syrup?'

Jim reached into the fridge and pulled out a couple of beers. He plunked them on the table, next to a big saucepan, right in front of Ned. 'Please, Ned, just cook it, OK? And stop calling me Jim lad.'

Ned said nothing and laid out the contents of the bags in a line. He kept his eyes on Jim, but raised his eyebrows higher and higher with each item.

Turkey pieces.

A fresh pineapple.

Bird's-eye chillies.

Syrup.

Instant coffee.

An artichoke, reduced.

Noodle Doodles, reduced.

After Eight mints, reduced.

Ned's eyebrows were now hidden in his shaggy brown fringe. Jim made a grab for the mints, but Ned held them out of his reach and placed them at the end of the line.

'I don't think Ainsley Harriot would thank you for this little lot, Jim.'

'You know Tamara's availing herself of my shower facilities?' said Jim, banging the button mushrooms on the table and removing the coffee.

'She is?' Ned took away the artichoke and replaced it with a bunch of asparagus from his coat pocket. 'Ta da! I have asparagus, if you don't mind having smelly pee?'

The bathroom door opened and they both swivelled round as if on castors.

Tamara walked across the hall and into the big kitchen, still efficiently rubbing her hair dry with Jim's Man Utd gym towel. As she massaged her scalp, the towel swished about, revealing tantalizing flashes of her long neck, and her silver necklace, a chain so fine it was almost invisible, glinted in the light from the patio doors as her toned arms moved up and down. One spaghetti strap of her black vest top had slipped off her shoulder, revealing an egg-yellow bra strap beneath. Jim swallowed.

'Hiya, Tamara,' said Ned, without bothering to look up from the drawer he was rummaging through.

'Hi, Ned.' A graceful hand with a mercury-silver manicure stopped rubbing and waved hello at them. 'Sorry, the
showers weren't working at the pool.' Her voice was muffled
beneath the towel. 'My hair will go green if I leave the
chlorine in too long. Naturally blonde hair's quite sensitive
like that.'

'Mmm, right,' said Ned. Jim envied the way he could be so
casual in the face of so many natural attributes. 'Asparagus
all right for you for supper?'

She flipped her head the right way up and dropped the
towel over the radiator, shaking her hair out. 'Great. As
long as you do that fantastic hollandaise sauce. And as
long as Jim gets that window unjammed in the bathroom
for ventilation afterwards.' She slid down into one of the
new chairs and began twisting damp strands into ringlets
around her fingers. Tamara had big blonde hair – like
Farrah Fawcett or Jerry Hall or Heather Locklear. She was
a Charlie's Angel from West Sussex. Iona had met her at art
school, during her post-grad degree, and it showed. Tamara
didn't look like anyone Jim and Ned would have met under
normal circumstances.

'But obviously – only if you're cooking them, Ned.' She
gave him a big smile. Even with no make-up in January, she
had a kind of glow. Jim's insides wilted like spinach. 'I
don't want to risk food poisoning so early in the year.'

Ned gave her an offhand grin. 'Jim's got to learn, you
know. There are no scurvy clinics in Westbourne Grove.'

Jim banged his turkey pieces on the table in an attention-
seeking way. 'I have provided Ned with a challenging range
of fresh ingredients, from which he is going to concoct a
delicious and nutritious supper for seven.'

The doorbell rang. 'And that will be two of them.'

'Come in, it's open,' shouted Tamara, rocking back on
her chair.

'You didn't shut my door? Were you born in a barn?' Jim
tried to make his voice stern, but all he could usually manage

in direct conversation with Tamara was pleading or, at best, stunned.

'Nah, that's me, the barn lad,' said Ned, beginning to sweep some space on the table for a chopping board. 'Born in a byre.'

'Carlisle is *not* farmland,' said Tamara. 'Is it?' Her smooth brow creased, as if troubled by an unwelcome thought. 'Your dad's not a *farmer*, is he?'

Jim slipped out into the hall, envying Ned for the easy way he could wind Tamara up. Lucky Sod. And she didn't even seem to mind.

'Look, even Marie and Chris are already here,' said Angus, slowing down outside Jim's flat. There were cars parked nose to tail down both sides of the street as far as Iona could see. 'There's their car. God, I hate London. I told Jim to look for somewhere with decent parking, but did he listen?'

The Integrale came to a halt and Iona looked out of her window at the space Angus seemed to be considering, since she was nearer than him. The gap between cars looked unpromisingly small and someone had left a Vespa at the end of it. Possibly Tamara.

'Can we get into that?' she asked nervously. There was a large tree lining up with her door. Being two-thirds the size of Angus had its advantages when confronted with his idea of ideal off-road parking (inevitable squeezing out through partially open doors required), and also for when Male Front Seat Privileges meant she was shunted into the back of his car like a Labrador to make room in the front for Ned or Jim. If she had known how much time she would spend travelling in the back seat of a car little bigger than a laundry basket, she would not have allowed Angus to restrict her input to the colour of the bodywork.

'You tell me, Iona, you're nearer.'

'It was a rhetorical question, sweetheart. I have no idea.

Reverse-parking is as a closed book to me. Do your wheels turn ninety degrees so you can slide in?'

He gave a tetchy sigh. 'Then watch and learn.' Angus turned in his seat and swung the car into the space at about twenty miles an hour, pulling right lock off, throwing left lock on, with one hand on the wheel and the other on her head for balance.

Iona kept her eyes shut until all movement had ceased and when she opened them, they were parked. Right next to the tree. She unbuckled her seat-belt and tested the door. About ten centimetres' clearance.

'And mind the door!'

Angus was more protective of his car than he was of her, and that was saying something.

Iona squeezed herself out, holding her stomach in as far as it would go, trying not to catch her belt on the lock. She managed one leg and then came to a painful stop at her groin. She could feel bone grind against top-quality beige leather interior.

Angus was rummaging in the boot, pushing escaped mangoes back into the plastic bags of groceries. 'Which is our shopping and which is emergency supplies for Jim?'

'The bag with the knot in is for Jim.' It would have to be a climb over the middle. Iona hated climbing over the middle. She gritted her teeth and extended one foot in a snakeskin boot (brought in a bag and swapped for her comfy waitressing Vans at home-time) in the direction of the driver's footwell, then arched her hips upwards to clear the handbrake. This had to be good for some part of someone's sex life.

Iona had a small but curvy bottom and would have cleared the handbrake easily if her foot hadn't slipped on the fire extinguisher (so necessary in a rally-based road car) beneath the driver's seat. Not that that was a problem in itself, apart from the painful angle of the handbrake. It was the panicky reaching out to grab hold of something that did the damage.

'Angus! *Angus!*' she yelled. Too late.

Angus had just slammed the boot shut. 'Good job you remembered Jim would be cooking and not Ned. He never has anything . . .' Then he realized that boots weren't meant to slide away from you as you slammed them. And then the car slammed gently into the Vespa.

'Hello, Marie.'

Jim bent down and kissed Marie's cheek. As usual, she smelled of chalk and small children. Not her own.

'Hi, Jim. How are you?' Marie gave him two careful kisses, one on each cheek. 'We brought extra, since you're cooking.' She handed over an Oddbins bag, just about containing three bottles of red wine.

'Jim.' Chris extended a hand and Jim shook it as heartily as he could, seeing as he didn't like Chris all that much. But since Chris didn't seem to like them that much either, he didn't feel obliged to feel especially bad about it.

'Great to see you. Thanks for all this – you didn't need to bring three. My cooking's not *that* bad, is it?'

'Er?' Chris pulled an amused '*Au contraire*, I think it *is*' face. 'Either you can slosh it in the cooking to mask the burnt bits, or we can drink it all first and not notice them anyway.'

'Actually, Chris,' said Jim, taking Marie's big tartan school-bag and hanging it on the hatstand in the hall, 'not that I'm not perfectly capable of whipping up a fantastic meal myself, you understand, but I've enlisted some last-minute, basic-level help.'

'You've asked Ned to cook?'

'He's just going to chop things up. *I* will be doing the cooking.'

'Really, Jim?' said Marie, in her 'Are you telling me the *whole* truth about the hamster now, Brittany?' voice.

'Absolutely.'

'Well, I want you and your hands to be in full view all the time, OK?'

The doorbell rang again. Jim could see one tall and one short silhouette behind the stained glass. Arms were being waved around.

'You go through,' said Jim, 'first on the left.'

Marie had already walked through into the kitchen, her eyes skating up and down the hall, taking in all the details of the new flat as she went. Jim could hear her kissing everyone hello, exclaiming about his gas-fired hob.

'I don't know, he's here somewhere . . . Chris, come and look at this amazing oven!' she yelled over her shoulder. 'I could roast the whole of my year three in here and still have room for Yorkshire puddings!'

Chris stopped looking through Jim's unopened post and followed her through.

Jim took a deep breath and flung wide the door.

'. . . insurance will cover it, won't it? It's not even a dent, for God's sake, Angus! Hello, Jim!'

From his vantage point on the doorstep Jim could see over Iona and Angus's shoulders to the cause of Angus's Darth Maul expression. Tamara's Vespa was still partially reclining beneath the Integrale. Angus had one arm around Iona's shoulders, but he could easily have been attempting to strangle her.

'Not the Inty, Ang!'

'Yes, the Inty,' said Iona, striding inside before Angus could reply. 'It was me or a tree-shaped hole in the passenger side door, actually. I nearly ruptured my spleen and injured my reproductive organs trying to climb out of the worst parking space ever and, as a result, the car has a slight front-headlight deficiency, but not to worry. Angus nearly killed a cyclist on the way over and think what that would have done to the paintwork.'

Angus smiled icily. His curly blond hair was sticking up in chunks where he'd been running his hands through it in enraged disbelief, but he didn't remove his arm from around Iona's shoulders. 'I've had a very long day at work. Do you have anything I could drink? Some hemlock for my lovely common-law spouse here, perhaps?'

Jim stood back to let them come in. 'Bloody hell, Iona,' he said, as Iona trotted past. 'Where did you get those boots? Did Skid Row have a house clearance?'

They were oxblood-red fake snakeskin and the toes were nearly as spiky as the heels.

'You could have someone's eye out with those.'

'Or someone's headlights,' Angus added pointedly as he helped her off with her coat. 'Or someone's leather interior.'

Iona ignored him. 'They make me feel better after a day making coffee for stressed people. They're therapeutic. I bought them when I sold that last big collage at Spitalfields. Handmade. Unique.' Her stiletto heels clicked seductively on the bare boards of the hall passage as she walked down to the kitchen.

'Therapeutic? Ought to be telepathic too, at that price,' muttered Angus, handing the bag of food to Jim. 'Still, your money, darling.' He shrugged off his own jacket and draped it over the banister, loosening his tie as he followed Iona down the hall.

'Why does everyone bring food when I'm cooking?' demanded Jim, looking through the bag as he trailed after them. 'Oh, cheers, yeah, *onions*. I always forget onions.'

In the kitchen Marie had opened two bottles of wine, emptied the dishwasher and was distributing brimming glasses around the table, where everyone fought over the crostini Ned had knocked up to stop them eating the main course raw before he could cook it.

Ned had already made a start on the vegetables Iona had given him, starting with the garlic, which he was chopping with an enormous knife, rocking the blade back and forth expertly, just a breath away from his fingers. He stopped when Jim walked in and pushed the little heaps of garlic into piles on the board, next to Jim's ginger and peppers.

'Ah ha, the chef!' said Chris, rubbing his hands at the sight of Jim tying a pinny round his waist. 'Time for some Dutch courage, I think.'

Jim took a glass off the draining board and held it out.

'I meant for the audience rather than the chef, actually.'

'More wine, please, Chris,' said Marie, holding out her glass.

'More wine, please, Chris,' said Iona, holding out her glass and Angus's. 'Before Jim pours it all into the usual chicken casserole.'

'I do make *other* things than coq au vin,' Jim protested, swiping Chris's glass while he was refilling everyone else's. 'Just because it's very good . . . Ned, where did you put my cookery book?'

'You're not going to use one tonight, mate.' Ned waggled his hands and smiled scarily, widening his eyes into a tranced-out stare. 'Tonight I will bestow on you the gift of freestyle cooking.'

'And does that come with a special free gift of food poisoning for the rest of us?' asked Marie. She smacked Chris's hand away as he tried to sneak the last crostini off the plate. 'Tamara, will you have the last crostini?'

'No, you have it,' said Tamara, rubbing her flat stomach unconsciously. 'I had a colonic yesterday and I'm not eating wheat for a week to give myself a chance to, you know . . .'

'Oh, God, you might have said!' moaned Jim. 'How do you know I wasn't going to make a fabulous wheat-based dish? Wheat surprise? Wheat à la Turque? Wheat con molto bene Milanese ragazza?'

'What *are* you making, Jim?' asked Marie.

'Um . . .'

'Exactly.' Marie crunched into the crostini.

'What's a colonic? Or do I not want to know at the table?' asked Ned.

Tamara's blue eyes took on an evangelical sheen. 'It's brilliant, actually, you should try it—'

'Ned, why don't you sort out Jim and supper first, and we can tell you all about colonics afterwards?' suggested Iona hurriedly. 'Have you seen my new boots, Tam?' She urgently extended her ankle towards Tamara, who was gesticulating ominously with a spear of asparagus. 'Why don't you try them on? No, go on, they'd suit you. Here, have a look . . .'

Jim picked up the knife Ned had left out for him, then looked uncertainly at the pile of food in front of him.

'Where are my turkey pieces?'

Ned flexed his fingers. 'We're just going to pretend you didn't buy them. Now, Jim lad, here's the pile of chopped vegetables. What are you going to do with it?'

He made a sweeping gesture towards the food on the counter, most of which had been brought by other people.

Jim put his finger up his nose, contemplatively. 'Fry up all the stuff in a big pan, add wine and turkey and simmer for an hour?'

'No.'

'Put all the veggies in a big bowl and pour salad dressing on? Serve chilled?'

'No.'

'That'll do for me, if you like, Jim,' Tamara interrupted. 'I've been eating that all day anyway. Very good for your colon! You don't lose any enzymes.'

'And for the rest of us?' Marie tried to keep her voice straight.

Ned and Jim looked at the food again.

'No, you've got me there, Ned mate,' admitted Jim finally. 'I cannot guess what is going on in your head at all. Just looks like a big pile of veggies to me.'

Ned looked despairingly at him, and then at the food, and then back at Jim. 'That's your best offer? A pepper, carrot and onion salad?'

'With my artichoke, obviously. And turkey pieces in ginger scattered on top.'

'OK, you've convinced us,' said Chris. 'Ned has to cook. Please, Ned. Cook.'

'Right, but you're watching, OK, Jim?' Ned rolled his sleeves up and took a glass of wine off the table. 'Man cannot live on Pot Noodles and artichokes alone.'

'And Man will never entice Girl home for supper when everything on the menu has more chemicals inside it than Keith Richards and a sell-by date of three years in the future,' said Iona. 'And I mean that caringly,' she added, as Angus kicked her under the table.

'Yes, I want to help.' Jim waved his big knife. 'Let me help.'

'God help us,' said Marie, and refilled her glass.

'I've got a better idea,' said Angus. 'Why don't we go over the road to the Bunch of Grapes and have a pint while Ned's cooking, so we can be out of his way?'

'The Bunch of Grapes?' Tamara pulled a face. 'You do realize that at the moment I can only drink vodka and orange *without* the vodka?'

The Bunch of Grapes was a rundown boozer on the opposite side of the road from Jim's flat, and was the only pub in the area not to have been bought up, regrimed and given a brand-new 150-year-old Irish birth certificate. The choices locally were fake Oirish; minimalist, with bottled beverages; fake souk; dating fast cattle-market wine bar (used by the local single yuppies for fast dating); or stripped pine, Yummy Mummy organo-pub. In an area becoming trendy for being a backwater, all the backwater locals – fed up with being used as authentically grimy background in fashion shoots – had retreated from one pub to another until the Bunch of Grapes was all they had left. And even they didn't like it.

'Great idea!' said Marie. 'You can give us a ring when you're ready, Jim. *What?*' she demanded as Tamara frowned at her. 'This kitchen isn't really big enough for all of us and anyway, watching Jim trying to cook . . . I mean, it's a bloodsport, isn't it? You can't want to sit and watch, can you?'

'Fine,' said Jim, trying to regain control in his own flat. 'You lot piss off to the pub and Ned and I will cook supper.'

Ned grinned at Marie, who was already slipping her arms back into her jacket. 'Or something like that. I'll call, OK? Won't be long.'

Chapter Two

Angus pushed open the door of the Bunch of Grapes and, as usual, the three men playing darts by the men's toilets stopped, turned round, muttered something to each other and carried on throwing the arrows overarm at the board.

Tamara looked round with an expression on her face which very clearly said, 'How *interesting* that people can still look so like gargoyles in this day and age!'

'Mad Boy Sam's staring at you again, Angus,' murmured Marie. 'I think he likes you.'

Sam – whom they knew well by sight, but fortunately not well enough for a surname – was more of a bar fitting than the dartboard. None of them could remember a time when they'd come in and he hadn't been sitting with his back to the bar, staring out at the clientele like a bouncer. He was of indeterminate age, with a small amount of black hair arranged not unlike The Count from *Sesame Street*, and was permanently sporting some minor injury, which he would inevitably be explaining in gruesome detail to the bar staff whenever anyone went for a drink.

When Ned and Jim had been sharing a flat near by, Ned had tried to catch him out by calling in for cigarettes as soon as the pub opened, but he was already there. Supervising.

'Of course he likes me,' said Angus. 'I'm a regular. And so is he.'

'In fact, most of them are staring at us,' Marie observed.

'I keep telling you not to wear a Barbour jacket in here,' Iona hissed into Angus's shoulder.

'What would you prefer me to wear, a sheepskin football manager's number?'

'So *this* is where Marillion disappeared to!' said Chris, a bit too loud.

'What is it about you?' Marie thwacked him playfully with the flat of her hand for the benefit of the barmaid, who was giving them the evil eye. Rather, one of her eyes was. 'When we want to say something rude, what do we do? We *whisper*, don't we?'

'Depends how big your mouth is,' said Chris. Loudly.

'Or how small your brain is.'

'So, anyway, what will you two lovebirds have to drink?' asked Angus, making his way to the bar.

Iona flicked a quick sideways glance at Chris and Marie, saw they were glaring eloquently at each other, and she sighed. Another long night. She looked around for a table. There were several. In fact, there were many. It wasn't really a 'sitting-down' pub. 'I'll have a Diet Coke.'

'The usual, please, Angus, thank you,' said Marie.

'Oh, so, seventeen gin and tonics then, is it?' said Chris immediately.

Iona bit her lip and prepared herself for the onslaught. It would be charitable to say that Chris had a combative sense of humour, but more realistic to say that he was too insensitive to tell the difference between being funny and being rude. More to the point, what would sound like harmless teasing coming from Angus or Ned always sounded like character assassination coming from him.

Marie's eyes went wide with shock and then narrow with indignation.

'Come and sit down, will you?' said Iona before Marie could open her anger-compressed mouth, and dragged her over to the corner table.

Angus leaned on the bar and tried to get the attention of the barmaid, who had suddenly discovered a pile of peanuts that needed rearranging on the other side of the horseshoe bar. The trick was to get her attention, but not Mad Boy Sam's. 'Er, hello? Hello? Very good. Deaf as well as . . . Oh, right, hi? Can we get some drinks in?'

Over in the corner, beneath a precarious and ancient silk flower arrangement, Iona went to put her bag on the floor, saw what she would be putting it on to and decided to keep it on her knee. With a beer mat, she swept the light scattering of crushed cheese and onion crisps that covered the table into a pile, making it higher and smaller from each angle until she had recreated a small alpine range in salty crumbs.

'Tamara,' she asked, looking up, 'are you sitting down or what?'

Tamara's pert rear hovered over the grimy plush of a red velvet stool, while she weighed up the other seating options. The high wooden bar stools were usually the best bet at the Grapes, since they at least were wiped down every week or so, but when in a group of more than three people, sitting in a row at the bar like that did make it feel as though you were on *Blind Date*. On the other hand, there was something on the seat directly below her that she couldn't quite make out in this light . . . Her long thigh muscles showed discreetly through her grey work trousers as she hovered.

Chris swallowed audibly.

'Because people are looking at you,' added Iona.

'I'm sitting down,' said Tamara, swiping Chris's leather jacket off the floor and draping it over her stool in one fluid movement. 'Mind if I sit on your coat, Chris? Thanks.'

'Pleasure,' said Chris weakly.

For the millionth time, Marie wondered why someone couldn't invent a wedding ring that somehow encoded the attractions of your best friends, like cable stations you hadn't paid for. Tamara with a fuzzy face and diminished volume would be much less stress all round.

At the bar, Angus struggled on manfully with the barmaid, who kept wandering away from him. 'That'll be a pint of Theakstons, a Diet Coke . . . Tamara?'

Tamara almost asked for a bottle of water on account of her detox programme and then thought better of it. The only bottled water you got at the Grapes was the bottle you took to the doctor for analysis afterwards.

'Errr, Diet Coke?'

'Two Diet Cokes, a pint of Stella . . .'

'Iona, tell me again, why do we come here?' asked Chris. He mounted a stool, splaying his legs round each side. It was a game they played a lot.

'Because it used to be near Ned and Jim's old flat and is now directly opposite Jim's new flat, and because it isn't full of pretentious advertising executives,' began Marie. 'Tamara?'

'Because it has proper seedy local pub atmosphere and it isn't randomly festooned with shillelaghs or hop seeders,' said Tamara, and turned to Iona.

'Because,' Iona's eyes skidded over the karaoke-night posters, the filthy windows and the man in the corner talking aggressively to his dog, 'because underneath all the filth there are some very interesting late Victorian mouldings?'

'You what?'

'Because beer is cheap here and we are poor?'

'Oh! Oh!' said Marie, waving her hand. 'Because of the quiz night!'

Every Wednesday the Bunch of Grapes held a quiz (first prize: a case of beer) which seemed to drag in every out-of-work roadie in London, as well as the usual crowd of flatmates and solicitors out on the piss. Not many students. There was something too grim about the Grapes even for students. On account of the clientele, the quiz tended to rely heavily on questions about the latter line-up of Hawkwind and what the combined age of the Rolling Stones was in 1983, which meant that there was always a new unsuspecting set of flatmates and solicitors every week to replace the ones who had left in a confused huff after the 'What Did the Drummer Die of?' round.

Iona and Ned, whose childhood in Carlisle had resulted in listening to music ten years out of date as a matter of course, were deceptively good on hairy metal bands in particular and, with Angus's rather middle-aged subscription to *Mojo* filling in any gaps, of late they had hit something of a winning streak. There were now four cases of Becks sitting in Jim's hall and Angus had suggested that it might be a good idea to give the quiz a rest for a while. Nobody minded a winner in the Grapes, even if they did sound suspiciously posh when collecting the beer, but Chris had developed an embarrassing habit of hissing 'Yeesssssss!' and thrusting his arms around in what he felt to be an ironically heavy-metal way whenever they got a question right and, frankly, the pub was never so full that they were properly hidden from view.

It was when he suggested getting team T-shirts with 'Everyone Hates Us and We Don't Care' that Marie suggested he might be taking his own persecution complex out on them.

'There is the pub quiz, yes,' agreed Chris. 'Though obviously when I can actually tell the difference between the riffs in the "Name That Riff" round, I might start enjoying it more. Still, all sounds the same when you're a brain-dead heavy-metal fan with impaired hearing and a denim jacket that walks to the bar by itself, eh?'

Marie bit back a retort.

So did Iona.

Tamara remembered why she hadn't seen Chris and Marie for about a fortnight.

'In fact,' Chris went on, unaware of the mood closing in around him like horror-movie fog, 'pretty much everyone here's a bit of a deaf leopard, eh? Eh? Def Leppard!'

'Your husband cracked a joke, Marie,' said Iona. 'Can you make him stop before the man behind you with a mullet and a flick-knife offers to pick his teeth for him?'

Angus came back with the first lot of drinks. 'Diet Coke

for m'lovely lady in red, a supersonic for Mrs Davenport and a pint of Stella for Mr Davenport.' He stood up. 'I thought Jim was coming over?'

'He said he wanted to watch Ned do some of the cooking.' Iona looked at her watch. 'But I'll give it five minutes before Ned kicks him out of the kitchen.'

'Do you think Jim's going to manage feeding himself on his own without Ned to show him how to get the beans out of the tin?'

'More to the point, do you think Ned's going to manage on his own without Jim to get him out of bed in the mornings?'

Iona shrugged her shoulders. She had been at school with Ned in Carlisle; Angus had been at school with Jim. They were a flatmate-match made in heaven. Ned had initially moved in with Jim when his old flatmate went back to Dublin, and they had quickly become completely co-dependent. So much so that when the issue of Jim's godmother's flat came up, Ned decided that he had to make the break and move in somewhere on his own, before he and Jim became more of a married couple than Chris and Marie. And, more to the point, before *every* single girl in London asked Iona if Jim and Ned had had one of those new informal pledging ceremonies in Soho.

However, all in all, it was a sad fact that Ned and Jim, even with levels of household orderliness that had systematically destroyed the will to live of three cleaners, radiated more domestic tranquillity than anyone else Iona knew. Filth and an addiction to registering obscene Internet domain names had bonded them. It was a fine, old-fashioned friendship. One that Chris constantly had trouble understanding, despite his right-on credentials.

'You would tell us, wouldn't you, if they said anything to you about being . . . you know . . .' Chris jiggled his eyebrows at Iona.

'About being you know what?' she replied icily.

'You know.' Chris held up his hands and added hastily, 'Not that there's anything wrong with that sort of thing, and you know I'm a bit of trendy liberal, but it's the kind of thing that a man needs to know about his friends, before . . .'

'Jesus Christ almighty,' said Marie into her gin and tonic.

'Before what?' asked Iona, as sweetly as she could. 'You *have* known Ned and Jim for, what? Five years or more? Are you looking to move in on Ned?'

'Chris, being able to scramble eggs does not make you gay,' snapped Tamara.

'Did Ned move out because they had a bit of a tiff?' he persisted. 'Because of that holiday they went on in Greece?'

'No!' Iona's hands itched to slap Chris but she sat on them because Marie was there, and it wasn't fair to make her suffer by drawing attention to themselves in a pub where all fighting took place in designated areas.

'Angus! Thank you!' said Tamara, trying ineptly to create a diversion by reaching out for the rest of the drinks.

Angus, who had only just turned round from the bar and was still virtually on the other side of the room, looked a little surprised. He ambled over, trying, out of habit, not to spill anything on the sticky carpet. It was dark, so as not to show beer stains, but this only had the unfortunate effect of highlighting suspicious lighter patches. 'Theakstons for me, Diet Coke for Tamara, Theakstons for Jim . . .' He looked up. 'Jim not here yet?'

'Angus,' began Tamara hotly, 'for God's sake, tell Chris that—'

'It doesn't matter,' said Marie. She shot Chris an acid look. 'Chris is either being hilariously retro or perhaps, more simply, an arse.'

'So, no change there then,' said Angus jokily, and took a mouthful off the top of his pint. 'Very good.'

The door of the pub opened and Jim appeared. He

was still wearing a blue-and-white-striped pinny round his waist.

Iona cringed.

When he saw them, Jim raised his arm in recognition and walked over, oblivious of the stares.

'That mine?' he asked, picking up the pint and slipping into the velvet booth next to Marie. 'Supper should be about half an hour. Ned's just doing some kind of sauce thing for the asparagus.'

'He doesn't have to,' said Marie guiltily. 'Not for us. It seems really unfair that we come round to your flat for supper and Ned spends the entire time sweating over a hot stove while we're in the pub.'

'That's a good traditional marriage for you,' said Chris, looking at Marie.

'No, *that's* domestic slavery. That's why we wrote our own wedding vows, remember? "I promise to treat and respect Marie as an autonomous human being"? Ring any bells? A beach? Your horrible travelling sandals? The delicate bridal fragrance of mosquito repellent?'

'Ah, happy days!' said Angus. There was a pause so he could do the routine. 'Just think, Iona, this could be us!'

'Yeah, just *think*,' said Iona automatically, and sank her head into her hands in pretend horror. This was her usual reply. Which didn't prove that she meant it, or didn't mean it. She peeped through her fingers and saw Chris scowling into his beer, though whether this was about Marie or Ned and Jim or just the state of the beer here she couldn't tell.

'Really?' said Jim. 'Aw, no. Surely you two must be getting engaged by now? How long have you been together?'

'Speaking of togetherness, are you missing not having Ned around?' asked Iona to change the subject. 'Mind you, it's difficult to tell he's actually living somewhere else, the amount of time he spends round at yours.'

'There comes a point in a man's life when he has to accept that he is never going to pull unless he lives on his own, you know what I mean? And anyway' – Jim took a big slurp of his pint – 'no woman's cooking is ever going to come anywhere near Ned's, so the sooner I stop getting used to restaurant-quality food every night, the better.'

Even though it was dingy beyond belief, the Bunch of Grapes had a relaxing, familiar atmosphere, and it was very easy to spend an entire evening in there, complaining merrily the whole time. Marie, who seemed to be drinking fast, got another round in, and then Jim went up to the bar to see if the new barmaid was as grim as Angus claimed, and before long it was getting on for nine already.

Iona's gaze wandered from the bouquets of dusty silk flowers marooned above the bar – which always made her think of some Victorian bride chucking them up there and no one being bothered to get them down again – to a group of young Scandinavians crowded round a table by the door. They were furiously consulting guide books, then peering at their drinks and she wondered if she looked old to them. She supposed they must seem old by now – Angus and Jim were nearer thirty than twenty. They all were.

Thirty!

She shivered and turned her attention back to the table and the collection of glasses filling it. Glass-clearing was never a strong point at the Grapes. Usually because most people brought their own tankards. Marie was comparing her nails with Tamara's and listening to the stream of New Year Vitamin Complex bullshit coming out of Tamara's mouth. Angus was sipping his pint and staring critically at the crumbling plaster mouldings over the windows.

And Jim's knee was jiggling up and down urgently beneath the table. He was looking back and forth at the different glasses before him with increasing anxiety.

Iona caught his eye and raised her eyebrow. The jiggling stopped immediately.

'Problem?'

'Er, no, no, not at all,' said Jim. 'We'll go soon, yeah?' He removed his hands from their warm haven between his legs, crossed his knees tighter and went back to his conversation with Chris about tropical diseases.

Thirty seconds later, the table started jiggling again and Iona turned to tell Jim to stop it when she realized it was now Angus's leg bobbing up and down in an annoying *pas de deux* with Jim's excitable knee. And he too had his hands clamped between his legs.

'What are you doing under that table?' she demanded. 'Is there a reason why you and Jim are clutching yourselves like that? Or are you trying to blend in with the rest of the regulars?'

'Um, I'm going over the road now,' said Jim, gesturing vaguely with the hand that wasn't clutching himself. 'I need to, um . . . check up on Ned.'

A light seemed to go on above Angus's head. 'Great idea. I'll, er, come with you.' He knocked back the rest of his pint in one.

'Er, aren't you going to wait for us?' asked Iona in surprise. 'We're only going to be two minutes.'

'But I really need—' Jim began.

'When I've finished my drink,' said Chris firmly. 'It's your own fault for getting another round in.'

Marie gave Jim and Angus a diagnostic up and down glance. 'Oh, I recognize this one,' she said. 'OK, OK. You both have my permission to go to the bathroom, only come straight back and don't forget to wash your hands afterwards.'

Angus made a small moaning noise.

'You've never been in the Gents here, have you, Marie?' asked Jim. It wasn't phrased as requiring a reply.

'Only in a manner of . . . Well, obviously not. In the *Gents*.' Marie fished the lemon out of her gin and tonic and flipped it into the ashtray. 'What do you take me for?'

'Well, even if I *wanted* to squat over a broken loo bowl in the manner of a constipated downhill skier, or pee into a

receptacle that looks as though it's just been unearthed from
a Roman dig . . . Are you still with me?' demanded Angus.

'More or less.' Marie couldn't help staring at the door
of the Gents now, even though it was probably asking for
trouble. Now that they mentioned it, she'd never noticed
any of them go to the loo in the Grapes.

'And even then I wouldn't want to go into the men's loos
until that bloke comes out.'

'Which bloke?'

'The barmaid.'

'Er, right,' said Iona.

'And her friend. The one who's been mending the jukebox
with the blade in his back pocket.'

'Fine,' said Marie, finishing her drink in one. 'Why didn't
you say so? Why didn't you just slip over the road and come
back? You could probably use your own loo from here if
you left the bathroom window open.'

'Marie!' Tamara looked shocked. 'That's the kind of thing
Chris would say!'

'No, I wouldn't,' said Chris. 'At home maybe, but not
here in front of ladies.'

'That's Ned,' said Angus loudly, replacing his phone in his
suit pocket. 'He says, Come on over to his place, hey you,
we're having a Wimpy.'

'Wimpy, still very big in the north of England,' Iona
explained to Tamara. 'I didn't hear your phone ring, darling,' she added to Angus.

But Angus was already halfway across the pub, with Jim
close behind.

Chapter Three

'What time is it?' asked Tamara, some hours later, sprawled in a red velvet chair in Jim's sitting room. She was clutching a big blue cushion over her stomach and rocking gently back and forth in time to the music, which Iona kept changing every ten minutes.

'It's . . . ten to one.'

'Ten to one!' Marie groaned, on her back in front of the fire, toasting her rounded stomach gently. 'I shouldn't be here. I should be cutting our spare sheets into child-size togas. I am giving St Anselm's the Marie Davenport Full-on Roman Experience this term – cooking, fashion, road building, the real meaning of the word spread-eagled, all before Easter. When I start on the Egyptians. God.' She let out a long garlicky burp. Chris shifted a few feet away from his wife. 'I made a resolution to be in bed by half-eleven every night for a month.'

'And how long did that last?' Tamara opened one eye.

'Hasn't started yet.'

'Well, my New Year's Resolution was to be in someone else's bed before the next New Year,' said Jim.

'And that hasn't started yet either,' added Ned, unnecessarily.

'Why don't you make it your resolution just to stay in bed until the New Year? You do enough training,' said Chris. 'Is there any more wine in that bottle?'

Marie threw a half-hearted arm out to hit him. 'You can talk, smartarse. You don't have to be in bed to be asleep.

I know where you go every day at three o'clock for half an hour.'

'Oooh, where?' asked Iona.

'To do the recycling run,' said Chris, at the same time as Marie sat up and announced, 'He sleeps in the loos at work for half an hour. One of his *colleagues* from the office told me they found him out when he came back from "doing the recycling run" with this bright red oval hole in the centre of his forehead.' She paused for full effect. 'They thought he might have been abducted by aliens and had his brains sucked out for analysis, but it turned out it was from lying with his arm over his eyes, where his watch had been pressing into his skull.'

'Is that the time?' Chris looked ostentatiously at his watch. 'I think Marie is getting a bit tired and emotional. I should take her home now.'

'No!' she protested, hugging a floor cushion. 'You don't understand. This is adult conversation. None of you has got anything stuck up your nose, or started a fight in the toilets, or been sick in someone's lunch. This is heaven!'

'I think, to be strictly accurate, you'll find Ned and Jim have done all those things in the last year,' Iona pointed out.

'Fair enough.' Marie slumped back down in front of the fire and stretched out luxuriously, wiggling her bare toes into the sheepskin rug.

'Would anyone like coffee? Since that's about the only thing I seem to be trusted to make?' asked Jim, as he winched himself off the sofa, where he had been comfortably wedged next to Ned and Angus, who were going through photographs of Jim's New Year, making unnecessarily savage comments about his relatives.

There was an apathetic silence.

'I said, who wants coffee?'

Muttered agreement.

'Tell us about your colonic irrigation, Tam,' said Marie.

'Does it make you feel less sluggish and, you know, less January-ish?'

'I'll go and make some coffee then, will I?' said Jim to no one in particular.

Tamara leaned over the side of her chair. 'Honestly, I just feel so much cleaner inside – especially after all that *food* at Christmas.'

Iona and Angus exchanged a quick, secret look. Food was not the problem, as anyone with a clear view of Tamara's flat stomach could see for themselves. The problem was more toxic than just too many chipolatas: Tamara, the decorative centre of any party, always got totally wasted at Christmas and New Year, indeed at Chanukah, Diwali and both the Queen's birthdays, in the hope that it would give her enough confidence to deal with seasonal sociability and the crowd of men who felt they had a seasonal free pass to Have a Go.

Like all apparent blessings, Tamara's show-stopping looks came with small print: she was self-conscious to the point of paranoia. If men gawped at her, she worried that they were only interested in her for the contents of her bra, and if they didn't gawp, she worried that she was never going to *get* a man. So she drank Southern Comfort and lemonade until she couldn't tell whether they were looking at her or not, and then Angus and Jim usually had to carry her home, still looking like Marianne Faithfull. Looking *particularly* like Marianne Faithfull. Iona had tried to expound on the new-fangled concept of not needing a man, but as Tamara pointed out, that only works when you've *got* one.

'You should try colonics.' She was demonstrating the reflexology bowel massage on Marie's hands. 'Doesn't hurt *at all*. And I mean, it's so simple. All the nurse does is she asks you to lie on your side, then she gets this tube . . .'

'Jim, hang on, I'll come and help you,' said Angus, levering himself up with surprising agility for a big man.

'Tell me this won't make me go to the loo now?' asked Marie, looking anxiously at her hands. 'I can't face two accidents in one day. And no, it wasn't me before you say anything, Ned. It takes a lot more than snow in the playground to overexcite me that much.'

'So, anyway, Tam, they do use KY first, though, don't they?' asked Chris. He leaned in nearer.

'We've no clean mugs,' said Jim without turning round, when he heard Angus opening and shutting cupboards. 'I mean, I had seven when I moved in and I don't know where they've got to.'

'Oh.' Angus opened a cupboard entirely filled with baked beans and shut it again quickly.

'But there are some posh cups in the box by the washing machine. That unpacked box.' Jim spooned coffee into the cafetiere. Three, four, five . . . his hand hovered over a sixth. How much coffee were you meant to put in? 'Tamara gave them to me. Well, to me and Ned. I haven't dared used them yet.'

'Wise,' said Angus. 'They'd probably disintegrate if you put instant coffee in them.' He moved some 'pending' washing to one side to get to the boxes in the corner and stared at the selection before him. 'Jim, how long have you been moved in here? There are about *six* unpacked boxes by the washing machine.'

'Er, yeah, it's my New Year's Resolution. New flat, New Year, new Jim.' Jim recklessly added a sixth spoon and poured on the boiling water from his space-age kettle. 'I'm going to be clutter-free. It's a test – if I don't miss it, I don't need it. So in February I'm chucking the lot out.'

Angus thought that in Jim's case that could eliminate such vitals as washing powder, an iron, green vegetables and a sense of purpose, but he didn't say anything. Instead he asked, 'Why is everyone talking about their arses tonight? It's revolting.'

'I know.' Jim opened and shut drawers in search of the After Eights Ned had put away. Living up to his reputation,

Ned had taken Jim's random selection of groceries and produced an apparently simple supper that everyone felt they should have been able to make on their own, but knew they couldn't. It helped that he seemed to carry things like truffle oil around with him for a start. 'I don't like to think of Tamara *having* bodily functions, to be honest with you. It spoils this little parallel universe I have going on in my head.'

Angus murmured a discreet agreement.

'Still,' Jim went on quickly, before he could give it too much thought, 'I think it's that time of year. No one's got much conversation. I mean, you've been very quiet. I haven't heard you disagree with anything Chris said all night.'

'God, I can't be bothered.' Angus ran a hand through his hair. 'Had an ap-*palling* day at work. I even shouted at Iona in the car on the way over. Even before she squashed Tam's scooter.'

Jim looked surprised. Quite apart from the fact that Tamara hadn't noticed her foldaway transport yet, Angus and Iona didn't argue. Ever. They weren't married, unlike Chris and Marie, who squabbled constantly and were. Perhaps there was some pattern to it.

'That's the trouble with Christmas,' Angus went on. 'You have a fortnight off to get used to doing nothing, getting drunk, lying in, doing your own thing with who you want, when you want, and then without warning, when you're suffering your biggest annual hangover, you're forced back to work and compelled to listen to everyone's stupid resolutions about how they're going to work harder and file everything immediately, and you *know* that their real resolution was to get a better fucking job somewhere else and that the reason there's no paper in the photocopier is because everyone's been updating their CVs.'

Jim nodded. 'I know. I don't think I'm still going to be at Overworld this time next year. I kept thinking that all through the bells. Mind you, I hate that half an hour *before*

New Year strikes when you look back over what you've done and what you need to do in the next year . . .'

'Yeah, and you just think, what's the point?' interrupted Angus bleakly.

Jim looked at him. 'Er, I was thinking more along the lines of, um, how long is it going to be before I get paid again? Actually.'

Angus lined up all the cups on the tray. White cups, black saucers, black cups, white saucers. Typical Tamara present, probably from a design shop. 'No, before you ask, it *is* that bad. Bring the coffee through?'

Jim watched Angus wedge the After Eights expertly under his arm and carry the tray into the sitting room.

Tamara was still draped crossways on the biggest chair, with Chris now virtually lying at her feet, transfixed by the conversation. Sporadically, and perhaps unconsciously, he was clenching his buttocks in time to the music. Marie was lying with her head propped up on one elbow, some way from Chris, Iona was sorting through Jim's CDs by the window, and Ned was stretched out full-length on the sofa with his eyes shut, one arm over his eyes and both legs dangling off the end. The arm above his head pulled his old green T-shirt up so the muscle ridges of his brown stomach were just visible. Every so often, Tamara flicked a glance at the room from behind a thick hank of blonde hair.

'. . . and then the water pressure in your colon just sort of . . . flushes everything out,' she was saying.

'Yes, but *do* you get to *see* all the bits *afterwards*?' Chris said. From the tone of his voice, it wasn't the first time he'd asked.

'*No*, you *can't*,' said Iona and Marie together.

'Weren't you listening to the nice lady?' Marie prodded his lower spine. 'She said it all goes straight into a bucket.'

'OK, but could you if you wanted to?' persisted Chris.

'Chris mate, I think you need to see a psychologist rather than a colonic irrigator,' said Angus.

Marie took the tray off him and started rearranging the cups back into matching pairs.

'I don't know about anyone else, but I wish I could flush out my entire head, instead of just my bowels,' said Iona. 'I feel, I don't know, totally clogged up after Christmas. I've got no energy, no enthusiasm, no nothing. Can't even be bothered to do the January sales. Did I say no money, by the way?'

Marie's hand stopped over teacups. 'Iona! Not you as well.' She reached out to Jim for the coffee pot and tried to push down the plunger. 'Iona, we rely on you to be our little ray of sunshine! Depression and sarcasm are the only things some of us are really good at!'

'It's all the practice you get that makes you so good,' said Chris.

'From living with you, *darling*.' Marie leaned on the plunger with her entire body weight and only managed to get it halfway down the cafetiere. 'Jim, can we go through the whole coffee-making thing again some time? I don't think you're quite there yet.'

'I know what she means, though,' said Tamara. 'I always wish you could start the New Year on a completely new note, but you're really still dealing with all the leftover shit from the previous year that you'd like to forget but your friends won't let you.' She gave Jim a particularly hard stare.

'Look, I only gave you his number because I vaguely knew him from home,' said Jim defensively, raising his hands. 'And if you'd told me you were going on a date with him I would have told you about his mother.'

'And his other little problem.'

'And . . . his other little problem, yes.'

'I tried to get my desk clear before the holidays,' said Chris, taking a cup of viscous black coffee from Marie. 'But it all came back again within three days of being in the office. I don't know why we kid ourselves that Christmas is the end of the year, when we all know there *is* no real end to the great rolling calendar that is Life. Human suffering doesn't stop for bank holidays.'

'At least you have regular work,' Tamara pointed out. 'I'm back on contracts now.' Tamara was a picture researcher, sometimes relief picture editor, sometimes relief waitress at the same café where Iona worked during the day. She agreed that the talent was much better in the café than in her other places of employment, as it was right in the middle of Clapham.

'Eeh, and I 'ave to lick t'roaads clean in't morning,' whined Jim, more at Chris than Tamara.

'That's a crap northern accent, man,' said Ned. He didn't open his eyes. 'After all the quality time we had together I'd've expected more from you.'

'Aye,' said Iona in an Eeh-Bah Gum North Yorkshire drone. 'Me an' all.'

'Give it a rest, Iona. What we all need is something new,' said Angus unexpectedly.

Iona looked at her boyfriend with faint amusement, although she tried not to show it. Usually 'new' was a synonym for 'evil, disruptive and wicked' in their house. Angus worked for a big City legal firm, had wanted to since he was very young, had sailed through exams with terrifying efficiency and was doing very well, as far as she could tell. His talent was for seeing a messy problem and straightening things out. Angus was a legal pair of straightening tongs. He also owned a tweed suit. Angus didn't like new. He liked proven, traditional, reliable. He liked a history of past test cases. She provided the new in their relationship.

'New, like what?' she inquired politely.

'A new challenge. Something that we actually want to do, rather than what we have to do every day for someone else.'

'If you're trying to skirt around the issue of wife-swapping,' said Chris, 'can I say right now that that's fine with me and you can take Marie home with you this evening if you want.

I can send her stuff on later. She does a passable paella, but don't let her try to give you a back massage.'

'Angus, man, didn't we have all this out at New Year?' murmured Ned. 'Five minutes each before midnight for regrets and recriminations, and you spent yours going on about the firm you didn't liquidize properly.'

'Liquidate,' Angus corrected him automatically. 'But that's just it, I don't think I'm doing anything properly any more. I had a pretty serious relationship with the law, but we've not been talking much lately. I've not been as attentive as I used to be, thinking about seeing someone else and, quite frankly, I think it might be time for me to move my things out. I've been thinking about it a lot and if we don't do something now, whatever it is you really want to do, it will be too late.'

'Too late for me already. My whole life was ruined at six because I couldn't be a Mini-Pop,' said Iona, the only person sufficiently used to extended metaphors to be able to follow what Angus was on about. 'And it's been one long disappointment ever since.' This was, in fact, completely true.

'Take it from one who knows,' said Marie, 'the only proper place for a Mini-Pop is in a deep-freeze.'

'Is anyone listening to me?' Angus demanded.

'Yes, I'm listening,' said Chris, rolling on to his side. His face looked blank. 'I know what you mean. I've got to the stage now where, in a couple of months, I'll have to commit myself to a much bigger, longer-term project, which will mean being in the same job, the same office, the same country, for at least three years. And after that I'll be locked into the same kind of thing. I find that a bit weird, you know? After travelling so much before I started. It isn't exactly what they said it would be when I joined.'

Marie looked at him curiously. It wasn't like Chris to admit to finding his job at the charity anything less than totally satisfying and spiritually uplifting. For one thing,

it would deprive him of his best argumentative weapon –
the industrial-strength guilt trip he wheeled out whenever
he wanted to cut them all down to size.

'Anyone want to help Jim with tidying up the kitchen?'
asked Ned, ignoring him. 'It's a right sty.'

Chris drained his cup crossly.

'So, let me get this straight,' said Iona. She pointed at
Chris. '*You* don't want to get married to your job.'

'Well, I wouldn't say . . .' Chris backtracked.

She pointed to Angus. '*You're* thinking of some kind of
trial separation, let's not get too heavy here, possible split
from your job.'

He nodded with a grimace.

She pointed to Tamara. '*You* don't have a steady job,
you've got about three on the go at once and you're still
playing the field a bit.'

Tamara, who wasn't brilliant with metaphors, looked
affronted but Iona moved on swiftly.

She pointed to Marie. '*You* have a bit of a sado-masochistic
kinky thing going with your job – like you pretend you hate
teaching, but we all know you secretly love it.'

'Apart from the actual kids element,' Marie agreed.

She pointed at Ned. '*You* are brilliant at your job and
we're all very grateful, thanks, and *I* don't like to think of
waitressing as a job as such, I prefer to think of it as funding
for my vocation, which is Art.'

There was a display of groans, sick-making noises and
obscene hand gestures.

'Look, while there's loft space in Clerkenwell, there's
money to be had from combing poster paint over canvases,'
she protested.

'Quite a lot more than you'd think,' added Angus, giving
her knee a proud and slightly painful squeeze.

'And? And?' said Jim, pointing to himself.

Iona delicately loosened Angus's grip from her knee. 'Oh,
yeah,' she said, looking at him as if for the first time. 'Give

me a clue. What is it you do again? Is it bigger than a bread box?'

Jim rolled his eyes. 'I am a *property developer*.'

There was another display of eye-rolling, dismissive fart noises and obscene hand gestures.

'Show me a property that you have developed.' Chris lay back with his arms folded over his chest.

'That place in Kennington!' Jim protested. 'One horrible house, soon to be three lovely flats, and a live/work area!'

'Soon?'

'Ye-ee-es,' Jim said uncertainly, 'once all the legal stuff is sorted out.'

'Right.' Chris looked round smugly.

'Show us a starving African you've liberated,' said Angus. 'Oh no, you can't. They're all dead. Very good.'

'I wouldn't want to be the man who wakes up and has to face that kitchen,' said Ned before Chris could react. 'I know that hollandaise was good, but I just about used every pan you've got, mate.'

'Oh, God!' Jim rolled on his back and stared at the ceiling, the first one he'd rented that didn't have large, ominous cracks bisecting it. Most ceilings you could read like a palm. But without the potential for good news. 'If only the Bunch of Grapes served decent food, I'd just eat in there and leave the dishwasher for storing beers.'

'Well, it's funny you should say that!' said Angus.

Iona looked at him carefully and took a big mouthful of coffee. So this was what all his recent ruminative silences had been leading up to. And now Angus was showing all the signs of mounting his Big Argumentative Horse. Once he was on it, it was impossible to get him off without a stun gun. When Angus got an idea in his head, a red mist descended before his eyes and he was possessed by the spirit of Hannibal, complete with elephants.

'Jim,' said Angus, fixing Jim with a persuasive smile,

'every time we go to the Bunch of Grapes, you look round it and say—'

'In a *slightly* too loud voice,' interjected Marie.

'—how you should buy it, get some investment drummed up and turn it into the kind of pub normal people actually want to drink in. You know, with decent food, proper beer, none of your poncy fake Irish theme nights.'

Iona noticed with a sinking heart that Angus had put down his coffee. This meant the arms were about to waved. Next it would be pointy fingers.

'You know Brian's always moaning about how he wants to retire to the Costa del Sol with Lois. Last time we were in he was even showing people estate agents' brochures.'

'Oh, yeah,' agreed Ned. 'You wouldn't believe how much proximity to a crazy golf course can add to your average bungalow out there. And Lois has always tanned easily, apparently.'

'I bet he'd just about give that place away, if you made him the right offer. It can't be making that much money as it is at the moment. It needs a complete overhaul. And I mean, we've got all the resources right here.' Angus looked round the room. He conceded to himself that they didn't look like a crack team of youthful entrepreneurs, but even Richard Branson had worn crap jumpers to start with.

'Jim, you could sort out the finance for actually buying it and setting it up, and I've done a lot of property law. Tenancies, that kind of thing. Ned could run the kitchen, get the right people in, sort out a menu, and Iona could use her extensive catering experience to be in charge on the staff side . . .'

'*Thank* you, darling,' said Iona brightly. 'But didn't you mean to say, "Iona can oversee the design and decoration"?'

'Iona can oversee the design and decoration,' repeated Angus, 'with Tamara helping out, of course, on the "attractive big pictures in black frames" front . . .'

'Not forgetting the "attracting people into the pub in the first place" front,' added Marie.

'Thank you, Marie,' said Angus, not sure if she was joking or not. 'And Chris can . . . can be in charge of, um, publicity and stuff . . .'

'And what do you have in mind for me?' asked Marie sweetly. 'Can I be in charge of writing up the menu? I'm very experienced at writing straight on blackboards. It's my party piece. That and removing Plasticine from infant orifices.'

'Perfect!' said Angus. 'Orifices. Lots of call for that sort of thing, I would imagine. Very good.'

His face was flushed and shining, noted Iona. Angus was a genuinely sweet man, but recently he'd been a ratty whiner, and, privately, she missed hearing him sing in the bath. It was frustrating when he was unhappy at work and she didn't have enough experience of office politics to be really helpful to him. So what if this was Fantasy Investment League? At least he wasn't throwing his mobile phone around. And there was something about Angus's enthusiasm that was truly infectious. How would I redesign the Bunch of Grapes, she wondered idly. How would you even set about *cleaning* the Bunch of Grapes?

'You make it sound so simple,' Jim said. 'Would you like to come and work for Overworld?'

Jim was the least susceptible to Angus's bouts of fervid persuasion, having had exposure to them for the longest time. When Angus had suggested getting an old school cricket team together, Jim was volunteered to do the actual getting together of it. Iona had slaved over the cream tea with Marie, and Chris and Ned were roped in to play, even though they weren't actually Old Boys and, as Chris objected as he was pushed on to the pitch in a pair of pads intended for a much taller man, they had both been to comprehensive schools. Angus's contribution was a majestic seventy, all in sixes and fours, after which he retired (sunstroke). Three fielders had to haul him off the pitch and he had lain heroically in the darkened pavilion for the rest of the match while Iona fed him strawberries and cream and the rest of the team sweated away to a draw in the 100-degree heat.

Hence the general wary reception to the latest inspiration. Jim's legs were aching already at the mere thought of it.

'It *sounds* simple because it *is* simple,' said Angus. 'People do it all the time.' He raised his arms above his head and waggled his fingers.

OK, thought Iona, here we go. And next: the whiz-kid speech.

'You know, I'm *sick* of reading in the *Standard* about all these whiz kids making money hand over fist with ideas I could have had,' said Angus, prodding the arm of the chair with his finger. 'This is the last chance we'll have to do something like this before we all get bogged down in mortgages and babies and life insurance, and Middle Age comes after us waving a big stick. And I don't know about you, but I *really* want to see if we can do it.'

Iona quietly replaced her cup on the saucer so as not to distract him, or draw attention to herself.

'Between us, we've got a *huge* amount of potential.' Angus was well into his stride now. 'And, if it doesn't work, it doesn't work. We can go back to our horrible jobs that we all hate with our tails between our legs and resign ourselves to a life of humdrum wage-slavery.'

'It is a great location for a pub like that,' agreed Jim tentatively. 'There's nothing here that does good food that isn't really wanky.'

'And it would be so convenient!' said Tamara.

'For whom exactly?' demanded Chris.

'Oi, Iona.' Ned was nudging her discreetly with his foot and brandishing a glass. 'You fancy some more wine? I think this could be a long runner.'

She nodded and looked over at Angus. There were no signs of him wanting to leave in the next three hours: his sleeves were now pushed back and his eyes were glittering with the kind of zeal she normally saw on QVC. He was wasted in a law office, she thought protectively. There were churches all over the Midwest crying out for that kind of rhetorical conviction.

And since she'd heard it all before at least once, she wouldn't be missed.

'Go on, then,' she muttered to Ned. 'Let's get the bottles out of the way for when Chris tries to argue with him.'

'And as for the food,' Angus was saying, making huge circles with his hands, 'as for the food, well . . .'

Chapter Four

'That's one skinny decaff latte, one skinny blueberry muffin and an espresso to go?' Iona recapped the order written on the back of her hand. Half in ink, half in red scratches where her Biro had run out midway through.

'Yeess,' said the woman in the power suit. It was the 'yes' that Iona and the other girls translated as being an abbreviation of 'Yes, I have a degree and I bet you don't.'

'OK,' said Iona. That translated as 'OK, you might have, but you're still talking in meaningless Seattle coffee jargon that you think makes you look cool because *Friends* followed by *Ally McBeal* is your idea of a good night in.'

Normally she was much quicker, but the after effects of Chris's rough taste in wine were still draped over her brain like bubblewrap. The after effects of Angus's 'We Must Change Our Lives' speech were also niggling away. He had gone on until half-two before grinding to a halt, exhausted.

'Great!' She smiled. 'Coffee will be at the end of the counter and I'll pack the muffin for you.'

It wasn't that Iona didn't like working at Coffee Morning, because she did. She didn't see anything remotely unsatisfying about it. For one thing, you could have the radio on all day, and for another, it suited her short attention span to be doing ten small, easily completable jobs all at once. It was only her mates who thought she should be doing something with a suit. She *liked* dispensing caffeine to needy people first thing in the morning. She liked frothing milk, cleaning tables, spending someone else's money on big bunches of flowers, being really expert on coffee varieties. And most of all she liked taking off her pinny at three o'clock, handing the till to the owner's daughter, Sarah, and then going home to an empty house to paint.

Painting was the real part of Iona's day. All the rest was just research. Sarah envied the way Iona could remember who'd ordered what on each table – it got her good tips – but the reason she remembered was because she was already storing them in her head like a gigantic photo library of impatient scowls and distracted smiles and intent gossip. Iona's daytime customers made up big collages of faces and colours that she worked on at night. Maybe it was a good job most of them didn't know that.

All right, it was a bit of cliché to be working in a café so she could carry on painting, and deep down Iona knew it was a luxury she couldn't keep up for ever, so she loved it, rather guiltily, while she could. She knew she was lucky Angus had cannily bought his flat before Brixton went trendy and that her contributions to the household expenses were much less than they would be in a flatshare. And so far, whenever some dental insurance-type crisis had struck, the Divine Law of Jamminess had intervened and she had managed to sell one of her big canvases at Spitalfields Market. Iona knew she was temporarily blessed. It only felt odd now that all the rest of her friends were doing proper jobs.

In the meantime, making endless cups of coffee, listening to the radio and tidying up weren't all that different from being at home. What wasn't there to like?

Iona smiled at the next woman in the queue, who scowled back. 'Morning, what can I get you?' She pushed her long brown fringe out of her eyes and turned up the radio. It was playing 'Stairway to Heaven'.

Angus and Iona's home was as muddled and colourful as her paintings. For five years, Iona had been sharing Angus's

big flat in Brixton, which had a large garden, two Battersea
Rescue cats called Lady Cat and Creighton, and a shed
where Angus had once stored his impressive collection of
DIY tools and in which she now painted. For the past six
weeks, however, in her head, she had been living with Jimmy
Page. As in the guitarist from Led Zeppelin.

Iona fell in love once a month, on average. She fell in love
with colours, writers, food, shoes and, sometimes, bizarrely,
chunks of history. Iona had the brain of a librarian and the
heart of a shameless teenage strumpet, and when she fell,
she fell hard and willingly.

But the Jimmy Page thing was going beyond the usual
limits. For the past six weeks there had been a Led Zeppelin
song playing in her head at all times, like a jukebox hijacked
by a particularly unimaginative local bikers chapter. She
found her fingers drumming out 'Stairway to Heaven' on
the espresso machine, apparently of their own accord. She
was happy to bellow 'Babe I'm Going to Leave You', even
though she weakly objected to the lyrics on postmodern
feminist grounds. She even started parting her hair in the
middle, to Angus's private distress. He blamed himself for
having the albums in the first place, and was constantly
paranoid about smelling patchouli everywhere.

She knew exactly why she did it, though she was aware
that it didn't make her look particularly mature. Life with
Angus was a steady, good-natured hum, but once they'd
settled into their rhythms she missed the exhilarating mood
swings of dating. She knew each month would end with
them still together, as regularly as their joint subscription
to *Private Eye* and Council Tax direct debits. Mini-affairs
with random objects provided the falling-in-love rush of
hysterical consumption, the sharp sweet stab of loss: that
she would never be able to see Led Zeppelin play live,
for example, or that gorgeous, ethereal Jimmy Page now
looked like someone who played pub league darts at the
Bunch of Grapes. But in the grip of something she couldn't

really associate with her normal life, Iona didn't care about that. She was in love with the dizziness which lurched around her heart whenever she heard the music, and the desperation that sloshed around her stomach when she realized it had all been over before she was born. Falling in love. Over and over again.

Iona didn't mind being swept along by sudden passions, running like a current through the rest of her day-to-day existence. That was the way she was and it made her feel alive. She knew these crushes would last only a few weeks and that, unlike a real affair, when it was over she'd be wiser, better informed about the origins of heavy metal or novelists of the 1920s, and still sharing a bed with the man she adored. When Iona fell, she wanted to immerse herself in her new obsession, but she was careful never to neglect what was real. The happiness, luckiness, of her real life was what allowed her to plunge so hard – and come back again.

Iona thought people who were unfaithful lacked imagination. There was nothing she would do to risk seeing Angus look at her with hurt written all over his open, honest face. But when they even shared the same bathwater, these vivid infatuations in her head made her feel as though she was keeping a little bit of herself private, fenced off for her own private use. A part that no one would guess was her.

And keeping that part was hard enough when all her friends relied on her to be emotionally stable and open-all-hours to their problems. They approached her as she washed up after supper as they might approach a supplier on a street corner, slightly embarrassed, self-conscious, apologetic but needy: 'Iona, can I have a quick word after . . .' She sometimes wished that they'd keep a bit more of themselves fenced off too. Increasingly, there were things that she didn't want to know.

Like whatever was boiling up between Marie and Chris. Won't be long before I get the panoramic version of that one, thought Iona grimly, rinsing out the cleanest of the J-cloths.

She checked her watch – nine-thirty – and began to wipe down the emptying tables before the first wave of mothers came in from dropping their children off at school.

She didn't mind helping out when there was something she could do, but with those two . . . There were lines you had to draw, even with your best friends. Iona swiped at the first table, driving the flakes of croissant into the centre like dead leaves. The lads thought their squabbling was hilarious, but Iona thought only some kind of masochist could imagine that was a happy household. Not that Marie had said anything, but there were only so many 'theoretical' conversations you could have about soap opera marriages.

Iona swept the crumbs into her hand. It was hard to know what to do. She and Marie had made a pact never to say, 'I told you so' about anything. And Marie was bloody stubborn like that – she'd rather suffer than be wrong, be it bad sex or tight shoes. Despite the assertions of winsome feature writers, in real life there was a discreet but solid veil that you had to draw with absolute best mates, usually over problems you could admit cheerily to acquaintances. In the years that they'd been friends, Marie had come to her worrying over all manner of humiliating medical conditions, embarrassing repercussions of ill-advised cloakroom gossip and awkward, debilitating crushes on unavailable men, but she had never ever admitted that a relationship was on the way out until she was safely dumped and the matter was out of her hands.

Iona knew from experience knew that you shouldn't judge a relationship's Elasticity Rating by the number of quarrels the couple had. She and Angus barely passed a day without a brief private swipe about the state of the flat or her inability to drive, but it was more like two lions batting each other, claws in, than Chris and Marie's brittle bickering. Sometimes, listening to the pair of them exchanging tight little comments in the pub, Iona was convinced that it was only one short step from 'God, Marie, is that your third beer already?' to 'Yes, it is, Chris and, by the way, YOUR MOTHER BLOWS DONKEYS FOR CASH!!'

More recently they'd taken to simply ignoring each other completely.

She frowned. It was definitely a bad sign when couples couldn't even argue together. Forget the making up afterwards. From the outside it was so obvious: half the time Chris couldn't tell when Marie was lacerating him, which only aggravated her, and his retorts were usually more hurtful than he intended, through their sheer ineptness. Iona paused with her cloth above some jam and conceded that was a polite way of saying that Chris was just too thick for Marie.

Iona gave the table a final lash and moved on to the next. Maybe the Bunch of Grapes mightn't be such a bad idea, even if it went only as far as having a good discussion about what they could do. Nothing jumpstarted flagging attraction quite as much as seeing your boyfriend coming out with businesslike suggestions and generally looking capable. Many of her fantasies about Angus revolved around him seducing her over his office desk, but only after he'd given her half an hour's complex and extremely expensive legal advice. Even her Jimmy Page fantasies involved a two-hour concert and a backstage impromptu acoustic session.

And really Angus was right: any minute now they were going to find themselves fully strapped into pension schemes and serious-illness insurance. And kids. Iona paused. Maybe that was the problem with Chris – he couldn't handle the idea of settling down yet. Maybe you couldn't, with charity work. Much as she enjoyed waitressing, surely it would feel better to be working for herself, for Angus – the difference between renting a flat and making inroads on a mortgage.

But where would that leave guilt-free painting?

Iona started wiping again, harder than before.

Chapter Five

Angus watched the clouds drift across the sky above central London. His office was high up enough to have a blanket view of sky out of the window – he was pretty positive that the office allocation had been messed up somewhere down the line and that this fascinating panorama of London had been intended for someone more senior. That was the way it went, wasn't it? The more senior you were, the less building you had to look at. The closer your view of heaven. The further away your view of Liverpool Street Station.

Today the sky was pure clean blue, blue like the background on a Wedgwood urn, thought Angus, pleased that he'd managed to pin it down. The sun was hidden, uplighting the whole sky, dramatic edges of intense light outlining each puffy cloud, undarkened by any rain inside. The drifting was hypnotic. The crochet of nimbuli (was that the right word?) stretched into the distance in a Magritte-like regularity, but so perfect you wouldn't believe they weren't painted.

Angus's hand strayed to the phone. He'd never had himself down as a creative type, being more of a *doing* chap, hence law, but he'd really started noticing things like this – tricks of the light, the sun moving across the day, the number of police helicopters in the area – since he'd moved into the new office, and he suspected, ironically, that it was having a contributory effect to his general not-very-positive attitude towards work. Sometimes he found himself putting his phone on transfer because he was looking at the busy sky so intently – whenever that happened, he made himself stay an extra half-hour at work as punishment, which only increased the staring-out-of-the-window desire.

Angus wondered if anyone else in the building had noticed the incredible pattern of clouds and sun. That was what happened when you tried to work a ten-hour day in eight hours, most days. No time to stop and look out of the window at what was happening outside while he moved piles of paper around inside. I should ring Iona and tell her, he thought; she would appreciate it, she'd understand what I meant.

As soon as his hand touched the cold plastic of the phone, he remembered that at ten in the morning, Iona would probably be in the middle of making millions of low-fat lattes for the post-school run au pair scrum and their screaming, toddling, sticky-pawed charges and possibly wouldn't appreciate a phone call telling her how beautiful and paintable the sky was over central London when she wouldn't be getting back to her painting shed until it was all dark.

The phone beneath his hand rang and Angus stared at it stupidly for a moment before his mind caught up.

'Angus Sinclair?'

Don't I say that to them, thought Angus, confused, and pulled himself together. 'Yes, hello.'

'Angus, it's Margaret from Human Resources. You're taking a discussion this morning with the graduate intake?'

Angus looked at his watch.

'In about ten minutes?' she went on pointedly. 'In the Churchill Rooms?'

So he was.

God, the graduate intake. Silently, Angus closed his eyes and leaned forward until his forehead touched the desk. The graduate intake, who unwittingly made him want to run round the room like a chicken, screaming, 'Stop the clock! Stop the clock!' All fresh and enthusiastic, and smelling of brisk unisex aftershave, even the girls, with their new suits and their extension-of-university social life arranged for them by the firm. They made him feel about forty-five.

In a way, Angus was flattered that he'd been picked out to do these discussions, but the suspicious part of his lawyerly brain wondered whether it was because other people he knew at the same stage as him were otherwise occupied with more important responsibilities. Responsibilities that might lead to promotions.

But is that what you really want?

He raised himself back to a sitting position and looked at the nondescript painting on the wall opposite his desk. Every office had one. About twice a day Angus asked himself how he could get Iona cut in on the 'tranquil and yet purposeful' paintings for law firms racket.

The bottom line for Angus was that if Iona was going to paint, then he had to do the law ladder and that meant promotions. He'd be a partner in a couple of years, then if they got married, if she wanted to take time off to have children . . .

Their children.

Angus smiled stupidly.

As long as he had her, and time to do up the flat, and play the odd game of cricket in the summer, he'd be fine.

His smile faltered. Or rather, that's what he'd been telling himself for ages now, and yet the blue sky outside hadn't seemed so appealing this time last year. Maybe it was the pension documents he'd had to sort out a few months back, or it could have been the shocking realization over lunch with his mentoring group that some of the new graduate intake had never seen a pound note. Or maybe it was some quarter life crisis, but whatever it was, some of his more iron-clad principles about What Was Right had started to feel a bit wobbly, and now he'd started wobbling them, like a loose tooth, he couldn't stop.

The phone rang again and Angus stared at it. If it was

Margaret calling again, he should be in the lift by now. If it was someone from Nuttall Nichols & Co. calling about the property in Belgravia, he certainly wouldn't have time to explain the latest shenanigans and still get down to the Churchill Rooms in time – the solicitor handling it on their side couldn't run a nun hunt in a nunnery.

God, he hated running around for other people, Angus thought, as he checked his e-mails one final time. If he took the trouble to be efficient, why couldn't they? It wasn't as though he *liked* being right all the time.

He pulled on his suit jacket and flipped through his in-tray for the notes on Negotiating Business Leases he'd prepared last week. His tactic now after three such sessions was to scatter information on the waters and let the fragrant, eager graduates come up with the actual discussion bit. That made them feel he was listening and also allowed him to stare meaningfully out of the window under the pretext of following the discussion.

He stopped and looked at his notes.

Business leases. Hmm.

Chapter Six

Marie shook her watch out from under the fake leopard-skin trim of her gloves. It was still only half past four. She hitched her school bag higher up on her shoulder and strode past some more shops on the precinct, quelling, with a withering glare, a gang of teenage girls from the upper school who were popping gum and sniggering aggressively at any passer-by over the age of twenty outside HMV.

She tried to make herself walk slowly. Marie was not good at wasting time. It bothered her. Whereas Iona had a calorie computer built into her head, Marie had a stopwatch. And try as she might, she couldn't switch it off. She knew how long spin cycles took. She knew when to plant bulbs for spring. She knew exactly how long to leave depilatory cream on for without frying her skin. She knew the precise attention span of irksome Lauren Edwards in her year-three class. Marie's Swiss timing was a skill that made her an expert manager of children and an expert destroyer of her husband. When he noticed.

She knew now, for instance, that in the same time she was wasting wandering around Oasis waiting for Chris to finish work so he could meet her for an early film, she could have educated a class of seven-year-olds in the arcane ways of the apostrophe, according to the national guidelines laid down by people who had probably had to use the spellcheck on the word 'apostrophe'.

Marie decided, browsing through a rack of bright shirts that would gape in an unsightly way across her ample bosom and so annoy her husband, that the hardest thing about teaching was that you never stopped doing it. Even when you were miles away from the screaming infants and their screaming parents, you were still teaching in your head. How much is 20 per cent off? What fabric is this? Which animal does Lycra come from?

She pulled a purple and a green example off the rack and amended that in her head. There were *many* hard things about teaching. The pay. The parents. The sad fact that recorders had been banned by the PTA at her current school, after all the hard work she'd put in at teacher training college getting to grips with a plastic Aulos descant. Teaching was not a soft option, but she'd known that when she started. Unlike many of her friends, Marie had a very clear idea of what she wanted to do, and even though it was tough, she intended to do it. Marie was like that.

The shop stereo was playing *Abba Gold* very loud and it began to put her in a better mood. She gave the shirts a critical stretch and was pleased to find that they had a good bit of give in the front. Which they would need.

Marie hummed 'Dancing Queen' to herself, rocking from foot to foot, and debated whether or not she should bother trying on clothes she really didn't need. On the one hand, she knew she really couldn't spend any money so soon after her Christmas spree. Particularly when any such clothes would have to be two sizes bigger than the size she had promised herself she would be by March, which would give her only three months' wear out of them.

On the other hand, the side effects of spending her thinking hours exclusively with seven-year-olds and forty-five-year-olds were manifesting themselves in a new and unhealthy interest in clothes that were either Comfortable or Neon. The words 'Rod, Jane and Freddy' and 'dungarees' were never far from her worried mind.

And she had browsed an entire new season's worth of stock and it was still only twenty to five.

Marie told herself that spending twenty minutes confirming that skinny-fit shirts couldn't *ever* suit her was a better waste of time than doing nothing, and took three into the changing room, where she began divesting herself of the many layers she was wearing. Scarf. Big warm jacket. School jumper. T-shirt. Little vest. Cotton jersey and wool piled up in the corner, much like the growing slag-heap of washing which festered in their bedroom while the laundry stand-off continued.

She slipped a dimpled arm into one of the three-quarter-length sleeves and knew instinctively how big the rest of the shirt would be. The material had a limited amount of give. Generous, but not exactly munificent. Chris doesn't like me wearing tight clothes like this any more, she thought, as she buttoned up the front of the purple one. Now why might that be?

The tangerine lace of her bra glowed between the straining buttonholes, so she undid the top four buttons of the shirt until her beautiful shelf-like bosom was exposed. Marie had a full-on Gina Lollobrigida bosom. Her skin looked peachy even under the harsh changing-room lighting, speckled with little chocolate-coloured freckles down into the soft cavernous cleavage. Hers wasn't so much of a balconette bra as an extension under scaffolding.

'Mamma mia!' she pouted into the mirror. '*La dolce vita! Que sera sera!*' She turned her head and shook back her curly black hair, admiring her profile. Then she saw the line around the back where the tight shirt was adhering to her bra straps and she deflated.

Or rather, she wished she could deflate at will.

This was why Chris didn't like her wearing tight shirts.

Turning to the front again it looked fine. She upped her pout. Tight and sexy. Mediterranean. *Carmen.*

From the side, vertiginous (Marie made a mental note to use the word in class tomorrow). Even a bit *Grease* with the collar turned up.

But from the back, blowsy. The shirt of a Fat Woman.

She turned back to face herself. Sophia Loren had abandoned her face and been replaced by her mother. Her mother in a bad post-Weight Watchers mood too. Why didn't fashion spreads ever show you what models looked like from the back? Did it *matter* what you looked like from the back? Was it her fault her man spent so much time trailing around behind her?

The purple looked amazing with her orange bra, but . . .

But.

And, indeed, butt.

Too late, thought Marie. It's those buts again. She unbuttoned each smug little rubber button and replaced the shirt on the hanger next to the lime-green one and a black one with a frill.

It wasn't her fault that you could only hold genetics at bay for so long.

She stood for a moment, smoothing her creamy stomach beneath the tangerine bra with her flat hands, until she remembered something Chris had been watching on Carlton about cameras in changing rooms and stopped feeling herself up.

Mind you, she thought, rallying with each still-warm school-teacher layer she pulled back on over her head, a bit of evolution wouldn't harm Chris much. A bit of development. A bit less of the knuckles-on-the-ground attitude.

'Though you know I'm a liberal kind of guy,' she mouthed to herself in the mirror, and instantly felt ashamed.

Then she felt sick at the thought of being married to someone who had not only a catchphrase, but a catchphrase her own friends took the piss out of.

Marie pulled on her jumper before she could see the expression on her face.

The shirts had filled up a good twenty minutes, from sale rail to changing room, but Marie knew that before she saw Chris she had to shake off the bad mood that was settling in for the long haul inside her head. Seeing him would just make it all set like a jelly of irritability. She also had to go somewhere where she wouldn't – couldn't – spend money.

She browsed through the racks at STA – the only shop apart from Boots Opticians where she couldn't impulse-buy – and idly picked up some brochures for India and Thailand. Her first thought was that she could use them as part of the geography project for later in the term, and the second one was that – horror of horrors – teaching seemed to have usurped her entire personality and now took precedence even over her honeymoon memories.

Marie and Chris had been married for a little over five years. They had got married when it was a reckless, mad thing to do, while they were on their reckless, mad junket around the world before settling down to proper jobs in London. The ceremony had taken place on a beach, as the sun went down on a very calm sea and the sand was still warm beneath their bare toes. Despite the daytime heat, the nights went very cold, very quickly.

Chris and Marie had been travelling together for a couple of months and the exhilaration of being free to move from place to place, working in this bar or that café purely to get enough money for the next bus, was running through their veins like the most powerful amphetamine imaginable. After the constant pressure of university, the sheer size of the rest of the world was like a constant thrill to the system. There wasn't anywhere they couldn't go, anything they couldn't do. Including getting married.

A small part of Marie was sad that her big family weren't there to share in it but, as Chris had said at the time, weddings always ended up being about everyone except the two people involved. This way it was a memory they would have all to themselves.

Chris had whirled it all up out of nowhere, which had

made Marie shiver inside at his impetuosity and passion.
They had been walking along the beach one evening, drinking beer and discussing whether they should stay or move on
to the next country, when she had seen an American girl she
vaguely knew from the bar where she'd been working during
the day. Cally was strolling across the sand in a white bikini,
with a white sarong around her tanned hips, flowers tucked
into her bra top and a short white veil on her head. It had
looked so incongruous that Marie had called over and asked
her where she was going, dressed like that.

Cally had smiled lazily (everyone seemed constantly stoned
to Marie, who never touched the stuff) and laughed lazily
(and the constant giggling had, to be honest, started to get
on her nerves a bit), and had pointed over to the tide line,
where one of the surfer guys from the bar was standing, also
adorned in flowers and very little else.

'We just got married,' she explained hysterically. 'It was
just . . . kinda . . . y'know.' She made strange wavy gestures
with her hands and rolled her eyes, smiling and shaking her
head like a go-go dancer.

'Cool!' said Chris.

'Romantic!' said Marie.

And Cally reeled off to drink cheap rum out of coconuts
for the rest of the night, while her new husband made
discreet inquiries about work permits in the US.

Marie wondered at the time if it had been Cally's minuscule nuptial bikini which had made the impression on Chris,
rather than the vision of an endless summer of love together,
but the next morning she'd woken up to find him making
her a tropical fruit salad.

When he forced her to get up and take in the view from
the balcony, it became apparent that he hadn't just sneaked
out of bed, without waking her for once, for greengrocery
supplies.

Chris had written 'Marry Me Marie' on the firm white
sand (she noticed he'd missed out the vocative comma) and

before she knew it, in a sublime maelstrom of one sultry day and two nights, somebody joined them together in the eyes of a politely unspecified higher authority for all eternity in virtually the same place on the beach. Marie wasn't quite sure how he'd managed to organize it so quickly, but she was so drunk with the idea that he actually wanted to that she didn't care. Best of all, the heat and the preponderance of local fruit meant that one way or another her stomach had retreated to a level at which she could wear a bikini too, albeit one with a much longer sarong.

To be honest, being a fully paid-up Spouse didn't feel much different from long-term Going Out to begin with. They had been together at college for about a year, virtually living in Marie's rooms, which had been like Miracle-Gro on their relationship anyway, but Marie knew from the beginning that Chris had to be the one. The One. Principled, articulate, tall and rangy-looking, he was Action Man Charity Worker. For the first month she ran round college singing, 'He is . . . the one and own-leeee', until even Iona had told her to shut the fuck up.

It had taken about a year of flirting and hanging around the library in Maria Callas shades before he'd realized that she was interested in more than just his VSO vacation work; Chris was a college swimmer and didn't spend quite as much time in the bar as Iona and Marie and Angus. But Marie's precision timing meant that she was always in the right place at the right time in the right dress with the right comment and eventually, halfway through his daily 100 lengths of the town pool, it dawned on Chris that he was completely in love with her and, as she remembered to act 'pleasantly surprised' at his forthright approach, they were joined at the lips for the rest of their time there.

Marie loved university. She loved having her own living space, and her own opinions, and her own complete set of kitchen knives. But she knew that Chris was not one for domesticity and she cleverly spent a lot of time in other people's rooms, cooking immense suppers for them. Although he never came out and said it, Chris was wary of routine, she could tell, so she never allowed him to settle into one with her, despite the intensity of their relationship. Travelling was the reason he had studied languages, and he travelled as far and as often as he could. The further away from hot showers and the more painful the injections, the better. Marie liked seeing new places and liked talking to people (but was considerably less keen on the personal hygiene aspect). As time went on, it seemed natural that Chris's Kubla Khan-esque plans for his round-the-world, post-finals odyssey should expand to fit Marie, who conveniently managed to defer her teacher training, just in case they never came back.

And so Angus and Iona drove them to Heathrow in June and by August England seemed so small and trivial and so far away that marrying Chris on a beach in a bikini with no one there to see it seemed the only way to celebrate the new free people they had become. If university had been a door into a new vision of herself, then the four months she spent travelling with Chris almost scared Marie. She knew she needed him to be there while she did them – he *was* her life partner, because he made all these things happen. Without him she would be lying around at home, doing her nails and reading up on child literacy theory. *With* him she was jumping over waterfalls, and eating unspecified rodent meat, and seeing the kind of Cinemascope scenery and human geography she had previously been content just to read about in his *National Geographic*s. Yet when October came and their travelling had to stop, there was a small part of Marie that was very relieved to be going back.

But on the plane home, with a cheap and ineffective eyemask over her eyes (her dad had wired the money for more comfortable seats than the ones they could afford), Marie realized she was a different person not only in a 'Man,

I've had an experience' *Doors of Perception* sense, but also in a literal one. She was no longer Miss Marie Lynch. She was Mrs Christopher Davenport.

Marie closed the holiday brochure and stared at the cover without really seeing the barefoot couple on the front. It was almost a kindness that they couldn't afford to go to Goa on holiday any more, since to go there now, with the knowledge hanging over them that in ten days they would be back at work in London, would be torture after that open-ended, careless summer. Marie shook herself crossly. That's such a negative attitude, she snapped inside. Get a grip. Life is not all pina coladas and bikinis. Isn't that what you try to tell the seven-year-olds?

Chris had got a job almost immediately with an international aid charity, which he loved, and she had done her year's PGCE, switching courses to London so they could live together. Fortunately someone in his office had been moving out of a very cheap flat, and economizing had become a pretty fun game. Who could make the cheapest supper? What could be done with the sitting room using only the inside of loo rolls and sticky-backed plastic? No one could believe that they were so young and married. Chris had loved that, that you could be so unconventional by being conventional.

And now they had been married for five years. Sometimes it felt like much longer, and sometimes it felt as though she had barely met him. And still she couldn't work out where the Going Out relationship was meant to turn into a Spousal one. Maybe that was the secret lifetime blessing of not having a military-planned church bunfight. The change was never really brought to your attention.

Marie looked at her watch again and realized that it was now quarter past five. Chris had said he would ring her to tell her where to meet. She checked her mobile phone again in case she'd missed a call while she was trying on loud shirts in the loud shop.

No. No missed calls.

She breathed hard to release the band of tension tightening around her forehead. It hadn't been a vintage day – half the class off sick with some virus that was going round, the other half determined to produce symptoms by the end of the afternoon, bits of compulsory grammar to teach that she wasn't completely sure of herself – and she'd really felt like some good mindless entertainment to soften her brain for an hour or so. Or, at the very least, a film that didn't have English subtitles.

Actually, what she really felt like was an evening in with Iona, with a couple of bottles of wine, and some curry, and the chance to talk about nothing more taxing than Cliff Richard films.

'Can I help you?' asked one of the travel agents.

Marie looked down at the collection of brochures in her hands. God, it would be nice to spend the evening with Iona, just talking rubbish and having a laugh. How rude was it to blow out your own husband?

Her mouth twitched. In a manner of speaking.

'No, I'm fine, thanks,' she said, smiling firmly. 'Just browsing.' The last thing she wanted now was to be told how good for her it would be to take a break somewhere hot. Every time she read an article about Spicing Up Your Failing Relationship by Spending the Council Tax Money on a Tropical Second Honeymoon, she couldn't help taking it as a personal jibe.

Not her fault that her marriage and her honeymoon were inextricably linked. They had got married because they were already *on* their honeymoon.

Marie pushed that thought to one side, not really wanting to examine it too closely, and turned back to the display racks. She went through the selection like Carol Vorderman, one from the top row, three from the middle, some fly-drive

Florida ones, a couple of European mini-breaks. A project on holidays, on Europe, on weather, on international food, on national dress . . .

When she had got enough for the whole class, she smiled at the travel agent behind the desk and slipped out of the door, which clicked discreetly, recording her presence in and out, as she stepped into the street.

As she passed a fish and chip shop, a very specific longing for steak and kidney pie popped into Marie's head. She could make one: there was always some ancient frozen pastry in the fridge, wouldn't take long to drop into Sainsbury's (though by some arcane Delia Smith law, that was always twenty quid no matter what she went in for or how recently she had 'done a big shop'). It was ages since she'd done some home-cooking and she really felt in the mood for getting all the pans out in their small kitchen and making an enormous oven full of comfort food. It might even thaw the terrible atmosphere between her and Chris. She couldn't pinpoint when it had started, and God knows she'd tried to ignore it for ages, but now it was there all the time, like a ghost in their flat. She couldn't even look at photos any more, because it hurt her to see how happy they had been and reminded her of how much less happy they were now.

Marie shook herself and rummaged in her bag for her phone. But she was making an effort. They just needed to work at it, not expect it to be perfect the whole time. She called his office phone and waited. Chris answered after five rings and then dropped the phone almost immediately. Marie thought it was a good thing she wasn't an escaped Chechnyan refugee ringing from a phone box.

'Hi, honey,' she said, forgetting again that she was meant to call him 'love', like his mum. 'Listen, would you mind if . . .'

'Marie, hi, yeah . . .' Chris sounded distracted. 'Oh, shit – the film! I didn't say I could definitely make the film tonight, did I?'

'Yes, you did.' She left a precise pause, but Chris didn't hear it. 'I'm waiting in town.'

'God, are you? I'm sorry, um, it's all just a total disaster here. We've got a problem with one of our sponsors . . .'

Marie listened, tucking the ends of her scarf round and round until her neck was swaddled up and she felt partially choked.

'I need to stay until we can get through to them, and they're on Canadian time, and half of them don't speak English so I can't leave it with Cathy . . .' There was muffled clattering in the background, the screeching of a fax, the sound of someone smacking the side of a malfunctioning computer screen.

If he was pretending, someone was certainly making an effort with the sound effects.

'Hang on. Fucking thing,' said Chris, the phone pressed pointlessly against his shoulder since it didn't muffle a thing. 'Can't we get someone out to fix it? No, I'm talking to my wife. My wife. Marie. No? Well, hang on and I'll . . .'

Marie fixed her eyes on the flashing Christmas and Diwali lights that the council still hadn't got round to taking down. Ten years' bad luck for the entire borough of Wandsworth, sponsored by a variety of local dry-cleaners and estate agents.

The charity was all-important to Chris. It gave him something he could work for and respect at the same time. He hated the idea of effectively moving money around for other people, as Angus did. He had spent a lot of time polishing up his principles – the president of the University Campaign against Nestlé could hardly leave college and take a job with Schroeders. The communications post he had taken with ActionTeam was long hours, 'multi-tasking' and quite high-pressure but, he was always telling her, he didn't feel compromised. And that alone was worth them having no money.

'Chris?' she said as loud as she could, without looking

like one of the sad people who screech into mobile phones in the street to prove they have friends. 'Chris! Don't worry about it. Are you going to be home before . . .' She looked at her watch. Sometimes it was midnight before he got home. If she didn't know better, she'd be forgiven for waving her two-timed-wife rolling pin around. But she did know better. That at least would give her some real reason to hate him. But infidelity would spoil Chris's all-important sense of moral superiority, and his passion for charity work was far greater than his passion for anything else, sex included. Marie's lip curled at the thought. It wasn't really a surprise that their sex life was the bombed and arid landscape it was, when displaced minorities were uppermost in his mind the whole time. 'Will you be in for supper?'

There was a guilty pause.

In the silence, to assuage the sting of being rejected for inoculations, Marie tried to imagine him having sex with another woman, and gave up. At least that would be something to rage about. How could you get mad with lorry-loads of Kosovar refugees?

'Don't make anything for me,' he said eventually. Phones carried on ringing in the background. 'I don't know when all this will finish.'

She felt a leaden drop in her stomach. 'OK, well, I might go round to Iona's then.' Via Sainsbury's. Why shouldn't they have the benefit of her pastry enthusiasm?

'Er, right, OK. I'm really sorry, Marie. I'll see you at home, yeah?'

'Yeah,' said Marie. There was the faintest trace of sadness in her voice – but it was sadness that she was actually pleased to be going to Iona's.

Chapter Seven

The 'So tell me, Jim, what is it you do?' running joke had been running for the three years Jim had been working at Overworld Property, mainly because he'd never been able to provide them with a satisfactory answer.

Which wasn't all his fault, since he still wasn't entirely sure himself.

He suspected that it shouldn't really involve being sent out to 'an espresso bar of your choice' with £50 from petty cash and a ridiculously specific list of requirements, as he had been now. And though he made no claims to being the brightest torch in the toolbox, he also suspected that it didn't involve leaving the office for lunch at ten-thirty and spending the rest of the day 'researching Limehouse', as Simon, his sort-of boss was doing, in the new company Z8, which Simon had persuaded them to buy instead of a smaller BMW plus a Polo for Jim. Simon who claimed the new CD system in his car seemed to interfere with mobile phone signals, rendering him unobtainable even under transmission masts.

Sometimes even Jim wondered if they were taking the piss.

He ambled down Old Street, worrying away at a hole in the lining of his jacket pocket with his house keys. This was a quiet time of the day round Clerkenwell. At eleven the bustle of people had bustled into their offices and weren't due to bustle out again for lunch for another hour or so. By six it would seem as though there had never been anyone here at all. But now there were more couriers than cars on the road. Jim crossed to the other side, stepping deftly out of the way of a man towing a huge basket of sandwiches behind his bike.

There wasn't much to detain him in the windows as he walked down to the coffee shop – Marie, Queen of Consumer Durables, would have difficulty window-shopping in an area that sold mainly photocopying and advertising expertise. Even the accountants' offices looked like groovy TV production companies. For once, Jim didn't really mind going out for coffee. It was a Friday, was unusually bright and mild for January and the office had been pretty quiet all morning, which was just as well, since he was still feeling the effects of the previous night. Ned had come round with some leftover dim sum to watch the international poker finals on Sky Sports and they'd drunk the best part of a bottle of Jamesons between them. Ned hadn't left until getting on for half-two, even though he was on an early shift.

On more than that, thought Jim. Through long practice, Ned had perfected a state of chemical imbalance in which he was manically bushy-tailed for the five or so hours he was working, then in a blissed-out haze of vagueness for the rest of the time. Some of this colluded with his natural personality, honed with strange sleeping hours, and the rest was bought in. Carefully bought in. It didn't do to mix it up and be chilled out while chopping garlic at the speed of light.

Jim reached Benugo on St John Street and couldn't be bothered to walk any further. He didn't really mind Ned doing whatever he had to do in order to work weird chef hours; he just wished he could be a little bit more together when he wasn't doing it. Angus's business idea for the Bunch of Grapes had been going back and forwards in his mind since the weekend and he had to admit that the more he thought about it the more it was growing on him, apart from the nagging worry that in order to get money out of potential sponsors they would have to exhibit their star chef,

Ned. And would you give thousands of pounds to someone who looked as though he had just stumbled out of the Happy Mondays' tour bus?

'Now, hey there a minute, come on, not that bad yet,' Jim reminded himself firmly, raising a hand in self-admonishment. A traffic warden, in the middle of ticketing a white van parked on the pavement, gave him a funny look, but Jim didn't notice.

'Got to think positive.' He pushed open the door to the café and looked up at the board of coffees, then down again at the list in his hand. Amazing how the number of people in the office seemed to double when you announced you were off on a coffee run.

Ned did look pretty ropy, but he'd always looked a bit, well, bohemian. Was that the best word? Even in the old school photos Iona had in the loo. He got too little sleep, drank too much strong coffee, smoked too much, went running at bizarre times, ate the weirdest things at the weirdest hours, and listened to The Cure too much.

But wasn't that what chefs were meant to do?

'Help you?' asked the girl behind the counter. She sounded Australian and was, at a rough guess, nineteen. Jim wondered automatically whether she was the sort of girl he might stand a chance with. He couldn't help doing it. Since his twenty-fourth birthday it had become a habit, and as it was now over three years since he'd had a bona fide girlfriend, and suddenly he was looking at the near end of thirty, it had become a necessity.

'Erm, yeah, hi. Can I have' – he looked down at his list – 'four grande cappuccinos, two skinny and one with normal-fat milk, one double espresso and a hot chocolate with soya milk and no whip?'

And were Ned's habits necessarily any less weird than getting in coffees like a sodding work experience boy at the age of twenty-eight and not being able to define your job to your best friends?

'I need a break,' said Jim aloud before he could stop himself.

One of the girls behind the counter held up a Kit-Kat. She looked Italian – way, way out of Jim's league.

'Yes, yes, very good,' said Jim. 'Ho ho ho. I'll take a couple of almond croissants as well, please.'

The first girl – short blonde plaits, nose stud, probably way too trendy for him on closer inspection – bagged the croissants up and pointed to where the coffees would emerge. Jim thanked God that at least he didn't have to do such a mind-numbing job and sloped off in that direction, making way for the person behind him, who also had a long list of office caffeine requirements, but was noticeably five or six years younger than him.

Jim Waters had built an entire personality around mindless optimism, but not even he was under the delusion that his career was doing 130 m.p.h. on the motorway of success. It wasn't that he thought he was wasting his time at Overworld, because they did at least do the kind of property development he was interested in doing. The trouble was, he didn't get to do it often enough.

Though he didn't like to talk about it, Jim had quiet romantic dreams of spotting rundown terraces and turning them back into beautiful places to live, waving a magic cement mixer over old buildings, filling them with people and light again. He had grown up in London and loved watching it regenerate, changing all the time within the same shells. Since he was little, that was what he'd always wanted to do: take faded old buildings and make them appreciated again. And, naturally, make huge amounts of cash in the process. Sort of like Chris's charity work, but with money at the end of the month.

As time had gone on and he spent longer at Overworld, Jim had wondered whether he was tough enough to do really well – although his parents were both accountants, he didn't have the piranha-like instinct for profit that men such as Simon had, for instance – but he'd stuck it out, watching deals, observing the tactics and strategies the other developers used, amassing snippets of information for the day when he found something he could regenerate by himself. But despite all this observation, what he actually knew just didn't seem to add up to much. Because no one ever told him *anything*.

Apart from whether they wanted skimmed or semi-skimmed milk.

Part of the problem was money. Overworld liked to do big deals, big factory conversions, big schools, big warehouses, and that meant being responsible for a big, big budget. And who would trust him with millions of pounds, when he hadn't completed a proper deal yet? And would he ever get to do a proper deal when they only did big ones? Jim felt, with some wounded pride, that it was a stinker of a situation to be in, and it didn't help his wavering confidence that the most money he usually got to handle was a £50 coffee float.

It didn't help either that all his mates were so keen to assist. Angus kept phoning him up to tell him that he'd seen another tumbledown factory from the train, just begging to be turned into luxury live/work units. Tamara too, always buzzing round town from one job to another on her Vespa, kept noticing little warehouses down side streets in the middle of town to make into studios to die for. These days, most phone calls from Tamara and Angus bypassed pleasantries and went straight into, 'Jim! Page 43, B4! Codpiece Mews!' They were on the phone a lot. In fact, Angus nearly all the time. Everyone was desperate for Jim to find just the one gem that would make his career and Jim really, really tried, made persuasive presentations and spent hours on projections, but in the end the answer was always the same: Sorry, mate, not enough profit in it for us, and can you get some more espressos in?

*

He collected the coffees, anchored in their cardboard tray, and tried to find enough pockets in his suit to put sugar, croissants, napkins in. Lately he had begun to wonder if he shouldn't try getting a job in a smaller company. Somewhere where he'd actually be allowed to do something. The scale of Overworld's acquisitions was beginning to depress him and he wasn't sure if it really fitted in with his true vision of developing anyway, ridiculous as it was.

The previous week, for instance, Simon had sent him to check up on the site work on a big house conversion in Holloway, as was his habit, and after he'd chatted with the foreman, seen some plans (Jim was never completely sure what he was meant to do, but was very conscientious about it), he'd grabbed a hard hat and wandered through part of the building they hadn't made a start on. Underneath a loose layer of plaster he found a whole original section of crimson kitchen tiling, beautiful vibrant Arts and Crafts tiles, glowing like fresh nail varnish out of the chalky plaster.

He stood there for a moment, running his hands over their cold, smooth surface, trying to imagine what the original kitchen would have looked like, scrubbed and hot, and how he would have developed it into one big studio flat. Instead of the three rooms he knew it was going to be from the plans.

'They staying?' he asked one of the lads breaking up walls nearby.

'Nah, going, mate,' said the workman. 'Could do them for you for £50 the lot?'

Jim had been tempted, debated whether it constituted stealing from his own company, and if Tamara hadn't phoned at that moment to tell him about some Deco garage she'd stumbled upon in Maida Vale, he'd have walked away and let history lie. But he couldn't help mentioning the tiles, at which she squawked in outrage down the phone and made him buy them; they were now in her bathroom, gleaming with layers of Bathroom Flash, as though they'd always been there. She had been hugely grateful (however, not unfortunately grateful in the reciprocal sense that Jim had hoped she would be). But it had made him sad to take them, as though he were stripping the last finery from some old lady whose beauty was all in the details she had lost.

If only sensitive girls like Tamara knew what a romantic he was, deep down.

That would be Tamara with the killer acquisitive instinct and no scruples about ripping photographers off for usage fees.

Jim walked more quickly back up the road to his office so everyone's coffee would still be drinkably hot when he got back. He hovered at the door, trying to catch Rebecca's eye on reception so she would open it for him, but she was so engrossed with a cycle courier that he was forced to push the door open with his hip and shuffle in backwards. Warm froth spilled over and down his hand, over his cuff and splashed delicately on the bit of his shirt not covered by his tie.

'Oh, arse and feck,' said Jim feelingly. This was his last clean white shirt. And he'd had only one day's wear out of it. Damn. He'd been planning to see a film with Ned tonight, but he'd have to go round to Mum's now and get some washing done.

'Ah, bless,' cooed Rebecca. Rebecca had gimlet grey eyes and spectacles with clear glass in them. Jim was pretty sure she didn't talk quite so much like a receptionist after five thirty, and it was unnerving. In fact, it gave him a bit of an *X-Files* feeling. 'Mine was the non-fat double latte, wasn't it? Yes, that one.' She carefully tugged the fullest-looking paper cup from the nearest cardboard tray. 'You are a sweetie, Jim,' she said, and blew some kisses from the safety of her desk. Her lips pursed like a luscious Revlon raspberry on her flawless face. 'Mwah! Mwah!'

Jim blushed and hunched his shoulders automatically. Rebecca, even with her sitcom receptionist act, was so ridiculously out of his league that only a random FA Cup tie could bring them together, or maybe the camouflage of someone else's office party.

She waited, little finger on her lips, hopeful as ever for some repartee.

Jim opened his mouth, couldn't think of a single thing to say, then blushed deeper and shuffled through to his own small office, dispensing coffees as he went.

Rebecca smiled sadly at Jim's departing back and answered the phone. In a business run on supply and demand, it never failed to amaze Rebecca (BA Hons, Business Administration) that Jim hadn't noticed he was the only single man under thirty in an office full of women.

Overworld Developments was run by three senior partners – Kyle, Michael and Martin – who had lunching stitched up as a fine art and who owned significant secret chunks of London which they played close to their chests until property went completely mad in those areas, whereupon they whipped them out and created market havoc. Jim had seen what they had done with a warehouse they'd been covertly holding in Clerkenwell since 1981 and it frankly beggared belief. Overworld's bosses were cash-cow cattle ranchers.

The secrecy element, though obviously essential, was a bit problematic for Jim in terms of sourcing new places, given that no one told him anything of even vague importance: at least three of the hidden, falling-down gems Angus had found turned out to belong to Overworld already, but not before Jim had spent hours trying to unravel the tortuous ownership registration details, which were as tightly knotted as a Morman family gathering.

The rest of the staff consisted of Simon, who specialized in warehouses, wore fashionable spectacles and drove the

Z8, and a bunch of secretaries, all of whom, Jim had been assured very early on by Michael, the most senior senior partner, were far too busy to waste their time running round for coffee. With so much time on his hands to think about office politics, Jim often wondered where he was meant to fit into the plan. More and more, he was wondering whether it wasn't time to start making some plans of his own – so, without realizing it, Angus had dropped the germ of his idea on particularly fertilizer-enriched ground.

Although he felt obliged to show more outward pessimism about the pub than he really felt, since he was the only one who was meant to know about property deals and therefore felt honour-bound to rubbish the idea, Jim had been thinking about it a lot. He'd made vague inquiries in the office about similar businesses and looked at new restaurants in the area on his way round town and, despite everything, he was starting to get a flicker of excitement in his stomach the more real, the more possible it began to feel. And it had been quite some time since the idea of buying somewhere had done that.

Every night that week he had lain awake mentally slapping himself about the face and telling himself that the time had come in his life to start being more proactive about things, and if he couldn't even assert himself in front of his friends, then what hope was there for him at work?

And at that point every night he had rolled over and wrapped a pillow round his head and tried very hard to summon up the image of Tamara washing her hair in his bathroom while wearing a full wetsuit.

While Jim had been out, Michael and Kyle had apparently gone for a meeting with the company accountant, so he left their coffees with their secretaries, who frankly never looked so busy they couldn't pop to Benugo instead of him, and checked to see if anyone had phoned him. No one had. Not even the estate agent who had been phoning twice a day for the past three months, begging him to confirm the rumours that they were holding an enormous ex-London Underground property in Clapham with plans for conversion. (To which Jim had repeated and quite truthfully claimed he had absolutely no idea.)

The door to Martin's office had been ajar as Jim went past. Martin, the third leg of the triumvirate and the relatively human face of Overworld (flushed and slightly sweaty), tended to have his lunch in his office, since it was the only time of the day when all the people chasing him wouldn't expect him to be there, enabling him to get two hours' work done before getting back into his car and returning to whatever it was he did for the rest of the time. His secretary, Svetlana, was coming out with an empty tray covered with expensive-looking take-out leftovers from the Montignac Boutique. Since Janet (The Wife) had slipped off to a health spa in Jamaica with their personal trainer, he had been on a serious low-cholesterol health kick. And when The Wife stopped sending postcards and got her lawyer to call instead, he'd resorted to kicking everything else.

Jim hesitated, then, before the impetus could slip away, he picked up a spare espresso and knocked on Martin's door, pausing for a moment before pushing it open.

'Martin,' he began, as winningly as he could, 'erm, is this a good moment to have a quick word?'

Martin looked at his Rolex. 'Good as any, I suppose.' He patted his stomach thoughtfully, as if weighing up how much more would fit in. 'That coffee for me?'

Jim looked down at the cup. 'Er, yeah.' He handed it over and settled himself as comfortably as he could in the leather architect's chair.

'Fire away then.' Of all the partners, Martin was the most reassuringly clichéd when it came to talking to junior employees. Which suited Jim, because he had no idea whatsoever how he should talk to Michael and Kyle. They didn't seem to speak a variation of English he was accustomed to.

'I've found an interesting property,' Jim began, and suddenly wondered whether he should make this an 'on-behalf-of-a-friend' inquiry. But Martin, unlike Simon, was not the type to run straight round to the Bunch of Grapes and make a counter-offer. Indeed, chances were Martin probably wouldn't remember the conversation in half an hour.

'I know Simon's been looking at various properties recently, with a view to turning them into gastropub-type restaurants . . .' This was a slight distortion of the truth. Simon had been looking at various NCP car parks recently, with a view to turning them into Conran-style gastrohangars.

'Quickest way known to man to get rid of all your cash, restaurants,' said Martin jovially. His face darkened. 'Apart from divorcing The Wife. Christ, I thought Janet cost me enough when she was living with me. Getting rid of the silly bitch's even worse. Half of her assets were paid for by me in the first place and we're not talking holiday homes here, Jim. Good God, no. I'll not be getting that little investment back in the settlement, put it that way. In fact, you could say her best assets were actually my—'

'Um, right, OK,' said Jim, unsure whether he should be agreeing or not. 'Well, this property I've found could be a bit of a winner, since it also has a couple of flats on top which you could offset against the initial costs of the business . . .'

'Just tell me where.'

Jim wished he'd done his usual sheaf of paranoid research before marching straight in. He was feeling somewhat naked. He knew from experience and ill-advised holiday videos that unguarded enthusiasm made him sound like one of the Famous Five's gaucher younger brothers. 'It's on Ladbroke Grove. The, um, less developed end.'

'And what, you think it's a goer?' Martin knocked back the coffee in one and pulled a face.

'Er, yes,' agreed Jim.

Martin sat back in his chair and gazed meaningfully at Jim over his hands. Jim tried not to look at the crumbs all over the desk and the stack of receipts for Svetlana to process in the in-tray, all of which seemed to have Conran logos on them.

With every silent moment that ticked by, Jim knew he was losing credibility, yet he didn't dare open his mouth and let forth a stream of drivel, because he knew from experience that, despite appearances to the contrary, Martin was the sharpest of the lot and would see through him like a Plexiglass bra.

'I find the acid test is, Jim' – Martin leaned forward suddenly – 'would you go home with record blood pressure and get completely rat-arsed if someone else beat you to it?'

This could so easily be one of their twisted trick questions, thought Jim in panic. 'Yes' means you're not chilled out enough; 'no' means you didn't want it enough and didn't deserve the money.

He looked into Martin's face for clues, but he was always bright red around the nose and had a permanent half-smile that could be reassuringly friendly or plain scary depending on the time of day.

Jim hazarded a guess based on the nineteen previous conversations he had had with Martin on a similar theme.

'I think . . . it could be . . . a sound investment opportunity . . .'

Martin smiled at him and threw the empty paper cup at the metal mesh wastepaper bin without looking. It bounced off the rim, but his attention was now occupied with steepling his hands and smiling knowingly at the tips of his fingers, secure in the knowledge that the gesture was the most important element of the cup disposal, and also that Svetlana would pick it up and place it in the bin when she returned with dessert.

'Thing is, Jim, as I may have said to you before now, there are times in business when you need to take a gamble and not worry about it if the dice don't roll your way. To take a throw for the hell of it. And this is a time when Overworld could afford to take a gamble, if you see what I mean.' He raised his eyebrows and inclined his head very slightly.

Jim recognized that this was meaningful, but didn't have a clue what it actually meant. So he nodded.

'I know you've been trying hard, Jim and, believe you me, it hasn't been going unnoticed. But this is the first time you've come to me without an armful of irrelevant crap about crime rates and council repair times and, frankly, it makes me that much more inclined to run with whatever your idea is.' Martin made a wave gesture with the hand that wasn't scratching his stomach between the buttons of his shirt. 'We like to go with the flow, get a gut instinct up and running. That's why Simon is such a fabulous guy – he gets an instinct, you know?'

He gets dodgy tip-offs from his mates in the council, thought Jim bitterly, but didn't let that show too much in his face. A faint trace of contempt was probably a good thing; outright disgust wasn't showing enough admiration for Simon the Operator.

'So, look, you get some stuff together – not too much,' Martin added hastily, 'I don't want all that bollocks about dog shit per pavement slab that you usually come up with, just enough to put it through a meeting. We'll have a chat at the end of the week, OK?'

Jim was lost for words. It might have been because he hadn't already run the conversation through his mind several times to anticipate all outcomes, as he had done before attempting to get backing for his other projects. The outcomes had been getting so predictable that he hadn't run through an 'OK, Jim, you've got the green light' conversation for about a year and a half. He thought about falling on his knees, managed, 'Fantastic!' and then fortunately Svetlana arrived with a crème caramel the size of a dustbin lid and he excused himself backwards.

Before he could forget any of Martin's pearls of wisdom,

and for a limited amount of evidence later, Jim sat down at his computer and typed as much of the conversation as he could remember, saving it in a new file called Bunch of Grapes. Then he kicked his office door shut and started to make some phone calls, biting his nails furiously all the while.

Chapter Eight

'Think of the question you want to ask the cards,' said Carena the medium in the traditional impassive medium voice, placing the deck in front of Tamara. She then shut her eyes like a magician waiting while the cringing audience volunteer selects a card, in order to underline her professional detachment from the outcome. Whatever cards came up had nothing and yet everything to do with her.

Tamara realized that she too was looking away from the deck on the table. For a transaction of information designed to unpick the most tender areas of your personal life, this was, Tamara always felt, a rather British squeamish delicacy on all sides.

However, she didn't need to think. The Question was one which occupied her mind at all times, even while she was thinking of other things, like spelling and shopping. It was a regular squatter. A squatter she had grown too used to to throw out.

Where is the man of my dreams?

Which could be abbreviated to *Where is a man?* if it meant getting a quicker result.

Or even, *Ned: when?*

The tarot card reader woman extended her hands, and automatically, through long practice, Tamara held out her own so they could be inspected for pre-reading psychic messages.

'What beautiful hands.' The medium took Tamara's long white fingers in her own cool, papery hands, turned them over and looked critically at the palms.

'Thank you,' said Tamara, folding her nails over the top of the bit the woman was inspecting. She looked down at her manicure. About time she took that red varnish off before it started chipping and making her look too much like Madonna *circa* 1983. Very fine line between Grace Kelly and Kelly Marie. Tamara spent a lot of time on her manicures, since she and her nails had an uneasy truce: fifteen years of insecurity, nervousness and what Iona called "nowtiness" had been chewed out on her nails. They were the only part of her that wasn't immaculate and she hated that everyone saw her insecurity each time she scratched her nose. Marie and Iona had cured her. Eventually. Iona bribed her with lavish home manicures and Marie phoned her mobile at random intervals to shout at her to get her fingers out of her mouth. But they cured her. And now Tamara twisted her hair and had chronic split ends.

'You have the power to make someone very happy with these hands,' intoned the medium significantly. 'A man, I think.'

Tamara was glad Iona and Marie hadn't come with her after all. That was exactly the kind of comment they liked to seize on as evidence of Tamara's gradual departure from the gates of normality. Not that Marie had ever thought she was normal. Tamara's lip curled very slightly. Like she could talk, anyway: a woman who still played the recorder, out of choice.

'Really?' she said, studying her hands and trying to keep the irony from her voice. Tamara trained herself to be completely impassive in tarot readings and the like, unreadable and unreacting. Clueless, as Iona would have said, had she been there.

'Huhmmm,' said the medium.

Just tell me where he is, Tamara willed her, but she was still staring engrossed in her palm.

'How odd. I can see glasses . . . lots of glasses . . . Wine glasses, maybe?'

Tamara snatched her hand back. If this was going to be another lecture about her drinking at New Year, then she didn't want to hear it. It was all very well being wise after the event, but what did any of them know about being stared at all evening as though you were some kind of sideshow? And waiting for them all to come up to you with their cheap lines, talking to your breasts while their girlfriends gave you death looks from the other side of the room?

It was all right for Iona and Marie, with their *men* there to stop it all. They didn't even *need* to meet people at parties.

The medium gave her a funny look and picked up the cards.

'Would you like to shuffle the deck?' The medium offered her a large deck of tarot cards, which Tamara shuffled fast and neatly. They were battered with use, which was a good sign. As she racked through the cards, she tried not to think of the combinations she was moving around in the deck; every time she had a reading, she spent all the time she should be focusing on her question worrying that she'd unconsciously done herself out of a happy ending by shuffling three seconds too long.

Though that was hardly the point, she reminded herself. It's *meant* to be out of your hands. If it was up to you then . . . then . . . It went beyond your control some time ago now. And yet the cards were there in her hands and it disturbed her that her subconscious was moving them towards some result and she couldn't know what that would be.

As a result of all this agonizing Tamara never knew when to stop. Her long white fingers moved in rhythm with her thumbs, pushing and separating the cards, back and forth, in and out.

Think of the question, think of the question.

The medium coughed discreetly.

Tamara abruptly made her final adjustments to the deck, hoping that it wasn't Death that she'd just seen, and promised herself that if it was a depressing or moralizing reading, it wouldn't count as her final shuffle since she'd been told when to stop.

'Now, remember that question you wanted to ask the cards.'

Can I forget? thought Tamara. *Before Easter or what?*

The medium began to deal out the cards in a wide shape on the red silk cloth that covered the table.

'Pick one,' she said.

Tamara's hand hovered over the half-moon of cards. She tried to feel a sense of pull towards one particular card, like a proper psychic should, but as usual she didn't, and so instead she pulled out a card which seemed hidden behind another.

'The Empress, good, good.' Carena studied the picture, holding it close to her face and turning it this way and that. 'This is a lady, a creative lady, a lady who nourishes.' She looked up at Tamara, as if to match the two together in the light. 'Pure emotion, full of love like a river. A river that flows and flows, always nourishing and refreshing all around. And kind, very kind. Is that you, my dear?'

Was that her, Tamara wondered. She wasn't self-deluding enough to say yes immediately. Creative? Sort of. She was as good at photography as anything else. Certainly better than she was at picture research. And she had the best nourished skin outside the Estée Lauder Institute. Full of love like a river, she didn't know about, unless it was a very heavily dammed one.

'The Empress is about healthy relationships, happy homes,' Carena went on without taking her eyes off Tamara's face, and was rewarded with a twitch, which slipped through her usual impassivity net.

'No, that's not me, then,' said Tamara heavily. 'That'll be my friend, Iona.'

'She's a good friend. She cares very much for you.'

Iona did care about her. She was the best friend Tamara had ever had in London, and she frequently thanked God that she'd run out of money in the art school caff so Iona could come along and bail her out and start up a friendship that had made her time there so much funnier. But then Iona cared about everyone, and sometimes in her darker moments Tamara wondered if Iona really cared about her as much as she did about brisk, confident Marie, who frankly didn't seem to need quite as much reassurance as she did, given that she was married and had the kind of repartee you only saw on American sitcoms with nine scriptwriters.

But then, when you had blonde hair down your back and men leaving their phone numbers under your windscreen wipers, other women tended to believe you didn't need any help at all.

That was why she spent so much time with astrologers and mediums.

'Another card?'

Tamara snapped her attention back and focused her whole mind on the right man for her. He was somewhere in this deck of cards. He was . . .

There, right on the edge.

'Hmm. The Hermit, reversed.'

Tamara had had enough of these readings to feel a sense of panic at this. But she tried not to let it show.

'I can see loneliness here. Oh dear, I can see painful isolation. There is . . . so much caution, holding you back like a bar. You have been hurt. This friend of yours, she tried to give you good advice, but you wouldn't take it?'

Tamara didn't meet Carena's eyes. This was more like it. Unfortunately. The last boyfriend she'd had, the one she'd spotted in her last monthly chart, had turned out to be married. It hadn't been nice. How was she to know he'd *meant* all the usual heat-of-the-moment rubbish about leaving everything for her? It wasn't like he'd ever told her exactly *what* he had to leave. Fighting with heavily pregnant women was not her thing at all.

'Yeah, yeah,' she said. 'Um, but what about the future?'

Carena gave her a searching look. 'You are a very pretty girl,' she said. 'Why are you so worried about the future?'

Because I won't be a pretty girl for long and then no one *will bother to talk to me* or *my breasts.*

Tamara forced out a smile. 'No reason, just curious.'

'OK.' She swept a hand over the deck. 'Another card, for your future.'

Tamara's hand wobbled. She always got nervous at this one.

Please be the Chef card. Or the Cute Northern Man card.

'Ah!' Carena's face broke out in a smile. 'The World! How interesting, you are picking only major arcana!'

'Mmm,' said Tamara. The World. Good. About time.

'Now this card, this card is good for those who have self-destructive natures,' said Carena. She looked a bit too knowing for Tamara's liking. 'I can see a new job here, a job with friends. Such a good feeling about this! It will be a wonderful time. There will be sacrifices' – she looked over her horn-rimmed glasses – 'and you may have to give something, or someone, up to get what you want. And it will be hard. But you will make that sacrifice happily, because what you will have in the end will be worth it to you. But be sure it is.'

Tamara looked at the rest of the cards, still spread out in a fan. Somewhere in there there had to be something definite to hope for. All she wanted was for some higher force to say, no, don't worry, Ned's just biding his time, you won't have to hang around with married couples for the rest of your life, it won't always just be cuddly seals on your bed.

But Carena seemed to be shuffling the cards back together.

'Hang on, was that it?' demanded Tamara.

Carena shrugged. 'The cards didn't want to tell me any more,' she said. Then she adjusted her glasses and gave her a sharp look. 'Are you a Gemini?' she asked suddenly.

'Um. No, Aquarius,' said Tamara. 'With Capricorn Moon and Venus. And Libra Rising.'

Carena raised her eyebrows. 'Do you have a twin?'

'No,' she said crossly. Not that much of a clairvoyant then.

'Odd, I can see twins.' Carena plucked at the long jet necklace that dropped down to her waist. 'I can see another you, very beautiful and blonde, holding your hand. A sister, maybe?'

'No!' Tamara was starting to get annoyed. Much more of this inaccuracy and she would devalue that World. She'd been waiting a long time to get one of those for her future and she didn't want it written off as fluke.

'How strange,' said Carena. 'It's so clear and spirit is so rarely wrong. And your mother,' she went on, still fiddling with her beads, 'I can see her in your garden, by the roses.'

Tamara stopped putting her scarf on and looked open-mouthed at her. Her mother's ashes *were* scattered in their garden at home, right next to the rose bushes her dad had planted when she was a baby, thus forcing them to live in that house for ever, or perish with guilt.

Oh, my God. Had she had a baby sister she didn't know about?

But Carena was off again. 'And I can see pictures.' She frowned. 'Terrible pictures. There is no colour.' She squinted. 'No colour, just black and white, and I can't see . . . can't see a focus.' She shook her head. 'I would love to see those pictures, but it is all cloudy. Can't make them out.' She shrugged apologetically. 'Sometimes it comes like that.'

'It's OK,' said Tamara shiftily. She knew exactly what those were. So much for her plans to do a joint exhibition somewhere with her photojournalism and Iona's paintings in the New Year.

Still, plenty of good stuff there. And some of it could be Ned.

She wrapped her scarf around her neck and smiled at the medium, who was tying her cards back up in the black silk and looking distracted.

'Thanks very much,' said Tamara, smiling winningly. 'That was very helpful to me.'

'Enjoy that new job.' Carena smiled and then stopped smiling. 'But remember that friend of yours,' she said. 'Spirit reminds you not to allow that river to dry up through neglect. And make sure that choice is the right one.'

The cards sounded a lot like a spiritual headmistress, thought Tamara, but she made all the right agreeing noises and zoomed off on her Vespa to Coffee Morning to tell Iona all about it.

Chapter Nine

'I want to grow a moustache,' said Angus unexpectedly.
'No, Angus. No moustaches.'

The moustache conversation took place about once a month – more so recently for some reason Iona couldn't fathom, but increasingly felt she should.

Angus put the crossword down and stroked his top lip thoughtfully. 'Just for a month or two. Iona?'

'Angus, if you grow a moustache, I will too, OK?' Iona carried on flicking through the channels. It was half-nine and she knew she should clear the pasta bowls from supper off the floor before Angus kicked them over and trod tomato sauce into the carpet, but she was too comfortably wedged into the sofa. She nudged him with her toe instead.

'You've already got one.'

'Have not. You're thinking of Marie.'

'Well, I'm going to get a false one then.'

'No, you're not.'

'I'll just wear it when I feel like it. And I won't tell you when. It'll be like an accessory.'

Iona flicked through two lots of gardening makeover shows and finally settled on Channel 5, for want of anything better. Halfway through one of their macabre *Serial Killers from Hell* specials. Most of the serial killers had cultivated big serial-killer moustaches. Possibly even before they had decided to become serial killers.

She shook herself. A false moustache. This was a new one.

'So you're saying I could roll over in bed one morning and wake up next to Freddie Mercury?'

'That would depend,' said Angus thoughtfully. 'Would you prefer to wake up with Errol Flynn? Because that could be arranged. I might have a range of moustaches, anyway.' He covered his upper lip with his fingers, as if practising the feel of it. 'For different occasions. Proper ones with spirit gum. Not the clip-on kind. They're a bit ugh.'

Iona unfolded her legs from beneath her and swivelled herself round on the sofa to give him her full attention. The time might have arrived to get to the bottom of this moustache business before it turned into a full-beard issue.

'Angus, I think you need to talk to someone about this.'

'I just want a moustache!' whined Angus. 'Is it so much to ask? If you wanted breast implants I wouldn't give you such a hard time.'

'If I ever say I want breast implants, quite apart from the fact that you would have to pay for them, I hereby give you full permission to use my arse as a trampoline. You can write that down if you want to.'

Angus paused. 'Do you *want* breast implants?'

'No!' said Iona exasperatedly. 'I just don't want to find myself being picked up from work by George Formby.'

'Does he have a moustache? I don't think he does actually.'

'In my head he does. He's exactly the kind of creepy little bloke who would have had one.'

'Whaat?'

'Like Stalin. What was wrong with *his* upper lip? Or Peter Mandelson – you remember those early photos? Cree-eepy. Angus, I have to tell you this. Women *wonder* about facial hair. Facial hair is always used as a disguise for something. Weak chins, spotty lips, dimples . . .' It occurred to Iona that Jimmy Page had had a full-on beard for most of the early 1970s and didn't look that bad at all, but before she could let this slip she forcibly reminded herself that she was meant to be coaxing Angus's deep-seated psychological need for a moustache out of him and skidded to a halt.

'Why do you want one anyway? You look perfectly gorgeous without a moustache.'

Angus stroked his face sadly. 'I don't know. I think it would make me look older.'

Iona swallowed a mouthful of tea carefully. 'I thought you were *worried* about looking older. What about your—' She was about to say 'receding hairline', an endless source of bathtime woe for Angus, but managed to substitute 'reading glasses' at the last minute.

Angus looked at her suspiciously. 'I know what you were about to say. I thought it might balance the hair thing out. I might even go for a full Romanov.'

'Romanov.' Iona looked at him seriously. 'Tell me, though I'm sure I don't want to know.'

'You do know. A big full-on beard. All round.' He demonstrated. 'Like Santa, but not grey.'

'Angus, what's the *matter* with you?' demanded Iona. 'You're twenty-*eight*. *No one* is doubting that you are now capable of growing facial hair. For God's sake, you've been shaving for nearly fifteen years. You even make me buy you that grown-ups' shaving cream from Truefitt and Hill.'

'I just want a moustache!'

'Why?'

Angus's lip twisted crossly. Iona carried on staring at him until he came out with what it was that he really meant. It was a trick his mother had passed on one Christmas.

'Oh, for God's sake, I just want people to take me more seriously at work!' Angus blurted out.

Iona bit her lip on the observation that Hitler had probably said the same thing and put her head on his knees.

'Sweetheart, people *do* take you seriously at work. Aren't you doing those seminars for the new trainee intake? Do you think they'd entrust you to indoctrinate little lawyers if they didn't take you seriously? Do you?'

She had to turn upside down to see his eyes. He was hanging his head like a sulky child, and for a moment she experienced a scary amphetamine rush of fierce protectiveness and a terrifying desire to march into Pryce Riley Riches and slam some heads in filing cabinets. This must be the Maternal Rage that Marie dreaded. The kind that made mothers barge to the front of parents' evening queues, flattening collages and caretakers with all the finesse and devastation of a speeded-up glacier.

Then, as all that shot through her system, it was overtaken by a more familiar sense of frustrated impotence that she had very little idea of what exactly Angus's colleagues were doing to annoy him, because he wouldn't ever tell her, and even less idea how she could practically help.

'Angus, what's the matter?'

'Everything.'

'No,' said Iona calmly. 'You can't have "everything". If you want to sort this out, you need to break it down into bite-sized chunks, OK?'

'Nothing is bite-sized at work,' sulked Angus. 'Bite-*marked*, yes. I can't break it down. It's just everything. Like a big brick wall in front of me.' He crossed his arms and leaned his head back on the sofa, his eyes shut in tired resignation.

Fear rattled in Iona's chest. She was so scared of losing touch with him when this happened, when he pulled away from her and dropped the curtain. It was too easy to have a good relationship when things were going well; sometimes she lay awake at night, listening to him snore, worrying that their lives had been going *too* well together, beyond what they deserved, worrying what dreadful event was going to test their love properly, instead of the mild panic of a red gas bill or whether next-door would notice if they chopped down the tree shading her shed studio.

And if her love wasn't strong enough to help him through his moments of frightening silence? How would she know until it was too late? Starting a life again without Angus was unthinkable. But balancing her life now depended on Angus not changing all of a sudden.

You start with a moustache, you finish up . . . well, in Motorhead?

'Has something happened at work?' she probed gently.

'Nothing happens at work. That's the whole point.' Angus let out a long deep sigh of exhaustion and started counting off on his long fingers. 'You just have no idea how dull it is. It's driving me mad. You want me to narrow it down? I hate my boss, I'm working in a team with a bunch of idiots, my clients have nothing better to do than to throw their toys out of the pram eighteen hours a day, our e-mails are monitored by a team of ex-Nazi war criminals and, just to rub my nose in it, I'm having to run training seminars for the new intake, who just remind me how much enthusiasm I used to have for everything. And which I don't have any more.'

'Oh,' said Iona weakly.

'I just . . .' Angus began, and broke off, rubbing his head distractedly. 'I don't know. I just feel that if I don't do something now, this will be the rest of my life, you know? I don't feel that I have options open in the same way that you do.'

'Which options are those?' asked Iona sardonically. 'To do two shifts a day or just one? Or to give up my fast-track waitressing career to concentrate on painting and having no money at all?'

She bit her lip before she could say any more. The selfish thought had occurred to her that if Angus did throw in the towel at Pryce Riley Riches, she would have to start paying for her share of the TV licence with money she didn't have at the end of the month. It was only because Angus was able to cover most of the bills that she was able to paint at all. Not that that should affect his decision. Or her support.

Iona blinked with embarrassment at herself and shoved the unworthy thoughts to the back of her mind to worry about later. She hoped it hadn't shown in her face. She left a pause and tried to catch his eye, in case he was going to explain more, but he was silent. She didn't want to let him slip into a silent mood. Once Angus went silent, getting any kind of communication out of him was like getting beans out of a tin with a skewer. And she *was* going to support him through this, because he'd encouraged her so generously and because – well, their lives could hardly be more closely knitted up together than they already were.

'Angus, is there someone at work you can talk to about this? You know I want to help you, but I don't feel I can, not as much as I want, and I don't want you to think I'm just trotting out platitudes I don't understand.'

Angus absently stroked the hair off her face as she lay in his lap, looking up at him with concern creasing her blue eyes. He hated making Iona worry about him.

'OK, fine, so let's forget the moustache if it's going to bother you so much,' he said. 'I'll concentrate on growing really bushy eyebrows instead.'

'Don't pretend to be fine when you're not,' said Iona. 'Do you want to give up law? Is that what you're saying?'

Angus opened his mouth to say something light, but then changed his mind. 'I don't think so,' he replied slowly. 'But I have this overwhelming . . . *fear* that this is my last chance to do something before . . .' He was going to say 'before I make commitments' but that would branch off into all sorts of areas he'd only really explored in his head so far. Angus liked to have ideas well thought out before he put them into words and risked them in public, hence his terrifying sudden torrents of fully formed schemes.

'It's not so much that I want to give anything up. As such,' he went on slowly, looking for the right words. 'I just feel there are other skills that we all have that are being wasted. Honestly, I think we should think more seriously about doing something like the Bunch of Grapes,' he said. 'I know you think it's just another idea that we can all get drunk and make plans but do nothing about, but it *could* really work. All the talent's there. Ned cooking, and you running the place, and I could handle the legal side . . . And we can *learn* so much. There's no flexibility any more. Everyone's so conditioned into imagining that you *have* to do this job or that job in order to fulfil yourself. Well, you're a case in point, aren't you?'

'Erm,' said Iona. 'Yeah . . . No, no, what are you talking about?'

'Your painting, you big div.' He held his hand over her mouth as she began to protest. 'You *know* you're really talented, shut up, and you're not ashamed to do some waitressing during the day so you can get yourself off the ground. You know, give yourself a chance to see what you can do. You've got a degree – so what? You know you could get a tedious pen-pushing job like mine if you really wanted to, but you haven't, have you?'

'I've never thought of waitressing as being so noble.'

'You know what I mean.' Angus poured himself some more coffee from the pot balanced on the PlayStation. There was no milk left in the jug, so he swigged it back without.

That he was prepared to drink black coffee immediately told Iona exactly how bad a mood he was in.

And he'd only paused to draw breath.

'What drives me mad about Jim and Chris and that lot is that they moan and moan about how much they hate their jobs, but when you give them an idea – an idea that could work and be really good for all of us – they love it for about twenty minutes and then just come up with more and more defeatist reasons not to give it a try. Then in the space of half an hour they've convinced themselves that doing the mindless shit they hate so much is a much safer option, and they go home depressed and cheered up at the same time.' His cheeks were flushing. 'They're such . . . *sheep*.'

'I know,' soothed Iona, stroking his hair to try to get him to calm down. The coffee probably wasn't improving his heart rate much either.

'They just can't deal with anything new.' Angus threw his arms over the back of the sofa crossly. 'Bastards.'

Iona phrased and rephrased her next comment quickly in her head. On the rare occasions when Angus lurched into one of these moods, he tended to feel everyone in the world was against him, so it was crucial not to give off signs of Being One of Them.

'Honey,' she started tentatively, 'I understand what you're saying, but security is usually quite high on your . . .' She stopped and started again. 'Normally, you're the one who goes for the . . .' No, that was heading for disaster. Iona blinked. 'Um, I know you'll have thought all this out carefully, but . . .'

Angus raised his eyebrows as she stumbled for the right phrase, then cut her off before it could get worse. 'Iona, don't you think *I'm* allowed to want to do unpredictable things too? It's not exactly fun being the one who has to remember when to pay the water rates.'

She flinched.

Then he flinched when he saw her flinch.

There was a significant silence where difficult thoughts hovered obviously in the air between them. More obvious in their unpalatability than if they'd been spoken aloud.

Iona opened her mouth and shut it again. Angus *had* always been the one to remember stuff like that though. Even at university he'd made sure they all had their loans sorted out properly. Obviously he'd managed to invest some of his and make a small profit, while she'd had to work two jobs every holiday to pay hers off, but if he hadn't helped her, she'd have been in even more trouble. People trusted him with things like that. It was his talent. Just as they trusted her with their problems, they trusted Angus with their money.

'But . . .' she began, thinking of all the restaurants in the area that seemed to close down before she'd even had a chance to try them out. Surely it was a mad risk?

'Anyway' – Angus's tone softened – 'I *have* thought it out carefully. It's not as stupid as it sounds.'

'No?'

'Would I knowingly do something stupid?'

'Are you asking me that seriously, moustache boy?'

Angus cuddled her closer to him and Iona's body relaxed into his strong chest, even though there was still a floating, panicky feeling in her stomach. The fabric-conditioner smell of his handwash-only woolly jumper was comforting, but Iona could sense invisible walls moving around her and was unsettled by her own nervous response. And she'd always prided herself on being good at adapting to new things. She pushed her nose into his jumper. Had she got too comfortable? Was this the Big Test at last, hovering on the horizon like a distant cyclone?

Angus was murmuring into her hair, his breath making little hot spots on her scalp. His voice sounded quite far away, talking to himself as much as to her.

'You're always telling me that there's no point in doing things that you don't feel passionate about, aren't you? Well, I could be *so* passionate and proud of making the Bunch of Grapes into the kind of pub I'd want to drink in – and know that I'd used my own abilities to make it work, instead of spending all day pushing some legal hamster wheel for corporate clients who don't even meet me. I want a chance to see what I can do in a *practical* way. We all do.'

'And you'd rely on Jim and Ned?' Iona privately doubted whether Angus's management skills would be able to contain Ned and his flexible approach to working practice. Though he might respond to bribery.

Angus tutted. 'That's what I mean. While we're all so negative about each other, no one will ever do anything.

If you expect Jim to be a helpless donkey, then he will be, because it's easy. But if you had to rely on Ned, and if he had to rely on you, then it's half-teamwork, half-self-preservation, isn't it?'

'Or half-paranoia, half-megalomania.'

Angus ignored her. 'It's like that thing they always used to do on *Record Breakers*, where you have a big circle of people and tell them to sit down when you blow a whistle. It doesn't collapse because everyone supports each other. It's just like that. If you had to rely on Chris—'

'Heaven forbid,' said Iona.

'—then he would *have* to pull his weight.'

There was a brief silence while each contemplated relying on Chris. Not even Marie relied on Chris. Outside a police car sped past, siren wailing. Then another, maybe an ambulance, close behind it.

'Is it a straight choice between the Bunch of Grapes and a moustache?' asked Iona.

'Kiss me and tell me you love me,' ordered Angus. 'Or I'll be sad.'

'You *are* sad, you sad man,' said Iona, climbing up to kiss him. 'Haven't you shamelessly revealed that to me this evening?'

'I haven't even discussed my plans for a complete set of Noddy Holder sideburns yet,' he murmured, nuzzling into the hollows of her throat. 'They will join up with my beard at the sides.'

'Oh yes, well, that'll be sure to have them taking you seriously at work. Absolutely. No, really, they'll be promoting you in days. *I* would.'

Iona shut her eyes to savour the sensation of his lips on her skin. She felt safe and warm with Angus to look after her. Safer than she'd ever felt in her life, safer than she ever thought she deserved to feel in exacting post-feminist times. And yet through the gentle pleasure of their slow and familiar kisses, there was a disturbing sensation at the back of her mind, like a muffled tune played in a different room which she could hear but not identify.

It bothered her.

Chapter Ten

A few days passed, in which Iona got up early to make sure that Angus shaved every morning, and nothing more was said about either the office or the Bunch of Grapes. Knowing him as well as she did, Iona didn't necessarily see this as a good sign one way or another. But he did seem to be tied up on the phone more than usual at work, and he seemed distracted at home, and didn't even react when she yelled at him about the display of spanners in the sitting room. The weekend seemed to come round very slowly.

'What time did you tell people to come over?' Angus shouted above the sound of Iona frantically hoovering cat hairs off the sofa.

His biggest kitchen knife flashed through chopped onion very quickly, spraying flakes around him like snow. Entire cows could be dismembered with a smaller knife. Angus had not only bought the biggest knife in the range – after he'd satisfied himself that it was the best one Peter Jones did, by leaving the apple he'd brought for testing purposes in minuscule pieces all over the department – he'd even bought the sharpening steel that went with it. Before all major cooking operations he spent a ritualistic five minutes sharpening, just standing in the kitchen slashing and sparking away like a bloodthirsty Victorian paterfamilias with a jam-eating grin all over his face. Iona suspected that it was a Celt warrior marooned in south London thing.

'I don't know.' She put down the Hoover and paused to think. 'No, no, you e-mailed them from work, didn't you?'

There was an indiscriminate grunt of assent from the kitchen, followed by the sound of high-speed dicing.

Iona tried not to think about the vulnerable tips of Angus's fingers, and instead stood back from the sofa and looked despairingly round the room. It was as though someone had tried to spread their entire possessions evenly across the floor. There wasn't a square foot of carpet visible under all the clutter.

'Angus, pet, do you think you could stop doing that for a moment and help me tidy up?' She paused. It was critical to get the pauses right so she didn't sound like a complete nag. 'It doesn't matter what time we eat, but the sitting room's still full of your toolkit and I don't know what goes where to put it away.'

No response.

She pressed her thumbs into her temples to stop her voice from going any higher. Living with Angus was like presiding over a keenly fought jumble sale. She could tidy a room, leave it to make a cup of tea and when she came back it would look freshly burgled. He'd offered to get a cleaner but, although Iona considered it fair dos to give someone money to do something she wasn't very good at – she didn't, after all, give Angus eye tests on the basis that it would be cheaper to do it herself – she hated the thought that she would then become one of the appalling yuppies at parties who talked about what a complete gem their cleaner was and what a blessing it was Margherita didn't speak English so couldn't spend hours talking to them in the kitchen when she should be scrubbing down their i-Mac. She was far too young to feel that old. And her grandfather would be horrified.

'*An*gus?' she said again.

In the kitchen, Angus responded by sticking his tongue out of the corner of his mouth in concentration and showering an arc of onion over the hob.

Once again it was her, alone, against the flat.

As she picked things up and dumped them in the bag,

she reflected bitterly that over the time they had been living together, Angus had perfected an infinite delaying tactic for tidying up. If Iona wanted him to hoover the sitting room, he would take all the videos out of the video cupboard, wipe it down and then rearrange them in order of age and nationality of the director. If she wanted him to clean the bath, he would measure up the wall above it for a new shelf on which to store the cleaning products. This method provided Angus with a bullet-proof excuse which he could wheel out with hurt puppy-dog eyes whenever Iona's mother was due any minute and the floor of the sitting room was still covered with plates and dishes and glasses that he'd gathered about him to watch the football with.

'Tell me again why we're cooking supper for that lot?' Iona shouted down the hall. She dragged all the cushions off the sofa, removed the pagan offering of pens, coins and remote-control batteries revealed beneath, and started to pound some life back into the flattened cushions. A small cloud of cat hair rose with each weak thump. 'Can you remember ever being offered so much as a round of toast at Tamara's?'

Her arms ached from hoisting the week's delivery of sugar, coffee and cleaning stuff into the café. It had been a very long day, longer than normal, since due to widespread flu there had been no one to take over at the end of her shift, and all she really wanted to do now was to collapse on the huge squashy sofa and slip into a comfortable coma of exhaustion with a nice video in the background. *Top Gun*, possibly, or *My Fair Lady*. *The Jungle Book*. *Footloose*.

Iona's eyelids started to droop at the thought of Kevin Bacon and an early night.

Muriel's Wedding. A mug of proper hot chocolate. A foot spa . . .

'They're coming over because Jim's got some news about the Bunch of Grapes!' yelled Angus above the sound of onions hitting very hot fat.

'No! Has he?' She was momentarily surprised out of her sleepiness. '*Jim* has? What's he done?'

She put down the throw that she'd bought to disguise the wine stains on the stupidly white sofa and walked back into the kitchen. Angus was ripping leaves off a basil plant as though he expected it to put up a fight.

'Angus, what's Jim done?'

'Oh, er' – Angus spun round and put the basil down – 'he says he might have sorted out some kind of finance for it. I'm not too sure actually, but he sounded pretty excited on the phone. He's picking up Tamara and coming over when he finishes work, he said. Don't know when that'll be, but . . .'

'Really? No!' said Iona again. 'He's really got something moving at *Overworld*?'

Angus nodded. His eyebrows were sharing her disbelief.

'You're kidding.' Iona opened the fridge to see if there was any beer or water chilling. 'You know what this means, don't you?'

'No, what?'

She took out a bottle of wine and began the long slow process of finding the corkscrew. 'It means that this could finally be Jim's big chance to get a proper company car out of Martin. After all this time with that crappy C-reg Polo. If we can make this work for him, that could be it. He might get a new one. He might get promoted. Stranger things have happened.'

Angus shuffled his basil into a small heap on the board. 'Well, that's one way of looking at it.'

'It's the only way of . . . Oh no. What way were you thinking of?'

'Well, I mean, the one that goes, if we screw this up then he'll never get—'

'Angus! What do you mean, *if* we screw this up?' She jabbed him with the corkscrew. 'For God's sake, it's *your* idea! You're the one telling us we have to grab this last freedom moped out of Nowhere City!'

Iona rammed the corkscrew into the bottle and poured herself a large glass of wine. An unexpected sense of the goalposts moving before her eyes filled her with indignation.

'Don't imagine you can quote crap song philosophy at me.' Angus went back to shredding his basil. 'I wouldn't say it to anyone else but you. But let's be realistic. It might not even come off. Jim might have misunderstood. They might have been talking about the photocopier budget. They might have been saying, "Yes, go ahead . . . and set up an account with Starbucks, Jim!" for all we know.'

Iona said nothing but continued to look at him sceptically. He was avoiding her eyes. He had been in a funny mood since he'd picked her up from work. He was behaving like a woman, for crying out loud.

Angus's big knife made dull chopping noises on the board. Ker-thunk. Ker-thunk. The basil didn't stand a chance.

She took a big swallow of wine and waited for him to explain the furrows appearing on his brow. He carried on chopping with a steadfast, rather pained expression.

'What have you done?' she asked eventually.

Angus sighed. 'I spoke to Kathleen in personnel about taking a sabbatical.'

Iona's indignation was overlaid with a faint beating of excitement. 'And?'

'And she said that since I've barely had any holiday and if the time off was tied up with something vaguely useful . . . I don't know. She's going to look into it for me, let me know. There's some new scheme they're launching where you can take an agreed period of official leave and then come back in again. Think it might be meant for women, but there's bound to be some EU regulation about offering it to men. I just made some tentative inquiries, that's all.'

'Ang, that's great!' said Iona. She paused. 'Isn't it?'

Angus carefully transferred the tiny green pile of chopped basil to the pan on the broad blade of his knife and wiped it on the side. 'Um, I don't know. It would give me a chance to see if it could work out. And even if I decided to go back, they could get another manager, or at least Jim would have a business he could sell.' He jutted out his lower lip. 'I just don't know if that's the right attitude though. If we're going to commit ourselves to doing this, we have to do it properly, and I've got more at stake than the others, haven't I? I don't think I could bear to start off with so many good intentions and invest so much in it – and I don't just mean money – and then have it all fall to pieces around my feet. Even if I did have a job to go back to at PRR.'

He gave the onions and basil a stir with his wooden spoon and turned down the heat. 'Do I need more olive oil in this?'

Iona went over and hugged him from behind, her arms slipping round his waist and his bottom pressing into her soft stomach. They fitted together like stacking chairs.

She leaned her cheek against his back and could hear his breath filling and emptying inside.

'This is my last chance to do something different,' said Angus to the fan extractor. 'I've put off doing different things all my life until now, and I'm going to get one go at doing something which isn't part of my career plan. If it all goes wrong . . .' He stopped.

Iona could hear his heartbeat speed up. She didn't say anything. The air felt very fragile around them; and she held her breath, the thought ringing like a red fire alarm in her mind that this could be it, the payback for being so happy. For once she didn't know what he would say next and it was scary. She tried to bury the thought under a reciprocal wave of concern for his concern.

'Then there's the other side of things,' he went on. 'The whole "Don't go into business with your friends" side of it. Like, I know it's amusing that Jim is the worst property developer since Noah omitted to convert the ark for business use, but *can* he actually manage properties? If I'm going to risk my future it's got to be on something worth doing, and I need to know that everyone else is taking it seriously too, you know? Otherwise it'll just end up with me being Mr Dad and everyone taking the piss as usual and, I'm telling you, that's not as much fun as it looks.'

'You're just doing worst-case-scenario thinking. It doesn't have to be like that,' said Iona. Talk about U-turns. Or was that part of his tactic, to make her sell the project back to him? She pressed on regardless. Too scary, too scary. 'But that's part of taking risks like this – you don't know what people will do until you ask them.' She paused. Would that make her somehow legally responsible when it all went wrong? 'Come on, Angus. *You* told me all this the other night. *You* were the one telling me how Jim and Ned would only learn how to take pressure if it was actually applied.'

'I know.'

'So? What's the matter?'

Iona heard a long sigh escape from deep inside Angus's chest. His stomach deflated accordingly beneath her clasped hands.

'He's actually started to *do* something. We're in unknown territory already and we haven't even found out whether Brian's actually put the pub on the market.'

'Well, isn't that proving your point?' She gave him a squeeze. 'You've already galvanized him into action! God knows what else he can do now he's got going!'

Angus swivelled round within her grasp until he was facing her. Iona lifted her face up for a kiss but he put a finger over her lips so he could carry on talking without interruption.

'I know. I know. But before it was all dinner-table chat and now . . . you know, it could be real? Iona, I can't tell you how important this is to me. Running my own restaurant – it's something I've *always* wanted to do, but never been able to. This is the last time I'll be able to take a sabbatical without seriously affecting my client work, and . . . who knows where it could go? There's no point doing this at all unless we've already decided it's going to be a success – but . . .'

He rolled his eyes at himself and shook his head. 'Look, I'm only going to try this once. I just want to give it the best possible shot. I don't know if that's what everyone wants, or is willing to do. And it might mean more pressure on us, it might mean changes here at home, I don't know. But I've been giving this so much thought and I've got such a good feeling about it, I . . .'

'Don't say anything else, piglet,' said Iona. She scratched her fingernails up and down his back and he wriggled with pleasure despite the serious expression he was trying to sustain on his face.

'Iona . . .' he began warningly.

She gave one final flourish of a scratch along the top of his shoulders. 'Of course I know what you mean. But if you want everyone else to get behind you on this, you're going to have to be much more positive than that.'

'Obviously.'

'Better you get it all out for me first so you can be extra-enthusiastic for Chris, eh? It's not me you have to persuade. You know I'll support you whatever you want to do. I've got the cats to think of. And my shed.'

Angus nuzzled his lips into the curve of Iona's neck. She smelled of coffee.

'You are just the best,' he said into her neck. 'Where did you come from? I don't deserve you.'

'No, you don't,' Iona agreed. 'Are you going to put some mince in that pan? Or are you just caramelizing the onions?'

'I think the onions can wait a bit, can't they?'

'Not if Jim and Tamara and Ned and that lot are going to pitch up any minute.'

'Well, what if I changed the menu from spaghetti bolognese to onion tart?' Angus's hand was working its way up the back of Iona's shirt.

Iona looked over his shoulder at the wall clock. It was already five to seven. With a supreme effort of duty over pleasure, she pulled back her shoulders so he couldn't undo her bra strap. 'Angus!'

'Iona!'

'No!'

'Please!'

'I said no!'

'Why?' He had both his hands behind her back now and it was turning into an undignified tussle. Iona knew it took him at least a minute to undo her bra behind her back, even on a good day, with her helping and with the use of a mirror, so it wasn't as though she was about to be stripped naked in seconds.

'What part of "Your friends are about to come round for dinner and probably won't want to see two elderly married people grappling with each other over the breakfast bar" don't you understand, Angus?'

He gave up with a groan and went round the back to see how it all fitted together. 'Oh, very good. A double fastener. Can't you start wearing those vest things? They'd be so much easier to get off you. You'd just have to put your hands in the air and I could whip them off, no trouble at all.'

'Men don't want to have sex with girls who wear vests,' replied Iona, ripping open some bags of salad while he examined the mechanics of her bra strap. 'Unless they're Gary Glitter or Jimmy Page.'

'Oh, I see. Three pack from M&S OK for you, then?'

'Make it Muji and I might consider it.'

Angus snaked his arms round her waist. 'In that case I'll get my Gibson Les Paul down from the attic.'

'Mmm. Well, you've seen the concert video. "Good

evening, New York!" Nice pair of very tight jeans, touch of patchouli behind the ears . . .'

'And you know I've got the chest hair for it . . .'

Iona's eyelids drooped and shut as Angus slipped his strong fingers into the belt loops of her jeans, pulled her closer and began kissing her neck again. His breath, syncopated with gentle laughter, was hot and he smelled of lemons and basil. Iona was disturbed to find herself becoming distinctly aroused and hoped it was Jimmy Page-related and nothing to do with Gary Glitter.

More to the point—

'Angus, you're not turned on by little girls in vests, are you?'

'No! Just big girls in little vests . . .'

There was a loud knocking from the front door and Marie's voice yelled, 'Stop snogging and let us in!' through the letter box.

'How?' said Angus, pulling away with disbelief written all over his face. 'How can they tell? Have they got radar? Why do they always come round exactly when you don't want them to?'

'Because you phone them up and ask them to?' Iona disentangled herself and straightened her shirt. 'Do the coffee, will you? We'll talk about these jeans of yours later.'

'You just let me know when you want them to go and I'll slip into them,' Angus shouted after her as she went to answer the door. 'Leave it until we want to clear the house of unwanted guests.'

The hall was a dumping ground for random rubbish on its way in and out of the flat. Iona kicked some stray shoes under the hall chest as she went past and in one bending movement picked Angus's jacket up off the floor, hung it on a hook and opened the door.

Marie was standing on the step with Jim and Tamara. Jim and Marie were holding bottles of wine; Tamara was holding two bottles of mineral water and one of Tooth-kind

Ribena and twisting on the spot as if on an invisible Space Hopper. Jim was looking slightly pained. They were all standing beneath Marie's NUS umbrella. Iona realized with some surprise that it was pouring with rain. She hadn't noticed over the radio in the kitchen. Are the cats in, she wondered.

'Come on in,' she said, swinging the door as wide open as she could and reaching out to take their coats.

'Gotta use your loo,' said Tamara, pressing the bottles into Iona's hands. 'Follow-up colonic.' Iona stepped aside immediately and Tamara dashed to the bathroom. 'Hi, Angus,' she yelled on her way past.

'*What*?!' Iona mouthed at Marie.

'What goes up . . .' Marie flashed her a look.

'Can't they give her a cork or something?' asked Iona.

'Stop!' protested Jim.

'Jim made her sit on a Tesco's bag on the way over.'

'Shut up, Marie,' said Jim, and walked through to the kitchen, where Angus had gallantly turned up the radio to disguise the fact that the kitchen was right next to the bathroom.

'Jim, you look a bit sick, mate.' Angus stopped stirring and squinted at him.

'Don't ask me,' said Jim. 'It was traumatizing.'

'Do we have a *sommelier*?' asked Marie. 'Or shall I just pull out the cork with my teeth and drink it from the bottle? I warn you, it's been a long five days – I've done the entire Roman civilization this week.'

'Give it here,' said Iona, and put the bottles in the fridge. 'There's some cold beer or some coffee. Why don't you go through and take off your wet shoes and I'll bring you something in?'

'Crisps would be nice, Pringles if you've got them,' Jim shouted over his shoulder as he stepped over a pile of dry-cleaning which had escaped Iona's instant tidying operation.

Angus waited until Marie had left the kitchen clutching a bowl of biscuits and then mouthed 'No Chris?' at Iona, widening his eyes with implication.

Iona glared at him and mouthed 'So?' back. It was a complicated urge – an urge to defend Marie's right to defend Chris. Even though she unequivocally disliked him. She made three cups of coffee and tipped a packet of Kettle Chips into a bowl.

'Only asking,' murmured Angus.

'Well, don't.' Iona opened and shut cupboards looking for the chocolate Fingers she'd hidden from him after the last major shopping expedition. 'Because I'm the one who'll have to *do* the asking.'

'Fill me in when I'm good and drunk.'

'If there's anything to tell,' said Iona, and took the tray through.

Jim had put on Iona's Guns N' Roses live CD and was standing in the middle of their sitting room, with one foot up on Angus's laser printer, eyes tight shut, crotch pointing as near the sky as he could manage, windmilling his right lead-guitar-playing arm to 'Paradise City'. Tamara was still in the loo.

'"Oh, won't you plee-ee-ee-eease—" Ah, cheers, Iona. Great, coffee,' he said, taking the mug off her and placing it carefully on the desk. "—take me hoooo-oooooo-ooooome?"'

'Irony has never visited the small town where you live, has it, Jim?' said Marie.

'Where's Chris?' Iona handed her the mug of coffee and slumped into a big easy chair. She kicked off her shoes so she could tuck her feet underneath the cushion and noticed too late that it was covered in white cat hairs. It only took the little feckers a minute while her back was turned.

'Working late. Again. I'm thinking of having NATO invade me illegally and set up new border checkpoints on my arms so I can justifiably claim some of his attention.'

'I think you're self-funding, so you can forget that.'

'You're right,' agreed Marie. 'I think I have adequate defences too. Not that he's worried about leaving me alone for great long periods – there's no chance of having my own office affair to get his attention when I'm surrounded by seven-year-olds with all manner of contagious skin infections.'

'There you are – there are all *sorts* of hidden perks in teaching,' agreed Iona. 'Enforced fidelity, as much sugar paper as you can slip under your jumper of an evening and just *think* of the Copydex-sniffing habit you can develop.'

Marie frowned. 'Excuse *me*. The only Copydex habit I have is the one where I glue my fingers together during break then spend a slow afternoon peeling the fake skin off.'

'Lerve-ly,' said Iona, pulling a face. 'And for supper . . . ?'

Tamara emerged at the door, flicking drops of water from her hands. Iona remembered that she'd forgotten to put a hand-towel in the bathroom again. 'Is Angus cooking?'

'Well, we thought it would be rude to ask Ned over and then hand him an apron as he walked in. I mean, I know that's what Jim does, but Angus can usually be relied upon not to buy turkey pieces. And he does have that big knife.'

'Hello?' said Jim. He looked wounded. 'I am still here, you know. And I made a really good pasta sauce last night.'

'Yeah, yeah . . .' Iona flapped her hand affectionately at him.

'Oh, fine, yeah, it's just that I'm, erm . . .' Tamara made a cover-all gesture in the region of her lower stomach.

'Oh, God, stop with the gut-flushing, will you, Tamara?' said Marie. 'Can't you just drink the odd Actimel once in a while and feel guilty like the rest of us?'

Tamara shook back her hair, which was falling in shampoo-advert waves around her face. 'It's more complicated than that. Human beings aren't designed to process so much saturated fats. And Angus always cooks like he's employed by the British Dairy Council. Anyway, I brought some fruit in my bag. Can't you tell the difference it's making to my hair and skin?'

'Not really, given that you look like a Nordic princess at the worst of times,' observed Marie. 'But there is a lot more shit coming out of you at the moment, I'll give you that.'

Tamara frowned. 'If your villi could talk, Marie . . .'

'They do talk. They say, "Feed me more of that nice gunky stuff and wash it down with coffee!" That's when I can hear them over the sound of my stomach wobbling around like a happy hippo.'

'Enough!' said Jim, flushing. His air-guitar arms wind-milled on even though he had stopped singing. 'There's only a short step from villi to periods and there aren't enough other men in the room to protect me. Can we talk about cars instead?'

'No, we can't,' snapped Iona. 'Don't even go there. It is a very short road with a great big roadblock on it.'

'Angus started on about you learning again?' asked Marie sympathetically.

'Yup. He picked me up from work and, just my luck, we hit a traffic jam almost immediately, so I got an unbroken three-quarters-of-an-hour-long monologue about how Angus wasn't a taxi service and what would we do if he slumped dead over the wheel with a heart-attack? Would I just leave us to die in the middle of the Westway because I wouldn't know which pedal to press? The usual.'

'Ah, dear,' said Marie, slurping off a mouthful of coffee and making room for Tamara on the sofa at the same time. 'Well, you know my offer still stands. I'd be more than willing to take you out, and so would Jim, wouldn't you, Jim?'

'Er, no,' said Jim. He rolled his eyes. 'Not if your driving's anything like Tamara's.'

Tamara looked wounded. 'I passed.'

'Yeah, and the examiner begged you to buy a scooter.'

'Well, it's all academic, because I don't want to learn,' said Iona. 'End of discussion.'

'I'm sure there's a really interesting psychological reason behind that,' said Tamara.

'No, it's just that until I went in a car driven by you, I never knew you could say the Lord's Prayer thirty times in ten minutes. Now, is there any sign of Ned?'

'He said he'd be round after he'd finished up at the Uxbridge, but I don't know exactly when that'll be,' said Jim. 'I told him to get a move on, but you know what he's like.' He put his air guitar down and changed Guns N' Roses for something more conducive to conversation. Iona didn't have a lot. Her CD player went up to 11. 'Is this your Dire Straits CD, Iona?'

'Certainly not. But isn't the Uxbridge just down the road?'

'Erm, well . . .' Jim pulled an explanatory face. 'He did say something about a friend of his in Shepherd's Bush and some new mushroom thing . . .'

'Oh, fantastic,' said Angus coming in and catching the end of the conversation. 'So he's going to be arriving around midnight, hallucinating dwarfs in my pantry and wanting to eat an entire packet of chocolate digestives with four of his eight hands?'

'You're so hard on Ned,' said Tamara reproachfully. 'Just because he doesn't have a nine-to-five job.'

'He does so,' said Iona. 'Nine-to-five on that he won't turn up. And I should know, I went to school with him. The only lesson he was ever on time for was detention.'

'What time's supper?' said Jim.

'Whenever you want in the next hour,' said Angus. He helped himself to a handful of crisps and put them all in his mouth at once. 'Earlier if you want to go out and order pizzas. Come on then, Jim. Do we have to wait until we have food on the table to hear your amazing news?'

'No!' said Marie. 'What amazing news? You've finally got a girlfriend?'

'No,' said Jim, blushing.

'You're having a baby? You've been promoted. You've decided to give things one more try with Ned. You've finally got on to *Blind Date*. You're . . .' She snapped her fingers trying to think. 'You're going to get a proper job?'

'I've got a proper job, thank you,' said Jim. 'Let me tell you how proper it is.'

'No, no, let me sit down first,' said Angus. 'Budge up, Marie.'

'Shouldn't we wait for Ned to come over? And Chris?' asked Tamara. She squashed herself into the back of the sofa to stop Marie's ample right flank crushing her.

'I don't think I could bear the suspense.' Marie finished off her coffee and put the empty mug on the table. She leaned forward expectantly. 'Well, come on. This is probably your optimum audience. Chris will only whinge at you and Ned probably knows what it is already, doesn't he?'

Jim fiddled with his cuff buttons. 'Well, OK,' he began slowly, a hint of deeper pink spreading across the tops of his ears. He wasn't used to being the focus of such avid attention. 'Well, I've been speaking to Martin, one of the directors at work, floating the general idea, you know, about buying the Bunch of Grapes for a pub-restaurant-flat conversion and, um . . .'

'*And*?' demanded Iona and Angus.

'And we went through some case notes and, uhm, he seemed to think it was quite a sound idea.' Jim couldn't quite disguise the surprise in his own voice. 'He told me to come up with some kind of formal proposal in the next few days, but *I think* he more or less said that Overworld would put up the money. If Brian still wants to sell.'

'That's brilliant!' exclaimed Iona, leaning over to squeeze his arm. 'Well done, you! I hope you're going to make sure everyone at work knows it's your baby!'

'As it were,' added Marie archly.

'Um, well, yes, I suppose so.' Jim flushed and looked pleased.

Iona flicked a glance at Angus from underneath her eyelashes. He was quietly triumphant, excited. Something bubbled up in her stomach again and she couldn't tell if it was fear or exhilaration.

'So, if we're going to do this,' Jim went on, 'we need to have a really serious talk this evening about who's in and who's not. And what our proposal would basically be. Thing is, sometimes these projects move at the speed of tectonic-plate shift and sometimes you need to make decisions immediately. I think this might be a fairly immediate one.'

'We do need Ned here then,' said Tamara, 'if he's going to be in charge of the kitchens.' She looked around. 'I mean, we can't really make decisions about the kind of food it's going to be without him being here, can we?'

Marie seemed to be about to say something and then stopped herself.

'Fine,' said Angus. 'We'll have to wait for them for supper anyway. What time are you expecting Chris to pitch up, Mazza?'

'Oooh, I don't know. What time does the UN shut? About eight? I'll give him a ring, see where he's got to in the old world peace stakes.'

'Phone's in the kitchen,' said Iona.

'But don't touch that sauce,' Angus added, as Marie unwedged herself from the sofa and got up, her skirt now laced with cat hair. Suddenly unsupported, Tamara slumped into the cushions. 'Oh, and bring some more beer through.'

'I suppose there's no way we can get hold of Ned, is there?' Tamara asked hopefully.

'Not unless one of you has better telepathic powers than me,' said Iona. 'We'll give them until half-seven and then start. I'm ready to drop anyway.'

'No luck?' said Angus as Marie reappeared in the door-way, expertly carrying six bottles of pub quiz Becks.

'No, but that's good, it means he's left.' She handed out the beer. 'If we all put our heads together and politically oppress Tamara, he'll probably turn up before Angus has time to put some pasta on.'

As she spoke, there was a long ring on the doorbell. As though someone had slumped against it. It was Ned's trademark.

'I'll go,' said Tamara, leaping up off the sofa.

'Oh, shame. I was all on for a bit of oppression there.' Marie dunked a biscuit in her coffee and tried not to drip on Iona's white cushions.

'What form of oppression were you going to go for?' asked Iona. 'Tell Tam her highlights were looking a bit faded, or something?'

'Oh yes, I had a whole string of them lined up. I was going to mention her puffball skirt and everything.'

Ned appeared in the doorway and waved a bag at them. The more dishevelled he got, the more he looked like a model, albeit not one that *Just 17* would use. Today, even though the rain was still lashing down, he was wearing a black sleeveless body-warmer and a faded Stone Roses T-shirt, from which his skinny brown arms protruded, the muscles standing out like knots in rope. His jeans looked as though he'd nicked them from a skip. 'Hiya. Got some whitebait – I'll put them in the fridge, yeah?'

His hair needs a wash, thought Iona protectively. And he's looking tired. Maybe he needs to be taking multi-vitamins or something. Maybe I should just give him some. Would he take them? Can you get speed with added Pro-Vitamin B complex?

'Ned, there's a bottle of wine open in the kitchen if you want a glass,' she shouted through.

'Oh, charming. Don't remember being offered that when *we* arrived,' said Jim.

'I was saving it for the grown-ups.'

'Hey, Ned? Get me a glass while you're at it, will you?' yelled Marie.

There was some banging and crashing as Ned opened and shut cupboards and the dishwasher in search of glasses.

'Has Tamara gone to help him?'

'I think she has.' Marie arched a dark eyebrow. 'It can be pretty tough for a professional chef to open a bottle of wine and pour it out, you know.'

'Miaow!' Angus scratched a paw in the air.

'Yeah, well, *whaddever*,' said Marie darkly, and held up her hand like a traffic policeman. She spent far too much of her school holidays watching American confessional TV. She had all the hand gestures. 'Why don't you start doing whatever you have to do to finish up supper? There's no point waiting for Chris – he'll only want to know why the food isn't on the table when he arrives.'

'OK.' Angus got up and Iona coughed. She hated to do it but it was part of the house-training.

'What?' he demanded.

She nodded at the empty coffee cups and with a reluctant grunt he collected them up and took them through to the kitchen.

Iona turned to Jim, who was flicking the CDs back and forwards in the rack. He kept pushing up the sleeves of his jumper as they slipped down and over his wrists. Jim was a compulsive fiddler. He hadn't yet cracked simultaneously looking cool and keeping his hands still. On one blind date she'd set up for him with a school-friend of hers, he'd managed to set fire to the tablecloth during an awkward lull in conversation. He looked a bit rattled now. Maybe he was getting it from Angus.

'It's really exciting, Jim, finding this backing from Over-world. They really think it's a goer?'

'Yeah.' Jim shrugged and smiled. 'Feels a bit weird, to be honest, now I've actually got to get out there and do it. I keep wondering what the catch is that they haven't told me.'

'You'll be fine.' She smiled encouragingly and hoped she didn't look like her mum. 'Angus is dead excited.'

'Well, there's a lot to do yet. Bridges to cross. You know.' He fiddled with the CDs.

'God, you lads are so miserable!' exclaimed Marie. 'You've been going on about this for ages and now it's actually happening you'd think you'd all been forced to sell your houses to pay for it! What are you *like*? I think it's fantastic news and if you do all the stuff you said you were going to do, I promise you I won't ever eat anywhere else! Jeez . . .' She turned to Iona. 'Honestly, I'm really excited about this, aren't you?'

'I am, yes,' said Iona. 'Erm, yes, I am.'

As Marie predicted, Chris turned up just as Angus was rinsing out the pasta in the sink. He had brought a bottle of cheap Bulgarian red wine and didn't apologize for being late.

'Hello, Christopher,' said Marie, waving from her chair. 'Hard day at the office?'

'It's international relief work, Marie, it's never exactly a bed of roses,' said Chris. He leaned over and gave her a peck on the cheek, helping himself to a handful of nuts from the bowl by her side on the way up.

Iona looked at Angus, but he was talking to Jim about the 1954 Protection Act and its relevance to the site. She didn't bother to eavesdrop. If she didn't understand one word in five, Iona had an automatic zone-out facility on her brain.

They ate supper round the big collapsible table which almost filled the sitting room. The windows that opened on to the garden in the summer were tightly shut and the rain drummed and trickled down the panes. Iona checked now and again to make sure neither of her cats was trying to get in and then, as the wine flowed and there was no sign of them, assumed they were inside somewhere and asleep on some carelessly exposed dark fabric.

Angus's rich bolognese sauce was very good. Jim gave a pitch-perfect round of burps in tribute. Ned did something unreal to some part-baked baguettes and nobody believed it was just garlic and butter. Iona then did a professional demonstration of plate-clearing up both arms, and Tamara made some coffee and a hot Tooth-kind Ribena for herself.

Then they started planning the pub.

'OK,' said Angus. He pulled the cap off his fountain pen and shuffled the paper in front of him. 'Brainstorming is go.'

The animated buzz of chat around the table stopped dead on cue, just as if everyone's batteries had simultaneously fallen out.

'Come on,' said Angus in the same voice he had been using that morning to kick-start a discussion about squatting rights with a diffident bunch of trainees. 'Who's going to set the ball rolling? Iona?'

'Can I smell burning?' asked Iona, sniffing the air. 'Let me just go and check the oven . . .'

'Well, I say traditional pub food,' volunteered Chris, with a wink at Marie.

The cold hand of dread at what he was about to say gripped her, but she made herself smile back.

'*Great* start,' said Angus with a blast of enthusiasm so strong Tamara had to move her chair slightly away from him. He wrote 'traditional' in the middle of the paper in his precise handwriting and drew flow-chart lines coming out of it.

'That's . . .' Chris paused to let Angus's pen catch up. '. . . crisps and . . . dry-roasted peanuts.' He delivered his punchline with a punchable grin and, at Angus's filthy look, raised his hands defensively and added, 'Pork scratchings. Vegetarian ones, though. Organic, if you can source them. Don't want to upset your fashionable clientele, do we?'

'Thank you, Chris,' said Angus. He was really trying hard to be patient, if only because an all-out screaming row even before they started would be too predictable. 'Always good to get the lowest possible common denominator gags out of the way first.'

'Are we going to have a theme for all this?' asked Jim. 'I mean, presuming we're going to keep the pub element of it, you could make it an . . . um . . .'

'Please don't say an Irish pub,' Marie interrupted. 'It would be bad enough us having to drink in yet another Mary Ellen's Poitin Palace, without knowing we were responsible for inflicting it on everyone else. If you're going to think about keeping it as a pub,' she went on, 'you have to think about the cultures that *have* pubs like that. I mean, there's no point making it into some kind of Texan roadside diner inside if it's still going to look like the Queen Vic from the outside. You're not going to get planning permission for a nine-foot diner-style stainless-steel wave-effect frontage on a nineteenth-century public house, are you? I bet it's listed.'

She looked round for agreement and noticed that, out of long habit, everyone was staring somewhere into space, trying not to be picked. For a bunch of bright, talented people who could debate the precise payment breakdown of a Chinese set meal bill for over an hour, it was depressingly like trying to extract contributions from her year three, even down to Tamara chewing the ends of her hair. Marie thought about telling her the Furball Horror Story that had cured the gaggle of hair chewers overnight, then decided it was too unpleasant for the table.

'Are you?' she repeated. She turned to Iona, who had sat down again next to her, bringing a draught of cold air in her wake. 'Iona, I can hear my voice in my head, but is it not coming through into the room?'

Iona seemed to take a moment to focus. Her hair was dripping wet and the shoulders of her dusty pink T-shirt were soaked deep crimson with rain drops.

'I only went outside to put the bin-bag out,' she said before Angus could translate his look of horror into words.

'And you slipped and fell head first into a swimming pool, is that what you're saying? You'll catch your death, you big donkey.' Angus threw her a towel from the basket of laundry that neither of them had got round to putting away yet and which Iona had temporarily shoved behind the sofa three days ago.

'Iona? Ideas for the pub?' asked Jim. 'Surely Angus got you to make a list?'

'Well, yes, quite. Um, OK then, I did have one actually. What about a Lake District bar? Like one of those climbing pubs in the middle of nowhere? Décor would be cheap, because you wouldn't have to do much to the interior, maybe even strip it back a bit, get some bare walls exposed. You could have Jennings bitter as the house ale, Cumberland sausages as a main menu feature, er, climbing boots on the walls . . .'

'Can we veto things on the walls?' said Angus. 'I hate them. Freaks me out, sitting there, waiting for them to fall on someone's head. Or in their beer.'

'And you have to dust them,' added Tamara, looking disgusted. 'Think of the airborne filth in the Bunch of Grapes! All that spitting for one thing. Eee-yuch. No, absolutely no hanging things.'

'Why not?' Chris asked. 'You can't beat a bit of junk hanging up. Gives the punters something to look at while they're drinking, doesn't it? Some of the best bars I ever went to in Durban had the most amazing stuff on the walls.'

'Brains, mostly, and the occasional wall-mounted chick, as I recall.' Marie drained her glass. 'Very *Thelma and Louise*. Is there any more wine, Iona?'

Chris gave her a stern look. 'I thought you were driving home.'

'No, you are. It's Friday night,' she objected. 'I don't have to be bushy-tailed and full of educative zeal tomorrow morning. I don't have to *explain* anything. Anyway, I agree with Angus, things hanging up is very dated now, isn't it? Unless it's something completely surreal and yet appropriate. Like if you had a tractor suspended from the ceiling. Long as it didn't drop on anyone. Unless you made that a feature, you know: "Drink t'yard of ale and drop t'tractor".'

'I wish you lot would practise your northern accents before you inflict them on native speakers,' Iona said. 'It's distressing.'

'Yee-ee-ees.' Angus scribbled 'tractor' on his flow chart. 'Not bad, not bad. I like the northern bar idea, I know the beer is fantastic . . . It might be possible to get some kind of exclusive beer supply if we made it the house ale . . .'

'And you could theme the food around good country produce, couldn't you?' Iona arranged her kirby grips in a line in front of her and started to twist strands of wet brown hair into knots, pinning them round her head like little molehills. 'Lots of sausage, lamb, free-range steak . . .'

'Oh, wow, Iona, those big Yorkshires with whole Cumberland loops inside and onion gravy you can get in that pub near your mum's,' said Marie dreamily. 'Do you remember . . . Can we have those?'

Ned twitched into life for the first time. 'No, no, stop it right there now. Are you wanting an indoor barbecue, or what? I *can* do more complicated things than sausages. I haven't spent the last ten years working in London restaurants to do sausages in Yorkshires. I could have stopped in Stanwix and done that.'

'Anyway, back on planet Earth,' said Chris, 'if you're going to have a northern theme pub, you'd have to arrange break-ins and ram-raiding contests and synchronized glassing displays, and "Shag me Mam, Fight me Dad" nights. I mean, come *on*! Who down here would want to go to a northern theme pub, for God's sake? Unless provincial is the new cosmopolitan.'

'*What* did you just say?' asked Iona incredulously.

'Chris, do you have *any* positive contributions to make?' inquired Tamara. 'I mean, just out of interest?'

'Oh, listen to yourselves,' he replied huffily. 'Quite apart from the lack of real originality, all these heritage theme pubs – it's pure tokenism. Patronizing tokenism. No better than all those American theme bars you're so snotty about. I'm surprised you even suggested it, Iona. Shows how far you must have come from your roots if you're prepared to theme up your background for a bunch of southerners to buy into after a hard day in the City. Now if you want a real cultural experience, why aren't we talking about highlighting proper country cooking from somewhere like Yugoslavia or Namibia? Somewhere where your regulars won't have holiday cottages, anyway.'

'Chris . . .' said Marie in what everyone else could tell were warning tones.

Everyone except Chris. He sailed on in the vacuum of stunned silence and folded his arms confrontationally. 'Well, come on, Iona, you know exactly what I'm driving at – you *do*, or else why are you looking so guilty now, eh?'

Jim looked round the table and was horrified to see the makings of a real row staring back at him. Chris, with his random and yet self-righteous approach to arguments, had an infallible knack of blowing these things up out of nowhere, since he inevitably managed to end up insulting everyone around the table, no matter what opinion they held on the topic under attack. Angus, intensely protective of Iona, was looking thunderous, Iona looked shell-shocked and Marie was ominously testing the sharpness of each red nail against the soft pad of her hand.

'Hey, hey, hey,' he said quickly. 'Hey! Stop it! We're just trying out ideas. It's not *Question Time*.'

Iona opened her mouth, nothing came out and so she shut it again quickly. As usual, Chris had hit unknowingly and unerringly on her most sensitive spot. He was the unintentional Jeremy Paxman of south London – if he'd known how easily he could wind people up, God help them, he would probably be even more of an arsehole than he already was. Chris had Teflon confidence and didn't seem to take arguments personally; they were just arenas for playing one idea off against another. And yet there was nothing she *could* say – how much she missed home, how much she *did* fear 'selling out' – without sounding defensive and playing straight into his hands.

'What? *What?* I don't know why you're so touchy,' Chris went on self-righteously. 'I'm only being Devil's advocate. God, you can tell you don't work in a high-pressure industry if this is what you're like every time someone expresses an alternative viewpoint.'

'That'll be why you work with starvin' refugees and the like, is it?' asked Ned, in his offhand, faintly sarcastic manner. 'Bet they're always dead grateful.'

Chris pulled an outraged face and drew himself up to retaliate.

'Enough!' said Jim, banging his hands flat on the table. 'That is enough. Why can't you just get a gym subscription or something, Chris, if you're under such pressure? Jesus, you have no idea when to stop, you lot . . .'

'I like the idea,' continued Ned, addressing Angus as if nothing had been said. 'I like Iona's idea of being able to get decent beer in London, and it would be great to have a simple, no frills, no gimmicks pub, but I think we need to have more ambition with the food side of things. You have to make people *want* to come out here to eat, you know? Though we can have some Cumberland sausage on the menu if you want, pet,' he added to Iona, deliberately flattening his accent to annoy Chris. 'Proper food, like, instead of poncy squid ink and lemongrass cookery.'

'I wouldn't bother about him,' observed Marie, catching the glance that passed between them. 'When you have the glorious heritage of Milton Keynes running through your veins, something deep inside can never allow you to sell out.'

Angus put his hand on Iona's thigh beneath the table and she jogged her leg up and down gratefully. It made her feel a bit stronger. Less likely to ram the peppermill down Chris's neck, anyway. She clipped the last of her hair twists on top of her head and tried to breathe regularly. Tension made her feel sick.

'OK, well,' she said, trying to keep her voice careless, 'the reasoning *behind* my suggestion was that you could keep the exterior as it is and make a virtue of the, er, roughness inside. I'm assuming that the budget for this is going to be pretty tight. As long as it's clean, it would look simple and honest. And it's not as pretentious as going for a theme that none of us has any real connection with.'

'And themes are a bit tacky,' agreed Marie. 'Whereas *treatments* – *treatments*, if you will – are rather chic.'

'Right, great,' said Angus, reverting to his management voice. 'Thanks, Iona. That's certainly a lot to think about.'

'Yes, go to the top of the class,' muttered Chris, just loud enough for Marie to hear.

Her face flushed red but no one noticed the sudden clench of her jaw. Not even Chris. She forced herself to keep quiet, not to stamp on his foot beneath the table. That would provide the diversion he wanted; an opportunity to stop the discussion, look wounded, demand to know where her sense of humour was, throw up his hands, dismiss the lot of them, maybe walk off, force her to leave to go after him . . . Marie felt the click of an invisible handcuff on her wrist. Maybe she should start worrying when she *didn't* care what he did.

'Did anyone else have any burning inspirations?' Angus looked round the table. 'Iona, are you warm enough in that wet thing? There's a jumper of mine behind you on the floor if you want. No, go on, put it on, *put* it *on*, you'll freeze otherwise!'

God, Iona's lucky, thought Marie, biting her lip enviously

as Iona slipped the big green jersey over her head. Angus had
a tick-sheet full of top boyfriend assets, as approved by top
glossy mags. He was so caring towards Iona, so watchful.
She'd noticed that every time he left the room, wherever they
were, he would touch Iona briefly when he came back, a little
caress of her hair, a brush of her hand, as if he were checking
to see she was still real. It was pure romantic fiction. And
once she'd noticed that, she couldn't help but see it every
time – and though she was pleased for her best friend, every
time it gave her a bitter nudge.

She and Chris didn't go in for public displays of affection. Or private ones, much. Right from the first day of
her marriage, the best part of which had been spent on
a cross-country bus to a prehistoric shrine on top of a
mountain, Chris had made a point of treating her as if
she were still single, which at the time she had considered
generous and forward-thinking. Now she was beginning to
wonder if he actually wanted people to think of her as his
wife. The way he spoke to her in public, anyone would be
forgiven for mistaking her for his annoying younger sister.

After an hour of circular discussion about lager versus beer,
Tamara interrupted things to make some fresh coffee. Marie
watched Angus scribbling down the initials of everyone
round the table at the top of his notes. Like at a real
meeting. Automatically, she kept one eye on Chris, who had
gone unusually quiet, tensing herself to drown out any more
carping with an extrovert diversionary comment. Maybe it
was Angus's pen and paper, and the way he was leading a
discussion, rather than just writing down ideas, but it felt
very real life all of a sudden, she thought, almost surreal.
When they'd talked about this in the comfort of Jim's flat,
it had been really easy to throw ideas out, when there was no
need to think in terms of cost or even basic practicality. And
now it was quite serious everyone seemed to be rising to the
possibilities for once. Just in time to have Chris wilt them.

He's a miserable git, thought Marie, studying him over the top of her glass. In her head, she heard his voice chorus, 'You've got to be realistic or else everyone ends up disappointed.' Chris said that a lot. He said it was an all too unusual attitude in charity work, although those colleagues of his that he'd risked introducing her to seemed like happy, practical, principled people. She didn't remember him saying it at all at university. In fact his unquenchable idealism had been one of the most exciting things about him. The rows he'd had with cynical Law Boy Angus had even been entertaining, and she'd fancied him even more when the light of battle started flashing in his eyes and he got so wound up by his own beliefs that words tumbled out of him like water shooting from an out-of-control hose.

A long time ago.

Jim pulled himself up in his chair and leaned his elbows on the table, trying to catch Angus's eye.

At which point Tamara made a modest coughing sound and put down the coffee jug very precisely on Iona's unpaid Visa bill.

'Tamara?' said Angus politely, as she seemed to be waiting for an invitation to enter the discussion.

'Well, I can't tell you much about lager, but I have been playing with some ideas, you know, about décor and so on,' she said. She reached down into her pristine and very fashionable courier bag. 'I went to a very good psychic, you'll remember, Iona, the one who told me about my mother in . . .'

'. . . in the garden of your new flat, yes, I remember the one,' said Iona.

Tamara looked pleased. 'Yes, well, she seems to think that there are some fantastic omens about this project and she really wants me to involve myself in it completely. She sees' – Tamara tapped the wooden part of the table three times and lifted her crossed fingers in the air – 'a real romance in it.'

Marie and Iona exchanged quick, discreet and completely despairing glances.

'Excellent, so there's hope for us yet, eh, Tam?' said Jim.

Tamara's porcelain brow briefly creased in confusion. 'No, romance for *me*, she said. Anyway, I had a think about all the places I liked going to and all the bits I like about them and' – she pulled out a spiral-bound folder from her bag – 'I made a kind of presentation thing.'

Marie swallowed. Tamara really would benefit from more full-time employment – or just generally getting out more.

'Very good!' said Angus. 'Very, *very* good. Let's have a look then?'

Tamara passed her folder down to Angus.

'I agree with Iona that you can't really do anything to the outside – and I don't think you'd get planning permission anyway, these crumbly old pubs nearly always have people jumping up and down about historic significance and all that rubbish. I think we should keep the outside as it is, maybe with some, ooh, I haven't really thought about it in detail,' – she waved her hands around vaguely – 'some terracotta boxes, or maybe hanging baskets, of single-colour cyclamen, maybe in white, lots of them, maybe red in summer for a bit of variation, some ivy trailing down to cover that dodgy brickwork round the front, then inside you could strip everything out and make it very bare and very stylish, get rid of that filthy germ-trap carpet and polish up the floorboards, very clean, not *too* All Bar One, but a sort of ironic pub treatment . . .'

'An ironic pub,' repeated Marie. 'Just explain that to me, will you, Tamara?'

'Well, you know, you would have those beer . . .' Tamara waved her hands some more. 'What do you call them? Those . . .'

'Glasses? Kegs? Monsters?' supplied Jim.

'Goggles?' Ned put his head on one side innocently.

'Ned!' hissed Iona and kicked his shin under the table.

Tamara definitely had beer-impaired vision but almost certainly had beer contact lenses.

'You know.' Tamara mimed what looked to Iona suspiciously like Angus's all-purpose road-rage hand gesture, used to imply that the other driver had either been drinking or attending to the contents of his pants. 'Oh, what are they called?'

'Beer pumps!' said Marie in a flash of inspiration.

'Yes, beer pumps,' agreed Tamara. 'You'd have those, but instead of the appalling tacky pictures on them, they would be brushed stainless steel.'

There was a pause while everyone tried to understand what she was getting at.

'Er, if you mean the pictures of galloping foxes that you get on the operational *china* bit of the handle, then I think they're unique to the Bunch of Grapes and, fair enough, they're pretty grim, but if you mean the little labels on the pump bit . . . that's so people can tell what kind of beer it is. Isn't it?' said Marie slowly.

'Oh,' said Tamara. 'They're different? All tastes the same to me. Anyway, it would all be stainless steel, and instead of a dartboard you could have a sort of ironic dart-operated jukebox . . .'

'And what would you have as double top? "Diamond Life" by Sade?' suggested Chris sarcastically.

Jim leaped in before Tamara could unwittingly make things worse. 'Yes, well, you wouldn't have to hear it that often, would you? Not if the standard of your darts is anything to go by. You could have the entire top ten on the wall around the board and still fill the pub with top chart action.'

Tamara looked at Chris and Jim, trying to work out whether they were taking the piss or not. She decided they weren't and let it go. 'Anyway, to go back to what I was saying, I thought about all the detailing on the sort of *iconic* eating and drinking places . . .'

'Just remembering at the same time that we're talking

about a rundown local boozer in a dodgy area of Ladbroke Grove here, Tamara, and not a Soho club,' Iona warned.

Next to her, Angus was turning page after page of Tamara's folder, with ever-heightening eyebrows.

'Yes, yes, yes.' Tamara rolled her eyes. 'What? Why are you all looking at me? I just put a few ideas together, you know, the wall mirrors from Bar Italia, some retro stained glass like in the Ivy, that would fit in nicely with an ironic Victorian treatment, those cute little retro bar stools from . . .'

She ground to a halt when she realized that everyone was staring at Angus, who was noisily sucking air in and out through his teeth without knowing it. He sounded like a carpet sweeper.

'Bloody hell, Tam,' said Angus finally, unaware of the audience his whistling teeth had attracted. 'Things been a bit slow at work lately? No one can say you didn't do this comprehensively.'

'What? What? Let me see.' Marie reached for the spiral-bound file.

Inside the neatly typed cover were pages and pages full of cuttings and Photoshop images, all annotated in the precision print of Tamara's Rotring drawing pen, little arrows coming out to link ideas and pages, cross-referenced like lab specimens. She had gone through style magazines, source books, IKEA catalogues, picture libraries and pulled out hundreds of examples of brushed stainless steel, white glass, clean, airy lighting – there were even sketches of which walls could be pulled down in the Bunch of Grapes to make it look as though it was actually seven floors up in a loft conversion, rather than a ground-floor, end-of-terrace pub.

Flipping through somewhat faster than Angus, Marie noted that there were only two elements missing from Tamara's research: the real-life clientele and the prices.

Rather critical elements, she would have thought.

But incredibly imaginative all the same, even if Tamara

had basically ignored what was actually there, in favour of what she would like to erect in its place.

Story of her life. Story of all their lives, come to that.

'Have you done the toilets?' she inquired politely.

'Er, no. I did food too.' Tamara leaned over and flipped through to the back of the file, in which she had compiled some menus, illustrated inevitably with full-page bleeds of glossy recipes from the back of *Cosmopolitan* and *Hello!*, all soft-focus arugula and tiny bead-like tomatoes scattered everywhere.

'Riii-ii-ii-ight,' said Marie, raising her eyebrows and nodding encouragingly. So they would need to source a wholesale balsamic vinegar shipper as well as a brewer.

'Though obviously it would be up to Ned what he decided to do with the food, ultimately,' Tamara added quickly. 'These are just . . . ideas. You know. Themes. But not themes, no, sort of, well . . .' She looked at him quickly and looked back at her file and shut it.

'Ned?' Angus stopped scribbling notes and turned to him. 'Seems like a good point to bring you in.'

Chris snorted just quietly enough to make anyone who pointed it out sound paranoid.

'OK,' said Ned. He rubbed his eyes with the balls of his fists as if he were trying to keep himself awake. 'Well, if it were up to me . . . I've been thinking about the kind of kitchen I'd like to run and in the end I don't see the point in wasting time on fancy gimmicks or specialist food for a place like this. You want something that people can trust and keep coming back to week after week, not just when they fancy Turkish, or Thai, or whatever. Because there are proper places they can go for that, you know what I mean? And it's not that cheap. You want something that the kitchen can put out easily, because it's going to take a while to get a team up and running, and cheaply, because specialist ingredients cost money and you have to have the right bits. And speaking for m'self here, I can't be doing with all that theme stuff. I wouldn't eat it, wouldn't cook it. It's really false. All that fannying around with curried parsnip fronds and what-have-you. So what I'd suggest is pretty similar to what I think Iona's suggesting, which is to have a pub that serves the best beer and the best possible simple, English but perfectly cooked menu. Really good organic meat, organic vegetables, hung pheasant, proper game – country food, cooked as it's meant to be, not like pork with chocolate, you know? But with a bit of room to be creative with it. So it's not boring, like.'

'But not to start adulterating steak and kidney pies with Puy lentils,' said Angus.

'Exactly.' This was the longest Ned had spoken for ages and he looked exhausted. His hands fluttered around his pockets, possibly in search of whatever was keeping him awake these days.

Jim nodded.

'Unless you wanted me to, Tamara. Bit of roughage for your villi, like,' Ned added slyly.

Tamara blushed. 'Vegetables are perfectly sufficient, thanks, if you have them raw.'

'I suppose you would make quite a bit out of the organic thing, wouldn't you?' Angus asked, sketching a plan of the Bunch of Grapes underneath his notes, marking in tables and walls.

'How innovative,' said Chris sarcastically.

Marie immediately started talking before he could go on. 'It's a bit funny that we're all thinking along the same lines, really. I mean, I suppose what Ned's saying basically fits in with Tamara's ironic pub idea too,' she said. 'You'd have "traditional" pub food, but it would be with the best possible ingredients – really good steak and kidney pies, and big fat Maris Piper chips, and fabulous fresh North Sea cod in real-ale batter, and pheasant casserole with the lead shot still in, and great steaming apple pies with that fabulous chilled double-cream vanilla custard you used to do at the Red Arrow . . .'

'You're dieting again, aren't you?' said Iona.

'Yes, I am. Is it that obvious?'

Iona grimaced and nodded.

Angus numbered all the tables he'd drawn in on his plan and lifted his head sideways from the paper to address Jim, like a swimmer coming up for air between strokes. 'We'll need to go through some figures, won't we, about profit per cover and all that? How much detail will you need for your presentation?'

'Well, I'm not exactly sure, but I copied a load of files from the last place they bought.' Jim passed him a file from beneath his chair. 'This would be a lot smaller, I think, and it takes some time to start getting any profit back, but the figures would have to work, definitely.'

'OK . . .' Angus flipped through the pages. Jim watched him anxiously. 'OK, that's another issue. No need to get completely depressed just yet.' He turned a page in his notes and started sketching out another spidery plan. 'Let's talk about our fabulous team!'

'Hurray!' said Marie, at exactly the same time as Chris did. Except her 'Hurray!' wasn't quite so sarcastic as his.

'Ned,' Angus said, mid-scribble, 'Ned Lowther, our star-chef-to-be, can you give me a list of all the places you've cooked at since you started working in London? You'll need that for the presentation, won't you, Jim?'

Jim nodded. 'Yes, and make sure you include all the places they're likely to have eaten at in the last year. That won't narrow it down though. This flat is probably the only place they haven't eaten at in London.'

'And Iona, you're another star catering player.' More cryptic notes. 'Obviously we'll be promoting you to manager of Coffee Morning.' Angus drew a line down the side of his crowded page and began adding their names. 'Tamara, you've done bar work, haven't you?' He didn't wait for her to reply. 'Let's make you . . . an . . . experienced front-of-house manager too . . .' He gave her a conspiratorial wink. 'After all, once these people have met you . . .'

'Meaning?' demanded Tamara.

'Meaning you look like the sort of person they're sure to have seen in the Bluebird or wherever all the gorgeous people are that week,' Iona explained quickly.

Tamara pouted, but seemed vaguely mollified the more she thought about it.

Angus's notes were now on to a fourth page. Iona tried to read upside down but couldn't make out his writing. She thought she could read 'llama' but couldn't see how it would fit in with what had gone before. Unless he was taking the quality-meat thing a bit far.

Chris looked round the table in amazement, trying to catch someone's eye so he could speak with a proper audience.

'Staff?' Angus looked up at Jim. 'How many do we need? Stroke can we take on? Stroke can we get away with?'

Iona noticed that Jim had abandoned the cutlery he'd been fiddling with earlier and was now fiddling intently with the bowl of sugar on the table. Small silvery crumbs were spread like tiny hail around his cup and saucer. Apart from one or two animated bursts, he'd been lapsing into thoughtful silences all evening. She'd imagined on earlier evidence that it would be Angus going quiet (which, she realized now, was wishful thinking), while Jim cartwheeled round the room, making this new project flicker into life from their discussions and suggestions.

But he had seemed subdued. Was he annoyed at Angus for taking over the discussion? Or was he too nervous about the whole thing to push himself to the front? Or was this just what Jim was like when he was – shock horror – thinking?

Stop doing Angus questions, she told herself, or at least give yourself time to answer.

'Jim?' she asked gently. 'Staff?'

No, that's worse. That's motherly. You'll be cutting up his food for him next.

'Well, I suppose I'll be overseeing the place, so I can be there whenever at the beginning.' Jim scratched his nose with a spoon. 'Can't see Overworld falling apart if I spend the odd morning helping out. Angus will have to be there full-time as manager, and you'll need at least one person behind the bar all the time, I guess, depending on how popular we get. Another two on floor service.'

'And we *are* going to be *really* popular!' urged Marie in her 'We're having fun, aren't we, Year Three?' voice. 'Especially if you do brunch on Sundays! Ned's kedgeree! Onion marmalade! French toast! Sorry, that's my stomach using me as a mouthpiece again, sorry. But come on, guys, let's have a bit of enthusiasm!'

'Yeah!' said Iona, banging a coffee spoon on the table. 'Get with the programme or get on the bus, guys!'

Angus gave her one of his looks.

How come it's just me and Marie getting behind this, wondered Iona, trying not to laugh at the 'Angus' face Marie was pulling behind his back. She could feel a lifting sensation in her stomach, a bubble of excitement that began to expand inside, pushing up her heart rate to coffee-overdose levels. The more they talked like this, the more real it was beginning to seem. Maybe they really *could* make the pub work and create something between them that other people would come to and enjoy and talk about, and even if they ended up working twelve-hour days for a year, it would still be theirs. Something tangible to show for working hard. And how hard was it to transform a pub like that? Angus had knocked down two walls in their flat alone.

'Tell you what, Angus,' she said brightly, 'you know that wall running along the back of the main area?' She leaned over and marked it on his plan in red biro. 'I can do a full-length painting to go along there. And let *me* think about the toilets. I hate pub loos. We can have the most fabulous loos in west London.'

'Whatever . . . just no horse brasses, OK?' Tamara shuddered.

'Awww, really?' said Ned. 'Not even a couple of small ones? And signs saying Mares and Stallions?'

'Mares and Studs, surely? And a separate loo for geldings?'

'And areas called Troughs and Nosebags. Marked out with ropes.'

Chris cleared his throat, managing to make it sound pitying at the same time. 'I hate to be the bearer of bad news here,' he said, 'but you haven't actually bought this place yet. In fact, you don't even know if it's still on the market. And don't think I'm being personal, because I'm not, but what serious property developer is going to lend money to a bunch of amateur punters with no catering experience at all? They're not stupid. You're all getting far too excited about something you don't really know anything about, and have no real business plans for. Will one of you please get real before we all get very disappointed?'

There was a pursed silence round the table. The rain continued to slide against the windows. Iona suspected that Chris wasn't including himself in the 'we'.

'Oh, come on, think logically for a change,' Chris said. He had never been afraid of a significant conversational vacuum. 'It's not as though I like being Mr Nasty here.'

'Yes, you do, darling,' said Marie. 'You love it.'

'I'm only trying to be the voice of reason, because the rest of you are getting carried away on your own little flights of fancy, aren't you? Just because you're always eating out doesn't mean you can run a restaurant. I mean, *you* don't talk about setting yourself up as a hairdresser just because you have your hair done every month,' he finished, looking smug.

I wonder how long he's been sitting on that one, thought Marie. Metaphors weren't Chris's strong point: they wasted time. She fixed a smile on her face and tilted her head to one side so Iona wouldn't see the irritation in her eyes.

'No,' she began, in the same patronizing tone he'd used, 'but it happens that my friend here is a top hairdresser who has worked with the Charles Worthingtons of the catering profession and that my other friend over there is a part-time stylist in a small but very exclusive salon, and another close friend here' – she pointed to Jim, who concentrated on crushing the sugar crystals into fine powder – 'specializes in finding top locations for much bigger multi-million hairdressers to set up shop in.'

Marie made herself stop before she started squawking and took a couple of deep breaths. Her smile had gone a bit skew. God, he was annoying. 'So while I *myself* am not a top hairdresser, I do flatter myself that, due to my infrequently indulged but deeply cherished passion for fine hairstyling, I know one when I see one, and that perhaps, by assisting in some way in the establishment of a particularly exciting new salon, I might be able to offer some help and pick up a few tips. Is that all right with you, or do you need the metaphor explained?'

'I bet you can't even remember how it started, the amount you've drunk this evening,' Chris said, looking pointedly at the glass in her hand.

'Oh, hang on now, Chris, that's not . . .' Angus murmured.

Marie looked at the two remaining mouthfuls of wine in the glass, fixed Chris squarely in the eye and swallowed them both.

There was another loaded *Cat on a Hot Tin Roof*-style pause round the table while she wiped away the tiny dribble of red wine on her lip with the back of her hand.

'I'd save the worrying for when I start *declining* the wine,' she said darkly.

Chris glowered some more. Even the rain now stopped raining, out of sheer embarrassment.

Everyone desperately searched for something, anything, to say that wouldn't sound like Alan Bennett following Tennessee Williams in a game of Consequences.

Jim cleared his throat, presumably to make sure it still worked after so long without use. 'Look, um, now we've got these ideas on paper, what we really need to do is to sit down and work out the figures. And that's something Angus and Ned and I can run through over the weekend, isn't it?' He looked round at Angus and Ned for support and they nodded enthusiastically. 'We can get hold of Brian at the pub.'

Everyone else took this as a signal to start nodding enthusiastically. Iona felt a strange compulsion to get up and clear the table, which she assumed was some Doctor Who-style telepathic vibe coming through from her suddenly-desperate-to-leave guests. That or a protective instinct to get all the cutlery off the table as soon as possible.

Angus seemed to snap back from wherever he'd been and the solicitor in him regained the controls. He shuffled his papers into order and fastened them at the top with a big paper-clip.

Tamara offered her file across the table to him. She was trying to look as though she didn't really mind whether he took it or not, but her eyes kept darting between him and Ned and back again, although she was trying to keep them casually focused on Iona's candelabra, which was making Gothic drips on the table and forming immovable compounds with Jim's powdered sugar.

'*Thank* you, Tamara,' Angus said, taking it and tucking it into the plastic wallet he'd found under the sofa. 'That's going to be really useful. Thanks.'

Iona froze halfway to the sink with all the coffee mugs, waiting for Chris's sarcastic response, but none came. She turned round to see that he'd left the table while she'd been loading the dishwasher, to go to the loo presumably, and Marie was sitting with her hands clutching her thick black curls, which spilled randomly over her fingers like hanks of treacle. The skin round her eyes stretched them up at the sides, and Iona could see a shiny layer of tears round the green cat's eyes, but they looked more like tears of rage than anything else. With her *Dolce Vita* winged eyeliner and straining red blouse, Marie appeared to be on the verge of a messy explosion, all hormones and crimson lipstick and anger.

Not that anyone was risking involvement in the fall-out. Tamara was buffing her nails with some kind of sponge vegetable, and Jim and Ned and Angus had already started to lay the framework of their costings argument. It looked like being a runner. Even Jim was frantically scribbling things down now, using one of her sketching pencils. Chris's timely intervention had served only to kick-start his enthusiasm at the last minute. He'd better not pocket that pencil, she thought absently. Or chew it.

Iona put down the cloth she was using to wipe the kitchen surface (not that it needed doing) and steeled herself to go to Marie. She would have to work out what to say when she got there. That was the problem. Iona wavered. What do you say? It wasn't meant to happen like this. She wasn't equipped with the appropriate articles from magazines yet. Or rather, the ones she read were still on 'From "Give us a ring" to "Give me that ring!"'. 'When your friends divorce' was still a couple of steps away, surely? Like magazines with knitting patterns?

Words probably weren't the important thing anyway, and Iona had an indefatigable instinct to clutch things to her bosom, which she often wished was more on Marie's scale. She should do it before Chris came back. Just as she had her whisper all poised on her lips, Marie gave her hair one final desperate tug and rearranged her face into its usual ironic pattern. And looking up she caught Iona's eye and shook her head, as if she could gently shake everything out of her hair like confetti.

'I was just saying,' Marie said, though she clearly hadn't been saying anything at all, 'time we were making a move. You'll be wanting to get off to bed.' She pushed her chair away from the table and stood up, just as Chris walked back into the room. He was affecting the air of the man who had suggested that the lifeboat provision on the *Titanic* might be a tad optimistic.

'Are we ready to go, Chris?' Marie asked brightly.

Tamara, on the ball for once, backed up this impression of imminent departures all round by wriggling into her tight leather jacket and picking up her crash helmet. Just as she had it raised to nearly head height, one of Iona's cats fell out, having been clinging on to sleep until the last possible moment. Tamara squealed.

'Show's not over till the Cat Lady swings,' Marie observed.

'Very good,' said Iona.

Lady Cat skulked off into the airing cupboard, leaving a faint cloud of cat hair floating in the draught. Some of it immediately attached itself to Jim's big blue jumper. Marie looked at Angus to see if he'd caught Marie's joke, but he and Jim were drawing charts of profit margins and squabbling about beams. Or beans.

'Iona?'

She almost jumped at Ned's hand on her shoulder.

'Ned? Are you off then?' She turned and he was standing right behind her.

'I am.' He leaned forward – barely needs to, thought Iona, he's that close – and kissed her cheek. The only southern mannerism he'd picked up in ten years. 'I'll see you tomorrow, round at Jim's, when Jim and Angus cook the books – tee hee.'

'Angus does occasionally go out on his own. We're not joined at the hip,' Iona said.

Ned raised his hands. 'Woah, Scary Mary! I was just

going to suggest making you some lunch – no need to get all aerated.'

'Sorry.' She flashed a smile quickly to get rid of whatever terrifying expression was evidently on her face. 'I'm a bit weary tonight.'

'Iona's a bit weary,' announced Ned, putting an arm round her, 'and I think we know what that can mean, don't we? So let's all go and let her put her feet up, eh?'

She blushed and pushed his arm away, but not before she'd seen Angus's head swivel like an alien from Jim's notes straight to her.

'No, no, no,' she said, 'I am not with child. But piss off anyway, will you? Some of us have got things to do in the morning.'

'Just when it was getting interesting,' Jim grumbled.

'It's not the first time you've sat up all night discussing this flaming pub.' Iona gently pushed Jim towards the door. 'Have you forgotten all the plans you made before Christmas?'

He looked blank. 'Angus?'

'You remember, all those numbers you did when you thought you were going to make it into a lap-dancing bar. Should come in handy now.' Iona opened the front door and arranged herself so people could get past her. A biting wind had now replaced the rain and there were dead leaves plastered all over the windscreen of Angus's Integrale.

Jim turned to Angus with a look of horror on his face. 'Angus! You didn't tell . . .'

'Don't blame Angus, just because he never tidies up,' said Iona cheerily. 'It's amazing what you can find under a sofa these days. Think you might have been underestimating the cost of your dancers a little bit though.'

'No, well, yes, that's the clever idea we had, to begin with—'

'Jim, no!' Angus raised a warning finger.

'And *wasn't* it a clever idea?' Iona turned to Tamara and

Marie, as Jim and Angus jostled unsuccessfully to cover her mouth. She squirmed out easily from underneath them. 'Yes, that's the really entrepreneurial part. To begin with, guess who they were going to employ as part-time pole dancers? Just to get things going? I'll give you a clue – it was a cunning tax fiddle to get their money going out of the till and straight back home.'

'Jim!' howled Tamara.

Jim moved swiftly to the door.

'Get out! Get out! Please just piss off home and leave us alone!' pleaded Angus.

Marie laughed. 'I'd look like a pork satay on a stick, wrapped round one of those poles.'

'You'd look gorgeous, Maz,' said Ned. 'Proper-shaped woman like you.'

'Well, I'm not going to get better than that, am I?' said Marie. 'So I'd better get home quickly before he spoils it.' She kissed Iona on the cheek and moved on to Angus. Her usual chalky classroom children smell was pungently overlaid with wine. 'Thanks for a lovely supper.'

Chris slouched out after her.

Tamara offered to give Ned a lift back on her scooter, since the last tube had gone an hour before, but he gestured towards Jim, who was now gouging wax off the table with his car keys.

'Might as well stop over at Jim's, since we'll be there all tomorrow. But ta, though.'

'It's perfectly safe, now all the repairs have been done,' added Tamara persuasively.

'Bloody should be. You could have bought a whole new scooter for that garage bill.'

'Angus!' Iona leaned against him to try to shut him up. 'Can we not have that conversation again? Can you let these nice people *leave*?'

'Can you *make* them leave?'

'We're going, we're going.' Ned and Jim shuffled past,

delivering quick kisses to Iona's cheek and manly punches to Angus's arm.

Tamara hung back, obviously hoping for some last-minute change of heart from Ned, but as he and Jim launched into their eternally reheatable debate about the best guest stars on *The Simpsons*, she let out a delicate sigh and fastened up her bag. 'See you soon.' She kissed Iona on the cheek.

Iona noticed sleepily that Tamara rarely smelled of anything, unlike Marie, who had a permanent fragrance of something about her. Maybe it was all the rampant pheromones Marie had pumping round her system, vibrating so close beneath her skin, instead of Tamara's papery translucence. Iona wondered what she herself smelled of from the outside.

Finally, Angus closed the door and did up all the bolts. Iona leaned against it and shut her eyes.

'Jesus Christ almighty, Iona, how long is that going to go on? It's like having supper with Elizabeth Taylor and Richard Burton having those two over. Except they still fancied each other.'

'And other people wanted to shag Richard Burton. And he regularly dished up sizeable gifts of jewels to make up for all the shouting. And he didn't wear travel sandals.'

'They have got worse, haven't they? I mean, it wasn't always as bad as this, surely?

'No, it wasn't. I don't know when they started rowing in front of other people though. That's not nice. I know Marie's not very happy.'

'She didn't look happy when she came round the other night.' Angus blew out the remaining candles and switched on the main kitchen light. They both flinched under the sudden hard brightness. He switched it off and relit a few more candles. 'She looked miserable when she came round, got gradually less miserable while you filled her with wine and let her watch MTV, and then Chris phoned to ask where she was and she looked bloody miserable again. And then you made me drive her home.'

'I came with you.'

'Too right you did. I'm not equipped for sudden drunken girlie confessions.'

'No, well . . .' Iona pushed herself off the door and started to make herself a bedtime cocoa. 'It doesn't look like Chris is very happy either. Do you want some cocoa?' She had already spooned the cocoa powder into his mug because she knew he did. But she asked anyway so they could pretend that they didn't know each other's minds inside out.

'Yes, but is it that they're not happy with their relationship, or not happy separately and just taking it out on each other?'

'I wouldn't like to say.'

'Don't ever call me names in public, sweetie-loo,' said Angus, coming up behind her with a bear hug. 'Or I'd be very sad.'

'You'd be very dead if you did.'

'No, I'd be very sad and I'd have to go away.'

Angus said this a lot and meant it as a joke as far as she could tell, because it would take them about a year to split up, logistically speaking. That wouldn't count the negotiations about the cats. But every time he said it, a little voice in Iona's ear asked her what *would* she do if he left? Where *would* she go? How *would* she cope? But then everyone in a relationship thought those things. For the same reason people watched *Jerry Springer* to remind themselves that though their own relatives were pretty grim, they didn't all live in the one trailer.

'How could you ever go away? You've no clean clothes. Make the cocoa before that milk fries on the hob, will you?'

'I think you should talk to Marie and find out what's going on,' said Angus, stirring the milk into the cocoa paste. 'But don't get involved.'

'But come back and give you the gossip, is that what you mean?'

'Absolutely.' He handed her the other mug. 'Don't quote me on that, obviously. I don't think it would come out with the caring, sincere intention with which I meant it.'

'No,' Iona said. 'It wouldn't.'

Chapter Eleven

Tuesday was Iona's half-day and she liked to celebrate it by not waking up before nine. While she was still pleasantly semi-conscious beneath the duvet, Angus had reminded her that tentative negotiations were now under way about the pub tenancy and made her agree to go to the Bunch of Grapes before her afternoon shift at the coffee shop to do some sketches, in her capacity as Chief Design Consultant. In case she conveniently forgot about it on waking, he had left a note on the fridge for her, reminding her too that he would be going over to Jim's after work to thrash out the final details of the presentation, so she needn't bother with supper, unless she wanted to make something and then bring it over. And also that they were out of cat food.

The day was so fresh and spring-like by the time she got up that Iona failed to take offence at any of this Dad-style organization and was on her way to the tube station with her sketch-book before it dawned on her that although the pub would be nice and easy to draw at this godforsaken hour, it would also be very empty and very obvious what she was doing. She would need cover.

So she phoned the only person she knew who was a) free in the mornings and b) not averse to visiting pubs before noon. Fortunately he had just got out of bed.

Ned pushed open the dirty frosted door of the Bunch of Grapes and Iona ducked beneath his arm and walked in as confidently as she could manage. She felt like a Health and Safety official.

Entering pubs during the day had a strong whiff of dissipation to her which she could only attribute to lingering traces of northern Puritanism that had slipped unnoticed into her education. The Bunch of Grapes had many strong whiffs, of which dissipation came a very poor fourth, behind Stale Beer, Elderly & Incontinent Yorkshire Terrier and Ingrained Tobacco. Shake 'n' Vac wasn't really an option, Iona thought, looking round at the filthy upholstery with a sinking heart. Lots of people had shaken, but there was no evidence of any recent vaccing. It was more Rip Out 'n' Chuck.

A small radio behind the bar was tuned badly to Radio One and there were vague signs of life in the back. Mad Boy Sam had already installed himself on his regular high stool and was nursing a fresh-looking pint, staring out into the emptiness of the bar area like the captain of the *Marie Celeste*. He nodded twice to acknowledge their arrival and carried on staring at them. Iona tried to smile back, but found something strange was happening to her face. Mad Boy Sam was freezing her from the neck up. She wondered how much time he actually spent out of the pub and if indeed he had a home to go to.

Ned ambled over to the bar and leaned across it so he could catch the barmaid's attention. She was wiping the Britvic bottles with a J-cloth and checking them cursorily for sell-by dates. Every so often one would be hurled over her shoulder in the vague direction of the black plastic bin at the end of the bar, where the dull clank indicated that anyone ordering a Bloody Mary in the past week had had a pretty mature tomato juice. Cocktails weren't a house speciality, to be fair. Asking for a Bloody Mary in the Bunch of Grapes would probably get you a blank stare or a fist in the face at best. Asking for a Virgin Mary would probably get you a list of phone numbers.

Iona sat down carefully on a banquette and tried to look somewhere other than at Mad Boy Sam. It was hard, given that they were the only people in and he had been refining his total bar domination techniques for about twenty years.

'Are you not open yet?' Ned asked over the bar.

'Soft drinks only,' said the barmaid without looking round.

'But he's got a drink,' Ned pointed out, shrugging a bony shoulder in the rough direction of Mad Boy Sam and his nearly full pint glass.

The woman straightened up, checked and went back to her shelves. 'Nah, brought that himself, din'e?'

Mad Boy Sam lifted the said glass and half drained it, keeping his eyes on them the whole time. Today he was sporting a long cut just underneath his cheekbone and a series of small scabs along his forehead. Iona tried to look at him, found she couldn't meet his gaze and returned her eyes to Ned with some relief.

'Do you do coffee then?' asked Ned persuasively.

'In what way do you mean, coffee?' Another tomato juice joined its friends with a crash.

'I mean, if you'll not serve beer, will you do us a coffee?'

The barmaid threw the J-cloth into the sink and turned round to Ned, pushing chunks of dyed blonde hair out of her eyes. 'I'm about to stick the kettle on for myself, as it happens, so I can make you a cup of Nescafé if you want, love, but none of that fancy espresso stuff. This isn't one of them Internet cafés, you know.'

'Sounds great,' said Ned. 'Nothing like a bit of instant.' He dropped his chin on to the bar and gave the barmaid a cheeky smile. 'Nescafé's OK for you, eh, Iona?' he called over his shoulder.

'Yeah, yeah, fine.' Iona pulled her bag on to her knee and rummaged for her pencil case. She opened up her sketch-book to a clean page, trying to ignore Mad Boy Sam's continued laser stare, and started drawing the rough dimensions of the main bar area.

Looking at it in daylight, it was simultaneously better and worse than it looked at night. Underneath all the tatty beer-promotion posters, there were some nice details on the walls and if you took down the boards that currently covered three of the long windows, you might even be able to recreate the feel of natural daylight, instead of the foggy Stygian look Brian seemed so keen on. The only thing missing from the darkness, grubbiness and general atmosphere of resigned despair was Charon the Ferryman and Cerberus the Three-headed Guard Dog of the Underworld.

Ned continued chatting casually to the barmaid while Iona drew in lines and shading. The bar itself seemed original, decorated with faded gold carved finials and etched mirrors which murkily reflected the jewel colours of the spirits lined up in front. All that would have to stay. Tamara could pull it out and replace it with stainless steel over her dead body. Unless of course Chris suggested making it a Jack the Ripper theme pub, in which case her dead body would no doubt be required by Angus for decorative purposes. Tamara's certainly would.

Iona thought as she sketched that, apart from about twenty years of dirt, there wasn't so very much wrong with the place physically; it was just a building that was unloved, that had no expectations of it, a pub that people drank in because they couldn't be bothered to walk further down the road. There was a kind of skankiness that was entertaining in a traditional, self-deprecating British way, but not very good for it in the long term. And despite all the jibes about the Grapes, she was quite fond of the place; she'd come here when she'd first moved to London and she'd had some fantastic (terrible) nights. The very last thing she would want to do would be to make this into the kind of place that Mad Boy Sam wouldn't be let into because it was full of braying estate agents.

Though she hadn't said anything at the time, Iona suspected that Tamara's meticulous design treatment had a whole 'Customers' section, made up of Photoshop models from *Esquire* and *Wallpaper* – people who would like stainless-steel bartops because it reminded them of their own bathrooms. What was the point in helping to create a pub that even she wouldn't want to go in? There were enough of those round here anyway. Mad Boy Sam made her feel a bit uncomfortable, but then so did herds of merchant bankers.

Ned returned with two dimpled pint glasses of coffee just as she finished detailing the mahogany surrounds of the bar. He tilted his head sideways to see what she'd been doing and nodded approvingly.

'Sorry, no sugar,' he said with a serious face. 'Charm's only got Canderel because she's on the Cabbage Soup Diet.'

Iona pulled her gossiping face. 'Ooh, Charm, is it?'

'It was Charmianne, but that's only her stage name now.'

'Don't tell me, she's the lunchtime meal deal.'

'Mee-ow.'

'Meow yourself.' Iona drew in a series of bar stools but omitted Mad Boy Sam, even though he was clearly a fixture and fitting.

'Maybe I've decided to go for the older woman,' Ned teased.

'Yes, well, there's vintage and there's antique.'

'Have you been getting on with that sketching or have you spent twenty minutes making up rudeness about my new friend?'

'It doesn't take twenty minutes to state the bleeding obvious. If you want rudeness you're better off waiting for Chris to turn up.'

'I'd rather wait for Marie and get top-quality laceration and whiplash, thanks.'

Iona took a sip of coffee. It was milky and very strong. Despite being served in a pint glass, it would still pass as a latte in most cafés she'd worked in. 'I've been thinking about all this décor,' she said in a low voice, so as not to offend Charmianne or Mad Boy Sam, 'and I think we should either stick to the original plan and strip it all back – bare floors, bare walls, lots of mirrors and *no* stainless steel – or we should just gag Tamara and go for the full restoration job.'

'Which is?'

'Paint all the walls deep, deep oxblood red, or get some of that old-fashioned red wallpaper with little gold fleurs-de-lis on, gild everything in sight, get some massive crystal chandeliers from second-hand shops, fake up some stained glass, polish everything until you can recognize it as wood, rip out the carpet, obviously, bring in some good old-fashioned prostitutes, stuff Brian's horrible little dog and mount it in a glass cabinet behind the bar . . .'

'You been in the wars then, Sam?' Charm shrieked across the counter. She had moved on to chopping up lemons and was swearing gently into the bowl.

'Doan' arsk, darlin',' Mad Boy Sam replied in a tone which clearly indicated that he was about to go into some detail whether she arsked or not.

Iona tried to pretend that she couldn't hear them, and hoped that they couldn't hear her either. 'Yeah, er, decoration, I can't decide whether that would cover up the dirt better, which is the plan Brian obviously had, or whether it would just be harder to clean.'

They both sipped their coffees and looked at the carpet. You could have ridden a horse round the bar and not been able to prove it afterwards.

'I'd say it must be pretty hard to clean,' Ned said.

'Fell off my bike, din' I?' said Mad Boy Sam. 'Going rahnd the soddin' 'Ogarth rahndabahd.'

Charm clashed some glasses on to the overhead glass holder and made sympathetic noises.

'There *is* a kitchen, isn't there?' said Iona. She knew there was a kitchen, because you couldn't cook scampi and chips behind the bar, but was desperate to say something quickly to blot out the grim details of Mad Boy Sam's injuries. Which looked very much as though he'd been dragged through Chiswick underneath an HGV.

'Yes, there's a kitchen out back, but I don't really want to have a look at it yet,' said Ned. 'It might put me off altogether. Anyway, we can always pull stuff down and put stuff up.'

'One of them mini-cabs,' continued Mad Boy Sam with some relish. 'Bleedin' awful red thing. Knocked me off my bike and right into the path of a—'

'Tell me about the Uxbridge,' Iona said as quickly as she could. Squeam was her middle name. She couldn't even watch *Casualty* all the way through. 'What sort of stuff are you doing there? And could you do it here? Does it involve fresh vegetables? Are your knives as big as Angus's? Will you be able to get decent suppliers? Will they try and rip us off like they do on television? Do you know Jamie Oliver? Do you think you'll be able to get your own cook-book deal off the back of this? Could you call it *Cooking with the Grapes Bunch*?' As she rattled through all this she cast an anxious look in Mad Boy Sam's direction. His mouth was moving almost as quickly as hers and she could see a look of revulsion and then sympathy pass over Charm's face and then he stopped, so she ground to a halt with relief.

'Course you can't see all the stitches from the ahtside,' Mad Boy Sam added, almost as an afterthought. 'But the places where my teeth came through were a right bleedin' mess.'

'Well, they would be, wouldn't they?' shrieked Charm.

Iona swallowed hard and Ned's shoulders shook with laughter.

'Is there anywhere else we can go and sit without looking rude?' she murmured.

Ned leaned very close to her ear and said, 'No.'

'Oh, bollocks.'

He rearranged himself on the banquette and flicked through her sketch-pad. 'Isn't that a drawing of your Maxi?'

Maxi, or Maxine as she was known theoretically, was Iona's younger sister, still resident in Carlisle and only slightly socially damaged by a childhood of being baby-sat by Iona and Ned.

'It might be.' Iona grabbed it back. He'd been winding her up for years about fancying Maxi, and she knew he was joking but couldn't quite stop herself rising to the bait every time.

'Quite the young lady, now, isn't she?' said Ned, trying to look sideways into the sketch pad. 'Those sexy Crosby eyes. Has that . . . hmm, what's the word, *starlet* look about her . . .'

'She does not,' said Iona forcefully. 'And she'll hardly have time for you with your big girl's job now she's going out with a lad who plays for the Border Raiders.'

'Ooh, controversial!' crowed Ned.

'Yes, well.' Iona drank a mouthful of coffee. Real Men weren't her speciality, and she'd have taken a chef any time, but that was where she and Maxi were very different. And Iona didn't ever ask about Maxi and Darren, because that was a whole set of worries she didn't have room for, or indeed feel qualified to advise on.

Ned put his feet back up on the banquette and nudged her leg affectionately, in case she was going into a mood. 'So tomorrow's the big day for Angus and Jim, then?'

'Jim's doing his presentation at Overworld, if that's what you mean, yes. He was round our flat until about four in the morning. Still, beats playing Tomb Raider all night, I suppose.'

'I know. He woke me up when he came in. Bastard put all the lights on looking for some Weetabix.' Ned took a big mouthful of coffee and grimaced. 'Like I'd be hiding it in my room.'

'Oh, aye? Your room?' Iona tucked her foot under her leg and turned to look at him. 'You're back at Jim's flat again?'

'Only for a couple of nights. It's nearer work and there's all sorts of shit going on in Archway. Not great karma there at the moment, I have to say.'

Iona tutted protectively. 'I told you it would be a disaster moving in with other chefs. And in Archway, for God's sake! Where's that meant to be near?'

'It's handy for the M1 and Rowan's Bowling Alley.'

'Fantastic.'

'Anyway, I don't think Jim minds me being there. I left him a whole plate of sushi in the fridge last night and he ate it for breakfast. Rice all over the floor. It looked like—'

Iona held up her hands. 'OK, OK, I don't think I want to know any more of your domestic arrangements.'

'When you due for your stitches out then, Sam?' yelled Charm conversationally.

'In me lip or in me leg?'

'Do you think Angus realizes that all his top-rate tax is going on keeping Mad Boy Sam in butterfly stitches and spray-on skin?' muttered Ned.

'No, he likes to pretend that every single penny is going directly to Marie and her crusade to educate the savage offspring of Wandsworth. You know he asked her if he could see some school-books the other night?'

'So what'll happen at this meeting then?' said Ned, changing the subject. Tax was something that happened to other people. And he could see Sam rolling up a trouser leg and thought it best to distract Iona's attention before he got on to the guided tour of his latest injuries.

'Well, I guess they go through the figures, talk about those menus that you did for them, discuss bar staff, discuss overheads . . .' Iona trailed off. She was definitely improvising now; she wasn't really too sure what they were going to do, but out of the corner of her eye she could see the trouser leg being rolled up and found herself being unwillingly hypnotized by it. 'Jim should really be taking Tamara in with him, shouldn't he?' she said quickly.

'Aye, she has her uses.'

'I meant she's good at presentations.'

'Presenta*tion*.'

They exchanged knowing looks.

From what Jim had told her about his bosses at Overworld, Tamara would have distracted them nicely, thought Iona. And the more she did her painfully sincere 'Take me seriously with my picture-editor black-framed glasses and my sensible mini-suit' routine, the more distracted they would get. She had seen it with her own eyes and could never decide which was more tragic: Tamara's touching belief that men would take her seriously if she dressed up in that 'Why, Miss Jones, you're beautiful' style, or the blatantly glazed look which passed over their faces as they imagined whipping off her glasses and undoing her Jerry Hall mane. It would be quicker all round if she just turned up in her usual clothes and cut out the imagination bit.

'It wouldn't surprise me if she did come and work here full-time, you know. I don't think things are going too well at the agency,' she said, sipping gingerly at her pint of coffee. This was a generously abridged version of a long conversation Iona had had with Tamara at Coffee Morning in which Tamara had sat at a corner table, nursing an endless procession of non-fat soya lattes while throwing problems at Iona as she whirled past delivering other people's orders and wiping tables.

'Really?'

'She wants to do more photography, I think. Or less running around for no money on short-term contracts. She was muttering something about getting a joint exhibition with me in some venue she knows.'

'To which you said?' Ned's face made it clear what he would have said.

'To which I said, "What a good idea, Tamara." Of course.'

'I'd like to see the venue that stages your collages and her out-of-focus pictures of trees and lipsticks in the one room.' Ned looked at his watch. 'But then I only did two terms at art school, so what would I know?'

'Same as John Lennon. And Jimmy Page. John Taylor from Duran Duran. All the greats drop out of art school after a few terms.'

'I won't tell Angus you said that.'

'No, don't.' Angus had insisted that Iona move into his flat while she did her art school year, rather than move back to Carlisle and live at home. She had repaid him by fresco-ing his bathroom, struggling with the laundry and surreptitiously ruining all his short-sleeved shirts on purpose.

'So when do you think we'll know what's going on?' Ned asked. 'How fast do these things move? I'm just a kitchen hand, me.' He leaned over again to whisper in her ear, close enough not to be overheard and close enough for Iona to feel his breath on her neck. 'And will Charm still be in a job this time next week?'

'Oh, so *that's* what you're worried about,' she said, pulling away in pretend disgust. 'Well, she can have a pint pull-off with Tamara and we can see who's the best, eh?'

'It's all in the wrist action, I hear.'

'In which case, I'd be hard put to say who'd be better,' said Iona archly. 'Or, to put it another way, does that not mean that you and Jim are probably the greatest undiscovered barmen London hasn't yet known?'

Ned grinned. He had slightly gap teeth, which was apparently very sexy to other women. 'Probably. Why don't you give Jim a call on your mobile and tell him about your change of design plan? He's probably desperate to talk to someone in words instead of legal jargon. I mean, I'm quite happy to sit here talking rubbish with you all day, but I've got to be off to the Uxbridge quite soon and God knows when I'll be knocking off there. We're not allowed to take personal calls, as you know.'

The head chef at the Uxbridge confiscated mobile phones at the door and fined the chefs each time they rang on their shift. He also had the Bad Chef's habit of branding them with oven trays. Even skinny Ned, who prided himself on moving faster than a fat man with a red-hot oven tray had a small white equals sign on the back of his right arm.

'Can we go outside?' Iona slipped her sketch-book back in her bag. 'For one thing, mobiles are probably the sign of the Devil in here, and for another, I don't think mine works underground.'

'We're not underground.'

'Aren't we?' Iona looked up and around for any sign of direct light. 'How can you tell?'

'I can just about see my hand in front of my face.'

'Maybe Tamara could install some ironic canaries at the door. You could serve on, wearing a miner's lamp. She'd like that.'

Ned finished his cooling coffee in one gulp and took the pint glass back to the bar. Mad Boy Sam regarded him with a look that made Iona's flesh creep.

'You putting the eye through me, marra?' said Ned cheerfully.

'Not from rahnd ere, are yer, son?'

'Not at the moment, no. But you never know your luck. Cheers, Charm!' Ned waved into the back room and amazingly Charm appeared with a pot cloth and a smile recently replenished with watermelon-coloured lipstick.

'Take care now,' she beamed.

'I will that,' said Ned and held the door open for Iona, who felt startled as the sunshine outside suddenly washed her face with light.

Chapter Twelve

'And then he just said to me, OK, you're on. Like I was pitching for a car-parking space.'

Jim's eyebrows hadn't yet recovered from the shock of the meeting, being still lodged halfway up his forehead. He always looked faintly surprised, as though he couldn't quite believe life was letting him get away with this, but even Angus, who had witnessed Jim's record look of amazement, sustained for a record six weeks while Tamara moved into his and Ned's flat during the subsidence work on her own place, hadn't seen him maintain an expression of such pure shock for so long.

Angus frowned. 'You gave him all those figures? All the projections and things?'

Jim nodded, and resumed biting his cuticles.

'And the set menus?' added Iona. She checked her watch and forked up the rest of her tagliatelle. It would take her a good half-hour to get back to Coffee Morning on the bus and there was only so long an 'emergency dental appointment' could take. 'And my sketches?' she asked through a mouthful of over-cooked pasta. 'You did include all the revised costings for the redecoration, didn't you?' She didn't ask if he'd broken it to Tamara that they weren't going to Tippex the pub after all.

'Yes, yes, yes.' Jim ruffled his hair distractedly. He was wearing an orange shirt with his black suit in an effort to look more Overworld, and his evident discomfort was springing out all over. Iona and Marie had helped him buy the shirt, much against his will. Like Angus, Jim's preferred work look was so traditional that most shops didn't stock it any more. 'I know how to do a presentation, thanks. I had all the info laid out like one of those really upmarket glossy gym brochures, and video footage of the building and everything. I did the whole thing myself.'

Iona gave him a searching look. She knew where he had been the previous evening. Ned had told her. 'Any excuse' was an approximate, polite translation, although Ned had been a little more descriptively creative.

Jim stopped with his fork halfway up to his mouth. 'Well, Tamara helped me a bit,' he conceded. 'With the computer stuff, you know. She's got one of those photographic-quality printers. Anyway, everyone had a copy for reference and they looked pretty impressed, if you ask me.'

Including Simon, who had come in halfway through and commandeered Janis, their shared secretary, who was taking notes, to collect his Z8 from the clamping people before his two o'clock at a reclaimed bingo hall in Clapham. Other than that, it had gone very well. Really very well.

'Iona,' he said, looking furtively over his shoulder, 'tell me honestly, are people staring at me because of this shirt?'

'No.'

'Do I look gay?' he demanded.

'No! You look . . . well dressed.'

'Fuck,' mumbled Jim.

'So, tell me again,' said Angus, as if he'd missed something significant the first three times Jim had run through the discussion. 'You presented the site, the current state of it, the plans we had, the projected budget you would need . . .'

'The whole spiel about Ned and how he was the next big thing on the hot young London cooking scene,' Iona went on, 'all that heritage side of things from the Land Registry . . .'

'Excuse me,' Jim interrupted, 'but were you two there? Who is telling this story? Or should I just give you a set of minutes and save myself the bother?'

'Jim lad . . .'

'Can you stop calling me that now I'm your boss?'

'Not after twenty years. Look, Jim lad,' Angus continued, 'if I'm using up my one and only chance of a sabbatical from Price Riley Riches – because they won't give me a break like this again, believe me – I want to make sure this is actually going to go the full six months I've got off.' He wiped the last of his sauce round the plate with a piece of bread. 'And yes, if there are any minutes going, you could give them to my secretary here . . .'

'Did you not keep a presentation thing for yourself?' asked Iona. 'Jim, are you listening to me?'

Jim's head flicked round from where it had been staring at Angus in amazement. 'Aren't you going to hit him for that?' he said, with wide eyes. 'Calling you his secretary? Marie would have had Chris's balls halfway to Penge for even mentioning that she was his wife.'

'Don't worry,' said Iona. 'Your friend here has an account which he will be settling in full very soon.'

'Oh yes, indeed,' said Angus. 'At LK Bennett, I believe, and also some kind of standing order at Majestic wine warehouses?'

'You know us secretaries, we get through Chardonnay like water.' Iona reapplied her lip gloss and started gathering her stuff together. 'But, much as I would love to sit around chewing the fat with you two' – she looked down dismissively at Jim's hacked-about lamb chop – 'some of us have to get back to work.'

'I'm lunching a client,' Angus pointed out.

'And so am I,' said Jim. 'So actually, if you don't mind, since you volunteered, I'll put you down as Angus's secretary when I send this through accounts.'

'Can I not be *your* secretary?'

Jim considered. 'Why would you want to be my secretary?'

'Because he's about to downsize and become a barman, whereas you're sprinting up the left-hand side of the escalator to gastro-barn success?' Iona wound her scarf around her neck. 'Only joking, lover boy.'

'Restaurant manager,' said Angus. 'That is my new job title and you'd better start getting used to it. My new business cards will be in your in-tray when you get home.'

'You're getting them done that quickly?'

'No, you and Tamara are designing them. Along with the new letterhead. You're the creative team. It says so in Jim's notes.'

'If she knew that men were only after her for her print facilities,' said Iona. 'Poor Tamara.'

'I know,' said Angus cheerfully. 'It's not her big green eyes at all, it's her big green i-Mac.'

Iona turned to Jim and pretended to lower her voice. 'Where did you find him? And, more to the point, did your boss not ask, at any point before handing over this wad of virtual cash, what other major gastronomic delights your man here had managed before now?'

Jim shook his head. 'Actually, no. Martin just looked at the business plan and projection I did, and we discussed all the notes Angus made about the kind of place he wanted to set up, then Martin talked about the area in terms of their current acquisition schedules and, er, everyone seemed pretty impressed.' Jim blinked knowledgeably and undid the very tight collar of his orange shirt, loosening the tangerine paisley tie – a fashion aberration that he had agreed to take home in a bag only because at the actual point of purchase he had been lost in a dream (craftily initiated by Marie) of Tamara removing it for him while perching on the end of his desk in her navy pinstripe mini-skirt.

'Well, that business plan must have been good,' said Iona.

'Oh yes, it was,' said Angus. 'It was a cracker, if I say so myself.'

Iona sank her head on to her hands and looked up at Jim from between her fingers. 'Jim. Please. If this is all an elaborate wind-up, you've *got* to tell us now. Because I really can't face a repeat of the birthday when he thought he'd secured a driving day at Silverstone and it turned out to be a day at the Jack Nicklaus driving range at New Malden.'

'No, honestly,' Jim said, giving her hand a reassuring pat, until he met Angus's ominous eyebrow and swiftly withdrew it. 'They think it's a real winner. They wouldn't let me go ahead with it if they didn't, believe me.'

He gave her a crooked smile. Iona's round blue eyes searched his face in a way he had always considered unsettling and found nothing. She smiled, and Jim felt a sense of relief almost equal to that which had flooded the parts of his body he hadn't even been aware of when Michael and Kyle had finally nodded tacit agreement – as much as he'd hoped for – and paged their PAs to get their lunch appointments.

To be scrupulously honest, from the point at which the directors had started to discuss their holdings in that area, the meeting had gone very cryptic indeed and he'd had a little trouble keeping up with some of the more abbreviated references, and without Janis's ample shoulder to look over, his own notes had gone quite sketchy from then on. And then suddenly everyone else apart from him and Martin was getting up to go for lunch – it being half-eleven and all – and he was left with instructions to talk to the Overworld solicitors before the end of the day to get the finance moving.

Though Overworld moved in mysterious ways, none of them so far had ever been in his direction. Until now, and it was moving very fast indeed.

Weird.

'Jim?' said Iona. She was looking anxiously at his hands.

Jim looked down and realized he'd wound his tie round his wrist like a bandage.

'Oh, er, yeah, guess I'm just a bit nervous, you know?' He swallowed. Understatement of the year. 'It's a lot of money.'

Angus flapped his hands dismissively. 'Oh, come on, Jim, this is the best bit,' he said. 'If Brian is as keen to get rid of the place as he's been making out—'

'Have you actually spoken to Brian about buying the pub?' asked Iona.

'Not directly,' said Jim. Without realizing it, he started winding his tie round his wrist again. 'Well, I have, but I, er . . .'

Angus too seemed to be looking down at his plate, though his was much more empty than Jim's and Iona thought she could see him sizing up Jim's leftovers out of the corner of his eye.

'No,' said Iona, holding up her hands in front of her face, 'no, I don't think I want to know why you don't appear to have done this very simple and straightforward thing, OK?' She hitched her bag on to her shoulder. 'It's obviously Big Business. I would just be confused.'

'See you later, Iona,' said Jim, raising his hand in a wave.

'Bye, darling,' said Angus, reaching out a hand to touch her face. Iona bent to kiss him. 'Maybe we should all go to the Grapes tonight for a bit of a celebration drink?'

'As long as it's very, very – *very* – incognito,' said Iona. 'I don't want Chris getting drunk and standing on a table, shouting, "You're all first against the wall now the revolution's coming!" and then having Mad Boy Sam disembowel him over the table football.'

'Ah, the pub of my dreams . . .' said Angus.

Jim frowned. 'No, you're right.'

'So get on the phone to Brian and sort it all out!' said Iona. She flicked Jim around the back of the head with her gloves. 'Then you can drink warm beer from dirty glasses with a clear conscience! Go on, get back to the office, both of you! Jeez . . . Call me,' she said to Angus, making a phone sign with her little finger and thumb, pointed sternly at her watch, and ran to catch her bus, which had conveniently slowed down at the traffic lights outside.

As soon as Iona was marching up to the top deck, Angus turned back to Jim and raised his eyebrows knowingly. 'So, you printed off your presentation at Tamara's, did you? Eh? Eh?'

'God, there are no secrets round here, are there?' Jim looked disgruntled and turned up his collar to put his tie back on.

'Jim, you just told me yourself . . .'

Jim tried to summon up some dignity. 'She helped me with the layout—'

'You wish!'

Jim glared, mid-knot.

'Oh, come on,' Angus wheedled. 'I'm a married man, I get no gossip these days. No one tells me anything, they're too busy telling Iona. All I've got these days is a fertile imagination that doesn't get much exercise at work.'

The coffees arrived before Jim could make any response and he morosely stirred two small bags of sugar into the froth, while Angus hovered, waiting impatiently for an answer.

'Well? I have to be back at the office before close of play. This is meant to be lunch, not a long weekend for two.'

Jim looked hopelessly over the top of his coffee. 'What's the point? I don't think I'd be able to remember what to do with her even if all her clothes had got stuck in the printer. It's been so long.'

Angus tried to look as sympathetic as he could, given that it was perfectly obvious to anyone with eyes in their head that Tamara had the hots for Ned like some kind of out-of-control Icelandic geyser. 'Have you talked to Ned about it?' he asked tentatively.

'I thought I did, one night. He was in pretty late – I was watching late-night poker, so it must have been way past one – and we sat down with a bottle of vodka and had a chat, and we did eventually get on to . . . the subject. And I tried to explain about Tam, and he sounded as though he was taking it all in, you know . . .' Jim shrugged. 'But he, ah, he wasn't much help.'

'No?' said Angus, wondering whether this was a good time to mention how much help Ned was likely to be. Maybe Jim was leading up to it himself. Maybe Ned had pointed it out in his usual oblique way. Though, short of writing it in Alphabetti Spaghetti on the fridge, it would take more than a few dry hints and references to the interior décor of Tamara's boudoir to get the message across if Jim didn't want to know. At a very early age Jim had mastered the technique of hearing as little as possible about anything which might subsequently bother him. The right-hand side of his brain now went 'La, la, la, I can't hear you' for him.

Still, thought Angus, you never know . . .

Jim sighed heavily. 'No, when I looked round to get the remote control off him, he'd passed out. Anyway, there's no point. I might as well carry on admiring from afar. It's probably safer all round.'

'Oh, come on,' said Angus, feeling it was time he offered some (non-specific) help, seeing as Iona wasn't here to bail them out. 'If I'd taken that attitude I'd still be hanging around the college bar waiting for Iona to fall into my arms. You've got to *do* things in life, not just talk about them. Like the pub – we talked about it and now we've done it.'

'Started to do it.'

'You know what I mean. If you want Tamara, you'll either have to stop talking and start doing, or start looking and stop whining.'

'Yeah, well.' Jim started the long process of catching the waiter's eye. 'Easier said than done, mate. Ah, yes, can I . . .'

The waiter glided past with the grace and casual disregard of a greased cat.

'D'oh!' Jim muttered, waving his fingers ineffectually.

Angus finished off his coffee and caught the attention of the waiter. He raised his eyebrows and made a writing sign in the air. The waiter nodded in agreement and even threw in a brief obsequious smile that could have doubled as a smirk, directed at Jim's tie.

'Anyway,' Jim retaliated, 'I don't see a ring on Iona's finger. You don't want to lose *her* down the back of your sofa. Hadn't you better get her properly fiancée-d up before someone with a full head of hair sweeps her off her feet?'

Angus ran a defensive hand over his skull and said, in hurt tones, 'Iona and I couldn't be much more married than we are already but . . . I hope that before the end of the year we will be.'

'What? Married?'

'Something like that.' The bill arrived and was presented to Angus.

Jim breathed an inward sigh of relief but immediately went for his inside pocket. This was something of a poker move, as he didn't have a very big credit limit on his company card and had already had to lunch the lawyers and some heritage woman from the council this week.

Fortunately, Angus pulled out his wallet and tossed his gold company Visa card on to the saucer. 'Better use it while I still can,' he said wryly. 'God knows, it's going to miss me.'

'So?' Jim leaned forward, aware that he might be getting the first line on some gossip. 'When are you going to do it? Get married?'

The waiter reappeared and swept the saucer away.

Angus brushed his hair back nervously, dwelling, Jim

noticed, on his thinning temples. 'If the business works out OK. If I can get the house sorted out. If my parents can stop rowing long enough to actually meet her. If I can get her weaned off Led Zeppelin before she has to pick music for the wedding. If she'll have me,' he added, almost as an afterthought.

'That's a lot of ifs.'

'Marriage, my friend, is a very iffy thing.'

'Ah, but I don't want marriage. I just want some hot sex.'

At this point the waiter reappeared with Angus's receipt and gave Jim a supercilious look as Angus scribbled his signature.

'Preferably with *Tamara*,' Jim added with unnecessary emphasis, in case it had sounded like a passing suggestion for the rest of the afternoon's entertainment.

'Very good,' said Angus, passing up the bill.

Jim wasn't sure who that was directed at. That was the beauty of Angus's 'Very good's. They were omni-directional.

The waiter removed the saucer with a final pointed stare at Jim's tie. He definitely had the fashion advantage. It was the type of restaurant where the waiters were dressed slightly better than most of the clientele, which meant that you could never confidently order without risking offending another customer who was merely passing your table on his way back from the loo.

'You have coffee froth on your tie, Jim,' said Angus, replacing his wallet in his inside pocket. 'But, no, marriage may be iffy, but hot sex is a different matter altogether. That's just a load of butts.'

'Oh, ho ho ho.'

'No, I mean it,' said Angus. '*But* you're my friend. *But* it'll never be the same again. *But* I'm a man. *But* you're my best mate's boyfriend. *But* I'm in love with your best mate.'

He paused to see if Jim would take the bait.

Jim was trying to mop the coffee off his tie with the remains of Iona's mineral water.

Angus sighed and pushed back his chair. She would have to tell him. He couldn't.

'Jim, phone me when you've phoned Brian, OK? Then, if you want to, come over to ours for supper?'

'With Ned?'

Angus considered. 'Er, yeah, good idea. Very good. See you both later.' He stuffed his newspaper and phone into his briefcase. 'Er, Jim?'

'Yeah?'

'Don't, er, mention to anyone what I've just mentioned to you, will you?'

Jim looked confused.

'About Iona. It's not . . .' Angus shrugged appealingly.

'Oh, yeah, right, with you,' said Jim. 'No, won't say a word. As long as you don't mention about the thing I just mentioned to you.'

Angus gave him a pitying look. 'Jim, the only person who doesn't already *know* about the thing you just mentioned is Tamara. So don't you think it might be time to mention it to her, instead of me? Your thing, I mean?'

Jim looked anguished and Angus could see him retracting into himself like a tortoise. He'd been doing the same amazing retracting trick since he was about nine. Jim Waters the Human Telescope. Angus sighed. If it hadn't been for Iona, he sometimes wondered if he'd have been the same. He hoped not. He really hoped not.

'Erm, I don't think . . .' Jim was floundering. 'I just don't want to, you know, screw things up with Tamara while we're trying to organize the pub and everything. I mean, we need everyone to help out and it could end up being really difficult, couldn't it, and I just don't want to lose her as a friend at a time like this, and . . .'

'Jim,' said Angus, 'be honest with yourself – how much of a friend is Tamara to you? Really?'

Jim didn't answer. A glow of awkwardness spread over his pale face and he dropped his eyes to the table, looking about twenty years younger than he was dressed up to be.

Angus stopped himself from pushing the point home, the way he would have done at work with a difficult client. There wasn't any fun to be had here and it was only because Jim had been his best friend since school that he felt obliged to put him out of his misery. Well, help him to put *himself* out of his misery. It was more Angus's instinct to tell Jim about her crush on Ned and then tell him to look for someone with a fuller personality allocation, but knowing Jim as he did, he also knew that there were some things he simply wouldn't believe until he found them out for himself. The stubborn git.

He sat back down again and dropped his voice. 'You don't want Tamara to be your friend, you want to . . . to . . .' Angus hesitated over the right word, discarded the sentence and started again. 'It's a different thing altogether. And you don't have to be someone's friend to start a relationship with them. And Tamara isn't . . .' He thought of Iona and bit his tongue before he could say anything snide about Tamara's idea of friendships.

He looked up and Jim's eyes were fixed on him, hungry for his words. Oh, the guilt.

'Jim,' he said carefully (why was saying someone's name such an easy trick to play for time and why did it always signal bad news?), 'if you really want to start something with Tamara, you'll just have to *do* something or *say* something. It might be that she doesn't think of you that way, because of what you've just said about being friends . . .' Now he really was clutching at straws. When all the signs were this ominous, surely it was just better not to get into these situations? If it was that hard to get into them, didn't that tell you something about getting out?

'We're all grown-ups,' he finished lamely. 'You've got to deal with this and then move on.'

Angus realized, as Jim's face fell, that that sort of gave the ending away.

He opened his mouth to try to recover, found there was nothing he could say without perjuring himself, but then, just as quickly, Jim's obvious disappointment was replaced with a hurt resignation. Angus longed to give him a good shouting-to. Jim hadn't always been like this. When they were at school, he'd been just as docile and nice, except for cross-country running. Mud, blood, blisters and, in one case, a broken rib hadn't come between Jim and the finishing tape. Heroic, some people called it. He'd gone for mental, himself. But then at some point after the age of seventeen, Jim seemed to have been involved in a Spiderman-type lab disaster with some contaminated breath fresheners and suede shoes, and had turned into The World's Nicest Man. Which was great for meeting people's parents, but not exactly a hidden weapon in the cunning world of property development. Or women.

'Anyway. Brian, yeah? We need to talk about staff and stuff,' said Jim. His voice carried a faint trace of wounded pride. 'Better if we go together and present a united front.'

Angus kicked himself and vowed to do an extra half-hour on the treadmill at work in penance for handling this so badly.

'Fine.' He tucked the underneath bit of the receipt into his wallet and made a quick note in his Filofax about leaving amaretti biscuits on the bill saucers. Or a good-quality mint. Ned would know.

'Fine,' Jim repeated, holding the door open. 'I'll call you later.'

Chapter Thirteen

Marie did what she always did when she felt as though her life was being remote-controlled by some invisible hand: she went home and made fudge.

There was a tin of condensed milk permanently in the cupboard for emergencies, hidden behind the leaking, unlabelled plastic bags of spices Chris bought in fits of enthusiasm from Tooting Market and then left to stain the Formica shelves like pungent powder paints. If it was a really serious emergency she could eat an entire tin with a spoon while achieving a trance-like misery state. She had to scrape the label off first, so she couldn't see the Nutritional Values box, then if she could wait she boiled it for forty minutes so it went thick and then sat licking it off the smallest spoon she could find while listening to Verdi's *Requiem*.

Marie ditched her school-bag, shrugged off her hat, coat and scarf and left them in a pile by the door. The more she thought about it, the more she realized that condensed milk was her best friend, in the absence of Iona. She ran a careless hand through her hair, ruffling up the flat curls after the bus journey home under the furry hat. Today had been bad at school and she knew that this evening could only go worse, since the cause of her preoccupation and tetchy mood with the kids would now be coming home from work on the bus. Only condensed milk could save her. Only Nestlé stood between her and the most enormous Chinese takeaway imaginable.

It wasn't fair on the kids that she was so grumpy, she

thought, slamming the nasty 1970s kitchen cupboard doors open and shut as she looked for all the fudge ingredients. It was no good getting into school earlier and earlier to avoid breakfast conversations when, for one thing, Chris was doing that too, so they ended up meeting awkwardly in the kitchen at half-seven, grabbing slices of unbuttered toast and old bananas in a frantic rush to be out first. For another, being in school for eight hours a day was just too much. Marie liked teaching. Up to a point. The point at which the scaled-down smallness of children and the holes in their mouths where their milk teeth had been started to freak her out.

She wiped down the work surface which never seemed to get clean, however many times she scrubbed at it, and lined up all the ingredients. Butter, brown sugar, proper Madagascan vanilla essence (from Ned, a gift), condensed milk. Weighing them all in *Blue Peter*-style glass bowls calmed her as well, the clunking of the wooden spoon on the solid glass when she scraped everything into the biggest pan she had. Melting the butter, pouring in the condensed milk and vanilla and sugar, and stirring it all up until the molten golden mixture began to bubble and boil gradually made her feel better. She shut the door of the small kitchen so the sweet steam would fill the room and switched on the radio so she wouldn't hear the phone ring or Chris come in.

She didn't want to have to talk, or pretend to talk. She didn't want to think about him, or how good it used to be, how bad it was now, how much worse it could get – she didn't want to contemplate anything to which her conscience would require an answer.

All she could think, as she stirred down the caramel bubbles in a regular figure-of-eight movement, was that it wasn't meant to happen like this. The situation between her and Chris (she heard the US Military resonance of the word 'situation' and grimaced to herself) was roller-coasting towards a conclusion that she hadn't ever considered happening to her. No one in her family got divorced. That was for people on the *Jerry Springer Show*. For people who didn't have happy childhoods. For people who cheated and threw things and kept rabid dogs in cages in their backyards.

However, as life at home descended into fogs of silence, punctuated only by sniping when they were with the others, Marie was beginning to realize that throwing things and arguing were good signs. They showed you were still touching the other person, even if you did want to insert your entire CD collection into their lower bowel. You were angry that they weren't living up to the personality you fell in love with. You had a nasty sense that the stock you had invested in had suddenly plummeted or been revealed to have been dodgy all along. While you were still fighting it meant you passionately wanted your old life back, even if the fight you were having only confirmed it had gone for ever.

No. They'd whistled through that stage, with barely time to notice the depressing details. It was her lack of worrying about Chris that concerned her now, not any worries about Chris himself. What scared her most, as she lay in bed night after night, their feet no longer touching, having learned to share the bed too well, was the thought that if Chris just didn't come home one night, she would be relieved. Not worried. Relieved.

It would let her off. Allow her to wake up and get on with her life as if the past five years had been a dream. Even thinking about it now gave her a guilty flicker of excitement. What if he just disappeared? Just wandered away? Went on a mercy mission to Angola and never came back?

Marie stirred harder with her wooden spoon and allowed for him to be so engrossed in saving lives that their bourgeois existence in Tooting could never satisfy him fully again. That would give him the jaw-clenched, eyes-fixed-on-faraway-point charity-hero image she had always loved and would let both of them come out of it without losing face. Chris would phone, on a crackling line from the Red Cross post, full of solicitous apology and burning idealism. *I'm so sorry, Marie, but they need me here, I don't know how long for. I know you're selfless enough to support me and not make a fuss, so the kindest thing I can do is grant you an unconditional divorce.*

She paused for a moment, lulled by the generous simplicity of it, and of her own supporting (but still commendable) charity-hero role, until the fudge took advantage of her lack of stirring and immediately boiled up the pan in a seething, scalding mass.

She stirred it back down crossly and conceded that that scenario was unlikely, to say the least. Chris as she knew him would more likely be phoning to get her to wire money and to check that the *Wandsworth Evening Herald* had an up-to-date photo to go with the piece he'd be wiring on the Red Cross fax.

She knew they had been happy once because she had the photos to prove it. Lots of photos. They were all in albums in the sitting room, on the bottom row of the IKEA bookshelf which she had measured specially. For about two and a half years, which covered the happy span between finally netting Chris, travelling, getting married and setting up home here, she had photographic evidence of all kinds of Davenport merriment: joy, excitement, lust, companionship, adventure, a paint-chart spectrum of shared happiness. She looked at the same photos these days with mild disbelief, guilty that she had let it all drain away somewhere without noticing, leaving only the caricature of a sitcom marriage they now inhabited. Sometimes it wasn't even that.

The trouble was, as Iona had tried to point out the last time she was over, no one takes photos of themselves trying to balance the accounts, or having a snit fit over the one sheet of loo paper left clinging to the roll. So, Iona pointed out – 'apropos of nothing, really' – over a tub of Loseley Vanilla, looking back over these images of a freshly-in-love couple didn't mean they'd always been in a state of permanent ecstasy, it just meant that they'd taken photos of themselves while they were.

Marie was so glad now that she had done, because even though these photos were barely three years old, she couldn't remember what it was like to be happy with Chris – and for her to be where she was now, she bitterly wanted to remember. Or else she was suffering for nothing.

The sugar was crystallizing on the wooden spoon and the little shards of sugar above the thick coating of fudge glittered in the kitchen strip-lighting. Marie held the spoon up for inspection. There was something satisfyingly scientific about making fudge, waiting for crystallizing points and setting points and catching the boil. It made her feel skilled that she didn't need a sugar thermometer to tell.

She got a glass out of the cupboard and filled it with cold water. This was her favourite part: the set test. Depending on how miserable she was, she would sometimes test a little too early, knowing the hot fudge wouldn't set hard, so she could scoop it out of the cloudy water, mouth hot and soft. Fudge-making could go on for hours – the longer it boiled the better it was and she'd already been stirring this for nearly an hour.

Today she knew the fudge was more or less there, though she didn't actually want to be finished yet. Maybe she would make some more. Marie sighed and noticed that the cupboards could do with a wipe down. It was coming to something when she genuinely wanted to shut herself in the kitchen with the radio and do her cupboards out, rather than slump in front of *EastEnders* with her feet up and a large glass of wine in her hand. The thought of being in front of the television when Chris came in, leaving herself open to his 'Oh, you've been watching TV while I've been saving the world' gaze, trapping herself there all evening, saying nothing and thinking too hard, made something inside her twist painfully.

Marie scooped a spoonful of liquid fudge from the pan and, holding it high above the glass, let it coil thinly into the cold water, like the little sandworms on the beach. It looked set, but she knew it wasn't and, taking a teaspoon from the drawer, she scraped out the fudge and blew on it to cool it down.

Then she heard the front door open in a gap between songs and put the spoon into her mouth automatically. It was nowhere near as cold as she'd thought and it seared a small brandmark into her tongue. She fanned her mouth ineffectually and felt ill.

He was back unusually early from work. Only half-five? Had the world ended? Did famine have half-days?

She waited quietly in case he was shouting hello, but there was no sound other than the bedroom door opening and the screech of the unoiled runners on the built-in wardrobe. Normally he just threw his clothes on the bed and walked around in his boxers until he felt the need to put some clothes on. The only thing he ever hung up in there was his suit, of which he was bizarrely proud, given that it was a symbol of capitalist oppression.

His suit?

Marie stopped stirring and let the spoon slide down the side of the pan while she listened. Chris virtually *never* wore a suit for work. That was part of the job for him: only puppets of commerce wore shirts and ties. Saviours of the planet wore Converse All-Stars and no socks. She hadn't had the heart to tell him that her brother worked in IT and wore exactly the same trainers to corral the planet in a giant Web. And yet, now she thought about it, he had definitely left for work in a suit this morning, but she'd been so busy sidling out of the door before him that she hadn't really noticed.

'Has it come to this?' she mouthed to her indistinct reflection in the steamy window.

He didn't even yell through to ask if the kettle was on

these days. They only ever seemed to talk when they were with the others.

Marie gave the pan of fudge a final angry beating with the wooden spoon and poured it all into the ceramic dish she had bought under the pretence of making more quiches. She made elegant trailing designs with the last thin dribbles.

. And then the phone rang and, knowing he wouldn't answer it, Marie dumped the fudge in the fridge, took a deep breath and, feeling like Lara Croft, went through to the Sitting Room of Deathly Silence.

Since neither of them had had a significant pay rise since moving in, they were still living in the one-bedroom flat they'd initially rented in a long terraced street in Tooting. When they arrived, their street had been slightly scuzzy, but since then clamouring hordes of Yummy Mummies who couldn't quite afford Clapham had moved in and hiked up all the prices, and their landlady, a ditzy ageing hippie with a small private income which allowed her to pretend she was still a student, despite having had an ample thirty years to come to terms with adulthood, had hiked up the rent accordingly each time they had come to renew. But whereas the rent was bang up to date, Maisie's adamant refusal to change a single thing in 'a house full of happy memories' (or out-and-out meanness, depending on your point of view) meant that everything else was about thirty years old, and smelled as you'd imagine. So much for hippie values.

Marie stood in the hall with the phone and turned away from the sight of Chris picking his toes on the squashy red sofa she had bought with the money she had sweated for after school, tutoring Katie Wilson though the entrance exam to a prep school out of the area. It had been a straight choice between educational principles and something to sit on, and once she had discovered something crawling on the arm of the old sofa ('No, I can't possibly throw it out! So much *happened* on that sofa!') there was no contest.

'Hello?' she said, careful not to give her number, in case it was a weirdo call.

But it was Iona. Hearing her voice made Marie want to run straight round to their house, where there was conversation and proper coffee, but she forced herself to sound cheerful. Perhaps too cheerful. She looked at herself in the hall mirror and tried to moderate the desperate note in her voice down to mere enthusiasm.

'Oh, that sounds great. Chris,' she yelled, 'Iona and Angus are going over to the Grapes for a drink. Do you want to go?'

'No,' said Chris without looking up.

I could go without him, she thought. I've got the car outside. But that would just be advertising the fact that I no longer think in terms of 'we'. Maybe we do need a night in together. Maybe that's it. More time to talk without all the others there.

'It's OK, Iona,' she said, sweeping a line of dust off the top of the mirror with her finger. 'I've got some Roman coins to counterfeit for tomorrow morning and I think Chris is a bit tired.'

She twisted the phone cord round her fingers while Iona commiserated. Seven feet away, she watched him turn up *The Weakest Link* and brush his toenails pickings on to the carpet.

Marie tightened the cord. 'Still, count me in for all the decorating,' she said. 'I've got half-term coming up soon and I'd love to help out with the old roller and brush set.'

Chris made an indiscriminate noise of dissent on the sofa, which may have been directed at her, or at the woman onscreen who didn't know the capital of Cambodia.

'OK, yeah. OK, see you soon. Love to Angus . . .'

Another snort.

'OK, bye!'

Marie made herself put the phone down carefully instead of slamming it against the wall, or, more satisfying, down

Chris's throat sideways. As soon as the receiver clicked into place on the unit, Chris turned up the television again.

Then Marie made herself go and sit down on the other side of the sofa and made herself pick up the TV guide in an interested manner.

'Can't remember you ever volunteering to do any painting here,' Chris observed in a tone which Marie knew from experience was intended to mask some outrageous barb in a cloak of lightness, so she couldn't object without being accused of a sense of humour failure. Their first words to each other since half-eight this morning. Charming.

'Well, there doesn't seem much point, does there, when it's not our flat?'

Oh fuck, thought Marie, as the words came out of her mouth. He gets me every time. No matter how much I try to avoid this, I *always* end up falling into the same trap. I *must* be tired.

'Ah, not again, Marie,' said Chris, with a whole body gesture of weariness. 'You know what I think about the housing market in London.'

Marie certainly did.

'And even if we did have the money to buy round here . . .' He trailed off because they had had this conversation so many times in the past year that it was almost like being in a Harold Pinter play, going through all the lines again. A play no one else was watching, with less dialogue and more silences each performance.

Chris's original reluctance to buy somewhere was based on his assumption that this was merely a stopover in London, while he got his bearings, got his shorts washed and did a year's work at ActionTeam, after which he would be globe-trotting on their behalf like a stubbly Geri Halliwell, with Marie in tow, teaching Roman cooking and right angles to little Rwandans. His disgusting open-toed all-terrain travelling sandals were still in the hall shoe-rack, primed and ready for action.

When it became clear that globe-trotting wasn't on the immediate agenda (and that they weren't even going to run to a company bus pass), he had clung to the dream even more. 'A mortgage is a big commitment, Marie,' he kept saying in reply to her desperately waved estate-agent brochures for increasingly remote or dangerous areas of London, apparently ignoring the passably big commitment he'd made to her already.

Once the property around their flat starting creeping up in price like a locked cellar filling ominously with floodwater, there was the question of if not here, where *can* we buy? Unless one of them had a massive unexpected pay rise, or found an immediate superior shagging the managing director while snorting cocaine off the fax machine, their combined salaries would just about buy them a luxury flat in a shed in Deptford, as long as they didn't mind sharing a bathroom with the refugees next door. Then there was the matter of a deposit which neither of them had, in response to which Chris went through a phase of arguing that the French had the right idea: rent all your life and go on major holidays with the roof-repairing money. He once tried to throw in a bit of communism 'property is theft' as well, which Marie knew he'd got from a Manic Street Preachers album – an accusation he denied right up until she produced the sleeve insert.

So each time the tenancy came up for renewal, despite Maisie's incongruously bread-head interest-linked rent hikes, they'd never got any further and now Marie too was avoiding the issue, not because she wanted to buy a flat – though God knew she couldn't afford to – but because the thought of financially roping herself to Chris for the rest of her life was something that made her feel weak and despairing.

She looked at him now, doing the quick crossword in the *Evening Standard* with a stunted pen, obviously lifted from a National Lottery stand. How could a mortgage feel more binding than a marriage? That had to be wrong.

He met her eye briefly and she had an instinct from the slightly ashamed expression that he had had the same thought. His wide grey eyes blinked nervously and he put down the paper.

'Oh, Marie, you're not . . .' he began and then his gaze fell to her waist.

Marie looked down too. Her tight red shirt was stretching over a bulge and the dark material of her skirt was showing through the gaps, highlighting her roundness. Her hands instinctively covered her stomach and she blushed.

'No, God, no. I'm just well fed.'

An expression crossed his face which he tried to hide so quickly she couldn't make out what it was, and, sensing it would be hurtful, she turned away too.

Not the time to start the Virgin Marie cracks.

Even if the immaculate conception bit would be true.

She got up and hovered by the bookshelves, pretending to look for a book, until he went back to scrawling out anagrams over the weather report. Then she gave it another minute to be safe and sat down on the other end of the sofa. The grim beauty of their tiny flat, as far as marital communication went, was that even if she had wanted to flounce away from him, there was no conservatory to down a moody vodka in. Only seriously rich people could afford to throw tantrums in London and then come down to dinner as though nothing had happened. And she didn't want to give him the impression that cleaning the kitchen was something he could trigger simply by being rude to her. The flat was too small for meaningful sulking. Togetherness was compulsory.

Marie looked across the sofa at Chris while he chewed the pen and stared at the crossword. Physically he was no different from the man she had had such a raging crush on at college. He was still rangy and tanned-looking, still able to do all those yoga positions. As far as she knew. And she knew more about him now than she had ever thought she would. Maybe that was the problem. How unfair it was that your instinct was to be with the object of your desire all the time, and in doing that you end up destroying your need to be with them.

Very metaphysical, thought Marie, reaching for the open packet of chocolate digestives next to Chris on the sofa. I must tell Iona that I've started to have grown-up thoughts again.

A hand snaked out from behind the newspaper and slapped her fingers as they closed round the top biscuit. Marie realized guiltily that she'd actually been about to prise the top three off without thinking about it.

'Oh, what *now*?'

'Said it yourself, you're too fat.'

'I don't believe I *did* say that.' Tears prickled at the back of Marie's eyes – not at the words but at the tone. Once he would have said that as a joke, so he could reach over and insinuate his long fingers between the buttons of her shirt and tickle her soft stomach to make her laugh. Six months ago, it would have been said with spite, a cheap retaliation to some cleverer barb of her own. Now it was said with total objectivity. As you would correct someone's English. Fat wasn't even deliberately rude. It was frank.

It's not even that he sees me as his sister, she thought bitterly. We're like stepbrother and sister. Who've only just been introduced.

'You did. Anyway, these are mine. They're Fairtrade.'

'Really?' said Marie, gritting her teeth. That had to be a classic feedline, but she ignored it and ploughed on. She had probably lost too many opportunities for conversation by cutting him off with a quip and any conversation they had now was proof that things weren't irredeemable. It wasn't in her nature to give up. Besides, she didn't remember reading anything about 'What to do when your marriage stops working' in *Company* recently. You couldn't really take 'How to put the sparkle back into your squeeze' and multiply it by a factor of ten.

'Maybe we *should* paint in here,' she suggested brightly. 'We can get Maisie to pay for it. God knows, she's had enough rent out of us in the past four years without bothering to redecorate. We could do it ourselves. What do you think – a nice bright yellow, to catch the sun? Or' – her eyes skittered across the room for something less Mediterranean, something Chris might like – 'or a pale blue? I read somewhere that that's peaceful. Lots of classrooms are blue now. Meant to be calming.'

Chris grunted noncommittally.

Jesus Christ Almighty, this is hard, thought Marie, biting her lip. No wonder people choose to go on national television in order to come out to their partners as transsexual animal abusers – at least you've got their undivided attention for ten minutes.

'It's not a big flat, it shouldn't take too long,' she went on. She'd helped Iona paint some of her flat when Angus had knocked the kitchen through to the sitting room. This was half the size and it could do with some fresh paint. Preferably over that hideous psychedelic mural in the bedroom for a start. Lemon yellow on two walls would bring out the sunshine, and pale cream on the others might open it up a bit . . .

'Oh, for God's sake, it always has to come back to this,' said Chris. He shook his newspaper out self-importantly, as if she had interrupted his critical study of the political leader column, even though he was quite obviously now reading the football pages. 'You should be happy we're living in London. You should be happy we even have a house. A lot of people in the EU don't.'

'No, they have *Häuser* and *maisons* and *casas*, don't they?'

'No, they live on the streets and *beg*.'

Oh, stop making me feel so bad, Marie wailed in her head. Even if it's making you feel better, how can you have so little idea of what it's doing to me!

She tried taking deep breaths, but her heart was racing, banging away in her wrists. And that would be just typical, wouldn't it, she thought, rile me to death and then walk away with everything I own and no murder weapon to hide in the canal. In fact, he'd probably point out the crème brûlées and the full-fat lasagne in the fridge to the police on his way out and inform them that she had been warned. He'd only been stating the obvious. 'God, it's getting hard to talk to you!'

Chris threw his paper on to the floor and stood up. His knees clicked.

Good, thought Marie, now *he* can deal with the problem of where to storm off to effectively in a flat the size of the average bathroom suite.

'Well, maybe I don't want to talk!' he spat. 'Maybe I've had a hard day at work and the last thing I want is more nagging from you about the state of our flat! Jesus Christ, Marie, will you get off my case?'

'Excuse me?' Marie threw up her hands with a baffled expression. Baffled underlaid with a strong hint of sarcasm. 'Your case? I wasn't aware I was *on* it. I wasn't even aware you *had* one . . .'

This was lost on Chris, who had opted for staring out of the window as the only reasonably dignified move. Marie now had the high ground of the sofa and, to mark this, she slipped off her shoes and kicked her feet up on to the far cushions to occupy the whole lot. But her heart wasn't slowing down much.

As long as they were talking it was OK. Even baiting like this was better than the long silences which had crept in lately. Iona had always maintained that long silences were OK too, and had even invited her round to Brixton, where she and Angus apparently had regular long silences (Sunday mornings with papers, during *Top Gear*, Saturday morning hangover breakfasts), but Marie knew they were the kind of long silences in which you felt safe and warm because you didn't need to talk, since you knew the other person still found you lovable when you weren't being amusing. The long silences she and Chris had were the kind usually experienced in prison cells when a serial strangler with temper issues is locked up with a serial poisoner who snores and bites his toenails.

'Don't try to be funny, Marie, I'm not in the mood.'

'Well, I can spot two deliberate mistakes in that sentence,' said Marie before she could stop herself. 'One, I don't *have* to *try* to be funny, and two, you are, it would seem, clinically *incapable* of being in the mood. Lesser women would assume you'd had some kind of pleasure bypass. A vasectomy of the humour lobe.'

'Did I say funny? Sorry, I meant stop trying to be a smart arse. I'm not one of your seven-year-olds. It really doesn't matter to you, does it, that I might have something serious to worry about?' His voice, to Marie's distress, had returned to that matter-of-fact drone which, as far as she could see, a lot of his colleagues had adopted as a means of talking about endless famine and racial persecution in the pub without engendering inappropriate displays of emotion and mass collapses of cheery atmos. 'As long as you can make a joke, you don't care about anyone else.'

'That's not true,' said Marie, wondering guiltily if it was.

'It is.'

'It *isn't*.'

In reply, there was a fresh bloom of condensation on the window to indicate that Chris was doing his trademark argument-ending dismissive breathing. The sort that indicated that there was nothing sensible left to say to her. He'd been doing it more and more in the past month, to the extent that, until she realized that it was just a sneaky way of getting the last word without the effort of thinking of something devastating to say, Marie had begun to wonder if he had some kind of respiratory problem.

'Chris?' Had that huff counted as a response? Was it now incumbent on her to reply to that? 'Chris!' Marie recognized the sense of sinking desperation that the conversation was getting out of her control – either it would go down one of their familiar routes, in which case actual participation was unnecessary, or it would go into totally unexplored territory, in which case they would be forced to say some very unpalatable things. She shivered, despite the central heating.

'You just . . .' began Chris, and let out a traumatized sigh that would have dislodged a small cat from the window-sill, if they'd had one.

'I just what?'

There was a pause long enough for Marie to note that, far from being the lead-up to a demonstration of soul-baring from her husband, this was exactly the kind of conversation she was required to break up in the playground before hair got pulled. Suddenly she had renewed sympathy for the hair-pullers.

'I don't think there's any point in discussing it.'

Her stomach lurched.

'In discussing what?' Make him say it.

'Nothing, no, forget it.'

'Come on, what?' Had he been to a solicitor? Marie's brain spun. Was that why he was wearing his suit?

The suit was now taking on scary significance in her mind. He couldn't have been wearing the suit . . . to *meet* someone? *Could* he?

'Just fucking get off my case!' He spun round and cast her a brief, contemptuous look. 'I suppose I should be grateful that you're making it easier for me!' Then he strode across the messy floor that separated the window from the door and Marie heard him wrench his manky old leather blouson from the hatstand.

She scrambled to her feet, feeling sick and as though she were going over Niagara Falls in a barrel. She couldn't control whatever was going on and she certainly couldn't see where it was going. She could only dread the drop.

'Chris! Where are you going?' she yelled, hating that her voice sounded like a cartoon nag, a cliché. But she didn't know what else to say. She'd never been in this situation before, never imagined that this would be how her marriage would end up. Like a bad Catherine Cookson novel, as it turned out. In the hall, the hatstand toppled over as he slammed the door.

He didn't reply. In her mind, she supplied the 'Out! Just out!' that cliché demanded. The banality of it made her ache worse.

Marie slowly pushed the hatstand back upright and started to pick up the hats that had been thrown off it. Knitted earflap bobble hats, all red and orange, her bright fake-fur band, berets and sunhats. There wasn't really room for it, and she should really chuck most of these out, but the hats made a splash of colour in the dark hall and, though she didn't wear them, they were excellent for dressing up.

Marie could feel big tears running down her face, smearing her mascara, but she wasn't aware that she was crying. She felt more scared than angry. More sad and more confused. Marie's hand hovered over the telephone in the hall. Maybe if she told Iona, Iona could rearrange it all to make sense. She nearly always could.

Her hand stopped. But if she told Iona, that would make it all real, and they would have to think about what Chris had meant when he said, 'You're making it easier for me!' And it would mean admitting that her marriage, which she'd insisted was so sweet and romantic and modern, was really just some nasty power-trip nightmare.

Marie sank down on her beautiful sofa and hugged her knees. All the sofa to herself at last and she was cramping herself up in to a ball, and still she longed to be smaller.

Chapter Fourteen

I ona thought Angus looked pretty good stripping paint.
Much as his smart investment suit was usually an integral
factor in his fanciability rating, there was definitely something alluring about his scruffy Levi's, for DIY use only, and
the skanky, paint-splattered rugby shirt that was slightly too
small for him now. Maybe the combination made him look
younger, more like the man out of the Diet Coke advert.

Or maybe it was because Iona now free-associated skanky
DIY clothes with a better kitchen or fresh paint in the
sitting room.

Whatever it was, Iona angled her sand-papering stance
on the window-sill so she could look at him raking the
scraper up the filthy wallpaper opposite. Angus did a lot
of DIY at home and he was unexpectedly good at it,
for a solicitor. Her mother, who specialized in finding
evidence that she and Angus should get married as soon
as possible, reckoned that he was nesting. Iona preferred
to think he was concerned about the resale value of the
flat.

She smiled affectionately at him. Huge chunks of grimy
red paper were flaking away and falling in ribbons by his
feet, revealing the surprisingly white plaster underneath. He
was scraping in rhythm to the *Top Gear Driving Anthems*
CD she had put on the pub system, furrowing his brow in
concentration.

How nice it was, thought Iona suddenly, to be able to
watch him doing something simple instead of the usual

pacing up and down, worrying violently about the decline of the British legal system.

'Are the loos working yet? Because you know I haven't used the loo in here for about five years on principle and I don't want to start now unless I know they're completely gutted. In fact, if they're reduced to a European-style hole in the ground, that's actually ideal.'

Iona turned to Marie, who was sweating visibly in a bright violet T-shirt which had 'St Anselm Primary Sports Team' printed on the front. She had customized it, hopefully for out of school use, in a most unteacherly fashion by removing the arms and deepening the V at the neck into a lascivious plunge. Understandably for a garment intended for a seven-year-old netball goalie, it stretched over Marie's lavish bosom in a manner which made the straining school logo rather ironic.

'Are the loos working yet?' Iona repeated. 'I don't know. Have you asked Jim?'

'Jim's gone home to get his marker pens and plans,' said Marie, drawing the back of her hand over her sweaty forehead. She adjusted her tight jeans, which looked as though they were effectively crossing her legs for her, in bladder-control terms. 'And a tenner says he won't be back for about an hour. I think he's suffering from delayed reaction horror at what he has to do, and who he has to do it with.'

'You think?' asked Iona, although it wasn't really a question. The sheer scale of what had to be done to the Grapes before they could reopen it was pretty staggering, once you removed all the punters and tables and switched on the lights. Even that hadn't been easy. When Jim, Angus and Iona had let themselves in that morning, fully equipped with the DIY big guns hired from someone Jim knew 'in the trade' (which trade exactly Angus disputed), Mad Boy Sam had been waiting on the doorstep with his four-pack of Tennants Special, and had offered to come in and help.

Only Iona, to whom he had taken a particular shine, could persuade him that he would get dust in his beer and might be better going down the park with the rest of the hard-core regulars, who were hanging around mournfully like displaced gypsies.

'I do think.' Marie put down her scraper and looked around. 'You three have been here since eight this morning, I've been here since four-thirty, we've worked straight through, and it still looks like an unconvincing set from a Blitz sitcom. This' – she banged the wall with her fist – 'is probably the original wallpaper, locked in place by a potent combination of fifty years of smoke, beer, grease and body odour. Filth being nature's own hairspray, as certain children of my acquaintance have demonstrated to me.' She stroked a dangling curl of wallpaper for illustration and it gently peeled away from the wall, taking a sprinkling of loose plaster with it.

'Careful with that, it's listed.'

'Under what?'

'E for effort?'

'I'd give it a D for decay.'

Marie tucked her scraper into the back pocket of her jeans, leaned against the wall with crossed arms and surveyed the brightly lit bar. Someone had gone through the whole pub and replaced all the missing bulbs with 100-watt new ones and suddenly previously unseen areas were appearing, along with lots of other, less desirable stuff which frankly would have been better hidden. Tamara was noticeable by her absence.

Angus was still steaming away down the opposite wall, pushing and pulling in time to Steppenwolf. He seemed a long way away. Marie rubbed her eyes wearily and smeared her black eyeliner. Now she had stopped the mindless hard work, her brain was catching up with her, waving a big bag of Bad Vibes. It was so good to be legitimately out of the house for as long as she wanted. 'Iona, I just don't remember this place being so *big*. It's like the Tardis. How come it always looked like the Black Hole of Calcutta when we drank here, and now we're having to decorate it it's turned into Wembley Stadium?'

'But you've done loads.'

They looked back at the wall Marie had been stripping down. Marie did a double take when she realized how fast she'd been working. Her muscles barely felt warm and, apart from drinking about four pints of Coke, she hadn't noticed the time going by. But now she looked back, she'd done about twice as much as anyone else and, since she'd arrived last and got the least desirable (i.e. most prehistoric) tools, it was even more amazing.

'I have, haven't I?' she said admiringly. Why bother with dodgy speed when you could just have caffeine and a row with your husband?

'Blimey, Marie, let me know when you do go to the loo,' said Iona, running her hands along the newly exposed wall. 'It's about time you had some kind of urine test for steroids. If this is how fit you get teaching, you should be running mixed classes at the gym.'

Marie wondered whether Iona had guessed that her blistering efficiency had been based on imagining each roll of wallpaper as the skin on Chris's back which she was removing with long, hard, unflinching strokes. That had covered most of the first wall. The high fireplace, which she had done in only three-quarters of an hour, she had imagined to be her own personality, which she was stripping of Chris, removing each hang-up he had installed and set working, each layer of defence, each allowance for his behaviour which had reduced her expectations to pathetic levels. Sadly, this only seemed convincing while she had a scraper in her hand.

He still hadn't told her why he had been wearing his suit twice in the past week. On the way to and from work, Marie had come up with many, increasingly baroque reasons, but not a single one which provoked feelings of relief. She was itching to ask him, if only because it was starting to irritate her, in the same way half a song lyric would. Not that she could begin to imagine how she would frame the question. 'You're not *honestly* telling me you've found someone else?' – still the least believable and so the least scary scenario – wasn't exactly going to get things off to a good start, and she wasn't at all sure what she would do, or even how she would feel, if he calmly informed her he had started divorce proceedings.

It was not a happy situation all round. The stress was manifesting itself in her usually flawless complexion and Marie knew that Iona had sensed something already, without her two new zits having to flash it out in Morse code to the rest of the world. She had noticed Iona carefully discouraging Angus from his usual patting and stroking routine when they stopped for coffee, underlined by the cautious glance Iona threw over her shoulder, to check if there was any negative reaction, any quick departure to the loo, or stifled sob.

Marie huffed to herself. Chris, on the other hand, had made no comment about her spots or the fact that for three nights now she had pretended to sleep while he moved unhurriedly round the flat, lying there waiting until he was snoring like a pig in muck, and then moved her pillows to sleep alone and cramped on the sofa. It was the only place she *could* sleep now.

'Marie?' She felt Iona's hand on her arm and shook herself before Iona did. At least it was better to work out her aggression on the pub and not on her year three, the gin bottle or, more satisfyingly, Chris.

Especially not if he was going for a divorce.

Iona was looking concerned.

Marie smiled ruefully. Iona always looked concerned, as though her wide blue eyes were inviting you to share the heavy burden of your problems, a walking, talking, concerned agony-aunt head-shot. Poor Iona. Marie had realized a long time ago that gentle concern was Iona's natural expression – she couldn't help the fact that her face fell that way when she wasn't concentrating, and she was just too kind to turn away the sorrowful hordes who interpreted that as a red light to dump their inner turmoil like so much toxic waste into a river.

Marie's own natural expression was one of outraged incredulity, which served her well as a teacher.

'Is there something up, Marie?' Iona repeated in a low voice.

They scrutinized each other's faces like fencers.

Maybe she already knew, Marie wondered. Maybe Chris had said something to Angus.

Somewhat unlikely, since the last time Chris and Angus had had a serious conversation had been about six years ago.

'Marie,' Iona persisted, 'I'm not being funny, but you keep switching between the Incredible Hulk and Penelope Pitstop right before my eyes. Your *expression*, I mean,' she added very quickly. 'Not your . . . Is it something to do with Chris?'

'Er, yes,' said Marie. The need to go to the loo was even more pressing now and was distracting her. 'He keeps going to work in his suit,' she said to get it over quickly. 'Something's up, but I can't ask him what because we're not talking.'

Panic widened Iona's eyes to Disney dimensions and she reapplied her concerned grip to Marie's lower arm. Somewhere far away Angus started singing 'You Ain't Seen Nothing Yet' while his scraper dragged along the wall, providing the rhythm guitar line. 'Marie!' Iona whispered urgently, 'you don't think he's after . . .'

A divorce? Going abroad? Someone else?

As the pressure of Iona's fingers tightened on her skin, it occurred to Marie that she had no idea at all what her husband wanted, and didn't really care either way, as long as it fitted in roughly with what she wanted. She wondered how Iona might feel about the best guesses so far, in no particular order: 'My husband wants to shag someone on the side,' or 'My husband wants to divorce me' or, from her own point of view, 'I hate the man I've married so much that I can't bear to see him eat' or 'I pray every night that he will be transferred to some very dangerous part of a distant subcontinent overrun with guerrillas so I won't have to pretend that we have nothing in common any more.'

Just because thoughts such as these had been haunting the darker parts of her mind for the past year or so, without ever being invited into the bright lights of her front brain, didn't mean they wouldn't be a shock for anyone who wasn't actually living in the scary parallel world that was her marriage. The world which looked so feisty and alive to everyone else looking in, but which went silent and cold when they stopped looking.

They probably think we have a foul row in front of them and then go home and have passionate, angry sex, thought Marie. A sardonic smile twitched the corner of her lips. *As if.*

Iona was shaking her arm now, scared at her lack of response and the strange smiling. As Iona pumped it up and down, Marie realized her arm was beginning to ache in a delayed reaction from all the scraping.

'Marie! Don't just say things like that and then go silent! What's going on?' Iona turned round to make sure Angus hadn't heard and then whipped her head back to her friend, who had apparently gone into a completely out-of-character trance state.

Marie sighed and squeezed her bladder muscles. She hadn't meant to tell Iona like this. She hadn't meant to tell anyone at all, not until she knew herself what was going on. All she could think of now was how quickly Coke went through her. The biological desire to pee overrode all other thought processes and suddenly she had burning sympathy with some of her more easily panicked pupils.

'Things are not good with Chris, and I'm pretty positive that something is going on, either with his job or with someone else, and all in all that adds up to . . . well, I don't know. It's not as easy as dumping someone, is it?' She stopped short of the word 'divorce'. Much as being legally separated from Chris was precisely what she wanted, something inside her shied away from the whole idea.

'No,' said Iona slowly, trying to read Marie's tired eyes.

'Can I go to the loo now, please, miss?'

Iona released the pressure on her arm, but stroked her fingers up and down. Something in Iona's eyes – an unusual steely determination – informed Marie curtly that it was pointless trying to shrug this one off with her best friend.

'You have to tell me what's wrong,' said Iona in a light voice, 'or else I'll let Tamara get her cards out and we'll all find out that way.'

Her voice was light, but her expression wasn't.

Marie felt sick and stumbled off to the toilets, acutely aware that her fake smile probably wasn't cutting any ice.

The state of the toilets at the Bunch of Grapes, and the fact that the Ladies was a definite afterthought, had been a running joke for so long that Marie hadn't actually been in for about two years. Neither had the cleaners, by the look of the loos now. They were humming.

She pushed open the door of the second cubicle, which was living up to her worst suspicions, flushed the unflushed loo and sat down. Her legs were really aching now, as well as her arms, and she wondered if she might be going down with some juvenile virus. Perfect. That would be the last time she let either of the Holroyd twins breathe so close to her when she heard them read.

Outside she could hear Jim return with his plans and demand to know what had been going on. From the relative silence, it seemed that Angus had either switched off his electric steamer or Jim had brought takeaway for them.

Unusually, Marie didn't feel like eating. Which was an unexpected bonus.

Friday night.

She let out a tiny laugh, despite herself. Not just staying in on a Friday, but staying in and *doing DIY* even. The Ghost of Marie Past stood up in the back of her mind and howled. Friday nights for her and Iona at college had always involved drinking half a bottle of gin (to get things going), then half a pint of milk (to line the stomach) and then hitting the town in their lucky pulling knickers. After which, since they nearly always came back together anyway, Iona made her drink the Preventive Hangover Cure; no matter how pissed she was, she always managed to get a pint of water, two paracetemols and three Berocca down them.

Marie ran a hand through her sweaty hair. Friday nights with Chris, when they were still playing their Cheap Life game, had been fun too: the cheapest possible wine, followed by the cheapest possible supper, followed by the cheapest possible entertainment (sex or a night bus round town).

The wine and supper had stayed, but the entertainment had fallen by the wayside some time ago.

Marie gripped the bowl beneath her. Why did all that seem so long ago? How was it all going so wrong so quickly? And could Iona make it stop?

'You know why they call it KFC, don't you?' said Jim, waving a piece of deep-fried chicken in the air.

Marie immediately got the Fucking Crap bit and searched for an adjective beginning with K.

Angus paused in his systematic shredding of a corn on the cob. 'Is this a joke?' he asked. 'Because I've now been here for over twelve hours, stripping the wallpaper off the pub equivalent of the Forth Road Bridge, and frankly I could do with some amusement. If it's one of your disgusting Man

Eats Dog stories, however, I'm not sure Iona will want to know.'

'Er, not exactly a joke, I read it on the Internet.'

Iona could anticipate where this was going and got ready to stop it by putting down her own piece of breaded leg, which she suddenly didn't want any more.

'Jim . . .' she warned.

'They call it KFC because according to EU regulations' – Jim's eyes gleamed with the thrill of having a new conspiracy theory to wheel out and, by happy chance, a visual aid to hand – 'and all those genetic modification laws, you can't actually call it . . .'

'Jim, a) that's slanderous and b) we're eating,' Iona snapped quickly. Bile lurched up into her throat and she put her palm up to her mouth. 'Oh, cheers. You know I can't walk past a kebab shop without retching, you arsehole.'

Marie looked at the bit she was eating and dropped it into the paper carrier bag. 'Thanks, Jim. And I hope that bit you're eating now was the leg of a puppy.'

'Doesn't bother me,' said Jim, gnawing at the bone. 'I've lived in France.'

'Thank God Chris isn't here,' said Angus, unwittingly echoing exactly what Iona was thinking. 'He'd be telling us about the range of flattened domestic animals you can eat by the roadside in Namibia.'

As soon as he realized what he'd said, he looked down at the congealing tub of beans. Angus rarely blushed, but the speed of his apology reflected how embarrassed he was. 'Sorry, Marie,' he said quickly, 'didn't mean to be rude, it must be the paint stripper going to my head.'

'You're all right. I'm in complete agreement with you. Saves me having to say it.' Marie tried to divert Angus's embarrassment by looking round the tattered walls, dirty white and bare like chicken bones where the plaster was seeing the light for the first time in many years. Moving her eyes away from Iona's concerned glance, she said, 'What time are these builders coming in the morning?'

'About nine.' Angus looked optimistic. 'Whenever they get here basically. Depends how long it takes them to get off the dirt tracks and on to a main road. Ow! What?'

'Nothing,' Iona said, picking up some more chips. Angus gave her a retaliatory nudge. 'Oy! Don't make me get food on the nice carpet!'

'They're setting off from Carlisle as soon as they finish today's job, Ned said.'

'I can't *believe* you've hired Ned's mates,' said Marie, returning her attention to the chips. She picked idly, wishing there was a bottle of wine there instead. 'Don't tell me you phoned Scoot and the nearest builders they could find for you were in Carlisle. I mean, I know west London is a bit remote . . .'

'They're very cheap,' said Jim knowingly. 'In a *very cheap* way.'

Angus nodded too.

'No, you're losing me. Are they losing you too, Iona?' Marie turned to Angus and gave him her hard look. The one that produced missing reading books. 'There are plenty of cheap builders in London. Entire north London economies are founded on them. Is this some kind of bloke language for "They're a bit dodgy but you don't need to know, little lady"?'

'In one,' said Angus, helping himself to a fistful of chips.

'But I thought Overworld had given you sacks of cash to spend on renovations?'

'Well, they have,' said Jim. 'But Ned's mates can do it cheaper. And besides, we're going to need to start stashing some of that money to balance out any cock-ups later. And there will be some.'

'But are they any good?' asked Iona. She toyed with a corn on the cob and then held it up for general inspection. 'And are these all right?'

'They're fine,' Angus said. 'And I'm sure Ned's mates are fine too. Don't you know them?'

'Why would I know them? We didn't hang out with a big decorating crowd at school. Where are they from?'

Angus consulted a piece of paper in his top pocket. 'The Raffles? Raffles Decoration? Sounds quite upmarket.'

'Raffles? Er, no. And no, I don't think I would know them.' Iona stretched her arms behind her head until the joints cracked. 'You think we can get all this stuff off the walls before they arrive?'

'That's the idea,' said Jim, relinquishing the chicken thigh. It was stripped shiny. He wiped his hands on his dirty jeans and got out the plans he'd drawn up with Angus and Ned. They bore no resemblance whatsoever to the plans drawn up by Tamara for decorating the place.

'God, it's a bit depressing now, isn't it?' he said, looking round at the ragged walls.

They sat in silence for several minutes, as this was indisputable.

Iona tried to rank the depressingness of the walls, Marie-and-Chris and the imminent arrival of seriously dodgy builders, and found herself walking over to the bar to see if they had left behind any stray miniatures.

Marie could only think that grim though the pub might be, at least Chris wasn't there to spoil the rather comforting family atmosphere.

Angus was thinking exactly the same thing, but including Tamara alongside Chris.

Jim was adding up paint and labour costs in his head and coming up with different numbers every time.

'How are they getting here, these lads from Carlisle?' asked Iona as her hand closed triumphantly around a dusty bottle of Diamond White which had rolled behind one of the soft-drinks fridges.

'They've got a van, by all accounts.'

Iona straightened up abruptly to see if Angus was taking

the mick out of her accent. He had started again on the nearest wall, stripping and steaming, and had his back to her, innocently.

'How come we're in a pub and there's not a drop to drink?' demanded Marie, flipping through the CDs Iona had brought to alleviate the silence. They were largely the album versions of the Bunch of Grapes jukebox, and a lot of Led Zeppelin. She waved a Free album at Iona. 'It's sheer *torment*. I can't drink any more Coke – I spent a whole science lesson last week demonstrating what it could do to a dirty twopence piece. I must have the cleanest bladder within the M25.'

'Did Tamara not tell you?' said Iona conversationally, picking up her own stripping tools. 'She's put you in charge of the toilets. Since you're the one with the most specific views on them.'

'Great.' Marie flinched at the amount of work needed to make the toilets even sanitary, let alone decorative. 'Is that a compliment?'

'Um . . . I'm not sure.'

'So what's she in charge of? The bar? Or the mirrors?'

Marie rolled her eyes as Iona turned and changed the CD.

'Ah, no. Please, no. Iona, *please* not "Houses of the Holy" again,' begged Jim. 'If I hear that "Hey, Lady" song again, I'm going to turn into a feminist.'

At eleven, when there were still acres of wall to go and the Raffles lads had phoned to say they'd be there by seven in the morning, Angus made the decision to work through all night.

'But we've got very little time,' he said in response to the howls of protest. 'There is a reason why we're attempting the world's fastest pub refurbishment, you know. It's not because I *want* to spend every waking moment with you lot and a bunch of builders.'

'No, but I might want to,' said Marie. She had done another big wall and now had so much paint and plaster dust in her hair that she was looking prematurely grey, but Iona could tell from her shiny eyes that she was on some kind of weird high. A high unlikely to be derived from power tools.

'But I'm knackered!' whined Jim. 'I've had a busy week. I've been—'

'For God's sake, Jim, you're the one who came up with the figures we're working from! If we don't open those doors again to paying punters as soon as is humanly possible . . .'

'Yeah, yeah, yeah.' Jim rubbed his eyes. 'Yeah, yeah, yeah, yeah, yeah. Can we take it in turns to sleep in the corner?'

'No sleep till Brooklyn. As Posh Spice would say.'

'You are a slave driver.'

Marie toyed with an extension cable and said, 'Far be it from me to introduce a sour note into proceedings, but there are only four of us here and apart from the four lovely professionals who will be arriving in a few hours to demonstrate exactly what we've been doing wrong, could we not call upon some assistance from our friends? I understand that Tamara is no stranger to a Black and Decker Workmate.'

'That's an evil slur,' said Angus, poker-faced. 'And you didn't hear it from me.'

'Very good point,' said Iona, reaching for her mobile phone. 'Very good point indeed. Besides, when I tell her we're all over here without much to talk about, she's bound to whiz round just to stop us getting into a good bitch session about her.' She dialled and started listening.

'That would get me over in ten seconds,' Marie said.

'Ned said he'd come over as soon as his shift finished,' Iona added. 'And he'll, er, be a little bit more wide awake than we are. Which could be a good idea in the circs.'

Marie and Jim exchanged glances. They were unlikely to get anything stronger than Red Bull past Angus. He raised an eyebrow and she raised one back. Before they could get into the eyebrow semaphore for 'Don't fancy going into a pub round here and trying to score much', Iona waved her arms around to signal that she'd got hold of Tamara.

'Tam! It's Iona. We're at the pub. No, the pub we're redecorating. Have you finished your osteopath appointment yet? Your *osteopath*?'

'So she cancelled her friend with the gallery opening in Bow?' Jim asked Marie in an innocent whisper. 'She told me she was—'

'If you don't wake up and smell the coffee soon, Jim, I'm going to put your head in the percolator,' Marie muttered back.

'Well, that's *very* late for an osteopath,' said Iona. 'Are you sure he's properly qualified? Oh. Oh, right. He's seeing you at *home*. Tamara? You'll have to shout up a bit, pet, it almost sounds like you're in a restaurant!'

'Fancy that,' murmured Angus.

'Yes, I can *see* how stripping wallpaper would put your back straight out again, yes, but you could come along and keep us company,' Iona persisted. 'Angus says we'll be here all night . . .'

'Ned, Ned,' muttered Angus in her other ear, as Tamara's muffled voice went off on a long explanation. Iona pulled a 'What?!' face at him. 'Mention Ned.'

'Who's we? Er, me, Angus, Jim and Marie and, oh yeah, I think *Ned's* coming over when he's . . . Oh, well, then, that would kill two birds with one stone, wouldn't it? We'll see you then then.' Iona's face registered 'surprise' then real confusion. 'Who? Chris? Um, no, he's . . .' Her eyes flicked over to where Marie was sitting, biting paint out of her nails, and her voice dropped unconsciously. 'I don't know if he's . . . OK, fine, we'll let you in when you . . . OK, fine, if that's the bill coming . . . Yes, the osteopath's bill, of course . . . Bye.'

Iona checked that the call was disconnected and looked

up at everyone. 'She's having her lower back manipulated at the moment, but as soon as the petits fours arrive, she's going to come over, via the Uxbridge, and pick up Ned.'

'Hmm, convenient,' said Angus and Marie, simultaneously putting their fingers on their chins.

'You want to call Chris, let him know where you are?' Iona offered her phone to Marie.

Marie noted that she had not said, 'And see if he wants to come over to help.'

'Might as well,' she said. Might as well keep up the pretence, in front of the lads. The lads who still thought The Crazy Davenports were a comedy double act to rival The Two Ronnies and who wouldn't notice a marital breakdown if the RAC arrived to fix it.

The phone rang and rang at home, as she knew it would. A heavy weight rolled around in the pit of her stomach, just as her mind was telling her that at least this was better than him being at home and raging piously about her unexplained absence and the washing machine full of shirts that she hadn't been home to empty and which would now be nicely perfumed with mildew.

'Not in,' she announced, when she heard her own voice on the answering machine. There were no messages, from him or from whoever he was out with now.

A small, cowardly part of her was glad that the inevitable confrontation had been delayed once again.

Iona gave her another sympathetic look when she was sure that Angus and Jim were busy squabbling over the floor plans.

'Good,' said Marie breezily. 'OK, pass me that scraper.'

Ned arrived half an hour later, on his own and with a bag full of Red Bull which he had 'borrowed' from work.

'No Tamara?' asked Jim, with what Iona hoped wasn't disappointment in his voice.

'Tamara?'

'She was going to pick you up from the pub on her scooter. After her osteopathy appointment.'

Ned raised his eyebrows. 'I've not seen her all night. Mind you, I knocked off about an hour ago and went for a late-doors pint with a couple of mates from the kitchen, so . . .'

'Ah, that'll be it then,' said Iona. 'She'll have shown up, seen you'd gone, and not wanted to risk putting her back out and making herself unavailable for opening night next week by coming over here to help with the decorating. Thoughtful.'

Ned shrugged his eyebrows and shoulders simultaneously and gave Iona a secret grin. 'Can't be doing with girls who worry about putting their backs out. Shows a lack of adventure.'

'Ned!' No wonder Tamara was so completely lust-dazed about him, thought Iona. He was probably the only man she ever met who didn't care whether the person he was talking to fancied him or not. If she didn't know him so well, even she would think it had to be a carefully constructed act, but he gave off the hypnotically sexy impression that he really didn't have any idea how attractive he was. All he cared about was whether you appreciated his bearnaise sauce.

But then Iona had always thought that that was Tamara's problem too: she honestly had no idea what she did to men. Tamara's was the sort of offhand beauty which disarranged the rational part of men's brains, then disarranged their lives without her noticing – but whereas Ned was smart enough to realize the effect he had on his admirers, Tamara simply couldn't understand why hers left their girlfriends, which she hadn't noticed they'd got, and turned up on her doorstep wanting to move in. She was the sort of girl who could go from object of deified desire to object of total loathing in ten seconds – the ten seconds in which she finally noticed the poor sod had fallen in love with her and she freaked out at him.

'Stop thinking about putting your back out, you little hoor.'

Ned was still grinning at her like a co-conspirator. She batted him on his shoulder and reached over into his bag for a can of Red Bull. It was pathetic. Ned only had to wink to make her smile back, even if deep down she was wishing that he'd knock Tamara's crush on the head before something bad happened. And that Tamara would knock Jim's crush on the head before something even worse happened. Not for the first time, Iona privately reflected how unfair it was that beauty should be dished out so randomly to maladjusted women who couldn't deal with it. It should come with a licence, like a handgun, or a Rottweiler. At least Ned had the sense to make his excuses when he saw they were necessary. Though frequently such displays of gentlemanliness only made things worse with the terminally smitten.

Bloody northern charm, thought Iona. Thank God I'm immune.

They worked on through the night, with no sign of Tamara, until finally Ned, Iona and Angus were all concentrated on the final stretch of wallpaper, which, being in the regulars' corner, seemed to have been welded to the wall by constant exposure to unknown pollutants.

At half-two Marie had suddenly fallen asleep in a corner, curled up on some dustsheets. Up to that point, she had worked as if she was possessed by the entire *Home Front* team, singing loudly and gyrating all the while. Now she was flaked out in a ball, with her hands wrapped defensively around her head, as if to ward off some unexpected blow. She didn't wake when Iona pulled off her boots, and she noticed that Marie had ruined her beautiful red nails without a single whine. The way she'd been going at the wallpaper, she may not even have noticed herself.

They had all drunk freely of Red Bull and when that ran

out, Ned had gone over to Jim's flat and brought his own
espresso machine over, which Iona took as a further sign
that Ned and Jim were back together, in flatmate terms.
Where Ned's kitchen equipment lived, he lived, regardless
of where his duvet nominally was.

In an unusually wired state, Angus and Jim had been
outlining to each other exactly how successful the pub
was going to be, and Ned, who sounded as though he
was chilling out as fast as they were speeding up, had
run through some of the menus he had in mind for the
first few weeks, until Marie, clutching her stomach, had
begged him to stop. In an attempt to stop herself going
mental from caffeine overload and arm ache, for the past
hour Iona had been conducting a silent interview with
herself and a journalist from *Rolling Stone* about what
it felt like to share her life with guitar maestro Jimmy
Page.

'And that is *it*!' Angus prised off the last of the paper.

They stood back to admire what they'd done.

There wasn't really much to admire.

The big main area of the pub looked much bigger without
the dark paper, and much smaller at the same time, with the
dustsheets making dirty puddles in the corners. Angus had
taken down the boards which covered some of the lower
windows, and scrubbed some of the filth away, and now
orange streetlight filtered in and bounced off the brass
rails of the bar. The effect was dramatic. Iona could see
now how the dark paper had absorbed any natural light
and already the bare walls were reflecting much better.
They were also reflecting the dirt brilliantly. And if they'd
thought it was dirty before . . . The whole place looked like
a Hollywood actress without her make-up. Or indeed her
support underwear.

A sinking feeling gripped Iona's lower body: a much
bigger version of the sinking feeling she'd had when she
and Angus had knocked down a wall in their flat and

wondered why the electricity had gone off. We've ripped all this stuff down, she thought, and . . .

'I don't know about you,' said Ned, before she could voice her panic, 'but I could eat a raw cow off the bone.'

'Very good!' bellowed Angus. 'Food! Great idea!'

'Remind me never to give you stimulating drinks again,' said Iona. 'You've turned into Field Marshal Haig with a power drill.'

Jim stopped staring worriedly at the walls. 'Before you say anything,' he said, biting a hangnail, 'there's nothing to eat in the flat. Sorry. I meant to go out and buy stuff, but I've been so busy at work I just forgot.'

'Not even for our *Ready Steady Cook* friend here?' barked Angus. 'A carrot? A pint of milk? A tin of sweetcorn?'

'Not even any milk.'

'You're such a bloke,' said Iona, 'never having milk. Is it part of your plan to make women feel sorry for you and move in to sort your life out?'

Jim was tapping nervously on the walls like a diffident spirit in search of Doris Stokes and didn't reply.

'Anyway, I don't feel like cooking any more tonight,' said Ned. 'Let's go out and find takeaway.'

'Very good!' Angus flexed his fingers. 'Might as well get started on some more sanding while I still feel up to it!'

'Yes, er, good idea,' said Iona. 'I'll come with you, Ned.'

Ned jangled his pockets. 'And you're in for a treat, bonny lass, because I've got the car.'

Ned's Mini was in and out of the garage more often than a Kwik-Fit fitter's overalls. Often because he simply forgot where he was meant to put oil in.

'I *am* honoured.'

Angus broke off from refitting his sander and gave Ned a hard look.

'You are fit to drive, aren't you, Ned?' said Iona quickly before Angus could ask.

'Me? Oh, fine, yeah. Do you want me to do a straight line for you, Angus?'

'Bit of an unfortunate choice of words, isn't it?'

Ned rammed his hands into his back pockets. 'I don't do that.'

Angus raised an eyebrow which clearly said, 'Noooooo?'

'Angus, it's three in the morning, there's nothing on the roads and we're only going to the nearest takeaway.' Iona realized that this sounded like plea-bargaining and added, 'Ned's fine. Aren't you? Besides, I can watch him do gear changes and everything. It'll be practice.'

A cloud went over Angus's brow and she kicked herself for even putting the idea in his head.

'Angus mate, apart from four cans of Red Bull and a pint at midnight, I swear I'm absolutely sober.'

'Be careful,' said Angus, pointing his sander at Ned like a stun gun. 'I can always get another chef. She's irreplaceable.'

Ned held up his hands. 'You're telling me.'

Getting back took a little longer than planned, since not much was open and they took it in turns to reject out of hand whatever suggestion the other made, and by the time they had driven east in a straight line, on pleasantly empty roads, with Ned's car radio working for the first time in about four years, it seemed like a good idea to go to the all-night bagel bakery in Brick Lane, where Iona queued behind fifteen cabbies and loaded up her shopper with smoked salmon bagels, still soft and pliant from the oven.

They scoffed the warm baked cheesecake out of the bag on the way back and agreed not to tell Angus that they'd bought any.

'Lights are still on,' said Ned, pulling up outside. 'Don't ever let your man take drugs. He'd invade Poland and repaper it.'

'I think you'll find that I would do the actual invading and he would shout at me from time to time to get the tank divisions' ironing in.'

Ned twisted round in his seat. 'Iona, will you stop talking like a housewife! You think Michelangelo kept having to stop painting to unload the dishwasher?'

Iona said nothing, because she knew from experience that whenever she tried to be flippant about the organization of living with Angus, Tamara in particular managed to twist it into an admission that she lived as a Filipino slave in the cellar.

'Look, forget I said that.' She made a final gesture with her hands. 'Just because you and Jim are content to live in squalor doesn't mean that all cohabiting couples have the same arrangements. We share housework, OK?' Iona shook her head. 'Why am I even discussing this with you at this kind of hour? I must be getting boring.'

'Iona, please tell me he's not getting you to learn to drive because you're . . .' Ned gave her a close look.

'Because I'm what? I wish people would just say what they mean instead of making me guess all the time,' she said testily.

He opened his mouth, then shut it. 'Because you're ridiculously old to be a learner? That'll be it.'

'Well, he's certainly keen enough for me to do it. I sometimes wonder if he's selling the whole experience to Carlton Television.' Iona undid her seat-belt and removed all evidence of cheesecake from the bagel bag. 'I'd check the car for hidden cameras if I were you. He's got you all lined up as practice tutors. Drugs tests and licence points permitting, of course.'

'I don't mind taking you out,' said Ned, patting the fluffy steering wheel. 'You wouldn't have any trouble getting insured to drive this.'

As if for illustration, the radio suddenly stopped working and the interior lights went off.

'Yeessss,' said Iona, in her best Angus impression. 'I'll get back to you about that then.'

Ned fiddled in a practised way with the leads, shaking them about randomly until the radio came on again. 'Suit yourself. I'm about the only person you know who wouldn't have a coronary, though. And I can teach you how to do handbrake turns.'

'You don't know how to do handbrake turns.'

'You remember that big car park by the Sheepmount Stadium?'

'I do. Or rather I don't. Can we go in now? You're scaring me.'

Inside, there was initially no sign of Jim and Angus. There were, however, a series of strange symbols on the walls in black marker.

'Get away,' said Ned, running his fingers over the arrows and sketched capitals. 'We've been burgled by the Rock Steady Crew.'

'What's going on?'

Ned put his finger to her lips as the sound of impassioned conversation started again from the other side of the horse-shoe bar.

'OK, so I think that we should take out this wall and that would lighten things up a bit.'

'Right.' There was the sound of felt tip squeaking on plaster. 'And you could put in lights *here*, which would take out that slimy thing.'

Iona pulled a disbelieving face at Ned. He pointed to the nearest wall marking, which read, 'Fab. lighting FX to go here.'

She turned round and pointed to 'Nasty stuff to be removed'.

'Oh, Christ, Angus,' came Jim's voice after a pause. It was higher than normal and bordered on the hysterical. 'Christ, Christ, Christ!' Then there was a thumping sound, which

Iona assumed was Jim's head hitting the wall. 'This is all horrible. The whole pub is horrible. We've made a terrible mistake. It looks even worse than it did with all the shit in it.'

Ned and Iona nodded at each other frankly.

'Nooooo,' bellowed Angus, clearly still under the effects of caffeine overdose. 'We'll just put in some . . . stuff here.' More squeaking of the pen.

'Ang, these builders are going to take one look at this place and just laugh at us, mate!'

'Oh, very good!' Squeak, squeak. 'Will you just shut up and start thinking positive for once in your life?'

Even without seeing him, Iona knew exactly which expression would be on Angus's face as he said this.

Ned nodded vigorously and pointed to 'customer overflow area to go here'.

'Now, where do you want the wine cave to go, eh?'

Ned picked up a red pen Angus had left behind when he was delineating the 'new' door. Iona assumed this was for the benefit of the builders, since there was nothing wrong with the door, and she didn't imagine they would be allowed to do anything with it even if there was. However, it wouldn't do the builders any harm to know they had Ambitions.

'Stand here so I can draw round you,' Ned instructed in a whisper.

'Why?'

'You're a happy customer. I'm drawing you in. That's great, where you are. Now, can you lift your left hand like you're drinking a pint, please? Fantastic . . .'

Iona shifted and giggled as he drew between the legs of her jeans. 'You're going to make me look as though I'm . . . Ned!' She stopped and laughed.

Ned, crouching to outline her boots, held a finger to his lips and nodded his head towards the other side of the bar, where Angus and Jim were now agonizing frenetically about telephone sockets. Iona forced herself not to look down.

'Are you not worried about the state of the kitchens?' she asked in a whisper. He shook his head. 'Shouldn't you be?'

'I know the guys who are going to come in and do them. They're quick and good, and I know Jim has spent a lot of money on decent equipment, so . . .' Ned shrugged. 'You can't worry about everything, can you?' He stood up, but continued in the same low voice. He was giving her his serious look, and Iona knew, uncomfortably, from experience, that this was a dig at her, in a throwaway disguise. 'You tell people what you need, where you need it and let them get on with sorting it out. I mean, someone orders steak and chips in the restaurant, they don't follow me into the kitchen to check I'm doing it rare enough, do they?'

'No.' Iona took the pen off him and added the outline of a small dog, cocking its leg next to her outline.

'Just because you give people advice doesn't mean you have to take it for them,' Ned persisted in an undertone.

'Thank you, thank you,' said Iona. 'I get the picture.'

'Sometimes them as give advice,' said Ned in a thick Carlisle accent, 'are the wust at tekkin' it.'

'Your granny.'

'Herself.'

'By, it's a long time since I've heard from your granny,' retorted Iona, feeling unreasonably stung. 'Just think what you could have made of yourself if you'd taken half the advice you passed on to me from her.'

'I'm just saying.' Ned lifted his hands. 'You start wading into Marie's life to sort it out for her and it won't just be her and Chris getting a divorce.' But before she could reply to that, or demand to know how he knew about Marie, or even, heaven forbid, why he thought she and Angus were married, he was slipping away round the corner, as light and lithe and silent as a cat in his battered Converse trainers.

Iona rubbed her tired eyes for a minute, as an excuse to

recover from what he'd said. Ned rarely bothered to interfere in or comment on anyone's life. In fact, most of the time he gave off the distinct impression that he didn't actually notice what was going on; a tactic, Iona thought, and a pretty useful one, as tactics went.

But when she tried to organize her thoughts, she found she was too tired to work out what was lurking behind Ned's unusual interest, since all the instincts in her brain were telling her to lie down and sleep.

And when she stumbled round the corner (now enigmatically labelled 'Snug here' in Jim's erratic capitals, with intricate but hasty partitions criss-crossing the wall) Marie was still snoring away as she had been when they left her earlier, while Ned drew carefully round her curved and inert outline, having sketched a meaningful line of pint glasses next to her.

At that point it seemed logical to draw round Ned, in darts-throwing pose, to illustrate the ironic facilities Tamara was planning, and frankly either there must have been something in the biscuits she'd found underneath the passenger seat of his Mini or her caffeine tolerance was seriously shot, because it followed on as totally essential to draw a wardrobe with 'Passage to the other world to go here' next to Marie, who didn't wake up despite their badly muffled sniggering.

When Jim discovered them beginning an outline of Mad Boy Sam on his bar stool, it was only the sudden lighting breakdown crisis in the cellar that stopped Angus braining them both with a Black and Decker Strip Mate.

Chapter Fifteen

As promised, the decorators crashed in during the very small hours of Saturday morning. Iona and Marie (who had woken up with a migraine and mysterious red pen marks on her jeans) beat a hasty retreat, and after about three hours of thrash metal and asides about wallpaper paste delivered in an impenetrable garble which always seemed to end in a question mark, Jim and Angus left too and let them get on with it. They were a crack team, though Iona suspected that there was more of a speed feel to them than anything else.

The only minor hiccup in this otherwise seamless arrangement arose when Tamara arrived on her scooter at eleven on Saturday morning to see how they were getting on with implementing her plans for a pub apparently created entirely from easy-roll royal icing. Seeing that the place was full of builders, she had dragged Jim out of bed for protection before she went in; Ned had been skulking around the kitchen eating bacon sandwiches, but had disappeared as soon as Tamara hammered on the back window.

Jim hastily tied up his scraggy bathrobe as he staggered through to answer the window. He'd often thought Tamara had found the ultimate form of travel on her scooter, since it meant she could lift off the very bloke-ish helmet and shake out her mane of golden hair every time she arrived at her destination, in the manner of a 'gender-bending' shampoo advert. His pulse quickened when he realized she had waited until she was in the kitchen before doing just that.

He was scurrying round, rinsing out some cups for coffee

(anything to stall her from seeing the pub in its current state) and still thinking about the beautiful fountain of Timotei hair when she casually delivered her first question.

'Where's Ned?' Her short fingernails clicked on the helmet.

It was to be the first of many questions that morning, most of which would begin with 'Why?'

'Er, seeing a fishmonger? He said something about talking to some people about kitchen jobs today.' Interviewing was perhaps too strong a word for Ned's approach to the staff issue.

'And when *is* the kitchen arriving?'

Jim slopped some coffee on to the table and, once Tamara's attention was diverted by some unopened mail, wiped it up with a spare pair of cleanish pants that were waiting to go into the wash.

'The kitchen fitters are coming in as soon as the decorators leave on Sunday night. Is the plan.'

Tamara hmmmed, put down the letters and got out her notebook. 'I gave Angus a copy of my decorating schematic to give to the builders. Did they get it?'

Jim swallowed. It was so hard to lie to someone he so wanted to impress. He was good at outrageous lies, being essentially an estate agent, but very bad at small ones. It also seemed rather unfair that Tamara had the monopoly on questions and he was getting stitched up on the answer front.

'I know Angus gave them some plans, so they might have been yours, yes. Biscuit?'

'No, thanks, I'm only eating raw vegetables at the moment. And coffee.' An involuntary twitch made her blink a couple of times. Tamara could give up meat and dairy products and alcohol for the sake of her detox programme, but she could not give up coffee. Caffeine was the only thing distracting her from the lack of white wine in her system. 'What kind of coffee is this? Is it organic?'

When Jim could delay her no longer, which coincided nicely with Tamara's realization that the front door slamming probably meant that Ned was no longer in the flat, they walked over to the Bunch of Grapes, Tamara's long legs striding in front, Jim hanging back slightly so he could fully appreciate her Emma Peel leather catsuit.

Tamara didn't see the funny side of the instructive graffiti, which even Jim could have predicted, but then she hadn't had the benefit of all the artificial stimulants they had had the night before either. In fact, her first reaction was one of ominous silence.

'Y'areet, pet?' inquired one of Ned's mates, whom Jim had learned earlier was called Lewty. Most of them seemed to be called Lewty as far as he could work out.

She just stared at him and said, 'Will this show through white paint?' She flicked Ned's bulbous outline rendition of Iona on the first wall in with her finger.

'Nah,' said the decorator rather too quickly, then added, 'Mind, that won't matter, willit, since we're papering an' all.' He waved a paste brush by way of illustration.

'Nice paper too, eh?' observed another one, slopping up some paste in a bucket. 'That'll've set yer back a bit, eh?'

'Paper?' Tamara did a double take and flinched. 'Jim.'

She didn't need to say any more until they were both safely out of earshot on the pavement.

Then she said quite a lot.

'You told her what?' Iona demanded when Jim turned up forlornly at their flat some time later. Angus had gone to have another last-minute question and answer session with Brian about maintaining cost-effective stock levels before the taxi arrived to whisk Brian and Lois to their bungalow of paradise, via Stansted Airport. Iona imagined they would be *very* pleased to see him.

'I had to tell her *something*! She was going spare right

there in front of Lewty and his mates about how she hadn't spent hours creating architectural plans for perfect white walls to have someone screw the whole thing up with the Laura Ashley Home Decorating Catalogue. I was *scared*.'

'Oh, thanks.'

'She didn't mention names.' Jim helped himself to a chocolate Hobnob, wedging it into his mouth without biting it. 'She probably thought they'd decided to do it themselves. Or that Angus and I had suggested it,' he added indistinctly. His cheeks bulged outwards, like a hamster swallowing a plate.

'Nice try, Jim lad, but I don't think so, as they say on *Jerry Springer*.'

'You watch too much of that stuff.' Crumbs sprayed from his mouth and scattered on the table. 'Too much trailer trash isn't good for you.'

'It's light relief from you lot. They don't eat my biscuits and they don't ask for answers. And I can switch them off when they start fighting.' Iona sighed and emptied more dried pasta twists into the pan. 'You staying for your tea then?'

Jim looked at his watch and hesitated. 'I think Ned might be cooking something, but I don't know. What are you making?'

'Just bolognese. I'd hold out for Ned if I were you. He was muttering something about a new lime marinade earlier.'

'Don't know when he's getting in.' Jim dislodged a sleeping cat from one of the chairs round Iona's messy kitchen table. 'Jeez! Feel the weight of that! What do you feed those animals, Iona? Body-building milkshakes? Anyway, he said he was going to see one of his suppliers.'

'Oh, really?' Iona stopped crushing garlic and arched an eyebrow. 'Don't tell Angus.'

'*Fish!*' huffed Jim. 'One of his *fish* suppliers down at Billingsgate! God, moral majority or what? Ned isn't . . .'

Iona said nothing but calmly added some salt to the pan and poured boiling water over the pasta.

Jim prised another chocolate Hobnob out of the packet and wedged it into his mouth.

'So, come on, don't tell me half a tale.' She turned up the gas ring. 'Has Tamara freaked out and ripped off the paper with her nails then?'

'She calmed down eventually, sort of. I got Ned to talk to her. Well, she demanded I phone him up. She's in charge of the kitchen redecoration. Ned says it can be as white as she likes.'

'And the loos?'

'Still up to Marie.'

Iona imagined the loos of the Grapes were either Marie's first or her absolute last priority at the moment, and she sucked the inside of her cheek thoughtfully while she shredded the basil for the sauce.

'I should get back,' said Jim suddenly, and left.

By Sunday night, the entire bar-room of the Bunch of Grapes was completely papered in deep red wallpaper, with gold fleur-de-lis details. Tamara was slightly mollified once Iona showed her all the historical research she'd done into period pub décor. And once two of the Lewtys had demonstrated exactly how many coats of white paint it would require to obliterate Iona's lumpen silhouette from the door, which hovered like a ghostly 'You have to be this tall to drink here' fairground sign.

Angus and his DIY crowbar had discovered windows where no one had ever suspected light could fall, and the weak sunshine made the place much airier than anyone could have reasonably expected. With the stained glass Jim had found in a salvage shop, it would be almost church-like. As long as it stayed empty. Already, with a good clean, the breathing air in the place seemed freer of dust. Tamara pointed out that you no longer had to inhale someone else's pint with your own. All the paintwork was shining, creamy white, Jim had got one of his architectural salvage people to source some glazed tiles for the fireplace and the elaborately organic plasterwork on the ceiling was restored to something approaching fresh. The rest – lights, gildings, mirrors, carpet, tables and chairs – had to wait until the kitchen was sorted out.

And Ned was sorting out the kitchen faster than anyone believed possible.

The decorators departed for Carlisle at around two on Monday morning, cash in hand and glowing with the satisfaction of a job well done. The kitchen installers arrived at nine the same morning. Jim had been prowling around throughout the weekend, observing and checking nervously, not wanting to get in anyone's way, but unable to leave for more than half an hour.

He went over to the pub at half-nine, having established that he wasn't needed at the office, and found Ned already there, organizing the workmen fitting the state-of-the-art kitchen, who were transferring the contents of two large vans into the designated kitchen area and marking things out with chalk. There was a dustbin full of ice by the bar, with three dozen cans of Diet Coke in it, and it seemed that the Carlisle lads had wired up the ailing stereo again, because it was working loudly and spreading the Black Crowes through the whole pub. Ned actually seemed to be making a list.

Jim rubbed his eyes and wondered if this was some kind of hallucination. He rarely saw Ned up by ten, let alone issuing precise instructions and questions at the same time.

'They're going to get all that in there?' he asked doubtfully.

Ned cracked open a can of Diet Coke and drank about half of it in one go. 'Jim, you hired these lads. You're meant to have answers to questions like that.'

'Yeah, right.' Jim rubbed his eyes again. Sometimes it was hard to make the leap of faith from employing people to do things to believing they would actually do it. Angus was much better at that. But then Angus was much better at making origami men out of them when it didn't happen.

'I'm going to see some people today,' Ned went on, finishing the rest of the can, his scrawny Adam's apple bobbing as the liquid went down. 'Aaahh. About starting here as soon as it's done. When d'you reckon that'll be?'

Jim tried to sound like Angus, as far as he could. 'We've timetabled to open at the beginning of next month. Which doesn't give you long to try things out, I know, but we might as well make mistakes as we go along before all the regulars find another pub to drink in.'

Ned pulled a face. 'Well, it's not ideal, like, but if that's the way it's got to be . . .'

'They are good, these fitters,' said Jim earnestly. 'Over-world have used them before for pub conversions. I went and looked at some of the places they've done. And you went through the plans with them, didn't you? I mean, it *is* going to work out and—'

Ned rested a hand on Jim's shoulder. 'Jim lad, go home, make yourself some breakfast and calm down, willya?'

They pressed themselves against the wall as a stainless-steel work surface went past.

'I'm just, you know, a bit stressed,' said Jim quietly.

'You're stressed, I'm stressed, we're all stressed,' Ned replied in a bad Yiddish accent. 'Well, actually, no, I'm not stressed. But I am taking a day off work to interview people with Angus, so I could well be stressed by the end of the day. Especially if— Oh, Jesus, you only have to think of her and she bloody appears. What is she, some kind of witch?'

Jim turned to see what Ned was staring at and saw Tamara through the newly translucent leaded windows at the front. She was wearing what looked suspiciously like full leathers and still had her biker's helmet on as she peered in to see who was there and consequently was doing a good impression of a bank robber. Then a huge sink went past and she disappeared from view.

'It's not as though I'm saying I'm irresistible,' said Ned out of the corner of his mouth, 'but she is turning into some kind of stalker.'

'It might not be you she's turning up to see,' said Jim staunchly.

Ned looked at his flatmate in surprise and then mentally slapped his head. Jim's blind spot.

'Look, Jim lad,' he began, but was interrupted by a tall blond man wandering into the pub, gazing around him as though it was the first pub he'd ever seen. His scruffy jeans and could-be-retro, could-be-bad-taste shirt made him look like one of the regulars and Jim automatically stepped over to kick him out.

'Ah right,' said the man, extending a hand to shake. 'You must be Ned? I'm Gabriel. Here for the kitchen interview?'

He had an accent that Jim couldn't work out and looked far too muscled to be a chef. His handshake was like a blood-pressure test.

Jim found he couldn't actually release his hand, but nodded towards Ned, who was rummaging in his rucksack for something, Jim didn't want to know what. 'Ned, your staff are arriving.'

Ned stood up and seemed to recognize him. 'Ah right, Gabriel, I'm Ned,' he said, extending a hand. 'Ta for coming.'

Jim flinched on Ned's behalf as the tanned fingercrusher engulfed Ned's delicate guitar-playing fingers and squeezed.

Incredibly, there was no sign of pain on Ned's face. Jim was yet again impressed by Ned's seemingly sky-high pain threshold.

'No worries. See things are still a bit in progress round here.'

'We're having the whole kitchen refitted,' said Jim, feeling that in Angus's absence he ought to provide a suitably Angusy response. As opposed to his own response, which was still to kick the guy out.

'Do you want to grab a Coke and we'll go and sit down and go through your CV?' Ned firmly removed his hand and gestured towards a table that didn't have building materials on it.

'Great, yeah.'

Jim watched as Ned leaned over the bar to grab a pint glass for his Coke and slid his wiry frame sinuously into the nearest chair without pulling it out. Gabriel, on the other hand, seemed to ripple as he walked and his golden rock-god hair shone ludicrously healthily in the dim London sunlight. Jim suddenly felt like Brian Epstein.

'But I've got the cheque-book,' he said fiercely to himself and forced his legs to move to the table and sit down with them. Ned's impression of a business manager could only go so far and while it might be interesting to observe, it wouldn't be great if he ended up staffing the bar with people who could be relied upon for a steady supply but couldn't actually make chips.

However, try as he might to keep up with the conversation, Jim couldn't focus on anything other than Gabriel and his incredible hair and unplaceable accent. An A–Z of London pub names flashed past, along with names of chefs and managers and restaurateurs, which seemed to satisfy Ned, whose grunts of approval became more frequent. He was making notes behind the crook of his arm, hiding his paper like a schoolboy which, although Jim thought was very immature, obviously worked, because he was now dying to know what Ned was writing. Only Gabriel, legs spread wide in archetypal rock-god pose, seemed totally unconcerned.

A pause emerged in the discussion while Ned made a couple of extended notes. Gabriel suddenly turned his head and Jim, who had been trying to work out where ears fitted into the golden mane set-up, was faced with Gabriel's very blue eyes, which appeared to be asking where he fitted into the gastro-pub set-up.

'So, do you have an, erm, speciality?' Jim asked diffidently.

'Pastry.' The eyes crinkled into a smile.

'Oh, lovely,' said Jim. 'Cold hands?'

The tanned brow crinkled. 'Sorry?'

'Do you have cold hands?' Jim was teetering on the very edge of his cookery knowledge now and he hoped it wasn't showing too badly. 'My mother always used to say that you need cold hands to . . .'

Gabriel and Ned were both staring at him now.

'. . . make good pastry. Right, another Coke, anyone?'

Jim stood up too quickly and nearly overturned his chair. Clumsily, he caught it before it started to fall and then stumbled over the leg as he tried to tuck it under the table. A hot flush of embarrassment began to burn from the neck up.

Jim hated the way he fell to pieces just when he needed to be impressive. He wanted to be cool like Ned, or competent like Angus, but always ended up looking as competent as Ned and as cool as Angus.

And even Ned was looking competent at the moment, asking relevant questions about Gabriel's experience of running sous chefs, while keeping an eye on the equipment going into the kitchen area and yelling to them about drainage every so often.

A drill started up in the kitchen. Jim sighed and wondered if it was a good time to phone Angus and see where he'd got to with the suppliers. Checking the hand temperature of all the potential kitchen staff probably wasn't on Ned's list of interview requirements. The other two seemed to have forgotten he was there, which was slightly unnecessary, he thought. A bit pointed. They might at least defer to his vast experience of eating at these places.

It was only when Jim stood up to go, and nearly brained himself on a hanging rack, that he realized Tamara hadn't actually come in. Then, as he disentangled himself from the hanging rack and the two men carrying it, he saw her, standing in the doorway, blonde and pale, looking more like Marianne Faithfull than ever in her leathers, just staring at Ned and Gabriel, as if she couldn't trust herself to speak, or come any nearer.

For a second, Jim tried to persuade himself that she could be looking at him, but the angles were all wrong and the expression on her face was something he hadn't seen before. It was utter absorption, hypnotized concentration. With a heavy heart, he turned to follow her gaze, a tiny desperate voice in his head suggesting that she could be marvelling at a perfect piece of moulding picked out by the sunlight.

A shaft of sunlight was falling through one of the new high windows, catching the swirling motes of dust and framing Ned and Gabriel, their heads bent over one of Ned's scribbled sample menus. They looked incongruously glamorous in the dark pub, glamorous because they didn't care what they looked like, being illuminated by something else, a skill, a passion he didn't have, and suddenly Jim felt himself being swept away from them on a tide of resentment and inadequacy. Even as he struggled with himself to stem such old feelings, feelings he thought he'd mastered by now, he couldn't stop the little voice wishing, hoping, that it was Ned Tamara was so transfixed by, because then at least he stood a chance later on, when she discovered Ned wasn't necessarily all that she thought he was.

Immediately, he hated himself for being so mean.

But he didn't know what Gabriel was. He wouldn't even know where to start with Gabriel.

Chapter Sixteen

Marie's mobile rang at ten past eleven. Halfway through literacy hour and at a crucial point in the simile poems she was trying to create with her basically imagination-free class.

'The *moon* is *round* like a . . . ?' she was punting hopefully.

The phone rang in her bag, underneath the chair she was rocking on. It was set to *Für Elise*, so she knew it was Chris. Everyone else was *The Flight of the Bumble Bee*. Marie felt rudely invaded, and found she didn't want to think about why he would be ringing her during the day. She only left her phone on for emergencies. Still, she pushed her panic and the sound to the back of her mind, as if both could fade into the background if she tried hard enough.

'Round like . . . ?' Her eyes skimmed over the class, looking for a brief spark of response in one of them, so she could distract their attention from the ringing.

She noticed three of the lads from the slightly smarter end of the catchment area checking their school bags to see if it was their phone.

'Katie?' Katie Archer was usually good for a smart-arse comment. Marie hoped they couldn't hear the desperation creeping into her voice.

But it was obvious that the entire class was now fixated on her rucksack.

'Katie!' snapped Marie. 'The moon is round like a what?'

'Like a moon? Miss, your phone's ringing.'

'So it is. Right, I want you all to write down three things

that the moon is round like and then we'll all read them out
and see who's is the best.' Marie scrabbled in her bag, turfing
out the scruffy free-with-*Cosmo* novel she was reading, her
purse, her diary, her Walkman on to the desk.

'Starting from now,' she added, looking up to see thirty
pairs of curious eyes on her, thirty pencils in mouths, up
noses, behind ears – anywhere but applied industriously to
the page. 'And there will be house points for the best.'

Immediately they got to work. Very easily bribable, this
year, thought Marie. Maybe Tamara could cast some light
on in it astrological terms. Maybe they were all Rats or Pigs
or something.

The phone stopped ringing before she could locate it in
the mess of old notes, pens, chocolate wrappers and she
breathed a sigh of relief.

'Who are you having a one-to-one with, Miss?' floated
from the back of the classroom.

Seven-year-old titters.

'Not you, Jake,' said Marie firmly. 'My future's bright,
my future's orange. Unlike yours.' It was disturbing, their
precocity sometimes, making jokes she hoped they didn't
quite understand. Sometimes it was hard not to quip back
at adult level.

She looked at the mobile display. The call missed was
Chris's office number; the charity was too small to have a
switchboard. She thought about switching it off, but then if it
turned out to be an emergency . . . She wondered whether he
would leave a message. Whether he was calling to explain the
lunar-landscape silence of the previous evening, when he had
come in at ten past seven, sat in front of the television and
remained motionless until she went to bed, unable to stand
the atmosphere any longer, at eleven. No questions about the
pub, no questions about the pile of scrumpled-up tissues in
the bathroom and certainly no answers to her own unspoken
questions about his uncharacteristic suit-wearing.

He hadn't come to bed himself until two. As the mattress

had shifted under his weight, Marie had rolled over to her side of the bed, pretending to be asleep, and seen the luminous hands of the alarm clock. Their bodies no longer touched by accident, even when they were asleep. It was as if the bed had a Perspex screen down the middle.

'Miss?' A hand went up by the window. It was Conor Johnston. His nose was permanently crusty and he had slightly gnarled hands, all scaly and peeling. Marie knew this from the amount of time she spent laboriously reading with him. 'Miss, how do you spell . . .' His eyes cast about him suspiciously, protective of his potentially valuable simile, arm curling around his rough book. He beckoned her over with a grubby hand, while Paul Brady next to him, interest piqued, tried to sneak a look.

Almost immediately the ringing started up again.

It had to be an emergency. Maybe something had happened to him at work . . . Maybe he'd been run over . . . Maybe the Hand of God had intervened after all . . .

'Does anyone know what this tune is?' asked Marie, making her way back to her bag as quickly as she could. Panic and guilt were starting to bubble up and spread at the back of her mind.

'My nan's got it on her mobile too, Miss!'

'Is it in an advert, Miss?'

'It's called *Für Elise*,' said Marie, fumbling with the buttons. 'No, not about a car actually, Matthew. About a lady. Hello?'

'Marie, I need to talk to you very urgently.'

She was by the door now. 'Right, Katie, you're in charge, and if Mrs Simon has to come in, you *all* automatically lose *all* your house points for today, OK?'

Marie shut the door behind her and went over to the far side of the corridor, where she wouldn't be seen by any passers-by but would be able to spot any teachers barrelling out of their classrooms to suppress the inevitable riot.

'Is everything OK? What's so important that you have to

ring me in the middle of morning lessons? Couldn't you have left a message with the school secretary?' She clutched her elbow, the other hand pressing the phone right in to her ear. Marie knew she shouldn't start like this, but couldn't help it. Chris was habitually dismissive of her job, just because it didn't involve an office.

'No, I couldn't.'

Irritation began to get the upper hand over the initial panic. His voice was flat, grating, not the sound of a man in the grip of a disaster that made all conventions of politeness irrelevant. Whenever the kids' parents phoned during the day, it inevitably signalled a family crisis, unable to be contained in school hours: illness, a collapsed granny, a car crash. Marie's breath caught. Maybe Chris had some kind of serious illness, maybe he'd been hiding it from her until the check-up today, maybe that's why he didn't want her to touch him any more, maybe . . .

'Chris, you aren't in hospital, are you?'

There was a familiar tut and sigh of irritated contempt. 'No, of *course* I'm not in hospital, I'm at work. You can see that on your phone, can't you?'

Marie bit down anger that he could push aside her concern so carelessly. 'I *am* right in the middle of Literacy Hour. Can't this wait until I get home?'

There was another gust of resentment. 'You're so self-centred. I need to talk to you very urgently.'

'Well, I can't talk now.'

'I didn't mean now, I was wondering what you were doing at lunchtime.'

Marie wondered what Chris thought she had been getting up to at lunchtime in all the years she had been teaching at this school. He saw her prepare her low-fat lunchbox every night – or morning, if she was too depressed to deal with fat-free yoghurt before bed – and he saw her shove her latest trashy novel into the bag after it. There were no fancy restaurants to swan off to, not even a gym nearby.

Lunch was taken in the staff room, recovering. How much of her routine was he actually aware of?

She thought about making a snide reply, but reined herself in with some effort. 'I *imagine* I will be sitting in the staff room eating my sandwiches and perhaps doing playground duty. I don't have long though.'

'Fine, I'll meet you outside the school.' There was a pause. 'When do you have lunch?'

'Half past twelve.' Sounds of unrest were now filtering through from the classroom. Marie judged that she had about a minute to get in and nip it in the bud. 'I'll see you at half-twelve then.'

Another pause, a brief intake of breath, as if he were about to say something. Knowing him as she did, Marie guessed that Chris was on the verge of arguing out of habit, to make the arrangement suit him. But there was no arguing with school timetables, even he had to concede that.

'Half-twelve then.'

'Aren't you going to tell me what this is all about?' asked Marie. She tried to keep her voice light, but instead it sounded panicky.

Yet another pause. Whatever happened to unguarded conversation? Marie's voice yelled in her head.

'Um, let's wait until we're alone,' said Chris. 'See you then.'

'Bye . . .' Marie's voice trailed away as he hung up, and she stared out of the window into the street beyond the playground.

With a sudden vivid stab of anxiety, she remembered how she used to fear the weekly cross-country running her own school made compulsory, every Wednesday games lesson. Each week would pivot around her paralysing dread, each day special in its proximity or safety from the Wednesday afternoon misery. But the hour before it all happened was different; even now she could remember the terrible calm that would descend on her, knowing that she couldn't stop time, and that the moment furthest away from the next bout of escalating dread was four o'clock that afternoon, only a few hours away.

Never mind the small matter of the run in between.

As Marie swallowed and tried to rearrange her face back into one which would silence the rioting class next door, she acknowledged that the same calmness was spreading through her now like horse tranquillizer: whatever it was that she was so terrified of Chris saying would all be over by this afternoon.

He could do no worse than tell her. Even if it was something painful she still needed to hear it. Maybe wanted to hear it, deep down.

Marie swallowed hard.

'Right,' she yelled, pushing the door open with the flat of both palms. 'Let's have those similes, starting with . . . you, Conor!'

Chris waited at the gates, aware that he was probably giving off child molester vibes. Those two concerned-looking parents were probably calling *Crimewatch* right now, hovering around the gates with their mobiles, a pre-school child tucked under one arm their passport to being there.

He didn't have such a passport. Thank God, he added mentally. He was married to the teacher. But he didn't feel old enough for that either.

He saw Marie come bounding out of the main entrance, pulling on her tacky fake animal-print gloves. She was talking to a little girl, one of her class maybe, and stopped suddenly to retie the child's flapping hat, tucking the ends of the scarf into her collar. Chris supposed he should feel an attack of broodiness at the glimpse of his wife nurturing someone else's baby, but to be honest he didn't feel anything. It was her job, just as supplying vaccines to starving, homeless, hopeless, Godless people was his job. Of course he cared, but if there was one thing he'd learned in the last few years (and here he gave himself a bitter smile, since there was precious little else he seemed to have learned) it was that you had to separate what you felt in your private life and what you felt in your work. Or else you went mad with frustration either way.

Marie saw him standing at the gates and bent down to speak to the little girl. Rather than bending from the waist, she squatted right down so their eyes were level, and her thighs spread in her dark blue jeans. They both looked at the little group of chatting parents, the child leaning into her hip very slightly, until the girl's yellow gloves pointed at someone and Marie gave her a gentle little shove towards her mother. She really did just look like another teacher.

Then she stood up and walked towards Chris. She wasn't bounding now, he noticed.

Marie found a sandwich bar nearby, after ten minutes walking in the bracing cold.

'I don't know where there's a coffee place round here. I don't normally have time to get out,' she explained, setting off at a teacher's pace, as if there was an implicit criticism lurking in the silence.

He had been about to suggest getting a cup of tea and sitting in a park, but something in him shied away from the memories it triggered off, of a time when conversation just seemed to happen between them, instead of being mined out laboriously like coal. And Marie was pushing open the door of a noisy Italian greasy spoon.

Chris was happy to let her order the coffee for them – she knew what he liked – while he went to scare off some kids from a table by the window. He knew immediately that they'd finished their one Fanta ages ago and were now flicking toast at each other, squealing in disproportionate horror as the crumbs landed in the crevices of their green school jumpers. He had no idea how old the kids were. Could they be from Marie's school? Would she know them?

He looked up to see her threading her way through the queue for takeaway sandwiches, wiggling her hips between customers so as not to spill the coffee. She shouldn't really wear jeans, not with her stomach. Jeans were for skinny girls like Tamara. They should gape at the sides, to demonstrate a toned stomach, or be buckled up with a man's belt. Not be filled to bursting point all over, as if she could erupt at any moment. No wonder everyone was staring at Marie's arse.

'Miss,' the kids chorused as she arrived at Chris's side.

'I don't think you're meant to be here, are you?' she said, pretending to purse her lips disapprovingly.

'Is that your boyfriend, Miss?'

'Why aren't you at school, Miss?'

'Are you kicking us out, Miss?'

Chris could see Marie nibbling back a smile on her lips. 'Well, if you get back to school now, I won't tell Mrs Henderson where you spent your lunch money. But I should tell you that I did see her in the hall with her register when I came out . . .'

He noticed she didn't mention him and felt a slight chill inside.

There was a scramble to gather bags and coats together, and Chris slipped into the window seat, pulling the hot mug towards him by the handle.

'You shouldn't enable them like that,' he said.

'Like what?' Marie unwound her scarf from her neck. 'It's an age-old teacher-pupil ritual. I'm younger than their mothers. Didn't you ever bunk off out of school at lunch? At least they're going back.'

'But they're only eleven!' He swept the crumbs off the table.

'Have you never seen *Crimewatch UK*? There's a lot worse they could be up to.'

Chris let out a deep cross breath but tried to keep his temper. It wouldn't help to get into a pointless row now, even before he told her what he'd come to say. But he hated it when she got like this, leaving him with nothing that wouldn't escalate the discussion into an argument. Marie never had been able to tell the difference between an exchange of views and a personal attack. It had been fun teasing her, at first, and now it was just frustrating.

'I didn't come halfway across London to talk about modern teaching methods, Marie.'

It came out too formal, his voice too hard with concentrating, and he could see the tightness return to her face. She said nothing, sipped her coffee delicately and waited.

'Um,' he began, pressing his fingers into his temples. The lunchtime noise was making it difficult to remember the careful phrases he'd constructed on the way over. All neatly balanced like a bridge, to lead him from this horrible situation into the new, improved situation. As long as Marie didn't argue and he didn't look down.

He took a deep breath and didn't chance a look at her. 'Where to begin? Without going into too much, er, detail, the reason I've been working so late is a massive problem in Kosovo. There's been a collapse in the aid network, nothing's getting through to the supply centres, and they've had a terrible winter on top of all that. You know I've been coordinating our contribution to the multi-charity aid package that's going out.' He looked up to see how that had gone. If she'd understood.

Marie's face was unreadable and he felt a surge of annoyance that she never took these things seriously enough. 'It looks like there might be a flu epidemic. The emergency hospitals are at breaking point, and if there isn't a concerted effort for medical supplies now from developed nations, there's going to be an appalling crisis.'

'So you're going out with the charity to do aid work,' said Marie.

'Yes.' Chris's momentum dropped like a roller-coaster. He stared at her. It was freaky sometimes, how much she knew. 'How did you know?'

'I didn't know,' said Marie. 'I was guessing.' She paused. 'I'm not sure what to say. What would you like me to say? "Oh dear" seems a bit loaded in the circumstances.'

Chris looked at Marie over the table, holding her coffee cup like a child, warming her hands on it. He wasn't sure he knew what she meant. She still looked nearer eighteen than thirty, wearing the bright colours of a teacher. Her body was blooming into that of a teacher too, soft and yielding like a dairy cow. That's what she reminded him of now, a Friesian cow: milky-white skin, brown hair, huge brown eyes, swaying flanks, totally, thoroughly sub-urban.

Her ring clinked on the mug as she lifted it to sip.

His wife.

He started gabbling, raising his voice over the hubbub of lunchtime. 'I only heard this morning. The organizers phoned me at ten to say that one of their team leaders has dropped out and they need someone reasonably experienced to take over.'

'And you're experienced in aid work?'

'I did VSO in my gap year. I'm good at picking up languages— God, come on, Marie, I've already had one interview for this!'

'So it's *not* "only this morning" then. Why didn't you tell me you'd been interviewed?' asked Marie. A pained look of understanding passed across her face. 'Why didn't you tell me you were having these meetings? I thought you—' She stopped and glared at him.

He kicked himself mentally and furrowed his brow. 'I didn't tell you because I wasn't sure it would happen. And it's not the sort of thing where you can take partners. It's not some school reunion with chalets for wives, you know.'

Though this was a white lie. You could take partners, and in fact the interviewers had asked about Marie, asked whether she had any interest in teaching in the makeshift schools for displaced children. He'd said with some assurance that she was too committed to her inner-city teaching programme. That had recovered the situation nicely. The truth was he didn't want anyone with him, let alone her. He wanted to be absolutely on his own.

'Oh. Right.'

Chris tried to see what her reaction was. Now Marie knew and she hadn't gone ballistic, he wondered why he hadn't told her from the start. She seemed OK about it. Well, it was pretty obvious that she wouldn't exactly be sad to see the back of him. Someone had to get hold of the situation. And going out to Kosovo would give the pair of them some space to think. He wasn't actually sure what his own feelings were any more, now they were here, talking about it. Apart from anything else, this was the longest non-aggressive conversation they'd had in about six months.

Around them the queue pushed and shoved, shouting random ingredients at the sandwich makers, learned from New York deli scenes and made bathetic by English ingredients. 'Double Cheddar on white, no Branston!' 'Egg mayo on Hovis, hold the cress!' The initial exhilaration Chris had felt when he'd leaped at the chance to go was fading into a slightly uncomfortable sensation he couldn't pinpoint. He'd hoped she'd be impressed, at the very least delighted that he was at last able to do something practical for the charity he'd worked his fingers to the bone for. God knows he'd been stuck in that office long enough to wilt the most burning vocation.

And he wasn't going to delude himself, the opportunity of being free to travel – and more to the point, travel *on his own* – was too good to pass up. He had to go. These people needed volunteers like him more than Marie did, here with her cappuccino and her unnecessary scarf.

'Face it, Marie,' he said, emboldened by her silence and the thrill of guilt-free rucksack fantasies, 'you wouldn't want to come, would you?'

'I couldn't,' she said, staring out of the window. 'I'm going to be OFSTEDed at the end of the term.'

'You're what?'

'School inspectors.' She stirred another spoon of sugar into her coffee. 'I did tell you. It's my first inspection since I started teaching. The whole school is being assessed.' The spoon clinked slowly and deliberately round the cup.

Like an Irish navvy, he thought, unconsciously echoing his father's phrase in his irritation.

'Is that all you think about? Your job?'

'God, you've got a nerve!' Marie's head snapped up as if a restraint had broken and her eyes were hard and cold with anger. 'Can you *hear* the words coming out of your mouth? I could say exactly the same thing to you, but I haven't! What *else* do you think about *apart* from your job? Me? The flat? Our friends? Jim's pub?'

She started drumming the spoon on the table. He made to snatch it off her and she rapped him savagely on the knuckles with it.

'I'm not going to give you the satisfaction of stopping you from packing your bags to help these starving people, of course not. Who am I to stand in the way of St Christopher Davenport and his International Charity Task Force? But *don't* just turn up at lunchtime, inform me that you're leaving London for a war-torn state in the morning, without knowing when you're coming back, and expect me to say, "Oh, fine, yeah, Chris, let me know what you need ironing."'

Chris pushed himself away from the table to disguise his flinch at the razor-sharp delivery of her anger. The more words she used, fluent and flying at him, the more angry he knew she was. The total opposite of a man. When he had been able to spar with her, this kind of thing had been invigorating, but now he couldn't defend himself with words, it felt like shrewishness. He tried to rally himself with something witty, but, as usual now, nothing would come. 'Oh, control yourself. There's no need to get hysterical. You've obviously been spending too much time with seven-year-olds.'

'Well, God knows I haven't been spending much time with my husband recently!'

He saw her blink, as if in pain at her own words, and was surprised not to feel much response.

What else could he say? Chris stared out of the window at the people and buses going past. The lunchtime rush into shops and banks. All he felt was this terrible longing to go away, and it was blotting out everything else.

They both sat and listened to the jostle and chatter of the queuing office workers. Chris wondered idly what she was thinking, but realized he didn't care as much as he should.

'Are you going soon?' Marie's voice was calm, but he could tell she wasn't. He knew this calmness, indicating the very eye of a row. It meant she was holding herself under control.

'I have to go in the next forty-eight hours, yes.'

I have to go.

'They want me to fly out with some vaccines and documents,' he added, belatedly trying to take the edge off his 'I'.

'And how long do you think you'll be away for?'

At least six months, maybe a year.

'I don't know at this stage,' he lied. 'I wouldn't like to say for sure.'

'And the rent?' she went on, still dead calm. 'Are Action-Team going to pay your rent while you're out there? Because I can't afford it on my own. And council tax and stuff? And your student loan?'

Chris bridled. 'Oh, for fuck's sake, trust you to think about money at a time like this.' He let out a breath that carried all the contempt he daren't put into words.

The eyes flashed up again from the table, but her voice was still crystalline. There wasn't a trace of bovinity about

Marie now. 'No, *let's* think about it now. One, someone has to deal with money while you're racing around like Bob Geldof, and two, what do you mean, *at a time like this*? Exactly?'

'I mean . . .' Chris rolled his eyes, so he could avoid that gaze. 'I mean, at a time when we have to make some quick decisions and arrangements. At a time of crisis. God, Marie, however bad you think this is for you, think about all those poor sods out there, desperate for some aid, just to carry on living!'

Marie caught his gaze and held it for a moment longer than he felt comfortable with, and he was reminded of the girl he used to be so scared of at college, before she had opened herself up to him and led him into that core of friends who always hogged the pool table in the bar.

He swallowed the rest of his cold coffee.

'I thought that's what you meant,' she said, and Chris had the sensation of being spoken over like a child.

'Of course it's what I meant,' he went on, more confident now the rage seemed to have passed. 'What else would I mean?'

Marie played with her spoon. 'OK,' she said, and the pleasantness in her voice was an effort, he could tell, 'so you're going out with the aid workers tomorrow, and you don't know when you'll be back. You haven't asked about your financial situation meanwhile, and you don't have any details of where you'll be when you're out there. Is that it?'

'Yes.' He looked at her, and considered whether explaining the aid situation would make things worse. He knew her well enough to know that a scene in a public place couldn't be ruled out, but then they were close enough to school for it to be unlikely.

'Well, what can I say?' She lifted her eyebrows. 'You're going, aren't you?'

'I need to go,' he said.

'Yes,' she replied, and they sat and looked at each other.

Chris knew that one word over the brink and it wouldn't be the aid work they would be talking about. But it was as if an airbag had gone off in his mind: the desire to be on the plane, travelling in a place where no one spoke English and no one talked about their Christmas bonuses, was filling up his brain and nothing, *nothing*, could be allowed to jeopardize it.

Marie seemed to be doing yoga breathing. He couldn't discern any breath from her at all.

'Well.' She shrugged. 'Congratulations. You get to save the world bare-handed.'

He stared at her face, moving his eyes around each feature, trying to detect any sign of the old Marie in her, Marie Lynch who had leaped at the chance to travel with him. Marie Lynch who had agreed to be married on a beach by themselves, millions of miles from home.

'Single-handed, don't you mean?' he said, attempting a smile.

There was a flash of something in her eyes, but it wasn't anger, and for a mad second he forgot to be elated at the rare opportunity of correcting her and thought she was about to demand to come with him.

'Bare-handed,' she said, and her tone was unreadable again. 'In the manner of a horny-handed son of the earth. From Milton Keynes. Or Superman.' She glanced down at her watch. 'Look, I need to get back to school.'

Chris knew from the tone of her voice that this was exactly how she spoke to parents at open evenings. Like Angus, but confidently dispatching grades and progress reports and literacy levels. Not Marie Lynch.

They both stood up awkwardly, bumping into the tables around theirs as Marie rewrapped herself. But a warm feeling started spreading through Chris, as he realized that he'd brought up the topic he'd been dreading and, instead of going ballistic, she seemed to have taken it almost well.

And now he could get back to the office and put all the arrangements into action.

Arrangements already drafted on your computer.

He stopped walking, his own body underlining the sudden stab of guilt. He blinked and realized that Marie had stopped too, and was giving him a close look.

'Chris, one thing about this project.'

'Yeah, sure, what?' Home and dry, thought Chris, shaking himself. Part of his brain was already working out which bag he could take. If he got home before Marie, he could use the nice holdall she'd bought for them to go home to his parents last Christmas. That would hold enough and she wouldn't need it – it wasn't like she'd be going on holiday while he was away.

'Why did the man drop out? The man you're replacing?'

Chris's hand hesitated on the door. 'I don't know. I think his wife had a baby or something. Haven't you got to get back to school?'

Marie was wrapping her scarf around her neck and had her back to him. He couldn't catch what she said.

Chapter Seventeen

Confidence, Jim had encountered long ago with Angus. Angus was confident because he didn't expect things to go any differently from the way he'd planned them, and generally they didn't.

But Gabriel had something beyond confidence.

Perhaps, thought Jim, watching as Ned and Gabriel glided around the finished kitchen as if on castors, effortlessly wielding an array of cast-iron pans and narrowly missing each other like a pair of figure skaters each time, it came from cooking – knowing you could add certain things to an ingredient, spice it up, cook it for so long, and it would turn out as your instinct told you it would. That must be reassuring. Maybe you could transfer that to people as well, that skill of touch, not rationale.

He corrected himself. Gabriel *was* transferring that skill. Very well indeed. And possibly the touching as well, for all he knew.

He breathed heavily as Tamara came into view in the kitchen, unnecessarily rearranging a bristling rope of garlic by the serving hatch.

'More wine, Jim?' Marie nudged him with the bottle.

'No, no, stop that. Let me,' said Iona. She swept over from behind the bar and replenished their glasses for them.

Jim wondered sourly whether Angus had had his staff fitted with silent roller-skates.

Iona flicked her wrist expertly to stop the final drip of wine dropping on to the table and looked at the empty bottle as if she had just seen it. 'Oh, look. You've finished the bottle, you pair of lushes. Shall I bring you the wine list for the little lady to peruse?'

'I hope you're not going to speak to all your customers like that.'

'Only the ones I like.'

'Anyway, shouldn't you be showing the wine list to me?' Jim prodded the table with his finger. 'I'm the bloke. I'm the one paying for her hangover.'

Iona looked at them critically and made a note on her notepad.

'What?' Jim demanded. 'What are you writing?'

'Well, for a start, you're not her husband, are you, sir? And I also know you're driving because you've got your car keys there on the table. Oooh, big man, you've got a VW.'

'Polo,' Marie corrected, patting his hand. 'Almost. Never mind.'

'Make this place work, baby, and it could be a Z8.'

'Anyway, back in real life,' said Iona, rolling her eyes at Marie. 'You've been drinking beer all evening and you're having a steak and kidney pie and she's having lamb with flageolet beans. And also, knowing this particular customer as I do, she has expensive taste in wine when someone else is paying.'

'That's right,' beamed Marie. 'I only start looking halfway down the list.'

'That'll be why Chris is working late again, I suppose?'

Marie's eyes clouded for a second and Iona felt herself lurch forward, the same way she would instinctively reach out to stop a child running into the road. She held herself back and let her spare hand fall gently on to Marie's soft shoulder. 'Actually, Jim, international charity work doesn't knock off at half-five, unlike London property scamming.'

'Anyway,' Marie swallowed, 'when I go out with my husband, I'm only allowed half a bottle of house white, so when I'm dining on my fancy man's business account, who can blame me?'

'If you turn that wine list over, madam, you can see our extensive and very reasonable selection of sparkling wines and champagnes,' said Iona, combining her most persuasive voice and her most innocent expression.

'Oy! No!' shouted Angus from behind the bar. 'This is meant to be a dry run, not a drink the pub dry night!'

'Darling, I'm just practising my sales technique. You're the one with the "We must sell lots of wine to maximize our profit margin" campaign.'

'Yes, but you're not selling it, are you? You're pouring it down the neck of two of the most wine-absorbent people we know!'

'Oh, I'll put it on my expenses,' said Jim.

'Yeah, you big meanie,' added Marie. 'Just be grateful Tamara's now a kitchen fixture, or you'd be looking at half a case gone.'

Their eyes swivelled as one to the kitchen, where Tamara was now perched on the side of the big chest freezer, ostensibly adjusting the positions of the Amaretti tins, and coincidentally demonstrating the disproportionately long split in her mini-skirt at the same time.

'Is it me, or is that a netball skirt?' asked Iona.

'I'd send you home if you tried to do gym in that,' said Marie.

'So would I,' said Angus.

Only Jim was silent.

'There won't be room for her to carry on like that when we open,' observed Iona, without letting her eyes drop to Jim's strained face. 'Ned's got another three lads coming in from the Somerset Arms and I don't think he lets anyone who can't lift a stock-pot over the kitchen threshold when he's got full service up and running.'

They paused and watched as Tamara stretched up to reach a bunch of sun-dried tomatoes and narrowly missed it, though the split in her skirt extended by some five centimetres, revealing the full length of her lean thigh. She turned to Gabriel with an apologetic smile and he handed the tomatoes down for her, reaching the upper shelves casually and flashing a tantalizing glimpse of tanned stomach muscle as his lairy Hawaiian shirt rode up.

'Oh, very good,' said Angus. 'The mating habits of chimps. All that's really missing now is David Attenborough.'

'I'm going for a slash,' said Jim, unnecessarily loudly. 'Gippy tummy.'

'You know, the truly fascinating thing, from a psychological point of view,' Marie observed as Jim stumbled across the bar, 'is that if you asked her what on God's earth she thought she looked like, giving it leg like Ru-bloody-Paul, she would flash you that Bambi-eyed stare and ask what you were talking about. She'd probably tell you that all she was doing was advising them both on the best kind of space arrangement. She honestly has no awareness of what she's doing. Total denial.'

'Oh, come *on*,' said Angus. 'You can't believe that.'

'No, really.' Iona nodded her head in agreement. 'It's true. I've seen her. It's like sleepwalking. She doesn't have any idea what she does to blokes until they're turning up at her flat with their suitcases and decree nisis.'

'Oh, please,' spluttered Angus. 'Don't give me that "It's a girl thing" nonsense. Tamara is the most *unbelievable* flirt. I mean, look at her!'

Iona noticed that Tamara kept putting her hair in a ponytail band and then shaking it out again in a golden wave once every ten minutes or so – or whenever Gabriel was chopping something up. She decided not to point this out, as it probably wouldn't strengthen her argument much.

'She's a nice girl, yes,' Angus went on, doing his best to be generous, 'but she gives prick-teasers a bad name. Look at poor Jim. He's had a permanent hard-on for the last three years and she's never even . . .' He ground to a halt. Frankly he had little idea what someone like Iona saw in Tamara. The deal was all in Tamara's favour, as far as he could make out.

'Be worse if she had, though,' Iona pushed on regardless. 'Wouldn't it? Then you'd say she was just playing with him. God, the double standards at work in male reasoning.'

'Double standards?' said Jim, who had reappeared behind Iona's back. He had run his hands through his hair to dry them and it was sticking up in gingery tufts. He looked a bit like a barn owl. 'Great bogs, Marie, by the way.'

'Thank you. All my own work. Tamara recommended me.' Marie tipped her head on one side and looked up at Iona. 'Now, would you like me to stay in character and be an impatient customer, rather than a friend who is keen to be nice to you so she can have some cheap nights out, albeit at a location far from her home?'

'I thought that was half the point,' joked Jim.

Marie's face froze again, as if someone had paused her on video for an instant, and then reverted to its usual sardonic expression. Iona wondered if she was the only one noticing the split-second changes in Marie's face, for the brief moment when she wasn't concentrating on not showing any fracture in her personality. Something must be going on. She was sure of it now. But if Marie wasn't telling her, then it had to be something so terrible that she didn't want to talk.

And Iona knew what that was likely to be, and wasn't sure if she wanted to talk about it either.

When had they all got so touchy?

'Excuse me.' Marie pointed at Iona and spoke too loudly. 'Are you serving?' She waved her hands as if she was guiding Iona into Heathrow Airport rather than over to her table. 'I've been here since half-seven and I haven't even been offered any hot bread with unsalted butter and Maldon sea salt. What are you going to do about it? I know someone who lives near Anne Robinson from *Watchdog*, you know.'

As she spoke, Ned rapped hard on the metal serving hatch and yelled, 'Service!' at Iona.

'Go, go, go, go, go!' said Marie, pretending to set off a stopwatch.

Iona collected the big white plates, flinched and yelled, 'Ned, you bastard, you didn't tell me the plates were hot!' as she swept over to Marie's table without letting go. 'Lamb for the lovely lady, pie for the bloke. Gaaaahhhh . . .' She shook her scorched fingers and sucked them to get the feeling back.

'Aaaahhhh,' said Marie and Jim, inhaling the fragrant steam like the Bisto Kids.

'Er, hygiene?' demanded Angus.

Iona wiped her thumbmark off the plate with her bar cloth.

Tamara had selected the plates to complement Ned's scaled-down simple menu: enormous white chargers which framed the food with broad clean margins. Marie looked at the glistening beans surrounding the pinky-perfect disc of lamb, crisp parsnip wafers framing the top. They were beautiful. It was difficult to know where to start. Sudden tears percolated up like coffee from a dark part of her mind and she bit the soft inside of her lip. It didn't help. The tears still flooded her eyelashes.

'Marie, Ned must have seen you coming. You've got yellow food,' said Jim. 'Like Play-Doh.'

'Saffron mash,' explained Iona. 'Under your lamb.'

'Sounds amazing,' Marie said, dislodging some beans to inspect the mash. She thought of her sofa and the tears subsided. Romans. Literacy Hour. Monday's spelling. 'Looks amazing. *Smells* amazing.'

But in truth, she was talking theoretically. She hadn't had any appetite for three days now, and was only eating because she knew her body needed fuel to keep going. And also because she feared drinking recklessly on an empty stomach. In company.

'Well, tuck in then,' said Angus cheerily. 'Iona, can I talk to you about the glass washer?' He gestured towards the bar. 'Finally got it working.'

'I thought the idea was that we would pretend that they were customers, serve them and then share whatever Ned came up with?' said Iona, her fork hovering over the segment of lamb Marie had eased away from the silvery bone.

'Yes, but I need to show you how all this works before tomorrow morning.' He gave her a flat stare.

Iona stared back.

She didn't like Angus when he was being someone other than her boyfriend. For the first time, it dawned on her that working with him – or rather, *for* him – might not be ideal, given that she also lived *with* him and was, to all intents and purposes, married *to* him.

And if Marie was toying with her food, Iona could certainly think of someone who'd appreciate it. Someone who had been cleaning the pub and painting out the loos since nine this morning. All right, so Marie had come round after school to help her, but she'd done so much cleaning this morning she had a Mr Sheen headache.

She eyed the lamb hungrily.

In fact, she could probably tell Marie a thing or two to watch out for, as far as aerosol sniffing went.

'Iona, for God's sake, the sooner I show you this, the sooner we can have something to eat. I need to know you know what you're doing with it.'

There was something in Angus's voice that made Iona's feet automatically walk to the bar, though she was definitely still thinking about the lamb. She frowned to herself. That couldn't be good, could it?

'Budge up,' said Ned, coming over with a large plate of pie and mash. Gabriel and Tamara followed him. Gabriel had gone for the lamb and Tamara, despite her usual protestations about red meat and pastry, had a sizeable slab of pie and enough potato to feed Cork for a year.

'Are you going to eat all that?' Jim stared at her plate, reminded of all the times he'd offered to cook her a bacon sandwich and she'd practically heaved.

She looked at him with angelic astonishment glowing all over her face. 'Jim, have you *tasted* this pastry yet? It's just . . .'

'It's fantastic,' said Ned, and they all knew Ned didn't throw compliments around to other chefs. 'Fucking spot-on.'

Jim forked some pastry into his mouth. Steak and kidney was his favourite, but somehow knowing that the Golden God of the Grill had made it took the edge off the flavours. Not exactly turning it into ashes in his mouth, but certainly dampening his appetite.

'Organic beef and all organic veg,' said Ned, stealing a hunk of steaming steak from Jim's plate. 'Cooked in Jennings beer. Fabulous. You barely need to do anything to it at all.'

'Fabulous,' murmured Tamara, flashing a quick look from beneath her long lashes over the table at Gabriel.

'What is going on with Marie? She's barely touched that lamb,' said Angus from behind a pile of cloudy pint glasses. As an observation hide, glasses weren't really up there with twigs and mud. 'Do you think there's something wrong with the meat? Should I try to find out? Is she not saying anything in case she upsets Ned? Because we need to know if it's not up to scratch. I mean, we'll have to get on to the suppliers. If you don't get them whipped into shape now, we'll be getting duff meat for the rest of the year . . .'

Iona let him go on, while she watched Marie. She seemed oblivious of the drama going on around her, as Gabriel and Tamara exchanged smouldering glances like some Aryan Mutual Appreciation Society, and Jim played glumly with his mash, forking it up and flattening it down like a toddler.

Ned seemed focused purely on the food, tasting it and everyone else's, his brow furrowed in concentration.

Iona didn't mind admitting that she found that kind of passion for flavour very sexy in a man. It was one of the things that had first attracted her to Angus: his flat-out, near obsessive pursuit of perfect pesto, even at university. Iona didn't mind admitting that she hadn't seen fresh basil before the age of twenty-one, much less a pine nut.

'She's looking a bit peaky anyway,' Angus went on, skulking behind the optics. 'Don't you think? I mean, it might be that the lamb is fine, but she's not well. Hmm? Iona? Iona.'

Iona dragged her attention back to Marie. She didn't look well, but then if she mentioned anything Marie would just pass it off as a cold. More to the point, she had turned up on the dot of three-thirty, and Iona knew that school finished at half past. Marie never left early, and it took a good three-quarters of an hour to get over London at this time of day – so where had she been if she hadn't been in school?

'Iona? Are you listening to me?'

She lifted up her eyes blankly without turning round.

'Did you get the name of the meat supplier's assistant?' Angus stared more closely at her. 'Oh, never mind. Now you're sure about working this glass cleaner?'

'I thought Jim's boss was coming in too,' said Iona, fiddling dutifully with the glass cleaner, just to show willing. 'To sample the fabulous wares of Ned Lowther's kitchen and generally marvel at the transformation we've wrought on the pub of a thousand infestations.'

Angus looked at his watch. 'Martin? He was. Was meant to, that is. Called Jim at about six to say he couldn't make it. He's going to drop in tomorrow maybe, have a quick look around.'

Iona raised her eyebrows to herself. 'Well, we *must* have been doing Jim down all these years.'

'Meaning?'

'Well, no one from Overworld's been in yet to check on how things are going, have they? Jim's supervised the whole thing. And all that money!' Iona wiped the bar with one of the brand-new bar cloths delivered wholesale that morning. They were temporarily almost as white as the freshly painted ceiling. 'I'd want someone handcuffed to the bar in a supervisory capacity if I'd put up that much cash. Or at least someone on site that I really trusted.'

'Mmmm,' agreed Angus, noncommittally. 'Do you think most people know what crayfish are? Or should we just not be fancy and go with prawns?'

Iona looked at him. He was scribbling on one of Ned's sample lunch menus, jotting rough sums in the margin, with the calculator which now lived in his shirt pocket where his comb used to be. Her fingers twitched to grab the pen and over-scrawl all his calculations with the huge lump sum Overworld had paid into the pub account the previous week – she still couldn't fit the reality of that much money into her mind at once. Jim and Angus seemed pretty casual about it, and Ned didn't seem to care about finance as long as all the terrifyingly frill-free equipment in the kitchen worked.

Iona's mouth watered automatically, remembering the saffron mash. Those kind of figures scared her. They were out of her reach, dealing as she did in tips and cash deals on her paintings. It made the project serious, very serious, somehow unconnected with the kind of dabbling she was used to being part of. But for Angus . . .

A cold finger of fear traced down her spine.

Ned was banging on the metal serving hatch again.

'Service! Service! Table three! God, Iona, wakey-wakey!'

She looked up and saw Gabriel standing behind Ned, shaking a fine dust of icing sugar on to a plate of chocolate-dipped strawberries. There was another huge white plate with a gleaming crème caramel poised in the centre, sur-rounded by a pool of dark sauce and thick cream. Marie and Jim seemed to be engaged in bagging it, though with her experienced eye Iona could see Marie's heart wasn't really in it. She was making too many hand gestures for it to be real.

Angus jolted to attention and she wondered if he had noticed too.

'Honey, don't,' she said, putting a hand on his arm, 'let me talk to her . . .'

'Strawberries? In winter?' said Angus, momentarily distracted from his maths. 'No no no no no. No no no no no no. We said only English seasonal products . . .' He dropped the pen and marched round and out of the bar. 'Ned, you can't have strawberries! They're foreign!'

Iona ran to get the service.

Chapter Eighteen

'**M**orning, sweetie!'
Jimmy Page raised a long-fingered hand in farewell and slung his Gibson Les Paul over his shoulder. He blinked in the strong setting sunlight and crinkled up his crinkly brown eyes as he smiled. Iona reached out a hand to stop him going and saw that her nails had gone blue again. So had the rest of her arm.

There was some kind of shadow hovering over her. It felt far too early to be waking up. It was a Tuesday, wasn't it? She was on afternoons and evenings, Tuesdays.

Jimmy Page, who kept mutating from his 1968 rock-god incarnation into, by some cruel twist of Iona's subconscious, his current, well, less ethereal incarnation, accompanied by that one from the Yardbirds who she didn't know by name but obviously now recognized by sight, was definitely walking further away from her in the car park, both of them blurring a bit because she'd never actually seen pictures of them from behind and, shit, Jimmy Page kept morphing into her Uncle Edwin, and . . .

'Wake up and smell the coffee!'

. . . and she was still standing there at the door of the diner in a ridiculous Deep South waitress uniform, which may or may not have been a hangover from her *Twin Peaks* fixation, but which was definitely too tight and unflatteringly checked, holding a Cona jug of freshly brewed coffee, which . . .

A hand which certainly didn't belong to either Jimmy Page

or the other one from the Yardbirds pulled back the duvet and tugged on her vest.

She batted it away, trying desperately to cling on to the tail of the best dream she'd had in ages, but it was too late. Her eyes had opened in irritation and once the bright morning sunshine bouncing off her white sheets had bleached all images from her mind, there was no getting either of them back, guitars or no guitars.

She sat up and tried not to look too outraged. Angus was perched on the edge of the bed with a cafetiere of coffee and some toast balanced on the plank he'd been using to stand on while he painted the kitchen. He had even decanted some jam into a bowl and some butter on to the dish she and Marie had made when Marie was test-driving pottery as a possible year-three project. It was in the shape of a spaceship. After a succession of bad meteor collisions.

'Happy bi-ii-ii-ii-ii-rthday!' sang Angus, and spread his arms wide.

Iona discreetly picked a lump of sleep out of the corner of her eye and noticed that the bed was speckled with Cadbury's Mini Eggs. In all the late nights and early mornings of the past few weeks, for the first time in her whole life, she had genuinely forgotten about her birthday. Individual days were running into each other like so much wet paint at the moment – she honestly thought it was later in the week. So this is what it felt like to be old.

'I even waited until your exact birth time – 6.47 – to wake you up,' said Angus proudly.

Iona smiled dopily. Bless him, thought one side of her brain.

It would still have been my birthday at eight-thirty, grumbled the other. Then I could have had Jimmy Page in, or indeed on, a Cadillac *and* fresh coffee.

She opened her mouth to thank him and smelled burning. She didn't like to start her birthday by yelling at him for burning down her house, so tilted her head towards the kitchen and lifted her eyebrows. Angus slapped his head, ran back to the kitchen and returned with a stack of pancakes over which he had poured what looked like an entire bottle of maple syrup.

'Sorry, left them in the oven to keep warm while I did the toast.' He searched around for something to put them on, pulled an old blue shirt out of the laundry basket and arranged the breakfast spread on the bed. 'Very good.'

'Top breakfast, chef boy.'

'Sorry for waking you up.' He settled himself on the bed, absent-mindedly picking a couple of Mini Eggs out of his boxer shorts. 'But I've got to get off to the pub pretty early. I need to talk to Ned about lunch, and there are some deliveries coming in that I've got to check.'

'The fish people?'

Angus nodded, folded a pancake in half and put it all in his mouth at once. Ned's rage at slightly rubbish fish hadn't had the required effect on the suppliers, so the big guns were being sent in. And if Angus couldn't get results, they would have to resort to Marie.

He licked the syrup off his fingers. 'Aren't you going to demand your presents?'

'Presents? You got me presents? On my birthday?' She leaned over the side of the bed to see if there were any large boxes on the floor. Big Disney ones with large bows and air holes. 'Is it a puppy? Did you get me a puppy? Oh, go on, you did, didn't you? A tiny little puppy we can take for walks and leave in the bar so he can pee all over Tamara's ironic spittoons.'

'Better than that.' Angus grinned smugly and larded some more butter on a fourth pancake.

'There's something better than a puppy?' Iona sat up more in bed and looked round the room. No immediate signs of gifts. 'Two puppies?' She swung her legs out and padded across the room in her tartan pyjama bottoms.

'Is that the post?' said Angus, cupping one hand to his ear in a hamateur dramatic fashion.

Iona scuttled out into the hall, where there were three envelopes leaning casually against the door, apparently unaware of the deluge of bills that would be hitting them in about half an hour. She grabbed them and went back into the bedroom, where Angus was pouring the coffee, turning the thermostat up as she went. It was not warm.

'Ah, no, stop. There's an order to opening,' he said, snatching them off her and giving her a mug. 'You can have . . . this one first.'

Iona took the white envelope and snicked it open with the butter knife. There was always an order to Angus's presents. He planned them like military operations. Even the cards were sourced.

This year the card wasn't exactly festive, featuring as it did the R-101 shortly before it burst into flames, but did score highly on the topical side, especially as Angus had crossed out R-101 in silver pen and written Pb over the top.

'Oh, very good,' said Iona, wriggling her cold feet back under the duvet. 'A lead Zeppelin. And what's that?' She inspected the little card which had fallen out. 'Oh, wow! A year's free pass to the V & A! Thank you!'

'And the Science Museum and the Natural History Museum,' Angus pointed out. 'Joint adult membership. You can take Tamara. They have a great section on housework through the ages, I believe.'

Iona gave him a big hug over his coffee. 'Well, she needs to start somewhere, I suppose . . . Honey, that's so kind of you! You know I haven't been since they started the entry charges!'

For a while they had spent nearly every Sunday there when Iona first started her art course and moved in with him; Angus read the papers in the café while she tramped round the entire museum with her notebook, sketching for inspiration. Every time she saw curly ironwork railings

now, she thought of Angus. It was typically thoughtful
of him to notice that she couldn't really afford to go any
more. And even nicer to buy a present they could share,
specially since they didn't seem to have that much time to
spare these days.

'Moving swiftly on . . .' He held out the next envelope.

'There's more?'

Angus looked at his watch and made fishy flapping
movements.

Iona took the brown manila envelope and stuffed a
pancake into her mouth at the same time. The envelope
was bendy and didn't seem to have anything in it.

Angus was now looking at her with barely contained
excitement gleaming in his eyes.

Feeling a faint sense of trepidation, Iona slit open the
flap and shook out the contents. Then her faint sense of
trepidation came into full focus and started flashing on and
off for good measure.

L-plates.

'Magnetic, so you can stick them on anyone's car,' Angus
pointed out proudly.

The pancake seemed to be swelling and sticking in her
throat. And there was still another envelope.

'Thank you, darling,' she managed. 'Do you want to . . .'
She meant to say '. . . pass me the other envelope?' but the
urge to say, '. . . kill me, you bastard?!' was so strong she
clamped her lips shut and nodded at it instead.

Angus was now unable to stop grinning with delight as
he presented it to her on a pillow.

Iona tried to gather herself together as her fingers fumbled
with the flap.

It was truly sad that this was Angus's dream gift, and
her worst nightmare. She could honestly say that the idea
of learning to drive filled her with about as much excitement
as learning to stuff dead pets.

'Hurry up!' beamed Angus. 'The suspense is killing me!'

'Mmmnrph,' Iona mumbled. Her fingers seemed to have turned into sausages.

There was no logical reason why she should be so petrified about driving, especially when she was the archetypal 'cars and guitars' girl. For most of her teenage years she had lived in a strange New Jersey hinterland in her head, inhabited solely by herself and Bruce Springsteen. Her teenage fantasy had been to drive across America in a Corvette, with a loud radio and a crate of Budweiser in the back. She had never been out with anyone who had had a crap record collection or a Nissan Bluebird. And even Iona had to concede that there was, after all, only so much of a speed kick you could get while you were being driven around by other people.

But there was a much deeper survival instinct in her that made her feel physically sick every time she sat behind the wheel of a car. She was OK on the theory of why she should want to drive, and could even chip in her own genuine passion for certain sexy cars, but once behind the wheel, something animal took over and she got out again immediately. Sometimes she wondered if she'd been a crash test chimp in a past life.

'Come on, open it,' said Angus. 'Or I'll open it for you!'

Iona opened the envelope with a hairgrip, since the butter knife was now coated in Lurpak. There was another card inside, of a sharp-looking silver Jensen Interceptor. Inside that – she had stopped her hands shaking by biting her lower lip until she could feel the pulse of her blood against it – was a voucher for fifteen driving lessons.

'Though why you couldn't have done this eight years ago and got your dad to pay for it, I'll never understand,' said Angus, helping himself to the last pancake. 'You have no idea how much driving lessons cost these days. Used to be about a fiver a go when I was learning.'

'He did pay for lessons,' said Iona weakly. 'A lot of them. Anyway, there were only about ten cars on the road when you were learning.' Angus was the sort of man who had been born with a driving instinct. He had passed his test within moments of his seventeenth birthday and had been driving so long that several speeding offences had already been on and come off his licence.

'I thought there were only forty-two cars in Cumbria, full stop.' Angus slathered butter on another pancake and Iona glared at him. 'Yeah, well, the people at the driving school reckoned you should be able to do it in fifteen lessons, if you practise with us in between. First one is at the end of the week. I am officially giving you time off to attend it.'

'The end of this week?' said Iona. Her heart sank somewhere deep and dark inside her. She hadn't felt this kind of inexplicable, back-pedalling-on-the-edge-of-the-cliff reluctance since she'd found out about communal showers in her first week at school. 'But . . . I don't have the right shoes.'

'Well, far be it from me to spoil the surprise, but I think you're going shopping with Tamara this afternoon. You do have the day off, don't forget, whereas she only has this morning. So you'd better get a move on, eh?' Angus put the plank on the floor and lay down on top of her, over the duvet. His body made a pleasant dead weight on her legs.

'Don't you like your lovely presents?'

'Thank you for my lovely presents, Angus. You've spent far too much on me . . .' Iona's mind was already running way ahead, somewhere around the end of the week. Where were these lessons going to be? Surely nowhere round here? Surely? There were cars double-parked down both sides of the road.

'It's about time you learned to drive, sweetie-loo. You'll love it once you get over the initial shock.' He buried his head in the duvet over her stomach. 'Once *we* get over the initial shock.'

'I heard that. And the eight years I've been putting this moment off?'

'You'll be nicely prepared for Friday then.'

'Angus . . .' She looked at him with the best puppy eyes she could summon. They had worked nicely up to now.

'Iona,' he said firmly. 'Do you want to present *Top Gear* or not?'

'Yes,' she admitted weakly.

'Well, they're not going to push you into shot, are they?' he said conclusively. 'Coffee?'

'He means it too,' said Iona glumly. She dangled the loafers off her toe and then added them to the spreading pile of discarded shoes around her. 'He even got the L-plates.'

'Well, he has been giving you a copy of the *Highway Code* for the last four Christmases, hasn't he? I mean, it had to happen sooner or later,' said Tamara sympathetically. She was systematically working her way around the tastefully sparse shelves of LK Bennett, Iona having lost interest even more quickly than normal. 'Have you tried these ones?' She waved a toffee-coloured flat pump.

'Doesn't come in my size.' Iona regarded her long toes crossly. 'How come I have the feet of a six-foot supermodel and yet the legs of an Eastern Bloc shot-putter?'

'Northern genes. Designed for survival in cold climates. Better grip down the mines and in canal tunnels and that kind of thing.' Tamara slipped a delicate shell-pink mule on to her right foot and admired it in the mirror.

Iona slit her eyes enviously at Tamara's slim ankles, which protruded gracefully from a pair of Capri pants that Iona knew from crushing experience made her look like one of the Seven Dwarfs. Tamara had only tried them on to prove to her that they would look appalling on anyone – and they'd suited her so much she had to buy them. But, fair play, Tamara looked so incredible in them that Iona couldn't really be jealous. It was like envying red setters for having such great natural auburn tones.

'And you've got what?' she asked. 'Half southern English,

half French genes? Ideal for shopping and sitting around drinking.'

'That's about the size of it,' said Tamara cheerfully. 'Can I try a pair of these, please? In a six?' She handed the kitten heel over to the assistant and joined Iona on the plush trying-on seat. 'Cheer up. It's your birthday. And you're still not as old as Angus.'

'The first lesson's at the end of the week.'

'Where?'

'I don't know. I haven't brought myself to look at the vouchers yet.' Iona half-heartedly pushed her foot back into one of the suede loafers. It pained her to have to buy a pair of shoes and condemn them to a life of misery by association. Having to acquire a pair of flatties was bad enough, let alone shoes that someone else was buying for her as a treat. Shoes that could have been satin and frivolous. Shoes that could have been firm and comfortable for standing serving behind the bar.

'Give me your bag.' Tamara scrambled through it to find the envelope with the vouchers in. 'Your phone's ringing, by the way.'

'Well then, why don't you answer it?'

'Would you like to try anything else?' The assistant returned with Tamara's elegant mules, stepping round the pile of Iona's rejects.

'I don't think so.' Iona tried to smile, but couldn't quite manage. Everything about driving was like a big slap. Even the bloody outfit.

'It's Marie,' said Tamara, passing her the phone. 'Thank you,' she beamed, slipping the shoes out of the box and on to her feet. Small pearls of pink varnish peeped out of the open toes. 'You know, I think I could drive in these. It's a smallish heel.'

Bloody Doris Day lives, thought Iona, envying her badly. 'Hello?'

'Happy birthday!' said Marie. From the muted squeals

and yells behind her, it sounded as though she was phoning from the playground. 'I hear Angus has given you the present that goes on giving.'

'I thought that was something that Chris caught in Malawi?'

'Oh, ho ho ho. One shoe is from me, so don't fall into the chasm of self-pity going shopping with Brigitte Bardot and get anything frumpy, will you?'

Iona looked at the Capri pants next to her and marvelled that Tamara had non-spread thighs. 'She's more Doris Day today. And everything is too small. My feet are too big to drive. Why don't you phone Angus and tell him I won't be safe? My foot could spread off the brake and on to the accelerator at any moment.'

There was a gusting sigh, followed by the shrill blast of a whistle. 'Archie!' shrieked Marie. 'Get down off Charlotte right now or I'll confiscate your mobile!'

Tamara flinched as Iona held the phone away from her ear.

'Now give the phone to the shop assistant right away,' Marie went on, forgetting to change tone back for Iona.

Iona dutifully handed it over.

'Do I really need these shoes?' Tamara asked, regarding her feet plaintively. 'I'm worried that I'm starting to use shoes as a boyfriend substitute. But my wardrobe is full and my diary is empty.'

'Have you been reading *Bridget Jones* again?'

'No, *Confucius As Made Relevant to Modern Living*.'

'I think you should stick to the *Daily Mail*, Tamara love.'

'Yes,' said the shop assistant. 'Right. I think we can . . . Yes. OK. Yes, I will.' Her hand crept up to her polished hair and started twisting it nervously into ratty strands. 'Thank you. No, I won't.' She handed the phone to Iona looking shell-shocked, and almost ran into the back.

'He doesn't understand that I just don't *want* to drive,'

Iona went on sadly. 'He mistakes my interest in cars for enthusiasm to drive one myself, and just doesn't see that most of it stems from *Thunderbirds*. Lady Penelope had the fab outfits, the fab car and the fab if dilapidated faithful retainer to drive it for her while she Aralited her false eyelashes on to her face.'

'I see,' said Tamara, taking a few elegant steps and spinning confidently on one toe while observing her other foot in the mirror.

'Oh, fuck it, why don't you just buy those for yourself and get me some new mascara or something?' said Iona. 'I won't tell Marie, and face it, I'm not going to drive, so I don't really need new shoes, do I? You could get me some of those knickers that hold your stomach in. Marie would approve of those. And I need some new cleavage-free T-shirts for serving on in the pub.'

A faintly guilty, faintly excited expression flitted across Tamara's face, at exactly the same moment the assistant reappeared with a box.

'I think she's tried those ones al—' began Tamara quickly, but the assistant was shaking the tissue out of the toes with the fervour of a woman who has Been Told.

Iona took the proffered shoe: soft brown suede, studs down the back, small wedgy heel. It fitted perfectly. It even gave her a discreet lift. Incredibly it also made her feet look smaller. It was indeed a magic shoe.

'Why didn't I see this before?' she demanded, as she slipped the other one on and it fitted just as well. She practised depressing the clutch and her calf muscle started to twinge immediately.

'You did. Only it was lilac on the shelf.' Tamara gave the perfect mules one last regretful look and slipped them off. 'Unlike some, I don't know all the colour specifications off by heart.'

'Well, that'll teach me to go shopping without the oracle.'

'Oh, cheers.'

Iona stood up in the shoes and looked at herself in the long mirror at the end of the shop. 'No offence, Tamara, but she knows. She dedicates her life to it. She's an example to us all. Can we take those, please?'

'No, you're meant to go, "Bag it, charge it!" if you want to shop like Marie.'

Iona slipped off the shoes, rolled up her jeans and put her boots back on, trying not to look at her prickly shins next to Tamara's smooth skin. 'How do you find time to wax your legs?'

'I don't. I know someone very cheap in Bow who does it for me.'

'Naturally.'

'Yes, with sugar. I don't like all that chemical stuff, you never know what's in it.'

'I meant . . .' Iona began and stopped. Tamara's world was different from the one she was used to living in. It had the same basic characters, but revolved on entirely different principles. A bit like the relationship between Dallas and *Dallas.*

'Angus seems to think you can all take me out practising,' she said, zipping up her boots. 'Don't think you can escape. He's under the impression that this is some kind of a community project. Rehabilitate Iona into the world of petrol poverty and road rage.'

'Oooh, actually, now you mention it, I think I've only got a scooter licence.'

'Nice try. He says he took you out before your test.'

'Anyway, don't pretend you've refused to learn to drive because you have some kind of environmental objection.' Tamara stood up and reluctantly put the mules back on the chair. 'We all know it's because you like Angus driving you around.'

'Is not.'

Iona stopped. She did like Angus driving her around,

it was true: partly for the convenience factor and partly because it left her entirely in charge of the music selection. But recently Angus's spiralling inability to control his contempt for other road users meant that, at best, she got the full impact of his shrieking inside the car. At worst, the windows were open and everyone else did too – including the offenders. Who, to Iona's mind, if they were scary enough to drive like that without feeling paralysing guilt and shame, were probably scary enough to take badly at Angus pointing it out to them in his red Italian rally car and lovely posh voice. Which carried much further than he imagined.

Iona shuddered involuntarily. 'No, it's because I can't stand all that little-lady stuff people do when they know you're learning to drive. All that "You only learn to drive once you've passed your test" drivel.'

'But you do . . .' Tamara began.

Iona held up a hand. 'No, don't say any more. You're obviously one of them.'

'You need to talk to Marie,' said Tamara, as they left the shop and headed back down the King's Road towards Heal's so Tamara could run her hands lovingly over some beige pottery things. 'She's a terrible driver. And she's got lots of time with the school holidays coming up. *And* she lives in south London, so she could teach you a thing or two about avoiding crashes.'

'Marie is a fantastic driver,' Iona corrected her. 'She failed her test three times in two and a half months before she was eighteen and then passed after her dad took her to one of those demolition rallies in Essex somewhere.'

'I didn't want to know that.'

'Well, she's first on my list of potential tutors.'

'Chris can drive.'

'He's last on my list of potential tutors. Just before my dad and Lord Voldemort.'

Tamara gave her a look of pure pity. 'It's not hard, Iona.

Unless there's some deep-seated reason that you don't want to do it. Did your mum have a crash with you in the car? Or something like that?'

'Nothing like that.' If only everything could be explained by Tamara's one-size-fits-all trauma theory. 'I'm just not the right sort of person to drive. I have no coordination,' said Iona, neatly side-stepping a double pushchair.

That she had to barge Tamara into the road to do it took the edge off the precision timing somewhat.

'Ned can drive,' said Tamara, rather too casually.

Iona's head swivelled, causing her to tread on the back of someone's heel in front. She had been expecting a torrent of abuse, since she could see a long smear of pavement dirt on Tamara's white boots (which Tamara obviously couldn't), but come to think of it, she should have been expecting this just as much.

'Almost seamlessly, she brings the conversation round.'

'What?'

'Never mind. Yes, I know Ned can drive. But you have never been in a car with him, or else you wouldn't make that suggestion.'

'Do you think he likes me?' said Tamara suddenly.

'Do you think we are sixteen?' Iona stopped at the road crossing outside Chelsea Town Hall and stared at the traffic. Tamara was pretending to gaze at the Teddy Bears' Picnic window display of Daisy and Tom's, but as Iona knew that Tamara's idea of hell was being locked in her flat with ten children, the Rolf Harris back catalogue and twenty choc ices, it was hardly convincing. Iona could feel a headache coming on.

'And you can forget that,' she said over her shoulder. 'The only kids Ned's into are the French ones that do divine little cheeses. Are you going to let me cross?' she demanded rhetorically of a blonde woman driving a 4x4 as if it were a runaway elephant. 'Are you? *Thank* you, madam.'

'God, Iona, what's got into you?' Tamara had to run to

keep up with Iona's long strides, her high heels clicking daintily on the pavement in counterpoint to Iona's determined clumps.

'Nothing!'

'It's not like you to be so merdy.'

'Mardy. Don't think you can get round me by using northern dialect. You mean mardy, but merdy probably isn't far off what you were intending.'

'Well, come on, it's your birthday and you're behaving like it's the last day of the tax year.' Tamara bit her tongue about Ned and stowed him away for later. 'It's all right for you – you're already living with the man of your dreams.'

Iona slowed down and pushed open the glass door of Heal's. 'Sorry.' She wandered in and started picking up random pieces of cream tableware. 'Sorry, I didn't mean to snap.' She sighed, turned over a sponge-printed teacup to see the price tag and flinched visibly. 'God, I should start doing pottery. The splodgier you are the more you can charge.'

Tamara scrutinized her from behind a display of shiny saucepans. Iona's brows were creased up and she was obviously breathing hard from the way the cup was vibrating in her hands.

'Is it . . . romantic problems?' Tamara hazarded. She wasn't used to offering Iona advice. It was always the other way round. In fact, she hadn't really thought about Iona having problems. She'd known Iona for about three years now and for all that time Iona had had the boyfriend, the talent, the solid bunch of mates and hair that didn't need highlighting. Barely a problem in sight. Which, in Tamara's faintly envious eyes, made her all the more qualified to sort out her lack of all of the above.

Iona toyed crossly with a blue plastic pasta server. '*Romantic* problems? Hardly.'

'Then what?' Tamara persisted, not quite sure what she would do if Iona spilled.

'I just *wish* you would all get off my back about learning

to drive!' Iona burst out. She had picked up the pasta server without realizing and was pointing it at Tamara like a semi-automatic machine gun. 'Maybe, just maybe, I know better than you lot, just for once, about what's best for me! And you, of all people! I mean, at least you treat me like an adult most of the time, even if the others don't. So if I *say* I don't want to do something, then at least do me the courtesy of believing that I know what I'm talking about, and respect my decision that I don't want to do it! *Jeez . . .*' She stumped off fractiously towards the glassware.

'OK. OK.' Tamara held up her hands and took a step back, then quickly stepped forward again to guide Iona gently away from a pyramid of chi-chi champagne saucers. 'OK, forget it. Let me buy you a tulip vase.'

Chapter Nineteen

Never had a week gone more quickly for Iona. And never had she had a more unpleasant journey than the one in which Angus drove her to Bromley in an apparent attempt to break the record for collecting speeding fines.

Naturally, they were late. It had been a shoe issue, although Iona suspected that it was really her subconscious trying to take control by making her unusually indecisive about what she could wear with the new flat shoes, which she hated on principle, even though they were quite nice as flat shoes went. And naturally the lateness brought out the best of Angus's track-day driving and the worst of his casual road rage. It was like being trapped in a car with a Jensen Button stricken with Tourette's Syndrome.

'Don't do this in your lesson,' he kept stressing, racing up behind a trembling Sierra in the fast lane, 'you *fuck wit*!'

'Or this,' undertaking an Eddie Stobart rig, and then looking back to return the two-finger gesture the driver was waving at him with both hands.

'Or this,' phoning the instructor to say they would be a bit late while undertaking a school bus. 'You have to drive with consideration at all times. Oh, for fuck's sake, get out of this fucking lane! This is for cars, not prams! Bloody hell . . . Are you watching how I'm changing gear, Iona?'

Iona wasn't watching anything. She had her hands over her head.

'OK, now, Iona,' said the nice man in the cable-knit sweater to whose tender mercies Angus had left her, given that he had to break the sound barrier the other way to get back for a meeting with the brewery rep.

Her new instructor's name was Ron. He talked to her as if he were a children's entertainer and she was the sole, sulking audience. Iona thought his almost eerie calm and full-on jolliness might be covering up for something. Tranquillizer addiction, very likely. She smiled politely and fidgeted with the seat-belt. She liked to check they worked early on.

Ron did a strangled sort of 'Ah-ha!' half-laugh and pushed up his jacket sleeves. '*Whenever* you're ready.' And he settled back into his seat in the manner of a man preparing himself for a relaxing Indian head massage.

Iona cut a glance at him and tried hard to keep the incredulity out of her eyes. Most driving instructors she'd known – all of them recommended to her by friends who had listed their unflappability and flowing kindness as if pitching for them on Esther Ranzten's *Hearts of Gold* – literally had to be strapped into their seat by the third lesson with her. It was a matter of mutual gratitude that she had rarely made a booking for the fourth.

Iona wondered how Ron had enveigled her into the driving seat. She didn't remember agreeing to change places; normally she could put off the evil moment for up to fifty-five minutes by asking ever more complex questions about the engine management systems in Vauxhall Corsas. And she knew that she knew more than they did. Thanks to Angus's loo-side copies of *Top Gear* magazine, she could talk about gas-flowed heads and slip diffs for about twenty minutes minimum.

Iona gripped the wheel and marvelled anew how she could love cars from the passenger seat and yet be so bitter about them three feet across the transmission cable. It was only fair to warn the man. 'I should say before we start,' she said, breathing calmly through her nose, as recommended by Tamara's reiki teacher, 'that I really hate driving and it really does scare me.' The nose breathing made her sound rather horsy, but Ron didn't seem to notice.

In fact, an amused smile – not dissimilar to the one which played about Angus's mouth when they 'talked' about Iona's 'fear of driving' – appeared. 'Well, Iona, ah-ha! If I had a pound for every new pupil who said that . . .'

And if I had a pound for every cliché I'd heard from a driving instructor, I'd be able to pay for a full-time chauffeur, thought Iona waspishly. But she pressed on, in her nicest possible voice.

'My friend Tamara . . .' She stopped and corrected herself. 'My friends do honestly think I should have had some kind of aversion therapy before I started these lessons but, as you know, my boyfriend has taken it into his head that I have to learn to drive, and I wasn't really given much option . . .' Her voice trailed off and hung in the silence of the car.

Ron merely carried on smiling encouragingly. Given the humour-free nature of the situation, he looked only slightly deranged.

She sighed and glanced at the clock while her stomach churned on as though stricken with food poisoning. Driving to this remote area of London (so remote, she'd never even been here before, and so far from public transport that every single drive had at least one car equipped with some kind of GPS navigation system) had taken up six minutes of the lesson.

Nice Ron increased the smile, which had now wrinkled up his eyes with sympathy, and flexed back the pages on her brand-new progress book. All the stages from 'Is That Buttton Meant to Do That?' through to 'Driving Proficiently with the Radio On' were tantalizingly empty.

Ten accusing dots, thought Iona. Ten levels of imbecility to wade through. How long is that going to take?

'Now, Iona, as I say to all my nervous learners, I don't *expect* you to know everything. Why would you be here if you already knew how to drive? Ah-ha! Now, I'll shut up and you show me what you can do, so we can decide where to begin.'

Angus had filled Ron in a little too well. Iona regretted telling Angus how many instructors she'd had – just as she frequently regretted arming Angus with any kind of verbal weaponry. He had an alarming habit of snatching whatever she came out with and using it straight back on her, a bit like a mugger whose eyes light up when you weedily brandish your car keys through the fingers of one hand as a makeshift knuckle duster. The trouble was, she'd inflated the numbers of ruined instructors at the time in order to persuade him she had a) given driving a fair go and b) was unteachable. Angus and Ron, though, saw it as a challenge.

Iona thought she might as well claim total ignorance while she still could.

The sick feeling had started in her stomach the minute she and Ron had swapped seats and she didn't think it was entirely due to the clammy cushion he'd left behind. By now, she was seriously considering vomiting, and even though she was trying desperately to pinpoint where all this animal-like fear was coming from, she just couldn't. Iona felt about four years old and wished she could just get out of the car, give back her provisional licence and go home on the bus.

'Iona? Are we going to start the engine?'

'I really don't want to do this,' said Iona, her voice wobbling treacherously.

I don't care if I have to use public transport! I don't mind waiting for the Northern Line! I don't even care about paying for taxis south of the river! Or getting mini-cabs!

'Are we in gear?' inquired Ron, waving his right hand around.

Iona turned her head to look at him without taking her hands off the wheel. He was either about to count out the moving-off drill on his fingers or had resorted to signing the whole lesson.

She swallowed and gave the gear stick a desultory wiggle 'No.'

'What *might* happen if we were in gear when we started the engine?'

'The clutch would be engaged and if the handbrake wasn't on the car would lurch forward when the engine turned over on ignition.'

'Very good!' exclaimed Ron. His kindly expression showed signs of grateful relief, Iona noted. He looked as if he desperately wanted to give her a Smartie. 'I can see we've been here before!'

'Oh yes,' said Iona heavily. 'We have.'

Iona firmly believed that there was nothing stupid about driving instructors – apart from the fact that they chose to make a living being driven around London by people who, on their own admission, couldn't drive. And that was down to either a Christian-like philanthropy, coupled with a fearless acceptance of the afterlife, or just plain arrogance.

Stupid people would not be charging £20 an hour, for a start.

Ron, she quickly discovered, was not only a model teacher – the driving instructor equivalent of the very docile learner pony – but specialized in Driving Instructor Philosophy. Everything about life was part of an endless series of questions to Ron, questions to which he knew the answer and yet still felt the need to involve Iona. He explained, unprompted, that his constant stream of inane chat was specifically designed to prepare her for driving girlfriends round town – and not, as she had imagined, to provoke her into doing an emergency stop and testing the passenger-side airbag. Because he *was* the passenger-side airbag. When she got a bit better, he promised, he would let her put Capital Radio on.

Iona didn't point out that they were so far away from central London as to be out of transmission range.

'What might be round this corner?' he would say, breaking off from another hilarious anecdote from his dog's obedience training programme. (*'Poor Colin! He wasn't to know it wasn't his squeaky toy! He'd never seen a dog that small before! Good job I had my pliers with me!'*)

How would I know what's round this corner, thought Iona, who was trying to overcome the worryingly dislocated sensation of driving an arcade simulator car. The car refused to feel real. Maybe it was something Ron was pumping through the air conditioning, but she found it almost impossible to concentrate on anything.

'Iona? What do we think might be round this corner?'

She could think of three spiky answers off the top of her head, viz: Wales? How far have we gone? What am I, psychic?

But since she didn't have Marie's brazen confidence, in the spirit of the game she said, 'Erm, an old lady crossing the road in a very stupid place?'

'Exactly!' Ron shoved his sleeves back up. 'Or an elephant! Or Colin coming at you off his lead to say, "Hello, Iona, how good are your servo-assisted brakes?"! Ah-ha! It could be anything! So what do we do?'

'We slow down.'

There was a pause.

'Right. Iona? We're in Catford, not Brands Hatch, aren't we? So, let's slow down, shall we? Shall I help you? Lovely. Now, what do we do when we see parked cars?'

The world was a series of barely avoided disasters for Ron.

Luckily, Iona could encounter only so many in an hour.

Chapter Twenty

Jim sloped in to Overworld with the tray of pre-lunch coffees, carefully holding the door open with his foot for the departing courier, who, in his haste to get away before the parking warden outside finally closed in on his bike, accidentally let the heavy glass door bang shut on Jim's heel.

'Fuck, ow!' yelled Jim, unexpectedly arrested in mid-stride. This made the tray jog, which made a thin stream of hot milk jet out of one of the cups and land on his bare arm, and that made him let go of one side of the tray.

'OW!'

Rebecca's bright smile, which she had been holding while Jim propped open the door, slipped into a disappointed twist of the lips. She had had a nice, lightly flirtatious witticism all ready for him, which she didn't now feel like delivering as he stood there with his mouth clamped to his forearm like a self-molesting vampire, and a trail of dirty-coloured milk spreading down the inside of his leg. After three years at Overworld, Jim still looked like the work-experience lad. She bit her cherry-red lower lip. Simon would have hurled the coffee six feet in the air and risked mass scaldings rather than get coffee on his trousers. Kyle would have hurled the coffee at her and sued the courier by the time it landed. No disaster management, that was Jim's problem.

'I'll call for a bucket,' she said heavily, picking up the telephone for the maintenance men.

Jim unsuckered himself from his stinging arm. 'No, it's

OK, I'll . . . Oh, cheers,' he said. He made a half-hearted attempt to salvage some of the more tightly packed espressos, chasing milk froth around the marble floor with the hopelessly inadequate recycled napkins. They didn't absorb much but were highly effective in redistributing the coffee to the new areas of reception dedicated to the acquisition of reclaimed playgrounds. Absorbency aside, from a cleaning point of view, Jim was mildly impressed to note that the coffee-soaked napkins remained an off-brown colour; last time he'd wiped spilled milk off his apparently white kitchen floor, the kitchen roll had come up black.

'Haven't seen you in much recently,' Rebecca observed, peering over the white desk, in the hope that her non-fat mocha might have survived.

Jim was on his hands and knees, chasing the spreading slick of double cappuccino under a model of a twelve-storey cinema/supermarket complex Simon had masterminded, and displaying a surprisingly neat rear view. As she spoke he straightened up awkwardly and banged his forehead on the controversial bungee tower.

'Er, no, I've been doing a lot of on-site work at the Bunch of Grapes. In Ladbroke Grove?' He rubbed his head, which seemed sticky, and made a mental note to wash his hair before the weekend. Since Tamara had nailed her colours to Gabriel's apparently substantial mast – and since Ned had more or less moved back in to be nearer the pub – Jim's personal hygiene had gone to the wall. Not spending much time in the office didn't help; Ned wasn't such an exacting role model as lemon-fresh Simon.

'We've all missed you,' Rebecca cooed. She touched a red nail to her chin. 'It's been very quiet. No calls from your funny friends. And I've had to phone out for coffee. Their delivery boy is nowhere near as quick as you.'

Jim stopped rubbing his head and gave her a searching look. Rebecca stretched her smile expectantly and flicked a flirtatious eyebrow at him. She wondered if she could point out some milk he'd missed to get him back on his knees.

He took a step nearer. 'You mean you can get coffee *delivered*?' Jim spat.

Rebecca's face creased in confusion. 'Well, yeah, we have an office account with Espresso Bongo, and . . .'

'Oh, *great*! Sodding great! Do you realize—'

The glass door swung open again and Martin scuttled in, glancing quickly over his shoulder as he dumped his briefcase on Rebecca's desk.

'The wife's having me followed. God knows why, I pay enough for her personal bloody psychic. She should be telling me where I'm going, not Svetlana . . . Ah, Jim, just the man! Can we have a quick interface in my office about the Wheatsheaf? Need to run some rough figures by you.'

'Um, it's the Bunch of Grapes, actually, Martin.'

'Absolutely! Absolutely! Rebecca, my sweetheart, can you have Svetlana get this little lot typed up for me? And then call the Montignac Boutique for my lunch? I'll have it early today. Thanks so. Come, Jim!'

'I'll leave the coffee with you,' Jim said over his shoulder, taking the two undamaged espressos with him. 'Maybe you can *ring out* for fresh.'

'No problem!' beamed Rebecca. As soon as they were both safely out of sight, she put her lower lip over her upper so as not to smudge her lipstick and started thinking. The acquisition and merger of Jim and herself was presenting a whole new management problem for her. He was either a lot cleverer than he looked, or the only straight twenty-eight-year-old in London without flirt antennae.

'So, Jim, Jim, thanks for the new figures,' said Martin. He swung round in his chair and shut the blinds behind his desk. The light-sensitive ambience system triggered a gentle glow of compensating light from the wall panels. 'Can't be too careful, can you?' he beamed. 'Now, this project of yours . . .'

They both looked down at Jim's neatly bound folder of accounts and projections which sat on the desk in front of them. Svetlana had carefully put Post-it notes on the important bits. Jim knew this, because he knew where the important bits were, but he wasn't convinced that Martin did. Then again, despite all appearances to the contrary, Martin was slyer than Kyle and Michael on a bed of greased foxes.

'Do you know, in all my years of experience, I think this is the first time I've seen a new restaurant fail to disappear up its own arse in three months!' Martin guffawed heartily and looked at Jim to join in.

Jim managed a tight smile. He and Angus had sweated blood to make the books work out. The deals they had driven with the breweries, not to mention with the suppliers, had brought tears to Brian's eyes.

Brian kept phoning from Las Palmas. At night, so Lois couldn't hear. He missed London. He missed the pub. After a tearful whispered half-hour with Angus, he even admitted that he missed Mad Boy Sam. That was when Lois had come in and, to Angus's relief, the call had been abruptly terminated.

'So, Jim lad! How *have* you done it? I'm very impressed!' Martin swung from side to side in his chair.

Jim felt very conscious of his unspinning status, and more conscious that whenever bonhomie was rolled out at Overworld it was as a smokescreen for something more sinister. And, as usual, he wasn't sure how much of the truth was required, or even appropriate. 'Well,' he began carefully, 'we went for a low-cost, high-result decoration treatment, with an interior designer I've worked with in the past, and I've been talking to some of the local estate agents about the flats upstairs and as long as we can get around the various security and insurance issues, I would think we'd be looking at a return of—'

'Ah, let me stop you – stop you! – there, OK? And you're off again, Jim. Pigeon shits per pavement slab, eh? Eh?' Martin shook his head and rubbed his stomach. It was, after all, his covert lunch hour. 'I had no idea that you could make this kind of thing work, which just goes to show, once again, that an old dog like me can be re-educated in the Trick GSCE department. Well, you've been handling this particular hot potato so well that Kyle and I want to give you a bit more to play with.'

Behind Martin's head was a large expanse of polished metal, bought at considerable expense from the graduation show at Chelsea College of Art. (Maximum style, minimum investment and, Jim had no doubt, maximum return.) With the funny angles of the feng shui'd desk, it had the unnerving effect of giving whoever Martin was interviewing a TV-sharp view of their own face, floating behind his. Before every single meeting, Jim steeled himself to use it to monitor his own stern, non-negotiable 'Make my day, fat boy!' face, but every single meeting Martin managed to steer the conversation so far away from whatever he'd prepared for in his head that all he could see in the reflection was his ever-widening eyes and bunny-like expression.

Today was no exception.

'More *money*?' he managed. 'But—'

'Oh, you know,' said Martin airily. 'Kyle said he popped in the other night with Catriona—'

'*Did* he?'

'Loved the décor, but wondered whether you might want to upgrade the wine list? Get some investment in the cellar?'

'Um, we're mainly a beer pub, to be honest. There's not really a great deal of call for wine in that area . . .' began Jim, thinking of Angus's plans for a quality wine list. Nothing above twenty-five quid, he'd said. Most of Angus's plans were based around what he'd be prepared

to pay in a similar place. ('Château Pétrus? Er . . . no.'
'Seventeen quid for squid ink pasta? Er . . . no.' 'Unisex
toilets? Er . . . no.' Etc, etc, etc. For a lawyer, Angus was
surprisingly immutable on the topic of negotiation.) Most
of the regulars refused to drink anything above two quid a
pint anyway.

'Well, it's up to you, Jim lad, but I've arranged a transfer
of funds. Spend money to make money, that's what the wife
always used to say.' Martin's brow darkened. 'Or spend
money to *get* money.'

'Right, well, brilliant!' said Jim, sensing that the useful
part of the interview was over and the marriage warnings
bit was about to start. 'I'll, er, leave that espresso with
you then.' He indicated at where the little pot of coffee sat
dribbling tarry liquid on to the desk.

'Good man!' said Martin automatically.

Iona yanked the heavy cellar trap door open and yelled,
'Angus, it's Jim on the phone!' down to where Angus was
repairing the magic spring of mineral water. She had been
refilling the frosty glass bottles early that morning (since
she could do it without having to unseal the sleep from her
eyes) and had been so intent on earwigging the sound of
Tamara and Gabriel through the ventilation shaft that she'd
filled three before noticing that the contents looked more
like Diet Coke than sparkling fresh mineral water from the
heart of Kent.

For once, Gabriel and Tamara seemed to have got off
the topic of how to treat chlorine-tinged highlights (yet
another shared interest of cosmic significance), and when
Iona finally tore herself away from Tamara's breathless
account of Marie's crippled aura and staggered up the
stairs to report the water problem, as luck would have
it Angus was trapped in suspended animation by Mad
Boy Sam's account of his sister-in-law's botched appen-
dectomy ('And, would you give it credit, it turned out

the one they put in 'er jar to take 'ome wasn't even 'ers!')
and was only too glad to get down there and sort it
out.

Or rather, as luck would have it for Angus. Gleefully, he
handed the listening and the glass polishing cloth to her and
legged it down to the cellar. He had been there ever since,
and so had she. So had Sam.

'Angus! Phone!' she yelled again. Gabriel and Tamara
must have done Marie and moved on to something more
juicy for him to be down there still earwigging. Maybe, in
fairness, she should tell Rick or Mark how much you could
hear . . .

'I mean, I coulda tol' her it wasn't 'ers, just from lookin'
at it, but I tol' her to go to one of them solicitors. The ones
you see on the telly during the breaks in *Trisha*. Stick another
pint in there, Ioner love.'

Iona privately wondered when Sam actually watched
television, given the amount of time he dedicated to supporting his local pub, but merely nodded at the phone she
was holding for Angus and smiled. Getting involved in a
conversation was fatal.

'He won't be a minute, Jim,' she said into the phone, more
to indicate to Sam that she wasn't available for participation
than to talk to Jim himself.

''Ave yoo been hurt at work? 'Ave yoo fallen down some
stairs?' said Sam in the style of the advert, a look of lawyerly
concern pleating his face.

'Is Sam doing one of his real-time anecdotes?' said Jim. He
sounded more light-hearted than he had done of late. Iona
wondered if it meant he was finally getting over Tamara's
defection to the Prince of Pastry.

'Yes.'

''Ave yoo slipped on your toilet pedestal mat? 'As your
wife annoyed yoo?'

Angus came steaming up the stairs with three screwdrivers
in his top pocket and a livid expression on his face. 'No, no,

no, no, no. I don't have time to talk to Jim,' he said, brushing Iona's proffered phone aside.

She flinched. This was the first time she'd seen his road-rage snarl outside a car. Gabriel must have said something really bad.

'Angus . . .' she began soothingly.

'Let me get that bloody little pansy by the fucking pony-tail!'

Iona wedged one leg under the mixers shelf and the other under the glass cleaner and blocked his way. 'There's no point. Service starts in ninety minutes. There are only two cold mains. You can't deck Gabriel. Talk to Jim.'

'I'm your boss and I'm telling you to move!' The mean, hard look flashed up into Angus's eyes, and Iona felt a steely retaliation in her own face. She didn't ask it to appear, but she could feel it creep over her like scales.

'And I'm your girlfriend and I'm telling you to leave it! You shouldn't have been eavesdropping!'

Angus carried on glaring. Iona didn't drop her gaze and felt her leg muscles tighten up. When he got mad, Iona observed, not for the first time, he lost the air of complete adulthood that he normally wore like a grown-up suit and regressed before her eyes to the hot and angry little boy he must have been once. She didn't like that. It wasn't part of their deal. He was meant to be adult, civilized and reassuring at all times. And – it occurred to her suddenly – she didn't like the 'I'm the boss' rank-pulling either.

Iona bit back the impulse to start yelling in front of the regulars. 'What are you going to do, sack me?' She tried to lighten the mood, but it didn't come out light, and then she remembered she was holding out the phone like a barrier, at roughly shoulder level, which meant that Jim would be getting concert-quality sound. Her lips twitched tight.

'I *could* do,' snarled Angus, obstinately. 'Sack you so I

can get through to the kitchen and sack *the pair of them*.
Then he'd be completely free to do this TV thing and not
have to put up with any of us . . . *time-wasters*!'

Damn. Iona could hear Jim distantly on the other end,
demanding to know what was going on in the 'We're all
going to die!' tone he usually adopted as soon as there was
the first hint of a raised voice. She hated anyone hearing
their rows. It was a good job too that Jim was there, waiting
to talk to him (now quite urgently), because she could feel
words and phrases bubbling under the surface that she'd
been pushing back down for too long.

Like, *I'm not your employee, you fascist!*

And, *Don't think you can order me around like that!*

Who the hell do you think you are?

Maybe you love the pub more than me!

Why do I only deserve one hour's quality time a week?

*Do you think I want to live with someone who smells of
pubs day in, day out?*

*Maybe I don't want to marry someone who's so psychotic-
ally bossy!*

Maybe . . .

Her hand tightened on the phone until the knuckles
went white.

Angus gave her silence another sharp squeeze of the eyes
and before she knew it, 'You'd better think a bit harder
before you talk to me like—' had spat out of her lips and
he was opening his mouth to yell back.

'Hey, hey, hey, what's going on?' Ned swung through the
doors with three vegetable boxes stacked on one another.
His biceps were standing out on his lean arms and his
Nirvana T-shirt still hung as loosely from his shoulders
twelve years on from its first outing. 'Lads? Do I detect
an atmosphere?'

Iona swung round and felt dizzy, her heart was racing so
fast. But she felt indescribably relieved to see Ned. 'No, you
don't. Jim's just phoned to speak to Angus.'

'No, it's OK, I've changed my mind,' came Jim's voice distantly from the phone.

'I don't *want* to speak to—'

'Speak to Jim!' roared Iona. 'Now!'

Shocked, Angus took the phone and retreated to the other side of the horseshoe bar.

'Didn't know you two were married,' said Sam conversationally.

'We're not.' Iona sealed her mouth shut before something bitter came out.

'Nah, mate, just looks that way,' said Ned, hefting the boxes on to the bar and going out for the rest. 'Shouting, yelling, ordering around . . .'

'Basis for a very happy marriage is that,' said Sam, aggrieved. 'Now my Kathleen . . .'

'You were after a pint, weren't you, before we were so rudely interrupted?' said Iona, opening the glass cleaner with trembling hands.

'If it's not too much trouble.' Sam slid off his stool and announced confidentially, 'I'm just going to point Percy at the porcelain.'

Iona's shaky grip rattled the dirty pint glasses stacked inside.

''S'broken, pet,' said Ned gently. He dumped the box of custard-yellow courgette flowers on one of the tables and removed Iona's hands from the wire basket. 'Will you be a pigeon and get some more ice up from the cellar for me? I need to chill some soups. I'll get Sam his pint. Speckled Hen, was it?'

Iona nodded and let herself down into the cellar.

Though the cellar was cleaner than Jim and Ned's old bathroom, it still smelled as musty and as old as the building, despite Angus's best efforts with the pressure hose. The walls were chilly even on hot days and in the bricks there were old marks and scratches, partially rubbed away with dust and time, where previous potboys had skived a couple of spare minutes. Iona sank on to the stacked crates of mixers and, propping her chin on her hands, looked up to the coal chute, where a few shafts of natural light fell through the heavy Victorian glass. The only noise coming from the kitchen now was the clunking and muttering of the prep work, filtered through Radio One on loud.

Why was it that the moments you really needed to tell people home truths always came when you knew they could least deal with it? There were so many things Iona felt she needed to say to Angus, but now wasn't the right time. She knew him too well – she knew his worries about the pub, about his career, about his lack of career, about the effect of any change in his career on his pension plans – he had told her none of this, but she had inferred it from the anxious dreaming hugs he now clamped her with, in the middle of the night, and from the way he told her only safely brilliant news about the pub. Financial headaches he shared with Jim. Iona's instinct was to be grateful she didn't know the half of it, but not knowing upset her even more.

She needed to tell him that in all his efforts to make everything work, he was pushing her away, making her feel like a controlled problem instead of a girlfriend – but she didn't, because she knew that would add yet another worry to his list.

And would that worry come before the weekly brewery delivery or after the problems with the drains?

Not fair.

Iona sighed and checked her watch. Twenty to twelve. People started coming in for early lunch around now. There wasn't time.

No time. No time for me, no time for him, no time for anything except other people.

So this was why the glossies always told you your man shouldn't be your best friend, and vice versa, then.

'Jim, I heard him.' Angus looked round crossly as one of

Mad Boy Sam's pungent mates banged his froth-cobwebbed pint glass on the bar. 'Be with you in a minute.' He turned back to his vantage point, half behind the bar but with a view directly into the kitchen, where Mark, the sous, was chopping up onions and arguing with someone unseen about the state of the freezer. 'You old git. No, I'm not talking to you. Will you listen to me, I heard Gabriel and Tamara in the kitchen having a— No! I don't mean . . . God, Jim, you're just obsessed. Will you get a grip on yourself . . . No! Oh, for God's sake, of course I *didn't* mean it like that . . .'

Iona slapped the table service list in front of him and pointed to a young couple who had installed themselves on table 3 with a bottle of house white. 'Yes, thank you, I can see them. Thank you, I have got eyes,' he said irritably. She gave him a look and stalked off.

Beneath the bubbling rage, Angus felt a stab of guilt. It wasn't on, being rude to Iona. How could he make it up to her without climbing down? Bloody Gabriel. 'He just infiltrates *everything* without doing anything specifically wrong,' muttered Angus. 'I can imagine how Pontius Pilate felt about Jesus now. He's upsetting my staff, the women follow him around to wash his feet and I can't sack him because people keep telling me he's the Son of God.'

Somehow it made him feel a lot better just saying it aloud.

Angus mopped his streaming brow with a glass cloth and yelled, 'Tamara! There are customers waiting to be served out here!' into the kitchen. 'No, I'm not overreacting,' he went on to Jim, in slightly lower tones. 'The hag who wrote the piece was back in here this morning with her mates, and they went through the whole thing again. Tamara was going on about it.' He wasn't going to mention how he had heard her going on about it, though. 'Apparently they had a good old chat about the possibilities of Gabriel's television potential and then they were . . .'

He hesitated. To be scrupulously honest, he wasn't sure

exactly *who* they'd been talking about, but it had been muttered and low and he had caught various keywords like 'bitch' and 'bossy' and 'domineering'. He wasn't paranoid, but he was a lawyer and admitting to the possibility of guilt was terminal.

'No, I didn't . . . no . . . but you know what I mean. That low voice he does when you can't quite make out what he's saying.' Angus didn't add that Gabriel didn't use this voice in direct speech; they heard it only when it floated out of the kitchen in conversation with Tamara's equally tantalizing unspecific murmur, while the rest of them were swabbing the floors and cleaning the coffee machine for the night. 'Yeah, you could be right, I think he's up to something.' Angus caught sight of himself in the mirror behind the spirit optics and stopped again. He sounded like Jim.

This couldn't be good. Angus didn't think he had a hysterical nature. But paranoia spread. It was turning into a nasty version of *Big Brother* – no one seemed to want to admit they didn't like Gabriel, for fear of looking jealous or cliquey, and yet there was no opportunity to vote anyone out without seriously jeopardizing the financial stability of the next quarter.

'Jim, what *did* you phone for?' he asked, feeling much calmer for having spoken to someone who didn't think the sun shone out of Gabriel's piping bag.

At that moment, Tamara appeared from the kitchen, strands of blonde hair shimmering around her dishevelled French pleat. Her coral lipstick looked freshly reapplied. Tamara's sitcom Barmaids Through the Ages tableau had reached 1958 this week. Along with the lipstick and a lot of liquid eyeliner, she had a beatific look on her face, which Angus had seen before, usually about two days before the man she 'had really made a spiritual connection with' left his girlfriend and year-old baby. Tamara had the mating instincts of a Black Widow, no matter what Iona said. 'Oblivious of her effect on men', his arse.

'Tamara, can you serve . . .' He nodded at the scrum forming around the bar. Worried squawking came from the phone. 'No, Jim lad, there's no problem. Yes, it's busy . . .'

Tamara carried on jetting Coke from the post-mix into an ice-bucket so she could clean the chalkboard, which annoyed him. And then she breathed, 'Of course, Angus!' in what he recognized as her über-Tamara voice. It came out when she was concentrating on being Tamara. The falseness of it, the deliberate 'I'm away with the fairies, me!'-ness, dragged down the back of his head like nails down a blackboard. Presumably in art college they'd all talked like that and Iona hadn't noticed how irksome it was.

'Hang on there, Jim lad, let me just walk round the other side of the bar,' he said, lifting the cord over Iona's head as he squeezed past her. She had three pints of lager pouring on the taps while she topped up a Guinness. Sadly, Iona did not have Marie's precision timing – and the ullage was going to be about five pints over at the end of the shift, he noted. 'Remind me to tell Ned about doing cod in bitter batter tomorrow,' he said to Jim. 'Excuse me, Iona, can I wriggle past?'

'Angus, I've got five people waiting here. Don't you think you could sort this out and phone Jim back?' she said. The measured tone in her voice was a dead giveaway. She evidently hadn't simmered down.

'I'm talking to Jim about *finance*, darling,' said Angus.

'Angus, for fuck's sake, this is the lunchtime rush! What do you want me to do? Get Mark out of the kitchen? Operate some self-service drinks thing?'

Angus narrowed his eyes at her and spoke into the phone without breaking the stare she was boring into him. 'Right, fine. OK, Jim, I'll have to talk to you later about whatever critical development you have there, because there are four punters here without pints. Very good. OK? Right, I'll phone you back.' He slammed the phone on to the wall bracket.

'Happy now?' he demanded of Iona, who scowled at him,

and he turned to the first shocked man at the bar. 'What are you having?'

He nodded weakly at the Guinness Iona was finishing up. 'Er, being served . . . thank you.'

'Very good.' Angus swivelled on the balls of his feet. 'Next?' The man behind the Guinness man was wearing a Hackett polo shirt and had been trying to queue-barge for ten minutes by leaning on those around him and getting out his mobile phone to make unnecessary calls and create elbow space. Iona wanted to tell Angus this, but didn't want to talk to him either, in case she accidentally dumped him. 'You?'

Two other people opened their mouths, but Hackett Man cut across them. 'Two Kronenbourgs and a packet of crisps. Do you take cards?'

'Ten pounds or over.'

He shrugged. 'You don't take cards?'

'I just said we didn't. Are you eating?'

'No.'

'You don't have cash?'

'No.'

'Right. Very good. You came out for a drink but you didn't think to—'

Tamara shimmered up and put a long hand on his bare arm, beneath his rolled-up shirt sleeve. 'Angus, bitter's off,' she breathed portentously, as if reciting horoscopes for a chatline.

'Oh, for God's sake!' Angus glared at the man, then glared at Tamara, then, for want of anyone else, glared at Iona.

'That's the danger of being so anal that you won't trust anyone with the pressure taps things,' Iona pointed out. 'Oh dear. If only I were intelligent enough to understand how to—'

'OK! OK! Christ!' Angus dropped his voice to a mutinous mutter. '. . . do fucking *everything* round here . . .' With a final all-encompassing glare, he hauled up the cellar trap door again, disappearing into its depths like a Santa's pissed-off elf, chuntering darkly all the while.

Iona rolled her eyes at Tamara, once he was safely out of earshot. 'He's been like that all morning, ever since . . .' she began, then remembered who she was talking to and ground to a halt. Tamara didn't seem to have noticed, though, and carried on taking the nearest order. Iona let out a cross breath. God, it was complicated. Having to think what you could say to who. At least with the Chris and Marie shenanigans you only had to deal with one of them at a time.

'Has he?' breathed Tamara. 'Really? I thought he was looking rather sweet this morning in his little red shirt. Four pounds twenty, please.'

'Four ninety, actually, Tam. With the crisps.' Iona made a conscious attempt not to get mad with Tamara. Poor Tam was going to need all the allies she could get if Gabriel did get the TV thing mooted in last night's unofficial fan column in the *Standard* Diary, and God knew she didn't have a big fanbase already.

'Oh, right, sorry, four ninety. Doh!' She slapped her head and smiled in a goofy, conspiratorial way at Iona. There was a sweet side to Tamara that she tried to keep well hidden so as not to spoil the groomed exterior. 'So this is what you meant about love turning you dozy! Never thought it would happen to me!'

Iona tried a smile but, checking in the bar mirror, it didn't come out quite as well as she'd hoped.

Jim turned up at one and Angus motioned him over to the bar. With Tamara and Iona now running around on floor service and the restaurant area full, there was no choice but to come out of the cellar and deal with the bar. His mood had cooled down to a mild simmer.

'He really is going to get that TV thing,' said Angus, throwing Jim the electronic key that would operate the till. Jim attached it to his belt loop morosely, realizing that his plan for a swift half and a masochistic look at Tamara wasn't going to happen. His ankle was still aching from being trapped in the office door too.

'And I know I should be really glad for him,' Angus went on, squirting post-mix lemonade into a pint glass for Ned in the kitchen, 'but I just can't be. He's that kind of bloke. You know what I mean?'

'Yes, I do,' said Jim, who didn't feel glad for Gabriel on any score and whose thoughts had turned more than once recently to the validity or otherwise of his work permit.

'Even if it means this place getting publicity. And that could really make it, you know?'

'I know.'

'It's hard. Isn't it?'

Angus stopped filling the pint glass and looked at Jim.

Jim looked him squarely back in the eye, and knew that Angus, who'd known him for so long, could guess what he was thinking. That after years of being taken for a prat in the office, the Bunch of Grapes was his one chance to prove to everyone – Overworld, Tamara, his friends, his parents, the food critics at *Time Out* – that he was A Man. And no sooner had he got things up and running than Gabriel arrived, apparently with the sole purpose of proving by comparison that he was actually A Mouse.

'Yup,' said Angus, clapping him manfully on the shoulder. 'It's hard.'

Chapter Twenty-one

Angus's horrible squawky alarm clock went off at six and beeped once before Iona's hand shot out from under the covers and banged it upside down to stop the broken-off button on top. She had left it on the drawing board in the painting shed once, to remind herself not to miss *Top Gun* on late-night television, and her too-powerful Anglepoise lamp had melted the ringer, so it now required physical turning, not just a sleepy hand, to knock off the sound, and there was no longer a snooze facility. Just a Get Up Now or Sleep On and Be Late for Work option.

Waking and waiting for the horrible squawk was a self-enforced torture she couldn't side-step. She invariably drifted into consciousness five minutes before it went off and this morning she had lain awake waiting for the final bell, breathing in rhythm with Angus's comfortable big-dog-like snuffling, listening to the intermittent sounds of early-morning traffic and thinking about priority on roundabouts. Iona's internal clock always beat the real thing, no matter how tired she was. Worry and guilt won over exhaustion every time. And this morning she felt both. All night she had dreamed of standing in an art supplier's, unable to decide which colours to buy and then finding her handbag was full of various shop-lifted black oils.

Unlike, say, Tamara, Iona didn't give too much credence to dream psychology, but she suspected black oil paints might have something to do with the wedding commission she still hadn't really started.

While Angus snuffled on, lagged in the white duvet like a fat larva, Iona slipped out of bed, pulled on her painting kit and went down to the kitchen, where she scribbled a quick note for Angus to explain that she hadn't run off, fed the cats, took a couple of slices of Hovis from the bread bin, then stumbled through to the shed.

She was already a week behind with the commission she'd blithely taken on before Christmas, before she'd realized that working at the pub would end up occupying virtually every spare minute she had. This was a wedding present: a huge collage of faces and 'bits' which she could assemble as she wanted from the shoebox of ideas the client had given her. In the interests of diplomacy, Iona wanted to get something roughed out and checked well before the delivery date – how was she to know if the mother-in-law was actually intending to lose quite a lot of weight before the day, or if the cow (bride's favourite animal) shouldn't for reasons of tact be anywhere near the groom's uncle (disgraced Young Farmer)?

The shed was cold, but Iona had several thin layers of clothes, which she usually peeled off as she got going and the blood returned to her extremities. She pushed back the long sleeves of Angus's school rugby shirt, flicked on the kettle and stood back to assess what she'd already done. It was a scarily big canvas. One shed wall was entirely covered with a pinboard, itself now covered with photos and notes. Through the window on the other wall, she could see the house, and their bedroom window. The light was still off. She could virtually still hear the snoring.

She sighed and made a cup of coffee. Starting was always the hardest bit. Iona switched on the radio and picked up a soft sketching pencil; it helped if she could get a rolling start while pretending she was doing something else, like listening to the news, or cleaning her brushes.

She looked hopefully at the sink, but all the brushes were clean and the paints were arranged in an attractive spectrum display, much like an art shop window. The sink was also fresh and sparkling, having been comprehensively debunged last time she was in, and all her paper was pre-sorted into filed piles. She hadn't actually started the painting yet, but the palettes were cleaned to a surgical standard.

Iona sipped her coffee and wondered whether she should measure all her paper again.

Angus's brain woke up when the radio came on at 7.25, and the rest of his body lay slackly absorbing the news on Radio Four while it adjusted itself to the prospect of getting up. This took five minutes, out of habit.

The first conversations of the day at Price Riley Riches were always the most competitive; the object of the exercise being to imply that the breaking news was old news – because they'd heard it either before they went to bed at four a.m. or as they got up at four a.m. It didn't bother Angus in the slightest that he no longer had to be abreast of current affairs just so he could make small talk about the economic collapse of Italy at the same time as making his morning coffee at work.

Running the cellars and dealing with the brewery was actually more complicated than the sort of stuff he was used to at Price Riley Riches, mainly because he no longer had a secretary to filter out all the tedious bits. If only he still had Margaret to sit at the bar, buffering Mad Boy Sam's endless discussions of Accident and Emergency Wards I Have Known. But at least he'd had training for that. These days he could listen to Sam compare and contrast the top ten casualty departments in central London and make exactly the right sympathetic noises (regret tinged with revulsion and admiration) that convinced Sam he was actually listening.

Should a man that accident-prone be allowed to sit on a bar stool, wondered Angus, seeing if he could still touch all four corners of the bed at once.

He noticed, when none of his limbs came into contact with warm flesh, that Iona had got up. He didn't really enjoy lying around in bed without her, so when the traffic news came on, with a heave he got up and stood under a hot shower, shuffling the day's tasks into order in his head.

Angus had reached an age where he washed his hair carefully, with the special aromatherapy shampoo Tamara had found for him, which promised to inflate each remaining follicle individually, endowing each one with a special pro-vitamin glow of personal attention. Angus was not a vain man, and certainly not a stupid one, and he knew all this was total rubbish (well before Jim pointed it out), but he felt an irrational responsibility to all his hairs, a dwindling bunch of stalwart survivors at the best of times.

He peered out of the shower and inspected his hairline in the steamy mirror. Wet-look was not the most flattering style for him, highlighting as it did the increasing advance of the pink stripes beneath. With a sigh, he ruffled up the straight furrows of ploughed hair. Brave chaps, clinging to the scalp equivalent of a sinking ship – a bit of made-up hydro-protozine was the least he could do for them really.

Angus rubbed in the conditioner. It felt better when Iona did it. He loved the way her fingers could go hard or soft, depending where she was in her massage. She knew all the pressure points on his head, where he liked to be touched, and exactly how long to spend humouring him by massaging the Hair Growing Points. That was the beauty of relationships, he thought, trying to find the right temperature for rinsing without frightening his newly fat hair down the plughole; the longer you had them, the better they got. Like fruit cake. Or port.

Iona twisted a strand of hair round her pencil until it made her scalp sting and decided that, now she had had a good go at all the windows in the shed with Mr Sheen – something she had never done inside the flat – she really had to take desperate measures to start work. At this rate, the couple – Matt and Lynn, she knew by heart from the top of the shoebox – would be divorcing before she got her paints out.

That's very negative, she berated herself sternly. They look very happy from the photos in the box. For a couple with over a foot and a half in height difference.

For the seventeenth time, Iona started to unpick and rearrange the photos on her pinboard to see if inspiration would follow if she magically got them in the right order.

It didn't. It all looked the same as before, but with more pin holes.

Resolutely, she put the bride and groom in the centre. Matt was in his late twenties and was in either the army or a uniformed stripping troupe. Lynn was younger and, in Iona's rural experience, had the look of a Jacob's sheep. Tight blonde curls and a bit yellowy round the eyes. All she needed was some horns and Matt could take her to work as the regimental mascot.

Stop it!

Maybe another cup of coffee . . .

Iona found herself halfway across the shed, being pulled back to the kettle by some invisible cord. With some effort, she marched to the easel, where she drew two large ovals and began to sketch Matt and Lynn inside them, resisting the temptation to have her standing on a prostrate pageboy.

The figures in Iona's paintings were stylized, round and soft like Russian dolls, leaving the strong colours she used to play with the subtleties of personality and life. Everyone smiled in Iona's paintings, no one wore shades, and everyone was just as fat as the next person.

Her eyes flicked between the photos and the paper. The eyes were the important bit for her: if she could get those right everything else followed. Matt had wide-apart brown eyes, a bit like a Jersey cow.

What came first: the favourite animal or the boyfriend?

Iona frowned at herself and concentrated on making Lynn's eyes less sheep-like, while remaining reasonably true to life. Not much point if no one could actually recognize the bride.

She stood back from the easel. Still wasn't right. She got out her big soft eraser and they vanished. Iona's pencil hovered over the paper. Should she try again? It really wasn't working and too much rubbing out would ruin the paper. Maybe if she worked from the outside in?

Once she started, she found it shamefully easy. Her pencil flew lightly over the paper, marking out areas for bride's side and groom's side, and the strange symbols which she assumed were regimental emblems. Obliquely, and perhaps inevitably, that put her in mind of Led Zeppelin for the first time that morning and she allowed her mind and imagination to part company as she studied the photos of the bridesmaids (most taken with a flash in disco darkness: presumably *not* how they would be appearing at Little St Martha's, Upper Dwindling, unless the red eyes were symptomatic of something more interesting than a college ball and a Canon Sureshot).

Iona wondered idly who she would have had as her bridesmaids, had she been able to marry Jimmy Page. Not Tamara. Not even Marianne Faithfull would have been generous enough, or stupid enough, to have had Anita Pallenberg standing beside her at her wedding. Tamara would have to be somewhere well away from direct comparison. A female usher maybe. Handing out orders of service with the rest of the Yardbirds.

She'd like that.

Marie would have to be matron of honour, now she was married.

How appropriate was Marie as an advert for marital bliss?

Iona bit her lip and pinned the two bridesmaids on to the side of the easel for ease of reference.

Anyway, she reminded herself, marital status notwith-standing, Marie would hardly agree to be your bridesmaid in a fantasy rock'n'roll nuptials (set in 1970). Iona curled her lip at her own stupidity. Not when she knows you're secretly engaged to Angus.

It was a while now since Angus had asked her to marry him. Or at least, if he had actually asked her. This sounded more dramatic than it really was: they'd all gone up to Scotland for New Year, and when they had reached terminal crush point up in Princes Street, half a million wrecked people counting down from thirty with the reformed Bay City Rollers playing in the background, her nose rammed into his shoulder and Tamara's elbow rammed into her upper spine, he'd shouted something in her ear about *getting married.*

At least she thought that's what he'd said.

He was wearing a soppy grin on his face at the time, which seemed to accompany most marriage proposals (except those on *Jerry Springer*, which were delivered in a high-pitched whine shortly before the other party announced the restraining order) and although she'd roared back something reasonably acquiescent, she could just as well have been offering to take his suit to the cleaners, given the deafening hysteria which had greeted the New Year and drowned out everything except Tamara shrieking 'Auld Lang Syne' in her ear.

That was the Scots all over, she thought grimly. Always disproportionately amazed at the arrival of another day.

It had surprised her at the time how light-headed it made her feel. The first thrill of their shared secret on the bone-chilling Edinburgh night had been like nothing else she could have imagined. It warmed her up from the inside out, like a hot toddy laced with anti-freeze. Angus had made so much of her life make sense that she couldn't imagine being without him anyway. She wasn't even sure whether she would still be able to operate with her Angus batteries removed.

Neither of them had made much reference to it since. Although Angus liked to give out the strong impression that he was a serious and dynamic young businessman, at home he liked to eat his food out of bowls and got upset if she wouldn't throw the cats off her knee to cuddle him. Even if they hadn't actually set a date, a new permanence had subtly manifested itself in their relationship: they'd gone halves on a new stereo in the sales and, flicking through his diary for the new year, Iona had found their anniversary written in already. In December. With 'Paris?' scribbled next to it.

She frowned and drew a long oval for the least squat of the three bridesmaids, tactfully omitting the sling.

By unspoken agreement, they hadn't mentioned anything to anyone; it was a bit of a novelty to know something about their relationship that none of the others did. No ring had materialized yet. That had made Iona wonder for a while whether she'd just misheard the proposal ('Sorry, but, er, did you ask me to marry you last week?' not being a question that sprang readily to her lips); however, around Valentine's Day, inspired by Tamara's hysterical three-dayer with an inbred silversmith, she had dropped vague hints about having something made. So vague that they'd gone straight over Angus's head, and she'd been too embarrassed to point them out. That was as far as they'd got on the official engagement front, although they had recently talked about getting a dog, and he had, obviously, put her on the insurance for his car.

Which probably cost more than an engagement ring would anyway.

And the trust implications! Iona thought, working in a border of red and white roses (the notes in the shoebox specified Yorkshire and Lancashire, though from the rest of the evidence Iona imagined that this referred to the location of their country houses, rather than their actual birth places). The Integrale was more than just a vehicle to Angus. It was every aspiration he had ever had about himself

– sportiness, exclusivity, idiosyncratic styling, mysteriously expensive maladies – made car.

She took a step back from the easel and wiped the hair off her forehead.

For some reason, it just wasn't looking right.

There was a large space where the happy couple should have been, for a start.

Iona sighed and fought back the strong impulse to make another cup of coffee. The height of the bride wasn't something she could do a lot about, unless she made a big thing of having the bride sitting on the groom's shoulders. Or seated on a bridal cow.

She scribbled this on a rough pad, just in case.

Taking another step back, Iona threw the pencil into the comfy chair in the corner, chewed her little finger, and conceded that she just wasn't in the mood for drawing happy couples. What with Chris and Marie and now Tamara and Gabriel throwing everyone into seething moods, the human ability to form lasting and mutually supportive relationships wasn't up there on the popular topics of the day list.

For a couple that exuded Love's Young Dream like a fragrant strain of poisonous gas, Tamara and Gabriel were having a far from euphoric effect on everyone else. After all, whose sex life was so perfect that they could dismiss the couple from the DKNY ad cavorting everywhere like a pair of demonstration dancers? Quite apart from Jim's permanent expression of perplexed dismay, even she and Angus were snapping at each other more than usual. The odd bark in the context of a relatively happy day was fine – even oddly consoling: Iona came from the school of thought that said Better to Squabble and Make up Than Not Row for Forty Years and Then Kill Each Other with Axes.

But these days they were so busy that there wasn't much time to sit together all comfy, watching television, letting the bickering happen in the reassuring surrounds of their large sofa. You couldn't have a serious argument lying down.

Most of it now took place when they stumbled in from a long night at the pub. Or worse, at the pub itself. If there was one thing Iona really hated, it was people telling her what to do at exactly the moment she was doing it of her own accord. It turned out that Angus was a genius at catching that moment. And suddenly it really pissed her off that they could do exactly the same day's manual labour in the pub, and yet she was still doing all the housework at home.

No, no, no, Iona yelled at herself (internally) as her heartbeat started to quicken.

Yes, yes, yes. The voice broke through. 'It's not fair!' Iona heard herself say aloud.

But he is doing all the driving, pointed out an over-reasonable voice in her head, which she felt sounded a little too much like Angus for her liking.

Iona pulled her gurning face, which she saved for quiet (and solitary) moments of extreme stress.

Maybe this was what marriage was: constantly having the other person's voice in your head as well as your own.

Overriding her own, in her case.

She looked at the main picture she had of Lynn and Matt, in which they were either singing a duet at a ball or having a screaming match, and got out her pencil sharpener.

Hair dripping down his collar, Angus drove west to Ladbroke Grove, thinking about Madras curry. Ned had been talking about putting some old colonial dishes on the menu, as a way of avoiding a permanent pie rotation in the continuing cold weather, and they had argued for an hour after closing about whether Empire cuisine was a fair interpretation of their British food only policy.

Like most arguments, it had turned into a massive free-for-all, with only Ned sticking to the real question of whether it would be practical or not. By the time he and Iona had left, still squabbling about when India actually left the Empire, Jim and Marie were slogging it out by the bar over whether you could include Pacific Rim fusion cuisine by the same colonial argument, and Sam, still there after a long day attempting to burst his new butterfly stitches by rage alone, was having an argument all on his own about mice.

Tamara had objected to the pub reeking of curry, then left with Gabriel. On the back of his motorbike, naturally.

Nothing like a good argument to get the ideas flowing, thought Angus, quite satisfied with the night's work. He prided himself on knowing the difference between a proper argument and a frank exchange of views. Not many of the others did. It had been Chris's only strong point.

Funny how it was just a short mental step between Argument and the Davenports, he thought, pulling up at the never-ending roadworks three blocks away from the Grapes.

Would that happen to him and Iona if they actually got married? Angus drummed his fingers on the steering-wheel. Part of him doubted it, but it was hard to dismiss the evidence so close to home. His mind flicked to the ring: he had the diamond, had had it for about six months now, in fact. He'd been lunching an old law-school friend from another firm and they'd wandered back to the office via Hatton Garden, where an engagement ring was under construction for his girlfriend, who, it turned out, worked in the litigation department at Price Riley Riches.

They had a long chat with the jeweller about the creative benefits, not to mention the economic advantage, of design-it-yourself, and he'd shown them a tiny velvet pouch which turned out to contain a bright shower of glittering gemstones. Being in possession of a bonus, Angus had gone back later in the week and bought the single diamond that had caught his eye. The fact that its preciousness was bound up in its tininess had fascinated him, and the terrifying ease with which you could lose something so valuable reminded him of the draining fear he felt when he thought about ever losing Iona.

Six more months and the pub should be doing well enough for him to make a decision about his future. Their future. He stopped drumming his fingers. No point in proposing properly until he knew what he could give her. And as soon as she had the ring there would be no going back.

And in the meantime? What if it took three months to make the ring? What if the ring wasn't right? In his mind, the bended knee, the proposal, the hesitant opening of the tiny box, the gasp, the sudden tears, the hug, were all part of the same scene. And it all had to be perfect.

Angus made a snap decision. He would phone the jeweller at the weekend. Might as well get things under way. It would be a double incentive to him.

He smiled in the rear-view mirror as he found a non-residents' parking space without a meter on it and carried on smiling down the street to the Bunch of Grapes.

Inside, the pub was quiet and wore its habitual stale morning smell like an accidental fart. Angus made a mental note to talk to Jim about air conditioning for the summer. Radio One drifted through from the kitchen, and there were faint banging sounds. He guessed at meat tenderizing, but couldn't help hoping for Ned tenderizing Gabriel with a cast-iron skillet.

Angus straightened up the bar stools as he walked round to the office, admiring in passing the jewel-like shininess of the reflected spirit bottles in the mirrors behind. Iona had been exactly right about the deep red walls. And getting rid of the skanky carpet. It really was on the way to being somewhere to be proud of.

'Morning, lads!'

The sous were already in, going through the vegetable delivery with Ned, who grunted a greeting. From his unshaven chin and puffy eyes, it didn't look as though he'd been to bed, or even left the pub since clearing up last night.

Angus went through to the office behind the kitchen and shrugged off his jacket, hanging it on the rail of hooks he'd put up himself. Hygiene and tidiness hadn't ever been priorities for Brian and Lois.

Jim was at the desk going through some receipts with a calculator and barely looked up. There was a crumb-laden plate next to him, with two empty cans of Red Bull beside it.

'And good morning to you, Jim lad,' beamed Angus. Good old Jim, getting the numbers crunched before work. 'Iona about?'

'Haven't seen her, no.'

'Oh.' Angus frowned and bit into the apple he'd picked out of the vegetable box. 'She'd already gone when I got up. There was a note on the fridge saying something about having an early start to get on with things, no sign of her in the house. I thought she might have been looking at the rough new wine list. You know I've got a meeting at eleven with the guy from the suppliers, maybe about getting some new house wines?'

'Nope, I haven't seen her. Sorry.'

Angus finished his apple thoughtfully. That wasn't like Iona. There was only her on shift for the morning while he went out. And she knew he had to go out and that Jim had to be back at Overworld before lunch. She wouldn't forget that. And she was rarely late for anything. Could she have been in an accident?

A cold hand of fear gripped him. Someone would have phoned, surely. If she'd been run over, someone would have found her bag with all her diary stuff in, all her contact details. Unless it had been thrown away from the accident scene. Or lost in the chaos of a tube accident. Had she changed his phone number from the old office one to here? Maybe there was something awful on his voicemail at work. How would he tell her mother? How would he . . .

'Angus, are you all right?' said Jim suddenly. 'You've gone all sweaty.'

'No, no . . .' He took out his spotty hanky and mopped his brow. 'Has Iona phoned to say where she is?'

Jim shook his head. 'No. Ned might know though. They were talking about her learning how to make sauces this morning, if she wanted to. Ned!' he yelled.

Irrationally, it annoyed Angus that Ned might know where Iona was when he didn't.

'Yeah?' Ned appeared at the door with a massive handful of parsley. He looked unaware of it.

'Seen Iona this morning?'

Ned shook his head. 'Is she not in the cave with the magic spring?'

'No, I did the bottles this morning,' said Jim. 'Maybe she's gone to the shops first, Angus. Get the shopping in.'

Rational though this was, it didn't quiet the panic rattling round Angus's chest. 'She doesn't go shopping on her own. We always do it together.'

'Why?' asked Ned.

'Because if she goes on her own she always gets the wrong toothpaste,' explained Angus. 'I can only use Macleans. The rest hurt my mouth. No, no, no, no,' he said suddenly, 'don't sidetrack me! I'm worried about her!'

'Haway, Angus, she's a big girl,' said Ned, turning back into the kitchen. 'She'll be here any minute. I don't know why you get into such a state about things.'

'As long as she's in before Mad Boy Sam, she'll be fine,' said Jim, stabbing at the calculator. 'I don't mind waiting till she gets here. But I can't stay for long. I want to talk to Martin at the office about those flats upstairs. And I need to see him in person or as soon as he sees my number on the phone, he'll pretend that he's gone into an underpass and can't hear me.'

'He does that to you?'

'Does it to everyone. You'd think the man was a main-tenance engineer on the Dartford Tunnel, not a property developer.'

Angus leaned against the filing cabinet. He had gone white. 'God, Jim, you don't think she's been abducted, do you?'

Jim finally looked up properly. 'No, I *don't*. And I don't know why you get into these hysterical fits.' His face softened as he took in Angus's pained expression. 'Look, make a cup of coffee. She normally comes crawling out of the woodwork as soon as she hears the espresso machine going.'

'OK,' said Angus reluctantly. 'But I'll just make a few calls first.'

Iona found that after three cups of coffee a weird sense of bonhomie settled on her brain and she could feel more or less benevolent towards everyone. She had discovered this after a week working at the café where she could achieve a state of graceful tolerance in less than five minutes, such was the strength of the espresso there. No jitters, or panic attacks, or anything. Just full-on philanthropy. By home-time, averaging a cup an hour on bad days, she could put up with almost anything and wore the peaceful suffering expression of a background saint in a medieval Italian ceiling fresco.

She finished the last mouthful of her fourth cup and took a step back from the easel, tilting her head for a critical appraisal of what she'd managed this morning. Given the complete lack of enthusiasm she had for this commission, things weren't coming along too badly. She still couldn't get the bride and groom right, somehow her pencil always shied away from drawing them in, but most of the background – sheep, cows, roses, red-eyed friends – was now sketched into place, and it didn't look too bizarre. How much of this was down to the coffee and how much was actually true she didn't know, and now she'd actually got started, she didn't care. At least it was begun.

Her shoulder muscles ached from stretching out and drawing and she rubbed them absently, hugging herself with her arms and letting the feeling of soreness and relaxation fill her head. While she worked, her mind tended to run along entirely different lines from what she was drawing, and after God knows how long wondering whether Angus really had brainwashed her into thinking exactly like him, it felt good to allow all thought to drain out of her brain.

In the minute's pause that followed, she heard the familiar jingle for the half-hour news on Virgin and checked her watch automatically.

'Oh, shit.' It was half-ten.

Iona would have got a cab if she'd had any money, or if she'd been able to find one. Getting into work wasn't easy at the best of times and now she was in a rush, running round the house getting dressed with the radio on to check for transport crises; it seemed that all the underground lines had delays and the Honda Highway patrol bikes were reporting major traffic jams all over the capital. Possibly due to car pile-ups caused by Honda Highway patrol bikes weaving in and out of the crawling traffic.

In the end, in desperation and panic, she dragged Angus's mountain bike out from its resting place in the junk cupboard and cycled in, cutting corners and going through a couple of no-cycling parks.

And when she arrived at the Bunch of Grapes, sweat pouring off her, it was hard to say who had the redder face, her or Angus.

He was standing behind the bar, on the phone, hair dishevelled from running his spare hand through it and the faint beginnings of sweat marks on his shirt. As soon as he heard the door swing closed, his eyes, which had been squeezed tightly shut, snapped open, registered her arrival and narrowed.

Bad sign, thought Iona, her heart sinking. Very bad sign. How much must have gone wrong already for him to be this stressed about me being late? Had the pub been repossessed?

'Ang—' she began quickly, hoping to get her apology in first to stall him.

'Do you realize I've had to call all the hospitals in London!' he roared, without bothering to hang up the phone in his hand.

'Why?' she asked, surprised. Surely that was a bit dramatic. She was only an hour and a half late. The four coffees had started a samba rhythm going at the front of her head.

'Why?' he repeated, even louder. The woman on the end of the phone finally yelled loud enough to get his attention and he put it to his ear, crossly. 'Yes, I'm sorry, she's just turned up. Very good. No, I'm *not* going to apologize for wasting your time. You should *know* who you have and don't have in your hospital. And frankly, you might want to keep that register open and a spare bed waiting!' He slammed the phone back on the wall bracket and it bounced off. Jim appeared from the office, slunk round, replaced it and slunk back to safety again.

'Angus, will you get a grip of yourself?' panted Iona, trying to keep her voice reasonable in the vague hope that he would respond in kind. 'I'm really sorry I'm late, I lost track of the time while I was painting. You should have phoned me.'

Angus was showing no signs of calming down. 'But you left a note saying you'd gone into work early! What am I supposed to think when I get here and you're not here!'

Iona pulled a face of extreme control. It was very, *very* hard not to get mad at Angus when he started yelling at her like her dad, but she knew as soon as she started shouting too, it would be like throwing petrol on a barbecue, and while the odd shouting match at home was fine, having one in the pub might give the place more of a Den and Angie Watts feel than Tamara would think decently ironic.

'But that's why I left the note, to *say* I was painting in the shed. Angus, please will you stop shouting? If Tamara was a bit late, you wouldn't assume she'd been run over, would you?'

'I could but hope!'

'Angus!'

'It's only because I worry about you, you stupid, stupid woman!' Angus was leaning over the bar now, hands firmly planted on the drip trays, knuckles whitening, eyes bulging, vein on his forehead throbbing. A vision of angry publican-ness straight from Hogarth. 'You could have been lying in a gutter somewhere, bleeding to death! Are you wearing your blood bracelet?'

'Angus,' Iona said in warning tones. She scanned the pub for signs of life. It looked like London during Princess Diana's funeral. As in: she knew that despite the deserted appearance of the place, they were all in there somewhere, watching.

'Well, are you?' he demanded. 'Thirty pounds that cost!'

Something snapped inside Iona. The combination of being spoken to like a child, an errant employee and an imbecile, possibly. 'Angus, you really scare me sometimes!' she yelled back. 'I don't *want* to wear a fucking dog tag the whole time! I'm a grown woman!'

'A grown woman with a rare blood group! And don't swear!'

Iona turned away and clenched and unclenched her fists. She told herself that he was angry because he was worried, and he was worried because he loved her. It wasn't like he was Chris and just enjoyed making her look stupid in front of everyone else.

Summoning up all her self-control, and one or two tips

for talking to small children which Marie had passed on, she turned back and looked him in the eye.

'Angus,' she said, very slowly and quietly enough that it wouldn't travel through to the kitchen. 'I don't want to get into a row here. I am sorry I am late. Please do not talk to me like that in front of all these people. You sound like Hitler.'

'You're not, are you?' he persisted. 'Wearing it?'

'Do you want a slap?' Iona yelled. She banged her hands down on the bar and stared him in the face. 'Why can't you just let well alone? Why don't you have any idea when to stop? Jesus Christ!'

Before he could reply to that, she dragged in a deep breath, which shuddered ominously, and said, 'I'm going to go outside for a moment to calm down. And you're going to calm down too. When I come in again, we'll start this morning again, OK? OK.'

And she walked slowly and deliberately out into the sunshine, where Ned sat waiting for her on the kitchen steps, smoking.

'God!' she hissed. 'I swear he is worse than my dad! He'll be wanting me to get one of those pet chips implanted in my neck next!'

Ned patted the step next to him and offered her his cigarette, which she declined.

'He only does it because he loves you.'

'I know.' Iona shut her eyes and tipped her head back to the sun, so it bleached everything pale blue behind her eyelids. Matt and Lynn the Sheep were still hovering there in their duet/slanging-match pose. 'I know. But it doesn't make me want to kill him any less.'

'That is the way of married couples, you know.'

'Is it?' It was on days like this that Iona really wondered if she could face pointless rows for the rest of her life. Not being allowed to do things independently because everything she did affected her other half. That was how she felt sometimes with Angus, as though he was the Siamese twin with the lungs and control over the legs and all she could do was wave her arms impotently while he decided where they walked.

'Only start worrying when you don't yell back,' said Ned, blowing out a stream of smoke.

'Why's that then?' asked Iona. 'Because I'll be too busy sharpening the kitchen knife? Or because I'll be gagged and bound to the Hoover at home?'

Ned snorted with laughter and slung an arm around her shoulders. 'You want to listen to yourself. Come on, leave it. Some people would kill for what you have with Angus.'

'As opposed to just killing Angus?'

'Iona! Yes!'

'Hmmmm.' She gave him her 'not convinced' face.

'Oh, come on, it's not worth having rows about, is it? You're both just tired, and under pressure, and . . .' He paused and looked at her, as if debating whether he should say what he was thinking.

'What?'

Ned flicked his eyebrows up in a 'never mind' gesture that had infuriated her for years, most recently because Tamara claimed it made him look like a young Sean Connery. Which it didn't at all.

'No, nothing.' He held up his hands and smiled winningly. 'Nowt at all. Come on, let me show you how to make a gurt big bowl of mayonnaise. If you promise not to curdle it with one of them dirty looks you were giving your man,' he said in an appallingly bad all-purpose northern accent.

It had started out as their joint impression of Jim trying to 'do' a northerner, and it had stuck because it was fun to do. Sadly Jim's grasp of irony was about as strong as his regional accents and this only reinforced his belief that he could save himself from a beating in Carlisle with the magic disguise of glottal-stopping. 'By 'eck as like,' Ned added, getting no reaction out of Iona. 'An' all. An' all.'

Iona remained on the step, staring up at him. She was trying to achieve the stern, fixated glare dogs use on cocky sheep, but it didn't have any effect on Ned. Nothing did. 'Don't distract me with comedy accents. What were you going to say?'

He only shook his head at her, smiling his crooked and impenetrable smile.

How come men never feel they have to explain themselves, when women always do?

'No, no,' said Ned, offering her a hand up. 'You're the one who does advice. I don't know what you're meant to do to stop him pissing you off. But it's so obvious he loves you. And he's always been like this, you know that. If you ask me, the problem's more with you than anyone else.'

'And what's *that* meant to mean?' she demanded, springing to her feet.

'I don't know. You tell me.' Ned looked enigmatically at her.

Iona felt an uncharacteristic desire to punch her fist through the newly etched window, and Ned apparently sensed it too, because he opened his arms to her and squeezed her in a big hug.

It was nowhere near as all-enveloping as Angus's bear hugs, due to Ned's inherent skinniness, but for the moment it was oddly preferable.

'That's all I wanted,' she muttered, pressing her clenched fists into his scrawny chest. 'Why can't Angus just do that? Instead of shouting at me all the time?'

'Because, you silly cow, he can't deal with being Angus your permanently concerned boyfriend and Angus your stressed-out employer all at the same time.'

Oh *yeah*, thought Iona, and hated herself for having to be told.

'Haway then,' said Ned, and released her from his hug. He slung his arm round her shoulders, leading her back to the pub, as if they'd just met on the street. 'Let's get on with lunch. I have a lot of vegetables to deal with. And so do you.'

Ned always made it sound so reasonable. And without making her feel stupid either. God, thought Iona, I'm lucky.

Chapter Twenty-two

It was a Friday night. School had been out for four hours. The weekend was meant to start here. In Tooting, however, it was already Sunday evening and looked like remaining so for the next forty-eight hours.

Marie, leaning against the wall with the phone lead twisted round her hand, noticed how her bookshelves could do with a serious dust. It didn't say a lot for the continuing influence of quality literature in her household. Perhaps it said more about the quality of British television and/or the quality of her social life. She wiped the nearest ledge clean with her finger and dragged her attention back to the conversation. Iona wasn't really putting her back into it. Anyone would think she was being distracted by something.

Against her will, Marie's eye fell once again on the letter that had arrived that morning from Kosovo and she forced herself to care about her dusting.

'Now you're *sure* you don't want me to come in?' Marie asked again, raising her voice to be heard over the racket of the pub. She curled the phone lead around her other hand, pivoted on her heel so she didn't have to look at the dust and leaned against the hall bookshelf. IKEA, like most of their furniture. It was the one she had assembled, so it was safe to put big books – and weight – on.

Luckily for Chris's carpentry skills that he only bought paperbacks.

She frowned at herself.

Which he threw away after reading.

Marie wasn't having a good night. By unfortunate contrast, at the other end of the phone it sounded as though
the Bunch of Grapes was full of vibrant, interesting young
people having a *great* time. Restlessly, she turned back round
to face the dusty shelves. 'I could have a quick bath and be
there in an hour.'

'No, no, you're OK.' Iona sounded in high spirits; a laugh
was bubbling through her voice. Not the hysterical one she'd
been developing lately, either.

Marie felt jealous, then guilty for wishing turmoil on
other people, and then gave up. She never knew exactly how
she felt these days, which was disorienting and didn't make
for consistent teaching. She opened her mouth to demur, but
Iona was off again.

'Oh, hang on. 'Scuse me, Marie.' There was a muffled
inquiry about eating and she heard Iona allocate the table
in the corner. Her favourite. A two-seater. The one with
the view straight into the busy kitchen – where no doubt
they would be hoping to catch a glimpse of London's
favourite rock-god-cum-pastry chef. Marie turned round
again, disengaged her foot from the telephone wire and
found herself staring at a thinner version of herself grinning
out from the framed wedding photo opposite.

She swallowed hard. Any photos featuring Chris, or her
and Chris, were now in a box under the stairs, wrapped in
the manky T-shirts he hadn't bothered to take with him.
How had she missed that one? She tucked the phone under
her ear and yanked the photo off its hook. There was another
pale frame of dust on the wall where it had been.

For a long moment she stood looking at the photo in
the frame. Was that really her there under the banana leaf
canopy, holding Chris's hand? It wasn't her hair, her face,
and it certainly wasn't her stomach.

'Marie? Still there? I've got Mark on floor service tonight,'
Iona went on, her voice all bright and unaware. 'The
kitchen's quite quiet for once. Ned's only doing fish, because

he got such a good deal from the fish man, so there's just four mains on the board, and Mark's helping me and Tamara out on the bar— Ned! Get back in there, will you? And take that haddock with you!'

Marie thought sourly that, as threats went, that one had a very low threat content.

'I don't *mind* coming in,' she offered again, revolving the other way. Her eyes unfocused on her collection of Thomas Hardy Penguin Classics, arranged at a height that people would notice them as they walked through into the sitting room. 'There's just me versus a bottle of cheap red wine from the school Christmas raffle and a packet of Hobnobs. We'll be at it all night. I mean, you'd be doing me a favour really, just keeping me away from them.' She tried to make it sound like a joke, although it wasn't. The nights she worked at the Grapes, nothing passed her lips; on the nights she stayed in she was a human Pacman, going round the house, her mouth opening and shutting until everything was eaten and she could start on the next level, which took place in Sainsbury's and saw Pacman equipped with a trolley.

'Noooooo.' Iona's voice still had a distinct quiver of a laugh in it – a private-conversation-type laugh too; as though she'd been caught in the middle of a big running joke.

Marie had an unpleasant flash of how her mother must have felt whenever she phoned home from a party to get one of her brothers to fetch her. Pretty pissed off, as it turned out. The photograph felt heavy in her hands and she put it down. Then pushed it behind the bookshelf with her foot.

'Honestly, Marie, there's no need for you to come over – it's so under control even Angus has gone home.'

'You're kidding? I thought he slept on a pile of newspapers in the kitchen during the week so he could be there for the vegetable delivery?'

'Yeah, well.' Iona made a lavish snorting noise. Or opened a bottle of wine on the big bar corkscrew, Marie couldn't quite tell. She tried not to feel peeved that she still wasn't getting Iona's undivided attention. But then maybe that was her own fault for underplaying the extent of the Chris situation. She'd told Angus he'd gone to Kosovo on a short-term project – not that anyone had actually noticed his absence for about a fortnight. Marie ached to pour everything out to Iona, but something made her feel that she should be dealing with this on her own. It *was* her marriage, after all, her adult's problem, and she felt traitorous even thinking about involving other people. The last thing she needed was Iona's sympathy, because deep down Marie knew that it would just confirm how bad things had really got, and she dreaded her advice – sound as it would be – even more.

Iona was still fiddling with something, holding the phone under her chin. 'Angus? Oh, he's got one of his bad migraines, so I made him go home and lie down. But I know he'll be reading *Caterer* magazine in bed, though, so it's not like he'll get any rest. The man's obsessed. I keep finding brewery reports in the loo at home. I can't tell you how boring it is. Don't tell him I told you that.'

'No, course.' Marie could sympathize with the migraines – she got them a lot herself. She had cut out chocolate and caffeine as much as she could bear, but didn't seem able to cut out Chris, who triggered them off more than anything else. And Angus was working like a demon; Marie now couldn't recall a time in which they'd had a conversation that didn't revolve exclusively around cover charges. 'Well, look, give me a ring if it gets busy and you need a hand. I'm just at a loose end here.'

As soon as this came out of her mouth, she regretted it; that would set alarm bells ringing. Not that it was Iona's style to be leaning on the bar, rolling her eyes and going, 'Oooh, I bet Marie's heading for a breakdown, she's that lonely on her own,' but she wouldn't put it past Tamara to start a bit of kitchen gossiping, under the convenient guise of sympathy.

Paranoia! The kids shrieked it all the time in the playground to one another, usually with some justification.

'Ah, poor Marie, are you missing Chris?' asked Iona politely. 'Must be quiet without him.'

'Oh, you know . . .' Marie tried to keep her voice vague, but she knew Iona wasn't fooled.

'When's he coming back, did you say?'

'Um . . .' Sickness started to spread through her stomach at the thought of Chris coming back and she felt horribly mutinous without actually knowing what she was feeling mutinous about.

Marie knew enough about eight-year-olds to recognize a hissy fit when it started brewing. She pressed her tongue against her front teeth to stop the whine coming out and coughed to get Iona's attention. 'Fine, well, look, you're obviously busy, I'll speak to you soon.' Her eyes flicked round the sitting room. If she stayed here, she'd go mad. Really mad. Redecorating in the middle of the night mad, even.

Iona's voice was sharp in her ear. 'You're OK, aren't you, Marie?' she asked. 'You would tell me if there was a problem?'

Tell the perfect friend, with the perfect boyfriend and the perfect life? I don't think so.

Marie felt a chill of self-inflicted isolation so painful she knew she had to get off the phone at once. 'I'm fine,' she lied. 'Fine. Bye.' And she put the phone down before Iona could check.

So. It was either read Chris's letter, which would make her feel guilty and decadent, or tackle the dusting.

Marie ran herself a bath and got in, holding the unopened letter above the water level. She could only face opening it in the bath, and only then surrounded by talismans – candles, glass of wine, CD player as near as the cord would stretch from the kitchen, playing her *Frank Sinatra Sings for Only the Lonely* album. She loved her imaginary Rat Pack Moll at the Sands persona even more than the Gina Lollobrigida one. No skinny dames for Frankie, she thought, slipping off her robe and hanging it on the back of the door to block out the hard strip-light from the hall. No skimmed-milk nagging about wiggling hips from Jack and Sammy.

She lowered herself carefully, stopped halfway down, bit the letter between her teeth and scrubbed viciously at her thighs with the body brush hanging balefully from the shower attachment. When her skin was stinging (from all the little cellulite families packing their bags in panic, she trusted), Marie allowed herself to sink into the water. She'd run a huge slug of baby bath oil under the hot tap and the resulting froth hissed around her as the little bubbles burst on her skin.

I'll open it when I've had half the wine, she thought, picking up the cool glass from the bathmat. Not that I'm putting it off.

Marie loved drinking wine in the bath and rarely had the chance to indulge. Chris had once happily told everyone that, incipient alcoholism aside, he'd knocked her student wine-in-the-bath habit on the head in case she 'got drunk and slipped and bled to death like Janet Leigh'. She'd pointed out (with an unattractively furrowed brow, he informed her later) that poor Janet hadn't exactly stubbed her toe on the shower rail, but he'd bluffed and Angus had saved him with a well-timed cry of horror about how drinking any half-decent white in such steamy conditions would ruin the bouquet. Marie knew all along that Chris hadn't the faintest idea about *Psycho*, or was perhaps confusing Janet Leigh with someone from *Crossroads*, but she hadn't corrected him in front of their friends. But it annoyed her that yet another moment of his correcting *her* had stuck in the collective memory. No wonder Iona hated him.

Their whole history was littered with incidents like that, she thought, letting her first sip of wine spread across her tongue. They must all wonder who the bloody teacher is.

Marie lay back in the froth and let the external warmth from the bath meet the internal warmth from the wine. She ignored the mould on the grouting. The envelope sat on the bath rack, propped up with a nailbrush. She tried to look through the paper, blanking her mind to see if anything would pop into her head. What had Chris said in his letter? As a rule, it helped her cope with unwelcome post if she could guess in advance what she might have to read. She liked to err on the pessimistic side, to be safe.

Marie stared at the letter, addressed in Chris's thin, backward-sloping hand. *I'm working so hard they've promoted me to UN Roving Ambassador?* Some inevitable undisguised dig about the refugees having nothing while they all agonized over the provenance of organic sausages? And another dig at right-on Tamara, probably; the only one of them who claimed to have a Social Conscience to compete with Chris's – according to him, Tamara's take on it was to go out socially, giving free voice to her conscience.

Not far from the truth.

Maybe he'll say how much he's missing you, said a small voice inside her, and Marie felt her skin shiver. That wasn't an insight from the letter, it was an automatic thought. They *ought* to be missing one another. But her mind chased it away again, with a worrying swiftness, and she realized she didn't actually *want* him to be missing her. Because she wasn't missing him. Missing each other (or not) just muddied the nicely flat surface his absence had managed to create.

Sometimes she felt the most tremendous sense of relief that the horrible situation had just gone, as if some higher magic force had heard her wish over the fudge pan: one day she was shackled to a man she couldn't stand and the next he had disappeared, through no fault of her own, and she could watch whatever soaps she liked on television and order in takeaway three nights in a row.

Then as soon as some kid called her Mrs Davenport in the playground, it would hit her like a slap – that she had screwed up her chance at marriage and that was it. Wrong man, wrong time, wrong stupid place. And she had to live with the consequences. Marie hated feeling stupid. How could she have been so *stupid*? She frowned at the letter. And more to the point, how could she have been so *tacky*? *How* had a child who had planned her church wedding down to the individual choirboys managed to convince herself that there wasn't something deeply suspect about making eternal vows while wearing a bikini? For God's sake, her one abiding memory of the service wasn't so much the promises she was making but the nagging consciousness of what kind of rear view everyone else was getting of the bride.

Don't be bitter after the event. There's nothing you can do about it now.

Marie sank further into the bubbles and had another big mouthful of wine. She couldn't keep pushing this away. She really had to deal with how she felt. He was going to come back at some point, wasn't he? With a frown, she stared at the letter for something to focus on and tried to pick apart the mess of conflicting emotions in her head, each one of which seemed to twist away like a fish every time she got near it. She hoped the gradual effect of the wine could slow them down and let her see her feelings for what they were before her conscience could put some kind of gloss over the ugly truth.

She grabbed the first one quite easily after another glass of wine and three songs: she actually loved being on her own. The first time in her life she'd felt truly free, in a faintly miserable sort of way. Being with all the others at the Grapes was easy – they all assumed she must miss Chris like mad, and didn't talk about it, and because they were all *imagining* her loneliness for her, it didn't make her feel a fraud, for some reason, when she kicked off her shoes at night and thanked God that her boring flatmate wasn't in to tell her her feet smelled.

Though she knew she should feel guilty.

She topped up the wine, and Frank turned himself over on auto-replay.

This could be easy, she thought, letting her eyes unfocus on the painting hanging on the wall opposite: a present from Iona, big, bluish and restfully unspecific. Decide how I feel before I open the letter and then it can't hurt me whatever it says.

You don't even like him.

It swam so fast out of nowhere and echoed so loud in her head that Marie almost swallowed her wine the wrong way.

But it was true. She didn't. She didn't really feel much for him at all, one way or another.

Irrationally, Marie waited for a moment for the finger of God to poke through the bathroom ceiling and impale her, but nothing happened.

She let out her breath. It wasn't that she was missing him so much as feeling that she *ought* to be. And what was she living with: a real man or the theory of marriage? The thought had been hanging around the back of her mind for so long and she'd steadfastly refused to define it. And now she had, she was back at the top of a long, swoopy water slide and she'd just kicked off. There was no stopping, no turning, no clambering up the slippery sides back to where she had been before.

She felt the loss more of his empty role as Husband than she missed him as a person, and that was just coming from a sense of social guilt. As a person, she was glad she didn't have to deal with the guilt of opening her heart and finding it shamefully empty.

Marie felt a bit sick. And she still hadn't got round to the letter.

Her brain searched on relentlessly now she'd tacitly given it permission to go into the dark, slimy tank and have a root about. It was like trying not to look at a car crash.

For all he tries to behave as though you're just his girlfriend, you've made a far bigger emotional investment than that – and he is never going to match it. So do you want to spend the rest of your life having him remind you of that, just by being there? Or not, as he sees fit. Do you? Is that what you're prepared to accept for the rest of your life, just to have that ring on your finger?

Her skin crawled in the cooling water.

And that's without him being the most irritating man in the world.

Marie snatched the envelope before she could hear any more. What was the point in torturing herself if he only wanted her to send more socks out? She slit it open with the end of her tailcomb.

Dear Marie

Sorry about the ITN note paper – we are getting very short on supplies.

You will have seen from the news that things are not getting easier here. (If, that is, the BBC ever bothered to broadcast anything we sent them.) Some of the volunteers have had to go home and I have agreed to stay for another six months at least, though it could be more, depending on funding.

It is not easy to write this, but I have reached the conclusion that since there is no chance of you coming out here to be with me, we should separate. I have thought for some time that our lives have been going in different directions, and now I know how bad the situation is out here for displaced peoples, I do not think I will be coming back to England for some time. Many of the things I used to think are important in life (e.g. decent music, nice car, etc.) I now realize are totally irrelevant.

I know this must seem very sudden, but this has been quite a catholic experience for me.

Hope you are well.

Luv, Chris

Chapter Twenty-three

'Can I come in?' Marie stood on the doorstep and felt the rain go down the back of her collar. She could see herself in the hall mirror, dripping. Ergh, cliché. Very *Four Weddings*. She winced as she heard herself say it; it was the first thing she had said aloud since she'd spoken to Iona on the phone – before opening the letter. Not the most stylish of starts to the rest of her life.

She supposed Angus was in his pyjamas – a warm pair of tartan trousers and a worn old white V-neck T-shirt from which the dark hairs on his upper chest were just visible. He had his wire-rimmed reading glasses on and a copy of *Caterer* magazine dangled from his left hand. Just as Iona had predicted. How nice to be able to do that. Predict things about your boyfriend.

'Yeah, yeah, course,' he said, running a hand through his half-squashed curls – he'd obviously been lying on his side all evening – as he stared at her own soaked hair. 'But you're . . .'

For the last two hours, walking around in the dark and barely noticing the steady rain, words had streamed silently through Marie's head with a fluency she had never known: raging, crying, demanding, yelling, she'd gone through the lot to an imaginary and silent Chris. 'Luv', indeed. What the hell did he know about it? Sharp little shards of resentment cut through the dull pain she felt all over, and hearing a voice that didn't sound like hers bawling fresh and yet somehow wearily familiar accusations in her head, Marie realized, with a terrible lurch of fear, how black and bottomless the whole thing was. Because it wasn't just about Chris leaving, it was about her too.

Suddenly she had no idea who she really was. None of this seemed to be happening to her. What was she going to do? And how could she imagine that she knew herself when this reaction could leave her so totally paralysed?

As she stumbled along the paths, her emotional compass swung round constantly, sending her spiralling off into totally different areas of fresh hell. It had felt scary, disconcerting, to be swept along by emotions you didn't realize you had, like being caught by a series of strong winds on open land – and more scary, standing here on Angus's doorstep, to realize how far she had walked, alone, in hopelessly inadequate shoes and with so little sense of where she was going. And, more to the point, on her own in the dark.

Behaviour so out of character freaked her out and, from the look on Angus's face, freaked him out too.

He stood there in his bare feet, wearing his reassuringly puzzled expression like a sturdy lighthouse of normality, and Marie's brain, relieved to be back somewhere it recognized after the blindfold roller-coaster of free association, started running on autopilot again. For some reason she was so glad it was him, and not Iona, who answered the door that, at the thought of burying her head in that strong chest, she felt the tears start up again in her throat. From somewhere outside her own head Marie despaired. They were honestly beyond her control. Someone must be flicking them on and off with a remote from the comfort of their own sofa.

She swayed dangerously on the step with the effort of keeping the tears in.

At that, Angus seemed to spring to life. 'Marie, for God's sake, come inside, you'll catch your death.' He opened the door wide and started hunting about for a towel. 'Where've you been?'

She shuffled over the welcome mat, all her energy suddenly draining away as the warmth seeped back into her extremities. Angus and Iona's house might not have been the ideal place to come. From the front door in, every surface was covered with pictures of the pair of them, taken at arm's length by Angus, the man with the longest arms in London.

She sank on to the sofa, which was covered with a duvet and full of pillows and papers, stock orders and letters with brewery headed paper. Marie shut her eyes and probed the hollowness that had opened up inside her, as you'd probe a hole where a tooth had recently fallen out. Suddenly, there was nothing there. Where had it all gone – her intestines, her heart, her stomach?

'Kick your shoes off, you're soaking,' ordered Angus. He lifted cushions and moved piles of paper until he finally found a towel on the radiator. 'Sorry about the mess, we've both been working late. Come here.'

'I'm not going anywhere.'

'Manner of speaking,' said Angus, and dropped the warm towel over her head, rubbing her hair dry as if she was a wet dog. The wine that had insulated her outside was wearing off and making her dizzy as he ruffled her hair about, but somewhere underneath the normal Marie began to swim slowly back to the surface.

'What's happened?' he said briskly.

Marie opened her mouth but couldn't find words.

'I know you don't normally go tramping around the streets of London at this time of night, and I know you wouldn't ruin those shoes for no good reason, so there must be something wrong, hey?'

His lovely posh voice, thought Marie. How could you not be reassured by that? Lucky Iona. But still nothing came out.

Angus finished towelling her hair and whipped it away to demonstrate his handiwork. Marie could see herself in yet another big mirror over the fireplace. Her hair was standing on end and her mascara had smudged down her cheekbones. Somehow she looked much thinner than usual. Deflated.

It occurred to her that she should maybe apologize for interrupting him, but she pushed it away. She wasn't sure if opening her mouth wouldn't release the tidal wave of tears again.

'Hang on.' Angus rushed out and came back with some Wet Wipes. 'Your face . . . you might want to . . .' He made scrubbing gestures.

Marie smoothed the tissue against her face and automatically the mantra that had got her through a hundred messy dumpings at school passed through her mind: this is your first cleanse of your new life. You're wiping him off your face. All mascara you put on now will be free of him.

Free of him. How could it ever have been that simple?

Maybe it hadn't actually got her through that well, she thought, as a huge lump rushed up her throat and threatened to spill out.

'Sit down here,' said Angus, patting the sofa next to him.

She stood still, her brain flitting from the irrelevant sensation of water dripping down her arm to the drowning feeling in her chest. Her thoughts whirred and spun like unengaged gears.

'Marie!' Angus grabbed her by the shoulders. 'For God's sake, Marie, you're not breathing!'

She looked at him with baleful eyes. Couldn't he tell that she was trying to suffocate a huge childish sob?

He changed tack. 'Right, we need to get you warmed up again, don't we? You take that wet stuff off and put some of this on.' He yanked a washing basket full of clean but unironed clothes out from behind a chair. 'I'll go and get you something hot to drink.'

He's such a *coper*, thought Marie, still standing up and dripping, but now managing small controlled breaths. Her

legs felt like jelly. What she really wanted was for Angus
to stand in front of her like her mum: 'Arms up!' to strip
off the jumper, 'Legs out!' to pull off the sodden jeans.
But that would be hard to explain to Iona if she walked
in unexpectedly. Without really knowing what she was
doing, she managed to get her jeans off and dragged on
a pair of tracksuit bottoms – there was no point picking
out Iona's size twelve clothes and getting Arse Guilt on top
of everything else – and found a warm college rugby shirt.
Obeying distant orders from another side of her brain, Marie
tried to put her wet clothes on the radiator but all hand-eye
coordination seemed to have deserted her and they slipped
off on to a sleeping cat.

Angus came back in as she was dazedly rotating in the
middle of the floor, her eyes flinching away from photo after
photo of Angus and Iona squeezing their noses together in
various parts of the world.

'Drink this,' he said, and pressed a warm mug into
her hand.

'Drink *me. Alice in Wonderland.*'

'You can stop teaching now, if you want to.'

'Can't. It's the only time I don't get answered back.'

Angus pushed her gently on to the sofa and covered up
her knees with the duvet. 'I know I'm no substitute for the
Great Agony Aunt but, uuuhm, if you want to tell me what's
happened, I'm happy to let you get it all out.'

'But you've got a migraine . . .' She was stalling and she
knew it.

Angus plumped up a cushion and put it behind her head.
'I've taken all the painkillers I can without topping myself
– and someone has to be in a fit state to see the man from
the brewery tomorrow. You know the pumps are playing
up again in the cellar? I just can't seem to get the pressures
right and . . .' He saw Marie's face glaze. 'Come on, get it
off your chest.'

Marie noted that he didn't make his usual joke about

that being quite some chest she had there. He must really be trying. Or else she must look seriously bad.

'Umm,' she began. As soon as she told Angus, it would be real and she would have to deal with it. She clenched the duvet up in her fists and squeezed. Better him than anyone else she could think of. Not Iona. Something in her wanted to run away at the thought of telling Iona. It would be like confirming every quiet hint Iona had dropped about Chris, every cautious inquiry about the marriage she had defended so stoutly. Telling Iona would be like admitting to herself that she'd been wrong all along.

Angus passed her a glass of water and didn't say anything.

Marie took a deep breath. 'I got a letter from Chris this morning. You know I told you he was in Kosovo. Well, he wants to stay.' She swallowed. 'He, er . . . He wants us to separate.'

She looked up at Angus for a reaction, but his eyes were deliberately fixed on the wall, on a huge photograph Iona had had enlarged to poster size of the sun setting behind a lacy suspension bridge. He waited a couple of seconds to make sure she'd finished and then circled her hand with his own, stroking her palm gently with his thumb.

The silence felt a bit disconcerting, conditioned as she was to expect the immediate storm of female sympathy, commiseration and denunciation that usually followed that kind of admission. But Angus's reaction made her feel weirdly calm, as though whatever it was that was breaking her up, he would sort it out, make everything make sense. It wasn't something she imagined Jim, Mr Panic, could ever pull off; and then it popped into her head like a speech bubble that in all the time she'd been with Chris, he'd never ever made her feel as though he could control things. He'd rugby-passed decisions at her like lead weights, and she'd always carried them because she thought she had to. And that was what he was still doing now, making her make the decision.

'Oh, Marie, I'm so sorry,' said Angus at last, and she shut her eyes at the undisguised sadness in his voice. 'Come here.' He stretched out his arms and she slumped into them, squeezing up her eyes to hold in the tears.

'Is this the letter?' She could feel him reaching into her handbag.

She nodded, not wanting to look.

'Shall I read it? Save you telling me?'

And that would be why too – Angus had no interest in prying. She shook her head against his armpit, and felt all the muscles in her body go limp. Her legs began to feel heavy after tramping across the common and the pulse in her head throbbed. Even though she must be crushing him, slumping boneless on his side, Angus didn't protest or try to rearrange himself, he just radiated comforting warmth and solidity like a three-bar heater. A distinctive aroma of Dormant Male hung around him, a very blokey smell, just on the turn of being sweaty but mixed with a faint lemony top note of shower gel. Angus didn't wear aftershave, no matter how hard Iona tried to make him, but he washed often.

There was a long silence while Angus read Chris's letter and Marie tried to stop herself drifting off into unconsciousness. She thought she could hear him murmuring, 'Git!' at intervals, but it could have been her own spasmodic hiccuping. Finally he let out a long breath, which she could hear from inside his chest.

'What does he mean, "a catholic experience"? Does he mean lots of different things are happening to him? Or that he's seeing visions of the Virgin Mary riding donkeys all over the place?'

'I think he means cathartic.'

Angus huffed through his nose. 'Well, I'm not even sure if that's the right . . . Yeah, well, there's certainly a lot of guilt washing around here.'

They sat for a few moments in silence while faint noises from cars, hissing on the wet roads, drifted in from outside, the hard rattle of the overground trains going by. The cat flap banged in the kitchen and Lady Cat wandered in, still silky smooth apart from her spiky legs, which were slicked into cowboy fringes where she'd run through the wet grass. She stalked over and settled behind the radiator.

'What are you going to do?' he asked eventually.

Typical man. Marie's lips smiled into his chest, even though she didn't know she was smiling and her eyes were still full of tears. Iona would have asked *how* she felt, Tamara *why* it had happened.

She blinked. What *was* she going to do? What was the point of doing anything? The End. Game over.

For fuck's sake! This isn't like you to be so spineless.

Marie was startled by the words that came to her lips from nowhere. 'I think he's right, we should separate.'

And she knew that was the right thing to do, despite the clamouring in her head. Somehow it was much easier to say this to Angus than to anyone else. He knew about honourable failures – not everything could work out in business the way you wanted. It didn't mean you didn't try. 'You know, I never imagined marriage would be like this. It doesn't feel like a marriage anyway – it feels like the sort of relationship where he does exactly what he likes and I'm the one doing the worrying for both of us.'

There was a pregnant pause.

'I mean, I know that's a traditional patriarchal marriage in reverse,' Marie skittered on, 'but I wanted something a bit more modern. Like having both partners in the same country. And in love with each other.' She bit her lip.

'You don't need to be glib,' said Angus. 'You don't need to say anything at all.' He stroked her hair and they sat in silence again.

Marie didn't know what to say, because her feelings seemed to be changing every twenty seconds, like traffic lights. As soon as she thought she was relieved, it turned

out she was actually devastated. And then she was angry.
Very angry.

They sat in silence for a long time, listening to the rain.
Eventually Angus said, 'People keep asking me why Iona and
I aren't married, you know. All the time. You lot, people at
work . . .' He paused. 'Her mother.'

Marie looked up. That was true. She didn't understand
why they weren't either. In a deeply unworthy way, it
stung her that Iona and Angus had the kind of marriage
she wanted, without actually being married. And it was
about the only facet of their relationship that Iona didn't
mind discussing – she was usually more than happy to fill
Marie in on the little anniversary dinners, or her slight
irritation at Angus's pet names for her. Being Iona, and
more considerate than most, she'd toned all this down a lot
recently. But Angus didn't ever talk about his relationship
in front of other people. Marie was touched. Maybe he was
trying to make her feel less stupid. He carried on stroking
her hair rather absently, as if she were Lady Cat.

'I know I'm boring and old-fashioned, but the whole idea
of what marriage *means* is really serious for me, and I think it
is for you too. It's not just a load of words and a few hymns,
it's about changing your life. And if you're going to give up
all the joys of being single, you have to believe you're doing
it for something much better, and that means you can't look
back. Ever. Because it can't be the same. People forget that
you have to sacrifice *something* to get what you want. The
way you both live has to change, and I really don't believe all
those people who say it's no different. It has to be, doesn't
it? Or why bother?'

Marie couldn't think of an answer to this, because it was
exactly what she had thought herself. Creighton, a cat who
never went out in the rain, stalked round the sofa and stared
up at her, gathering himself to leap up in search of more
warmth. Marie closed her eyes slowly at him, trying to win
his trust. He stared back, inscrutable.

'You know, and I'm sorry for going on here, I really believe that if you're going to live by a set of rules, you have to know what they are and *want* them,' Angus went on softly. 'And to be honest, I don't think you and Chris have been playing by the same set of rules. Or at least only one of you takes them seriously. Don't you think? If you don't mind me saying. Being unfaithful to a marriage doesn't just mean sleeping around.'

He fell silent again and Marie wasn't sure if she was meant to reply. The hair-stroking was making her feel sleepy. The thought of having to leave the warmth and calmness of Angus's house was making her feel sick. She temporarily forgot about Iona, distracted as she was by the long-forgotten experience of talking to Angus on his own.

'I mean, it's not *just* hurt pride,' she said. 'I almost don't care about that. It's what it means to all the things I believed in. I feel like I'm letting everyone down. I keep thinking,' Marie mumbled, speaking the words aloud as she thought them, 'that because he obviously didn't get married in the same sense as I did, there's not really a sacred bond there, and that it wouldn't be so bad if . . .' She stopped. Oh, God, if only she could get into a time machine and stop all this happening in the first place!

'Marie, don't answer if you don't want to, but why *did* you and Chris get married?' Angus's voice was very gentle.

She swallowed hard and pressed a hand to her forehead to stop another burst of tears. 'In ten words or less? Erm . . . Because . . . Because we . . . .' Marie managed a rueful smile. 'I don't know.' She cast her mind back, trying to winkle out the exact sensation she'd felt on the beach, but it had all gone. All she could see in her mind were the too-familiar photographs, not her memories, and they were static.

She groped around, trying to think between the spaces in the photograph album. Any thought of Chris was now impossibly painful and her mind kept twisting away from recalling anything nice about him. Angus's slow hand kept stroking her hair – she wondered if he had forgotten he was doing it, but it was too soothing to risk making him stop.

'Ah,' said Angus meaningfully.

Marie frowned. *I don't know why I got married?* This was what she'd been afraid of, confirming every snipe and dolorous prediction about her marriage. Self-respect made her dredge something up. 'No, no, we got married because it really felt like the right thing to do at the time. So we just did it. There was no one there to stand up at the back of the church and stop us, and I suppose that was the whole point. I always knew we had to come home. I thought he realized that too at the time.' She let out a short laugh of breath. 'As you do. And when we got back, you know, the novelty of it kind of distracted us for a long while. I was doing my training, he was starting his lifetime's work to save the world . . . None of you lot were married, so it wasn't as if we knew what we were *meant* to be doing. And we were happy to begin with. Honestly, we were.'

She'd rehearsed this in her head for ages. Now she came to speak it out loud, it didn't feel like her own past any more. The hand scratched her head gently, pressing down on what Marie thought must be her reiki points from the waves of relaxation that went through her.

'Well, there aren't any rules for a good marriage, are there? Have you got any other married friends?' asked Angus. 'People at Chris's work?'

She bit her lip from the inside. She knew what he was getting at and she knew very well how marriages were meant to work, thank you. Hadn't her parents been married for thirty years at the last countback and weren't they still able to talk in full sentences and with normally pitched voices?

But out loud she said, 'Not really. A couple of teachers at school, no one we'd go out with.' She could hear her voice go tight and defensive.

'Well . . .' Angus politely let her make the connection by herself.

'No. *No.*' Marie mentally pushed her parents to one side. Bringing them into it would make her sound like some sad little bimbo who even delegated responsibility for her own marriage. Bringing Chris's parents and their long-running alimony wrangles into it would make her sound vindictive. And hadn't she always fought her own battles? 'No! It's not that . . . I just don't think . . .'

Tears filled up her eyes again and she struggled to keep them back in front of Angus. '*Don't* make excuses for him. I'm not. Marriages can work. If one in three ends in divorce, then there are two that last, aren't there?' she said fiercely.

She felt him nod above her. 'But Marie, you know, no one's blaming you for—'

Marie twisted herself up and looked Angus in the face. He looked back at her, took off his glasses and squeezed the bridge of his nose, wise blue eyes full of concern.

She hurried to speak before he could. His lovely male sympathy was pushing her towards the edge of a complete Scarlett O'Hara crying fit. 'Angus, I'm not asking you to say it can all be made better. I know what the truth is, even if it's really hard to say. If I liked Chris, I could come to terms with the fact that I don't fancy him any more. There would be a relationship there, with other rewards. But I *don't* like him. I think he's a self-centred, self-deluding, self-serving, *boring* arsehole. That's the easy bit. The hard bit is knowing that he feels exactly the same way about me, and that, being brutally honest with myself, I'm too proud to let him dump me, because he promised to love me for ever, and I won't let him treat those promises so lightly. If I let him do *that*, it means admitting that he didn't mean them when he made them. Which means admitting I've been stupid all along. So I can't let him walk away. God, even when I was fifteen I wouldn't let a lad dump me by letter.'

There was another longish silence. Angus seemed to be choosing his words carefully, picking his way through the tangle of what she'd blurted out. In the wine and the confusion and the shock, even Marie had lost track of what she was thinking, and she didn't really fancy having all the contradictions of it rationally presented to her by Angus the solicitor. A couple of times, he opened his mouth to say something and then stopped. But when he did speak, it wasn't to sum up her argument, and his voice was soft and worried.

'You'll refuse to divorce him, if it means being miserable yourself?'

Marie nodded miserably. 'That's what I'm scared of. Knee jerk. I didn't know I could be such a cow. This morning I just wanted him to vanish, I prayed that the last five years could be erased so I wouldn't have to deal with the way I feel now. And now he's making me *do* something, I just feel mad and vicious.' She laughed bitterly. 'You know, I prayed for this to happen – for him to vanish magically from my life! And look how I've taken it! I must be losing my mind!'

Angus sighed. What could he say? *It could have been so much worse?* 'You're not mad, Marie. It's the hardest thing you've ever gone through. Poor, poor you. Come here.'

Angus tightened his arms round her and hugged her, grateful beyond belief she wasn't Iona and scared that – in the future he couldn't predict or prevent – she could be.

Marie buried her head into the soft darkness beneath his arm. How bad would it be if she didn't have her friends? How would she get through this without someone to absorb some of the pain? If she didn't have them, she really would be no one at all. A flood of warm feeling overwhelmed her, meeting the rising tide of misery, and as they met she burst into tears.

All that time, all those *allowances*, all for *nothing*.

'Hey, hey,' said Angus, stroking the length of her spine. Marie knew he could feel the babyish sobs jerking through her, but she had known Angus too long to feel embarrassed with him, and she cried in a way she knew she never could with Iona. Iona. God! The thought of her sympathetic eyes and her well-meaning concern made Marie feel ashamed and stupid and humiliated, but deep down she knew that was nothing at all to do with Iona, and everything to do with herself.

'Come on.' Angus's hand stopped between her shoulder blades and rubbed the small hairs on the nape of her neck. 'Marie, I'm no expert, but sometimes things go wrong no matter how hard you try. Shit happens. It's not your fault. It's not anyone's fault. But you may find that later you're grateful for all this. That it happens for a reason. Hmm?'

I knew you'd say that, thought Marie. No fake promises of overnight salvation, just practical reassurance.

She groped for words to express how she felt, how grateful she was for his comfort, but all she could think of was floating in this reassuring darkness for as long as possible. Not letting go.

But Angus was tipping her chin up, to check she hadn't passed out, probably, and the sight of the concern written on his tired face made her heart contract for what she didn't have herself, and she clenched her eyes shut against the tears she could feel squeezing through her eyelids again.

'Oh, poor Marie,' he murmured.

Before it could occur to her what she was doing, Marie lifted her head and, still hiccuping faintly with tears, kissed Angus on the mouth. The darkness was velvety behind her eyelids and it felt as though she had no sensation anywhere but her lips; reaching blindly, she brushed his chin before hitting the soft firmness of his mouth. His skin was bristly with late-night stubble, and his lips softer than she'd imagined

—*when* had *she imagined what Angus's lips would be like?*—

parted in surprise and kissed her back. The swimming in her head seemed to stop as she touched him and Marie shut her eyes and ears to every other sensation, feeling the blackness rush up and envelope her. It was a relief to drown, knowing that it wasn't just her who was wrong any more, and she sank willingly into Angus, all her senses converging on his mouth; he was all she could taste and smell and feel. Nothing of her remained. She just wanted to be somewhere safe inside him, carried in his pocket, hidden in his hand.

But clearly, in the front of her mind, Marie knew as soon as she felt the soft wetness of his mouth that this moment would have to stop, and even if she felt a million times better now, she would feel worse, *much* worse than before, when it was over.

She had no idea how long their kiss went on for – and it reminded her painfully how long it was since she'd been kissed by anyone half decent – but she broke it off before she realized she had. As her lips pulled away from his, she was swept by the same sense of chilly loss as when she'd stepped out of the hot shower that morning into the cold bathroom.

Marie kept her eyes closed. 'God, I'm *so* sorry, Angus,' she said, meaning it. 'I honestly don't know what . . .'

Her mouth smiled at the cliché, although absolutely no part of her felt like smiling at all.

'No, don't worry,' said Angus's voice. He sounded a long way away. 'It's . . . I wouldn't worry about it.'

Had that happened to him before? Was there a side of sensible, responsible Angus none of them knew about?

Marie opened her eyes in curiosity and wished she hadn't. He was staring at Iona's graduation portrait over the bookshelf. The 'big dog' expression had returned. And though he hadn't pushed her away – he was far too polite to do that – she didn't want to compromise him yet again, so she pulled herself into a sitting position by pretending to reach for the handkerchief on the floor.

In the silence, she noticed that the rain had got heavier and was drumming against the skylight like ball bearings.

'Uumm,' she began, feeling it was up to her to say something, but then stopped, not actually knowing what to say. She didn't want to go home, though she knew she should offer. She knew she couldn't really stay here, though Angus would feel *he* had to offer. Where else could she go, without having to explain why she couldn't go home? The spinning, hopeless feeling gripped her chest and she remembered that this was the real horror of splitting up, not being happy in your own space any more.

Angus made the decision for her. 'Marie, you can't go home tonight,' he said.

If the kindness of the offer hadn't been deeply reassuring, the warmth of his lovely chocolatey voice would have been enough, she thought.

He got up and ruffled his hands through his hair, making it stand up in tufts. Marie couldn't stop herself sneaking a curious glance at his pyjama bottoms for signs of guilt. 'You've had a dreadful shock and Iona would never forgive me if I let you go home now.'

They both spotted the irony of this and looked away.

Gallantly, Angus kept talking to spare her embarrassment, although she was very near to sinking into exhausted oblivion where she sat.

'So, um, look, why don't you sleep on the sofa tonight, and I'll run you home in the morning?'

'That would be really kind of you, Angus,' she said. Her eyes felt so heavy and trying to come up with proper sentences was like pushing her thoughts through treacle. She was drunk, but it didn't help.

'Fine, OK,' he said, 'no problem. Just give me a minute . . .' and he began to gather up the papers scattered on the floor. He looked at a couple and swore gently under his breath while he shuffled them into order. Marie wanted to do something, or say something grateful, or witty, or just anything to rub over what had happened, but she couldn't. Instead she let her eyes close, and the comforting sounds of Angus moving about the room started to lull her to sleep.

She heard him draw the curtains, switch off the main hall

light, softening the light falling against her closed eyes. She
heard one of the cats mew crossly for food until Angus went
into the kitchen and opened all the cupboards for cat food.
It was so warm on the sofa. She heard him talking under
his breath to the cats, calling them his little friends, or was
he murmuring her name?

'Marie? Marie?'

She managed to prise one eye open. It didn't focus at
first. Angus seemed miles away and all she could see was
blurry tartan.

Angus relented and bent down to speak to her. 'Marie,
what shall I say to Iona about you being here? Do you want
me to tell her? Or do you want to tell her yourself?'

She closed the eye and pushed away the unwelcome swill
of jealousy for Iona's lovely man and lovely life. 'Don't
know.' Then, with an effort, she opened both again and
chewed on her lower lip.

Angus thought how tiny and washed out she looked under
the spare green duvet. She looked about ten, all scared and
determined.

'No,' she said, with more of her old spirit. 'Tell her I'm
here because of Chris and I'll tell her the rest when I know
what there is to tell.'

'Right.' Angus tucked the rest of the duvet around her
feet. 'I've put a pint of water down there if you get thirsty
in the middle of the night.'

Oh, the tact of the man, thought Marie.

'Don't kick it over,' he went on. 'And don't worry if one
of the cats comes to sleep on you thinking you're Iona.'

'Iona sleeps on the sofa?'

'When I snore. Which is rarely.'

Marie managed a smile. 'And is that duvet kept behind
the sofa, by any chance?'

Angus smiled back. 'OK, OK. About twice a week then.'

There was a moment's pause while they smiled sadly at
each other, and Marie felt a sharp stab of gratitude for the

long, no-questions-needed nature of their friendship. But did it stretch as far as inappropriate, inexplicable snogs?

'Thank you,' she whispered.

'It's nothing,' said Angus automatically, and then cradled her cheek with his hand. The calluses – work? DIY? rowing still? – were rough against her skin. Like a man's hand. His eyes were very sombre. 'I really am sorry about you and Chris.'

'I know.' She had to say something; it couldn't hang between them like a ghost of an indiscretion, made more meaningful by its silent presence. But she only had single words in her head, no elegant, or even complete, sentences. And it wasn't exactly an easy social *faux pas* to cover in single words. 'Angus?' She let it hang in the air.

Angus made an indistinct dismissive noise and bent down and kissed her forehead. His lips felt like a gentle cat's paw, pressing softly on her head. Again the freshly bathed, sleepy male smell. 'Don't. We're friends, Marie,' he said into her hair. 'And we always will be. OK? Now go to sleep.'

Marie shut her eyes gratefully. Tomorrow is the first day, she thought, drifting off.

Because today was the last.

Chapter Twenty-four

Ned turned into a wide and quiet residential street off the main road and pulled up behind a skip. He had to yank hard to get the Mini's handbrake on, and there was an interesting grinding noise from the engine as it stopped turning.

A pale echo of the sick feeling returned to Iona's stomach as the radio went off and silence filled the car. Apart from the ticking of the engine and the spasmodic crackling of the prehistoric heater. But she breathed deeply and tried to distract herself with the home-made tapes littering Ned's parcel shelf. He seemed to be in no rush to let her take over.

'Ah, Bromley!' said Ned, winding down his window to smell the air. 'Just like being at home in the country. But without the cows.' He leaned his skinny arm out of the car and drummed happily on the roof.

Iona thought she could see a curtain twitching over the road. 'Ned, have you not noticed something about this street?' This was where all Iona's lessons started. It had taken her four lessons to work out what it was that was so deeply unsettling about it.

Ned leaned back in his seat. 'Er, no? As far as I can see, this is exactly what normality's meant to look like. This is the kind of road my mother dreamed about living in for most of her married life. Even the cats are trimmed regularly.'

'More than that.'

'Hmmm. This isn't actually a street? No one lives here?

The whole street was wiped out by a bad packet of tea in 1949? It's a Suburbia Theme Park?'

'What, like Terry and June Land?'

'Yeah!'

'No.'

'Tell us then.'

Iona fixed him with a serious stare of B-movie fear. 'There are *no cars* on the road. Every single house has off-road parking, and those that don't have concreted their lawns over.'

'Get away.' Ned looked up and down and realized she was right. Shiny new Fiestas and A-class Mercedes tucked away, safely installed next to the *leylandii*. 'Don't know why, though. You could park up on both sides of the road and still drive a tank formation team down here.'

'Ah, well, there's a reason for that.'

Conveniently, at that moment a red learner car swung round the corner on the wrong side of the road and proceeded at some speed towards them until the steering wheel was wrenched back by the instructor and the car swerved on to the left, narrowly missing another learner car, this one a Vauxhall Corsa, coming the other way. Also on the wrong side of the road.

'It's not easy, when you start, judging your road position,' Iona said defensively.

'You're not as bad as that, though,' said Ned. He left a masterfully timed pause. 'Are you?'

'No. Yes. I don't know. You know what I'm like about driving.'

'I do indeed,' said Ned. 'That's why I didn't bother to get the suspension redone on this until you'd passed your test.'

Though she was nervous about driving in front of Ned, Iona wasn't nearly as rammed full of trepidation the way she had been the previous weekend, when Angus had taken a precious half-day away from the pub and made her do laps around Richmond Park. ('You can only do thirty, there are no pavements, junctions, buses and only two roundabouts.' That hadn't stopped them having the biggest marital of their relationship in one of the car parks. Much to the consternation of the park-keepers who had asked them to keep it down, since it was the deer rutting season and the screeching was putting them off their stroke.)

Ned, on the other hand, had seen her throughout her inept school games career, had seen her drunk and staggering on cider before she learned to fall over gracefully, and had even watched as she kangarooed away from the school gates on her first abortive attempts at learning. She couldn't possibly embarrass herself further.

And more to the point, he didn't *expect* her to be any good.

'Angus thinks it's like swimming, you know,' she said, as Ned offered her half a Bounty. 'Er, no, I won't, thanks. Fat grams.'

'I'll put it there,' he said, laying it carefully above the speedo binnacle. 'And if you drive well, you can have it later.'

Iona smiled. This had been her father's final desperate measure, trying to bribe her with chocolate to get in the car. Most complicated lessons in her life had involved chocolate bribery at some point. Ned had eventually told her dad to try £5 notes, and her dad had confided that her mother was bribing *him* with fivers to get into the car with Iona in the first place.

'Driving's like *swimming*? How does your man work that one out?' he asked through a mouthful of coconut.

'He reckons, *if you will*, that if you put a non-swimmer in a car, strap 'em in, push them out into traffic, they will instinctively drive like bastards in order to save themselves from steering-wheel acupuncture.'

'Oh, right,' said Ned. 'That sounds like Angus to me. Which is why he's handed over the best part of a holiday for two in Majorca to that driving school. And where does your driving instructor fit into his analogy?'

'Water-wings.'

The red car swung round the corner again, this time on the right side of the road, but with all the hazard lights flashing. Iona caught sight of the driver: a seventeen-year-old girl, still in school uniform, looking completely relaxed and even cheerful.

One minute later, the other car emerged behind them, at a chastened fifteen miles an hour. The driver was also in school uniform and seemed to be tuning the radio. The instructor was wearing sunglasses.

'God, I feel so old,' sighed Iona. 'I'm the oldest learner on my instructor's books by about ten years. They're all teenagers who get picked up at school in their frees.'

'Excellent! I'll tell Jim,' Ned said drily. 'This could be the career opening he's been searching for.'

A woman came out of her house across the road and put out her bin in an unnecessarily elaborate manner. She looked as though she suspected Ned was going to try to flip his dilapidated car into the skip and then run off.

'Yup, the only things that move around here during the day have little pyramids on the top, and that includes people.' Iona scanned the road. 'This, apparently, is where every single learner driver within the South Circular starts their motoring career. Let's go before one of those two tries to reverse-park around us for a novelty.'

They unbuckled their seat belts and Iona slipped on her flat shoes, chucking her snakeskin boots in the back. As soon as she got out of the car, her heels unusually near the ground, she felt diminished and nervous.

'Why are they going round in circles?' asked Ned, adjusting the passenger seat backwards to make room for his long legs and opening a packet of crisps, as the red car reappeared at the top of the road.

'Well, one's obviously doing right turns today and the

other's doing lefts.' Iona buckled her belt, trying to keep her breathing normal, and fought her instinct to get straight out again. She gripped the wheel, trying to make her mind go on to autopilot.

First cockpit drill: mirrors, rear and side, adjust seat, seat-belt. MMSS . . . one more. What had she missed?

'Maybe you could go to a hypnotist,' Ned offered casually.

The door. D. That was the fifth. DMMSS. Shut the door. Who didn't shut the bloody door? That was just giving you something you could do, so you could tick it off your progress list immediately, even if you were still having trouble remembering where the key thing went.

Iona looked round at him. He was reading about the 'Win a Car' competition on his crisps.

'For what?'

'For your driving thing, dur-brain.'

'I don't have a driving thing.'

'Oh, come on, Iona, it's me you're talking to now, not Angus.'

Iona huffed and bit her lip, and noticed that her knuckles were white on the steering-wheel. The red car came round again and this time the instructor was looking at her as well as the driver.

'Look at the road!' she yelled at them. They lurched past, still looking and veering into the middle of the road again.

'I don't have a driving thing,' she said again when they'd gone.

'Fine, then. Great. Let's drive, baby.' Ned sat back in his seat and waited.

Iona fiddled with the mirror. It felt as though it might snap off in her hands if she was too rough.

Then she checked her seat-belt was OK.

'Does this car have power-steering?' she asked. 'Because I'm used to power-steering in the car I've been learning in.'

'Iona, love, this car just about has power, if you're going

downhill, and while the steering rack holds up, it has steering. That is all you need to know. Now, are you going to set off, or are we going to wait for Mrs Next Door to come out again and report us to the Tidy Police for littering her avenue?'

Iona made herself turn the ignition key and the engine hacked into life.

'Excellent,' said Ned encouragingly. 'Doesn't do that for me.'

OK. Gearstick in neutral. Handbrake on. Into first gear. Don't flinch at the sound of the engine revving. Breathe deeply. Check mirrors. Release handbrake. Clutch up . . .

'Iona, sorry to interrupt,' said Ned, 'but why don't you put it on full lock so you don't shoot forward and impale us on that skip? Just a suggestion. My fault for parking too close, I suppose.'

'Don't tell me things like that,' pleaded Iona, hauling the steering-wheel round as much as she could. 'Things I haven't even thought of getting wrong. I keep thinking of all the times I could have killed people without even knowing. I lie awake at nights, remembering junctions with old ladies unwittingly dancing on the edge of oblivion with their tartan pushalong shoppers, just because I didn't see the Give Way signs.'

'Get on with it, you big chicken.'

She checked all round before pulling out, as had been drilled into her by her instructor. This took about three minutes, given that Iona liked to give bicycles on the horizon a good head start before attempting to mow them down. Ned tipped his head and his packet of crisps vertical to get the crumbs.

'You're taking all this very calmly,' said Iona, as the Mini eventually limped up the road.

'What other way is there to take it?' Ned leaned over and released the handbrake. 'It's a bit sticky, the handbrake, you want to watch it.'

Iona wasn't really listening, but noticed that for some reason the accelerator started working better. She liked roads with no traffic, no parked cars and a good few metres clearance of the pavement. It diminished the sense of speed.

'Junction coming up, yeah?' said Ned, reaching in the back for a can of Coke.

'Er, yeah.'

At this point, Angus normally started making convulsive movements with his right foot on an imaginary brake.

Iona slowed to a stop at the line and swallowed. In an ideal world there would be only her on the roads. In order to pass her driving test, there would need to be either some kind of state funeral or a nuclear attack warning.

'Anything coming?' asked Ned.

'Not on my side,' said Iona, suddenly unable to remember whether she would stall if she moved either of her feet.

'Or on mine. So go on then.'

Iona saw a car appear in the distance and looked at her feet in panic. Which one should she move? Which one would make her stall? Could she get out before this car? Or if she stalled in the middle of the road, would she cause a crash?

Ned stopped drinking from his can. 'You can go, you've got right of way.'

'I'm, er, waiting for that car to go past.'

The Honda, driven by an old lady, with three other old ladies in the back, all wearing hats, lumbered past.

'OK, get yourself ready and . . .' said Ned encouragingly.

A bright-green VW People Mover loomed up very fast in her rear-view mirror and, disconcertingly, didn't seem to be slowing down. And the faster it moved, the slower Iona's brain seemed to work.

'Ready *and* . . .' Ned did a helpful 'and *through*' hand movement.

Iona was staring blindly into the rear-view mirror, as if frozen in a Dalek death ray.

Ned resisted the temptation to wave his hands in front of her face. That wouldn't look good from the point of view of the People Mover. 'Ah, yeah, people do that all the time. It's like Minis don't take up enough road space. But you're OK to go . . .'

Suddenly Iona defrosted. 'Fuck!' she yelled. Both her hands and her feet seemed to be shackled to lead weights. 'Fuck! Help me! Help me!'

'He thinks you're going, the road's clear,' Ned explained calmly.

Iona couldn't think of anything at all. Nothing to do with cars, nothing to do with driving, nothing to do with the fact that she was on a slope. Her mind was a total blank canvas.

'I'm happy to sit here all day, like,' said Ned cheerfully, 'but I think your man behind is on the school run and I can't afford to pay for a new rear bumper until Angus doles out the brown envelopes tomorrow.'

'Ned . . . Ned . . . I . . .'

The strident hooting of the People Mover's horn made something snap inside Iona. Other vehicles threw her. In panic, she yanked off the handbrake and slammed both her feet down at the same time. The car lurched forward into the road, Ned grabbed the wheel and steered it round the corner and the People Mover did a highly illegal overtaking at a road junction manoeuvre to get round, hooting aggressively all the while.

'Brake!' he yelled just before Iona slammed the car into a parked van and she braked hard, bursting into tears of shock at the same time. Then the engine, which had coped heroically with Iona's ministrations up to this point, finally stalled.

The Mini came to rest a breath away from the van, at a precarious angle from the kerb.

She closed her eyes and wailed, her head in her hands and her elbows firmly wedged into the struts of the steering-wheel. Her heart was hammering painfully and she felt as though she'd had a *Pulp Fiction* adrenalin special, including the punch in the chest. She remembered too late that there were no airbags, or indeed any safety equipment, in Ned's car, and another shock wave of panic went through her.

Ned finished his Coke, threw the empty can in the back and put an arm round her shaking shoulders, stroking her back. 'Ah, never mind, pigeon,' he said soothingly. 'Happens to everyone, that kind of thing. Your mind just goes blank, doesn't it?'

Iona moaned something inaudible into her sleeves.

'Don't worry about it,' he went on. 'No one was hurt, nothing got broke, just one of those things, eh? Better you do it now than in your test.'

'But I can *do* junctions,' Iona howled. 'I *know* what to do. But my brain just doesn't make connections fast enough! Why did I let Angus talk me into *doing* this again? I don't *want* to drive! I get in a car and turn into some kind of root vegetable! I hate it!'

Ned kept one arm around her and used the other to put the gearbox in neutral and secure the handbrake. 'Iona, can you turn the ignition for me?'

He felt her shiver beneath her T-shirt. 'No, I'll stall.'

'You won't stall. We're out of gear and the handbrake's on. Just turn the key to the first notch.'

Her hand was trembling as she reached out and when she touched the key her fingers recoiled from it, as if it was red hot. Then, with an obvious effort, Iona grasped the keyring and turned the ignition key.

'Brilliant.' Ned put the radio on quietly. A DJ was doing a phone-in quiz to win your weight in tequila on Virgin. The female caller was battling with avarice and pride regarding how much she actually weighed. 'That better?'

Iona managed a weak smile. 'Much better.' Then a mixture of shame and frustration crumpled her face again.

Ned said nothing, and they sat listening to the radio

together. Nine stones ten of Cuervo Gold was duly shipped off to Crawley, and the DJ went to the travel updates with 'Tequila' by Terrorvision.

'Yup, tequila makes *me* happy,' said Ned. 'Makes you pretty miserable though, if your eighteenth birthday was anything to go by.'

'There were other things making me unhappy on my eighteenth birthday, if you remember.' Iona's voice was dark and hiccupy from beneath the hands holding her head.

'Like what?'

Iona looked up, her face registering disbelief. 'Er, Gary Williams? Er, writing off my mum's Fiat? Er, our mock A-levels? I think you'll find that the tequila was bringing me *up* to a state of "Life can go on"-ness.'

'Ah,' mused Ned, putting a philosophical finger on his long nose, 'how soon we forget.'

'Well, you might have forgotten. My mum certainly hasn't.'

'Shouldn't think Gary Williams has either. Or the good people at Carlisle police station.'

Ned opened another packet of crisps.

'Should we not move the car?' Iona asked eventually. 'Am I not causing an obstruction?'

Ned looked round. 'Well, you're far enough away from the junction, and there's very little traffic on this road, and anyway, I don't care what they think about your parking. Do you?'

'Not really. But this doesn't look like parking. This looks like a breakdown still awaiting the AA.'

'It doesn't look as bad as you think it does.'

'I shouldn't be out on the roads,' she moaned. 'Should I?'

'Iona, I'm not going to sit here and congratulate you on your low self-esteem, if that's what you want. Your driving's nowhere near as bad as you think it is.' Ned gently took hold of her ear and pulled it, so she would be forced to turn her gaze away from the clutch pedal and look at him.

'If you're going to get the hang of this,' he went on, in his dry, amused voice, 'you've got to stop being so hard on yourself. I know it's a long time since you didn't know how to do something, but *no one* expects you to be able to learn how to drive without getting things wrong. *Everyone* gets things wrong. All the time. God, when I started working in London, it was two months before I was allowed to chop onions, and I still got things wrong then.' He laughed. 'Christ, only last night, it was that busy I sent out two covers without vegetables on.'

'Ah, well, that's where you're lucky with your staff,' Iona reminded him. 'Who notice things like that and go back with the veg on a separate plate.'

'Iona, you know I don't care if you make mistakes. I'm not going to let you kill us and write off my only asset, am I?'

'But *I* care if I make mistakes!' she burst out, banging her fists on the steering-wheel for emphasis. Angus wouldn't let her do that in his car in case she set off the airbags. 'I *hate* feeling stupid! I *hate* having Angus lecturing me and pointing out trees and nuns on bicycles and stationary objects on the other side of the bloody road! I *hate* the fact that this is yet another skill that I don't have that all the rest of you do! Like bowling!'

'What about bowling?'

'Oh, you *know* what I mean about bowling,' spat Iona. 'You lot can all bowl and I can't and everyone spends the whole night giving me patronizing advice about swinging my arm and standing in the same spot each time, and then having a good laugh when I can't hit the fucking pins. And bloody Tamara in her bloody tight bowling trousers whose teenage social life was so crap she went down the local alley every Friday, getting strikes all the time and pretending it's all fluke so you lads won't feel bad and stop fancying her.'

Ned said nothing. On the very rare occasions that Iona lost

her temper, she had to steam like a volcano before she could calm down; trying to stand in the way of this just resulted in instant boiling. It was Angus's only flaw in his otherwise perfect reading of Iona that he tried to stem the molten flow and couldn't understand why he ended up with singed eyebrows.

Iona lapsed into steaming silence again for another five minutes, punctuated only by involuntary gasps of anguish as the junction incident flashed up in all its horror before her eyes, like some kind of demonic subliminal advertising. She couldn't believe how calmly Ned was taking it. One slight misunderstanding in Richmond Park with another driver in a Polo and Angus had nearly removed his kneecap on the glove compartment like a bottletop in his anxiety to snatch the wheel from her dithering hands.

'It's his own fault for letting you drive that car,' said Ned unexpectedly. 'I couldn't drive an Integrale. It's a rally car, for fuck's sake.'

Iona murmured agreement. It didn't startle her that Ned had intercepted her train of thought – he did it all the time – and now he mentioned it, it *wasn't* fair that Angus was giving her guilt trips for practising in a car that was not only a bugger to control but was also his pride and joy. No wonder she drove it as if she was on television.

'Serve him right if you wrote it off,' Ned added.

Iona managed a smile despite herself. For all Tamara's much advertised telesympathy, she was nowhere compared to Ned. Maybe he just knew her too well. No one knew her as well as Ned did, not Marie, not even Angus.

Iona sneaked a glance at him in her mirrors. His eyes were half shut and the long fingers of his left hand were drumming on the roof. She could make a shrewd guess that he was thinking about something different, to do with the free-range chicken that had arrived that morning from the new organic supplier, but beyond that he could be thinking about anything. Carlisle United, legwarmers, shower gel. Probably not shower gel.

As always she felt a sadness flick at her heart to realize that she'd never have the same insight into the inner workings of his mind as he did into hers, no matter how well she learned to recognize his patterns; Ned had a transparent screen which came down over his private self, and it was so convincing that most people wouldn't even know he was sectioning himself off, leaving only as much as he wanted them to know of him. Tamara might have compiled one of her dossiers about his favourite colours and adolescent fantasy object, but she had no idea.

He had a very calming influence, Iona thought, feeling her own breathing return to normal. Sometimes she wondered how different her life would be without Ned there to put things in perspective. Sometimes, when she and Angus fell into bed physically exhausted after finishing off at the pub, her racing mind would keep her awake, endlessly rearranging worst-case scenarios, and piecing together the fragile daisy chain of coincidence that had led her to where she was now. It scared her a little: the same sort of quick, dispensable jerk of fear she got peering over a cliff edge. Things could have been so different if she hadn't met Marie on her first night at college, then Angus, then lost the first depressing secretarial job, then started painting, then met Tamara on her foundation course. But she would always have had Ned. And Ned . . .

Ned gave the roof of the car a final finger drum roll as the song finished. 'Haway then, let's get back to civilization, shall we?' His voice was casual, slightly amused, as if they'd just shared a private joke.

Iona realized that she hadn't even thought about driving for five minutes, and she was sitting in the middle of the most confidence-destroying cock-up yet. The sick feeling returned, bringing some friends for the ride. Like Embarrassment and Fear.

'Civilization? You can talk, coming from Brough,' she said, aware that she was playing for time. Stalling, if you will, ho ho not very ho. She grimaced again, reliving the moment at the junction.

'I think you'll find that you come from somewhere not too far away, so if you could start your engines, please, gentlemen?'

The lead weights reclamped themselves to Iona's wrists and she was filled with an animal instinct to get out of the car.

'I don't want to drive back, Ned,' she said in a small voice. There was no point doing the little-lady routine for Ned, though it would have worked with Angus, and might even have got a Chinese takeaway and a foot rub for its trouble.

'You *do* want to drive back.'

'I don't.'

'Well, how else are we going to get back for the afternoon shift?' Ned sounded so reasonable, she could almost believe him.

'I know this sounds hysterical,' said Iona, trying hard to make her voice as calm as possible to compensate for the twitching which had started up in her left calf, 'but my whole body is telling me to get out from this driving seat.'

'No.' Ned turned himself round to face her, as much as he could in the limited amount of space available. His face was serious. 'I don't mean to nose, Iona, but this, er, really isn't about the old driving, is it?' He rubbed his nose and looked at her over his hand. His grey eyes were concerned.

'What else could it be about?' She felt herself frost up again and couldn't really say why.

'Because you're not normally like this. I mean, refusing to drive because you get bad vibes from the car, that's a Tamara line, isn't it?'

'I'm not saying that. And please don't start suggesting that I had a bad experience in a car when I was in the womb and have never recovered, because we both know that's rubbish,' snapped Iona, wondering if it was.

'I wasn't going to say . . . Are you stressed about the pub? Have you had a row with Angus? Come on, Iona. You know I wouldn't ask if I wasn't worried about you.'

Iona sank her head on to the steering-wheel and made herself think hard. There was no point pretending in front of Ned, but she seemed to be carrying so many people's problems at the moment that it was hard to pull them apart.

A passing car slowed down as it came towards them, the driver and passengers staring horrified at Iona's slumped head and Ned's arm round her shoulders. It hooted concern and Ned waved it on.

'Oh, God,' wailed Iona into the steering column. 'Everyone feels sorry for me now! I look like a bloody road accident!'

'Shut up.'

Iona breathed hard through her nose and sifted through the dead weight on her shoulders.

The engine ticked, and Ned was silent.

If she was being honest, Angus's preoccupation with getting business things exactly right and Marie's obvious distress about Chris bothered her deeply, since she wanted to do whatever she could to help, but Marie seemed to be completely resistant to any attempts to draw her out about it. Either she'd pretend everything was fine, which it clearly wasn't, or fob Iona off with some promise to talk later. Which she never did. Iona wasn't stupid, and she knew Marie well enough to guess that was the only problem she'd be too proud to share with her. And whatever was going on with Gabriel and Tamara was really upsetting Jim, though he wouldn't say so in his new Maximum Efficiency persona, and since Tamara had met everyone because of her, she felt a certain responsibility for Tamara's actions towards her older friends.

And all this was without taking into account her own concerns about the pub, the paintings stacking up in the shed that she hadn't had time to take to the art market, the wedding commission which still didn't have a bride and groom in the middle because she couldn't bring herself to put them in, and some other, darker worries she didn't want to examine too closely. Like how the spectacular collapse of Marie's marriage was affecting her own ideas of what she wanted from life. Like how Angus might change if he never went back to the suit and the office. Like how she might change if all the old orders were shaken about.

Iona hoped she could think all this, painful as it was, too painful to put into words, and that Ned could pick it up without her having to speak it aloud. She didn't want him to hear those thoughts coming out of her mouth, since most of them were pretty unworthy and mean.

'Maybe,' she said suddenly, 'it's that driving is the only thing I do that doesn't involve work or the pub or Angus, and I'm just making it too important to allow myself to be this crap. And the crapper I am, the more it's going to cost.'

She sat back surprised, not realizing she actually thought that at all until it came out of her mouth. But it was true.

It would do.

Iona looked over at Ned carefully.

He tilted his head to one side, but his eyes were still wary and there was no smile at the corner of his lips. She knew from experience that it meant he didn't really believe her.

'Are you sure that's all?' His voice sounded loud in the car.

Iona nodded. That was all she was going to tell him anyway. He knew her well enough to guess the rest, and the other bits she wouldn't tell anyone. She barely allowed herself to think them. 'What is this, a driving lesson or a therapy session?'

Ned made a big show of looking back up the road. 'Well,

so far you've driven about a hundred metres, so I reckon it must be a therapy session. If you drive back to town, it *could* just about be a driving lesson, though.'

Iona gripped the steering-wheel until her knuckles whitened. If she could deal with driving, maybe she could sort out the rest.

She started the engine and the windscreen wipers sprang into life unbidden.

Or rather, if she could sort out the rest, she could deal with driving.

'Did I do . . .' Iona gestured nervously towards the thrashing wipers.

'This may sound too much like Angus for your liking but, honestly, the only thing you should be thinking about when you're driving is the car,' said Ned. He leaned over her and jogged some exposed wiring to get the windscreen wipers to stop. 'You're *allowed* to forget everything else. Believe me, the state of the cellars at the Grapes is not going to wash as a decent defence when you mow down a crocodile of brats. Can you chuck us another can of Coke from the back and get a move on?'

'You think I'm safe?'

'Stop trying to get permission for everything. I'm not going to let you crash, am I? Not before opening time. You think Angus is going to shut the pub to come and get us from Casualty?'

'No, you're right,' said Iona, and began the long process of checking all her mirrors.

'Anyway, I've got some fantastic wild salmon marinating and if I don't get it out in the next hour it's ruined. Pass me those Opal Fruits.'

'Starbursts.'

'You're in reverse.'

'I know.'

Iona managed to negotiate the rest of the drive without any major problems, and without going into fourth gear at any point, and they arrived back just in time to witness Angus erupting like a liquidizer with a badly fitting lid at the man who sent back the dessert wine.

Chapter Twenty-five

'Eeeeuurcchhh!' Marie slapped a tenner into the till. 'I hate Gabriel!'

'Hate is a very strong word,' Charm interjected sternly. 'You mean you dislike Gabriel. Or Gabriel just isn't your cup of tea.'

'No, I *mean* I hate Gabriel,' hissed Marie, removing £3.25 in change. 'I *hate* the way he gives Tamara that sexy, dirty look when she's picking up orders, and I *really* hate the way she looks so fucking radiant all the time. And, most of all, I hate the way she's started wearing those kinky boots with her suede belt-skirt all the time. It's like working with Sonny and Cher.'

'Before they started beating each other up.' Iona rang a bottle of house wine and three Kronenbourgs through the till. She had some sympathy with Marie. Tamara and Gabriel had taken to kissing in much the same way that prisoners and their wives kissed in *The Bill* when they wanted to exchange small parcels of hash without being seen by the guards.

'What's that programme where they chant, "You gots to go, you gots to go" in that moronic and yet chilling fashion?' Marie went on.

'Um, I know the one you mean. Why?'

'Because I feel like chanting it every time I see Gabriel strut through that kitchen like something's on fire in his pants.'

'Well, be fair now,' said Iona. 'It probably is. Charm, can you sort out the glass washer? There are no pint glasses left.

And you're the only one who knows how to work it,' she added in her best wheedling voice, spotting Charm's hands moving on to her hips in preparation for a good lecture while Marie, oblivious, replenished the mixed-nut trough.

A demonstration of superior bar skills struggled with Charm's deeply rooted 1960s beliefs, which had weathered thirty years of mockery despite – or possibly because of – being nurtured in Mile End's Summer of Love. 'Instant korma's gonna get you,' said Charm meaningfully, with a side look at Marie. 'You want to think about that, lady,' and she stalked round to the other side of the bar.

'She'd be funny if she knew what she was talking about.' Marie watched her retreating back. Charm didn't care about bra-strap delineation. She liked as much of her bra to be on view as possible, front and back. Value for money all round.

'Don't. Charm is the only thing standing between me and a nervous breakdown,' said Iona. 'I'm telling you, it's been so busy in here the last few days, and she's the only one who can do all those weird Guinness cocktails Sam's mates like.'

'I don't mind doing some more shifts, if you want,' Marie offered. 'It's coming up to half-term and God knows I'd prefer to be in here serving pints than reading up on nuclear physics for year threes in the dingy confines of my empty marital nest.'

Iona concealed her wince by wiping up some spilled ash and pistachio shells from the bar. She still hadn't got a full explanation as to why she'd almost crushed Marie to death the other night when she'd collapsed on the sofa at one in the morning in the hope of some Channel 5 soft porn to wind down to after scrubbing out the pub. Angus hadn't been much more forthcoming than 'it was something to do with Chris' – like, as if it *wouldn't* be. She bit her lip. She and Angus didn't have secrets, but he refused to tell her what had happened. It wasn't like she was prying – had Marie any idea how much it was hurting her, having to see her best friend so miserable? No, tonight Marie was going to tell *exactly* what was going on, or she'd have to get it out of Angus. No more stalling. There was no point suffering in silence, and Marie was clearly suffering.

'Are you going to come in tomorrow?' she said cheerily. Before Marie could reply, a man came to the bar with three empty glasses and she put a hand on Marie's downy arm while she turned to deal with him. 'Hello? No, sorry, can you hold on a moment? We're having a glass crisis. I can give you some peanuts to while away the minutes. No? OK, then. Sorry, Marie, what were you . . .'

Marie carried on polishing the wine glass. 'You're very calm about the whole glass thing. Are people nicking them? Or is Tamara breaking them? I saw Jim nearly reduced to tears yesterday by one of Mad Boy Sam's mates, desperate for his pint.'

'Well, what can I do?' Iona shrugged. 'I keep telling Angus to go and get some more. The washing machine just can't keep up. If I wash glasses by hand, everyone will complain to the Health and Safety, and if I try to serve Guinness in plastic glasses there'll be a riot.'

'Aren't there some old spares in the cellar?'

Iona rolled her eyes. 'Yeah, unwashed ones. I meant to put them through a glass wash, but it's been so busy. God knows what kind of residues are on them. Angus cleaned that place so enthusiastically he nearly gassed himself. It was like Chernobyl down there for a few days. No more of your pesky vermin for us, I can tell you.'

'Just vermin too out of their heads to do anything but listen to Pink Floyd albums.' Marie took a deep breath. 'I've been meaning to ask – has he sorted those flats out upstairs yet?'

Iona shook her head. 'No, well, the thing is that Jim's meant to be doing them up to sell off as part of their Big Finance Plan, but they can't spend any money on decorators, and they're too busy to do it themselves. Jim's here nearly every day and Angus . . .' Her voice trailed off. It was true that she saw Angus more than ever before, but despite taking Ned's advice to heart and trying to see concern rather than a world domination complex in his eyes, she still seemed to come up against the New Shouty 'I'm Your Boss and There are No Mixers in the Fridge!' Angus, and she wasn't sure she liked him all that much. Unsurprisingly, Jimmy Page and his magic fingers were still resident in her head, and she infinitely preferred the imaginary conversations they were having about open tunings and obscure Delta blues guitarists to the real conversations about stock levels and ullage that now seemed to make up her relationship with Angus.

'Because . . .' Marie looked hesitant. 'I was wondering if . . .'

'You've got to switch it on *twice*!' Charm dumped a crate of clean and steaming pint glasses in front of them as if it were a case of dead rats she'd found behind the mineral water spring.

Iona looked blankly at her. 'Twice?'

'The button. The orange one? Needs to be handled carefully. You want to wiggle it around. Didn't Angus tell you?' Charm gave her an incredulous look. 'You can't just ram it in and expect it to work first time.'

'You should know that, Iona, with your lifetime's study of women's magazines,' murmured Marie, taking three of the glasses and starting three belated pints of lager all at once.

'Well, I know it's been a bit temperamental in the past . . .' Iona started. Shifts were so hectic now she just put the glasses in and didn't think about it again. Usually someone had yanked them out and put another lot in by the time she remembered to look.

'You'll have to get the hang of this for when I go away.' Charm folded her arms.

Iona nearly dropped the glass in the sink. 'You're going *away*?'

Another piercing look of disbelief. 'That husband of yours don't tell you much, does he?'

'He's not my husband,' said Iona through gritted teeth. 'He's just my slave master.'

The till beeped and rattled open behind them. 'Off somewhere nice, are you, Charm?' Marie held a £50 note up to the light to check for photocopying marks.

'As it happens, no. I'm having my . . .'

Whatever it was that Charm was having done, the simultaneous arrival of Jim and Mad Boy Sam, one from the front door and one from the men's loos, snapped her mouth shut like one of the grabby claw hairgrips she wore and, flushing beneath her Maybelline 3-in-1 stick, she slid round to the other side of the bar, waving an admonitory red nail at the glass crate.

Sam and Jim both had their flies open.

'The usual,' said Jim, dumping his briefcase on the bar.

'Jim . . .' Iona began, but he shut his eyes at her. It had been a long morning already. A car bearing a suspiciously strong resemblance to Simon's BMW had been spotted on some 'Police, Camera, Action!' programme and Kyle was going berserk.

'Iona, I need some of those nice drugs you do? Quickly?'

Iona went to make him a cup of very strong coffee.

'Ah, Jim,' said Marie, a smile playing on her red lips as she very obviously weighed up which of a number of gags to go with. Thank God her sense of humour hadn't deserted her. On the contrary, she seemed to have got even darker of late.

'What?' he said warily, eyes still shut.

'I was just thinking – the wonderful thing about the close community of the Bunch of Grapes is that Sam only has to walk to the bar with his flies undone before someone tells him, whereas you've probably come all the way from Clerkenwell like that.'

Jim's hand went reflexively to his flies which were indeed

undone and exposing a thin tail of faded blue boxer short. He flushed. No wonder Rebecca had given him that lascivious grin as he left this morning. By the time Kyle had done his third round of the office reassuring the local police, there had only been him and Rebecca in, barring the secretaries, who never seemed to leave anyway and probably had little pens upstairs that they were allowed to sleep in.

Iona returned with the coffee. 'Jim, you didn't tell me Charm was going away?'

'Oh, God. No, I didn't, sorry. Couple of months, she thought.'

'Jim! It's bad enough running the bar on the staff we have without finding out that the only proper, fully paid-up member of the barmaids' union among us is leaving!'

'And what do you suppose that's called?' asked Marie, floating past with a bottle of wine. 'The Barmaids' Union and Serving Technicians Incorporated?'

'What?' said Jim, opening one bleary eye.

'BUSTI, she's being amusing.' Iona passed him the sugar bowl and milk. 'But I'm not,' she snapped. 'What are you going to do about it?'

'Oh, we'll get in a student or something,' said Jim, stirring in three lumps of sugar. 'An Australian. It's their national occupation, isn't it? Freelance bar work? Iona, honestly, there are people all over London gagging for bar cover work. Out-of-work actors, bored writers, struggling drummers. It won't be a problem, believe me.'

Iona snorted. Getting someone would probably be easy enough, but getting Jim organized to sort it all out was another.

'When's she going?'

Jim wrinkled his brow. 'Er . . . Angus would know. She only just told us,' he added quickly, seeing Iona's eyes narrow. 'Oh, come on, Iona. Angus has got a lot to think about at the moment. We all have.'

'I know, I know,' Iona interrupted. She didn't want Jim to know exactly how much she knew, or rather didn't know. 'It's just . . . We'll have to find someone before Charm leaves, just so they can get the hang of it.'

'Well, I'll put you in charge of that. I mean, you're the ones that'll have to work with her. Or him.'

'Him. Definitely,' said Marie. 'Jim, can I talk to you about something? Quickly?' She looked up at Iona, who scanned the bar for a possible charge of customers on the horizon and, seeing none, nodded.

Jim took his coffee to one of the empty tables in the eating area and sat down. Marie made sure he didn't get the chair facing into the kitchen, so he couldn't be distracted by the chefs cleaning up and recycling butter out of the table pats. She needn't have bothered, since Jim sank his head back on to the balls of his palms as soon as he'd downed his quadruple espresso.

'Jim, these flats above the pub,' she began.

He opened his eyes briefly to roll them skyward and then closed them again. 'Please don't go there. They're not ready yet, and I don't know when I'm going to get all the legal insurance stuff untangled, so . . .'

'Well, I was wondering . . .' Marie bit her lip. 'If I agreed to paint one of them and get it sorted out, would you let me live up there until you decide to sell?'

Jim removed his hands from his eyes and looked seriously at her. 'You want to move?'

She nodded. 'Um, Chris doesn't know when he's going to be back from Kosovo and our place is pretty grim, to be honest, and God knows we've loathed the landlady since the day we moved in. I've been trying to get up the energy to move for ages. And it seems like a good time . . .'

She stopped. It had taken her one minute and then a whole night to reach this conclusion. Somewhere at the back of her mind, Marie knew that there was a good chance Chris might never come back. And if he did, as he'd more or less said in that chillingly matter-of-fact letter, it might not be to live with her again. She flinched but didn't allow herself the euphemism. He *almost certainly* wouldn't be living with her. Being in their marital home, full of memories and now pointless compromises, when he got back to tell her would just make it worse.

And, being positive, if he did come back, it was time they did something new with their lives. Moving out of Maisie's grotty little terrace ('So many wonderful happenings took place here! So many fabulous creations came into being on that very window seat! Christ, no! I couldn't possibly redecorate that mural! It's in original Pucci fingerpaints!') would be a first step.

Not that Jim needed to know all this. Marie tilted her head encouragingly and a dark curl fell over one eye. She pushed it back with a smile.

'Er . . .' Jim's internal dilemmas were virtually external as they wrestled all over his boyish face. 'I don't know about the insurance liabilities. I wouldn't want you to be compromised, or put in danger or anything . . .'

'Come on, Jim, it's only for a little while. And think of all the extra hours I could do for you here!'

'What about school? It's not exactly round the corner.'

'I'm going to start cycling in.' Marie beamed. 'Good exercise. Oh, go on, it's bonus points for everyone. You get your flat decorated, and some rent if you want—'

'No, I can't not pay you for your hours here and charge you rent as well,' said Jim stoutly.

'Well, then!' She raised her eyebrow. 'Do we have a deal? We do? Excellent.'

He nodded weakly and reached into his pocket for a bunch of keys. 'Don't ever go into Overworld, will you? They'll give you my job. Probably give you Simon's job too, come to think of it.' He prised off a smaller ring of keys and pushed them across the table at her. 'And I don't want to hear you playing that bloody recorder, OK? Now, will you bring me another one of these, please?'

Marie's heart bounced in her chest as she pocketed the keys, but outside she frowned and took the little cup and saucer away. 'You want to watch your cellulite, Jim. All that coffee you drink these days. Terrible things, toxins.'

It was almost too easy. She dropped the cup into the dirty plate bin on her way to the coffee machine and watched Jim's back straighten in panic. 'Are they? Really? What's cellulite? Is it like cholesterol?'

'Marie!' murmured Iona, ringing through a round of drinks at the till.

Marie happily schwooshed the steam arm through a jug of milk. 'Oh, he loves it, really. Gives him something entirely new to worry about that doesn't involve the pub, his job or Tamara.'

'Yeah, winner,' said Iona sarcastically. 'Can you think of one for me?'

Making the decision was relatively easy; getting Jim to agree to it even more straightforward. Giving Maisie the smug hippie cow a month's notice was positively enjoyable. But actually moving out of the house was another matter altogether.

There was so much stuff, for a start. Well, stuff of Marie's. Chris didn't accumulate things the way she did – he tended to throw paperbacks away as soon as he'd read them and didn't keep magazines. Marie had a teacher's eye for possible projects, if not a housekeeper's eye for maximizing space in a small flat. As a result, she kept coming across things she hadn't seen for three years, including two remote controls and a Walkman previously written off as having been stolen by aliens.

Then there was all the other invisible stuff which filled up every room and ranged from things he'd taken with him in her good travelling bag, through all the things they'd bought together at some point in their lives, to all the things she thought were important to her but now she realized she could throw away without a second thought.

Right, thought Marie. *I will only take what I can fit in the car.*

She looked round at the sitting room.

What I can fit in the car in two journeys.

It seemed easiest to start in the bedroom, since it was so small that there was very little to pack anyway. Marie dragged the empty packing boxes in, tipped the drawer out of her bedside table and picked up the first thing that came to hand: a photo of themselves presenting a happily united front at a New Year's Eve party, one of the first she had hidden when he packed up and left. Bad move, she thought, even as her hand touched the cold silver-plated frame. Oh, shit.

It was her favourite photograph of them; Chris's favourite too. She was wearing a plunging red top and was partially draped in a very flattering shadow, which by the magic of camera angles rendered her almost waif-like, and he was going through the golden week in his tempestuous relationship with his appearance in which his hair was exactly the right length and showed off the shadows beneath his cheekbones. He looked beautiful. They both looked beautiful.

So why hadn't he taken it with him?

Marie swallowed back the wave of tears which surged up her throat and shoved the photo frame down the side of a box with spare towels in, but the image was printed on the back of her mind. She sank on to the bed and pressed the balls of her fists into her eyes, but it wouldn't go away, even though her eyes were now swimming with stinging tears. She longed to get a big scraper and scrape her head clean of all these pictures that popped up to torment her; it wasn't the images so much as the agony of knowing that they were once real in the past but would never be real again.

Three or four minutes passed and she sat unfocusing her eyes on another of Iona's unspecific green paintings to make her breathing go back to normal. Misery wasn't going to solve anything. Instead, she put on her dirtiest jeans (which also made her feel sexy), took off her bra, which was digging into her, and pulled on the old soft T-shirt she wore for bed. Then she put on her best shoes and sprayed a mist of Chanel No. 5 and walked through it.

Hard work always cleared her head. In this case she was searching for things to fill up her mind so full there was no room for anything else. She put on an old Madonna tape she found under the bed and turned it up loud.

All the posters and paintings came down off the walls, leaving recriminatory squares of dust behind. But Marie found she couldn't give a damn. Not even vaguely. Instead she threw open all the windows and let the wind catch the curtains and pull them outside. She went through the room systematically, singing all the time to stop herself thinking. And when Madonna finished for the second time, she put on Wham!

Iona came round at three o'clock for her hour's driving practice and was too shocked to say anything.

Marie stood back from the pile of boxes stacked around her and together they surveyed the sitting room, which looked recently and randomly burgled.

'Jesus, Marie,' Iona whistled through her teeth, and then suddenly caught the fleeting expression of desperation which appeared on Marie's face. She moved swiftly, throwing herself on the sofa and raised an impressed eyebrow at the decimated room. 'Congratulations! You have now achieved the Angus Sinclair homestyle. You must be proud and happy. Did you see it in a magazine or did you always want your house to look like Paddy's Market?'

Marie smiled ruefully over her mug of tea.

'I wish you'd said,' Iona went on. 'I mean, I could have

come round and helped.' She looked at the pile of bulging refuse sacks piled up by the door. 'Though I see you don't need any help on the ruthless chucking out side of things.'

'No,' said Marie. 'It's all going.'

'Won't . . .' Iona was about to ask whether Chris would go berserk when he saw the place, but stopped herself just in time. 'Well done, you,' she said instead, as brightly as she could manage.

'Do you want to drive round by the skips?' said Marie, searching for her car keys in the jumble of bits and pieces on an empty bookshelf. 'You can learn what to do in the event of having a car full of stuff. Should be useful if your examiner wants to bring his washing with him on your test.'

'OK.' Iona looked at her watch. 'Look, I can see if I can get someone in to cover for me if you want me to stay this evening and help you. I've been phoning round some friends of friends about covering for Charm and Angus is right, you wouldn't believe the people who've done bar work. Who *want* bar work. There are probably four solicitors on the phone right now, begging for some shifts.' She looked winningly at Marie. Going through Chris's stuff would be pretty miserable and she hated the idea of Marie doing it alone.

Marie let a long, deep breath out through her nose. 'No. No, I think it's something I should do myself. I don't want you going through my horrible undies for a start. But I'll ring if I need you.'

'Fine.' Iona gave her a careful look and then levered herself off the big red sofa. Out of habit, she puffed up the cushions behind her. 'You're taking this with you, aren't you?'

'Sleeping on it, I should think. The bed belongs to our landlady. We never got round to buying our own. It's been here since her happening hippie days, I'm told. Along with the small dust factory underneath. Dead skin cells of the artistic and celebrated, apparently.'

Iona pulled a face. 'Er. Grim.'

'Ah, you wouldn't believe the things that took place on that mattress, according to Maisie. Wild nights of drug-crazed poetry readings. Tripping, visions, spontaneous jams . . . Just like *Performance* . . .'

'But in Tooting.'

'That as well.'

'Ah, Marie,' said Iona, putting her finger to her cheek in admiration, 'the excitement that bed has supported . . .'

Marie's sardonic expression slipped a little. 'Well, up to the point Chris and I moved in.'

It was the kind of quip that she habitually snapped out, but now it was almost unbearably bittersweet. Iona heard the trace of defeat in her voice and she squeezed Marie's small hand until she felt the rings on her own fingers. 'Marie, stop pretending everything's OK. I *know* it's not, I'm not stupid. What's going on? When's Chris coming back from Kosovo?'

But Marie shook her head, with a look in her eyes that Iona didn't dare push, and said, 'Let's go to the skips, eh?'

After a few jerky laps of Wandsworth, Marie dropped Iona back at the Bunch of Grapes with some bags to take upstairs, and went back to finish off her packing. Iona noticed that the car shot off at about four times the velocity she had managed to get out of it.

There was obviously a knack, she thought, as she resignedly pushed open the door, and she still didn't have it.

It was quiet inside, with only Mad Boy Sam at the bar, reading the racing pages of the *Evening Standard* and marking things off with a pencil. A grubby TubiGrip was adorning his left wrist. It looked as though it had been thoroughly used before, not necessarily recently. There were a few other people sitting in the corner by the fire, nursing pints, and Tamara was behind the bar, apparently trying to read her own palm with the aid of a book propped up against the cider tap.

Iona dumped Marie's bags at the bottom of the stairs up to the flats and slid round to the kitchen to avoid being spotted.

There wasn't a great deal more life in there either. Mark and Rick were laboriously chopping up peppers and cutting out shortbread stars respectively, while moving in a vaguely arhythmic way to a Steps song on the radio. Ned, whose smart white upper half contrasted nicely with the grimy jeans and battered Converse All-Stars below, was at the gas rings, stirring a vast copper pan which Iona supposed contained his precious stock. Ned's stock was more carefully tended than Elizabeth Taylor's wigs and probably contravened nine separate Health and Safety regulations. The one time he'd let her taste some, it had been a revelation, but she didn't want to look down into the pan to see how it had got so good.

'Hiya,' he said, without taking his eyes off the ladle he was holding up to his lips.

'No Gabriel?' Iona helped herself to some uncooked shortbread mixture.

'Oy,' said Rick, pretending to stamp the back of her hand with the sharp star cutter.

'No. He's gone out for a couple of hours. With Tamara. And they took a box of crayfish with them. Make of that what you will,' said Ned. 'We've made quite a lot of it already. I say they've gone fishing, myself. Mark thinks otherwise.'

'I think they've gone for a shag in the park,' Mark piped up helpfully.

'Thank you, Mark,' said Iona. 'How novel. And Angus?'

'Angus doesn't know.'

'Right,' said Iona. She knew which explanation he would go for. 'But I think you'll find there's nothing Angus doesn't know, by the way. He has a certificate to say so.'

'Your new barman arrived while you were out,' said Rick. He slid the tray of biscuits into the fridge to chill and brushed the flour off his hands.

'Oh, very good. Only six days after I told them to get something organized,' she said. Bar*man*? Someone *else* to follow Tamara round the bar with their eyes and do Territorial 'I Saw Her First' Bloke Stand-offs with Gabriel and Jim, while leaving her and Marie to change the barrels. Something sank inside Iona like a soufflé. Not that Tamara could help constant male attention coming her way, even if she did have the world's most charismatic pastry chef dancing attendance on her. And at least Gabriel would knock any competition on the head. Probably literally.

Iona felt her stomach twist and she started throwing the dirty towels into the laundry bin. Not jealousy, surely? God!

'Hey, Iona, take a chill pill?' Ned stopped stirring and looked at her with amusement written all over his face.

'And while you've got them out, give one to Tamara,' added Mark. 'She's even more manic than usual today. I haven't seen her this narked since the day she fell off the chair and Angus told her to do the lunch service.'

Why would *Tamara* be narked, Iona wondered. What did she have to be narked *about*, apart from the occasional attack of cystitis – which was an occupational hazard with a boyfriend like that. Maybe the new barman wasn't paying her *enough* attention. *Miaooww*, she chastised herself.

'Pass us the butter, Rick. Might as well do something while I'm gossiping in here,' said Iona, though this was only half the reason. Ned would be starting to cook properly soon and, apart from delaying the evil hour of having to go and do some work behind the bar, she liked watching him chop and pick and taste.

Rick took out three rolls of Normandy butter and pushed them across the metal work surface. 'Dishes in the washing crate, yeah?'

'Got them.' Iona picked out the little white butter pats and started forcing the butter in with a warm knife. She wasn't very good at it and the wedge of butter tended to slip out the other side as soon as she got one bit flat. 'So Tamara doesn't like the new lad. Has he got the old 666 tattooed on his forehead? Or does he just have bad karma? Or is he not ironic enough?' She smoothed the first pat down with the flat side of the knife.

'He's not a he. That's your first problem,' said Ned, from deep within the huge kitchen fridge.

'No!' said Iona, looking up with glee and some relief. 'Is it "Jerry, my barman is a pre-op chick?" Does Angus know?'

'Jim did the interview.'

'Hello,' said Rick, in a painfully accurate impression of Jim's shy murmur. 'Can you take your, er, jacket off, please? Lovely. Are those your . . . own? Not, er, padding or . . . I see, mmm . . . Excellent, you've, er, got the job. Thank you. Thank you very much. Will you make me a cup of coffee, please? Very strong?'

'She's a babe,' said Mark, by way of explanation. 'Kelly, she's called. Brunette. It looked like Abba had come back to life this morning, when she and Tamara were on the bar together.'

'With Gabriel as the blond-ish one and Jim as the one with the beard. But without the beard, obviously. Nice. Very nice. Or at least, we all think so,' agreed Rick.

'Oooh.' Iona pulled a face. Women, she could deal with. 'And we all know what happened to Abba! How's that gone down in Love's Young Dreamworld then?'

'Not good,' said Ned drily. 'Mark went down to the cellar for ice and found Tamara doing a Celtic Cross tarot reading on the Kronenbourg barrel, muttering imprecations to herself the while.'

'Imprecations, eh?'

'Imprecations. And the cards must have told her to take Gabriel out for an al fresco quickie.'

'From which he's still recovering, since Tamara is behind the bar now,' Iona pointed out. 'And there's no sign of Gabriel.'

'Really?' Ned managed to look mildly animated and wiped the sweat off his brow with the back of his arm. 'Maybe, just maybe, they don't want to arrive back together in case anyone suspects there's something going on between them.'

'No shit, Sherlock,' said Iona.

'Well, he'd better get here in the next half-hour or I'll have him. There's still an apple pie to knock up before tonight.'

'And he's your man for that,' said Mark unnecessarily. 'Knocking things up.'

'Mark, you're getting desperate,' said Iona. 'I'd have said he was—'

'Ahem,' said Rick, nodding at Iona as Tamara swept into the kitchen.

Tamara, it seemed, had reacted to the new girl by ditching her usual glossy, shiny look on a grand scale, and Mark was right: she was looking narked. Her blonde hair was dishevelled into a bedhead, but rather than looking messy, as Iona knew it would on her, it just gave her a Debbie Harry-style angelic dirtiness, further enhanced by dark rings of smudgy black kohl around her green eyes. The overall effect, with the tight jeans and sleeveless T-shirt, was like a full-page Chanel ad in a glossy mag: ridiculously over the top, and yet on Tamara perfectly reasonable. Iona was glad Jim wasn't there to witness it. The kitchen was unhygienic enough as it was.

'Iona,' Tamara hissed conspiratorially. 'Have you seen Kelly?' She rolled her eyes to indicate that if Iona had, no further words were necessary.

'No, I haven't,' Iona hissed back. 'Why?'

'She's very, *very* bad news.' Tamara nodded meaningfully. 'I know. I've got this . . . feeling about her. And the cards predicted it.'

There was a muffled snigger from the corner of the room, only partially disguised by the oven door being opened loudly.

'Why?' Iona knew Tamara better than to argue with the cards. It only led to philosophy. 'Is she pouring flat pints?'

'No . . .'

'Has she screwed up the till?'

'Not as such, no . . .'

'Did she laugh when Mad Boy Sam tried to tell her about the Hogarth roundabout incident?'

'No! Iona, listen . . .' Tamara came very close to her, smelling of nothing, as usual, and whispered, 'She has a *grey* aura.'

Iona considered her options carefully. She liked Tamara very much, mainly because she was so different from all her other friends and was her only ally against the Cult of the Combustion Engine, but there were times when she honestly couldn't decide which tree she had fallen out of. Tamara in love – a new experience for both of them – was also testing Iona's already over-stretched patience.

'Tamara,' she began in a normal voice, 'if she can do all the bar work, then I don't think her aura comes into it. Most of our clientele have a visible aura, for a start, but we don't take them to task for their personal hygiene, do we? So I think . . .'

Iona was spared any further need for explanation by a round of 'Hi!'s and laughter ringing from the bar.

'Gabriel's back then,' observed Rick.

Tamara sprang to attention by leaning sexily against the serving hatch. Iona noticed that there was a faint hint of nervousness over her habitually blissed-out Gabriel expression. Maybe the competition was getting to her. Maybe Gabriel was living up to the 'love 'em and leave 'em' promise of those religion-revealing rock-star jeans of his. Maybe the traumas of going out with someone gorgeous were finally dawning on her.

'Mind that haddock, Tamara,' said Ned over his shoulder.

Tamara leapt off the hatch as if it were wired to the mains. 'Where?'

'Hey, babe,' said Gabriel, breezing in and winking at her. He didn't see Iona standing in the corner, her eyebrow shooting skyward. 'Looking . . . hot.'

'Looking pretty foxy yourself there, Gabriel,' said Iona shortly.

Which to be fair he did. He certainly looked more like Robert Plant than Robert Plant did these days.

'Oh, er, hi, Iona.' Gabriel pushed his long blond hair out of his eyes and reached behind the door for his white chef's jacket. Today he had abandoned the lairy surfer-dude image and was wearing leather trousers. He and Tamara looked more like half of Skid Row than Abba. 'I didn't see you there. Hey, is that a new T-shirt?'

Iona hated herself for feeling flattered but she did. Warmly flattered all over, like a piece of toast. And even more so because it was a T-shirt she had screen-printed herself, with Jimmy Page's Zoso symbol on the front and a drum kit surrounded by runes on the back. Angus, on the other hand, had just asked her which coven she planned to be affiliated to.

'Er, yeah.' She brushed some of Rick's stray flour off her sleeve, which was actually adding quite a rock'n'roll marching-powder effect. 'Made it myself.'

The warmth of Gabriel's approval was just terrifying, she thought, as his generous mouth twitched into a colluding smile and his blue eyes twinkled in obvious assessment – of her *and* her art school talents with a screen print.

Iona gulped. Scary Mary. No wonder Tamara was in some kind of trance half the time. She had to get away before she offered him head for a backstage pass.

'I'll, er, see if Kelly needs help on the bar, will I?' she stammered.

Behind her, Ned allowed himself a smile into the pile of fish entrails.

'Have you met Kelly yet, Gabriel?' asked Rick, all innocence.

A variety of emotions passed across Tamara's beautiful face, the most obvious of which were resentment, fear and jealousy, an unusually complex combination for her.

'Gabriel . . .' she breathed. Her hand strayed across to touch him on the arm, then she seemed to remember the others in the room and hesitated.

But she didn't need to say any more. He was already signalling all manner of complicated things with his eyes, which she had no trouble interpreting. Tamara and Gabriel were still in the delirious phase of requiring only the merest hint of invitation to molest each other – and believing, like drunks, that the flimsiest excuse would cover up for them.

'Tam, will you come and help me get something off of my bike?' he said conversationally.

Tamara's face lit up with joy. 'OK!' she said brightly, like one of the Mickey Mouse Club gang, and the pair of them slunk out of the side door like two leather-clad ferrets.

There was a momentary pause while Rick, Mark and Iona waited for Ned to yell at Gabriel about the apple pie. But he carried on gutting the fish, with confident, strong strokes of his knife.

'Get *what* off his bike?' Iona demanded eventually. 'It's a Honda, not a Harley.'

'I think he meant, "Get ma rocks awwwf, honey,"' Rick drawled from the sink, spreading his legs as far as they would go in his grubby combat pants.

Mark wrinkled his brow in confusion. 'What?'

'My rocks, Mark. As in "Get my rocks off."'

Mark shook his head and went back to the bag of potatoes.

Iona gave Rick, still spread-legged, a critical look. 'Not quite the same effect, I'm afraid. But good try, eh?'

''Scuse me?'

Rick's legs shot together as if the elastic had snapped.

Standing at the door was a life-size Sindy doll, of the 1980s vintage. Kelly, presumably. The only woman Iona had ever seen who looked as though she had been made in the same Mattel factory as Tamara.

Albeit one in Dagenham.

''Scuse me, but I can't make the soddin' lager work.' The Bambi eyes widened. 'And there's a man in the bar says 'e's got the blood pressure of a pensioner. Should I be servin' 'im, do you think?'

Much as she loved them, Iona often wished that her friends weren't quite so high-maintenance on the emotional front. It had been a long evening, even though she'd bailed out early to help Marie move. Coping with Tamara's simmering mood and dark mutterings about karmic fields, while simultaneously explaining Angus's intricate restocking system to Kelly – who was, by a very small mercy, too dim to be aware of Tamara's sniping – almost had her deranged.

Jim arrived at half-eight, suddenly very keen to spell her off behind the bar and wearing what looked like a brand-new shirt, complete with packet creases down the front, and Iona was too tired to start worrying about the perils of his tormented love life on top of everything else. At least with Jim it had been so long that he wouldn't know what to do with Kelly even if he did manage to get those unfeasibly tight jeans off.

To Iona's eye, the jeans looked sprayed on anyway. There certainly wasn't any room for a panty line, visible or otherwise.

So it was with a heavy heart that she arrived on Marie's doorstep, knowing that there was much more to worry about here than petty infighting. All the lights were on in the house and she could hear Duran Duran from three doors down. Not good omens for Marie who, as she knew from many sleepless nights at college, liked to soothe her troubles with loud music. Usually the kind of music that most people would play quietly and well out of earshot of anyone who might still have a reasonable opinion of them.

It took a couple of rings on the bell to attract Marie's attention, and when she did finally open the door, she was mid-dance step and there was a strong smell of dust and aromatic room spray. Part of Iona wanted to go straight home again, but she gritted her teeth. Tonight she had promised she would get to the bottom of things.

'No, no,' said Marie, covering her face with her hand, and then shimmying it across as though trying to flick a bogey off her palm, 'notorious, notorious.'

'Hello, Maz,' said Iona, taking off her jacket. 'Is that it?' She stared doubtfully at the boxes and bags stacked up by the door. Even looking down the hall into the sitting room, there seemed to be a lot left. About three car boot sales' worth.

'No,' said Marie, 'it's not it, but I *have* to move out tonight or else I never will.' She had her hands on her hips and her face was covered in a fine film of sweat and dust, which on anyone else would look revolting, but only conveyed a faint Mediterranean gleam to Marie. She didn't appear to be wearing a bra either, but with breasts like that, it was fair enough. Iona privately thought that, given a toddler slung on each hip and a rifle slung over her back, Marie could do a good Spanish Revolutionary, but she didn't say anything.

'What'll you sleep on? That sofa's not going to get in the back of your Golf, now, is it?'

'Jim's taking his camp bed over for me.' Marie's determined expression softened and for a moment she didn't look as though she was about to spray the room with machine-gun fire. She looked almost amused. 'Aaah, he's sweet, is Jim lad, isn't he? He phoned me this afternoon, all worried about whether I'd be safe up there on my own. You know, he even asked if I wanted Rick or Mark to stay.'

Iona hooted. 'And you said?'

'I said thank you very much but I'd feel much safer knowing they *weren't* within shouting distance.'

She dragged a dirty hand across her forehead and smeared her mascara.

And she still looks like she's stepped out of a production of *West Side Story*, thought Iona, even with those sweat marks on her T-shirt. Marie had that unselfconscious, sexy earth mother thing perfectly – and it wasn't something you could get in a makeover. Chris: what a tosser. 'Well, we're all worried,' she said, trying not to sound too reproachful.

'Yeah, well, typical of Jim to worry about burglars, without actually touching on the difficult fact that I'm moving out because my husband's abandoned me for a bunch of starving refugees.' Marie smiled ironically. 'Bloody typical men. The only way they can get out of domestic problems is by trotting off to war. He might at least have joined the Foreign Legion.'

She shrugged and Iona saw Marie's entire body droop for one split second. She immediately forgot about Kelly and Gabriel and Tamara and all the pointless bollocks. Her whole body ached to hug Marie, even more for the determinedly flippant way she had said it, and she stretched out her arms and grabbed her. 'Marie, don't,' she said, rubbing her back. 'Jim's very fond of you. He's worried. We all are, even the lads. Angus was only saying last night . . .'

Marie bit her lip and looked as though she was trying not to break down. Iona wished she would. It was really hard to force someone determined to cope into admitting that they couldn't, not all on their own. Certainly not when people *wanted* to help.

'Grab a bag and we'll start getting these down into the car,' said Marie, changing the subject abruptly.

If only they'd all tried to like Chris a bit more, maybe Marie wouldn't feel so defensive about him now . . .

Iona hoisted the rucksack and a gym bag on to her shoulder and tried not to look surprised at the sudden change in tone. At least she'd admitted there was something more to it than just Chris being sent out with work. That was a start. With the amount of stuff Marie needed to move, they were going to be here all night. She could wait.

Several hours and two car journeys later, they lay on the bare floor of the new sitting room, heads propped on Marie's floor cushions, drinking a bottle of red wine Angus had, after some foot-stamping, given them from the bar and staring at the cracks in the ceiling.

The flat Marie had chosen was pretty grim, but light, and not as smelly as Iona had anticipated. All the same, she thought, it had to be some kind of permanent rift with Chris if Marie would rather be here than in their house. Even if she wasn't telling her anything, Marie was displaying all the hallmarks of A Fresh Start. Apart from a new haircut and a night class in motor maintenance.

As promised, Jim had delivered the camp bed (hmm, handy, thought Iona, and then remembered that getting other staff up to the staff accommodation for routine appraisals probably wouldn't have occurred to him – yet) and on the way over Marie had explained her plans for getting everything else delivered during the week.

What little she wasn't chucking out.

Downstairs, Iona could hear Angus and Jim tidying up the pub and throwing out the last stragglers, still clinging on to their warm pints. The distant clunking and muffled voices felt surprisingly companionable, and Iona could see how, with some paint and some furniture, it would be pretty cosy up here. Not to mention convenient for the odd bottle of wine.

The first thing Marie had unpacked was her stereo, and until everything was dragged upstairs from the car (Marie wouldn't let Iona ask the lads for help), they had listened to a selection of music which had made Iona feel quite young again, until they worked out it was all about fifteen years old, at which point they felt very old.

Now everything was out, and the boxes were stacked on

the landing, and they were collapsed on the floor, knackered and dusty. They were listening, at Iona's insistence, to *Led Zeppelin III*. After fifteen minutes and two glasses of wine, all thoughts of the pub, her still-unfinished commission, Angus and his irritating new fascination with profit margins, Tamara and Gabriel's puke-making love circus, her inability to drive backwards, and everything else that made her feel she wasn't actually in charge of her own life, had drifted out of her brain, leaving her tranquil and somehow a nicer person. Iona put her feet up on a box and revisited a very interesting dream from the previous night which had involved Jimmy Page teaching her how to drive round the Wandsworth roundabout in Ned's Mini. Like Ned, Jimmy too had quaffed vast amounts of Coke while doing so. Waking up had been extremely distressing.

'Marie, what was I like before I became obsessive about Led Zeppelin?' she asked sleepily. It was such a luxury to be on her own with her best friend, not having to pull pints, not having to make allowances for Angus's short temper with Chris, or indeed having to be with Chris.

'You were obsessive about Bob Dylan.'

Iona frowned and awkwardly sipped some wine. Bob Dylan? That felt like a very long time ago. 'No, this is worse. It feels like splitting up with someone. All that sense of things lost and time you can't have back. You know what I mean?'

'Yes.' Marie sat up and rocked back and forth, knees tucked up, barely making a sound on the rug she'd thrown over the floorboards. 'Oh, yes, Iona. I am familiar with your thoughts on this topic.'

'But when you think about it, I suppose it's unfair to ask your idols to exist in that one moment for ever,' Iona mused. From where she was lying, she couldn't see the concentration on Marie's face. 'They get stuck in a loop of fans willing them to stay exactly the same, so that their own youth carries on. So that they can listen to the music and have a tunnel back to that moment when they remember being sexy and fresh and untouchable themselves.'

'Like a parasite,' said Marie. 'Can I distract you with more wine?'

'Ta,' said Iona, rolling on to her side and pushing her glass across. God, it was a relief to talk about something other than the pub, or stopping distances. 'But the memory the fans have isn't the same memory the band has, is it? The fans don't remember the pressure of having to live up to expectation, and all the drug busts and the wives going mad at you down the phone because there's a photo of you wrapped around Pamela Des Barres in the *NME*.'

'Oh, the pain.'

But Iona was too well away to notice Marie's expression. And Angus never let her talk about Led Zeppelin at home. He said she put the fear of God into him. 'I suppose they didn't have any idea of what was happening, just that they were there and this amazing music was coming out of them, and that they could make their world any way they wanted it. That must have been . . . well, scary, I suppose.' She dug into her subconscious to try to work out what it was that was making her feel like this, so desperate to cling on to something intangible. The wine made her thoughts slippery. 'Don't you think?'

Marie stopped rocking. 'You do get more obsessive than most people, Iona. I don't think everyone listens to "Stairway to Heaven" and wants to lie down and die because they'll never be able to sit through a live two-hour drum solo.'

'But there's something about the music that *makes* you feel that way. Don't you hear that?'

Marie shook her head. 'Iona, sweetheart, you're starting to sound like some kind of nutter. It's like you're going through a delayed adolescence. I'm just telling you.'

Iona's brow creased over her hands, which were propping up her chin. 'But now I know they're all old and John

Bonham's dead, and that even if they did play that music again it's not going to be the same, because it's like my dad doing it . . . It's so *frustrating*.'

'Yes, but . . .' Marie sipped from her wine glass – she had been here before with Iona. 'Remember how you used to nag at your mum for not going to see the Beatles just because she was twenty-four in 1962? And she pointed out, very reasonably, I thought, given the way you were carrying on, that she didn't like them that much at the time and that it was a long way to go to Liverpool from Carlisle just to stand and sweat with a bunch of dirty scallies. Her words, not mine.'

'I just want to be there,' said Iona simply. 'And I can't be. And I've read so many books and listened to so much music that I feel there's a bubble of time alive in me where Led Zeppelin are young and it's all going on for the first time.'

Marie topped up their wine with a liberal hand. She felt strangely calm now. It was a novelty to be the one talking sense. And hearing Iona talk drivel, like a lovesick teenager, was having the comforting side-effect of making her own problem seem at least grown-up. 'Iona, tell me when you're going to start your "We're all going to die eventually" pissed lecture, because I think I prefer it, to be honest.'

Iona rolled over on to her stomach and the room spun inside her head. Maybe it was delayed adolescence – it certainly felt like an illness. She could understand the footage of speccy teenage girls sobbing with frustration in the fifticth row at Beatles concerts because they had finally made it there, sharing the same air as the objects of fantasy, and yet as far as the objects of fantasy went, they needn't be there at all.

'Sometimes,' said Marie's voice from a long way from Iona's head, 'you have to accept that things were perfect in the past, but that this is a different time. And there isn't anything you can do to create that perfection again, even if you had the original line-up there, because they're all different people now, with different experiences, and sometimes it's not the specific songs, it's the vibe you can't recreate. You know, that horrible disappointment when you buy a greatest-hits album by some group that was long-haired and sexy and on speed in the 1960s and it turns out to be versions recorded in 1987 when they did their reunion gig in the Brighton Pleasure Gardens.'

Carefully, Iona propped herself up on her elbows. 'That sinking feeling when you hear the first chord and everyone starts clapping and they're having to pitch it an octave lower because it's not the original singer.'

'I hate hearing a song that means something to me done badly,' Marie said. Her dark eyebrows furrowed moodily. 'I hate seeing some bloke standing there, older, fatter, wrinklier, singing words that used to twist my stomach as though for him it's just Key Stage 3 History.'

'But it is, I suppose,' said Iona. She'd never thought of it like this before, that being a rock star was a job. 'That's what they do for a living. You don't ask an accountant to give it up and get a proper job when he's forty, do you? What are they meant to do? Retrain as traffic wardens?'

'I know, exactly. But I hate feeling so cheated, that the song means something more to me than just the person singing it, and when I feel like that . . .' Marie looked about to say something else and stopped.

'You feel dumped. I know what you mean,' said Iona, and they sat in silence while 'Since I've Been Loving You' played out.

Iona's heart lurched around her chest. Led Zeppelin truly were the only rock group where you fancied the singer – up until the guitarist started playing.

'He's just not the same person he used to be,' Marie said bitterly.

'I know.' Iona groaned with frustration. Not that she would have turned down the singer, if it had come to that.

'It all went wrong when he got a fringe and started wearing leather trousers instead of skin-tight jeans.'

Marie's head jerked up in surprise.

'Robert Plant, yeah?' Iona said hopefully.

'Iona, I'm talking about Chris.'

Iona put a hand to her head. Long day, red wine, driving lesson, bad idea. This was why she didn't get drunk. It was fine for slipping into weird Led Zeppelin trances but hopeless for dealing with your best friend's very immediate crises. 'When? God, I'm sorry. When did we stop talking about Led Zeppelin and start talking about Chris?' She only just managed to suppress the desire to demand how Marie could even think of them in the same mental breath. Which was the red wine talking.

'Loath as I am to encourage you in your disturbing adolescent meanderings about the nature of fame,' said Marie, all on one heavy breath, 'let me put it in terms you may be able to understand. Chris and I got together when he was young and passionate about saving the world, and I was stupid enough to think that it was sexy. Now I am older, I know that it is sexy in a way, but that way is really only when it is depicted in a Hollywood screenplay and starring Julia Roberts as the Angel of Mostar. In reality, it is hard and thankless, and now I think even Chris hates it.'

'But he's just gone to do it all! Hasn't he?' demanded Iona, rubbing her head. 'Or have I missed something?'

'Yeah, but Iona, I think even Chris hates it. He's painted himself into a corner. I think he's jealous of the fact that I can help people but for more money and in an office with wall-to-wall poster paints.'

Iona stared. Her concentration was lurching around her brain like her dad at Christmas and even though she really, really wanted to concentrate on what Marie was saying to her, her ears, clutching a pint of vodka orange, kept slinking back to the hiccuping drum pattern on 'Out on the Tiles'.

Iona dragged her attention back to Marie by putting a

thumb in her mouth and biting it. Time to get sober. The kettle had already boiled twice in the last half-hour, but when it came to it neither of them could be bothered to get up to make the coffee.

'Iona, Chris isn't coming back,' said Marie softly. 'He thinks we ought to get divorced and . . . you know, I think we should too.'

'Marie . . .' Iona stretched out a hand. 'Marie, I'm so sorry. But he was making you unhappy.' *And it made me feel like I was letting you down because I allowed you to be unhappy.* Iona thought it, but didn't say it.

'I know. But things change.'

They sat and looked at each other for a minute or so.

'Marie, I'm making myself a cup of coffee. Do you want one?' She had to focus quickly or else she'd start telling Marie about Jim and Angus's popular 'Chris chats to God' party double act. She stumbled to her feet and walked carefully to the kettle.

Marie ran her finger around the rim of her wine glass until it hummed weirdly. Her voice, when she spoke, was quiet but definite, as though she had been winnowing out exactly how she felt for a long time and had reached the definitive version. She'd been right – no point in telling Iona until she knew exactly how she felt herself. 'You know, the more I got to know Chris, the more I realized it was mostly in his head, all that Save the World stuff. He isn't that nice a guy. He might give out to you lot about buying Amnesty International Christmas cards, but he won't have Eastern European wine in the house. Thing is, being Mr Charity is what he does, like Ned cooking, or you painting. Or Angus being right all the time. And if he doesn't do that – what does he have?'

She lifted her eyes to meet Iona's.

Iona, coming across the room with a lukewarm four-spoon cup of coffee, didn't know what to say. Marie had scrupulously never criticized him before. 'He has you?'

'I'm not enough. He doesn't count me. Not *even* me.'

Blearily, Iona put the cup down and tried to read Marie's face. Sadness, she had seen there before. And pain. Maybe, on bad nights, this resignation too. But she sensed that there was something else there that she had no idea how to help with, something she couldn't soothe away, and a wave of panic that she couldn't make the last connection with her best friend rose up in her throat like sick. She stretched out her hands and grabbed Marie's in them as if she had to pull her out of sinking sand. 'Marie. I don't care how saintly Chris thinks he is, he didn't deserve to have you in the first place. And if he's put his work over you, then he's even more of a wanker than I thought he was, but it's not *your* fault! Do you understand that? It's not your fault.'

'Oh, Iona . . . He's . . .' Marie turned her lips under her teeth like a child and sighed heavily, hiding her face in her hands. 'Iona, I'm so sorry for not telling you.' She shivered in her T-shirt. 'I just couldn't talk about it to anyone, knowing you all hated him so much. I didn't want to have been so wrong all along and . . .'

'But I *wouldn't* have judged you,' protested Iona. That hurt. 'Why did you think that?'

Maria looked up at her. That was the trouble; Iona would have given her whatever reaction she wanted to hear, and it had taken so long to work out what she *did* feel. 'There are some things that you can't sort out for me . . .' She fiddled with the cork. 'I needed to be on my own.'

There was a pause. Iona felt the skin goose-pimple on the back of her arms. How would it feel if Angus left because he didn't love her any more? An irrational sweep of panic filled her brain. 'He's really gone?'

Marie nodded. 'Not coming back.'

Iona felt stricken, ashamed to be worrying about her own stupid problems. 'God, Marie, I'm so . . . I don't know what to say. I'm so sorry. I feel *hopelessly* inadequate.'

'Don't say that,' said Marie.

Iona came round behind Marie and wrapped her arms around her, cradling her legs with her own, pressing her head into Marie's neck. Her body was so soft and firm beneath the soft cotton of her T-shirt, so comforting to smell.

It occurred to Iona, after a long song's worth of silent hug, that Marie's warmth and comforting familiar smell were actually reassuring her too, probably more than her own weedy arms were reassuring Marie. She would finish the painting eventually. She would pass her driving test – didn't all sorts of total idiots manage to get through? Things would work out with Angus. This was just a phase of mutual dissatisfaction they were going through. If they'd got married as soon as they'd started going out, this would be the end of their honeymoon period, wouldn't it? As it was, no harm done. They'd get through it.

Unlike Chris and Marie.

Iona gave Marie a guilty squeeze. But that was no one's fault, no matter how much they all wanted to blame Chris and Marie wanted to blame herself. Chris and Marie were just a relationship that had simply assumed too much, nothing more. But though it was constantly on the tip of her tongue to say it, she knew it was far more than that to Marie. And she didn't want to give Marie a reason not to trust her.

'You're so *lucky*, Iona,' said Marie unexpectedly.

'Why?' Iona grimaced behind Marie's back as soon as she'd said it. Wrong answer.

'Because Angus is a lovely, *lovely* man.'

They habitually reached the 'lovely, lovely man' stage of the evening at around the two-bottle mark, but now Marie wasn't doing her usual pretend Irish accent and she sounded as though she was in real pain, deep down.

'I know he is.' Despite everything she'd thought seconds earlier, a mutinous voice popped up in Iona's head. Lovely was great, but it didn't wear tight black flares with embroidered poppies down the leg. 'Despite everything.'

'No, he's *lovely*,' said Marie fiercely. 'He's good and kind and you must hang on to him.'

And lock myself away from live music and dyeing my hair and getting drunk on Moscow Mules and never snogging anyone else again for the rest of my life? Iona could actually feel her heart rate speed up.

And then to her horror, she thought of Ned. In his old grey T-shirt that stopped just above his bicep, gutting fish in the kitchen this afternoon, throwing her cheeky looks as if they were the only ones in on the joke.

I've got to give up drinking, she thought, panicking.

'So come on, tell me what happened,' Iona said, trying to push Ned away with mental pictures of Chris lecturing them about why Live Aid was actually bad for the Ethiopians. 'You don't have to go into detail.'

Maybe it helped that Marie didn't have to look at her. Iona felt her tense up, then relax back into her arms. She increased the pressure of her hug as Marie spoke.

'Um. Chris went out to Kosovo to organize some relief work,' Marie began.

Iona nodded and said, 'Yes,' as encouragingly as she could.

Marie took another deep sip of wine. 'Well, he wrote to me – this *horrible*, impersonal letter – to say that he's decided he wants to stay, and because I don't want to go out there with him – *me*, you notice – he wants us to . . . separate. Or rather, that's his story. Alleviating the world's suffering is a more heroic reason to get divorced than just not fancying me any more.'

It amazed Iona how articulate Marie could be even after drinking vast amounts of wine. It had to be part of the PGCE course.

'I can't believe it's like that,' she said automatically, and then her brain ran up against a brick wall. Why couldn't she manage something more complicated? Why did the International Girlfriend Convention not allow her to say,

'Chris is a completely selfish, manipulative git and you're well shot!'?

Well, she could, but she sensed that for once it wouldn't help.

'Marie, that's ridiculous,' she said into her dark hair. Despite all the hard work, Marie still smelled of flowers. 'How could he not fancy you? You're beautiful. No, you are,' she insisted as Marie shifted around in her arms. 'You are. What are you wriggling for?'

'I'm redistributing my layers of fat so you can't feel them.' Marie stopped wriggling and sighed, dropping her head on to Iona's arm. 'So once I knew he wasn't coming back, I had to move. Being in that flat made me feel ill. Physically sick.'

'I can't believe you didn't tell anyone,' Iona marvelled. 'Poor you, keeping it all to yourself.'

Marie made an ambiguous noise.

'But how do you feel now?'

'I can't tell you how I feel because I don't *know*. Every time I think I finally *do* know how I feel, and what I want to do, it all turns upside down again. I only feel OK when I'm pulling pints, or teaching, or painting, or whatever will fill up my mind to stop me thinking about how endless and painful and . . . Iona, what am I meant to do? He made me feel so bad in that letter, just for wanting him to come home when he's helping all those people out there!'

'Oh, God, Marie,' said Iona, hugging her, 'I don't know why you married him in the first place!'

Marie's eyes flashed. 'Don't you?'

Iona paused and the wine she'd drunk suggested that it might be a good idea to tell Marie the truth for once, instead of what she wanted to hear. Because massaging the truth about Chris hadn't worked so far. She gave her a careful look. 'No! I don't, really.'

Marie's face twitched with surprise and Iona felt disoriented by the power of saying what she actually thought about Chris, instead of having to play along with Marie's pretence that acting like an arsehole was normal husband behaviour. 'He's *always* been self-righteous at the expense of everything else! And it's only a cover for his own inadequacies. Who in their right minds would try and make their wife feel guilty – in a *letter* – like that? It's *obviously* his problem! I mean, yes, he was OK as a boyfriend, but . . .'

'But what? If you were such a good friend, why did you let me marry him? Why didn't you say anything?'

'What could I say?' Iona retorted exasperatedly. 'Did you phone me from the beach? Did you expect me to come running up from behind a sand dune? "No, stop, Marie! It isn't a real vicar!"'

'Don't make fun,' said Marie. 'It wasn't like that.'

'Wasn't it? I couldn't *believe* it when you told me. After all those conversations we had about which hymns we'd pick and whether I would have had kids you could have for bridesmaids. What was I meant to say when you came back and told me you'd got married on a bloody beach?' Iona put a hand over her mouth, unsure of whether she'd gone too far.

'You could have . . .' Marie trailed off, as she realized Iona couldn't have done anything, given that she hadn't been able to either.

'I'd never tell someone they'd made a mistake *after* the wedding,' said Iona more gently. 'Or even before, come to that. You can't, can you?'

'All those conversations . . .' Marie laughed bitterly. 'They always stopped at the bouquet-tossing stage, didn't they? We never discussed how we would argue over the gas bills.'

Iona blushed and turned away. She was willing her whole brain to come up with ways to make Marie feel better, but all she could think of was her and Angus, and she hated herself for being so selfish when she was meant to be so compassionate.

I want you to tell me that marriage is right. I want you to tell me that you can promise to love someone for the rest of your life and mean it. I want you to tell me that it's OK to argue when you love each other. I want you to tell me that I'm doing the right thing even though you didn't.

I want someone to tell me what to do—

There was a knock on the door. Marie and Iona froze and listened, unwilling to be the one to break the intimacy of their conversation by letting whoever it was in.

Iona wondered whether Marie was wondering if it could be Chris. Some delicate guitar picking from the stereo sounded like needles of sound in the sudden silence and Iona realized that one ear had been listening to Led Zeppelin all the time. For Christ's sake, grow up, she thought crossly to herself.

The knock came again, this time accompanied by hesitant whispers and a much clearer, 'Oh yes, very good!'

Angus. Neither of them moved. The dirty light from the streetlight opposite fell through the curtainless window and threw their one bulbous shadow across the rug.

Iona heard Jim say quite clearly, 'Angus, how much wine did you let Iona have?'

Great, thought Iona. Quick, before he says something completely stupid and ruins everything. She squeezed Marie, who squeezed her arm back and began to lever herself to her feet. 'See? You've got visitors already. They're queuing down the stairs.'

'You let them in and I'll just splash my face.'

'Er, with the sink like that?' When they arrived, Iona had assumed it had been fitted with an unusual green-grey marble-effect bathroom suite. Then Marie had come in and squirted the whole lot with Mr Muscle and now it was only off-white.

'You know what I mean. If it's Jim . . .' Marie heaved meaningfully at her unfettered bosom and disappeared into the bathroom.

Iona got up and took a swig of her horrible cold coffee

on the way to the door. She felt pretty sober at last. Angus had known all the time, and he hadn't told her. She didn't quite know how that made her feel. Had he persuaded Jim to let Marie move in? So they could keep an eye on her?

'Lads,' she said, opening the door wide.

Jim and Angus stood there on the landing, obviously in the middle of an embarrassed discussion about something.

'Ah, very good,' said Angus, striding in. 'We were getting worried about you.'

'Well, don't be, it won't exactly *help*,' Iona hissed.

'Can I . . .' Jim peered round and, seeing Marie wasn't there, came in and wandered politely around the room.

'This'll look fabulous once it's done up a bit,' said Angus, hoisting up the window. 'You want to let some air in here. And, for crying out loud, Iona, is there *no* escape from that music of Satan?'

'No,' said Iona, setting her jaw at him.

'Hello, boys,' said Marie.

Iona was pleased, in a strange way, to see that she'd put on a clean T-shirt. Being in possession of the bald facts made her even more protective, and she didn't want Marie to fulfil their expectations of what an abandoned wife should look like. As it was, she looked tired and a bit drawn, but Jim had looked more tired and far more drawn when *he* moved house.

'I've come to take this one home,' explained Angus. 'If that's OK.'

'That's fine,' said Marie. 'We've done all we can tonight. Night, Iona.' She came over and gave her a big hug. 'Thanks so much.'

'Night-night.' Iona released her and gave her a firm look. 'See you tomorrow.'

'Come on, sweetie-loo, I'm knackered,' said Angus. He took his keys out of his pocket and waved them at her. 'You're driving back, are you? The L-plates are in the boot.'

'Can't. I'm *well* over the limit.' For a wild moment, Iona considered whether drinking three glasses of wine for breakfast for the rest of her life would convince Angus of her commitment to her non-driving status.

Probably not.

'Why don't you put your shoes on, Marie?' said Jim quietly, while Angus and Iona bickered amiably about whether she'd been so gormless as to leave her fleece in the pub.

'Why? It's too late to make me swab the floor downstairs, isn't it? Or is that part of my rent deal?' She gave him a bold look from under one dark eyebrow. Being predictable was quite comforting now she didn't really know what sort of person she was any more. It was like having lines to recite, without responsibility.

Jim blushed. 'Look, come over and sleep at ours tonight. You can't stay here. It's a bit miserable.'

'But you haven't got enough beds,' protested Marie. She tried not to let the temptation show in her eyes at the thought of a soft duvet and a clean pillow to cry into. 'Unless you and Ned are finally sharing for real?'

'I'll sleep on the sofa.' His eyes were rooted to the floor while he said it, but then he looked up and Marie could see genuine concern in his face. Concern from Jim. God. Things must be obvious. She wrestled with her pride, which was demanding that she stay here and lie on her bed right in front of them all, now she'd made it. Having Jim feel sorry for her was a new and not comfortable experience.

'I'd *like* you to stay over,' he said again, shyly.

He hasn't really changed at all in the eight years I've known him, Marie thought. *Nothing's spoiled him. And eight years is a long time.*

'Come on, get your girl bag,' he added, seeing her waver.

'My what?' Wrangling pride or not, Marie startled herself into laughing by Jim's best attempt at a masterful expression.

Or maybe Gabriel *was* having some kind of influence.

'Oh, I don't know, that rucksack of rubbish you girls need to take with you when you go somewhere.'

'You must be thinking of someone else. I only need a toothbrush and the merest hint of mascara to look this good.'

'Ah, well, he is, now you mention it,' agreed Iona, from underneath Angus's arm. 'You haven't met Jim's new friend yet, have you? Sindy Barmaid? Angus, you arse, you'll rick my neck.'

'My what?' Jim spluttered. 'You must be thinking of someone else.'

'Are we all going to have the same tedious bloody conversation all night?' demanded Angus, still headlocking Iona. 'Can I remind you bunch of selfish idiots what time it is?'

'Quick,' said Marie. 'Let me lock up and get out before you all make me cry with your tenderness and concern.'

Chapter Twenty-six

Angus and Iona had four pillows between them on their vast double bed.

One was Angus's 'special' pillow, a flat thing in a 'special' red flannel pillowcase, which he either clamped between his knees or screwed up into a ball and stuffed under one arm; apparently this was essential for him to get to sleep. Early on in their relationship, after a couple of months of waking up to see Angus snoring contentedly with a manky old pillow wrapped round his throat like a flaccid neck brace, Iona had cautiously consulted Marie about the normality of this and Marie had confirmed that all men had a 'special' pillow, and that she should be grateful it wasn't a dog-eared stuffed 'lucky' mongoose. Chris's 'special' pillow, for instance, was housed in a *Star Wars* pillowcase he'd had since junior school and which he insisted on her washing without fabric conditioner because fabric conditioner gave him a mysterious night-time rash.

Iona couldn't believe Marie had missed this gloriously appropriate opportunity to turn the tables and irritate Chris to death.

Two of the remaining pillows were expensive feather-stuffed beauties which Iona's mother had given her as consolation when she announced she was going to live in London, and the fourth was a pathetic specimen that Angus had acquired somewhere – he knew not where – and that had lost a tenth of its bodyweight every year until now it was, as Iona's mother would have put it, 'neither use nor ornament'. (Though, to be strictly accurate, she would actually have said, 'neither usenerornum'nt'.) They hadn't ever got round to replacing it; Iona felt she had made her pillow contribution, and Angus refused to throw away a perfectly good one.

And so every night they went through the pathetic routine of trying to grab both decent pillows and foist the flat one on the other, and whoever got it was more or less guaranteed a headache in the morning.

As soon as Iona crawled under the duvet and felt her head touch the useless fourth pillow, the nice two being wedged beneath Angus's head and his special pillow occupying the warm space between his thighs, she knew with a grim certainty that she wasn't going to get to sleep at all that night.

She lay on her back and listened to the cars still driving by outside. She could shut the window to block out the noise, or she could leave it open and keep the small room ventilated. A tough choice, which would result in irritation one way or another, and hinged on whether she could even be arsed to get out of bed in the first place.

Iona noted, with some animosity, that a major contributing factor to the heady aroma developing already in the room was Angus, who had crashed out without bothering to have a bath first and had consequently brought a fragrant hint of the Bunch of Grapes to bed with him. He was already in the deep-breathing phase of his snore cycle, indicating that he was now terminally inert and his body mass had effectively doubled, which meant that getting either of the two nice pillows out from under him was impossible. It also meant that there were about six minutes left before he moved into the full snore phase, which would fill the bedroom with white noise until forty-five minutes before the alarm clock went off – a frankly derisory amount of time for her to pack a night's sleep into.

Most nights she could forgive him for this kind of thing,

since he worked so hard and she alone could fit on the sofa, but tonight it seemed incredibly selfish and annoying. Iona turned on her side and huffed as hard as she could to see if that would wake him.

It didn't.

Her head was virtually on the mattress, the pillow was so flat, and she could feel a headache approaching from the back of her skull. Maybe that last coffee while they were finishing up had been a bad idea.

God, thought Iona tetchily, coffee never used to keep me awake before. I must be getting old.

The cold truth of that made her feel even less like falling into a peaceful slumber and her mind returned masochistically to the thorny topic that had been niggling at her and Tamara all day in the pub: the number of boy-band cover versions in the charts that they had bought first time round.

Was it finally time to start investing in a special night cream?

Next to her, Angus began to rasp ominously. Only about four minutes before the full snore.

How on earth were you meant to maintain a full and active sex life once you knew exactly when your partner would start snoring?

Iona tried fluffing up the pillow but it was like trying to fluff up a pitta bread. Selected parts of her body were desperate to get to sleep, others felt tightly wound up. A voice in her head observed dispassionately that this was a really bad night to spend tossing and turning – she had a full day at the pub tomorrow, with the first round of the pub quiz in the evening, her driving theory test in a couple of days . . . And the more her brain told her to fall asleep, the less likely it was to happen at all.

She turned her head to the luminous hands of the alarm clock on the bedside shelf. Half-one. Plenty of sleep left in the night. Trying not to hate Angus too much, Iona wrapped her head in the pillow and resorted to the only useful thing Tamara had ever told her: how to get to sleep by flexing each muscle group in turn. Or boring your body to sleep, as she called it.

In an hour, Iona managed to bore her body to screaming pitch and her mind to frightening new levels of hyperactivity, and still there wasn't the faintest hope of dropping off. So at three-thirty, after a fridge raid, she was in the sitting room, eating Weetabix and watching late-night television with the volume very low. The steady chain-saw whine of Angus's snoring was carrying operatically through the flat, which made her wonder why she was bothering to keep the sound down in the first place.

The time had not been wasted: since two-thirty she had absorbed two Learning Zone modules on Dorset life in the nineteenth century (why did schools programmes still last seventeen random minutes?) and sat through three minutes of American beach volleyball, as much as she could take while eating. Though all this was interesting, she was tempted to call one of the late-night chats on Carlton to demand why someone didn't capitalize on the captive audience and start showing repeats of *Mr & Mrs*, or *Jerry Springer*'s husband-killing classics. 'Jerry, ah stuffed his nose with mah foam ear plugs and he snored no maw!'

Both cats were asleep on Iona's knee, radiating heat in a circle, and normally, in front of *EastEnders*, that sent her dozing off in minutes, but her brain was still racing, despite the worsening headache banging away at her temples like something trying to get out of her head through her eye sockets. The only part of Iona that was even approaching a state of rest was her left foot, which had been tucked under her when the cats leapt on and was now tingling ominously.

The continuity man, who sounded about as bored as she was, announced the imminent arrival of another module about town planning, and with a sigh Iona looked out of the window into the dark garden. A mood was now settling on her. Maybe painting would help.

Carefully, she decanted Creighton from her knee and on to the chair. Lady Cat clung on tenaciously and Iona had to remove each claw from her pyjama bottoms before dumping her in her box by the radiator. Both slept through the entire operation. Bastards.

Then, rather than go back into the bedroom and disturb the incredible snoring man, she looked through the permanently full basket of unironed washing for some warm clothes.

As she pulled on an old pair of tracksuit bottoms, Iona was suddenly aware that something was wrong. What was it? She listened hard. The snoring had stopped.

A cold hand gripped her inside. Angus! He'd finally suffocated himself with that stupid pillow! She threw down the jumper in her hand and ran through to the bedroom, trying to remember how many chest pumps you were meant to do for every breath into the mouth (close off the nose first), but as she set foot in the hall, the rasping started up again, this time about a semitone lower than before and with an interesting rattle at the downstroke.

Iona stopped crossly. Bloody typical. Then she turned on her heel and marched out to the shed, without bothering to close the back door quietly.

In the shed, with the light on, it didn't feel like night-time. That was the beauty of the shed as far as Iona was concerned: it was the one part of the house where Angus wouldn't come in without knocking, and where she didn't have to be anyone but herself. If she hadn't had the shed, she was quite sure she and Angus would have been reduced to Chris-and-Marie-style scratching and gouging long ago.

The wedding commission was up on the easel, dominating

the room accusingly, and still missing the bride and groom in the middle.

Iona bit her lip as she looked at it, and put the kettle on. She had had an extended phone discussion about a delivery date with Lynn's sister Melissa, the chief bridesmaid – the only person she had ever spoken to who made Angus look tentative and flexible. For a while, Iona had wondered whether Melissa was in fact Matt's commanding officer and he really *was* marrying the platoon mascot.

They had agreed – or rather, Melissa had informed her and Iona had agreed – a delivery date at the end of the month, about three weeks away. By which time Iona would be a qualified driver and able to take it over to Fulham herself. Or not.

Just looking at the massive blank core of the collage made Iona's heart sink and settle somewhere at the pit of her stomach like chronic indigestion. That was the thing about worries like this: they just didn't go away. They collected at the back of her mind like gallstones. And it wasn't as though she hadn't been working on it: the border of roses was now so detailed that they were virtually photographic. Anything to put off the evil moment of starting on the bridal party.

Iona absently flicked off the kettle and poured water on to the tea bag. It wasn't that she couldn't draw Matt and Lynn, because she knew she could. It was just that – and she wished somehow that night thought didn't make her *so* clear-headed – for the last few weeks, she hadn't been able to think of marriage without feeling a profound sense of dread and she was scared that it would show up in the painting.

There, she'd said it. The more she thought about marriage, the more it made her feel weird, because suddenly all the things she'd thought she wanted, she wasn't sure if she wanted at all.

She stood in the middle of the silent, overlit shed with her hands wrapped round the mug of tea, feeling acutely alone. Iona didn't like reaching into her stock bag of familiar reactions and finding they didn't fit any more.

That's why you'll never be a good artist, nagged her conscience. The Voice of Bad Iona. She'd been hearing a lot from her recently. *You want everything to be the same all the time. You're not prepared to suffer.*

A shiver ran through her, because this was irrefutable. Wasn't that why everyone came to her with their problems? Because she was so good at putting everything nice and right again?

Rather than face up to whatever it was that was causing them in the first place? *Very good. You're not helping them, you know.*

It was at times like this that Iona wished she smoked, but she didn't and politeness forbade her from indulging in Marie's recommended stress relief and putting the radio on really loud. So she took the painting down and turned it against the wall so she wouldn't have to see it when she came back, marched up the garden, got the packet of cherry Bakewells that Angus thought he had secreted behind the bread in the bread bin, and ate the first one on her way back and started the second one with another mouthful of tea once she'd secured the door again.

The pretend jam and almond paste combo made her feel nicely sick, and cheered up by doing something annoying (on a small scale) to Angus for a change, Iona took out a fresh piece of paper from her folder and fixed it to the easel.

She stared at it, seeing all sorts of colours moving around on the whiteness, which seemed to be projecting from the churning in her own mind. It was impossible to stay on one thought for more than a few moments. Like, marriage, was it really possible? And to Angus? And what happened to someone like Marie who believed in it when it all goes wrong? And when did I stop believing in it? And how can you feel all those things about Ned and still know you love Angus?

Steady on, Iona reminded herself. This isn't one of your internal interviews.

Anything. You can paint anything.

Without thinking, Iona squirted some black on to her palette and started squashing it about with a brush. She didn't often use black and hadn't ever really thought about all the colours in it, blues and silvers that the overhead light was catching as she swirled the colour around with a big brush.

So, Iona, is it true that you and Jimmy met at the now famous Eel Pie Island R'n'B scene?

Iona smiled as if to a secret camera and flicked a petal of black paint round coyly. 'Well, yes, sort of,' she murmured, dropping into *Hello!* speak, but not too loud. 'I'd just sold a painting to Andrew Loog Oldham, and I was round at his house with Mick and Keith and Marianne for the grand unveiling, some magazine or other was there, and Andrew asked me if I wanted to sit in on some Immediate sessions the next day. Jimmy was producing. I told him I was pretty good with a pair of maracas . . .' (*Pause for indulgent smiles all round, as interviewer acknowledges Iona's own reputation as long-fringed guitar maestro.*) 'Of course, he didn't know then that I'd been playing guitar myself with . . .' Iona paused. The name of her own R'n'B group? Think of one later. '. . . for about a year,' she finished.

And he dumped Jackie de Shannon for you?

(*More indulgent smiles.*) 'Well, yes, I think so, although I never really met her.' Iona didn't like to be a troublemaker, even in pretend interviews. 'As soon as we saw each other, we just knew. I went back to his riverboat and he sat and played to me for hours and we talked about which restaurants we liked, what kind of food, he's a fabulous cook, you know . . .'

Iona paused again mid-swirl and frowned. She had a feeling that last bit might have been how Jane Asher met Paul McCartney, a nugget of typically obsessive information left over from her Beatles phase. Talking chastely in hotel rooms about custard. She wasn't sure she wanted to be Jane Asher, even subconsciously. And where had the fabulous cook bit come from?

She let out a deep breath through her nose, put down her brush and picked up her rapidly cooling tea. She knew where the fabulous cook bit had come from, all right.

The canvas was now covered in the outline of a curly, spinning circular thing. Iona tilted her head at various angles to see if she could see what it was yet. A cabbage? A rose? She swigged a mouthful of tea – which seemed to have some weird kind of truth serum in it – and squirted her darkest purple out on to the palette. The tea did taste funny, now she actually thought about it. The milk was fresh, so it couldn't be that. The tea hadn't come from Ned's, had it?

And as she began to squidge the violet paint around the black waves, her mind slipped seamlessly from The Swingin' Home Life of Britain's Top Session Guitarist to Ned. Iona didn't actually mind working at godforsaken hours like this; in fact, she found it helped her painting dramatically. If it wasn't for the hopeless pretension of working in the middle of the night (not to mention the inconvenience of it for her day job), she would have done it all the time. She had to dislocate her brain with something else – music, pretend interviews, large amounts of caffeine, sleep deprivation – in order to make room for whatever it was to flow out unimpeded by thought. Iona didn't like to say talent, it sounded too precious, but if she thought too hard about what she was doing nothing happened and that was when she had serious doubts about spending the rest of her life as a waitress, smearing paint around in the evenings for no apparent reason while Angus paid for everything, up to and including her dental insurance.

Iona stopped squidging and sighed. Made-up interviews with surprisingly knowledgeable journalists or not, it was about the only time she got to listen to herself think.

She frowned. Here she was with one of the biggest dilemmas she'd had to face and who could she talk to? No one. All
her friends were either too distressed themselves, too busy or
too loved-up to notice that she might want to talk about her
own problems for a change. No wonder she couldn't sleep,
or paint, or function properly, thought Iona angrily. She was
silting up from the inside with unspoken worry.

She could hardly tell Marie, in her current situation, that
she wasn't sure if she wanted to marry Angus any more.
Iona felt hot and guilty even thinking about it. And as for
Tamara . . . Iona shivered at the thought of asking Tamara
for advice. Even if she could get any practical sense out of
her, which couldn't be guaranteed these days, Iona was all
too aware that Tamara considered living with Angus to be
one step up from a boot camp.

Iona mingled some violet shadows around the edge of a
black petal. She *loved* living with Angus. It was just the
looking down the long end of eternity that bothered her.

For ever. How could she promise anyone that she would
be exactly like this for ever? Her mood slumped further and
she mixed up some gunmetal grey, a colour she hadn't used
since last year's 'child on donkey' christening portrait.

And she could hardly confide in her best friend, could she?
Not when her best friend – after Marie – was Angus.

Alone in the shed, no cats, with the night still dark around
her and the radio on so quietly she could barely hear it, now
she thought about it, Iona felt scared for the first time in ages.
Because she couldn't move her life on without disturbing
everyone else.

OK, Iona, she said to herself, trying to get in quick before
her sarcastic inner voice started making snide comments.
Go on, while you've got my complete attention. List the
lot. List all the reasons you're pissed off, since no one
else is going to ask you about them. Be as churlish as
you want.

Her hands trembled as she carried on swirling her brush

round and round and round the paper. Grey layered on purple, splitting and mixing into streaky veinage.

1. Angus is annoying me and we can't ever split up, married or not.

2. I don't want to be thirty, I don't want to be shunted up to the 'young parents' age bracket, and I still haven't sorted out a pension.

Iona felt a chill of terror run through her at that, but she pressed on.

3. My best friend is getting divorced from a man we all hate and she probably still loves, and I don't know what to say or do to help her.

4. I'm deeply jealous of Gabriel and Tamara and their outrageous sex life and the way it's making me feel old and tied down instead of young and tied up.

5.

A tear spilled out of Iona's eye and rolled down her cheek.

5. I think I've fallen in love with my oldest friend, and I can't ever tell him.

6. I don't think I can pass my driving test. I could kill someone tomorrow and Angus will be so disappointed.

7. I'm scared that the pub won't work out and Angus will be devastated.

8. I'll probably never go to a proper gig again and if we do Angus will get sitting-down tickets.

9. I'll never even meet Jimmy Page.

This was a reason too far. A huge sob broke out of Iona's throat before she knew it was coming and she stumbled across the room to the comfy chair, not caring that she was getting paint on the arms from the brush she'd forgotten to put down first. Without opening her eyes, she sank down and cried and cried until the radio news announced it was six-thirty, and she slunk back into bed. Angus was still snoring.

Chapter Twenty-seven

'Slow down! *Slow down!*' yelled Marie. 'For fuck's sake! This is a thirty-mile-an-hour zone! There are kids around!'

'Marie, will you give it a rest?' Iona checked her mirrors and put her indicator on. 'You'll split your blouse.'

'Pair of dykes *in your dreams*, mate!' Marie flicked a final V-sign, wound up her window and slumped in her seat. 'I hate it when men like that drive as though their testicles are part of the engine. They all do it. I mean, tell me why do men spend longer waxing and moisturizing their cars than most women spend on their legs, and then have this bizarre notion that the more wing mirrors they can collect, the bigger men they are? *Bastards.* You can go a bit faster if you want.'

'Marie.' Iona didn't take her eyes off the road. Marie's Golf GTI was a good deal perkier than Ned's Mini. It also drove in a terrifyingly straight line. 'Marie, I can see a crossroads.'

'Yeah, I know. Don't panic, but if you look you'll see there's a mini-cab office right next to it.'

'Auuuggghhh!' Iona felt her thighs clench in an animal fear response. She had been driving now for three months and still hadn't got mastery of her self-preservation instincts when approaching traffic hazards. Angus protested in particular over her skunk-like reaction to big roundabouts.

'I'll switch the music off, will I?' Marie leaned over, her red blouse straining across the widest point of her ample chest, and knocked off *Led Zeppelin II*, which she had been playing to calm Iona down after the Clapham Common interchanges.

'Marie, just tell me,' Iona's voice wobbled, 'am I doing all right?'

This was a part of London that she hadn't been in before, and the roads seemed to be constructed entirely from speed humps. The last two miles had been more like the assault course from *Junior Kickstart* than prime Wandsworth housing market, added to which everyone was driving either a Nissan Bluebird or a Toyota Landcruiser, and both varieties seemed to spend disturbing amounts of time arguing with passengers in the back.

'Yeah, you're doing very well, sweetheart. I wouldn't have time to shout at the arseholes if I was worrying about your driving, would I?'

'I just worry that I'm doing the wrong thing all the time,' wailed Iona. 'And when things are going OK, I worry that if something does go wrong, I won't know what to do because I'll be too busy trying to remember which foot goes down first in an emergency stop.'

'That's a bit like life, isn't it?' said Marie, her voice suddenly sounding far away. About three miles away. Streatham, roughly.

Iona frowned. Lately Marie had developed a habit of lapsing into random analogies, which she supposed was her way of rationalizing the Chris situation. She was glad – sort of – that Marie was happy to talk about it to her, though she was being very tight-lipped with everyone else, but her increasingly baroque analogies were tricky to manage along with clutch control and keeping to the speed limit.

'In what way, like life?' she asked, since there was a very long red light and two bicycles in front of her. The engine sounded scarily racy, idling in the comparative silence.

'Well, you know.' Marie leaned her elbow out of the window and propped her head up on it. 'You think you've got all the theory of how to do things, you've got your five-year relationship plan from *Cosmo*, you think you're a mature adult and at least you're not counting fat units like Bridget Jones any more, and then whoomp.' She slapped her forehead with the heel of her palm for emphasis. 'It all goes wrong and you don't actually do *anything* the way you thought you would. You slam both feet down at the same time, no mirror checking, and you wonder why you've stalled on the crossing with traffic still coming at you from both angles.'

It distantly occurred to Marie that perhaps this wasn't the most felicitous direction to take the metaphor, in light of Iona's fear of box junctions, but she was getting disconnected again, as she frequently was in class these days: too aware of what was inside her head and yet not aware enough of what was coming out.

'I blame magazines, m'self,' said Iona, her eyes still sweeping anxiously back and forth over the traffic. 'They give you a false impression of what to expect from other people. And just because you've read all the articles, you think you can cope. Ha! Real life does not come with a Posed by Models illustration. Says Iona, twenty-seven, waitress and barmaid.'

'Iona, twenty-seven, *artist*.'

'Whatever.'

'Are you watching me or the lights?' Marie demanded of the Nissan Bluebird next to them, then she turned to Iona and yelled, 'OK, lights are green! Car is go!'

Iona let out the clutch and the car sprang forward, revs straining against her like a Great Dane on a very short, non-extendable lead. Terrified of stalling, she changed up the gears as quickly as she could to get out of the yellow box junction. Iona had seen too many Public Safety Broadcasts in the *Tiswas* advert breaks involving cartoon cars and giant grabbing claws descending from on high to be entirely happy about box junctions at the best of times.

The engine whined in protest.

'Build up the revs before you go into third,' barked Marie, sounding unnervingly like the computerized voice in Angus's Formula 1 PlayStation game.

'Marie, it sounds like the engine's about to explode!'

'It's fine, it's just a bit tuned, that's all. You can go faster if you want.'

'No, I'm fine as I am, ta. And since when was this thing tuned?'

'Since Chris wasn't around to tell me not to, and since I took it to Aircool last month with my birthday money. Come on, you're going to be overtaken by that road sweeper unless you hurry up. And people know my car round here. Come on, pretend I'm Ned and impress me. Think skinny, dirty Naked Chef sitting here instead of bulging best mate.'

'And what do you mean by that?' Iona turned to look at her in guilty surprise and nearly swerved into the path of an oncoming Nissan Sunny which, as luck would have it, was also swerving in the opposite direction as the driver turned into the back to consult the passenger holding the *A–Z*. What did Marie know about Ned? How had she guessed?

'Oh, well, you've missed your chance now,' Marie said comfortably, sinking back as far as she could in the Recaro sports seats.

'*What?!*'

'With the overtaking. Get into the right-hand lane.'

Iona looked over her shoulder as a sense of dread fell over her like a wet towel. All thoughts of Ned disappeared like snow off a dike, faced with her traffic nightmare. Her heart was hammering. 'You want me to cross traffic.'

''Fraid so. Unless you want to get even deeper into sarf London. Have we got time for you to drive back to the pub, or do you want me to do it so we get there before night falls?'

Marie was on half-term and had volunteered to take over from Ned on the coaching front for a few days so he could concentrate on expanding the menu, according to

Angus's five-year plan. Iona was, according to Angus's strict timetable to ensure a first-time pass, having a minimum of three hours a week freelance amateur coaching, and just one hour's professional tuition to correct the resulting effects.

Iona tried to remember what Ron, her official instructor, had said about crossing traffic, then realized that she had automatically situated herself in the approved Marie position: halfway over the stream she wanted to cross.

Needless to say, this approach was not one recommended by the Driving Standards Authority.

'Well, didn't you say you were doing a shift tonight too?' Iona sheepishly raised her hand in a thank-you to the man who had let her go. He didn't have much choice, given that she was almost on the other side of the road. 'Drive aggressively or get the bus' was Marie's driving mantra.

'I am,' said Marie. 'Quick, quick, quick! Nip in behind the van! No, either I serve behind Angus's bar downstairs or I paint Jim's bathroom upstairs. I feel like I should be living in slave quarters.'

'You are,' Iona pointed out. 'And you love it. Jim being all masterful with your wages.'

'Oooh.' Marie jiggled her eyebrows in the vanity mirror. 'Now, should I offer to let the other little slaves sleep up there with me?'

'Sex with those two would be small compensation for having to listen to Mark's car porn for the five hours they're not being worked to death by Ned. He and Angus swap it. *Jeremy Clarkson's Unfeasibly Huge Cam Shaft Orgy! Hot Rod Coupes Go Wet and Wild!* And I know Rick plays the guitar because he tried to impress Tamara with his repertoire of Radiohead classics when he first started.'

'And she said?'

Iona pulled an eerily accurate impression of Tamara finding a piece of used chewing gum on her leather trousers. 'I don't think she actually *said* anything. Why bother with scrawny indie chef boy when you're riding on Jim Morrison's Harley to heaven?'

'As it were.'

Iona drove up to the next stationary trail of traffic and yanked on the handbrake. She could see Marie assessing the road ahead of her, which was blocked with blue flashing lights in the distance. Iona liked traffic jams. It limited the driving possibilities nicely. She settled herself into her seat and decided that this jam could actually be a good opportunity to find out whether Chris had been in touch again yet. Marie hadn't said what she intended to do, and Iona hadn't really pushed her. Neither of them had mentioned the actual word 'divorce', although Marie had made an appointment for a haircut and wanted Iona to come with her for moral support.

Iona still found it hard to believe that Chris could choose his charity work over someone as special as Marie. He'd never find another woman like her in a million years, much less persuade her to marry him. How could work, however charitable, be more important than that? But then Angus *was* practically doing double shifts at the pub to save money on bar staff, she reminded herself, then pushed the thought away. It was unworthy. At least she knew where Angus was. At least she knew who he was with.

That was the niggle at the back of her mind, niggling away every time she saw Marie. Was there some *other* incentive waiting for Chris in Kosovo?

Marie's voice shook her guiltily back to the traffic and she saw to her horror that she was so close to the car in front that she could actually read the headlines of the paper on the back shelf.

'There is a way out of here, if you double back on yourself and go down . . .' Marie's eyes were scanning along the traffic in front of them, and Iona could see her feet twitching. 'Put it on full lock and do a U-ey here . . .'

There was a high involuntary squeak from the driver's side

and Marie looked round. Without wanting to, Iona found herself doing her Frozen at the Wheel thing again.

'Oh, I'd better drive or we won't get there before Angus goes nuclear.' Marie sighed, and Iona didn't ask her why.

Iona was well aware that Marie's effectively working at the pub was keeping it all going, more or less. Whereas she and Jim were visibly fading under the constant pressure of trying to do two jobs at once, and Angus's temper was reaching Basil Fawlty heights of unpredictable wrath, Marie, despite everything, was working harder than any of them: a full school day, then straight back to the pub, or manic trips to pump aerobics (Iona went once to see what it was like and walked like a Cro-Magnon man for three days afterwards).

As far as the others went, Tamara seemed to be flourishing in the constant attention (big wow, thought Iona sourly, then bit her lip in contrition) of both her kitchen virtuoso surf-god boyfriend and the stream of lazy diarists who still came in to do little pieces on the place. That the cooking was getting better every day was undeniable, and even Iona had to concede that Gabriel had a lot to do with it. Ned was as he always was, partially illuminated from inside by a strange sub-human light force that might or might not have eaten out his brain. And since Tamara had finally frightened Kelly away – Iona hadn't told Angus that Kelly's verbal resignation had been prompted by a tarot reading involving dark warnings about beer barrels – there had been no replacement, despite Tamara's promise to find someone. And that didn't help the mutinous front of house, particularly as both she and Gabriel seemed to be researching some kind of magazine feature on impromptu sex.

'Pull in here and I'll take over,' said Marie.

'Pull in where?' There were parked cars down both sides of the street with no gaps as far as Iona could see and the traffic was moving about as fast as tectonic-plate shift.

'Oh, just get out and I'll slide over.'

'Marie, no . . .' Iona started to protest, and was about to cite the incident with Angus's car and Tamara's moped in abnormal motor mating shocker, but Marie was already swinging her right leg over the handbrake, short denim skirt riding high on her plump thigh. Resignedly, Iona opened her door and got out.

This was the official low point of learning to drive, she thought, sloping round the front of the car, eyes fixed on her feet in their hopeless flat driving shoes. Signalling to the traffic around you – confirming their early predictions, more like – that you're not fit to control the car in this complicated new situation. It happened every lesson she'd ever had with her dad. Once, her final lesson with him as it turned out, they had *both* got out of the car and her mum had had to come over and drive them home. Good job they were only at the other end of the street.

Iona buckled herself in as Marie started the car and revved the engine. Driving with Ned, though hair-raising at times, made her feel cool and sexy and actually quite competent. Driving with Marie made her feel as though they were in *Thelma and Louise* – not so much wild and free, as probably pursued by a SWAT team.

Through her red-hot blush of shame and the shiver of excitement the thought of Ned had generated, Iona reminded herself of her moral duty to sort out whatever problem Marie was trying to signal to her in complex literary code.

'Well, this is kind of like real life too, isn't it?' she tried, as Marie flicked on her indicators, leaned out of the window to make eye contact with the driver behind and put the steering on full lock all at the same time.

'In what way? Cheers, mate, that's kind!' said Marie ironically, somehow extricating the car from the stream of traffic and beginning a turn in the road.

How did people drive like that? Was there a School of Central London Driving that she should be going to?

Iona noticed that Marie, unlike fully accredited Ron, was

not using her handbrake and certainly wasn't checking her blind spot in the right order. She was also turning the wheel by holding it from underneath to get maximum leverage. Iona thought this looked very cool indeed and filed it away to use next time she was out in Ned's Mini.

'In that, er,' Iona improvised wildly, 'sometimes you get into traffic jams in your life where you can't move and you can't see what's blocking the road and the best thing you can do is get out and find a different route.'

'*If* you can get out.'

'Marie,' said Iona, forgetting her metaphor and bristling now she was safely on the other side of the car, 'if you'd told me what to do, I'm sure I could have done it.'

'Iona, you big donkey, you know as well as I do that you're terrible at taking advice.'

Iona stared at her. First she'd heard of it.

'You're fantastic at *giving* advice though,' Marie amended. 'No one better. But you're not one of nature's pupils, it has to be said.'

'But . . .'

Marie inched her way through the apparently solid wall of cars. 'And I know I'm not one of nature's teachers, despite my professional training, but I do know a difficult pupil when I see one. You're a much better passenger than you are a driver. No confidence, you see.'

'Can we get back to you and your metaphorical traffic jam?' Iona demanded.

'Sorry?'

'You and the traffic jam of your life. Have you been going to those creative writing classes again, by the way?'

'No, we're on to metaphors in literacy hour. But hold that thought.' Marie's Ricki Lake hand reappeared about an inch from her nose. 'I think we've touched on a *far* more interesting set of raw nerves. You are incredibly touchy at the moment, has anyone told you that?'

'Yes.' Iona huffed through her nose. Her tips were down,

though there was no way she was going to admit that to Marie.

She wondered, over the background noise of indeterminate panic in her head, what the best way of getting out of this problem headlock was, without having to examine any of those raw nerves Marie had twanged, now singing out in close harmony like a Welsh male-voice choir.

That was the trouble about having embarrassing crush problems: you couldn't exactly share them with your nearest and dearest.

Iona's face froze.

What did she mean, *embarrassing crush problems*?

Well, if Marie was starting to take an interest in her problems, that had to be a good sign, didn't it?

'Heard from Chris since you wrote to say you'd moved?' she found herself saying in casual counter-attack.

Marie was now sailing down towards Battersea Bridge, changing lanes at will. The last white rays of the spring sunshine were bouncing up off the murky waters of the Thames, piercing through gaps in the clouds and dazzling office windows flat silver. Iona put her sun visor down and tried not to meet her own eyes in the vanity mirror.

Embarrassing crush problems.

'Um, yes. I was going to tell you when we got back to the pub.' Marie scratched her nose. 'Didn't want to put you off your driving. I had a very quick call from the volunteers' pay phone the other night, at about three in the morning.'

'Sociable of him.'

'I wouldn't have heard it at all if I hadn't been getting up to go to the loo.' This was a lie. Marie hadn't had a full night's sleep for months and had given up ever wanting to again. She supposed getting by on four hours a night would be the closest she would ever get to feeling like Margaret Thatcher.

'What did he say?' Typical Chris, Iona thought: probably crossing his fingers that she wouldn't wake up, while retaining his self-righteousness for trying to get through at all. And what could he say, after a letter like that? 'What did he expect you to say, more to the point?' And what had Marie said in her letter back to him? Surely it wasn't just a case of putting a change of address card in the post?

'Er . . .' Marie put the radio back on.

Iona noticed that Marie's nails, normally neatly polished to match her shirt, were looking bitten and ragged.

'Er, not a lot really. Well, not a lot that didn't directly pertain to grain shipments and the problems of getting needles into toddlers. Maybe he thought that was my field of expertise, I don't know,' she added.

It crossed Iona's mind that, on the other hand, Chris mightn't have called at all and Marie could be making all this up to save his face, but she didn't say anything.

'Is he not missing you after all, maybe? In the manner of John Waite?' Iona made it flippant to give Marie the opportunity to be flippant back, but she watched her profile carefully for signs of distress or rage.

Marie laughed, in a dangerously hysterical fashion, and pulled her 1950s cat's-eye shades from the side pocket and slipped them on with one hand. 'Hmm, he didn't *say*, now you come to mention it.'

'And how are things . . . you know. Are you missing him?'

Marie slowed down, joining the queue to turn left, and looked at Iona over the rim of her shades. 'You want me to be honest? Or dutiful?'

'Always be honest with me.'

'No,' said Marie. 'I'm not really missing him. Not now I've got over the first shock. The thought of having to spend the rest of my existence with him used to give me panic attacks in bed at night. But now . . .'

She shrugged apologetically. 'Don't tell Angus, but flats without men in them are really fantastic. I tidy up and the rooms stay tidy. I make supper and no one complains about buying organic foods. I have a bottle of wine and don't get it in the neck about exploitative wine growers. Or about finishing it myself. Iona, there is a bar of Dairy Milk in the fridge big enough to lightly coat Wembley Stadium in melted chocolate and I can eat as much as I want to. I'm telling you, it's like having my own life back. Do you know how big a double bed feels when there's only one person in it? Bloody Sting and all that "Bed's Too Big Without You" shite – bed's fabulously roomy without you, thanks very much, and absolutely no discarded Y-fronts lurking under the duvet either.'

'Oh.' Iona tried to remember what that felt like, and realized that she hadn't lived on her own since her first year at university. Angus's discarded bed Y-fronts were just part of her tidying-up routine, like Toilet-Ducking. It cheered her slightly to know that other men left pants in the bed.

More to the point, *wore* pants in bed.

The (inevitable) erotic thought of sleeping with a man who *didn't* wear pants in bed shocked her. She didn't imagine Gabriel wore pants in bed. Was that something she could ask Tamara? Did Ned wear pants in bed?

Her brow creased. *Should* she know the answer to that?

Marie flashed a mother and toddler over the road. 'Maybe this is just the second round of shock. Maybe I will be much worse again next week. I don't know. I'm just enjoying not crying all the time. Keeping busy helps, although I hate to sound like my gran. This weekend's big task is going to be painting the sitting room . . . I thought a deep red, like your kitchen?'

'Does Jim know you're doing it red?' Iona asked, temporarily distracted by the question of Ned's bedwear. His back seat had been covered in laundry last time she'd been in the car. Had there been any boxers?

Marie made an unladylike scoffing sound. 'I don't think Jim will mind. It won't do him any harm to imagine that

I'm running some high-class den of sin up there. I mean, he hasn't even come up with any curtains, and you can virtually see into the flat from his bedroom window. Good job I'm not walking around in thigh-high boots . . .

Iona flinched.

'At the moment,' Marie added.

Iona blinked rapidly. This was not the grieving abandoned wifey, sobbing into her wedding album, that everyone had been imagining. Probably not the off-duty Marie Davenport St Anselm Primary School imagined either. 'Well, I'll ask Angus if he's got some paint left over for you to try first. He keeps all the paint in case he needs to touch things up.' She stopped, wondering whether it was politic to mention Handy Angus, the man of a hundred odd jobs, in such direct comparison with Chris and his multiple domestic failings.

A small voice in the back of her mind reminded her that she in fact had wanted the kitchen blue and white like a Wedgwood plate. It was Angus who had gone for the abattoir look – and had sneaked out of bed at three a.m. to get it all finished before she could protest. The fact that it looked fabulous had rather diminished her argument the following morning, although not her sense of being steam-rollered by a higher force.

A smaller voice then wondered belatedly whether Marie might be being a little *too* unfussed, but it was drowned out by the far-more-interesting strike mark on Angus's Similarities with Hitler list.

'Shouldn't you be trying to talk me out of this good mood?' demanded Marie cheerfully.

'Why? You seem pretty convinced to me.' *Why had he even bothered to let her choose paint cards if he was always going to paint it the colour he wanted?* seethed Iona.

'Well, you in your capacity as champion of married bliss.'

What? Iona dragged her attention back to Marie and held up her hands. She had the feeling she was on thin ice. 'Who knows the interior of other people's marriages? Who am I to say they're not an outdated medieval tradition with no basis in human behaviour patterns?'

Marie's darkly arched eyebrows rose above the rim of her shades. 'Now that's the best U-turn you're ever likely to perform in a car, mate.'

'What?'

'Nothing.'

'What?' Iona swivelled as far as she could in her bucket seat. Marie's lips were curved in a wide scarlet smile behind her shades. So pretty. What was she smiling at, though? 'What? Why are you grinning away like that? Does your seat do something I didn't know about?'

Marie momentarily took her eyes off the traffic and arched a quizzical eyebrow at her. She looked funny and cute, and much prettier than she had for ages.

'What?' wailed Iona. 'Now I know how Tamara feels when she doesn't understand jokes! What exactly are you getting at?'

'Oh, Iona, don't get so touchy. I just mean . . .' Marie let out a 'Let it go' breath and flapped her hands, still smiling. 'There's nothing so liberating as doing something you're not supposed to do and admitting you like it. I was in *pieces* when Chris first left – you saw what I was like. Couldn't talk to anyone, didn't want to tell my parents, didn't want to admit to myself that I was really glad he'd gone, because I thought admitting that made *me* a different person and I'd forgotten what that was like. But I *was* glad. Really glad. It was like a weight lifted off my shoulders, I'm telling you. And I lost about half a stone,' she added in a more conversational tone. 'Did you notice?'

'That's not healthy,' Iona said sternly.

'Oh, don't worry, I've put it back on. And some. God, the *thrill* of Wall's ice cream!'

'Marie, you're going to hit that car.'

'Am not. I feel so excited all the time, like there are so many possibilities out there that I'd forgotten about . . .'

The mention of Marie's possibilities made Iona feel inexplicably ill. 'What did he say about you moving out of the flat?' she asked, spurred on by some horrible inner desire to drag Marie down to the same level of turmoil currently and inexplicably seething away in her own chest.

The smile dropped.

'He didn't. I told you, it wasn't a long conversation. He was a bit vague about details, kept yawning and telling me how late it was there.'

'Did you point out that it was quite late with you too?'

'Yes, I did. But I don't have to carry sacks of grain so that was selfish of me.'

'Arse,' said Iona feelingly.

'I won't lie to you – I do miss him a bit,' Marie said, turning into Hyde Park and joining the stationary queue of cars. 'But not for longer than about a minute. Now he's not coming back, I keep remembering some of the better times we had together. It wasn't all misery and shouting, honestly. It's the small things that other people don't see, like the way he used to wait for me when we went running. And he was very good at making flat breads, you know? After all, he's my husband, isn't he? For the time being, at least.'

Iona said nothing.

They snaked through the park. Like quite a slow snake.

'Are you watching my clutch control?' demanded Marie, pointing to her feet.

Iona nodded and wondered how far she could probe, with Marie in this mood.

'You really don't feel like going out there and joining him?' she asked instead. 'If that was what he wanted you to do to save your marriage?'

'Iona, if Angus decided he wanted to go and open a pub in Grozny, would you go with him?'

Iona considered this. 'Yes, I think I would.'

'Fine. If Angus told you that you *had* to go with him, that if you *didn't* go with him, you were deliberately depriving the people of Grozny of your murals, and that you were a middle-class Grozny-hater who didn't deserve your education, would you still go?'

'No!' Iona flushed. 'Is that what Chris said to you?'

Marie was silent, as she concentrated on finding a gap to roar into on the Bayswater Road.

Iona was silent too, thinking that since she loved Angus, following him to the ends of the earth sort of came as a traditional part of the small print – and whether the fact that Marie hadn't apparently even considered it was significant.

'And more to the point, if, as soon as he walked out,' Marie went on suddenly, 'it came to you in a flash that you'd actually hated Angus for at least a year, but had refused to admit it to yourself because some random bloke in a *lei* had told you that you had to love him for ever, despite the fact that Angus made you feel like a worm, despite the fact that he clearly felt that saving the world was more attractive to him than you, and despite the fact that you hadn't had sex in over eighteen months, would you want to pack up your life and trot after him?'

'Arse!' said Iona again. 'Oh, my God! I think—' She flushed deeply and couldn't think of anything tactfully sympathetic enough to say. Marie hated people feeling sorry for her.

'I think we should stop talking about this,' said Marie firmly. 'I want to go and serve some Modern British cuisine so I can prepare for next term's project on farmyard animals and their culinary uses.'

'God, Marie,' said Iona and, not without a guilty sense of relief, left it at that.

Chapter Twenty-eight

'No Iona?' asked Jim, leaning over the bar to see if she was hiding next to the Britvic oranges. There were no Britvic oranges and no Iona either.

Tamara carried on polishing the pint glass she had in her hand. 'She's sorting out things for the pub quiz. And she's not in a good mood.'

Jim raised his eyebrows as Angus glided past with a couple of Guinnesses. Iona in a bad mood was something of a rarity, wasn't it? At least it wasn't just him who could cock things up with women. 'Oh, why?'

'She realized over the weekend that Led Zeppelin split up when she was only eight and it's hit her quite hard.' Angus casually showed him the pints. He'd finally perfected the shamrock on top and now tried to do it on everything, including lager. 'Says she can remember John Lennon being shot but can't remember Led Zep splitting. Shift over, Tamara.' He took the tenner from the customer and rang it through the till. 'She was even talking about asking you about being regressed to see if something had slipped into her subconscious on *Newsround*, but I told her not to be so ridiculous.'

'Well, I can understand the need for regression, because it's a wonderful way of getting to know yourself, but God knows why she's so upset,' mused Tamara. 'It's not as if she *could* have known them anyway. I mean, I'm not saying I'm an expert on rock music, but even I know Led Zeppelin didn't spend much time gigging in Carlisle.'

'Though the groupie scene was quite hot there, I understand,' Angus confided over his shoulder as he shoved a
glass under the vodka optic. 'Lots of girls with dogs, *if* you
know what I mean.'

'Really?' said Jim. 'I wouldn't have thought that there . . .'

'Noooo,' said Angus. 'Not really.'

'I don't see Iona as wanting to be a groupie,' sniffed
Tamara. She put the glass on the shelf and ran a hand
through her long blonde hair, smoothing it behind her
pretty ears, which now had small skull and crossbones
studs in, a gift from Gabriel. 'She's much too sensible. I
mean, shagging meathead bouncers to get backstage passes?
Ugh. *So* degrading. I hate all that cock rock wankery.'

Jim pretended to inspect the new wine list while sneaking
a lustful glance at Tamara, who had for years appeared
in his fantasies in full-on Aviator shades, leather mini-
skirt, dead straight blonde hair, lip-gloss groupie uniform.
Which was conveniently much the same as she had taken
to wearing most days in the pub now Gabriel – or the
style editor of *Loaded* – seemed to be in charge of her
wardrobe.

'Well, shows how little you know her then.' Angus tipped
a bottle of tonic into the vodka and dropped in a couple of
ice cubes. 'That's the last Slimline tonic, by the way. Let's
hope we don't get a rush of ladies' bridge clubs in later. Will
you go and ask Ned for some more lemons, Tam? We're all
out. Anyway, Ned says it's Maryport that has the groupie
scene going.' And he glided back round to the other side
of the bar as if on castors.

'I suppose they have to make their own entertainment
in the north of England.' Tamara watched Angus's broad
departing back, trying to work out if he was skitting her.
She hated it when everyone had these private jokes going
that she didn't understand, but she also hated looking as
though she couldn't take it. It was tough, not being as dumb
as you looked.

'Tamara,' said Jim on the other side of the bar, 'have you been to the Lakes much?'

'No,' she said. 'Why?'

'No reason.'

It was even tougher when someone like *Jim* looked down on you.

'Why were you looking for Iona anyway?' Tamara picked another pint glass out of the crate, stuck it on the end of her towel-covered hand and started twisting deftly with the other. Her wrist action looked quick and practised. Jim swallowed.

'Oh, I, er . . .' He forced his attention back to the wine list. 'I was talking to Martin this morning and he's given me some more money to spend on refurbishments. He was saying something about getting a mural painted, and I wanted to talk to Iona about doing it. It would work out much cheaper than getting someone in, and you know . . .'

He ground to a halt, wondering why he was bothering. It was a habit to overdo the old 'I'm more capable than you think' routine in front of Tamara, just to remind her that not everyone earned a living from rolling out pastry. Jim smiled ruefully at his hopeful, speccy-boy reflection behind the optics. But then evidence showed that she went for the pastry every time anyway. And yet he couldn't stop, just like he couldn't stop wanting her, even though he could see her and Gabriel daily becoming more and more of a couple. The habit was part of *their* relationship and to break it would be to give up at last.

She finished the glass and put it on the shelf with the rest, then turned back to him. 'The mural?' she said, her mouth smiling encouragingly, but Jim could see that her eyes were now somewhere far, far away.

It always was with Tamara.

'*Why* is there a chain around this?' Angus demanded. He

tugged pointlessly at the bench, which Brian had chained, perhaps over-zealously, to the ring on the wall. Quite some time ago too, by the look of the rusty padlock. 'Who is going to steal a manky old pub bench, for crying out loud? Actually, don't answer that, I bet Tamara would have it like a shot for her ironic flat. Jeez!' He gave the padlock a rattle. 'Where the fuck is the key?'

'Angus, how would I know? I didn't put it here. I just need to get it inside for the quiz. We don't have enough seats.' Iona aimed a kick at one of the legs and stubbed her toe. Solid wood. Tamara would have to round up at least three men to sneak off with that. 'And can you hurry up?' she added. The sore toe made her voice even more tetchy. 'I need to get the things for the pub quiz man. He'll be coming over soon to set everything up.'

'Oh, God, I'd forgotten about that.' Angus stood up and brushed the rust from his trousers. 'Right then, I'll go home and get the wirecutters.'

'Angus! You haven't got *time* to go home and get wirecutters!' protested Iona. 'The pub's going to start filling up soon and the bar will go crazy! Marie won't be here for another hour and a half and—'

'I can be there and back in no time,' said Angus. His face darkened, and Iona stopped and bit her lip. She could argue but it would only explode into another row.

'Fine,' she said.

'What do you mean, fine?'

'I mean, fine, go on, do that. I'm sure we can manage.'

'Oh, for God's sake, Iona, what do you want me to do?' Angus burst out. 'We need to use this – *you* wanted to use this, which is why you got me out here in the first place – and there are no wirecutters in the tool box, because Brian took them with him, presumably so he can dismember the lovely Lois when the sangria finally runs out, and there's no point in spending more money on new wirecutters when I know we've got some at home.' He paused. 'Somewhere. OK?'

'Fine.' Iona felt her lip go mutinous too late to stop it.

'Fine.' Angus stared at her. 'I wish I knew what was going on in your head at the moment, Iona.'

Iona wanted to say, 'Then why don't you ask me?' but she knew there was no point opening a whole family-sized can of worms with only three minutes to empty it before Tamara started squawking from the bar that the mixers had run out.

So she sighed, knowing as she did it that sighing always irritated Angus more than anything else, but still unable to stop it coming out.

That's what she hated most about the way things were at the moment: knowing that with a little more peace of mind, she could stop herself from inflaming situations.

'Fine.' Angus tried a weak smile. 'I'll be back in no time, OK?'

'And what do I do about the mixer situation?'

He thought. 'Ring up the brewery and see what they can do, and failing that send Jim to the cash and carry. And in the meantime, just get some oranges from the kitchen and tell any punter who asks for a vodka and orange that all orange juice is now hand-squeezed and consequently costs five times more than normal. That'll get them back on the lager.'

'Right,' said Iona heavily, and went back to the bar.

Angus knew he had a pair of wirecutters somewhere, left over from a tip-off he'd had from a journalist mate that certain councils had wheel clamps with a tiny Achilles' heel that you could snip through and the whole thing fell apart like an oyster. Over a long liquid post-cricket lunch one Sunday, they'd constructed their burning crusade to go around London in the dead of night, anonymously liberating drivers from the malicious attentions of the fascist traffic wardens, while disguising themselves with balaclavas and misleading football shirts. Angus had gone as far as visiting Halfords and Millets to purchase the relevant gear – until the journalist mate got caught on CCTV outside Waterloo and found a summons in his morning post. Not very Robin Hood.

And not the kind of thing the Law Society would look favourably on, Angus reminded himself. Or Iona. He hadn't even told Iona. She would have chalked it up as another example of his ridiculous alleged 'road rage' problem.

The wirecutters weren't in the tool box in the junk cupboard. Angus paused, hands on hips, looking at the stack of old ironing boards, cricket equipment, the ridgy snout of the vacuum cleaner. Where would he have put them, if not back in the toolkit? Could Iona have borrowed them for painting purposes and left them in the shed?

Reluctantly, he didn't think so. Iona hated DIY almost as much as she hated driving. That was his department. And he didn't like going into the shed without a good reason – when he'd handed it over to Iona for her painting, he'd promised her he wouldn't go in without asking her first, and Angus didn't break promises.

But they might be in there, and it would save having to buy a separate pair for the pub.

Angus wrestled with his conscience and with the manic sense of economy which seemed to grip him harder the more money Martin sent them. Then, with a stroke of inspiration, he remembered something he'd read in the *Caterer* magazine, about covering the top of the loos with spray glue to stop people snorting lines of coke off them. Angus didn't really think anyone bothered to do that in the Grapes – their clientele would be more likely to snort the spray glue – but it was such a cunning idea that he was desperate to try it out. And Iona was bound to have spray glue for her collages. And that was *bound* to be in the shed.

He shut the cupboard door before the contents could slip out and then hesitated. Should he phone her at the pub first? In case she was in the middle of anything she might not want him to see?

Angus looked at his troubled reflection in the hall mirror for moral guidance. Then he snorted. Phoning your girlfriend to see if it was OK to look in your own shed? He leaned further forward. And had his hair line receded *again* since last week?

'OK,' said Ned. 'You're on a country road. What might you expect to see coming towards you?'

Iona's knife paused halfway over the butter pat. 'Er, a herd of cows?'

'No, the clue is in the question.' Ned peered at the mushroom he was preparing and flicked experimentally at the skin. 'Although that's not wrong, given your country bumpkin expert knowledge. Listen again: coming *towards* you.'

Iona frowned. She should know this, with two days to the theory test. But she didn't. Not that she was worrying that much. If she failed the written test, she would officially send her GCSE certificates back. In fact, she could have just sat it at fifteen without ever going near a car and got it over with then. It wasn't hard. Half the questions weren't even about driving. 'Are you going to give me the multiple-guess options?'

'No, because I'm doing this off the top of my head from the questions we did last night and I can't remember.' Ned frowned at the mushroom and sniffed it.

'Please? Exam conditions? One right answer, one could-be-right answer and two blindingly obvious "Tick this and you fail instantly" ones.'

'Oh, OK.' Apparently satisfied that he hadn't accidentally let a death's head in by accident, Ned dropped the offending specimen into the glass bowl. 'Is it, er, a) gypsy travellers, b) nuclear protesters, c) pedestrians or d) horses?'

'Well, that depends which country road you're on, doesn't

it?' Iona began conversationally. 'If you were on a country road near Sellafield, you might see . . .'

'Can I remind you that this is a multiple-choice test and not a written question?'

'OK then, it's c) pedestrians, although that depends on them having read the *Highway Code* and knowing where their designated area is. Or having the sense to walk on that side in the first place. Or being sober. Or, in fact, living in the country and not having a car. I think people only walk on the road in the romantic daydreams of the DSA. Unless the pubs have shut and they can't get a taxi back home.'

'Have you quite finished?'

'Yes. Next question, please.' Iona opened another packet of butter, feeling reasonably pleased with herself. If getting a driving licence was a matter of theory, she could have had it years ago. Her conscience then reminded her that she was much better at *everything* in theory than in practice, which was why she ended up dishing out so much advice to everyone.

'You're walking around town when—'

'Why would I be walking? Wouldn't I be driving?' Iona interrupted.

'Oh, yeah, sorry, I forgot. Thinking of you too much there.' Ned got his big cook's knife out and tipped the mushrooms on to the chopping board. 'Right, you're driving around town when you come across a whole bunch of people, one of whom is waving a red light. What are these people doing?'

'You *are* having a laugh now, aren't you?' Iona demanded.

'No, it's a real question,' Ned insisted.

Iona sucked her lower lip. These were always the ones they used to revise first at school. The really stupid ones you wouldn't get asked because they were just too weird.

'No, no helping,' she said as Ned opened his mouth to give her a clue.

'But I can give you a visual aid, surely?' said Ned. There

was a hint of a smile twitching around his mouth that Iona recognized. They had always done visual aids, even when visual aids for their English A-level hadn't really been all that useful – at least not the ones Ned had devised. In fact, she had almost been thrown out of the hall for giggling through the entire Shakespeare paper while he mimed Bottom and the rude mechanicals.

Though that could have been a particularly good year for the mushrooms.

'Hmm,' said Iona, smiling, 'well, couldn't hurt, could it?'

This was really just like school. Revision sessions, the ability to get simple things right or wrong, Ned fiddling around with mushrooms, even down to Angus casting himself as Mr Scott, the psycho head of house.

'Great!' said Ned. 'OK, it's dark, right, and there are all these folk' – he lifted his cook's knife up like a placard – 'lasses, you know, but only biologically, like, and they've all got moustaches, and they all look like those women you used to hang out with when you did your Women's Rights thing at school and they're going . . .' Ned advanced on her, banging the knife up and down like a placard, and Iona couldn't help noticing, with a thrill of terror that she pretended was to do with the Sabatier, how you could see the long dark hairs in his armpit when he lifted his arm up at that angle, and was it her imagination, or was he looking at her like . . .

'Excuse me.'

Ned and Iona both swivelled and looked up guiltily.

Ned looked more guilty than Iona, given that he was apparently about to stab her with his cook's knife, but Iona knew she was looking more guilty than she should do.

'I'm looking for Iona? Or Angus?' said the man standing by the door. He looked familiar.

'Ah,' said Iona, recovering quickly and lifting her finger in recognition. 'You're the pub quiz man, aren't you?'

They *had* looked at him for four hours a week, for their six month run of pub quiz triumph, so he ought to be a bit familiar, although their tactic had always been to stay well out of his line of vision so they could carry on freely consulting the *Evening Standard* under the table.

'Yes, I'm Dr Keith. Hi there!' He put his antique ghetto-blaster down and clamped Iona's hand in his clammy grip and gave it a good shake. It felt like the handshake of a plague victim.

'I'll need to put this through your PA system,' he said, brandishing his tape, 'and have you got facilities for photo-copying question papers?'

'Er . . .' Iona looked blank. Had they? Wasn't that his problem? Where was Angus when you needed him?

But before she could reply, Dr Keith dissolved in a terrifying series of hacking coughs, his body shaking so violently that Iona half-expected to see his lungs appear through his mouth.

'Are you OK?' she asked, putting a very tentative hand on his shoulder.

He nodded weakly, still half bent over. 'I've had this terrible' – hack, hack, bleeraugh, bleeraugh, retch, retch – 'cough for a few days now and it just won't' – cark, cark, cark, curghacgh, curghacgh – 'go,' he finished lamely.

'You could be so good at Irish,' said Ned admiringly. 'One of the world's most complicated native languages, spoken by a total of . . .'

Iona gave him a look. 'Quiz starts at eight and don't think you can get early points now by showing off.'

Ned shrugged. 'Here's an idea. Why don't you take Dr Keith to our very own barside rare diseases expert and see if he's managed to contract something Sam hasn't? Or he could save it until tonight. Your starter for ten is a visual clue. What disease is . . .'

'Ned, just finish those mushroom tartlets, will you?' said Iona. 'Now, Keith, why don't you come through to the office!' she went on brightly, showing him the way. 'And I'll see what we have by way of Lemsips . . .'

Angus inched open the shed door and peered in nervously. It felt very wrong to be doing this somehow. He had a guilty paranoia that Iona would be waiting in there for him, having rushed back from the pub, guessing what he would do, already rising from her chair to yell at him.

But Iona was in Ladbroke Grove, pulling pints and setting up the crap PA system for Dr Keith the Pub Quiz King. She couldn't possibly have beaten him back – he'd come in the Integrale. A helicopter couldn't have beaten him back. Angus pulled himself together, pushed the door and went in.

It was spotlessly clean inside, which surprised him. Iona wasn't the world's most instinctive charlady and it had never been a very nice shed. It didn't smell like a shed any more either. It smelled like . . . Angus sniffed for a moment. What did it smell like? It reminded him of school: the school art room, that would be it. Paper, and paints, and a faint hint of turps and coffee.

It was all very Iona, he thought, standing by the door, taking it in. A small vase of pink and purple ranunculuses on the sink, a big mirror by the window, bouncing the light round the room, notes and sketches pinned on the wooden walls with bright silver tacks, and no visible clock. Beneath the guilt, Angus felt faintly excited to discover a new corner of Iona he hadn't previously been allowed in; he felt a bit shy. Maybe he'd never properly realized how professional she was about her painting. He took a step further in the room, drawn by the sketches around the wall, and a mixture of curiosity and shameful vanity. Were there any of him? Had she maybe seen a side of him that he might not have noticed?

But just as his hand stretched out to a pencil drawing of a familiar-looking man with his feet up on a sofa, Angus's attention was arrested by the easel by the window, and the startling black painting clipped on to it. He took a step back in surprise and his brow furrowed.

This *couldn't* be the wedding commission she'd been talking about, could it?

Angus stared at the easel for a few moments, unsure whether he ought to turn back now and just go before he saw something he really shouldn't, but then approached it tentatively, as if it were a poisonous plant.

It was so . . . dark. And angry. He'd never seen Iona do anything like this at all, even when she was at art college and she had to do all sorts of ridiculous stuff. You couldn't give *this* to someone as a gift on their wedding day – it looked like the kind of paintings tortured rock stars with artistic pretensions did, shortly before checking themselves into rehab and admitting that they were best mates with Satan.

What *was* it? The blacks and purples and greys swirled into one another like a vortex, or a spiralling, spreading bruise. It was mad, scary even. It reminded him, out of nowhere, of what his head felt like inside if he closed his eyes when he was pissed. Did *Iona* paint this? Unconsciously, he ran the tips of his fingers over the cracked and layered paint; it seemed as though it had been smeared on, rather than painted. Angus didn't pretend to know much about art at all, but he could sense the incoherent emotion that had whipped all the colours together. And no light at all in it, somehow, as though it was all imploding on itself. It was confused and out of control.

He snatched his fingers back. They tingled as if they'd been burned. Could Iona tell he'd touched it? There were traces of pigment on his fingers, so she must have done it fairly recently.

Iona. A flood of fear rushed into his heart. What must she be feeling if she could paint something like this? What was going on? Why hadn't she said something to him?

'I've got to talk to her,' said Angus out loud, shocked by his own reaction.

But how could he bring it up without admitting that he'd been in the shed in the first place?

He stuffed that away in the part of his brain he used for sifting legal problems. Come back to that. And until he'd worked it out, he'd just have to be as nice to her as possible.

Concern chewed away at Angus's breast. Was it stress about the theory test coming up? She refused to tell him when it was. Or even if she'd done it already, come to that. Should he try and give her more time off from the pub? She must be under a fair amount of pressure to get this wedding painting done, as well as everything else, and they'd barely had ten minutes together recently.

Maybe that was what he and Jim should use Martin's latest lavish cheque for – more part-time staff. Get someone in so Iona could have some free evenings. Angus's tension eased a little as he recognized an answer. Things were getting under control, and if at least he and someone else were there to see nothing went too badly wrong . . .

He looked again at the black vortex and shuddered. It was like something from *Doctor Who*. What if it *was* the wedding commission? What were you meant to say when your chief bridesmaid handed that over during the speeches?

Angus's face froze. What if *that* was Iona's response to the idea of marriage?

He could feel the blood run cold in his veins, although his brain scoffed at the cliché.

It couldn't be. It had to be something else.

But once the thought was in his head, it wouldn't let go and seemed to spread and shoot out roots, that curled around his brain and forced their way in. She *had* been very snappish lately, and maybe he'd *forced* her into driving, and he *still* hadn't taken her to the V&A as he'd promised and . . .

'Stop it!' he said out loud, wrenching himself away from the easel.

As he heard his voice in the empty shed, something clicked him back to reality. Talking to himself. Very good. One step closer to Jimdom. Very, very good.

Calling upon years of family tradition and a training in the law, Angus pulled himself together. You can't deal with imaginary problems, he reminded himself, in the manner of his old tort supervisor. Just deal with what's there.

And so he marched over to the bookshelf Iona had converted into a storage unit, taking a path around the easel, and quickly found the can of spray glue. She had everything, all arranged according to height, without a trace of dust on the shelves. Weird. Then he marched out of the shed, locked it and drove back to the pub as fast as he could, via a flower stall outside an underground station, where he negotiated a decent quantity of freesias for a tenner, and made a firm promise to let her go early after the pub quiz finished.

The whole point of the pub quiz had been to give Ned and the kitchen lads a night off once a week. Angus thought there might be some kind of EU law about working hours, and it would be cheaper to give them a night off than to get more chefs in – 'at this stage'. Which Iona knew meant 'ever'. So Ned, Gabriel, Rick, Mark and the YTS washing-up lad all did a half-day in the morning, preparing basic cold plates and nibbly things so there would be some food to soak up all the extra beer Angus had ordered, then they'd disappeared down the road for the rest of the afternoon.

Iona watched them go and wondered idly where they were off to. Well, she knew where Gabriel was off to, given that Tamara had delayed her lunch break until two-thirty and then legged it on to the back of his bike, taking a melon out of the kitchen with her.

But then at six, there they all were back again, Ned,

Rick and Mark, bagging a table in the corner and looking disturbingly normal without their checked trousers on.

'Round of Kronenbourgs when you're ready, Iona,' said Rick cheekily.

'Can you not stay away? And you can come up here for your lager – you know this isn't table service.' Iona barely looked up from the jug of orange juice she was pressing. Jim was still out at the cash and carry looking for mixers and she didn't expect him back for ages. Tamara hadn't reappeared and Angus was outside, sawing away at the chains on the bench. Still.

And for some reason he was treating her as if she was pregnant – a sure sign that something was up. Flowers, offers of early finishes, refusing to let her carry crates of water about . . .

'Ah, but we're so tired,' whined Rick. 'We are too tired to walk to the bar. Your husband works us so hard so he can buy you flowers. You are a pair of eighteenth-century slave traders. You are . . .'

'Three Kronenbourgs,' said Iona, 'and shut up. I'm not meant to know who you are.'

'What?'

'I wasn't born yesterday, I know exactly the way his mind works. Has Angus made you come back so you can win the pub quiz and we don't have to give away any beer?'

Three pairs of eyes widened innocently.

'Oh, I get it. Well, don't forget Dr Keith the Pub Quiz King has seen you, Ned.'

'Are you *sure* he's the guy who did it before?' asked Ned. 'He looks a bit more mild-mannered than I remember.'

'I think so.' Iona finished pressing the last orange and put the jug in the fridge. 'Angus got his number from Brian.'

'And will anyone turn up?' Rick looked sceptical. 'It won't just be us and Mad Boy Sam, will it?'

'Rick, people follow this man round London like the Pied Piper. It will be full. Believe me.'

Jim staggered in with two crates of orange stacked on top of each other and pushed them on to the bar with an exhausted huff. 'Give us a hand, lads. There's another five in the car.'

'You got the lot?' asked Iona, grabbing the Britvic oranges and ripping off the polythene.

'Ginger ale, diet ginger ale, bitter lemon, tonic water, diet tonic water,' Jim gasped. 'Get's a pint of lime and water, will you, Iona? I'm about to die.'

'Well, that's the last time Angus lets you deal with the brewery,' she said, aiming the post mix into a pint glass and shovelling some ice in.

'I know, I know, I know.' Jim held up a hand of defeat and doubled over to get his breath back.

'What I don't understand is why he hasn't gone schitz on you,' Rick observed, 'like he went schitz on Gabriel for dumping all that pastry without telling Ned.'

'Shut up, he's just outside,' warned Iona. 'Anyway, he's in a very weird mood this evening, so don't push it.'

'Iona,' gasped Jim. 'Forget the lime and soda and make us a coffee, will you?'

'Tsk,' Ned rolled his eyes. 'Drug addict.'

The first couple of rounds of the pub quiz seemed to pass without incident. As Iona had predicted, the pub had filled up steadily, so when Dr Keith started at eight there wasn't a seat left: all the roadies had come back in force, and some of the local estate agents were having to perch on the edge of banquettes and write on each other's shiny-suited backs. The bench that Angus finally managed to unchain, at the expense of his wirecutters, was covered by three huge men, all wearing Status Quo denim waistcoats, who greeted Sam like an old mate and turned out to be local ambulance drivers.

'Do you reckon it's safe to give Dr Keith another Lemsip?' asked Iona.

'How many's he had? That's fifteen ninety, please.' Angus

took the note and stuck his electronic till key back in to ring the sale through. Regular quizzers, some of whom he recognized as old rivals and, more worryingly, some of whom he thought he recognized from graduate intake training sessions, were starting to get the drinks in before the half-time rush, and Angus sensed they were already way ahead of the usual takings record for this stage in the evening.

'Erm . . .' Iona paused with her hand on the lager tap, trying to think back as far as the early evening. 'I made him a double dose, and I think Jim gave him a hot lemon and whisky before he started.'

'And I made him one about twenty minutes ago.'

Iona looked at Angus and pulled a worried face.

'He'll be fine,' said Angus dismissively. 'If he's the quiz guy who used to crew for Motorhead. Iona, listen, if you want to pop home early tonight, then I'm sure we can . . .'

'Angus, we're run off our feet!' said Iona. 'What on *earth* are you talking about?'

He raised his hands. 'Fine, fine, I just thought, if you were feeling a little . . . I don't know, *overwrought*, maybe . . .'

'Question seventeen!' Dr Keith's amplified voice croaked through the smoky pub. It sounded as though he was speaking through a straw from the bottom of a pond. 'Tottenham Hotspur lost their home match at the weekend.' (Pause for roar of contempt from crowd.) 'What was the' – cark, cark, caraught, heurch, as he managed to dislodge some small intestine from his throat – 'score?'

'Now is this where we go round and confiscate all the newspapers?' asked Iona.

They looked round the pub. In their privileged 'poacher turned gamekeeper' position, they knew this was the time of the evening when all the copies of the *Evening Standard* and the *Sun*, carried in very casually at the beginning, disappeared under the tables and were furiously rustled for results.

Only Mark, Rick and Ned didn't seem to have one. But

they had Mark and his photographic football memory. Mark had no girlfriend. And – Iona stretched up on to her toes to see – they seemed to have been joined by Mad Boy Sam. Great.

'Question eighteen!' The sound of a building being demolished came over the PA, but it was only Dr Keith having another hacking retch too close to his microphone.

'He's getting worse, isn't he?' observed Jim, who had appeared from the cellar with a couple of buckets of ice. 'Good job I took him that hot whisky over.'

'When?' demanded Iona and Angus together.

'Well, one at about seven and another one about ten minutes ago. I made him a treble so it would last him. Hot in here, isn't it?'

'Jim, you pillock, he's not going to get to the music round without passing out!' yelled Angus.

'That's if he doesn't collapse with Lemsip poisoning first. Because he's had four of those on top of the booze,' Iona pointed out, her forehead creased with concern.

'Guys!' said Jim, spreading his hands wide. 'This *is* the man who's done more drugs than Iggy Pop, isn't it? A little Lemsip and whisky and he's not going to be choking on his vomit in the loos.'

Marie weaved her way through to the bar with her hands full of empty pint glasses and dumped them by the glass washer. 'Not in my loos, he's not. Is he really the guy who used to do the quiz here? He looks a lot less tattooed to me.'

They all looked anxiously at the swaying man behind the Desk of Dilemma. He was wearing a large black jumper over any identifying marks.

'And now . . . the music round!' he announced.

'Oh, great. Name that Drum Solo,' groaned Marie and went off to collect more glasses.

There was an unrestrained cheer from the roadie contingent and the estate agents looked more nervous. Each team seemed to have brought a girlfriend for the pop music round, into whose trembling hands the question paper was now shoved.

'I don't think it is him, Angus,' said Iona slowly. 'I think Brian must have got the wrong guy. If he does bits from Andrew Lloyd Webber, there'll be a riot in here.'

'Now, I'm going to play you ten short excerpts from popular songs,' Dr Keith announced in a slurry croak, 'and I want you to tell me: in which rock songs do all these simulated orgasms occur?'

There was a vast 'Woooaaaarrrrgghh!' from a leathery, studdy corner by the men's loos.

'No, you're right, that's definitely the same guy,' conceded Iona, 'and the first excerpt will be the middle theremin section of "Whole Lotta Love", I bet you.'

'A fiver,' said Angus. 'There must be loads or else he wouldn't be doing ten.'

'Number one!'

There was a dull crackle from the ancient speakers and then, with a tape lurch, came an outer-space whine in stiff competition with a badly faked male orgasm, some Drums from Hell and a train crash.

'Uh, uh, *uh*, UH!' groaned Robert Plant.

'Swquuuueeee, squueeeee!' went the theremin.

'OK, cash at the end of the night,' said Angus in defeat.

Marie was outside, collecting glasses very slowly, surrounded by surreptitious-looking people muttering into their mobiles.

'Don't tell me, Angus put you on phone duty,' said Iona, cheerfully picking up three pint glasses with her three middle fingers from one of the outdoor tables.

Evenings when neither she nor Ned could make the quiz, Jim (usually) would be appointed to listen to the music round, then run outside and sing the excerpt, then run in

again and pass on whatever Iona could make of his flat
and hopeful paraphrase of the lyrics.

As if to confirm this, an embarrassed young banker was
mumbling, 'Come on, Carolyn, you must know it, it sort of
went, um . . . Diddly-diddly, doof, doof, uh, *uh* uh *uh* UH!
No, of course I'm not trying to harass you! That's what it
was!' Pause. 'No, I *haven't* been drinking.'

'Is Tamara meant to be on tonight?' asked Marie.

Iona pulled a face. 'I'm not entirely sure. She said she'd put
in an appearance if it got busy, but if Gabriel's got the night
off, they're going to want to be together, aren't they?'

'Mmmn.'

There was a moment's pause while both of them reached
back longingly to the brief period when being apart
was physically agonizing. Iona remembered stealing one
of Angus's shirts and burying her face in it every night
until term started again; Marie remembered the evenings
she had secretly watched Chris training from the balcony
of the college pool, length after length, her arms and legs
mentally moving with his.

It seemed like a very long time ago.

Lucky, lucky Tamara.

Iona shook herself crossly.

Lucky Iona, with the nice boyfriend and the fun job.
Remember?

'Yeah, but hey, Marie. Good news on the New Charm
front. Before she rode off with Big Metal Pastry God,
Tamara said something to me about finding a lad for the
bar, some student friend of her brother's?'

Marie flicked up a dark eyebrow and stacked a load of
pint glasses along her arm. She was getting amazingly pro.
'Well, that'll give Jim a whole new patina of maturity,
having a spotty student to boss around.'

There was a new burst of groaning and drumming from
inside the pub. 'Oh, I could have had another fiver off
Angus,' said Iona. 'I *knew* they'd do "Rocket Queen" next.

By Guns N' Roses,' she added for the benefit of the young banker, who wrote it down.

'I don't know how he'll follow this,' said Marie, clearing a table. 'Where can you go from Great Rock Climaxes?'

Iona looked at Marie closely while she tipped some pistachio shells into an ashtray. She seemed surprisingly level at the moment. She hadn't mentioned Chris all evening, or made any bittersweet wisecracks about joining Dateline. Maybe it wouldn't be too mean to ask her advice about Angus? Or would that set her back days?

'Marie,' she began, 'it would be really great if we could . . .'

And what exactly are you going to say to her? Please help me – I don't know if I want the big-white-dress-and-pageboy number any more?

Marie glanced up. 'If what?'

'Um, nothing,' said Iona. She did a quick 'nothing, really' smile.

'So next time we'll go to the Frog and Forget-Me-Not, OK? It's just that this is Charles's local,' the embarrassed banker was pleading into his phone.

'I'm going to have to speak to Tamara about this,' said Angus ominously.

The bar was going mad, as Dr Keith marked the half-time scores and everyone dispatched their girlfriends to get the lager in. Angus, Marie, Iona and Jim were all serving, weaving in and out of each other's way as best they could in a small space.

'About what?' asked Iona. 'We're out of pint glasses again. Jim, can you go round and collect some, please?'

'Yeah, yeah, hang on . . .' There were three pints lined up underneath the three lager taps and Jim was watching them anxiously, not least because Marie was standing behind him with three more glasses, wearing the sort of expression he imagined Michael Schumacher habitually saw in his rear-view mirror.

'About this absenteeism. She said she'd be in tonight, didn't she?'

'I don't know if she said for definite,' said Iona defensively. 'Just if it was busy.'

'And?' Angus waved the hand that wasn't pulling the bitter tap. 'What's this? A quiet evening in? She's just not pulling her weight, is she?'

'Angus, how's she supposed to know how busy it is? Telepathy?'

'I thought that's *exactly* how she would know. Shouldn't her tarot cards have mentioned something about it getting a bit *congested* in the sphere of work in the foreseeable future?'

'Well, I'll phone her then,' snapped Iona. She couldn't help agreeing with Angus – even a ditz like Tamara should have known that they'd be run off their feet. It was nights like this that she could feel the glue of friendship stretching very thin, and it pissed her off that she still felt beholden to keep it all together. In fact, if their little circle of mates was like a raft made of empty barrels, then Tamara was in severe danger of floating off on her own and the only thing holding her on was Iona's precariously outstretched leg.

There was a worrying crackle from the speakers and the crowd noise thinned immediately. 'OK, and the scores are as follows . . .'

Iona and Angus stopped chuntering under their breath and looked at each other. Dr Keith now sounded as though he had a blanket over his head and seemed to be talking in Welsh.

'He's not a well man, is he?' observed Jim, dumping glasses in front of them. 'For a doctor.'

There was a thud and a clunk as the microphone fell to the floor.

'Shit,' said Angus.

Iona took a quick look at the crowd still pushing at the

bar and decided that any resurrection would be best left to Angus. She didn't think she could cope with accidental death on top of everything else.

'Hi, what can I get you?' she asked the nearest weary girlfriend, but before she could start her list of lagers, Iona's attention was distracted by a hand waving from the back of the crowd.

Once the crowd shifted as one to retrieve their marked question papers, leaving a light smattering of girlfriends still at the bar, Iona could see that the hand was attached to Tamara, who was clinging on to a lad whom Iona guessed to be about twenty, twenty-one, and, naturally, since Tamara was hanging on to him, he had the sweet, dark-eyed gorgeousness of an underwear model.

'Oh, my *God*,' gasped Marie, following her line of vision.

'Who is that? And where is Gabriel? And does he know? Marie? Marie? Are you listening?' Iona turned to look at Marie, but she was staring so hard at Tamara's man that the pint of Fosters she was pouring was overflowing into the drip tray.

Oh, so she *had* recovered then. More so than Iona had previously thought.

'Do you know that man?' Iona asked sarcastically. 'Or, rather, boy?'

'Er, no, no, sorry, I don't,' said Marie. 'Oh, shit, look what you made me do. I'm hopeless at doing heads.'

Iona bit her tongue.

'Guys,' said Tamara breathily. She never had a problem getting to the front of the bar. Men parted to get a better look and women stepped aside to avoid the comparison. 'Hi, I can't stop, Gabriel's waiting for me outside. I just wanted to introduce Liam to Angus.'

'Hello, Liam,' said Marie and Iona in unison.

'Hi,' said Liam. He raised a broad hand and smiled.

Iona thought she heard Marie squeak, but she couldn't be sure.

'Um, Angus is just taking care of the quiz man,' said Iona. 'He's had a funny turn.'

'God, you're really busy tonight, aren't you?' Tamara observed interestedly. 'You know whatshername from *The Times* is in the corner with the pub and bar guy from *Time Out*?'

'Are they?' asked Iona. 'Where?'

'There, look.' Tamara pointed them out with a long finger. Iona noticed with a sinking heart that there was a new plaited silver ring on it.

'How do you know all these people?'

Tamara frowned. 'Um, everyone knows them. I used to work with *him* and a picture researcher I know shares a flat with *her*. You know, maybe I should make some kind of chart, so that Angus can learn who everybody is. It would be just like him to be rude to them about their choice of mains or something and ruin a good review opportunity. Should I have a word with him?'

'Well, we're all a bit hopeless with faces,' said Iona defensively. 'It does get very busy in here . . .' Sometimes Tamara really pushed it.

'But anyway, it's really great that they're in,' said Tamara, oblivious of any sudden frost. 'The cards were right about the quiz – it's going to be a real success. Isn't it, Liam?' Out of habit, she squeezed her companion, and then seemed to remember who he was and retracted her grip. 'No, so, anyway, Liam's a friend of my brother's and he's available to do some bar work, aren't you, Liam?'

Liam, to his credit, rolled his eyes amiably and said, 'I can speak for myself, Tam.'

Then he addressed himself to Iona, since Marie had been forced, much against her will, to go down to the cellar for some ice cubes by a girlfriend demanding four double vodka tonics. *Yes*, with ice and lemon. 'Yes, I've done bar work before, I've got references if you need them, and I can start whenever you want.'

'Isn't that great!' said Tamara, her eyes flicking round the pub in case Angus turned up unexpectedly and forced a till key into her hands. 'Look, got to run, Gabriel's cooking for me. See you tomorrow!' And she was off, her long black coat floating out behind her as she made for the door.

Liam was left at the bar. He cast a look heavenward and smiled apologetically. 'Sorry about that. She's a bit mental. Well, you would know. I think the peroxide goes to her head.'

Iona knew instinctively that he was going to be fine. He had a ReadyBrek glow of Decent Lad about him. And even if he had had nine tattoos, no front teeth and a pit bull in tow, the fact that he seemed totally impervious to Tamara's magnetic charm field would have been recommendation enough for her. 'Right,' she said. 'You've picked the perfect evening.'

'Iona.' Angus appeared at her shoulder.

'Ah, Angus, this is—'

'No, no, no, no, no. No time for that. Look, Dr Keith has collapsed. I've put him in the office and Jim's called for a doctor. Um, can you go and, er . . .' His voice trailed off hopefully.

'No,' said Iona. Sometimes couple telepathy was exactly what you didn't want. 'No.'

'Oh, come on, please,' he said, holding both her arms. 'I wouldn't ask if . . .'

Iona looked straight into Angus's blue eyes. He never looked away when she did that, which was one of the reasons she loved him. And his face was tired, and vulnerable, and she could see faint lines around his eyes. She didn't think she should tell him about the *Time Out* guy and *The Times* woman. As Tamara had pointed out, Angus never recognized journos or TV people, and it was probably better that way. It would only make things worse.

'Fine,' she said without thinking. *And* what *are you*

agreeing to? 'But I can't guarantee the questions will be as good.'

'Excellent!' He wrapped her in a hug. 'I think he left his list of topics. It's all in the folder on the desk. You might have to do some new Current Affairs ones though – he knocked the last whisky and lemon over those when he, er, passed out. Yes, can I help you?'

'Excuse me,' said the blonde nearest to the front. 'I've been waiting for twenty minutes here for a Fosters, two Becks, a Kronenbourg, half a Speckled Hen and a Blastaway.'

'A *what*?' said Angus.

'Half Castaway, half Diamond White,' explained Marie staggering up the stairs with more mixers. 'So called because you're in orbit if you have three and the top of your head comes off if you have four. Bitter's off, by the way, and there are no house whites left in the fridge.'

'We don't serve those kind of drinks,' said Angus firmly. 'Would you like a glass of wine instead?'

'And I ordered some food and it still hasn't come,' added the man next to her. 'Four lots of the mushroom tart platter.'

'Where exactly did you read that it was called a *platter*?'

Jim squeezed his way into the happy throng. He smelled and his tie was askew. 'Angus, he's been sick again,' he said, 'and can you pass me the mop from behind the bar? Cheers. Is that black jacket of Iona's washable, incidentally? The one she left on the chair?'

'Hello,' said Liam to Angus. 'I'm Liam. Tamara recruited me. Would you like some help behind the bar? Or would you prefer to see my references first?'

Angus pinged the till open to get Tamara's till key and handed it straight over.

'And now the final question in round six, the new Top Gear Round. If you break down on a level crossing, is your first action a) to get everyone out of the car, b) to jump-start your vehicle from the one behind, c) to ask your girlfriend to walk down the line to stop the train or d) to check your mirrors?'

Chapter Twenty-nine

'Iona, if you don't move soon, they're going to come and put one of those police incident tapes around the car.'

Ned took another loud swig of Coke. His voice was amazingly non-confrontational, unlike the voice of the man in the car behind.

As she wrenched the gearstick about, Iona wondered absently, above the general scream of junction panic in her head, how Ned managed to knot his bladder up for the duration of their driving lessons. He drank constantly and had never once asked her to stop in a petrol station. Whereas Angus's eyes constantly scanned the horizon for places where she could safely grind to a halt and let him out.

'Your teeth'll go yellow, you know,' she said, hauling the wheel round as far as she could while watching the speedway-style traffic zoom past on Balham High Road. Moving Ned's Mini at low speeds was like steering the QE2 on rollers. Iona could see the muscles in her upper arm flexing with the effort, and she hoped Ned had noticed too.

'Should I . . .' she began tentatively.

The traffic seemed to be slowing down and thinning out, which probably meant there was a police car coming up from Tooting Bec.

'Go, go, go!' yelled Ned and, bringing up the clutch as fast as she dared, Iona screeched out towards the next set of traffic lights, spinning the wheel back from full lock and narrowly missing an old lady with a shopping trolley who had optimistically seen her L-plates and hadn't banked on Iona's Jensen Button approach to cornering.

'Champion,' Ned roared.

'Ta, lad.' Iona beamed, accelerated and belatedly cancelled her indicator, just in time for the overwrought nanny in the Jeep behind to abort a reckless overtaking manoeuvre.

Impressing Ned had taken over from Avoiding Death as the uppermost priority in her driving lessons. Iona wasn't particularly proud of that, but as an incentive to better driving it seemed to work.

What bothered her more was the way she looked forward to her practices with him. Not looked forward, *yearned*. In the manner of a very bad ballad, probably one by Chicago. Iona hadn't felt so aware of time passing between brief meetings since her GCSE French set acquired the first male French assistant known in north Cumbria. It was disturbing, the passion now boiling dangerously inside her like hot fat (not a metaphor she could remember Peter Cetera using), and even more disturbing how much more it could build up in the time between the hour together; a couple of nights ago she'd had a dream involving Ned changing a wheel on his Mini while stripped to the waist, and when he didn't change into Jimmy Page, as normally happened, her conscience had stepped in and woken her up.

Well, either her conscience or the part of her brain in charge of being outraged that she'd absorbed the mechanics of how to change a wheel from Angus's 1975 AA *Book of the Car*. On which he was now testing her before bed.

But no matter how much she furtively longed for it, the illicit thrill of being alone with Ned still wasn't compensating for Iona's continuing fear of the steering-wheel, and the accompanying mechanics. Which, in a way, was good, as it stopped her enjoying it too much. Not even Ron, the reassuring, official instructor and constant fount of rhetorical questionage, had the answer for the panic attacks she still suffered. (Although had she slumped over the wheel, wailing, 'Why, Ron? *Why* am I so terrified of driving?' he would most likely say something like, 'Well, now, Iona, why do *you* think you are?')

The Mini continued buzzing down Balham High Road, veering indecisively between lanes.

'Yeah, the lane markings *are* confusing here, aren't they?' frowned Ned, as if reading her mind. 'Not that easy to see where you're meant to go.'

Iona couldn't agree more. She had no idea where she was going. Not just in the car either. This morning, instead of cracking on with Matt and Lynn's nuptial collage, she'd consulted her back-issue *Cosmopolitan* library about what to do when you fell in love with your best friend, and all she'd been able to find were a couple of slightly salacious self-help stories about part-time lesbians. *Elle* hadn't been much help, going mainly for the fashion aspect of putative infidelity, and there wasn't anything at all in *Marie Claire*. The Only Glossy with Brains was evidently too smart to get into such embarrassing predicaments. Not when there were limbless child prostitutes in Guadalajara to worry about.

Company and *New Woman* were probably better bets, she thought, spotting the traffic lights in the far distance and slowing down ready to brake. (The car behind her also jammed on its brakes, assuming she had just run over a child.) It was, in truth, thought Iona, a classic sixth-form dilemma. Except most sixth-formers didn't have a live-in boyfriend/arguable fiancé to factor into the equation. Would it be worth asking Maxi to flick through her own back issues for her?

'Can Maxi drive yet?' asked Ned, rummaging in the side pocket for another can of Coke.

Iona's head whipped round and she inadvertently slewed into the left-hand filter lane.

'Maxi? What about Maxi?'

'Maxi, your sister. Still lives with your parents. Looks a bit like you, less lippy. More hair.'

Iona swallowed and felt herself blush. Her cheeks stung. This was getting ridiculous. If he could pick up Maxi vibes, what else was he tuning into? The thought of Ned reading her mind appalled Iona, but didn't actually surprise her that much. He just knew her too well.

'What made you think of Maxi?' She was aiming for casual, but it came out about as casual as Rosa Klebb.

Ned creased his brow in surprise. 'Er, we went past a billboard for some festival or other, and I suppose I was thinking about the time we took Maxi to that concert in Bitts Park. Where you were shit scared she'd get stoned and be abducted by Hell's Angels.'

'She was only nine.'

'There *are* no Hell's Angels in Carlisle. And that was no excuse for grabbing that bun off her.'

'Mum didn't tell me she'd put chocolate buns in the lunch-box. I thought . . .' Iona stopped. The most obvious answer at the time was that Ned might have made hash cakes, but now she didn't want to say, 'And I thought you might have given it to her, you addled bugger.' She *had* said it at the time, though, repeatedly and loudly, until the crowd had been more interested in them than Satan's Wicker Pygmy on the main stage.

'Man, Maxi was pissed off, wasn't she?' Ned smiled and leaned over to put her indicator on for her before she took out an unsuspecting cyclist. 'She ended up missing Gobrats Five because of you. Dragging her home by the arm and all. Jeez.'

'Well, at least she didn't have her stomach pumped.' Iona's face darkened as she realized she was in the wrong lane and would have to sneak her way across. She dragged the wheel round as far as she could, given that the car was almost stationary, and someone in a terminally wounded Fiat Panda gave her a very dirty look. 'As Mum originally demanded.'

The traffic made her stop and she allowed herself a quick glance across at Ned. Of late, Iona was strictly rationing quick glances. Funny how taking drugs now seemed quite cool and dangerous when Ned did it, when it had been sad and irritating at school. So much for growing up.

Iona conceded that this might be as much to do with Led Zeppelin as Ned, and then reminded herself that Drugs Screw You Up. Look what happened to the *Grange Hill* Just Say No lot with their Live Aid one-hand-on-the-headphones stance and serious expressions. One short encounter with dodgy white powder and they never worked again, except sporadically on *EastEnders*.

'You know, I can't remember the last time I went to a gig,' mused Iona. Two years? Three? How old was she? Did you still call them gigs even? She moved swiftly on, in case you didn't. 'Have you seen anyone good lately?'

'Er, yeah, one or two. Don't remember much about them though.' Ned's preferred music tended to be performed in small, airless pubs with funny hours. Scratchy R'n'B – in the John Lee Hooker sense, rather than the Puff Daddy sense – lo-fi garage bands squalling with feedback. They used to go and see a lot of that back home, and not care what it did to their ears to be so near the amps, but Angus made it a rule not to go to pubs where you couldn't use the loo without making a purchase in there at the same time.

Ned is now my last official contact with Youth Culture, thought Iona, with a flare of panic.

'I never see live music any more,' she half-whispered.

'Aye, well, there is the small matter of most of the groups you like being dead anyway. Are you really going to take this corner in third gear?'

'Shouldn't I?'

'No.'

Iona changed down too late and heard the engine-braking screech of protest.

'Is it meant to make a noise like that?' she asked, fighting with the steering-wheel on the off chance that it did that for every corner.

He looked thoughtful. 'You know, I don't really know. Maybe there's something wrong with it.'

Ned was the only man she knew who really didn't have the first idea about cars. Which made him the perfect practice partner.

'I should ask Angus, I suppose,' he conceded, without much interest. 'Don't want him thinking I'm driving his little lady round in a total shed.'

Angus. Iona checked her conscience for guilt and found only annoyance. *Then* guilt popped in.

'The last band – group' – she floundered for the least geeky word – 'um, band, I wanted to see did three nights in London in two years and when I finally got Angus vaguely promising to go, they split up. And no, I won't say who it was, you'll just laugh.'

'You should have asked me, I'd've gone with you. Left, left!'

'You wouldn't.' Iona hauled the wheel round, crossing her hands with the effort. Ned didn't tell her off the way Ron did. In fact, he didn't even notice. 'Anyway,' she went on, once they were safely round, 'it's Angus's *job* to accompany me on these things, isn't it?'

'Not if it's the band I suspect it was. Are we talking sequinned mini-skirts and glitter eyeshadow here?'

'That's not the point. I go to his cricket matches. I sit through endless films about submarines.'

'Your indicator's still on. Have you got a test date yet?'

'No,' said Iona automatically.

This was a lie. She did have a putative test date. In fact, Ron had sorted one out for her the minute she'd showed him her theory test pass certificate. 100 per cent. Not even the questions about horses on the road had stopped her completing the whole thing in sixteen minutes, including checking.

Iona was pleased that not everything was slipping.

'Tell me when the test is, Iona. I'll not tell Angus.'

'I said I didn't *have* a test date.'

'Iona, will you pack it in? I know what you're like.' Ned finished off his can of Coke. 'More certificates than I've cooked hot dinners. You're the only person I know who could write your essay in blue and put your quotes in black and still walk out before I'd got my name on all the bits of paper.'

'Ah, shut up.'

'It's true. You'll always be an eleven-year-old swot to me, no matter how much of an adult you think you are.'

Iona flushed and the boiling sugar in her stomach spread up to her chest. Then it struck her, like a bucket of iced water, that he was only saying that on the understanding that both of them knew he was joking – and that made it worse than if he'd said nothing. An involuntary yelp of frustration stuck in her throat, helpfully masked by the whiny transmission.

'*So?* When's the test?'

'Provisionally twelve days' time.' It fell out of her mouth – honestly, it was impossible not to tell him things. Ned leached secrets out of her head. Only her own secrets, mind. Iona huffed down her nose at her own weakness. 'But I could still cancel it. I'm not taking it if there's even the remotest possibility that I could fail. Acts of God aside, natch.'

They drove down to the end of the street and Iona stopped to let some women with baby buggies cross.

'You don't have to stop unless they're about ten feet away,' Ned pointed out. 'Even if they sprinted with those buggies, it'll take them a good three minutes to—'

'OK, OK!'

There was a longer pause, as they waited. Ned drummed his fingers on a can of Red Bull, as if debating whether his system could take any more caffeine.

'Ned, please don't tell Angus about the test,' said Iona. 'I don't want him to know I've even taken it until I've got the pass certificate safe in my sticky little hands.'

Ned said nothing.

'He's very, um, confident that I'll pass first time,' Iona went on, feeling as she always did that having caused a silence it was her duty to fill it. 'And I'm not. That confident.'

'You don't want to let him down,' Ned said reasonably.

You don't want him to know you can fail things.

Iona furrowed her brow. Bloody inner voices. Bloody Tamara Effect.

'I just don't want all that, "Oh, no one passes first time in London" stuff. It's almost as annoying as, "You only learn to drive once you've passed your test." Which, in turn, is not *quite* as annoying as, "What might you have wanted to have done there?" I get that a lot. Why is it that as soon as people can drive, they immediately forget what it's like not to be able to? I *hate* qualified drivers. I mean,' she added, 'I'm only telling *you* because I'll need someone to fetch me back from the test centre.'

A car came up behind them and tooted. From their low-down Mini point, it sounded like a bull horn going off. Iona moved away as quickly as she could and nicked the kerb with a tyre as she cornered.

'Mind my bodywork,' said Ned affably.

If only.

'Back to the pub?' asked Iona hopefully.

'Nah, back to mine.'

Iona's heart lurched in her chest like a very bad gear change and her foot slipped off the accelerator and caught in the exposed wiring, which hung down carelessly underneath the steering-wheel, and the sudden loss of speed made the car bump against a sleeping policeman. She didn't dare look round at Ned. Whether he was joking or not, she knew she couldn't get away with the expression on her face the way it was.

'Nah, better get back to the pub,' said Ned, as if in an afterthought. 'I said Rick and Mark could take charge of the mains tonight for a bit of practice and I can't see Gabriel getting their noses to the grindstone.'

'How d'you get on with Gabriel?' asked Iona casually. She could feel a pulse in her palms and her hands were sticking to the steering-wheel with sweat. Ned was the only one so far to have avoided Marie's How Much Do You Hate Gabriel? inquisition, usually because he was swinging chef's knives around at the time. 'Small kitchen, that.'

Ned shrugged. He could shrug with his lips, which made him look very northern and rugged.

'He's OK. Good chef. Sticks around until the kitchen's clean, which is more than I can say for the rest of the little buggers. I hope he's not going to mess Tamara around, but then she's not exactly a little snowflake herself, is she?'

'Noooo,' said Iona. 'But don't you . . .'

She was interrupted by the sound of a car alarm going off, very loudly.

'Oh, I just hate those,' she said, turning up the car stereo. 'There's one in the street outside our house, goes off all hours. You remember the time Angus threw a pot of basil out of our kitchen window at four in the morning and it smashed the back window of—'

'His Integrale, yes, I remember.' Ned was hunched over the handbrake. Iona tore her eyes from the road for a risky moment. Ned seemed to be grappling with her ankles.

'Are you trying to grope me?' she asked encouragingly.

People were staring at them as she drove by. People often stared at Ned's Mini – usually in wonderment that it managed to get over the speed humps – so it didn't bother Iona unduly.

'Is my indicator still on?' she said, hoping that he couldn't see the hairs around her ankles that she always missed when shaving. 'God, car alarms, eh? No one takes the blindest bit of notice, do they? All that racket and it's not as though

anyone's rushed out to check on their precious car.' She
looked backwards in her mirror. People were still following
the car up the road with their eyes.

'No, I can't do it,' sighed Ned, straightening up.

'Do what?'

'Work out which wire it is.'

'What are you talking about?' Iona frowned as the tape
came to a quiet part and the alarm was still shrieking in
the background, a deeply irritating up-and-down, two-note
migraine-inducer. A small child with a recorder would be
less irksome. Maybe people should just leave their kids and
their plastic Auloses in the back of cars. That would knock
car crime on the head. 'Oh, my God, Ned, there's a mini
roundabout here. That wasn't here last time we came.'

'It was. Just go straight ahead. Um, I think you must have
undone the wiring loom or something, because I can't switch
the alarm off.'

'It's *our* alarm?' Iona felt the first hot flush of embarrassment flood over her, and tried to switch off the stereo
to confirm it. The tape wouldn't switch off. The two-note
wailing continued. The alarm also carried on roaring away
like the siren on Fort Knox.

'Oh, my God!' yelled Iona over the top of the combined
forces of the stereo and the car alarm. 'I am going to die of
shame! I'm going to have to crash this car just to end the
humiliation! We have to drive down Ladbroke Grove to get
back to the pub! Oh, my God!' Her eyes flicked back and
forth in search of somewhere to stop. Anywhere. A tree or
something.

'Iona, don't stop the car,' said Ned urgently. 'This happened to me once before – I pulled over and *everything*
went dead. Three weeks in the garage before they could even
work out what had been wrong to begin with. Don't stop
the fucking car!' he yelled louder as she passed a tempting
supermarket car park. 'And turn the tape down, we look
like Yardies with bad taste in music.'

'What's less embarrassing?' demanded Iona hotly. 'A car driving round London playing "Kashmir" as loud as possible, or a car with a car alarm very obviously going off?'

Ned tried a weak smile. 'Look, at least no one will think we've stolen it.'

'That is *not* a consolation.' Iona couldn't stop her voice rising to a squeak.

'We'll just have to get Kwik-Fit Angus to have a look at it,' Ned bellowed over the opening bars of a ten-minute guitar solo.

'No!' shouted Iona immediately, gripping the wheel. If Angus saw the state of the car he would terminate Ned's tutelage and that would be it as far as she was concerned. All round. 'I will drive back to the pub!'

'Through central London?' asked Ned, impressed.

'If that's what it takes!'

'Good on you!'

Iona gripped the wheel and felt the sweat prickle underneath her arms. Somehow, and she couldn't tell why, there was a little less fear when she was driving with Ned.

And she *could* drive back through central London.

She *was* driving back through central London.

Ned opened another can of Coke and smiled at her.

Chapter Thirty

Liam, for all his tender years, had a way of looking at Marie that made every muscle from her throat downwards tense with guilty desire, culminating in a sick feeling in her stomach. And after a few weeks of shifts, it became gradually apparent to Marie, despite her total disbelief, that pints weren't the only thing he was interested in pulling.

It wasn't even that he had a 'seductive' look, unlike the intense and apparently meaningful smoulder Gabriel gave Tamara every time he handed her a plate, and which, Marie felt, gave him a strong resemblance to a cow in need of urgent milking. Liam didn't do anything special, but simply looked straight at her, with something unreadable in his permanently half-closed brown eyes, and Marie knew he could see right into her head. It made her turn away in embarrassment, knowing without a shadow of protective doubt that he could see exactly what was happening inside her.

What was happening, of course, was a terrible churning desire, so mad that Marie had trouble associating it with herself, and it was made even more surreal by the fact that Liam – too young, too beautiful, too cool – seemed to be flirting with her.

Even though she knew it was wrong, for a whole line-up of pressing reasons, of which her marriage was only one of a bunch, Marie felt as if she were floating down a warm stream every time he spoke to her. And they spoke a lot; every time they did shifts together, the evening seemed to have disappeared after only twenty minutes of conversation

– conversations that she hadn't had in years, about music and books and what things meant to her. Marie felt her age, in the face of his earnestness, but she didn't feel it too much; some of the cute, naïve things he said made her smile, because she could remember saying them too, and meaning them.

More to the point – Marie's lips curled in a self-mocking smile as she stole a long gaze while he unloaded the glass washer – Liam was also nineteen and so flawlessly clean and fresh that it made her ache. There was something hypnotically touchable about him. Every time she was within arm's reach of his springy curly hair, or the delicate moles on his tanned forearm, or the softness of his old T-shirts, it was all she could do to stop herself stretching out a finger to feel. It was so hard not to touch him. And since he did evening shifts, and so did she, Marie had to spend more time with her hands in her pockets than was really convenient for a barmaid. Mentally, at least, it seemed a very short step from looking at the soft curve of his lower lip to feeling the soft curves with her own full lips, and it scared her that one day, when her brain wasn't looking, her own body might make real what was going on in her head.

It felt weird, this lack of guilt. Being honest, Marie felt more guilty about *not* feeling guilty in the first place. But she didn't feel bad, and she didn't feel that she was cheating on Chris. She tried so hard to drum up some lingering image of him being more attractive than Liam, more attentive, but there wasn't a single qualm there, only the dull sense that this powerful, almost choking attraction seemed so fresh and new, it must have been a very long time ago that she once felt it for Chris.

And that did stop her in her tracks. And it made her sad.

The body aside, which Marie could have looked at quite happily for hours, the special thing about Liam was that he really talked to her, which was a novelty. He stayed for hours talking to her, even turning up when he didn't have a shift, so he could lean on the bar and catch her as she went past. He wasn't even trying to be seductive, which made it even more delicious. They just had brilliant conversations. No shouting, no lecturing, no ignoring what she had to say in order to get his next point across as soon as possible. He simply wanted to hear what she had to say. Liam talked to her as though she was as young and idealistic as him, and after five years of being A Teacher or A Wife, Marie had almost forgotten what that felt like.

'Marie, where do you really want to be?' he asked her as they polished wine glasses right at the end of the evening. Mark was mopping the floor while Angus tallied up the till, but Marie was only vaguely aware that they were even there.

She had to think. Where *did* she want to be? What did she want to do with her life, outside paying rent and getting to the summer holidays? Not fairy-tale love any more. Not family. Not anything, really.

Marie smiled. If one of her own friends had asked her that question, she knew they would have expected the answer, 'Oh, somewhere in Wandsworth, if I can't afford Clapham any more. But with a garden, definitely.'

'I don't know,' she said, concentrating on getting a streak off the glass. 'I think here's OK, you know. Globally and literally. I don't have any big plans to travel. I'm not sure I really want to any more.' Chris was the one who had two rucksacks and no suitcase at the age of twenty-nine. She bit the edge of her mouth. For some reason, she had no desire at all to talk to Liam about Chris, and yet he managed to hover at the periphery of her conversation the whole time. Which was typical of the selfish little fucker.

'Don't you?' Liam sounded surprised. 'But you've done loads of travelling.'

Marie paused in her polishing and considered. 'Er, well, I suppose so.' She tried not to say, 'But that was with my husband, not because I actually wanted to.' There was something very easy and open about Liam that made her tell the truth and not lie flamboyantly to impress him, or even trot out the answers she guessed he would want to hear from her. All these novelties at once really were disarmingly seductive.

'Thing is, I don't really like travelling that much, because when I come back from the airport, go to bed and wake up the next day, I can't really believe I ever went away,' she said slowly. 'I'm too much of a real-life person, I suppose. Unless I can see the photos, it's hard to believe it actually happened.' She smiled her most Gina Lollobrigida smile at him. 'You know, I've never actually put that into words before. I suppose I'm more of a here and now kind of person. Short attention span. I can only deal with one thing at a time, and anything I can't see doesn't really exist.'

He tipped his head to one side. 'And that must make it easy on your conscience.'

'Ah no.' She picked up another wine glass from the crate and pretended to frown at him. 'Conscience is different.'

'You mean, being bad is easy, and the worrying comes later? Handy.'

'Liam, Liam, Liam, this is the terrible way of the adult world. I'm so sorry.' She turned away to hide her blush and smile. He was making her feel like Mrs Robinson and she wasn't even thirty.

'I wish you wouldn't go on about your age the whole time,' he said softly. 'It's not important to me. It's not important full stop.'

'Tell that to Estée Lauder.'

'It's what you've *done* that matters.' Liam put the last wine glass on the shelf and began to rinse out the bar cloths in the sink. 'You don't stop learning things just because you're not at school any more. You should have an experience every day that you can take something away from.'

Marie tried to think what could be gained from breaking

up a playground scrap over skipping/football territories.
'And do you?'

He gave her a flirtatious smile and a dirty look from under
his long lashes. 'I try.'

Marie forced herself to go on an extended glass collection
before she lost control of herself entirely. God! It was almost
as bad as Gabriel and Tamara! And who wanted to be like
them? Though from what Liam had told her about the
various previous weirdos he and Tamara's brother Josh had
encountered on Saturday mornings throughout the course of
their adolescence, Gabriel was a significant improvement,
being single *and* over six feet tall.

The Tamara gossip potential was yet another of Liam's
many shining virtues. Marie would never have had her down
as a teenage Goth.

She undid the bolt on the front door, which Angus
had locked to keep Sam out until morning, and began
to gather the glasses from the picnic tables outside. A
bit of cold air should do her the power of good. Just so
long as Liam didn't catch her out here with no defences
to hand.

'Oh, I *can't* fucking *do* it!' shrieked Iona. She turned the
ignition key off and yanked on the handbrake so hard it
nearly reached a ninety-degree angle.

She and Ned sat in silence while the engine ticked. It was a
good job they were in a quiet road, as the Mini was forming
a fairly effective roadblock. Fortunately no one had come
out during the course of Iona's ninety-point manoeuvre to
fit the car behind a skip. She had refused to risk another car
as target practice.

'You *can* do it,' Ned pointed out calmly. 'You did it five
minutes ago in Longford Road.'

'Yes, but that was with you telling me when to steer and
when to . . . Oh, fuck! Fuck, fuck, fuck!' Iona pushed her
hands into her eyes to stop herself crying with frustration.

She was going to fail. And there was nothing she could do about it. She just couldn't park a car. Even a really bloody small one.

Ned rubbed her back absently.

Through her rage Iona hoped he didn't chance upon the angry red spot she could feel coming on between her shoulder blades.

'You can do it, Iona,' he said in a soothing voice. 'You know you can. You'll most likely find, knowing you, that as soon as you have to show off for the examiner, it'll all come into place. And you'll do a test-perfect one. You big swot.'

'You know what's confused me?' said Iona, her head springing up. 'That arse Angus. He went through all this last night using diagrams. What angle you have to reach to turn left, what angle for reversing . . .' She breathed out heavily through her nose. *Angus*. God! Sometimes it would be nice if he could stop being her dad for ten minutes and be her boyfriend.

'You haven't told him it's on Friday?'

'No,' said Iona. 'I have not. Or my mum, before you ask. I'm not stupid. When I want a Happy Ad in the *Cumberland Times* advertising my late-starting driving habits, I'll put it in myself.'

'Come on, you're tired,' said Ned, squeezing her shoulder. 'It's really late. Stupid of me – we probably shouldn't be practising when you've already had a long day.'

'No, it's OK,' said Iona. *What you don't know is that I've been looking forward to this humiliating torture all week*. She looked at him and felt something burn inside her. The streetlight was casting shadows down from his strong cheekbones, making his eyes even darker than normal. There was nothing Dad-like about Ned.

'Thank *you* for coming out with me,' she said. 'After a long day sweating over a hot stove. You must be knackered.'

He smiled and chucked her under the chin. 'No problem. I want to help. You can pick me up from parties when you pass.'

'Yeah, right.' Iona felt a terrible row going on in her conscience, all slamming doors and half-heard threats. What was she meant to do about this? It felt so right to be with him. And yet it obviously wasn't.

She permitted herself another sideways look at Ned and felt her heart skip as he smiled at her.

Maybe she should just go to one of Tamara's psychics. Er . . . very good. Not.

'Back to the pub?' said Iona heavily.

'After you've reversed into that large space, yeah,' he said, as if it was the most reasonable thing in the world.

'Ne-ee-ed, no-oo-oo-oo!' she whined.

'OK. Look,' Ned put his hand on her knee and Iona felt the sensation tingle all the way up her leg. 'If you park in that space, I will make you a really amazing chocolate soufflé when we get back to the pub.'

A chocolate soufflé versus 'Oh, very good! Don't be so silly, Iona, of course you're capable. Mind my bumper! Oh, my God, what are you *doing*? *What* are you . . . ? *Can* you read? Shit! Shit!'

Not really a competition, as such.

Iona checked her mirrors, took a deep breath and started the engine again.

Maybe she should let her test results be her guide, said a little voice in her head. If you pass the test, it won't be any thanks to Angus. And it might mean that Ned gets the best out of you.

And maybe . . .

Iona flinched with guilt and let off the handbrake.

'Liam, you big fibber, there is nothing wrong with this pump,' said Marie. She shook the beer-filled tube as proof. 'You have got me down to the cellar under false pretences and even made me demonstrate the hideous extent of my arse by making me follow you down the ladder.'

'And beautiful it was too,' he said. His lazy brown eyes crinkled.

Marie swallowed a gasp and felt her heart rate speed up. *Be cool, be cool. You are twenty-seven years old.*

'Right.' She picked up her cloth from the stairs and brandished it at him. She had forced herself not to be alone with him – masochistic thought that had been – and she wasn't going to show them both up now.

Be grown up.

She tried to smile in a patronizing fashion, but it came out as amused and voluptuous. Damn. 'I have eighty-three pint glasses to clean and you have the wine stock-take to do. Or did you want some help with that as well?'

He took a step nearer. 'Maybe. But that's not why I got you down here.'

'Isn't it?' said Marie faintly, unable to believe what was coming next and yet positive that it would, because she knew from personal experience that it was what nineteen-year-olds thought was seductive.

'I got you down here because I want to kiss you,' he said simply, taking the bar cloth out of her hands.

Marie stared hopelessly into the brown eyes, which were now black with dilated pupils and very close to hers. She wanted him to kiss her too, very much, but she wasn't entirely sure she should.

'Liam . . .' Upstairs she could hear someone swabbing the bar floor, bad-temperedly hitting all the skirting boards.

He stretched out his left hand and ran his fingers along her jaw, stopping just behind her ear. With the tiniest pressure he pulled her closer to him, slid his other hand into her hair so she couldn't get away, and kissed her.

Marie breathed the scent of his skin before his mouth touched hers and immediately she felt weak. Despite the hand on the hair, she didn't want to get away at all, and wouldn't, couldn't, even if her body hadn't gone into total paralysis.

No one, in twelve years, had kissed her like this. Liam was truly, truly fabulous at it. His mouth was warm and cool at the same time, his lips firm against hers, and he moved his tongue in a positively sensuous exploration of her lips, her mouth, with no pressure at all, except from one hand tangling up her hair and the other sliding down to the small of her back. She felt completely weightless.

Liam stopped for a moment and pulled away and Marie was filled with the hysterical image of resentment and fear a baby must feel when its mother removes the bottle. But rather than stopping, with one swift, determined movement he wrapped an arm around her waist and steered her firmly to the door of the wine cave, pushing her up against it and nuzzling his mouth into the soft warmth of her neck while his hands carried on roaming around the rest of her.

Marie closed her eyes and tried not to think about how the bottle of wine apparently pressed between them, and now being ground gently and highly effectively into her groin, had got there. Or how her legs had spread like that. Or when she had stretched up on her toes, calves feeling no pain, to get the best angle of exquisite pressure. Or when his hand had slipped down from the small of her back to her buttocks to pull her closer, and which was now sliding, unstoppable, confident, inside her pants.

'Liam, don't,' she said, thinking of the horrible flesh-coloured knickers she was wearing with her white skirt, rather than horror at what he was doing. And she wondered how it was that these words still managed to come out, even though she really didn't mean 'don't' at all. Conscience, maybe.

'Why not?' His breath was hot on her neck and she was aware of her own hands tracing up his back, catching the wiry curls of his hair, scratching his scalp in long slow circles, and the thrill of finally touching him. Marie realized that she was rotating her hips at exactly the same speed and in the opposite direction to his, and there was nothing she could do to stop them. And if he carried on like this, she would come in about ninety seconds.

She twisted a bunch of curls between her fingers and pulled his head back up to meet her parted lips. That would give her time to think of a good reason to stop.

Or it would be too late anyway.

Liam kissed her more urgently and shifted his body weight, and Marie marvelled again at how light his touch was. She felt like laughing with each kiss. How could he be this good? How could she have gone for so long without snogging anyone so sexy?

Because she was married, maybe?

There was a sudden banging on the cellar door. 'Oi!' yelled Angus's voice. 'How long does it take to sort out the wine, Marie? I don't want an essay, just what's been drunk. And have you seen Liam? He's disappeared, the cheeky little slacker.'

Marie sprang out of Liam's strong arms with the invigorating power of guilt. Angus couldn't have seen them against the wine cave even if he'd come down the stairs to look, but still she felt hot and cold all over, and her heart was pumping.

Liam leaned against the ice maker and gave her a long, slow, sexy smile. He raised his eyebrows, amused by her teenage reaction.

Oh, my God, thought Marie. *How many cheesy things will he be able to think of to do with that ice?*

'Erm, I'm just coming, Angus!' she yelled, adjusting her clothes.

Liam raised his eyebrows further, even more amused, and stretched out a hand, running it down the dramatic curves of her waist.

'Indeed you are,' he whispered.

Marie, unable to drag her eyes from his despite his worryingly Barry White taste in 'Hey, laydeez' dialogue, tried to push his hand away, but her heart wasn't really in it and it returned and began caressing her breast, lingering accusingly over her tell-tale hard nipples.

'Tut, tut,' whispered Liam. 'You can't go upstairs like that.'

'Marie?' shouted Angus. 'Do let us know if you've fallen and broken your leg or something, and we'll break off from *cleaning the pub* and come and get you.'

'Yeah, yeah!' she shouted back, trying to redo the bra strap Liam had flicked undone, and while she was distracted, he suddenly pulled her back to him, slid his hand down the buttons of her shirt, undoing them all in one go and, bending his head to her breast, liberated and then sucked her swollen nipple. With precision timing almost as spot-on as her own, he silenced her groan with another long kiss and pulled her as close as he could while she arched her back against him and came.

Marie kept her eyes closed as long as she could, feeling the blinding burst of pleasure spread and fade and linger, nursing the sensations for as long as possible in isolation. Knowing that as soon as she opened her eyes it would all be over and would never happen again, *could* never happen again, and it would all be memory, not real life, inaccessible and gone, and instead of relishing the fact that it had happened, she would be filled with a sinking ache that she could only play back the thin film of it, and not the pulsing, erotic reality. And yet when she finally opened her eyes, Liam was still looking at her, still holding her, and his eyes were still black-pupilled with desire. He looked as dazed and aroused as she did.

'Don't know what to say,' she whispered into his mouth, unable to break the stare. She could smell the faint trace of the glass of wine he'd drunk on his breath, over the top of his own smell. 'You're too beautiful. Too good. Not real.'

He carried on looking at her, stroking the hair off her face.

'Oh, that's bad,' he said ironically.

'No, that's *good*,' replied Marie automatically, quoting from 'Theme from S-Express'.

Liam looked puzzled. Which made her smile.

'Oh, you beautiful boy.' Marie's hand rose without conscious thought to his jaw and stroked the faint traces of stubble starting to prickle the soft skin. 'You beautiful . . .'

'Marie!' roared Angus down the cellar steps. 'For fuck's sake! If you don't get up here right now and start going through the ullage book, I'm going to come down and get you!'

She bit her lip and reluctantly removed her hand from Liam's jaw. But they still couldn't tear their eyes away from each other.

'Oh, I feel so guilty,' she said. 'Or don't I feel guilty enough? I can't tell any more.'

Liam slipped a finger under her chin and stroked the hollows of her throat. Marie couldn't believe that he could make sensations run through her entire body with such an innocuous touch. It wasn't right. 'I don't know why you do all this guilt thing,' he said, fairly easily, to her mind. 'It's just an *experience*. That's what your man's doing in Kosovo, isn't it? Adding to his own experiences of life?'

Marie nodded, gazing transfixed with lust at the perfect softness of the skin under his collarbone, exposed by the opened shirt. Had she opened that?

'And has he asked your permission to go out there and leave you?' he went on. 'Did you try to stop him?'

Marie shook her head. He had a point.

'You have to take experiences when they come.' Liam pressed his lips against her forehead and spoke into her hair. 'I've always wanted to meet someone like you. Funny, and mature, and beautiful, and intelligent, and—'

'Now, Liam, stop right there,' said Marie. 'I may be old but I know when someone's trying to talk me into bed.'

But not so old as to have forgotten that maybe he wasn't.

That maybe he really meant it, untainted as he was by crap relationships and disappointments and clichés.

'Let me finish what I started,' said Liam suddenly. 'Let me stay and make love to you.'

'Er, no,' Marie replied automatically, and then remembered that she didn't live in Tooting with Chris any more, she lived over the pub on her own and could quite easily engineer a night of passion whenever she wanted to.

Her stomach lurched with excitement and fear and she had to put her hand on his chest to steady herself. As soon as she felt the hard muscles underneath the T-shirt, she felt even weaker.

'OK,' she said, before her brain could intervene. Liam was already taking the splayed-out hand as a signal to pull her close again. She flexed her elbow to try to keep him at arm's length.

Remember, he probably only fancies you because you're a cooler older woman. Stop trembling like a teenage virgin. Just think about your cellulite.

'When's your next shift?'

He pulled a face, but still looked like a Botticelli angel. 'Friday.'

'Stay Friday night.' She gazed at him, knowing her eyes were probably as black as his.

'I will.'

Fuck, thought Marie, how can I lose a stone between now and Friday?

Chapter Thirty-one

'Morning, Jim,' said Rebecca. 'Do you want some help with the doors?'

Jim nodded crossly. He was wedged between the heavy glass doors – again – because he'd foolishly tried to hold it open for some smart-arse courier – again – and then the tray of coffees had slipped and he'd pushed it up against the door to stop it spilling and now he was stuck. One false move and his suit would be fully latte'd.

Martin had now taken to calling him on his mobile on the way in to pick up the coffee. Apparently, Svetlana had his number on speed dial.

'Let me give you a hand.' Rebecca shimmied out from behind the huge marble desk and Jim noticed with a masochistic pang that she was wearing those sheer tights with a seam up the back. Her legs looked endless and finished at a pair of plum leather stiletto heels that made him swallow helplessly and wish that he could occasionally see her when he wasn't being crushed by Overworld and all its bastard fixtures and fittings. Literally *and* metaphorically.

'Careful, they're all hot,' he warned, as she gently removed the top two cappuccinos from the pyramid of cups. Up close, Jim noticed that Rebecca smelled the same as Iona. God, if only he could remember useful girl stuff like perfume names, he could make a suave comment about it. Not even suave. Even Angus would have the guts to roar, 'You smell nice!' if he thought someone was flirting with him. Even *Chris* would manage, 'You don't sweat much for a fat lass.' He slapped his head mentally and despaired.

'Did you get one for me?' she asked with a little smile.

Jim peered at her closely. She had that amazing film-star lipstick on, so red and glossy that it looked about to spill over the neat line. Tamara used to do her lips like that before she became Gabriel's in-house rock chick and just started slapping eyeshadow on all over like some kind of cack-handed panda. Everything about Rebecca was neat. Neat and just . . . right.

Was she flirting?

Or was that the same as being nice?

Or was she taking the piss about his coffee run?

The inner Jim shrank back. There was so little point. It had taken him three years before he could talk to Tamara without two others there for conversation insurance. It had taken nearly a year to get to this nervous banter stage with Rebecca and, frankly, attempting to *chat up* Rebecca would be like kicking off your mountain climbing career with Everest. OK, so if you managed it, the view would be incredible, not to mention the exhilaration of getting there, but the possibilities for frost-bite and accidental death were huge.

But if Iona or Marie could see this, they wouldn't let him get away without saying something. Not without breaking his arm first.

'Erm, well,' he stammered, 'I got myself a latte, which you're, er, very welcome to. It's full-fat milk, though, and you normally get skimmed, don't you?' It was a simple memory thing, an easy bloke fact, and God knew he'd done enough coffee runs to have the requirements of the entire office at his fingertips, but as he said it Jim realized that, with a swift smile, it could easily pass as a compliment Of sorts.

Or would she think he had stalker tendencies?

The smile faltered.

'How clever! You remembered!' cried Rebecca, as if he had whipped a bunch of flowers out from under his jacket. 'Oh, that's so sweet of you. Thanks so much! I'd love it!'

She gave him a dazzling red smile which made his ears burn and then she seemed to remember that he was still trapped in the front door. Quickly she divested him of the remaining tray of coffees and carried it back to her desk, allowing him to disengage his jacket from various parts of the door mechanism with relative dignity.

'So,' she said, peeling the top off one of the coffees. 'How are things going at that pub of yours then?'

'Oh, er, very well, actually,' said Jim. He tried not to look (too closely) as she licked the foam off the inside of the lid with a pointy pink tongue. 'You should, er, come over for supper one night. To the pub, I mean,' he added hastily.

'Where else would I be going to supper?' Rebecca raised a flirty eyebrow. 'Your flat?'

'Um, no, of course, yes.' Jim found an espresso among the rest and knocked it back in one like cod liver oil. Iona said they helped her concentrate, so it couldn't hurt.

The strength of it made him grimace, but he forced his facial muscles not to flinch.

Rebecca sipped at her latte and looked at him over the top of the lid. Her lipstick stayed glossy, Jim noticed. And it didn't seem to come off on the cup. How did they do that? Was it laminated on?

'Is Martin back in yet?' he asked, before he made some ridiculous observation about her make-up.

'I think so,' she said. Rebecca didn't think so. She knew so. She knew where everything was and was going and had been. She wasn't so much an office manager as Big Brother. Stealth, she had decided, was the key round here.

'Oh, good,' said Jim, without much enthusiasm. 'I've got a meeting with him in ten minutes. He wants to give me more money for the pub, I think.'

Martin kept giving him more and more money and,

frankly, it was starting to get a bit worrying. First it had been mildly insulting – that he imagined they couldn't manage their budgets – and then it had got a bit weird, with more and more meetings in which Martin casually handed him vast cheques and told him to go out and get great big chandeliers or more brandy for the wine cellar.

They hadn't gone out and got either of those things, naturally. Angus had used some of the cash to get another student in to take some shifts off him and Iona, and he'd bought in some decent wine for the top end of the list, most of which they'd sold at a good mark-up to the increasing number of media types who wandered in, platinum Amexes at the ready. They'd invested some of the rest in a share tip Angus's old boss at Pryce Riley Riches had given him. To Jim's amazement, they'd actually made money on it. The pub was actually starting to make money.

He and Angus had had many late-night discussions about this unexpected turn of events over the accounts books. Angus's feeling was that if Martin wanted to give them more money than they needed, that was fine. At the moment, they were actually doing a little bit better than their cautious predictions, and any surplus could only be a bonus. Jim, on the other hand, worried. Worried because he had a feeling there was something he should be worrying about but was missing. As usual.

Rebecca gave him a knowing look. 'More money, eh?'

Jim cut a look at her. What did she know? 'Er, yes. For a seafood and champagne night, apparently.'

She smiled with obvious amusement and Jim felt something curl up and roll over inside his upper chest.

'Oh, that's the best yet,' she said. A bubbling laugh gurgled up her throat. 'Oh, wow. I'd like to hear Kyle get that one past the Inland Revenue.'

Jim joined her in the laughter, which he found strangely infectious, but then he stopped short. Surely the funny thing about the seafood night was that most of the Grapes clientele thought crabs were something you got medication for? Far off in a distant corner of his brain, a penny was starting to drop. And ricochet around.

'What have the Inland Revenue got to do with it?' he demanded.

For once Rebecca's face lost its natural expression of superior knowledge and she looked confused. 'Um . . .' She raised her eyes appealingly to him, but Jim stoutly resisted the churning in his stomach. 'Um, well, come on, Jim, you know what I mean. When they see Kyle's books for this year . . .'

'They're not Kyle's books,' said Jim. 'This is my project. I do the accounts myself. And it's in profit, actually. Oh no,' he said, seeing his worst fears begin to emerge from the shadows and come into focus, armed with placards. 'Oh, you're not telling me that this is some kind of scam, are you?'

Rebecca nodded. 'Didn't you . . . ?'

'But it *can't* be! Why would it? The Bunch of Grapes is a functioning, successful pub! We're full every night and someone even wants to do a pilot TV thing with one of the chefs!' Jim never thought he'd be happy to tell anyone that.

'I know,' said Rebecca. 'Simon can't believe it. He's been trying to get someone to do a documentary here for years. That's why they spent all that money doing up the partners' offices.'

'But I don't understand,' Jim protested. 'Martin really encouraged me to take this project on. He's been so supportive. I mean, you've seen the financing he's given it!'

'Oh, yes,' she agreed, then remembered that she wasn't strictly meant to read company accounts and shook her head sympathetically. 'I mean, no. I mean, you said . . .'

'No, you must have got it wrong,' he said definitely. 'You must have misheard something.'

If Jim had known Rebecca all her life, he couldn't have

picked a more effective method of getting information out of her.

Her lips tightened in a reflex reaction. 'Jim, Martin keeps giving you all that money because he wants you to spend it, so he can write it off against the huge profit he made on that development in Spitalfields.'

'He what?' Jim demanded. All the blood rushed into his face.

'He *wants* you to lose lots of money on the pub. That's the whole point. It's a tax thing.' Rebecca hesitated. She liked Jim, despite, or maybe because of, his raging naïvety, and she wanted to help him out if she could, but she had read her Shakespeare. Shooting the messenger and all that. If she was going to get him to take her out for dinner, there was no point repeating Kyle's harsh but accurate e-mail observation that the best man in the firm for losing cash hand over fist was Jim, since according to the petty cash receipts the coffee shop had been short-changing him for the past six months.

Jim, meanwhile, appeared to be having trouble breathing regularly.

'Jim, are you OK?' she asked. The phone rang and she put it straight through to Agnetha, the group secretary, to deal with. According to Rebecca's phone-line monitor, she'd been getting her Internet horoscope for the last half-hour, so it was about time she did something company-based on company time.

'Jim?' She touched him on the arm.

'I'm . . . fine,' he said, loosening his tie. Fucking awful tie. He'd only bought it because he had a meeting this week. It was the first time he'd been in a suit for five days and he just couldn't get used to the constraining feeling under his arms.

'I mean, it's not as though Martin's *mad* at you,' she went on quickly. 'Otherwise he wouldn't keep giving you the money, would he? And it's been getting the most brilliant coverage in the *Standard*, hasn't it? I've been hoping for an invite! That sexy chef you've got – what's his name?'

'Ned Lowther,' said Jim heavily. He took the lid off the other espresso and downed it with another 'gaaah' face, not quite as bad as the first. They seemed to go down a lot better second time round.

'No, that's not the one I'm thinking of.' Rebecca furrowed her brow. 'Something biblical, isn't it? Jesus or something?'

'Well, that's what he thinks, anyway. Look, Rebecca, this is really important, are you sure you've got it right?' Jim leaned on the desk. 'Martin can't want me to *lose* money for Overworld. I had to do plans, presentations, the whole lot! He's been looking at the accounts since we started up! We even talked about selling the upstairs flats when the market hots up again in the autumn. He wouldn't have let me take it on if it was going to lose money. God knows, I've had enough projects turned down for that very reason. I mean . . .' He threw his hands up in bewilderment and slammed them on the desk. 'The whole *point* of this place is wealth creation. Christ, there's even that racehorse syndicate in the accounts department! Making money is all they care about!'

'But not making it for the Inland Revenue.' Rebecca gave him a little tilted, rueful smile. He was such a kid when it came down to it. 'I thought you *knew*, Jim.' This again was a fib: she'd seen it coming for ages, and it was part of Jim's cute and unworldly charm that she knew he hadn't. But it hadn't been until now that she'd actually cared enough to point it out to him.

'Oh, God.' Jim sank his head into his hands. 'Fuck, fuck, fuck. Fuck . . . fuck. No. No. No. Oh no, what time is it?'

'Half-twelve.'

'Oh, fucking hell.' His face was distraught, and Rebecca felt her first ever maternal instinct for a man. 'I've got to go and talk to Martin about another vast cheque. I suppose he wants me to get all excited and blow it all on crystal dishes of free coke in the Gents.'

'Is that what you get in gastro-pubs now?'

'No, it bloody well isn't.' Jim distractedly polished his glasses on his tie. He didn't care about being late for Martin now. O'ho no. *How* could he have been so slow? In fact, being late would probably be a good thing – it would make him look even more incompetent and stupid. Great. If that was what Martin wanted, that's what he would get. Jim stung all over with humiliation and wrath. Just because he didn't behave like an underhand shit, how was he supposed to second-guess people who did?

'Rebecca,' he said wearily, 'how do you know all this? I mean, I'm not saying you've got the wrong end of the stick, but where did you find it all out?'

Rebecca looked at Jim, who was gazing at her with the tragically hopeful gaze of an elderly pony being ushered into the horsebox for the final time *en route* to the vet's. Some people were just too nice. Why couldn't he have had a nice career as a stockbroker or a florist? Something without too many sharp edges.

'Well,' she began slowly. It wouldn't be a good idea to give away all her surveillance secrets too soon. She knew it was tactical not to seem too all-knowing with men like Jim. 'Well . . . you know as office manager I have to patrol the office e-mails . . .'

A separate, constipated expression shot across Jim's face.

'And there were a couple of meetings I had to minute when Svetlana was ill last week and you were out working on-site . . .' Was that enough? She gave him a quick glance under her long eyelashes. He was still looking worried about the e-mails. Rebecca smiled indulgently. As if she was bothered about those dirty jpegs he'd been getting from his web-designer friend.

'Is that . . .' he asked hopefully.

She nodded, and he looked relieved, whatever it was he was trying to get at.

Better not to let on about the excellent clarity of sound

carrying from the Gents into the Ladies through the state
of the art ventilation system, through which she had heard
Simon's harsh but fair assessment of Jim's ties.

Or the fact that, according to Kyle, the real beauty of
Martin's plan was getting Jim out of the office and 'on-site'
somewhere miles away from anything significant.

And definitely better not let on just yet about what Martin
planned to do with the pub site once Jim had 'proved' that
it wasn't financially viable as a pub.

'What really pisses me off,' said Jim, half talking to himself
in bewilderment, 'is that I honestly thought they were taking
me seriously at last. I honestly thought that I was getting
somewhere. And they didn't even bother to let me in on the
most important detail of my own project! God, it makes me
want to be sick. They must think I'm just some stupid little
boy they can push around . . .'

Jim told himself with grim finality that this had to be the
end of the line. How long could he carry on maintaining any
degree of self-respect while he was constantly being treated
as the intern, the office junior, the stupid one who never got
asked to the pub on Friday?

Asked to Mirabelle on Friday, Jim corrected himself.

A flood of shame and anger swept through his veins like
amphetamines. He'd never felt so mad, or so determined to
let everyone know about it. It felt almost as though a whole
new man was tearing at the inside of his skin, trying to break
out and wreak revenge.

Maybe this was how Angus felt all the time . . .

'But, come on, Jim,' said Rebecca soothingly. 'It is just a
project, at the end of the day. You can work on other ones,
now they've seen—'

'Rebecca, it *isn't* just a project!' Jim's eyes flashed angrily.
'Four of my mates work there! Real people drink there!
My best friend spends all his waking hours there, slogging
his guts out trying to make the place into a success. My
flatmate's working himself into the ground running the best

kitchen in west London. And all the time Martin doesn't give a fuck whether it fails or not because it's *just* a *project*!'

'You don't know that,' backtracked Rebecca, although she did know that *was* what the plan was.

'Oh, I bet it is,' said Jim. 'I bet there's loads more that I don't know about. Well, that's it. That's the last straw.' He wrenched at his tie and loosened it until it hung like a noose around his neck. 'You've *got* to help me, Rebecca. I need to find out exactly what's going on. And then I need to work out what I'm going to do about it.'

Since she could admit a growing affection for Jim, especially this new, sharp-focus version who might at last notice her, as well as the devious way of the world, Rebecca didn't point out that, as office manager, she didn't have to help anyone if she didn't want to. Instead she smiled as Jim slipped behind her desk with an A4 pad and biro, and she began to flick through the Rolodex in her logical, ruthless brain.

Chapter Thirty-two

'There it is.' Angus carefully lifted the lemon tart out of the Tupperware container and held it up for inspection. 'Bruléeing to follow, of course.'

Mark, Rick and the YTS washing-up lad stood back and admired the glossy, egg-yellow surface of the tart and the just-brown crinkle of visible pastry. Not a crack in sight. In fact, possibly Angus's best yet.

'You've a fine tart there, Angus, I'll give you that,' said Rick.

'And your lemon flan's not bad either,' quipped Mark.

'Ho, ho, ho,' said Angus, holding his sides, deadpan. 'What a double act you two are. However, that's my girlfriend you're talking about, and you'd do well to remember that she's got a black belt in sarcasm. But do not joke about my *tarte au citron* if you want to be working here next week.'

'Sir!' barked Rick.

'And, though I say it myself as shouldn't,' Angus went on, in his best impression of Iona's mother, 'I don't think Gabriel himself could make a better lemon tart than that.' Which was, of course, the whole point.

Mark made loud, job-insurance noises of agreement.

Angus gave the lemon tart one last, loving look and slid it in the fridge. He had to move a lot of Gabriel's stuff to get it in but that didn't bother him.

'Gabriel not around then?' he asked. Since Tamara wasn't, it didn't look likely, but Rick and Mark, caught off guard, were more likely to let something slip by accident than trot out whatever Gabriel had told them to say.

Angus gave Mark his best trainee-unnerving stare, but Mark just looked faintly shifty, which was nothing new, really. 'He came in early to sort out the vegetable delivery and he went out about half an hour ago. Said not to worry, he'd be back before service started.'

Angus snorted angrily. Jesus, it couldn't *get* more casual. 'He *is* in charge of the kitchen this lunchtime, is he not?'

Rick nodded.

'So is it just me,' Angus demanded, 'or is it permanently dress-down Friday round here?'

Rick and Mark looked blank.

Angus sighed. Dress-down Fridays were another world. The last time either of them had been in an office, it had probably been to sign on. 'Never mind. Where's Ned?' He knew Ned had the morning off, but he frequently came in anyway when the weather was too bad to go rooting about for wild fungi. He wasn't really happy when he wasn't fiddling around with food. Angus suspected that the mushrooms had saved Gabriel's bacon more than once. So to speak.

'Eh?' he said when answer came there none. 'Where's Ned?'

Mark was fiddling with a spatula and Rick's attention was being distracted by the clattering lid on a huge pan of boiling potatoes. 'Um . . . Ned's not . . .'

'Fine, OK, let's get on with it then.' Angus rubbed his hands together. There was no point going mad at them, especially not just before lunch. 'Did either of them bother to leave a menu for Iona to write up?'

'Er, yeah, Gabriel did . . .' said Mark, putting the spatula down for a moment. 'But I'm not sure he's finished it yet. I think that was why he went out, actually, said something about getting some more basil from somewhere.'

'Though I did offer to go for him,' added Rick, before Angus could ask why he hadn't.

'Oh, great,' said Angus. 'Well, give it here then.'

Mark took down a crumpled sheet of A4 from the pinboard and passed it over. Gabriel had done the menu on the back of the fish order and, as Mark had said, it wasn't finished. In fact, there were five puddings and no mains on it.

Angus rolled his tongue round the inside of his mouth to stop himself yelling at someone. He swallowed hard and forced a smile out at Mark (who flinched at the unexpected show of teeth) and walked deliberately out of the kitchen into the bar.

Iona could calm him down. She always did. That lovely calming smile. The gentle way she could drain the tension out of his neck with those long fingers . . .

'Darling,' he said, projecting his voice ahead of himself to the other side of the pub, where he'd last seen her slicing lemons, 'can you make me a coffee, please?'

As he rounded the corner he could see that Iona was standing facing the optics, gripping an invisible steering-wheel and chewing her lower lip as she reversed herself into the two lager taps. Except she was unwittingly steering in the opposite direction to the one she thought she was travelling in. When she heard Angus's voice, her head jerked up hard enough to give herself whiplash and a guilty expression flooded her face. She'd been jumpy all day.

'Just when you have a moment . . .' finished Angus limply.

God, it was coming to something when he looked forward to Jim's arrival from Overworld for a bit of normality.

At half-two, Ned and Iona sat in the Mini for the final time outside the driving school. They had been there for about ten minutes now. She could hear something ticking – not the clock, since it didn't work. It could be the engine, or maybe the fan belt, or possibly the tin worm, or . . .

'OK, Iona, let's be having you,' said Ned, breaking the silence for her. 'An hour and a half with your man, then the test will just fly by.'

'It will do if I crash the car before we get out of the test centre,' she said morosely. 'I give it three minutes. Less if I have to do the reverse-park straight off.'

Ned put his arm round her and squeezed. He smelt of basil and cigarettes. 'Come on, think positive. You've got the skunk thing, haven't you? And you've not failed an exam with that yet, have you?'

Ned had phoned Maxi and got her to post Iona's old exam mascot, the skunk thing, for good luck. The skunk, which Iona had made in second-year needlecraft, was much smaller than she remembered and, despite herself, she now wished she'd given it to Tamara to put some kind of luck-boosting hex on it. A sort of talisman refresher. The skunk was stuffed in her bag, along with her provisional licence, her 100 per cent written test certificate, her appointment card, her passport (allegedly for identification purposes but fulfilling a handy second use for fleeing the country and Angus's disbelief when she failed), two packets of Polos and an *A–Z*. For getting the bus home.

Iona wished her bare skin didn't tingle so much beneath Ned's fingers. She wished the tingling wouldn't spread through the rest of her body so much. In fact, pleasant though it was, she wished the tingling would stop already. It was distracting her from worrying about her driving test.

'I hope you didn't tell Maxi why I needed this?' she said meaningfully. 'Because if my mother gets wind of it . . .'

'Certainly not,' he protested. 'As far as Maxi is concerned, I was just looking for a reason to phone her up and engage her in conversation in the hope of securing a date when I next go home.'

'Hmm.' Iona let that pass for the time being.

'So, um . . .' Ned hesitated.

'What?'

I really don't want to get out of this car.

'You haven't changed your mind and told Angus about . . .'

Iona swivelled her head guiltily, wondering what he was referring to, and then realized from his concerned expression that he was talking about the driving test, not anything more inflammatory. She shook her head. 'I've got the afternoon off to paint. I just hope Angus wasn't planning on coming home early to surprise me with a bottle of wine and some romantic music.'

'He does that?'

'No.'

'Oh.'

Another tick- and tingle-filled silence.

Finally, with a huge effort, Iona leaned forward and unbuckled her seat-belt.

'Good lass,' said Ned encouragingly.

'Don't talk to me like I'm a sheepdog,' she replied, checking in her bag for the final time.

'OK, OK. Look, keep thinking of all the people you know who can drive. Eh? Me, Tamara, Jim – and if we could pass the test, it can't be that hard, can it now?'

'We all know how Tamara passed,' said Iona derisively. 'But you will see that I'm wearing a pair of jeans and flat shoes, so that tactic's out.'

'Iona . . .'

'Not that many people go to their test dressed as Daisy Duke, but it must work for some. Right.' She took a deep breath.

'Just remember to look in your mirrors *all the time*.'

'Oh, excuse *me*,' said Iona, putting a finger on her cheek, 'I was wrong about the hotpants – so *that's* why Tamara passed.'

'And don't speed.'

Iona gave him a look. 'That's your department, isn't it?'

Ned threw up his hands in despair. 'Aye, and *don't* be smart with the examiner. It'll come back on you later. Anyway, you'll be fine. You always are.' He patted her knee reassuringly.

'You're doing that sheepdog thing again. And hey, no pressure, eh?'

Ned laughed and took a can of Coke out of the capacious side pocket. 'Look, give me a ring when it's all over and I'll come and get you.'

Iona felt a brief and unreasonable flash of panic that he wasn't going to sit right here and wait until she came back. Angus would have done. But then Angus would probably have insisted on sitting in the back seat for the test to prevent any malpractice, and disputed most of her driver errors with the examiner.

'Please drive a long way away from the test centre in the meantime,' begged Iona. 'I couldn't bear the thought of seeing you gurning away in my rear-view mirror while I'm negotiating the Catford one-way system.'

'No, I was talking to a mate this morning, who says he's found a little crop of wild ceps in the cemetery,' said Ned, sounding suddenly animated. 'Very early, but they look fantastic. I thought I'd go and have a quick sken, check it out. Least, I think they're ceps. They might even be . . .' He remembered who he was talking to, and Iona's views on fungal ecstasy, and snapped back to reality. 'Long as we're back at the Grapes before evening service.'

'OK.' Iona let out a long breath through her nose. This was it. So much seemed to hang on what she could do in the next couple of hours. She looked across at Ned, sitting in the passenger seat, his long legs up against the parcel shelf, slurping from his Coke and raising his eyebrows at her.

It would have been so much easier to do this at seventeen. The driving test – and Ned. She could have got them both out of the way at the same time.

'Right, this is it.' Again the plummet in her stomach.

Weird, since she hadn't noticed it recover from the first plummet. It had been plummeting up and down like something from Alton Towers since they'd pulled up, about fifteen minutes ago.

'Right, I'm going.' If she said it again surely it would dawn on him to give her a good-luck kiss? They never normally kissed, being too good friends for that kind of thing.

Iona pulled at the door release, but nothing happened. She turned her body and pulled at the lever with both hands and still nothing happened.

So much for dramatic exits.

'Ned, I can't get out,' she said, her voice rising on each word, and since her brain was now firmly engaged in GSCE exam superstition gear, she immediately clapped her hand over her mouth and squealed through her fingers, 'Oh, God! It's a sign! I can't even get out of the car! I'm trapped!'

Trapped with Angus! Whether I like it or not!

'Give over.' Ned leaned across her and gave the door lever a special flick with a finger and a thumb. It swung open, with a grating noise as it skimmed the kerb: Iona had parked tightly. 'You should know it does that by now.' He didn't move back and Iona could feel the warmth of his body through his Therapy? T-shirt.

The moment seemed to hang in the air, as similar moments had done at school.

'Good luck,' he said, half upside down, and kissed her cheek.

Iona shut her eyes, hoping that by saying nothing she could quell her conscience without actively discouraging anything else.

There was a rap on the roof of the Mini.

'Ah-ha, ahoy there, Iona!' said a familiar voice. 'And will this be your boyfriend, is it, come to wish you good tidings for your driving test?'

Iona opened her eyes and saw Ron the driving instructor hovering outside the car with a clipboard. It was clear from the expression on his face that he realized he was looking at the explanation for some of her less sophisticated driving tactics. Like driving in the rain without windscreen wipers, because she wasn't used to them. Or revving wildly when starting up to stop the ignition cutting out.

'Er, yes,' she said. The flock of butterflies returned to her chest and a nasty fit of cramming panic hit her. If only she'd done index cards! What were those stupid angles for reverse parking? And Ron was looking very conversationally at Ned – the last thing she wanted to do was spend the next ninety minutes of last-ditch instruction explaining her domestic arrangements when she could be acquiring the secret of reverse-parking in a residential street next to the test centre.

'Lovely!' said Ron. 'Lovely . . . um, old car! I used to have a Mini! Great fun!'

'Yeah, right,' said Ned, and turned to give Iona a final squeeze. 'Give me a call,' he said cheerily. 'I might have to go back to the pub if it gets late, but whatever happens I'll make you a great big cep risotto – if I pick enough.'

Iona got out, suddenly desperate, for the first time *ever*, to start her lesson. 'Don't eat any,' she said warningly as he slid his skinny frame over the gear stick and into the driver's seat. 'You're driving home, remember?'

'Whether she passes or not!' added Ron helpfully. 'Although I'm sure she will! Because if she doesn't, she'll be breaking my run of successful pupils! Forty-nine so far without a fail! Ah ha ha! No pressure, Iona! And I've got my lucky jumper on too!'

'Iona's not failed an exam in her life,' said Ned, starting the car.

Iona fervently hoped the alarm wouldn't go off. Unless it meant Ron could get her some kind of special joker card she could play at the low point of her test.

'See you later, pet!' yelled Ned over the raw sound of the tiny 848cc engine, which was missing on one cylinder, although neither of them knew that. 'I'll be thinking of you!'

'Will you now?' she yelled back. 'Right, Ron, where's the car? I still don't feel happy about reverse-parking.'

'Steady on, Iona!' exclaimed Ron, pretending to hold his hands up in horror. 'Don't tell me you're actually going to get into that car and drive! Heavens above! What's come over you?'

'Fear of failure,' said Iona through gritted teeth. 'All round.'

Friday evening always started at about five at the pub: the lunchtime diners didn't hurry back to their offices the way they did the rest of the week, and since Gabriel was in charge of the kitchen, even after a heated discussion with Angus, there were still only four mains on the board, and seven desserts plus cheese. If anything, the vast array of puddings seemed to be keeping everyone lingering longer than usual.

The atmosphere in the bar had almost reached the relaxed warmth that Angus had always dreamed of creating in the Bunch of Grapes – the light was falling through the stained glass on to the wooden tables in rich shards of colour, a gorgeous smell of melting chocolate and oranges drifted through from the kitchen and there was a gentle buzz of conversation. If it hadn't been for one thing, Angus would have been doing his nearly perfect impression of a Proud Publican. As it was, he stood at the bar with a curdled feeling in his stomach, and watched Gabriel assembling a mixed chocolate plate in the kitchen, dusting it theatrically with icing sugar from a great height, while Tamara waited expectantly at the hatch with her mouth slightly open. It was impossible to say which she found more delicious.

Even more irritating, there were three women in the corner who, he suspected, were of a journalistic persuasion, cooing over the spectacle, no doubt with a view to a cute little piece in a weekend food column or perhaps a co-starring role for Tamara in the forthcoming biopic of Gabriel's glittering career.

'Hurry up, babe!' he heard Tamara breathe in her most kittenish voice.

'Almost there, hon!'

Bleaurgh.

Angus wished he could like Gabriel more, but he just couldn't. He wasn't sure his conscience would allow him to say why, either. It made him feel a little better that Jim obviously felt intimidated by Gabriel (but then Jim's inferiority complex was hardly limited to flashy, lady-killing chefs), and there didn't seem to be much rapport between Gabriel and Rick and Mark, who had had any latent animosity singed out of them in previous kitchens. But much as Angus didn't rate Tamara as a judge of character, there must obviously be something about the guy to reduce a woman like her – a woman who had nearly brought Jim to his knees with her glib disregard – to some kind of dribbling Barbie doll.

Now, now, Angus reasoned with himself, trying to get Iona's moderate tone. There must be lots of reasons to like Gabriel. Not any that sprung immediately to mind, but . . .

Without really being aware of it, Angus narrowed his eyes, as in the kitchen Gabriel shook out his mane of blond hair and tied it back tighter, then extravagantly fired up his flame-thrower to finish off the crema Catalinas for table three. Did he look brilliantly 1972 – or was he just a complete git?

Angus frowned. That was the trouble – he couldn't put his finger on anything about Gabriel. He just seemed to set off a chain reaction of feelings in other people that created an ambience of tension far greater than his relatively minor irritating character flaws.

It was a hard lesson of management, Angus thought, as he swept the bar with a clean J-cloth, that given half a chance he would have sacked Gabriel ages ago, on the grounds that he upset at least 50 per cent of his workforce, and yet even he, whom Gabriel barely bothered to speak to since he wasn't a chef, had to admit that in the kitchen he was something else, and for that reason alone he had to stay.

And that's the reason that this place is working, he thought ruefully: sometimes I seem to be the only one who can tell the difference between working *with* your mates and working *for* your mates.

Angus sighed and got the ullage book out. And now Iona was late. But then he knew she had to get that commission finished soon, so he couldn't be too mad. Might as well get this done for her before the evening rush started. He pulled a big Pimms jug out from the glass washer and started emptying the drip trays into it.

Speckled Hen – quarter of a pint.
Kronenbourg – a pint.
Kronenbourg 2 – a pint.

Angus frowned. That was a lot of spilled lager. Tamara obviously needed another lesson on pulling pints.

Recently, as the novelty of all working together wore off for them and Tamara's lunch breaks got longer, he'd wondered if the rest of them knew how important all this was to him. He only had another three weeks left before his sabbatical ended and he had to go back to work, and although he hadn't mentioned it to Iona, he'd had a couple of letters from the office wanting some details about his return. There was one in his jacket pocket now, wittering on about National Insurance contributions. But he didn't want to go back. He *really* didn't want to go back, and it wasn't just a 'back to school' knee-jerk reaction. Managing the pub had often been harder than the cases he'd been assigned recently, but for the first time in his whole life a real sense of achievement had cancelled out all the exhaustion and the setbacks and the difficult conversations.

The only incentive to return to his desk that Angus could think of – and he'd had to remind himself of it quite hard of late – was the fact that he needed to know his future was secure before he and Iona could get married. He realized how old-fashioned that was, but there was no point them both having unpredictable careers, and she was the talented one, after all; she had to carry on painting.

More to the point, if he left, who would run this place properly? If it was up to Jim, he'd be running it under Tamara's tarot guidance – and no doubt having them all dressing according to their star signs. Which would be funny, if Iona's job, and Ned's job, and Rick and Mark's jobs weren't at stake. If it wasn't making money, Overworld could close the Grapes whenever they wanted to, and Angus couldn't bear the thought of coming in here and seeing everything he'd achieved being lorded over by some new manager, brought in by Jim's bosses and no doubt wearing estate-agent shoes. It was like having a baby and then being forced to give her up for adoption.

Foster's – half a pint.

Guinness – half a pint.

I've got so little time to waste, so little time to work out what the right thing is to do, he thought, and his chest suddenly felt light with trepidation.

It was tiring, constantly having to make decisions, and with this it wasn't as though he could go to Iona and ask her advice. Well, he could, but gentlemanliness forbade him from asking her to make the decision for him, knowing that their relationship rode on it. If it wasn't for Iona . . . he thought, and smiled just thinking about her. But the smile dropped as quickly as it came. Angus knew she worried about the pub, though he actively tried not to dump his concerns on her – she had enough to think about with Marie and all that spreading disaster. And it wouldn't be fair. It was his problem.

'Hurry back, gorgeous,' he heard Gabriel snarl to Tamara as she balanced the finished crema Catalinas, now dusted and decorated with filigree sugar sails, up her arm. She responded with a blown kiss and nearly walked back-wards into table 7, unable to turn round and tear her eyes from him.

Angus thought about yelling something across the bar, but knew with a heavy heart that it would only make him look like a sad, jealous old man, and would more or less guarantee a work rate verging on calcification from Tamara for the rest of the evening.

No wonder Gabriel got his blood pressure up.

The frosted door banged and Marie rushed in and dumped her school-bag on the bar. Her nails were blood red and looked fresh, as though she'd just had a manicure or torn apart a small animal. 'Won't be a second,' she said, panting. 'I just need to have a shower, tidy up a bit first, you know . . .'

Angus looked at her, surprised. 'It's OK, Marie, you don't have to be here until six-thirty. And it's only nearly five.'

'I know.' She pushed the dark curls back off her forehead. 'But you know, I just thought . . .' Her eyes were glancing around the bar. 'I just thought I'd get here early . . .' Her gaze came back to Angus. 'Right. Shower, hair, be down in a minute, OK?'

'OK,' said Angus, 'but don't panic, it's not . . .'

He could hear her thundering up the stairs, two at a time.

Odd.

He checked his watch again in case the wall clock was slow, but it was right. Wishful thinking. Iona had said she'd be here by five-thirty. He'd hoped she'd come over early, so they could be together while it was quiet.

I mean, God, thought Angus, if Tamara and Gabriel are managing to fit a much-documented athletic love-life around the pub, why can't we?

His thoughts slid, as they often did, to the cellar; and the stability of the beer barrels. Iona was pretty flexible, all those yoga classes she used to do with Tamara. And in the beginning, they'd worked their way through every randomly animal-named position, from the Electric Grasshopper to the Resting Snail, in Iona's *New Woman Guide*, and then added some of their own. The Herdwick Sheep, for instance, had been particularly good, if hard on the backs of the legs. In the beginning! What was that, five, six years ago?

Angus assessed the state of the bar. Most people were drinking coffee, and the big rush wouldn't start until the offices finished for the evening. There was time for a quick phone call. He smiled, remembering the calls Iona used to make to the office when things were quiet. And if the call turned a bit saucy, he could always transfer it to the office, since Jim hadn't turned up when he said he would either . . .

Their home number was on speed dial. As it rang, Angus wondered whether she'd taken the portable handset into the shed with her. She'd sounded quite stressed when she'd asked for the afternoon off, so maybe she didn't want any distractions.

The phone carried on ringing, without an answer.

Angus frowned. She could be on her way over. That would be it. He hung up and surveyed the bar, checking for new arrivals. Three more people had arrived on table 21 by the window, arguing about who was getting the drinks in. Possibly media types, since they all had funny glasses. But then Tamara had laboriously pointed out to him that architects wore funny glasses too, and TV people. He had no idea, apparently – and he wasn't arguing with that.

He kept one eye on them and reviewed the staff situation so far tonight. Iona missing, Jim missing, Tamara receiving on one waveband only, Gabriel cooking as if to Madison Square Gardens. And on a positive note, Marie in a weird mood but early, the surprisingly competent Liam due at six-thirty, and Ned on mains for the evening.

It didn't get much better, or much worse, than that

Tonight, thought Angus suddenly. Whatever happens this evening, I'll make my decision about what to do tonight.

Upstairs, her hair in a high whipped-up towel, Marie was staring at all her shoes, which were lined up on their boxes by the window while the new paint on the wardrobe dried. All outfits began with shoes. Before she even started on the big seduction, she still had to get through a bar shift tonight, and it was no good transforming herself into Gina Lollobrigida – however effective that might be to a teenager born well after Elvis died – if the stiletto heels that were so vital to the finished look were trashed by the end of the evening. Or, more to the point, if they trashed her feet so badly Liam had to carry her up the stairs.

Do not let him attempt to pick you up.

Do not let him see your thighs.

Do not let him remove your bra without checking first for rolls of flab.

Do not . . .

Marie shoved all that to one side in her head and turned the stereo up. She was a complete bag of nerves, and had been since at least Wednesday evening. Even finding something to listen to had taken ages in her new state of heightened excitement and guilt (nothing that reminded her of Chris, nothing that made her feel old, nothing semi-recent but released before Liam was born, etc., etc.) until at last she had gone for the Beatles. Who had split up well before either of them were around.

The loud music began to settle her erratic heartbeat and ruthlessly she disqualified footwear with a practised eye. The only shoes she had that she could work in and weren't trainers and didn't look like orthopaedic soles were a pair of black M&S chunky wedges, so used that they didn't even have a box.

So that ruled out delicate florals.

  Good. She didn't have a lot of those anyway. And Liam
probably saw enough of those at college.
  At college. Marie's stomach flipped and a hot flush spread
through her whole body.
  So. Underwear. Marie pulled open a drawer and chewed
her lip. This was a whole etiquette minefield, and one she
hadn't even thought about for . . . ooh, getting on for six
years. Chris preferred 'sensible' underwear since you could
put it all in the wash together. (Theory only.)
  'Stop it!' she said incredulously to the tangle of off-white
knickers. 'I am *appalled*!' How was it *possible* to think so
dispassionately about Chris's laundry failings when she was
about to seduce a young man in the manner of a voracious
adulteress? And above a pub too?
  Actually, the whole thing smacked badly of *EastEnders*
when she thought about it.
  But then the sense memory of Liam's hand reaching down
her jawbone and finding the little hollow beneath her ear
played across her skin and she felt an electric shock tingle
through her whole body. And then the tiniest pressure he
had used to pull her to him . . .
  Who am I fooling, thought Marie, her heart banging
furiously. It isn't me doing the seducing at all. I've never
felt like this in my whole life. She pulled out a purple bra
and matching pants and slammed the drawer shut. Unworn
since being purchased to celebrate her fifth anniversary. She
still had the M&S receipt in a bag.
  Several different permutations of outfit rattled on their
hangers through her head, based on purple underwear and
those shoes and the far from ideal wardrobe situation.
  Dressing for a date was coming back to her, complete
with all its early 1990s nostalgic glory – the thrill, the
mental rehearsal of cute one-liners, the stern limits she
knew she'd override. But now it was vying with guilt,
preventing her from enjoying the preparations, wagging its
finger in a Chris fashion at sparkly body cream or lingering

deep-conditioning treatments. She felt a strange compulsion to sit on a spike or something. Endless tryings-on were definitely out.

It would have to be the old Eddie Cochrane Levi's ad approach, she decided, automatically slathering baby lotion on to her damp skin: Marie had long ago resigned herself to having a vast expanse of skin and now concentrated on making it soft. Nice underwear, old jeans, casual glam. Even if he was in primary school when that advert came out, at least he won't know what a cliché it is.

Her hand stopped on her hip, mid-circle, as a Male/Female Life Insight dawned on her. So *that's* how Mick Jagger gets away with it, she thought.

Marie's stomach rumbled blokeishly and she looked down at it, encased as it was in her tightest jeans. Rumbling wasn't sexy. Lunchtime had been spent waving her hands around at the local beauty parlour, willing the polish to dry, and Marie knew that, unlike other wafer-thin lovelies who simply couldn't contemplate food before a hot date, she *had* to have something to eat before the shift started or she wouldn't make it through.

If only she could get this tense on a permanent basis – her frazzling nerves really seemed to be burning off the calories a treat.

A quick search through the fridge revealed nothing beyond a jar of mayonnaise and some out of date sweetcorn. And a bottle of champagne in the door next to a pint of skimmed milk.

Doh, thought Marie, slamming the fridge shut. You're only living above a pub. Ned'll give you something out of the kitchen. And it's too late to try to be thin now, she thought, suddenly remembering that today was Angus's lemon tart day.

Mmmn, that Friday feeling was starting early.

At five to six, as things were beginning to start getting

Friday-night hectic as opposed to Friday-afternoon busy, Ned turned up at the side door in his scruffy combats and carrying a Tesco's bag full of mushrooms. He looked rather distracted, Angus thought, but he was in the middle of serving Mad Boy Sam and hearing all about his latest plan to rip off an insurance company with the Back Pain that Escaped Diagnosis. Getting away wasn't an option.

Ned disappeared into the kitchen – which Angus was pleased to see, anyway – and the wall phone rang.

'Where there's blame, there's a claim,' Sam was intoning. 'See wha' I mean? And I got evidence, me . . .'

'I'll get it,' said Marie immediately, and shimmered across the bar in a trail of perfume.

What was that on her face, wondered Angus. Apart from all the eyeliner. Panic? Surprise? Marie looked particularly vivid tonight, all red lips and white shirt and black lashes. He looked at the pint he was pouring, and wondered if it was a bad sign that his immediate thought was that she looked like a pint of Guinness. Did he need to get out more?

'Hello, the Bunch of Grapes?' she said brightly. Her expression changed and she turned her shoulder to Angus and faced into the optics. 'Yes, he is, I'll just . . . Where are you? What's . . .'

'Who's that?' asked Angus, handing over Sam's Guinness and leaning backwards to the till with a tenner.

'It's . . . um, someone for Ned. I'll just get him.'

'Oh, very good. He'll be in the middle of getting the service ready. Perfect timing. Who is it? One of his stoned chef mates? Someone with a new consignment of funny toadstools?'

Marie gave him an odd look. 'Um, yes. Yes, it is. Ned!' she yelled.

Angus widened his eyes. 'He isn't going to hear you from here, is he?'

'Ned!' yelled Marie, a bit louder, clutching the phone to her chest.

Angus shrugged his shoulders.

'And I reckon I can make enough out of that 'earing impediment inflicted on me when the council 'ad the road up ahtside 'ere to 'ave an 'oliday this year, know wha' I mean?' Sam grimaced knowingly and tapped his left ear.

'Have you heard of gurning, Sam?' asked Angus. 'Because you could be a natural.'

'Well, aren't you going to get Ned?' Marie demanded.

'No, as you can see, there are three people waiting at the bar for me to offer them drinks,' he said patiently. 'And Sam here is explaining how I can make a fortune from selective deafness.'

Marie looked down at the phone nestling in her cleavage and then towards the kitchen end of the pub, deliberated and then roared, 'NED!' at a playground-clearing volume.

Everyone at the bar apart from Sam winced.

Ned came rushing out of the kitchen with a towel over one shoulder and a potato masher in his left hand. 'Who is it?' he asked.

Marie turned her shoulder on Angus and rolled her eyes back towards him.

'Oh, fuck,' said Ned. 'Look,' he muttered, 'can you distract him or something for a moment?'

'What's going on?' Marie hissed.

'Later,' hissed Ned. 'Just get rid of him.'

She frowned. 'If this is anything dodgy . . .' Her face darkened. 'If this is *anything* to do with those mushrooms in the kitchen . . .'

'Oh, give over, will you? And get shot of Angus for ten seconds.' Ned gave her his best pleading eyes, the ones that had once turned Tamara to water on the rare occasions that she had intercepted them turned on someone else.

'You'd better tell me later,' said Marie in a low voice. 'Angus? Angus, sweetie, can you check the bitter's on properly? It won't stop frothing. Oh, cheers. Who were you serving? OK . . .'

It faintly occurred to Ned that Marie wasn't being as interrogative as normal, but as soon as he heard the cellar door being opened, he walked as far away as the phone cord would stretch from the bar and checked all round for Gabriel or Tamara listening in.

'Iona! What's happened? I thought you'd gone. I came round to the place and waited for half an hour, but the receptionist body said you must have gone already.'

'Oh, God, Ned.' Iona's voice sounded very small and scared.

'Well?' Ned didn't like to ask if she'd passed or not. It sounded as though that wasn't even relevant any more.

'Iona, pet, where are you?'

'Dulwich Hospital.'

'What?!' Ned looked up as Tamara went past, clutching the menu he'd knocked out in three minutes flat on the back of a vegetable invoice, a bucket of Coke to wipe the board and the pint glass of wet chalk to write it up.

'Ned, just come and get me, please.'

'I'm coming now, pet. Don't worry. I'm on my way.'

'Ned!'

Ned just caught her panicky yell before he hung up. 'What?'

'If Angus goes mad, I'll take the blame, I don't want you to—'

'Iona, shut up and get yourself a cup of sweet tea, OK?'

Ned slammed the phone down just as Angus emerged from the cellar and slipped back into the kitchen before he could say anything.

'Marie, do you *know* how to change the barrels?' Angus asked. 'Because there was nothing wrong with that. You just have to let the first few pints run through – they're bound to be a bit frothy, because . . . Look, it might be easier if I explain. The first pints you pull on a new barrel of beer will be full of air and therefore frothy because you've let out the gas in the . . .'

Marie carried on pulling her pint of cider and kept nodding, as out of the corner of her eye she saw Ned leave by the side door, pulling his manky fleece on as he went. She must have glazed, because Angus suddenly stopped, mid-demonstration, and stared at the swinging door.

'Oh, my God, he does *not* change!' Angus yelled furiously. 'Was that Ned disappearing? Was it?'

Marie nodded reluctantly and Angus spun round 360 degrees on his heel in a fit of impotent rage. First Gabriel bunking off, now Ned. At home he would have found something to hurl across the room – a remote control, his mobile – anything to release some of the sudden charge of anger. Here there was nothing and he knew he was in severe danger of punching someone, particularly without Iona here to soothe the anger away.

'Fucking hell!' he spat instead. 'Just when I thought he was *finally* getting reliable! Doesn't he *care* that we're about to start service in a few minutes? Does he have *any* idea about responsibility? Jesus Christ, I should . . .' Angus grabbed a lemon from the fruit tray and crushed it in his hands.

'Ang, calm down,' said Marie, flashing an apologetic smile at the startled punters around the bar. 'I'm sure he's just popping out for a quick . . . Um, well, he knows service is about to start, so he's not going to be going far, is he? And he's done the menu and the other three are in the kitchen.'

'That's not the *point*,' bellowed Angus, hurling the lemon into the sink. It pulped even more on impact.

Marie was shocked, not as much by the sudden rush of rage, which Angus often spewed out without warning, but by the strange note of distress in his voice.

'I'm *relying* on him! We all are! What's the point of doing anything like this if you can't *rely* on people to do what they say? I'm fucking *sick* of . . .' He stopped, his big hands splayed on the bar.

Hands that could cradle you or throttle you. Iona's big bear. Marie shivered.

'Look, Marie,' he went on more quietly, 'I'm worried that if . . .' He looked up and stopped himself again. 'I'm just worried, OK? It really matters to me that we do things properly here.'

No one took a shrieking publican seriously. He'd read that in *Caterer* magazine. This wasn't looking good. Angus shut his eyes and tried to will his pumping blood pressure back down. He visualzed a white room, a cool spring, all the rubbish they'd been taught by the HR manager in last year's staff relaxation training.

But whether he meant to or not, Ned – *Ned*, for whose benefit all this had been started – had just put a great big *Family Fortunes* cross on the 'Give it up and go back to proper job' side of the score sheet.

Marie stroked his arm. He was trembling. 'There's no need to get so stressed, Angus. Gabriel can cope fine. Just go outside and have a walk around the block. Get a breath of fresh air and come in again, OK?' She looked at him closely. 'You've been here too much lately, you know? You *are* allowed to give yourself time off. We can manage.'

Angus smiled weakly. Marie might be free with her opinions, but she didn't take things personally. Maybe it was dealing with small children that made her impervious to temper tantrums. She wasn't soothing in the instinctive way that Iona seemed to siphon away his tension with her fingertips, but Marie could put things in perspective, and that was a real gift.

'I will,' he said. 'Be back in a moment.'

Marie smiled and would have said more, but at that moment Liam pushed open the door and came in and her entire internal structure melted down to her feet.

'Hiya!' he said, shrugging off his jacket and walking round to the other side of the bar.

'Great,' said Angus, as cheerfully as he could manage. 'Two competent pairs of hands. Back in a tick.'

'Good evening, Marie,' said Liam. 'You look gorgeous,' he added in a lower tone.

Immediately, Marie forgot how to be cool. She felt about fourteen years old – which seemed appropriate. But she did feel beautiful, now he'd pointed it out, as though she'd been touched by a wand that had made her all sparkling.

'Um, thank you,' she mumbled.

'My pleasure,' he said, and gave her a smile that sent an electric shock through her entire melted body.

Outside, Angus stalked as fast as he could all the way down one side of the road, filling up his lungs with the cooler night air and listening to the sounds of Friday night cranking up on Ladbroke Grove, trying to walk the tension out of his muscles.

Marie was right, they could cope. It would be fine. He put a big mental tick on the opposite side of the score sheet: Marie. She was great, wasn't she? Sensible, capable and reliable. Apart from all the stuff with Chris. Angus frowned and lengthened his stride to step over some abandoned lettuce from an early kebab. Marie seemed fine, but then she'd been all over the place that night she'd come round to tell Iona. A hot blush prickled his neck.

But the legal side could all be sorted out easily enough, if divorce was what she decided. No kids, no house, no assets. Angus huffed down his nose. What sort of husband had that arse Chris been, after all? Shouldn't be too much of a wrangle, not with a decent solicitor. Hugh – what was his name? Played rugby. Welsh. Hugh . . . Pritchard, yes – from law school was a family law specialist. He could put Marie on to Hugh.

Angus crossed the road, feeling better already at the thought of having sorted something out, and strode back to the pub. As he went past the side entrance to the kitchen, the rattle of the dustbins made him stop in his tracks and swing round to investigate. If it was rats, he'd have to explain about the Health and Safety to Ned *again*, and if it was junkies using his alley for nefarious purposes . . .

'Oi!' he yelled, stomping towards the bins. There was a scuffle and, to his horror, in the yellowy streetlight, Angus caught a flash of a skinny pair of buttocks, before the owner could hoist their jeans up again, and the muffled squeal of whatever, whoever, had been beneath them.

'What the fuck is going on here?' he roared.

'Well, kinda answered your own question, mate,' said a familiar voice.

'Oh, my God,' said Angus, barely able to decide which emotion to go for first. He clenched and unclenched his fists.

'Angus, it's not what . . .' began Tamara, or at least Angus assumed it was Tamara. He stared at the brickwork gallantly while they adjusted their clothes. Gabriel, naturally, was taking his time.

Christ, anyone would think he was enjoying this, marvelled Angus.

'So you're telling me that *no one* is in the kitchen now,' he said to the wall, deciding to start with the factual before moving into more treacherous waters of rage.

Gabriel came out of the shadows with a mean yet smug look on his face, his golden mane of hair all dishevelled and his shirt open four buttons.

Very Robert Plant.

If only Iona were here.

Angus shook himself. 'I can't *believe* you could be so *irresponsible*!' he yelled. 'Halfway through service and—'

'Angus, will you give it a fucking rest?' Gabriel began in a belligerent tone. 'So Tamara and I were—'

'I really, *really* don't want to *know* what you and Tamara were doing!' Angus roared. 'Now get back in the kitchen before I say something you'll regret making me say!'

He spun on his heel and stormed back in through the swinging doors.

At the bar, Liam and Marie broke off a suspiciously intimate tête-à-tête and started polishing clean glasses furiously.

Jesus, I'm seeing it *everywhere* now, thought Angus. His pulse was racing with embarrassment and anger. They're all at it and I'm working so hard to keep everything together that . . . Maybe it *would* be better to kick all this into touch and get back to work. At least he never had to interrupt either of the group secretaries having sex in the photocopying room whenever he needed a fax sent. And he might have more conscious time with Iona.

'Angus, are you all right?' asked Marie, concerned.

'Oh, *Gabriel*,' Angus spat. 'And *Tamara*. In the back alley, like a couple of . . .' He screwed up his face to stop himself scaring the customers further.

'Eurgh,' said Marie. 'Not nice.'

'I will *not* have shagging on these premises,' spluttered Angus. 'What do they think this is, some kind of dating agency? Or some kind of *knocking* shop?'

Marie gurgled something and rushed off to the other side of the bar.

'That really isn't like Tamara,' said Liam. 'She's always been so fussy about her clothes, apart from anything.'

Angus gave Liam a close look and made a mental note that childhood friends of Tamara's brother could be very useful character witnesses later on.

At seven, with the table order list full and four people down on the waiting list, Ned returned with Iona. He had thrown an old jacket over her shoulders and shepherded her into the office as if he were shielding her from a hostile press pack.

Angus, mid-Bloody Mary, saw Ned's back apparently sneaking through the side door and dropped the Tabasco sauce in the sink. The delicate equilibrium he'd managed to achieve since breaking up the in-house floor show disappeared like froth off a Foster's and his blood pressure rose again.

'One moment,' he said to the startled customer and hurried through. He could taste the coffees he'd knocked back in the interim burning in his empty stomach with tension.

'Where the hell have you been?' he demanded, once he was within three metres of the office door, anxious to get as much in as possible before Ned could retaliate. 'If you weren't my mate, and you weren't Iona's best friend, I would . . .' He trailed off when he saw Iona slumped behind the desk, Ned holding her head between her legs in the faint recovery position. At least he hoped that was what was going on.

Could tonight get worse?

'Iona?' Angus came closer and saw with a shock of protectiveness that her brown hair had fallen out of the plaits he'd watched her tie while they drove into work, and was madly wispy around her neck where she had parted it. Her skin looked very white.

Ned looked up and his normally amused face was angry and worried. 'What?' he demanded. His northern accent was stronger than ever and turned the word into a spit.

'What's going on?' Angus rushed over and put his arms around Iona. 'Iona, what's happened? Are you OK? Has there been a burglary? Have you had an accident? Darling. I won't be mad, just tell me what . . .' He smoothed the skin around her eyebrows with his thumbs, but there was no response apart from faint moaning and anxiously he looked up at Ned. 'Has she been attacked? Ned, what's going on? She's been at home all afternoon, painting . . hasn't she?'

Ned crouched down to Iona's level. 'Iona, do you want me to tell him?'

She nodded.

'Tell me what?'

Ned straightened up and looked Angus in the eye. 'She had her driving test this afternoon. That's where she's been but . . .'

'Iona!' Angus sounded crushed. 'Oh no! Why didn't you tell me? I could have . . .'

Both men looked at each other above her head and decided not to pursue that line of conversation. Angus flushed angrily. Why hadn't she told him? He felt hurt and somehow ashamed, in front of Ned, who was now kneeling and looking up into her face, which she was covering with her hands.

'Iona, please talk to me, will you? You've got to tell us what's happened, pet. Why were you at the hospital?'

'*Hospital!*' repeated Angus incredulously. 'Oh, my God . . . Ned, is that where you've been?'

He nodded without turning round.

'Oh, for Christ's sake!' Angus exploded. 'Why didn't you *tell* me? *How* could you not tell me? I'm her boyfriend!'

Angus sounded close to tears, and Iona pulled her hands away from her face and said, 'I'm not hurt or anything, it was . . .' but a wave of hiccuping sobs broke up her voice before she could say more.

Angus and Ned both rushed to wrap her up in their arms. It was awkward, but neither wanted to give way, dangerously close as it was to hugging each other for Angus's liking. Iona leaned back against them and cried her eyes out.

After about five minutes of Angus stroking her back in a circle and Ned squeezing her hand, she managed to get the hiccups under control. 'I've had . . . a bit of a shock,' she said carefully.

'Brandy,' said Ned immediately. 'I'll get you a brandy.'

He sprang up and Angus said, 'Don't bother with the bottle on the bar. There's some proper stuff in the filing cabinet, bottom drawer, underneath the till rolls. Jim was slipped it by some contractor as a bribe. Said he's always felt too guilty to drink it.'

Ned yanked open the drawer, found the brandy and said, 'Mmn, nice,' as he examined the label.

Angus gripped Iona's hands in his. 'Iona,' he said in a low voice, 'sweetie-loo, why didn't you tell me about your driving test? I wanted to *help* you. We could have practised together. I would have given you all of today off to practise. I'd have *closed the pub* if we'd had to.'

Iona looked up at him and her eyes were brimming with tears. Angus felt as if he'd been punched in the stomach.

'I didn't want to let you do-o-o-o-o-own . . .' she said and put her hand over her mouth as the hiccups started again.

'Here, drink this.' Ned offered her an inch of brandy in a wine glass and she sipped at it tentatively while they both watched. The pathetic impression of deflated tinyness was rather undercut by Iona's stomach giving out a huge gastric rumble.

She tried a feeble smile. 'Haven't eaten since last night. I'm starving.'

Angus stood up, galvanized by being able to do something. 'Excellent. I know *exactly* what you would love. I've got your favourite thing right here in the fridge.'

'Lemon tart?' Iona's face brightened up from death to deathly pale.

'Yup. And Gabriel's done some fancy cream for his compotes . . .' Angus experienced a wave of revulsion for the fornicating Gabriel, but couldn't bear thinking about it. And didn't want to think about his tiny shiny arse either.

'Will I get it?' offered Ned.

'No, it's OK, I'll go,' said Angus firmly. 'My tart and all that. Back in a moment.'

Iona listened to him thundering through to the kitchen, brushing aside Gabriel's vocal protests about eating food off the menu. She shut her ears. She didn't want to hear a row. But then the last thing she ever wanted to hear was silence. Tears came welling back up her throat.

'Iona?'

She focused on Ned. He looked really worried and Iona's heart reached out to him. She could almost see it, stretching perfidiously out of her chest, beckoning to him. It made her feel ill on a whole new level and she shut her eyes again.

'Iona, will you tell me what happened?' Listening to his voice, he could still be eighteen. It hadn't changed; London hadn't rounded down his vowels as it had hers. Hadn't begun to lay a tissue of someone else over his voice.

She shook her head. 'Can't. Still too-oo-oo-oo . . .'

And then Angus was back. Or rather, she opened her eyes and saw one of the huge white dessert plates in front of her, with a large slice of butter-yellow lemon tart in the centre, about twice the serving size, surrounded by a pool of thick cream and brûléed to a deep caramel gold on the top.

Despite herself, Iona's mouth watered in anticipation of the tangy, thick sweetness. She very much wanted her head to be full of the flavour, and nothing else.

Angus handed her a fork and she cut off the pointy end of the slice, dipped it in the cream and popped it into her mouth before it could drip. She shut her eyes as her taste buds started to ripple around her tongue in a celebratory Mexican wave. Angus's lemon tart was superb, a structural triumph: light and rich at the same time; lemon-sharp and egg-velvety. Comforting beyond words.

Better than tranquillizers. Better than sex.

She opened her eyes and smiled at the pair of concerned faces staring at her like a prize heifer in a pen.

'Is it OK?' asked Angus anxiously. 'I tried a slight variation this week with different lemons and more egg yolk and—'

''S fine,' said Iona, shovelling more in. ''S lovely.'

'Can I have a taste?' asked Ned.

'Please do.' Angus looked on anxiously as Ned forked off a large mouthful. 'Tell me what you think about the sweetness.'

'Mmm!' mumbled Ned, with his mouth full. ''S *very* good, this.' He gave him a thumbs up. ''S excellent. Can I have a bit more, Iona?'

When they'd finished the entire helping (about four minutes), Iona wiped her mouth and drank half of the remaining brandy. Then she took a deep breath.

'What happened?' said Angus tenderly.

Being asked the direct question immediately conjured up an instinctive refusal to tell him, but Iona forced herself.

'I had the driving lesson as planned,' she began with a shudder, 'and it went all right to start with – I did a couple of reverse-parks that were better than normal, and then we drove to near the test centre and I did a turn in the road . . .' Iona swallowed but made herself go on. 'I did a turn in the road so bad that I mounted the pavement on both sides. And I nearly hit a woman with a pram because I was concentrating so hard on getting the handbrake on in time. And usually I'm really *good* at turns in the road, aren't I?'

She looked up at Angus and Ned for reassurance and they both nodded sympathetically. Angus temporarily forgot the 'hospital' element of the story and began to relax slightly. If she was just going to say that she failed on three-point turns . . .

Iona took another sip of brandy and went on. 'Anyway, we went and signed in and I got the examiner that Ron didn't like, which was a really bad start. Mr King. Apparently, when Ron first started here Mr King had to take Colin in the car with him for his initial assessment and he made a mess, which he couldn't help, because Ron hadn't trained Colin to go in cars at this stage and . . .'

'Iona, love, you're doing a real-time anecdote,' said Ned gently.

'Who's Colin?' demanded Angus.

'Oh, er, yes, OK, well, anyway, Mr King . . .' Iona looked flustered and swilled the brandy round, trying to get her train of thought back.

'His dog,' muttered Ned.

'Oh,' murmured Angus. 'That's OK then . . . I just thought maybe . . . Deep breaths, Iona. Good girl.'

'So we drove off,' said Iona firmly, ignoring the sheepdog tone in Angus's voice, 'and he made me reverse into a parking bay first time off and I'd never done that before, but I had a go, and *just* managed to park it *exactly* on the line, which he couldn't fail me on, but I could tell he had it in for me from then. He made me go round all the narrowest streets, the ones with double parking and speed humps, and the one with two schools on it, and then, then he made me go back to the street where I'd done that appalling turn in the road . . .'

She looked up for some more support and got a round of nods and sympathetic eyes.

'Is there some EU regulation about calling them a three-point turn now?' asked Angus conversationally, trying to ease some of the tension Iona was building up for herself. As if he would be mad at her for failing on a manoeuvre. OK, so it was a bit disappointing, but not as if she'd run someone over . . .

Ned was looking closely at her and squeezing her hand.

'Go on, pet,' he said.

'I suppose it was my own fault for not checking my blind spots,' said Iona, 'but I went forward, very slowly on clutch control, and put it on full lock, then handbrake, into reverse, clutch up, full lock . . . Anyway . . .' She saw Ned glaze slightly and shook herself. She was getting as bad as Angus. 'Anyway, I did three points and couldn't get round because there was a bad camber on the road, and so I did another two, and I thought Mr King had gone very quiet, but examiners do that, apparently, and I just turned round to apologize, like you said, Angus, to be nice, and I noticed that . . .' Iona clapped a hand to her mouth. She felt really sick all of a sudden.

'And?' said Ned and Angus simultaneously.

'And his eyes had gone all rolly in his head and he'd turned bright red!' she wailed. 'I thought he might be having a heart-attack, so . . .'

'Fuck!' breathed Angus, caught unawares.

' . . . so I tried to remember where I'd seen a hospital this morning, and I was driving round and round, and no one seemed to notice that he was having some kind of fit, and . . .'

'Iona, why didn't you stop and ask for help?'

'Aauuuuuggggh!' she wailed angrily. 'What would *you* do if your examiner had a heart-attack on your test? Ask him to direct you to the nearest A&E? I wasn't *thinking* straight! It was my *driving* test! I didn't want to stop in case he only had minutes to live and all I could think about was keeping to the fucking speed limit in case I got driver points because you're only allowed fifteen before you fail automatically and I was sure I had about ten already!'

'It's OK, now, pigeon,' said Ned, stroking her hand. He shot a cross glare at Angus. 'So you got him to a hospital all right then?'

'Eventually,' Iona said. Her hiccups were coming back and were now threatening to follow through. 'I couldn't remember how to park in the bays though and I'd had three goes at getting the car straight before a couple of nurses came past and saw him in the passenger seat. They had to carry him in, because he'd gone all rigid.' Her eyes misted up. 'They couldn't get his clipboard out of his hands, and I couldn't even see whether I'd failed or not.'

It occurred to Angus that she could probably have ticked the relevant boxes herself while they were winching the unfortunate Mr King out of the dual controls, but some automatic censoring device *just* prevented him from letting it slip out.

'But I came back to the driving school to fetch you home and you weren't there,' said Ned. 'I was really worried and the nasty old cow at reception wouldn't tell me what was going on. I thought maybe you'd come back here.'

Angus's face twitched in recognition as it all fell into

place. So *that's* why Ned had been looking so distracted. But it should have been him! He should have been waiting outside the driving school for her. And instead he'd been here, breaking up Last Tango in the Back Alley.

He hugged her guiltily. Poor little Iona. What a nightmare! 'All over now, all over,' he soothed into her hair. 'You were so *brave*, sweetheart!' he said, releasing her enough to see her tear-stained face. 'I'm so proud of you. You did so well. And they must have passed you for that, surely? Saving the life of a driving examiner?'

Iona sniffed and wiped her dripping nose on her T-shirt. 'No, the bastards. Not even that. I phoned the test centre from the hospital to let them know what had happened and they told me . . .' Her face crinkled up in a mixture of rage and misery. 'I got this complete jobsworth who told me that the test was invalid because I hadn't completed all the components under supervision!'

'Get out!' said Ned.

'And that I'd been driving without a qualified supervisor for most of my test . . . I could be arrested for that!' she wailed.

'Oh, *very* good!' said Angus, leaping to his feet and scrabbling for the phone on the desk. His face was white with fury. 'Where's the number? Where's the number for the test centre? Is it in your handbag? Iona? Where is it?'

'Angus, don't,' said Iona, between hiccups. 'There's no point.'

'Yes, there is! They can't get away with this! Bunch of fucking idiots! You saved that man's life!' He broke off. 'You did get him there in time, didn't you? I mean, he will live?'

Iona dissolved into loud tears.

Ned got up and prised the phone out of Angus's hand. 'Calm down, Angus man,' he said. 'You'll get nothing done now, will you? It's nearly eight o'clock. There'll not be anyone there on a Friday night. We'll phone them in the morning, and—'

He broke off as Iona started to make funny noises.

'Bucket!' she managed, her hands over her mouth.

Ned just shoved the wastepaper basket under her as she threw up noisily into it.

'Upstairs,' Angus decided as liquidized lemon tart hit discarded fliers for pub furniture. 'Why don't I take you upstairs and you can have a lie-down in Marie's flat? You've had a terrible shock and it's far too noisy down here.'

Iona nodded weakly.

'Very good,' he said, stroking her back in a circle like a baby. 'Right. Ned, I think Rick's started doing the mains, but I'd be grateful if you could go and salvage something from the jaws of chaos.'

'Fine.'

'And don't talk to that arse Gabriel.' Angus flinched at his own choice of words. 'I think he's finally gone too far this time.'

Ned raised his eyebrows curiously, but Angus shook his head. 'Tell you later. I'll get this one somewhere quiet first and then . . . Come on, sweetheart,' he said, helping her to her feet as she wobbled, Bambi-like, to the door, still clutching the wastepaper basket.

Angus followed behind as Iona carefully climbed the stairs to Marie's flat, noticing how dramatically a few well-placed framed postcards of red gerberas could lift a boring expanse of flaking wall. Maybe Jim should be hiring Marie to do up student flats for him. They could make a fortune.

'Hang on, I've got a key,' he said when they reached the top.

Iona gave him a quizzical look. 'Should you have?'

'Why not? What if there was a fire or something? I've got keys to everything. Marie won't mind you lying down for five minutes.'

Iona shrugged and he unlocked the door, pushing it open for her to go in first. She went straight through to the bedroom, grabbing a duvet-protecting towel from the bathroom as she went. Her stomach still felt weird.

The whole flat, once mildewy and dank, now smelled of Marie: fresh paint, hot recent baths, lots of perfume, and an undefinable smell of other people's children. When Iona's eyes adjusted to the low light in the bedroom, she was impressed by how tidy it was by Marie's normal standards. The walls were a deep blue, with full-length blue curtains, and there were no clothes on the floor. Although there was a rather spooky line of shoes by the window. The effect was somewhere between the Three Bears and the Seven Snow Whites.

'Take your shoes off, sweetie-loo,' said Angus, bending to undo the zips on her boots. He did a small double take. Surely she hadn't attempted her driving test in a pair of boots Stevie Nicks would have passed on as being too clumpy?

Iona sat down on the double bed and immediately felt like passing out. She had no idea how drained she was until she felt the sinkiness of Marie's brand-new double divan.

Angus pulled off her boots and swung her legs up on to the duvet. Iona felt as if she was dropping like a stone in a well, all the way through it. Her mind was full of nothing.

He leaned over her and smoothed the hair off her face. She looked so small and tired and beautiful. And zomboid. 'I'll come up and check on you later,' he whispered and kissed her forehead. It was damp. 'Look, there's some water by the bed here for you. I'll leave a glass here, by your arm.' Fortuitously, Marie had left a whole bottle of Malvern Spring by the bedside and a box of tissues. Angus used one to mop Iona's brow and, as an afterthought, picked up her bag and looked through it.

As he'd guessed, she was carrying *Led Zeppelin IV* around with her, so he put it on Marie's bedside stereo, very quietly, and crept out.

*

Downstairs, the atmosphere hadn't got much better but the general volume had got much louder. The pub was now full and when Angus checked the food order list, to his annoyance only the first four tables had been crossed off. He looked around the bar for Tamara, who was meant to be in charge of the floor tonight. She was talking animatedly to the group in the far corner he'd spotted earlier, waving her arms around and doing ridiculously exaggerated laughs.

If they didn't get everyone's order into the kitchen by eight-thirty, the food would be delayed and he knew there'd be a riot. Speed of service was the only area he knew they really had to sort out, and Tamara was demonstrating to the very people who would write sarky reviews about it exactly why it was so slack.

Angus checked the list, ignored Sam's demand for the name of a good legal aid firm, took orders from the next two tables and went through to the kitchen to see what was going on.

Normally at this time of night the kitchen was a mess of shouted orders, and jokes, and banging and scraping, but tonight all was terse, one-word orders, no laughing, no conversations, no teasing. Ned was flipping rainbow trout on the big griddle, sending up plumes of steam and flavour, while swigging from a pint glass of orange juice. Rick and Mark, unusually silent, were frantically constructing the warm salad starters, slicing up tiny shreds of glossy liver and deep black trumpets of death as if they were under a time limit. Gabriel, predictably, was looking mutinously into a deep bowl of cream as he slashed away with a whisk. Even the washing-up lad was concentrating on not breaking things.

Wearily, Angus slipped the orders on to the little pulley and went back out to take the rest.

'Liam, can you do another pint of orange juice for Ned, please?' said Marie as Liam came up from the cellar with a crate of waters. She was in the middle of a split-second-timed round of two lagers, a bitter and a Guinness all on adjacent taps.

'Another one? How many's he had now?'

'Four? Five? It can get really hot in there, and he's always drunk like a fish. It's why his skin is surprisingly good, despite his best pharmaceutical efforts otherwise.' Marie flicked off all the taps in a row, leaving the Guinness two-thirds full. 'Cheers,' she said, taking the proffered note, and rang the drinks through the till. By the time she'd done the change, the Guinness was perfectly settled for topping up.

'I love the way you do that,' said Liam admiringly. 'You've really got a knack for it.'

Marie squirmed pleasurably. When had she got so disused to compliments that the merest hint of praise made her feel so pathetically special?

'And timing like that is very sexy,' he added, dropping his voice. 'It sort of makes you wonder what else you're good at managing. Timing wise.'

Marie ignored the grating use of 'timing wise' and put it down to youth. 'Liam, do you make a habit of chatting up elderly women in pubs?'

He laughed at her. 'No, and you're not elderly.'

'I am married.'

'Er, yeah . . .' said Liam sarcastically. He looked around the pub in a significant manner and returned his penetrating gaze to her. 'To a man so stupid as to leave you here and piss off to suit himself.'

Well, that much was true, thought Marie. Can't argue there.

'You must have a really low opinion of me, if you think that,' he went on. 'I mean, if I did have a thing about older women, I'd have gone for Tamara years ago, wouldn't I?'

Marie was forced to agree that that would have been the most obvious first choice.

'I haven't felt like this about anyone before, honestly. It's so weird. Like a chemical thing.' He looked at her, and for a moment Marie wasn't aware of anything else at all in the room. There were so many different exciting things to take in at once right in front of her; the length of his dark lashes framing the eyes, the faint hollow at the open neck of his shirt, the musky smell of his aftershave, the hammering of her blood through her veins.

Then it dawned on her what he'd just said and she sniggered out loud.

To his credit, Liam laughed too and pulled a face. 'But it's true.'

'Very good,' said Angus's voice, and she swung round.

He clattered two handfuls of pint glasses on the bar. 'Oi, this is a bar, not bloody *Give Us a Clue*. If you look behind you, you'll notice that there are no pints left. Can one of you please go round and collect some glasses? If it's not too inconvenient? Sorry, sorry, sorry,' he held up his hands. 'Sorry, I'm not shouting, I'm not shouting, I'm just getting a bit worried about the kitchen and the staff we seem to be losing by the hour and . . .' Angus wandered off, still muttering to himself.

'He isn't always like this,' said Marie. 'Well, he is, but he's got a lot on his mind at the moment.'

'Haven't we all,' murmured Liam in her ear. His hand strayed to the small of her back – as luck would have it, the only cellulite-free area of her body – and stroked gently.

Marie marvelled at the fact that Liam could say the kind of things that would normally have her wriggling and shrieking with embarrassment, and yet when he said them they seemed unfeasibly sexy.

Get a hold of yourself, woman, yelled a voice in her head.

But then it followed up badly with a mental image of Liam

getting hold of her instead and she leaned against the bar for support.

They circled each other for about an hour while the bar was busy, brushing past to get to the till, quick gropes beneath bar level, and then at around nine Liam approached her from behind while she was laboriously setting up a table tab on the till.

'Marie, I don't know if I can wait until later on,' he muttered in her ear.

She could only squeak in response, since he was pressing very close to her and, from what she could feel through her jeans, was backing up his words with visual aids.

Marie closed her eyes and gave in to the wave of appalling lust that swept through her, closely followed by a sickening feeling of guilt. No amount of stern internal talkings-to could override the fact that she was desperately, desperately keen to go upstairs with him and let him do exactly what he liked with her, and she didn't feel a single qualm about it.

'It's very quiet at the moment,' Liam went on persuasively.

Well, that was true. It did seem to go quiet around now.

'We could just slip upstairs for five minutes and I could, sort of, um . . .' And he muttered something she couldn't quite catch but knew by the response in her jeans that it was something pretty dirty and inviting.

Oh, my God! He actually wants to have sex with me twice!

No, said Marie to herself. No, he is too young, you are too married, you are both risking being sacked by Angus the Boss from Hell . . .

'OK,' she murmured. Was that her voice? Or had her jeans now found a way of speaking independently? 'Quick, and we have got to be back down here by ten past or Angus will kill us both.'

Liam pressed a swift kiss into the back of her neck,

finding a tender, thrilling place that Chris hadn't stumbled on in five years, and turned round. 'Sorry, mate,' she heard him say to the punter at the bar, 'cider's off. Won't be a minute.'

Then she heard him lift the counter partition and then open the side door up to the flats.

Marie's heart raced. She hadn't done this since she was a student and it was more thrilling than anything she could remember. It didn't matter that he was gauche, and that she didn't think she could sustain an entire conversation with him without giggling or feeling about ninety; he was gorgeous and he wanted her. It felt so exciting that she could barely correlate it with her usual real life – maybe that was why her normally over-active conscience was giving her permission to do all this.

Or maybe her jeans had not only found a voice but had started stun-gunning dissident bits of her while they marched their way to total control of her body.

Whatever.

She checked her reflection in the mirror behind the optics: lips still red all over and not just on lip outline, eyeliner still smudge-free, hair still bouncy, cheeks flushed in attractive 'Catch me on the haystack, honey!' Jane Russell fashion. Not much more she could do.

Marie twitched her top for maximum cleavage value and slipped out from behind the bar.

Liam was waiting for her on the stairs, leaning on the wall with one long leg up on the banister to stop her getting past. Marie barely had time to notice the toned county-rugby stomach muscles this revealed before he pulled her into a passionate kiss, tangling his fingers through her hair with one hand and running the other one down her back and into her purple knickers.

He was just as good as she remembered, and she'd been remembering a lot, and with increasing suspicion that her memory had to be playing tricks on her.

Woooah! thought Marie, feeling her jeans respond enthusiastically to Liam's strong fingers. Fan-taaas-tic! So this is why all those older men go for younger models!

But something was churning in her stomach, and she thought she knew what it was.

Her conscience was starting to fight back. Not alas, her wedding vows, but her deeply rooted sense of guilt.

Liam broke off and pushed the dark curls out of his eyes. He was breathing heavily and his distended pupils made his eyes almost completely black. 'Upstairs,' he said thickly. 'Now.'

'You first,' said Marie, for the first time not thinking about the unflattering angle it would give her own arse – only because she wanted to see Liam's firm Levi'd behind going upstairs. She felt totally giddy, not just from the voice in her head yelling at her jeans, but also because, on a more practical level, she'd only consumed a large slice of lemon tart and about nine coffees since last night's supper.

'No, you.'

'Tick, tock, tick, tock,' said Marie, waving her watch at him.

'Fine.' Liam grabbed her in a fireman's lift and staggered up the stairs with her.

Marie could barely contain herself with excitement. A man so lithe and yet so strong and yet so gallant not to have mentioned the crippling weight!

Being turned upside down didn't help the dizzy feeling pounding through her head, and under normal circumstances she would have sloped off for a quick nap with her eye-mask on.

'Oooh, Liam,' she said, holding a banister for support as he put her down. 'I think I'm going to have to—'

'Lie down?' he finished for her, with a gorgeously raised James Bond eyebrow, and as she let out a tiny involuntary groan of lust, he started kissing her neck again, finding all the points that made her shiver with acute pleasure. Where had he learned all this? Did they do A-levels in professional seduction these days?

The tension building in her head was now so bad that, to her horror, Marie could feel a migraine coming on.

Jesus Christ, of all the times!

'Come in,' she panted, fiddling with the keys, 'my bedroom's just through here. First door on the right.' She pushed the front door open and they stumbled in, kissing hungrily at each other. Liam already had her T-shirt out of her jeans and was pulling at the button fly, running his fingers up and down her trembling stomach.

That's funny, thought Marie, in between yanking at Liam's shirt and tasting the deliciously salty skin on his neck, did I leave the CD player on?

'Now. Here,' groaned Liam, and pushed her against the nearest door, fumbling with his jeans.

Marie just had time to arrange herself into a seductive jeans-half-down, T-shirt off, look at my curves, position before he grabbed her by the waist and the combined weight of them sent the door flying open and them flying into her bedroom.

Normally this would have been enough to have her scuttling for a hole to crawl into at the thought of his crushed internal organs, but Liam's obvious passion was oddly liberating, and instead she used the opportunity to straddle him and began rocking back and forth in the style of some bimbo from the *Red Shoe Diaries*.

'God, Marie, you're so beautiful,' moaned Liam. His voice was incredibly sexy, all dark and strong. 'You're so *warm* and *real* and I want you so much . . .'

Marie shut her eyes and threw her throbbing head back, knowing that her neck would now stretch like a lovely white swan's in the dim light from the hallway. She *felt* beautiful. She felt weird, but beautiful. She felt . . .

It dawned on her at exactly the same moment that a) she didn't have any Led Zeppelin CDs, which was what she was sure she could hear now, and b) there was someone looking at her.

Her eyes snapped open.

'I'm going to put this duvet over my head,' said Iona, sitting bolt upright and looking very ill, 'and pretend that I haven't seen anything, OK?'

And she wrapped her head in Marie's brand-new purple Egyptian cotton duvet and began counting to ten.

Oh, my God, thought Marie, panicking and flushing with shame. She'll tell Angus I've seduced a helpless teenager, and Angus will tell her about that night I snogged him by mistake, and I'll look like some kind of nymphomaniac divorcée and, God, maybe I am! Is there no one I won't go for? What kind of slag am I turning into?

Marie put a hand to her aching temples and remembered that she'd bought three packets of condoms at Boots, but no Migraleve.

By half-nine, Angus had marshalled most of the mains out of the kitchen, with just a few stragglers on warm seasonal salads left. Gabriel had sent out a couple of puddings already and despite the atmosphere in the kitchen, which was frosty and over-heated at the same time, it seemed everything was just about under control again.

Angus moved from serving hatch to table on autopilot, worrying about Iona with one half of his brain, and what he should do with Gabriel with the other.

Why hadn't she told him about her driving test? How could she have imagined that he didn't want to know? What did she think he would do if she failed – dump her? His heart ached. And she must still be in shock to have thrown up like that; typical NHS hospital, to let her out without so much as a cup of hot sweet tea. Very good.

'These aren't our mains.'

He looked down at the pan-fried skate and the lamb chops he was about to put down, and then at the customer, who was rolling her eyes at her companion in a deeply unnecessary manner.

'I'm sorry?'

'We changed our order to the game pie – I did tell the girl.'

'Which girl?'

'The pretty blonde one.'

Angus longed to demand, 'As opposed to the ugly blonde one?' but didn't. He did his best smile instead, although it was starting to feel a little painful tonight every time he flexed his cheek muscles. 'I'm sorry, I don't think that reached the kitchen. Let me go and check.'

And how could he run this place with an arse like Gabriel – turning up when he felt like it, rendering Tamara even more useless than normal, casting some weird stiffness spell on Jim, who turned into Management Today Boy every time he caught sight of Gabriel's ponytail . . .

'Rick, this isn't the order for table 9,' he said, putting the plates back on the hatch. 'Have you got the original order?'

'On the spike,' said Rick, without looking up from the plate of water ices he was drizzling with ruby-red raspberry jus, spooned from a margarine tub. 'If it's done.'

Angus fiddled with the orders, and found one with several crossings out. Was that it? Tamara's writing was virtually illegible.

'Is there some kind of training school we can send her to?' he asked, half to himself.

'What's that?' Rick looked up. 'Tamara? She's really messing up the orders tonight – I think she's working from a different menu to us.'

'Or she's doing it by astral guidance,' suggested Mark. 'You are Taurus, you must have shin of beef.'

'Fuck off,' snarled Gabriel, emerging from the freezer with a huge catering tin of fresh ice cream. 'Don't you talk about my chick like that, all right?'

'My chick?' said Angus, before he could stop himself. Maybe it was a mutual sense of humour failure that had brought him and Tamara together. Then he remembered that starting a row with Gabriel would add more crosses to the score sheet than he could ever put right, and he held up his hands. 'Sorry, sorry, sorry! Forget it! Forget I said anything. Where's Ned?'

'Over there,' said Gabriel with an ambiguous grin.

Ned was leaning against the wall, looking deathly.

'Ned, are you OK?' Not another one. Angus felt the blood drain from his own face, just looking at him. He rushed over and put his hand on Ned's forehead. It was like feeling up a fish. 'Mark, get some water for Ned! All right, *do* the bloody trout first! Rick! Rick!' He waved at the griddle. 'Leave that tart and come and finish whatever Ned was doing!'

'But, it's a . . .'

'I don't care, it's a pudding and they can wait. Get Marie to give them some dessert wine.' Angus put his arm around Ned and ushered him out through the side door. 'Come on, Ned, mate, you need some fresh air. Are you going to be—'

In response, Ned lifted a dustbin lid and vomited neatly inside.

'Jeez, Angus, I feel really . . .' He swayed and put a hand to his mouth.

Angus looked away politely. Was he being paranoid, or could there be some connection between Ned being sick, Iona being sick, the pair of them conspiring about her driving test and . . . God knew what else?

A new sense of dread crept into his stomach but he pushed it away. No. If there was one thing he knew about Iona, it was that she was honest with him.

Apart from the driving test.

'Angus!'

'Oh, what is it now?' He turned round to see Tamara coming in with a smug look on her face.

'You know who's in the corner, don't you?'

'No, I don't, and I don't care. Look, Ned's been sick. Is there something we should know, Ned? Have you eaten something here that's made you feel ill?' Angus leaned over him and Ned vomited again into the dustbin.

Tamara looked at the plated-up game pie in her hands with horror.

'What is it, Ned?' asked Angus. 'Come on, because if it's something off the menu, we'll have to get it back.'

Ned waved a vague hand at the work surface next to the fridge.

They all swivelled to look at the work surface, on which there was a margarine tub of shortbread hearts, a large bowl of whipped cream, the lemon tart, his bag of mushrooms and a bain-marie of crème caramels that had just come out of the oven.

'Shouldn't all this be in the fridge?' Angus demanded testily. 'Surely there are health issues? Germs and stuff.'

Rick sniffed the bowl of cream. 'This smells a bit funny,' he said. 'Is it off, maybe?'

'Oh, did they teach you that in catering college?' retorted Gabriel sarcastically. He grabbed the cream and tasted it. 'It's fine. The reason it tastes *funny*, as you so elegantly put it, is because it's crème au beurre fucking mousseline!'

Ned managed to raise his head, and there was a certain degree of professional loathing apparent in his steely grey eyes, now somewhat bloodshot. 'I've told you before about doing French stuff, you *twat*. This is meant to be modern British, not some up-your-arse bluc riband—' Whatever else he was going to say was lost in a stream of retching, but Gabriel got the gist of it.

A thunderous expression darkened his handsome face and he threw his gaze around the kitchen. 'Well, it's pretty fucking obvious what's making everyone throw up, isn't it?'

'What?' demanded Angus. He could see Rick and Mark cowering, just out of his range of vision, and he knew they'd be no help at all. Adrenalin charged through his system. Rows were not a problem to Angus. He was a solicitor. He had trained for this! And most of all, he didn't care what Gabriel thought of him, because there was an ever-growing possibility that it wouldn't be his problem for very much longer.

'It's your fucking amateur lemon pie, isn't it?' Gabriel's sneer curled contemptuously. 'What happened? Did you use some eggs past their sell-by date? Or wasn't Delia's recipe clear enough for you?'

'You fuck off!' roared Angus, facing him off over the central work surface. 'And take that back!'

Tamara looked terrified and wondered if she should go and find Iona to calm things down before Angus rearranged Gabriel's lovely face. Although Gabriel had well-defined muscles, she knew the power of Angus's rage was like something from Masters of the Universe when he got really mad.

Marie wandered in from the bar, looking ashen and unaware of what was going on. 'Angus, have you got any Nurofen in the office?' she asked. 'I feel really ropey.'

'See?' said Gabriel. He widened his eyes smugly. 'Didn't I see her helping herself earlier?'

'What? To what?' asked Marie, massaging her temples. She'd never had a headache this bad and actually wanted to stay at work. 'Tamara, have you got any of that homeopathic nonsense you carry around with you?'

Everyone apart from Marie stared at the tart. It was half-eaten and glistening deliciously in the overhead striplight.

'Most popular pudding on the menu tonight,' Mark pointed out in his boss's defence. 'All those women in the corner ordered it.'

'Yes – but then throwing it up immediately afterwards does make it fairly low-calorie,' said Gabriel unpleasantly.

'There is nothing wrong whatsoever with that lemon pie,' repeated Angus. His voice was deepening ominously.

'I made a smaller one which Iona and I ate last night and we're fine.'

'*Is* Iona all right?' said Marie, who seemed disconnected from what was going on all round her. 'I've just seen her and if you ask me, she's . . .' Then she remembered that she shouldn't have been upstairs anyway, and from the glower on Angus's face, it wasn't the right thing to say at all.

'Marie, you look dreadful,' he said shortly. 'Maybe you should go and lie down for half an hour. Liam's OK on the bar on his own, is he?'

Marie nodded nervously.

'Fine, we're only three staff short then.' Angus rolled his eyes. 'I don't suppose there's anyone we know in the bar who knows anything about cooking, is there?'

'Oh yes, there is actually,' said Tamara helpfully. 'Fay Maschler and Charles Campion are in the bar. They're doing some *Big Book of London Pubs* or something. They seem to like it here and—'

'Right, that's it,' said Angus, throwing up his hands. He *had* heard of those two. This was the final big cross. Nothing else mattered now. It was all over bar the shouting. Or, in Gabriel and Tamara's case, pouting. 'Tamara, get all the puddings back that have gone out – anything with cream on it, anything that's got eggs in it, and yes, get the lemon tart back.'

'But . . .' said Tamara, looking horror-struck.

'I don't care what you tell them, just get it all back in and you,' he glared at Gabriel, 'either find something in the freezer, or think very, very quickly about the validity of your work permit.'

Gabriel's expression transformed. 'What about my work permit? There's—'

'We'll discuss that later,' said Angus darkly. 'Now, Mark . . .'

Mark looked as though Angus was about to demand his liver for a main.

'Angus! I need to talk to you *right* now!' Jim marched

through the kitchen and into the office. He looked uncharacteristically savage and was waving a sheaf of paper around. His tie was somewhere halfway down his shirt. 'I'm . . . I'm . . . just *furious*!'

'Come on!' said Angus to the stunned kitchen. 'Get on with it!' And he followed Jim into the office.

To his surprise, Jim was pouring himself a large brandy into a coffee cup.

'I thought you weren't touching the wages of sin?' said Angus. He couldn't believe that he wasn't crying. Somewhere, he wasn't sure where, tonight had moved from tragedy into complete farce. The dull realization that he really was going back to the office began to settle in the pit of his stomach. 'I thought that Christmas brandy bribes were below your sense of commercial integrity? Or was that for Tamara's benefit?'

Jim knocked back the brandy with a cynical grunt and loosened his tie still further.

'Pour me one, will you? And where've you been, anyway?' Angus went on, trying to ignore the glaring fact that Jim was behaving like a character from *This Life*. 'If you want to tell me that you've impregnated Charm and that's the reason she's packed in her job, that would round things off nicely. No, actually, why don't you tell me that you've impregnated *any* girlfriend and . . .'

'I've been at the office, getting evidence with Rebecca,' said Jim, tapping the sheaf of papers which Rebecca had put into a green plastic folder for him. He looked exactly like a nice guy trying to do a No More Mr Nice Guy face.

'Getting what?' Angus filed Rebecca away for later. If there was a later.

'Overworld. That bunch of scheming bastards,' spat Jim. 'I've found out why they wanted to give us all that money.'

'Oh no,' said Angus, sinking into the chair. Ker-ching – the final, final cross on the board. Part of him, the lawyery part, had been waiting for this for some time. It was just the happy pub managery part that had chosen to ignore the warning bells of suspicion calling time on their plans. 'Go on, tell me the worst.'

'Oh, *where will* I start?' asked Jim rhetorically. He looked livid, not an expression Angus had ever experienced on Jim before. 'First of all, giving me this place to run *wasn't* Martin taking me seriously after all these years – it's a fucking tax loss dodge. They *wanted* to lose a load of money for this year and next year, and they chose me to lose it because they all think I'm about as capable of managing money as a three-year-old. The bastards! There are e-mails here and everything!' He jabbed at the file with a finger. 'Having a good laugh at my shirts!'

'Oh, God,' said Angus, his heart sinking. He was starting to feel sick too now. 'So that's why they kept telling us to buy Bavarian crystal chandeliers. And get more staff in. Of course.'

'And then!' Jim banged at the desk. '*Then* they wanted to use the losses as proof that the pub was no longer financially viable as a pub, so they could override any local planning objections to turning it into flats at a later date and making a fucking fortune out of the fact that it was a converted pub! Simon even had a project name lined up – the Urban Vineyard, they were going to call it! God! I can't *believe* none of this occurred to me!'

Angus could, but didn't say anything. He just wanted to go somewhere quiet and weep. Overworld were always going to be about fifteen steps ahead of them. And he'd thought he'd thought of everything.

'You know they've got half the houses over the road?' Jim went on. 'It's just fucking Monopoly to them.' He stuck his fingers into his hair and frowned violently at the wall. Then he ripped down all the target projections he'd stuck on the noticeboard only the day before and hurled them in the bin.

'How did you find all this out?' Angus asked faintly.

'Rebecca told me. Everyone knew but me, apparently. I can't believe they've been laughing at me all this time! I'm fucking *sick* of everyone treating me like some kind of joke! Well, this is the final straw.' Jim looked up and there was a scary glimmer of determination in his eye that Angus hadn't seen since their Under-11 county running trials, the one Jim had finished with a broken rib and low blood pressure.

At bloody last, thought Angus, pleased.

'I'm going to get the money somehow and force them to sell me this place, or else I'll pass this little lot on to the Inland Revenue. There's loads more.' He snorted, and Angus was pleased to see that he looked a little deranged. Maybe there was hope yet. '*God* knows how much more. So, Angus, will you do it?'

Angus didn't reply. He was imagining what it would be like to get up every morning and not worry about Gabriel rowing with the vegetable man. What it would be like to go home at seven in the evening, instead of one the following morning. What it would be like to get his relationship with Mad Boy Sam back on to a purely nodding basis.

'Angus?' Jim repeated.

'Angus?' But that was Iona's voice. His head shot up, and he saw her standing in the doorway, bracing herself against the jamb for support.

'There's a riot going on in the kitchen and I heard shouting in here and . . .'

Angus stood up. 'OK, Jim, you're in charge.'

'But . . .' Jim began, the familiar harassed expression returning to his face.

'You're in charge. You want to run this place, you go ahead. Sort out the muppets in the kitchen, I'm going outside to talk to Iona.'

Leaving Jim floundering but determined, Angus grabbed Iona's hand and led her through the pub. Behind him, he could make out Jim's voice rising above Gabriel's in the

kitchen and was grimly glad. All he wanted was to get
out. OUT.

For a big lad, Angus moved quickly, and in passing he
unwittingly trod on Mad Boy Sam's mate Den's lurcher,
which was tied to a barstool, and Iona had to do the
apologies as she was dragged past.

Angus pushed open the frosted glass door and carefully sat
Iona down on one of the ropey old picnic benches outside.
He squatted in front of her, holding both her hands, trying
to get his breathing regular again. For some reason, beneath
the surface turmoil, he felt very calm. The three women
in office suits lingering by the door moved off, looking
backwards as they went, wondering if they were about to
miss something.

Angus took a deep breath of cool night air and looked
Iona in the face. She was slightly green, and her hair was
squashed on one side of her head where she'd been lying
down, and there was a bit of sick crusting on her T-shirt,
but she had never looked more beautiful to him now he'd
begun to entertain the reality of leaping into the unknown.

'Iona,' he began, not sure of what he was going to say
but feeling the words popping into his head, pushing each
other out of the way. Every time he thought he had a good
phrase ready, it seemed to vanish, only to be replaced by
some ridiculous legalese.

'Iona, it's all going down the tubes,' he said. 'The kitchen
is revolting and Overworld are going to try and close us
down to make a tax loss. If Jim doesn't do it, they'll get
someone else to. Did you hear him? He wants us to buy it.
Angus shuddered. 'But I don't think I can do it,' he said. '
don't know if I can deal with all these idiots any more, and
I certainly don't want to risk our future on them. I'm no
putting our relationship at stake. I'm going to have to tel
Jim no.'

'No!' Iona burst out. She looked horrified. 'But you can't
You've put so much into this place! Of course Jim has to

find a way of buying it! But if you don't run it, everything will fall to pieces! Jim won't stand up to Gabriel – Jim can't even understand the shift rota!'

Angus knuckled his eyes. 'But I'm so *sick* of being Mr Nasty the whole time, telling people what to do, chasing up suppliers, neglecting you because I'm sorting out Ned's bloody kitchen accounts. I just looked at all the disasters tonight and asked myself, is it worth it?' He looked up at her. His eyes were bloodshot. 'Well? Is it?'

'Yes!'

He shook his head. 'I'm not sure it is, you know. You and I have no time together. I didn't even know you were taking your driving test! And you hate me bossing you around behind the bar, I hate having to tell you what to do . . .'

'Angus,' said Iona, taking his hands, 'you've found something you love doing, and you're really good at it. You only have to look at the accounts to see that.' She shook his hands like a child's. 'And you mustn't stop just because there's one bad night – I mean, it's not the first night Gabriel's played up in the kitchen, is it?'

Why haven't you told me any of this before, you moron? 'Why haven't we talked about this, Angus?' she asked quietly.

They sat together in silence for a few moments, each wondering how to move on into dangerous waters, sensing the conversation getting deeper by the minute.

Angus looked up at her, and decided to put all his eggs in one basket and then break them into one big omelette. 'Um, Iona. This isn't quite the way I wanted it to happen, but it's happening, so there you go.' He pressed his lips together and tried to order the jumble of words. It was like shuffling a pack of cards with shaky hands; phrases and ideas kept falling out. 'There are just two things that really matter to me in the world – making this pub work and being with you. Well, actually, no,' he corrected himself, seeing Iona's eyebrows lift eloquently, 'the *only* thing that matters to me is being with you. But you know my sabbatical is almost over and I'd have to make a decision really soon and . . .'

'You *know* what the decision should be, Angus,' said Iona stoutly.

He took a deep breath. 'Well, OK. I know. I *thought* I could just take all this on for six months, and somehow it would come to me – as if by magic – what I should do with the rest of my life. But, er . . . that was a bit naïve of me. I mean, it's not that easy – I can't let this pub be run down, just to make a bloody tax loss for Overworld, not after everything we've managed to do in such a short time. But if I think up some kind of buy-out plan, with Jim's help and with your help, I want to do it *properly*, with *proper* investment backing, and then . . .' He trailed off and stared into space. 'Then maybe I'd get something *out* of slogging away at work, instead of just sitting in the office, watching the papers pile up in the out-tray.' He looked up at her and hoped for the best.

'But?' said Iona, and there was enough encouragement in her voice to make him gamble.

'But I won't do it unless you're absolutely sure you want me to. Us. Unless you want *us* to. Only if you don't mind that our future won't be as mapped out as it used to be. I wouldn't want to do it at all without you there with me. I wouldn't want to do *anything* without you.'

Angus's eyes filled up and Iona stretched out her hand and cupped his chin, which was starting to bristle with stubble. 'Why *wouldn't* I want to be there?' she asked. 'Where else would I *be* except with you?'

Angus tried not to think of who she'd been with when she took her driving test. Maybe that was just the beginning . . . Of not needing him there . . . 'But, Iona, think of the hours, and the commitment, and the money!'

'Angus, you're not exactly selling this to me. And I want you to do it! I want us to do it!'

Was that enough? Angus took her hand back off his chin and interlaced her smooth fingers with his. He hoped she couldn't feel his hands shaking with nerves. 'Iona,' he said, and cleared his throat. 'Um, I wanted to wait until, well, until I knew exactly how things would be, but I don't suppose you ever know exactly.' He paused and waited for her to look up. When she did, he held her gaze. 'Will you marry me?' he asked. 'Now? So we can go into this together?'

It was the moment Iona had been dreading and longing for in equal measures. Quick visions of Marie and Chris, and her own parents, several royal weddings, the video for "November Rain" by Guns N' Roses, and all the old plans she'd made whizzed through her head as if in a blender, and a panicky, undefined resistance emerged.

'Angus, aren't we as good as married now?' she asked with a shaky smile. 'Would getting married make a difference? It's not a guarantee, is it?'

The inner Iona wailed in despair at her lack of romance.

'I'm a solicitor,' said Angus wearily, 'and, believe me, I know there are no guarantees. *Nothing* lasts for ever. But sometimes I think that you don't know how *much* I love you, or maybe I forget to tell you, and we take each other for granted. And I know it's scary, promising to do something for the rest of your life when you don't know if that life will be the same by the end of the year. But it's when I think of what life would be like *without* you that I know I want to make sure you'll always be with me . . . if you want to be. Anyway, you know me, I'm not your man for taking risks. I only go for dead certs.'

'But the pub, Angus,' said Iona, wanting to be sure he understood what he was getting into. 'Isn't that enough of a risk to be going on with?'

'If it wasn't for you, I'd never even have *thought* about taking the pub on in the first place,' he said, oblivious of the pins and needles spreading up his leg. 'If it wasn't for you, I'd be making my twenty-year plan at the office now, boring myself to death and wishing I had the guts to get out there and do something. And where's the risk in us getting married? It's not like we're legally obliged to turn into Basil and Sybil Fawlty.'

'Or Chris and Marie,' said Iona automatically, and couldn't stop herself twitching with embarrassment as the surreal image of Marie and Liam falling through the bedroom door flashed across her mind. Now that was an image that would stay with her for some time.

'Or even Chris and Marie. Why would anything change at all? Iona, you know I love you, I've loved you for years. I mean' – he looked at her very seriously – 'you make me a better version of myself and, as far as I can see, that's exactly what a marriage should be. Two people helping each other to enjoy a life together. I don't want to be your other half – I love you because you're *not* some bloody tedious version of me. If I wanted that, I'd have got someone from the office. I mean, that's why I sorted out the shed, give you a bit of privacy . . .'

Mentioning the shed brought a startling mental image of Iona's black wedding painting to the forefront of his mind, and Angus stopped abruptly. Christ almighty. How could he have forgotten that, all scary and mad, even with the pub descending into chaos? He really had been spending too much time obsessing about this place.

But that would stop, he promised earnestly, bartering with fate. If he and Jim took it on, he would make sure there was more time for him and Iona. Walking in Richmond Park time, and going to museums time, and breakfast in bed time. Like it used to be.

Angus looked into Iona's face as if they'd just met, and suddenly it broke on him that she *could* say no. In fact, she hadn't actually said yes. Or sounded that enthusiastic. He panicked and, feeling there was little left to lose, let out the question niggling at him anyway.

'Iona, that painting in the shed . . .' he began.

Her eyes went defensive and embarrassed. 'Er, that? Um, how did you . . .'

'Iona, tell me it wasn't the wedding commission you were doing for that bossy woman, was it?' he asked hurriedly, before she could ask what he was doing in the shed to see it. 'It wasn't what you think marriage means to you?'

Iona didn't say anything immediately. *Was* it what she thought of marriage? Wasn't that what she'd been thinking about as she whipped all that paint around? How scared she was of the way her life was slipping out of control, and all the problems, hers and other people's, that were choking her up. And wasn't getting married part of that fear?

I just don't want to let him down, she thought wildly. I don't want to be the one thing he relies on when everything is going out of control and I can't even rely on myself. It's too much.

She closed her eyes and tried to dislocate her mind, to hear what her instinct told her, rather than a million old advice pages and other people's second-hand bad experiences.

It was as if she could hear Marie in the back of her mind, her hands on her hips, snorting in disbelief and straining her shirt buttons.

How exactly would marriage be different from what you've been doing until now? said the cross voice in her head. *You're there, and he's there, and although you might get sick of each other every now and again, where else would you like to be? You can't be a teenager for ever, flitting from one renting relationship to another, no matter what you might read in the glossies.*

But . . .

And don't try and wave Ned around as an example of your lack of fidelity. He's the most pathetically safe choice for a last-minute crush anyway. Yes, you fancy Ned, who wouldn't? He's gorgeous and sexy and terminally single. But you don't love Ned, not really; you just love what he is to you – your adolescence, and irresponsibility, and all the stuff you can't have if you swap it all for a husband.

But . . .

He is a teenage crush, Iona, just like Jimmy Page. And you don't use your lurid fantasies about Jimmy Page as a reason not to marry Angus, do you? And they're not going to stop, just because there's a ring on your finger, are they? Crushes aren't about people: they're only about what they stand for – freedom, or cheap thrills, or unattainability, or an echo of something they desperately wish they had in themselves.

But . . .

Love – real love – is different and you know it involves a swap: you have to accept that you can't have everything any more. Most people would cut off their right arms for what you have with Angus. And this shared life, this steady happiness and comfort and understanding, is where all the wine bars and dinner dates are meant to lead. And you're already there. You've won.

You silly cow.

'Iona, look, I'm sorry . . .' Angus began miserably. His voice sounded different from the one he normally used in conversation with her, more grown-up and sad, and Iona realized it was because he was talking to her about something they'd never talked about before, in all their long conversations over the years. He wasn't making assumptions, and she wasn't automatically agreeing with him. In fact, schizo inner voices aside, she was thinking about spending her life with him more rationally than she thought was possible at moments like this.

Who would have thought it?

'I shouldn't have said anything,' he said, starting to get up. 'I know it's all a bit much, and I don't want to force you to—'

He thought she was saying thanks, but no thanks.

'No, listen,' said Iona, putting her hand on his mouth. It was soft, and when he turned his blue eyes up at her, full of worry and hopelessness, she felt her heart melt. How could she live without this man? Sometimes she couldn't see where he stopped and she began.

'Angus, that was just a painting about . . .' She scrabbled for a credible topic and then didn't bother. All he cared about was that it wasn't about him. 'I was listening to "Kashmir",' she said, 'and I was trying to paint the sound. I was a bit drunk. It was in the middle of the night.'

'You can get help for this Led Zeppelin thing,' he said. The relief on his face was obvious.

Iona braced herself. None of this was easy, but it had to be said and said now, if they didn't want to end up sending each other snotty letters on headed notepaper and moving to different parts of Europe to prove points about marital independence.

Part of her wondered when she'd been planning to say this otherwise. When they were posting the invitations?

'I . . . I *worry* about what marriage means,' she said. 'And it's nothing to do with how I feel about you,' she added quickly, as his face fell. 'It's just the whole thing. You know, I see people promise to do things and be things they can't possibly know for sure, and then get hurt beyond belief when circumstances force them to break those promises. If I had Tamara's cards, and I could find out how our lives would go, and that I would be a good wife to you, I would marry you right now.'

'Much good Tamara's crystal ball's been in the past for her,' Angus pointed out. 'Or do you think she knows something we don't about Gabriel?'

'Angus, shut up, I'm talking.' She slapped him gently on his knee. '*I'm* talking. What I'm trying to say is that I can't bear the thought that I could hurt someone I love as much as I love you. I'm not saying I will, but I *could*. I can't *bear* the thought of hurting you. I mean, I don't mind having the odd row about line-up changes in Black Sabbath, but . . .' She left the Davenport Death Match unsaid.

'But, come on, Iona, isn't that life?' Angus, increasingly feeling that the romance had completely drained out of the moment and that they were getting into some kind of philosophical debate instead, got up off his knees and sat facing her on the picnic table, his long legs straddling the bench. 'No one can possibly know what will happen next – even me with all my safe bets. And I'm willing to try it.'

'Yeah,' she said, looking down at her hands.

'How come I'm having to talk you into this, when every other time marriage has raised its ugly head you've been all radiant?' he demanded, hurt. 'Just tell me, whatever it is. Go on.'

Iona looked at him, the man she had shared her life with for seven years. Longer than many marriages. Enough time to have a child in primary school. Enough time to have watched entire families come and go on *EastEnders*. Enough time to know whether it was right or not.

She didn't need someone else to tell her that – advice, or psychics, or friends, or anything. If she didn't know now, who ever would?

'It's different because now it's real,' she said quietly. 'I'm not giving you some stock reaction, I'm telling you things I didn't even realize I felt until now. And I wanted to be sure If you want to spend the rest of your life with me.'

Angus waited a few beats, while a couple of pissed estate agents staggered out of the pub and began to negotiate the pavement.

'Oi! Not against the wall!' he yelled as one of them started to fiddle with his flies.

'Mate!' slurred his friend, raising an apologetic hand.

'In the alley, if you must!' Angus gestured towards the bins.

He turned back to Iona and held her hands, and his breath. 'Well?'

Iona concentrated on his concerned eyes and on the pulsing of her heart. It felt like leaping off a cliff, like

jumping off the bridge into the deep beck when she wa
a child: the moment of flying through space so quickly she
barely had time to savour the feeling of being between one
safe place – and another.

'Yes,' she said. 'Go on, then.'

She hardly had chance to feel the smile spread across her
whole face before Angus had caught her in his arms and
they were hugging each other as if by hugging hard enough
they would mould together into one.

Epilogue

Tamara and Gabriel

'Oooh, that's it, more there. Yes. Aaaah, harder . . .'
Tamara's hair was pinned up in loose curls on her head, her cheeks were flushed pinkly and her face was wreathed in smiles, making her look like some kind of underdressed angel. She was still too scared to believe her luck, even after six months. Gabriel looked so beautiful with his eyes closed and his head thrown back like that. His whole face could have been sculpted from marble, the steep cheekbones, the sloping nose, the smooth eyelids. In fact, with his eyes closed and the tiny beads of water on his forehead, he could have been advertising any number of post-shave fragrances.

Ned was way out of line – how could Gabriel be vain? He'd have to be the only person in the world who didn't see how gorgeous he was.

So why was he with her?

'Oh, you're so good at that,' he moaned without opening his eyes. 'It feels incredible. Harder, mmm, harder. Ah, yeah.'

Tamara increased the pressure with her fingers and wiped her forehead with the back of her arm. It was getting really hot in here. She looked at her own bare shoulders in the mirror which stretched the length of the room and she smiled at their entwined reflection. They looked really good together. As though they were made as a pair, each one designed to complement the other.

She still couldn't get over how lucky she was. Meeting Gabriel had been a revelation for Tamara. It had shown her how she could have no idea what the future had in store and yet still be blissfully happy. All that pressure, searching the cards for a man, or for a sign of love, or scanning neurotically for a new heartbreak – she'd never realized how heavily it weighed down her shoulders until it was gone. No wonder she couldn't really believe how easy it could be. She hadn't had a tarot reading *or* a drink for weeks.

If she could only tell someone about it, it would be perfect. Tamara sighed very quietly, which Gabriel took as evidence of enjoyment.

For ages now she had really wanted to discuss this almost incredible lifestyle-mag-type bliss with Iona, but she wasn't sure it would come out right. Iona didn't seem to see Gabriel the way she did – not many people did, to be fair – and yet she of all people should appreciate how exciting it was to find your soulmate. God knew, she'd told Iona enough times how much she longed to find an Angus to make her complete, the way Angus completed Iona. And now Tamara was finally happy she wanted to tell Iona how jealous and sad it had made her, seeing those two so happy with so little effort, while she had to sift her way through every creep and dribbling idiot in London.

Tamara carried on massaging Gabriel with tingling finger-tips, letting her eye trail greedily over the chiselled muscles in his back.

He behaved as if he'd known her all his life and skirted around all the little things that irritated her as if by instinct. They were so similar. There was no showing her off in fancy restaurants, or making her go with him to parties just for the entrance and then leaving her by the drinks. They went together and stayed together. Gabriel didn't just want her as some kind of arm decoration. If anything, people stared at *him* more. Men and women. Tamara stopped massaging and a light frown creased her forehead, then disappeared as if an invisible hand had smoothed it away.

But that didn't matter: she and Gabriel were soulmates. He understood about destiny and the power of knowing where you were going. Her astrologer had agreed that they were a really powerful union, if you took Gabriel's rising sign into account. Aries weren't usually compatible with her own chart, but she was pretty sure he was a cusp. She'd have to check the time zones.

And things were even settling down at the pub, now Angus and Jim had made some kind of proper commitment to running it and given up their day jobs. In Tamara's opinion, it was really rude of Angus to have called Gabriel all those appalling names, even worse of Marie to have made that comment about his dark roots, but at least they'd got all that sorted out now. More or less.

'Mmm,' said Gabriel, opening his eyes. 'That was fantastic, babe. Hey, can I return the favour?'

Tamara's eyes widened in anticipation. 'Oh yes. Don't use the intensive conditioner for me, though, because I had that treatment put on it at the hairdresser's on Monday.'

'And I can leave this on while I do yours?' asked Gabriel fingering the conditioner on his long hair.

'It takes about ten minutes to develop after the initial massage,' explained Tamara. 'It's the coconut oil. Very good for highlights.' She ran some more hot water into the bath and curled her long, slim legs round Gabriel's. He had breathtaking thighs, truly breathtaking. Very Scorpio. Very Hugo Boss.

She smiled at their reflection in the bathroom mirror. Like a pair of flawless marble sculptures, carved from the same rock.

'And then can we do that facepack? The exfoliating one?'

Tamara relaxed as his strong fingers cradled her skull. 'Of course. We both can. It's hypo-allergenic.'

Her other half. What she'd always wanted.

Marie and Chris

Chris had told Marie to meet him at the airport at eleven.
Which was reassuringly typical – first, that he expected her
to drop everything at school and secondly, that he was too
mean to pay for a cab into town.

Charity, as ever, with Chris, tended to begin at home.

But where she was once willing to make sacrifices rather
than point out the unreasonable nature of his command,
Marie suddenly found it easy to tell him it wasn't convenient,
and so, even though part of her had argued to grant him
one last indulgence, just to make this hard conversation
slightly easier, they were now sitting in PizzaExpress and
the whole atmosphere was exactly as she imagined one of
those blind lunch dates for busy professionals would be
like. One where the conversation had run out before the
mains arrived but politeness prevented anyone else running
out before the coffee.

Chris had arrived first and was directed to the table Marie
had booked in their name – a corner one where they could
talk privately. He declined a drink and sat down to wait,
studying the menu for something he couldn't make at home
for a fraction of the price.

He was oddly glad for the impersonal setting, and not
sorry that this wasn't happening in their old flat, where
the debris of their married life had covered the place like
a snake's shed skin. Always old photos, old *stuff* that Marie
wanted to hang on the walls, nothing new. He hadn't been
too surprised really when she'd said in her letter that she'd
moved out of Tooting and in above the pub: Maisie had
always got on her nerves, and Marie wasn't great at being
on her own.

At least their old house wouldn't have to be sold and split.
Not that the money wouldn't have been useful now.

Chris allowed himself a small, bitter smile and conceded

ﬡat maybe Marie had been right about rent money being
ﬦoney down the drain.

He attracted the attention of the waitress and asked for
a jug of tap water and two glasses, then went back to
the menu, although his eyes were only skating across the
surface.

On the tiny plane on the way over, Chris had tried to
think of ways to explain to Marie how he had changed,
but nothing had come to him. He knew he wasn't much
good at expressing himself – living with her quick brain
had rammed that home constantly – but he felt he owed
her some kind of explanation for breaking up. He wasn't
going to say 'and ruining her life'. Not until she did.

Unfortunately, nothing came to him that he hadn't heard a
million times in crap American sitcoms, and he knew Marie,
with her high standards of verbal abuse, wouldn't accept
that. She would use it as the main plank of her attack, that
he hadn't even bothered to express himself honestly. 'It's not
you, it's me!' – no matter how true it actually was – would
probably get him a plate over his head. In fact, that was
probably why she'd insisted on meeting in a restaurant.

Chris sighed and rubbed his eyes. He couldn't cope with
histrionics from Marie. For the past three weeks he'd had
only a few hours' sleep a night, and not necessarily at regular
intervals. He had seen things he'd only read about, or heard
about; things he had blithely imagined he could deal with by
faxing letters and making the odd phone call to some other
warm London office. Only now he knew he couldn't deal
with the reality, and that his best was pretty second-rate
compared to what these starving, confused, angry people
needed, but, more than that, he knew he had to keep on
doing it, even if it was a million miles away from the job
he *thought* he had been doing all this time. Sometimes he
completely forgot who he'd been *before* he'd arrived at the
relief centre.

Chris knew it made him seem hard-faced, but, in the gran

balance, the small amount of good he was managing to do for some of these people weighed far more heavily than six months' misery of getting over it for a woman he shouldn't have married in the first place, and who would probably thank him for this in years to come.

Marie arrived dead on one-fifteen, as he had expected her to, and Chris half rose from his seat, unsure how affectionate he ought to be with her. She'd been fairly calm in her reply to his letter, and fairly calm on the phone, if a bit distracted. She looked fairly calm now – she certainly hadn't been wasting away in his absence – wearing a tight lime-green shirt which showed more of her ample cleavage that was really appropriate for a primary school teacher, swinging her handbag and walking confidently through the crowded tables, weaving her hips in and out of chairs like a large but graceful cat. There was nothing in her eyes to suggest that she was about to lamp him, although, as usual, her handbag was big enough to conceal a cosh.

The waitress showed her to the table and offered her a menu, which Marie accepted, turning to the woman and thanking her as she took it, flashing the kind of special, secret smile that had always had kids falling at her feet.

'Marie,' said Chris formally. 'It's great to see you.'

She leaned over and allowed him to kiss her cheek, and the smile she had given the waitress faded for a moment while she took him in. Then she smiled again, but despite the red lips widening in a generous bow, it didn't reach her eyes, which remained mistrustful and a little sad.

'And to see you,' Marie said. She sat down, unfolded her napkin with a flap and began to scan the menu, but he sensed that, like him, she wasn't really seeing anything. 'I'm sorry that it's a restaurant but . . .' She let the sentence trickle away and they sat and stared at each other's chests over the solitary pink tulip.

'So,' she said into the loaded silence, as he struggled for words.

Thank God, at least she isn't going to make this hard, thought Chris with tongue-tied relief.

He looked up to see where she would take it from 'So', and was hit by one of her private Mona Lisa half-smiles. The ones he could never work out and therefore hated. 'So,' she went on, 'a needle pulling thread?'

Chris looked blank and then felt a familiar irritation. '*What?*'

'Nothing. Forget it. You aren't staying then, I take it?'

'Er, no. I'm sleeping on someone from work's floor for this evening. I have to get back by the end of tomorrow, really. We're quite understaffed at the moment. It's a bad time.' He stopped, stiffly unwilling to turn people's misery into dinner chitchat. If he told her the truth, she wouldn't be able to eat her supper through guilt; if he tried to make light of it, he wouldn't either.

But then he owed her some reason for going out there, didn't he?

'I can't tell you how hard it's been . . .' Chris caught her eye and looked at her seriously. How was he meant to explain? How could she really understand? Was it really necessary to launch into this kind of thing immediately, or should he be asking whether the British summer had started yet?

Marie inclined her head, inviting him to go on.

'It has changed me, changed my life,' he said simply. 'I know that sounds like a cliché but it's true. I used to talk a lot of naïve bullshit before, about the kind of human suffering right on our doorstep, without really knowing how bad it could be. And now I do know, and even though I don't really want to go back, because all those scared, desperate faces give me nightmares, I know I have to, because if I don't, it could get worse.'

Marie bit her lip. 'Yes, I can imagine. Well, I can't imagine, no. But it must be . . . be . . . draining for you.'

Chris nodded. Now would be the time for most men to

say, 'Which is why I need my wife out here, damn it!' bu
he'd realized, almost as soon as he'd got there, that he needec
to be on his own. Theirs wasn't the kind of relationship that
would prop him up; he couldn't really think of one that
would. If you couldn't prop yourself up, then you shouldn't
be out there in the first place, trying to help people who
really needed it. People who had nothing at all.

'But what about you?' he said, trying to be polite. 'How've
you been?'

Again the half-smile. There was clearly something she
didn't feel she had to tell him, and it pissed him off, though
he knew it shouldn't. 'Oh, fine, you know. We passed our
OFSTED inspection at school. I'm helping Jim and Angus
at the pub while they sort out their new arrangements. Ned
is talking to someone about letting a docu-soap film in the
kitchens . . .'

Marie could tell he wasn't really interested. But at least
he was being cordial. After years of finely judging his moods
to avoid verbal explosions, she could read Chris like a
large-print book and suspected that he was torn between
telling her everything in gory detail to make her feel bad
and wanting to hoard it all to himself to make himself feel
martyred.

But then she tutted at herself for being harsh. What was
the point? At first glance across the room Chris had looked
the same as ever, but now they were up close she could see
that he had changed in small ways, indicative of changes that
probably ran much deeper. His eyes had bags and his hair
seemed to have receded by about two centimetres all round,
and midway through sentences his concentration seemed to
wander about the room, flicking impatiently at everything
that moved. He sounded distracted, as though part of him
hadn't even left the aid centre.

Funny that he now seemed more like the man she'd
originally fallen for than he had done during all the years
she'd actually been married to him.

Funny, in a wry, ironic sense, and only faintly painful.

'I've spoken to a solicitor,' she said, wanting to get it out of the way. No need to tell him it was Angus.

Chris's eyes snapped back to hers, surprised at her directness, and she swallowed, but didn't let her eyes drop to the table. Funny how they both knew they weren't here for a tearful reconciliation, yet still flinched from getting on with what they'd come to say. Marie belonged to the 'medicine, then chocolate' school of thought, although she didn't really expect much in the way of chocolate today, even if she managed to get the medicine to go in.

'Look, Chris, I don't want to make it complicated, and I'm sure you don't. We can just spend two years apart and then get a no-fault divorce. There's nothing much to divide, but if there's anything special you want, it's all back in my flat, above the Grapes. I don't have a lot of storage space, though, so I'd appreciate it if you could sort it out. I took some of your stuff round to your mum's.' She fiddled with her napkin. There *was* very little there of his, no goldfish or cat to argue over, no significant wedding presents to split up. Even the stereo was hers. That should have told her something about Chris's nesting potential. Calling round at Chris's mum's with the box of stuff had been an odd, taut experience. It wasn't difficult to see where Chris got his ability for working in an all-out war zone. 'Told her I was having a clear-out while you were away. I'll leave it to you to break the glad tidings.'

He looked at her. 'You're very calm about all this.'

'Why wouldn't I be?' Marie looked him straight in the eye. Her own mother, on the other hand, had taken it very well indeed. She hadn't exactly cracked open the champagne, but she'd immediately started talking about Marie coming over for Christmas, something she'd never offered while Chris and his disapproval of modern turkey-farming methods were a non-optional extra. In fact, it had been more of a shock that her mum *hadn't* wept and rended her clothes at

the news – another cherished childhood assumption dow
the drain.

She didn't know what her dad had said, though, and
wasn't looking forward to that little chat much.

'Just . . .' Chris floundered. 'I just thought you'd be
more . . . You know.'

'If it makes you feel better about yourself, I did cry solidly
for about a month,' said Marie drily. 'But now I realize that
it's actually a good idea, and we should have admitted it
wasn't working years ago.'

She had practised this with Iona, but hadn't planned for
the complete lack of nerves which now threatened to derail
her by their total absence.

'You are *sure* you want to get a divorce? Before we spend
all this money on solicitors?'

That was more like it. Manipulative arsehole. Marie
surprised herself by easily squashing the knee-jerk reaction
to shout at him. 'Chris, for God's sake,' she said, hoping
she sounded reasonable, '*you're* the one who wanted the
divorce! Remember that?'

He gave her a peculiar look. 'But do *you* want to?'

Marie tucked a stray curl behind her left ear. Somehow
it was easier to say exactly how she felt than to dress it up.
Maybe because she no longer considered herself contrac-
tually obliged to moderate his temper to a sociable level. 'I
didn't at first, no. I still hate the *idea* of the last five years
being for nothing,' she admitted. 'But the more I thought
about it, the more I realized that there was absolutely no
point in staying in a dead situation like this, and that at
least we're able to do this rationally and cleanly, without
fucking up any kids or fighting over a house. We don't even
have to go to court and argue. Just live apart for two years
and that's it.'

Marie stopped pleating her napkin and sat back in her
chair. Everything else she'd ever believed in about her
marriage felt as distant as a film; all her old opinions now

unded like a script someone else had written. Quite sweet,
in a sad way, but a bit dated. And ready to be chucked out,
like all the accumulated postcards, pizza leaflets and magazines she'd slung out of the flat. God, that had felt good.

She flicked a glance up at him. 'Unless you've found
someone else you want to marry?'

As soon as she said it, Marie held her breath and looked
closely at him. Could he? Had she underestimated him
all along?

Chris looked shocked. 'No!' Then he said, almost as an
afterthought, 'Have you?'

Marie's red lips curved into a broad smile. As if! She
didn't even want to think as far as the next college vacation
– but she failed to see why Chris should assume so little
about her appeal to other men. 'Ah. Hmm. I don't have to
answer that.'

'I think you do!' Chris snapped hotly. 'If it came to it in
court, I think it would be very relevant indeed!'

'Oh, take a chill pill,' said Marie. Then she relented and
tilted her head apologetically. There probably wasn't much
sex going out there, what with all the guilt and suffering
and late nights. And since her own nocturnal activities had
reverted to heights previously enjoyed nine years earlier, she
could afford to be generous. After all, he was the one on
the moral high ground, ostensibly giving up his marriage in
order to spend more time saving the world.

And Liam still gazed at her as if she was the first woman
he'd seen, even though he now knew every inch of the
cellulite relief map of her thighs, and he still talked to
her all night, even though she admitted that she'd never
actually read any of the Thomas Hardy novels stacked up
by the door, and he still pinched her bum behind the bar,
even though Tamara had given him a stiff warning about
his Public Displays of Affection.

But Liam wasn't the source of her new all-over gleam.
God, she wasn't that dumb.

'I've been so unhappy, Chris,' she said suddenly. 'But I only realized when you made me look at what we *really* had, that I've been unhappy – *we* were unhappy – for a long time, but didn't allow myself to believe it because I didn't want to admit that it wasn't working.' She held up her hand to stop him interrupting. 'I'm not saying it's your fault, or my fault. I think I've known we weren't right for each other for ages, but for some reason I couldn't forgive myself for screwing up something I'd believed in since I was little.'

And admitting the rest of them were right when they said you were a selfish arsehole.

'It meant a lot to you, didn't it?' said Chris.

Marie nodded, but didn't screech, 'So why didn't it mean anything to you, you bastard?' the way she had in her head, three months ago. They were simply two different people.

'I'm not sorry we did it,' he said, and scratched his head. 'It was a lot of fun.'

He didn't add 'while it lasted'. Neither did Marie. They both supplied it in their heads but politely kept it to themselves.

Marie sipped her water. She couldn't be mad, not when she knew there had been no burning, vicious decision on his part to divorce her. He'd just woken up one morning, as she had done, and known that it had already been over for a long time. The final absolution had come to her, almost abstractly, one morning after a particularly torrid night of passion with Liam, as she was drawing the thin black eyeliner across her eyelid, her concentration focused on making the flick-up at the end straight and swift: she actually liked being herself again.

It was stupid to grieve for something she hadn't even wanted when she'd had it, and pointless to hold herself back from enjoying what she had now. You were allowed more than one reinvention in life, and this wasn't even the first time she'd transformed into someone she'd never thought she'd be.

Marie looked at Chris, trying to fish the lemon out of his glass. He was slightly smelly from the long journey and unkempt. She couldn't think of anything to say; no recriminations at one end of the spectrum and no chitchat at the other. It was odd that there was so little to say, and yet maybe that was why they were there.

'What are you going to have?' she asked, indicating the menu. No one she knew ever bothered to look at the menu in PizzaExpress.

'Er . . .' Chris looked down as though he'd just seen it. 'Um, I'm not really hungry, actually.'

'Oh. OK.' Neither was she. And she didn't want to fill up on pizza when she knew for a fact that there was grilled wild salmon back at the Grapes, not to mention Angus's lemon tart, now back on the menu as part of the complicated peace negotiations Iona had brokered with Gabriel. 'Well, let's just get some coffee and then go.'

'Fine,' said Chris, rubbing his eyes again. They were red with tired shock, and unfamiliar. He looked up and managed a smile, and Marie was glad to feel a reciprocal smile curve her lips.

'Good,' said Marie, and immaculately caught the eye of the waitress.

Jim and Ned

'So I said to him, "Look, Martin," . . .' Jim finished off his beer, put his feet up on the arm of the sofa and folded a Kermit-green pea crostini into his mouth. His eyes closed in respect to Ned's fearless use of garlic and he wriggled further into the cushions. There had to be at least three cloves in this. If not four. Excellent. 'I just said,' he went on, raising his voice to carry through to the kitchen, '"You've got to be straight with me, if I'm going to be straight with you, mate." ' Jim brushed off all the crumbs he'd sprayed over his new work shirt. White and cotton. Back to normal.

'Oh, aye?' Ned didn't stop blitzing the food processor in the kitchen. On off. On off. On off. 'And what did Martin say to that?'

Jim was distracted by the choice of two large crostinis left on the plate. 'Um . . . Well, I didn't exactly say *that* . . .'

'No . . .' agreed Ned.

But then Martin hadn't been nearly as obstructive as he'd expected. In fact, he had been almost helpful. If Jim was in the market for worrying – which he had promised himself he no longer was – he might wonder why Martin had suggested various ways in which he might raise the money for the pub. Which didn't seem to be as ludicrously over-priced as he'd anticipated.

Still, leave all that to Angus and his lawyer's brain. All he had to worry about was whether or not to let Mad Boy Sam invest his long-awaited compensation money for the Hogarth Roundabout incident in the place.

'Yeah, well, maybe I'm paraphrasing a bit, but it was essentially the same thing.' Jim's hand wavered over the plate. Should he leave one for Ned? But they were so nice. And it was the end of the week.

'Right. But you've got the draft contract off of him?'

'Yeeees.' Jim hesitated and picked the marginally bigger one. 'Ned, are you going to make any more of these?'

'Did you remember to get another *ficelle* on your way home?'

'No.'

'Then no, I'm not.'

'Oh.' Jim ate the other one quickly.

Ned came through with a bowl full of home-made hummus, gleaming with golden pools of olive oil, and fresh crudités and some basil-mint-tomato spicy salad thing he'd learned from a Greek commis chef.

'Excellent!' said Jim, rubbing his hands.

'God, I'm ravenous. Has it started yet?' Ned put the nibbles down on the new coffee table and settled into his sofa next to Jim's. They had separate sofas. That was one of the first things they'd agreed on when moving into the other flat above the pub to save some money and get some rent coming in on Jim's flat. Separate sofas and a fuck-off great big wide-screen TV, with cable and an integral DVD player.

Loud enough to drown out any unwelcome noises from the flat next door, like sex or recorder practice.

'No, just about to.' Jim settled himself in arm's reach of the food and the television guide.

'Excellent!' Ned scooped up a load of hummus on a stick of celery and stuck it sideways in his mouth.

'How long till supper?' Jim inquired.

Ned looked at his watch and shrugged. 'Dunno, really. Any minute now, I guess. Pass us a beer, eh?'

Jim kicked the beer wagon towards him. IKEA was excellent for many things: sofas, coffee tables and children's push-along trolleys that could be packed with beer and ice, thus obviating the need to get up and go to the fridge.

'Is this a repeat?' he asked. 'Because I read on the Internet that Buffy's meant to have had implants, and I think that makes it a significantly better viewing spectacle.'

'I wouldn't know about that,' said Ned. 'I'm watching it for the modern reinterpretation of the vampiric co-dependency myth. Like.'

There was a ring at the doorbell and they both looked at each other, faking expressions of increasingly macabre exhaustion.

'Ah, get that, will you, Ned?' whined Jim. 'I've only just finished sorting out that wine delivery.'

Ned rolled his eyes into the back of his head and exhibited the whites to Jim. 'Yeah, and for the last two hours I've been thrashing round west London with Iona and she still reverses round corners like she's driving a tank.'

'I've had to bar that darts team.'

'Jim, I don't think you understand, man. Angus phones up every fifteen minutes for progress reports. He makes her do turns in the road on command. In my car.'

The doorbell rang again, but louder.

'OK, you win,' said Jim. 'But this is only going to work until she takes her test again.'

As he picked his way through the messy flat to open the door, Jim reflected contentedly that few marriages were based on a domestic situation and meeting of minds as skilled as his and Ned's. He wasn't even sure if he would want to move in with Rebecca, even if she asked him to. Living with Ned was about as good as it got as far as he could see, and he actually wasn't sure that in-house sex, unbearably exciting as it would no doubt be with a woman of Rebecca's high standards, was a fair enough exchange for top-quality food, silent support of a masculine, northern nature and a tacit understanding about dust.

'Cheers, mate,' said Jim, handing over the money – in exact change – to the pizza delivery boy.

'Haway, get a move on, Jim lad, you're missing the beginning,' shouted Ned. 'She's wearing those hotpants you like!'

'The red ones?' asked Jim, kicking the door shut.

'Ah-ah-ah, mind that painting of Iona's!' Ned warned as Jim's new suede Hush Puppies threatened to punch out the bride and groom at the centre of the canvas. They were wearing matching smiles and Iona had used the magic of perspective to bring their heights more in line with each other.

'When's she going to move that, by the way?' demanded Jim. 'It gives me the creeps.'

'Tomorrow, your woman said she was coming for it. If she doesn't Angus is going to hang it in the bar. As a warning about genetic engineering, he said.'

'Eurgh,' said Jim. 'Plates?'

Ned was already inching his chair nearer the television. 'Nah . . . eat it with fingers,' he said distractedly. 'Tastes better.'

'I don't want your half with the funny cheese on it.'

'You weren't getting any.'

'Good. Right, there you go . . .'

'Oi, oi, oi! Don't try and palm off the burnt bits on me. Or that manky pineapple.'

'I didn't order pineapple.'

'You must have done.'

'I hate pineapple.'

'Well, that's what a Hawaiian is, pineapple and ham.'

'Is it?'

'Yes. You big thick.'

'Fuck off.'

'You fuck off.'

Jim settled back into his chair and grabbed the remote, which was the size of a shoebox. 'No, you fuck off.'

'No, you.' Ned spread some hummus on to his slice of American Hot and put his bare, spindly feet up on Jim's sofa.

'Get your feet off my sofa,' said Jim in outrage.

'No.'

'Now!'

'Make me.'

'OK. When *Buffy*'s finished.'

'Yeah, you and your mum.'

'Fuck off.'

'No, you fuck off.'

'Fuck off yourself.'

Happy ever after.